Prologue

1807

A WHISPER WENT AROUND Mrs. Upton's Academy for Young Ladies soon after tea. A new student had arrived, and she must be of rare family and fortune. One girl caught a glimpse of the carriage waiting outside, glossy black with an escutcheon on the door, and soon the whispers grew fevered: it must be a duke's pampered daughter, or even a foreign princess.

They were wrong. Twelve-year-old Sophie Graham was an orphan, and she was the granddaughter of Viscount Makepeace, not a duke or a foreign dignitary. She also wanted nothing to do with him, and the viscount returned the feeling in full. Within a week of her arrival at his gloomy manor in Lincolnshire, he'd declared that she must go to school as soon as possible. Now she stood silently in Mrs. Upton's office, listening as her grandfather tried to browbeat the headmistress into accepting Sophie.

"The trouble is, my lord, I do not usually accept new students midterm," Mrs. Upton tried to explain. She was a moderately tall woman, fashionably dressed in subdued colors and devoid of embellishment, and she seemed utterly unafraid of Makepeace. Sophie respected her instinctively for that.

"You must. Her parents died of some gutter-borne fever." He glared at Sophie, who gazed back without expression. "They left nothing for her, but abandoned her to my charity. She needs feminine influence and proper instruction in some decent trade."

"Sir, we are an academy for young ladies," replied Mrs. Upton, laying a delicate stress on the last word. "We do not instruct students in trades, but in fine arts and social graces—"

Makepeace waved this aside. "I don't care what you teach her. She's a wild thing, neglected by her no-account parents. I have no use for a hoyden."

The headmistress glanced at Sophie, who remained still and quiet. She was not a hoyden, and her parents hadn't neglected her. But she did want very much to be accepted by Mrs. Upton, and so she did not argue with the hateful lies her grandfather was speaking. "My lord, our students come from the finest families in Britain. Our reputation rests on my personal assurance that every young lady here is of the best character and demeanor, in need of the instruction we offer for her future life."

The viscount barked with angry laughter. "I see your point! My son ran off with an opera singer— French, no less! Is that what you want to know? Good blood never does mix with common stock. Well, the girl is half wild and there's nothing to be done about it, but she bears my name and that, madam, is superior to whatever standard you maintain." He glanced around the understated room in obvious disdain. "Your establishment was recommended to me, and I wish to be done with the business as soon as possible. Name your price."

Mrs. Upton's face had grown expressionless during his tirade, but now she took another, more measuring look at Sophie. In the end, something—either in Sophie's expression or in her grandfather's final words—overcame the head-mistress's doubts. Sophie was sure it was the money. She didn't blame Mrs. Upton; in fact she hoped the woman extorted an enormous price. Makepeace would pay anything to be rid of her, as she had learned quite explicitly in the three weeks since she'd been left in his care, and she hated him enough to savor him being rooked for every farthing.

"Thirty percent, my lord," said the headmistress. "For a thirty percent premium on our usual tuition, I believe I can make room for her."

"Done." Makepeace reached for his walking stick and heaved himself out of his chair. "Her trunk is outside."

"Would you care to see the grounds?"

"No." The viscount led the way to the carriage, where Sophie's small trunk had already been removed from the boot and left on the gravel drive.

Makepeace yanked on his gloves, his thick white brows bristling in a ferocious scowl. "I'll pay the tuition until you're of age," he growled at Sophie. "Not a moment longer. You'd best try to learn something of value here, for you shan't be my responsibility."

"I never asked to be." She raised her chin and met his stare. "Goodbye."

He stared at her a moment before giving a contemptuous sniff. "A proud little thing, are you? You've no grounds for it. If you didn't bear my name, you'd be as insignificant as your mother." The viscount climbed into his carriage and snarled at his coachman to go. The carriage started with a jerk immediately. At no moment did Lord Makepeace look back.

"Let me show you to your dormitory, Miss Graham," Mrs. Upton said in the awkward silence. The pity in her voice was faint but detectable. Sophie had heard that before, but this time she also heard sympathy. "I'm certain your grandfather will relent once he sees how diligently you work to become accomplished."

"He won't. Nothing I ever do will please him, and I'm glad he's gone." She watched the carriage pass through the tall iron gates to be certain that he was in fact gone. "I wouldn't mind if he were waylaid by highwaymen and shot." She turned her forthright gaze on the shocked headmistress. "Thank you for accepting me, ma'am. I promise to be a very good student." And she dropped a flawless curtsy, worthy of the finest ballerina in Moscow—indeed, that was who had taught her.

Mrs. Upton took her inside and sent a teacher to fetch Miss Eliza Cross and Lady Georgiana Lucas. "You shall share their room this term," she told Sophie. "They are both kind and well-mannered young ladies."

"Are they my age, ma'am?" This interested her intensely. She had rarely had the chance to make friends with girls her own age.

"They are both in the second form. The girls your age are generally in the fourth form, but since I've had no opportunity to assess your education thus far, it's best if you begin there." She gave Sophie an uncertain glance. "I presume you have had some education, Miss Graham?"

"Yes, ma'am." It stung to be placed in the lower form, but Sophie refrained from informing the headmistress that she spoke fluent French and some Italian, that she loved math and geography, that she knew how to dance and had been playing the pianoforte since she was four. She intended to win over everyone at this academy, and it wouldn't hurt to hold some pleasant surprises in reserve.

Lady Georgiana arrived first, as tall as Sophie but fair and fine-boned. Miss Cross hurried in after her, breathless and a little flustered. She was shorter and plumper than Lady Georgiana, and every bit as ordinary in features as Lady Georgiana was beautiful. Sophie smiled at them both. "It is my great pleasure to make your acquaintances," she said to the two other girls. "I hope we'll be friends."

Miss Cross smiled nervously and Lady Georgiana gave her an appraising look, as if to say *we'll see.* Sophie didn't mind. She would be circumspect in the other girl's place, too. But Sophie had inherited her father's charm and her mother's drive, and so she set about befriending them.

She needed to. Under no circumstances was

she going back to Makepeace Manor, where her grandfather ruled in surly silence. Her youth had been spent in the capitals of Europe, following her operatic mother's career. Her parents' deaths had upended that happy if unsettled life, leaving her at the mercy of a grandfather who seemed determined to hold her accountable for every sin and slight her parents had ever committed—and in his eyes, they were legion. Sophie soon divined that dying was possibly her father's worst sin, as he had named the viscount her guardian in his will. If there had been a way to break that will and wash his hands of her entirely, Sophie was sure Lord Makepeace would have done it. Sending her away to school was the next best thing.

A young ladies' academy might not be as exciting as Europe, but it offered the one thing she hadn't had in all her twelve years: a fixed home. On the interminable drive to Mrs. Upton's, Makepeace had informed her that she would board at school during holidays if she didn't get invited home with another girl. Sophie could endure holidays at school, but she yearned for friends.

Eliza and Lady Georgiana had great promise in that regard. Eliza was shy and sweet, the sort of girl who would always be steadfast and loyal. Sophie admired that. Lady Georgiana, on the other hand, appealed to her high-spirited side, the sort of girl everyone else admired and looked up to. It didn't take long to discover that Eliza was the only child of a man with wealth but no connection, while Georgiana was from one of the most august families in Britain, being the much younger sister of the Earl of Wakefield.

After dinner the students retired to their rooms to study. Sophie was reading the French lesson—her mother's language—and feeling relieved there was one class where she wouldn't be behind, when her new roommates' whispering caught her attention.

"Try again," Georgiana urged. "You can learn this."

"I'm *trying*," said Eliza in anguish. "I am, I just can't—"

"Is it sums?" Sophie asked, spying the page in front of them.

"It's so difficult for me," whispered Eliza, shame written on her face.

Sophie smiled. "I can help." She rummaged in her trunk and drew out a pack of cards.

Lady Georgiana raised her brows. "Gambling?"

Sophie scoffed. "It's not gambling if there's no wagering. But cards are an excellent way to practice sums, and odds, and all sorts of mathematics." She dealt some hands. "This is a game where you add the value of the cards. You must do the sum very quickly and quietly, and decide whether you'd like to add another card."

"Ladies aren't supposed to play cards." Lady Georgiana came to sit on the end of her bed, studying the cards with fascination.

"Truly?" Sophie was surprised. "All the ladies in Paris play. And in London—my father said the only people more passionate about gambling than English ladies are English gentlemen."

Lady Georgiana snorted with surprised laughter. "No!"

"Oh yes." Sophie didn't add that her father

knew because he'd gambled with all of them. When her mother began to lose her voice to a suppurating throat condition, they'd left Europe and come home to England, where Papa put his charm and name to use playing at the card tables to support them. She'd helped him practice the art of appearing to play carelessly while actually calculating the odds of every move.

Eliza edged closer. "Will it really help with sums? I—I have such trouble."

"Of course!" Sophie lined up the cards of one hand. "What is this hand worth? Add the numbers."

"Six," said Eliza, staring at the four of hearts and the two of clubs.

"And now?" She flipped down a seven of hearts.

"Thirteen," said the other girl slowly.

"Good! Now?" An eight of diamonds appeared.

"Twenty . . ." Eliza hesitated. "One."

"Very good." Sophie beamed.

"That's far more fun than totting up numbers on a page," declared Lady Georgiana with a delighted laugh. "Where did you learn this?"

"My father." She caught the quick look the other girls exchanged. "He and my mother died," she added. "My grandfather didn't want me, so he brought me here."

"Oh, how dreadful," said Eliza.

Sophie mustered a smile. Her parents' deaths were dreadful. Her grandfather was dreadful. Mrs. Upton's was by far the least dreadful thing in her life at the moment. "I'd rather be here than with him. Would you rather be at home?"

"Oh." Eliza looked startled. "My mother also

died, when I was a child. My father sent me here to learn to be a lady. I miss him, but . . ."

"My brother wanted rid of me, too," offered Lady Georgiana readily. "But like you, I prefer to be here. He's an odd duck, my brother. I revel in being unwanted by him."

Sophie grinned. "Mrs. Upton's Academy of the Unwanted."

Georgiana burst out laughing, and Eliza gasped. "That's *terrible* . . ." But she joined Georgiana on the end of the bed. Sophie dealt more cards, and they practiced sums in happy camaraderie. Gradually Sophie began teaching them the rules of the game as well, and then how to calculate odds. Eliza's confidence grew until she was adding the cards almost as quickly as Georgiana.

"What should you do with this hand?" Sophie asked.

Eliza looked at her cards, a ten of clubs and a five of hearts. "Take another, because almost half the cards have values of six or less?"

"Precisely! You're doing very well," Sophie assured her, just as the door abruptly opened.

"Young ladies," said Mrs. Upton, aghast. "What is this?"

Eliza went pale; Georgiana winced and gave an audible sigh. All three girls scrambled to their feet.

Mrs. Upton crossed the room and swept back the fold of blanket Sophie had instinctively tossed over the cards. "Gaming," she said in a deeply disappointed tone. "This is improper behavior for young ladies."

"We were not gaming," said Sophie. "None of us have any money."

The headmistress did not look amused. "That is a very fine distinction, Miss Graham, and not one I accept. Not only is gaming immoral, it exposes one to people of low character and risks one's reputation and fortune. No respectable gentleman will wish to be connected with a lady who gambles. He will recognize that she harbors a dangerous susceptibility to wickedness, and he will not want to be held liable for her losses."

"What if she wins?" murmured Sophie.

Mrs. Upton gave her a look of warning. "Any gambler who thinks like that is heading for a loss. It is the lure of winning that drives people to risk ever larger sums of money until they have bankrupted themselves and their families. What are the chances of winning every hand, Miss Graham?"

Sophie said nothing. She remembered too well the nights Papa had come home late, in dismal spirits, not having won enough.

"Gambling has destroyed many a decent and eligible man," continued Mrs. Upton. "You cannot begin to imagine how much worse it is for a female. Mind my words, young ladies—gambling is the path to ruin. Avoid it at all costs."

"Yes, ma'am," whispered Eliza tearfully.

"Yes, ma'am," echoed Georgiana.

Mrs. Upton raised a brow. "Miss Graham?"

Sophie began to shrug, but caught herself in time. "Yes, ma'am."

The headmistress surveyed them. "Since you are unfamiliar with our rules here, Miss Graham,

I shall let this pass. But do not stray again." She collected the cards and left, dousing the lamp as she did.

"I'll practice sums another way," said Eliza as the girls got into their beds. "Papa would be so upset if Mrs. Upton wrote to him that I'd been gambling. He hopes I'll marry a gentleman, which means I must be a lady. If only sums didn't matter so much to gentlemen . . ."

"They don't," declared Georgiana from her own bed. "No gentleman I know can abide sums. They don't even like discussing them with their secretaries, who do all the work."

"A few hands of cards doesn't hurt anyone. And we were not gambling." Sophie said a silent prayer of relief that Mrs. Upton had confiscated her old deck of cards and not Papa's deck. She would have fought like a wild animal to keep that deck—or any of her few reminders of her parents—and that might have got her tossed from school and back onto Lord Makepeace's mercy.

A wave of heartsickness washed over her at the thought of her parents. Four months ago they'd been alive and well, their finances strained but their home happy. Then it all disappeared. Consumption, the doctor said; she was lucky she hadn't got it, too.

Lucky. How she hated that word.

Sophie forced herself to inhale evenly and deeply. Everything in life was a matter of chance. Happiness depended solely on one's own efforts, because Fate was rarely kind or generous. Sophie had learned that early, and she would never, ever forget it. One could never count on luck.

"But Mrs. Upton wouldn't teach sums if they weren't beneficial for ladies to know," Eliza insisted, unaware of Sophie's inner turmoil. "I'll have to find some other way to learn . . . although I truly hope I don't need to learn odds . . ."

Georgiana giggled. "That's because the odds are *very good* that you'll find a handsome and charming husband, Eliza, and he'll treat you like a duchess, whether you can balance your household accounts or not."

"I hope so," said Eliza wistfully. "Since I haven't got your beauty or Sophie's cleverness, I can't risk it."

Sophie tucked the blankets under her chin as they debated the question. That simple comment, calling her not only clever but by her given name, caused an unexpected warmth inside her. She was all alone in the world now, with Mama and Papa dead, her grandfather an ogre, and her mother's family a continent away. She vaguely knew she had an uncle or two, and perhaps even cousins somewhere, but none of them were coming to her aid.

She might not have any family worth knowing, but true and honest friends would be a good start. And she had a powerful feeling that she, Eliza, and Georgiana were destined to be great friends.

Chapter 1

1819
London

THE VEGA CLUB occupied a curious position in London. Tucked away on a dead-end street not far from St. James's Square, it sat precisely midway between the wealth and elegance of Mayfair and the brutal squalor of the Whitechapel rookeries. It made no bones about catering to both extremes; it was said that anyone—duke or dockworker, lady or lady of the street—could apply to become a member. There were only two requirements of those fortunate enough to secure the stamped silver token of membership.

Pay your debts. Hold your tongue.

It was rumored that members were required to take an oath pledging not to reveal anything that happened within Vega's walls. Rumored, because no one could, or would, confirm it. When confronted directly, members would claim not to know anything about it before quickly walking away. But since even the most determined scandalmongers were frustrated in their attempts to learn many details about the gaming club, the pledge of secrecy became part of Vega's legend, whether or not it was true. And that encouraged the spread of all manner of stories about what *did* go on.

Jack Lindeville, Duke of Ware, knew all about Vega's. It was the bane of his life even though he himself never went there. His younger brother, Philip, frequented the place, along with his crowd of friends. They invited him to accompany them from time to time, but Jack always declined. He knew why he was welcome at their tables, and it wasn't for his charm and wit. Young men on fixed incomes, even generous fixed incomes, were always in search of someone wealthy to play against, and as Philip often reminded him, Ware was one of the richest dukedoms in England.

Jack interpreted that to mean that he looked like a prime mark for Philip's friends with empty pockets. Unfortunately for them, he wasn't fool enough to go. One bit of bad luck, and a man's life could be ruined.

His lip curled at that thought as his carriage turned up St. Martin's Lane on its way to the Vega Club. Bad luck, Philip claimed, had been the cause of his most recent downfall: the two of clubs, when all he needed to win was any card higher than a three. Philip was sure he had calculated the odds correctly and the dealer had made a mistake, although he dared not say so and risk his membership. But the result was that he had signed a note for almost two thousand pounds, which he could not pay.

Philip was penitent. He apologized for asking

such a favor. He promised it would never happen again, even though it had happened several times before. But he also told their mother, who swept into Jack's study in a storm of indignation and insisted he settle the debt to prevent Philip being humiliated or impoverished.

At first Jack would have none of it. Philip brought it on himself, and if he was man enough to sign a note that size, he was man enough to work out how to honor it. But his mother argued, and then cajoled, and then she began weeping and bitterly accusing him of callous indifference to his family duty. At that, Jack relented. When the duchess made up her mind, there was no reasoning with her.

The carriage rocked to a halt. The footman opened the door and Jack stepped down. He'd pay this debt for Philip, but not without repercussions. His brother had an independent income—thanks to his mother—but he also drew an allowance from the Ware estates, which Jack controlled. For seven years he'd safeguarded those estates, and he'd be damned if his hard work would be siphoned off by Philip's bad luck at the card tables.

Thin-lipped, he strode into the club. A burly fellow in impeccable evening clothing appeared before he'd taken two steps. "Good evening, sir. May I help you?"

"I'm here to see Dashwood," Jack replied, naming the club's owner. He drew out one of his cards and offered it.

"Is he expecting you?"

Jack smiled humorlessly. "I daresay he won't be surprised by my arrival." Philip was not shy about trading on the Ware name. If Mr. Dashwood were half as canny as his reputation suggested, he'd probably been anticipating Jack's visit from the moment Philip scrawled his signature on that marker.

The manager gave him an appraising glance. "Perhaps not. Would you care to wait in the dining room?"

God no. He might see someone he knew and be caught in conversation. Jack wanted this over and done with as soon as possible, preferably with no one aware that it had happened. "I'll wait here," he replied in a tone that made it clear he did not expect to wait long.

The manager bowed his head. "Perhaps you'd rather play a hand or two in the meanwhile?"

Over the man's shoulder Jack could see into the main salon of Vega's. It wasn't tawdry or garish, as he had somewhat expected, but refined; it looked like a normal gentleman's club . . . except for the women. Not house wenches clinging to men's sides, but society ladies. Jack's brows went up a fraction as he glimpsed Lady Rotherwood playing whist.

"Vega's doesn't exclude the ladies," remarked the manager, following his gaze. "It's a bit of a surprise to some gentlemen, but they soon see the benefit."

Jack's mouth firmed. Empty-headed ladies could lose a fortune just as easily as reckless young men. "No doubt." He wondered if Philip had ever lost so dramatically to a woman and then decided it hardly mattered. Money lost was money lost.

Still, it piqued his curiosity. Ladies, gambling

with men. How novel. The manager left to inform Mr. Dashwood, and Jack took a step forward to survey the club through the protective screen of a tall stand of palms.

He recognized Angus Whitley and Fergus Fraser, some of Philip's mates. They sat at a table with another man and a woman in a vivid crimson gown who had her back to him. Her dark hair was swept up in a twist, exposing her pale skin. She wore a thin black ribbon around her neck, tied in a neat little bow at her nape, and the loose end curled enticingly, tempting a man to tug it loose.

Jack's eyes lingered on her. What sort of woman wanted to be a member of a gaming club? Every decent woman would shy away from the mere thought of it. Lady Rotherwood, for all that she was a viscountess, was known to be a bit fast. What were the requirements for membership, he wondered; did they differ for men and women? Not that Vega's could be very stringent, as Philip had had no difficulty gaining entry. Philip, with only his illustrious name and considerable charm and abominable luck at cards to recommend him.

Whitley made an exclamation, tossing down his cards. Fraser laughed, preening in victory. He reached for the pile of money in the center of the table, but the woman stopped him by laying her fingers on his wrist. Jack had no idea what she said, but from the way Fraser's face went blank with shock, he supposed it wasn't good news. The other man laid down his cards and began to laugh, a hearty bellow that turned heads. Clearly the woman had trounced them all.

And rather than being dismayed at being the focus of attention, she responded to it. She said something that made Whitley give a shout of laughter, and fellows at the next table chuckled. Jack couldn't see her face but he could tell she was pleased just from the angle of her head, tipped ever so slightly to one side as she collected her winnings and Whitley shuffled the cards for another round.

No wonder Philip liked the place. Jack wondered if his brother knew the lady in crimson.

"Your Grace," said a voice behind him. Jack turned, glad to shake off that thought. The manager was back. "Mr. Dashwood will see you."

He led the way through a door set discreetly beside the palms, down a short corridor to another door. He knocked once, then swept it open and bowed as Jack went in.

"Nicholas Dashwood, at your service, Your Grace." Dashwood bowed. He was a tall rangy fellow, his face all lean hard lines and angles. "I apologize for the delay. I didn't expect you."

"I've come about my brother's debt."

One corner of Dashwood's mouth lifted at Jack's cool tone. "He said you might."

Jack repressed a spike of fury that Philip had presumed that strongly enough to tell Dashwood. He should have known, though; Philip was shameless in getting out of anything unpleasant.

The club owner walked around his desk and picked up a paper lying on its surface. "Two thousand one hundred and twenty pounds."

Jack took a breath to control his temper yet

again. Philip had lied about that, too, claiming it was less than two thousand. "May I see?"

Dashwood handed it over with a faint smile. He must deal with this all the time. It took only a cursory examination to determine that it was Philip's handwriting, promising the large sum to Sir Lester Bagwell. "Is it customary for you to guarantee debts for your members?" Jack handed back the note.

"I guarantee nothing." Dashwood leaned against his desk. "Members are free to exchange notes or funds directly. On occasion they prefer to have me hold them—not as guarantor but as a favor. I am an intermediary, if you will. We have only a few rules at Vega's, the most important of which is to pay your debts."

Meaning Sir Lester feared Philip wouldn't pay what he owed, and wanted Dashwood to enforce the rule of the club. Grimly Jack wrote a draft on his bank for the sum, mentally excoriating his brother. Without a word he offered it to Dashwood, who handed him Philip's note in exchange.

"A pleasure, Your Grace." Dashwood went to the door. "If you're ever in search of a table to play, I hope you'll return to Vega's."

Not bloody likely, thought Jack.

Dashwood escorted him back to the front of the house. On impulse he looked toward the main salon again, through the palm fronds. His brother had solemnly promised to give up the tables for a month in penance, to retrench on his spending and learn some moderation in his habits. Philip would not be here. But the lady in crimson . . .

He had the strangest desire to see her face. Just to know what sort of woman joined a gaming hell.

To his shock, he did spy his brother's dark head at the center of the room, in a small crowd of people gathered around a table. Jack stopped short. Already Philip was back at it, placing wagers he couldn't afford, no doubt telling anyone who asked that his brother would pay his losses tonight, tomorrow, on into eternity. As he watched, a cheer broke out, and Philip threw up his hands and laughed.

Jack knew that mannerism. Philip was losing. He always lost with a laugh, a quip, a grandiose gesture. It was only later, when he had to contemplate the consequences of his loss, that he became contrite. Having just settled a very large gambling loss, Jack felt fully in the right dragging his brother out of the club before he could incur another one—which, Jack realized with fury, he was quite likely to do. Philip was playing hazard, a game of almost pure chance. He turned on his heel and brushed by Dashwood as he strode into the room.

"If I must lose," Philip declared gallantly as he drew nearer, "at least I'm losing to the most beautiful woman in London." The crowd around him laughed in boisterous appreciation.

Idiot, Jack seethed, barging through the crowd. *You don't have to lose, you just have to stop playing.* Dashwood would cancel his membership if Jack refused to pay this debt. In fact, Jack would have no qualms getting his brother's gaming privileges revoked across London. He had accepted that his life was to be given in service to the Ware estates, but damned if he'd beggar himself settling Philip's debts.

He reached the front of the crowd, unfortunately opposite his brother. Oblivious to his glowering presence, Philip gave an extravagant bow and held out the dice to a woman—the same woman in crimson who'd been playing cards earlier with Philip's feckless friends.

"Thank you, sir," she said, her words colored with laughter. "It's always a pleasure winning from you." She turned to face the table and raised the dice to brush her lips over them. "Five," she called, naming her mark and managing to make it sound seductive, before she made her cast. The crowd gave a boisterous huzzah, but Jack's gaze was locked on her.

Not beautiful in the classic sense, but mesmerizing. Her face was a perfect oval, her eyes the color of sherry. A silver locket hung on the black ribbon around her neck, and when she leaned forward to collect the dice again, Jack got a glimpse of her bosom, threatening to spill over the crimson fabric. She straightened and gave Philip a flirtatious glance as she made her second cast. Jack managed to tear his eyes off her in time to see the focused interest in his brother's face.

Two thoughts careened through his mind. First, that she was a siren of old, as brazen as brass and as wily as a serpent. Philip was so busy staring at her bosom he didn't even notice how badly he was losing.

And second, Jack wanted her.

Chapter 2

᭡᭡᭡

THE VEGA CLUB was very nearly Sophie Campbell's second home.

In fanciful moments she imagined Vega's had once been the home of a gentleman, perhaps even an earl or a marquess. It wore its dark wood paneling like a comfortable suit of clothing, inured to the elegance of its crystal chandeliers and plush carpets. Other gaming hells had a closed-up feel, as if sunlight were some sort of plague to be avoided, but not Vega's. Draperies were only closed at night, and there were windows built high into the walls to allow fresh air on warm evenings. Smoking was confined to a room at the back, and the dining room rivaled the one at Mivart's Hotel, presumably so the female members were more at ease.

That was the most important feature of Vega's: women were allowed. Not merely as guests of a man, but as full members in their own right. It was not easy to gain membership, but Sophie had recognized early on that it was the ideal place for her purposes. The Vega Club attracted all sorts of men, and they were all willing to lose to a woman. That was vital to her, for that was how she earned her living.

From the moment she arrived at Mrs. Upton's Academy, Sophie had known that she would be entirely on her own when she was grown. The morning of her eighteenth birthday, Mrs. Upton had summoned her to gently break the news that Lord Makepeace would no longer pay her tuition. Since the viscount's letter had arrived the morning of her birthday, Sophie could only imagine how long the bitter old man had been looking forward to sending it. The headmistress offered her a position teaching mathematics, but Sophie declined. At Mrs. Upton's, her chances of making a good life were small; in the great world, who knew? She'd always been one to play the odds.

It certainly hadn't been easy. Without funds, she'd taken employment as companion to a widowed viscountess. Anna, Lady Fox, had been a revelation. She was unconventional and bold, generous and witty, and she planted the seeds of an idea in Sophie's mind. *Every woman needs a fortune of her own*, she often said—making Sophie smile in wry agreement, wishing it were that easy. But Lady Fox meant what she said. When she died, she left Sophie three hundred pounds. *A good beginning*, she wrote in her will; a rare stroke of fortune, to Sophie's mind, and not one to waste. With that three hundred pounds, plus her own small savings, she invented a dead husband, changed her name, and went to London at the age of twenty-one to put her Grand Plan into effect.

It was a simple plan, really. Once she had secured her independence, she would be mistress of her own fate and able to chart her own course. If independence—which meant money—weren't the key to happiness, it was at least a very great factor in it, and accordingly Sophie set about gaining it with her one profitable skill: gambling.

At times she felt a pang of remorse for living off others' losses. She remembered well Mrs. Upton's lectures against gaming, and she knew that the headmistress had been correct about it being dangerous and ruinous. Even though she had developed iron-clad rules to prevent herself losing too much, there was always the matter of her reputation . . . such as it was.

Her friends worried about that, too. Ever since that first day at Mrs. Upton's over a decade ago, she, Georgiana, and Eliza had been inseparable. During the years when Sophie was with Lady Fox and her friends were still at school, their letters had flown back and forth weekly. Now that they were all in London—Eliza at her father's home in Greenwich and Georgiana with her chaperone, the Countess of Sidlow—they made sure to have tea every fortnight, usually at Sophie's snug little house on Alfred Street.

"Surely you could invest some money, as well?" Eliza often asked. "It must be safer."

"Never," was Sophie's firm answer. "Playing the 'Change is the riskiest gambling there is."

"Papa does quite well, and he's offered many times to advise you," Eliza reminded her. Which was no solace at all to Sophie; Mr. Cross could afford to lose a thousand pounds on a bad stock, while she could not.

Georgiana thought she should make a different sort of investment. "What you really ought to do is make one of the gentlemen at Vega's fall in love with you. Sterling says Sir Thomas Mayfield would be a brilliant match for you." Viscount Sterling was Georgiana's intended husband, and her most frequently cited authority on everything.

That made Sophie laugh. "Thomas Mayfield! A baronet? You must be mad."

"Mad!" Georgiana widened her expressive green eyes. She turned to Eliza. "Am I mad to suggest she set her cap for a tall, handsome gentleman? The sort of gentleman who could make most ladies in London swoon with just one devilish smile?"

Sophie rolled her eyes as Eliza laughed. "You sound quite smitten with him yourself. Should we warn Lord Sterling?"

"Of course not. Sterling's got nothing to fear. I've been in love with him for ages," said Georgiana with a flip of one hand. Viscount Sterling, whose property neighbored that of the Earl of Wakefield, had proposed to Georgiana as soon as she turned eighteen, and had been happily accepted. Lord Wakefield had dithered and delayed the match, but everyone knew he was an eccentric fellow, and her engagement left Georgiana free to enjoy two Seasons in London, buying an endless wedding trousseau while Wakefield and Sterling argued about the settlements.

"Perhaps that's why you should leave Sophie in peace about him," said Eliza gently. "You've found your hero so easily. Not all of us are as fortunate."

"Oh, but I want you to be!" cried Georgiana, contrite. She turned to Sophie. "Is Sir Thomas really that bad?"

"No," she lied with a smile. "He's just not for me." She hadn't missed how Sterling thought the baronet would be a brilliant match *for her*. Sir Thomas, with his wandering hands and flexible sense of honor, would be utterly unacceptable as a husband for Lady Georgiana Lucas, even for the heiress Eliza Cross. But for Mrs. Sophie Campbell, a supposed widow of modest means who spent her evenings at a gaming club, he'd be a marvelous catch. Sophie was not unaware of her standing in society.

"A younger son, then," said Georgiana, undeterred. "Lord Philip Lindeville."

"Who? No!"

"You must remember him, Sophie. You've been seen with him several times in the last month," said Georgiana somberly. "Sterling says he's a great fellow, and he's devilishly handsome."

"Papa says he's a rake," reported Eliza.

"In need of reform through true love." Georgiana winked at her.

Sophie laughed. "Far too much trouble for me, I'm sure."

Eliza looked shocked, and Georgiana snorted in amusement. "Only you would view a suitor as trouble, Sophie!"

"Lord Philip," she replied, "is not a suitor."

For some reason that conversation stuck in her mind as she reached Vega's that night. It was a cool and cloudy evening, with passing sprinkles of rain, and she wore her crimson gown, not for luck but for cheer; the bright cotton was her favorite. When Mr. Forbes, the club manager, carried away her cloak, she caught sight of herself in the mirror above the fireplace. She didn't feel old, but at twenty-four, neither was she young. She didn't want to turn up her nose at mention of a suitor. Sophie wouldn't mind at all finding a gentleman who would fall in love with her and win her love in turn. If only the men she met were interested in the same thing.

Assuming she kept winning at about the same rate, it would take her another six years to reach ten thousand pounds, the amount she'd decided meant financial security. Six years plus ten thousand pounds equaled independence. That was the equation she should keep in mind, or she'd find herself at the mercy of lecherous baronets who weren't even as handsome as Sir Thomas Mayfield. She squared her shoulders and strolled into the salon. It didn't take long to find a table of partners, and she took a seat with a confident smile.

At least an hour passed. She lost a little at first but then made up for it. She was ahead sixty pounds when someone exclaimed behind her, "Mrs. Campbell!"

Sophie started. She and her partner, Giles Carter, were happily trouncing Mr. Whitley and Mr. Fraser in a game of whist. Whist was not only perfectly acceptable for a lady to play, it was an easy game to win when one paid attention and didn't drink too much. Mr. Whitley wasn't paying enough attention, and Mr. Fraser was on his third glass of madeira. Lord Philip Lindeville's delighted greeting interrupted a winning streak of six tricks.

"What a pleasure to encounter you here." He gave her a neat little bow.

"And you, sir." She smiled and inclined her head. Her friends' teasing about Lord Philip wasn't all wrong; he was one of her frequent companions. He was charming and amusing even though he was a little too sure of his own charm. Sophie had meant what she said when she called him trouble—as a suitor.

"Won't you play a turn with me?" He grinned and lowered his voice to a conspiratorial whisper. "I vowed not to come tonight, but the chance of seeing you again was too tempting."

"I wouldn't want to tempt any man to break his vows," she said with a teasing smile.

He laughed. "It was a foolish vow! Come, you shall probably beat me, and that will be my penance."

"Oh, but we're playing here," she tried to point out, but Lord Philip had already exchanged a glance with his friend Mr. Whitley.

That gentleman promptly pushed back his chair. "Time for me to retire. You've routed me thoroughly, ma'am." He bowed, and Mr. Fraser followed suit. Mr. Carter, her partner, hesitated, but Sophie knew when Philip was determined and would not be thwarted.

She tamped down her irritation and laid down her cards. "Mr. Carter, I hope you will play with me again. I do believe we are an indomitable team at whist." As hoped, his face eased and he even wished her luck as Lord Philip tugged her away.

"I was engaged in a game," she reproached him as he tucked her hand around his arm. "Patience is a virtue, my lord."

Philip grinned. "No wonder I haven't any! I only came to speak to Dashwood, but then caught sight of you and utterly forgot my mission there."

"Should I be flattered?" The only reason to see Mr. Dashwood, the Vega Club owner, was to vouch for a new member or to see to a gambling debt—a large one. Twice Sophie had had the good fortune to be on the winning end of a wager significant enough that Mr. Dashwood had stepped in to oversee payment. Somehow she doubted Philip would have been so easily distracted if he'd come to collect winnings.

He looked down at her. His dark hair fell in romantic waves over his forehead, and a rakish smile tilted his mouth. "Yes. You should be very flattered. Tell me you are, and I shall be flattered as well."

He was so handsome and charming, it was a pity she would have to discourage his increasingly obvious interest. She pressed his arm. "Flattery is lightly given and so easily repaid."

"Not lightly given," he returned. "And please do repay it."

She laughed. "I see you're feeling lucky tonight. Shall it be hazard, then?" Hazard was quick. A few games and she would shed him, no matter what he said or did. Lord Philip had been growing too attentive of late.

It was unfortunate, that; unknown to almost everyone in the world, she *was* keeping an eye out for a husband, and it would have been very convenient if he'd been acceptable. Georgiana, for one, would have been so proud of her for snaring a duke's brother.

But as much as she liked him, Lord Philip Lindeville was most assuredly not cut out to be a husband—at least not hers. During her three years in London, Sophie had honed some very specific matrimonial requirements, and Philip barely met any. He was charming, but reckless; he was good-natured, but cocksure; he was almost sinfully attractive, from his wavy dark hair to his tall, lean form, but he was far too aware of that fact, as was every other woman in town. And even worse, what made him so appealing as a partner at Vega's—his utter indifference to losing money—was the very thing that made him utterly unacceptable as a husband. Sophie had no desire to marry a man who would gamble away their future. So despite his impeccable connections and unmistakable interest in her, she would have to turn him off.

Giles Carter followed them to the hazard table. She gave him a rueful glance as Philip called for dice. Mr. Carter was much more in line with her object. He was at least a dozen years older than she, but possessed of his own independent income. Philip, she knew, was largely dependent on an allowance from his brother, an income he thought insufficient for a bachelor, let alone a married man. Mr. Carter knew when to quit the tables, although of late he had played longer than was prudent . . . at least with her. Sophie hoped that was a good sign. He always lost with excellent grace, and seemed almost chagrined when he won. Mr. Carter would make an excellent husband, being neither cruel nor miserly nor ugly.

However, any hope of that would be irreparably scotched if she allowed Philip to tempt her across the line of respectability. Sophie knew she was clinging to the edge of it now, and she was determined not to slip off. She wasn't above flirting with gentlemen while she won their money, but never to the point of letting them think she wanted an affair.

"What shall we play for?" Philip held out the dice, his dark eyes gleaming at her.

"A guinea per round?"

He pulled a disappointed face as he dropped a handful of markers on the table, belying his claim that he'd only come to speak to Dashwood. "Oh. Money."

She made herself laugh lightly, aware of Mr. Carter at her other side. "What else?" Before he could answer, she turned to the table. "Seven," she announced, tossing the dice.

Hazard was a game of chance. A player called his main, from five to nine, and then rolled the dice. If the sum of his roll equaled his main, he had nicked it, and won the pot. If he rolled a two or three, he had thrown out, and lost. The rules got complicated beyond that, with rolls of eleven or twelve being generally losing turns, but often a player had an opportunity to roll again and again, until he lost three in succession and was forced to yield the dice.

It took her three throws to win. Lord Philip applauded. "A fine start!" He always lost so easily, as if he didn't care about the money, and he quickly racked up two losses in two rolls. A flash of pique crossed his face but only for a moment. He took up the dice and rattled them for several seconds in his palm.

Years ago at Mrs. Upton's, Sophie had figured the odds in hazard, burning her candle to a stub as she filled the back of her mathematics primer with calculations. After the headmistress's stern words, she never dared gamble with other girls at the academy, but the boys in the stables were another matter. She'd learned many card games from her father, but in the stables she learned dicing as well. She knew the odds of every play and throw. She learned when to be cautious and when to risk it all, and thus far she had employed these tactics splendidly—to whit, a saved sum of four thousand pounds, amassed slowly and painstakingly over three years in London, thanks mainly to the Vega Club.

Still, hazard was a fool's game . . . except against Lord Philip.

He never calculated anything. If he rolled too high in one turn, he called a higher main; if he rolled too low, he called a lower one. He would improve his lot considerably if he simply played the odds, as Sophie always did. She didn't like taking advantage of him, but tonight she was a little annoyed he had broken up her game with Mr. Carter. If she won a good sum, he'd leave her be. Some nights people practically insisted she take their money.

Giving her a sly smile, Philip rolled again and didn't lose. His eyes grew bright with triumph, even though he hadn't won yet. He dropped another marker onto his stake and played again.

A small crowd gathered around them, with whispered side bets flying around behind her. Sophie kept her demeanor poised and easy, watching her opponent's play. He was on the road to ruin, she thought. It was unfortunate but undeniable. Every toss of the dice exhilarated him too much. He raised his stake every time he didn't throw out.

In the end, it was a rather impressive eight throws before the fatal nine came. A little cheer went up as Lord Philip put back his head and groaned. He scooped up the markers and presented them to her. "Play another with me."

"You shouldn't," she tried to say, feeling a twinge of conscience, but he leaned closer and winked.

"One more? Be sporting."

She hesitated. Philip would probably remain here all night, from the looks of things. If she didn't win his money, someone else would. Perhaps after another round she could persuade him to try something less ruinous. "I'll play one more—but *only* one more . . ."

"She'll *win* one more, she means," said someone nearby, to laughter.

Lord Philip shot the fellow a peeved look as he collected the dice. "If I must lose, at least I'm losing to the most beautiful woman in London." He offered her the dice with an extravagant bow, ever the flirt.

Sophie also knew how to play to the crowd. This time she kissed the dice before she rolled them, and this time she nicked it—winning on the first roll, earning a huzzah from the crowd. She offered the dice to Philip. "Your cast, my lord."

His eyes were fixed on her in unblinking fascination, his lips slightly parted in awe. "Kiss them for me," he said, his voice dropping a register. "For luck."

From the corner of her eye, Sophie could see Giles Carter watching, expressionless. Drat. Philip was becoming a problem; she would have to start actively avoiding him. "Since you are in dire need of it . . ." She blew a kiss toward the dice. "*Bonne chance*, my lord."

"Stop this instant!"

Chapter 3

THE HARD, FLAT words cut through the air like a sword, startling Sophie so she nearly dropped the dice. Lord Philip released her as if burned, thrusting his hand behind his back. "Wait," he said, suddenly sounding young and nervous. "I can explain—"

"Stop, damn you," repeated the man who had interrupted, still hidden from her view by the crowd. He was furious. Good Lord, was there about to be a duel over the hazard table? Sophie sent a wary glance at Giles Carter; what should she do?

Mr. Carter stepped forward as the onlookers parted to allow the newcomer through. Comforted to have someone supporting her—Philip had retreated another step and wore a tense, uneasy expression—she stared with interest at the newcomer. Something about his face was familiar, and when Sophie glanced again at Lord Philip, she realized the two must be related.

Of course. Her shoulders relaxed. Philip had mentioned him. This was the duke, the dour elder brother who controlled Philip's allowance and scolded him for losing at the gambling tables. Philip had called him boring and dried-up, and said he spent all his days reading ledgers, and Sophie discovered she had unconsciously formed an image of the brother as far older and far less attractive.

She could not have been more wrong.

He was tall, golden-haired and austere in dark evening clothes. His face might have been carved by Michelangelo, so beautiful was it. Philip was of a similar height, but rangy; the duke's perfectly fitted evening clothes showed off broad shoulders, lean hips and well-shaped calves. If he were more than five years older than Philip, it would be a shock.

But there was no warmth at all in his blue-gray eyes as they flicked over her, a thorough but dismissive examination that made her feel very small and insignificant. He stopped in front of them, his attention on his brother. "Well?" he demanded, his voice low but hard.

Philip's jaw set but he smiled. "Fancy seeing you here. Have you come to play a round?"

The duke's eyes flickered toward Sophie again. "That was not my plan, no. Nor did I believe it to be yours."

She glanced from side to side beneath her lashes, but she was stuck. With the fascinated onlookers close behind her, Philip by her side and the duke in front of her, there was no easy avenue of escape.

"It was not." Philip's expression grew defiant.

"But I spied my dear friend Mrs. Campbell, and all my sense and intentions blew away like a puff of smoke. I was helpless to resist. Can you blame me?" He caught her hand and swept it to his lips.

Sophie flushed; how dare he blame her? "My lord," she murmured, tugging against his grip. "It grows late. We must finish our game another time." She put the dice on the table and bobbed a curtsy.

"Perhaps that would be best." Philip gave her a rueful smile, although with an air of intimacy she would have rather avoided, and released her. "Until another evening, my dear."

"Don't be ridiculous," said the duke. "That won't do at all."

"Oh?" Philip smirked. "Then you must excuse us, Ware—"

"I meant you shall not finish your game another time," snapped his brother. "Not with her, not with anyone. You're done, Philip. I've no more patience for these antics."

"Antics?" Sophie repeated in spite of her determination to stay out of it.

"I'm not a child, Your Grace," spat Philip at the same moment.

"If not, then you're a fool," replied the duke coolly. "A child may be reasonably expected to grow up and become a man of sense and dignity."

Philip flushed deep scarlet. "Ware," he said between clenched teeth. "Stop."

"*Stop*. The very thing I said to you, the very thing you promised to do," the duke said, every word as sharp as polished steel. "A month, you swore, away from the tables and the races. And yet here you are, the same night that vow was made. What is your explanation?"

"I only came to see Dashwood," muttered Philip. The crowd had withdrawn, but the room was quiet enough that people could hear their conversation. Giles Carter had slipped away and was nowhere to be seen.

"*I* came to see Dashwood," snapped the duke. "You came to wager away more money you don't have." He glanced at Sophie, this time with open disdain. "I see how firm your resolve is, if you're ready to be fleeced again by the first woman who smiles at you."

So Philip had promised to stop gambling and broken his word. Privately Sophie sympathized with the duke's anger; she'd already thought Philip shouldn't be at the tables, and if his brother had been even a tiny bit kinder about it, she would have added her own voice to his and urged Philip to moderate his behavior.

But she refused to be blamed and castigated as the cause of anyone's profligacy. "Let he among us who is without sin lob the first stone," she said lightly. "No doubt we all should contemplate our failings, but surely arguing them in public aids no one."

"Morality," the duke drawled. For the first time he gave her more than a glancing look, more contemplative than before. "How novel among your companions, Philip."

Philip's head had sunk on his shoulders, like a turtle's. His ears were red. "Enough, Ware," he muttered again. "*Please*, Jack."

Jack. What a carefree name for such a rigid man. Sophie began to feel rather sorry for Philip, being dressed down in front of his friends and companions. The duke's voice was not loud, but they had attracted notice. "Yes, *please*," she said to the duke in her most quelling tone. "This is hardly the time or place."

"Oh? There appeared to me to be no time to lose." Again his cool blue gaze slid over her. "No doubt you would have preferred I remain silent until you'd won a good sum from him."

She breathed deeply to avoid saying something she would regret. She should have put off Philip more forcefully when he interrupted her game with Giles Carter. "That is manifestly untrue. I've no interest in ruining anyone and am appalled you would imply it."

"Leave her out of this," said Philip. "My dear, perhaps you'd better go, so my noble brother and I can quarrel in private."

The duke's mouth curved darkly, and Sophie had a quicksilver thought that he'd be irresistible if he really smiled. "How much have you won from him?"

"That is absolutely none of your concern," she shot back in indignation. What did it matter how he smiled when he was such a coldhearted beast?

"It is when he pleads with me to pay his debts," the duke said. "Will you be the next creditor I must satisfy?"

Philip flushed purple with humiliation—and rage. He stepped forward, putting his hand on Sophie's shoulder. His fingers lingered, then slid gently down her back to her waist. She went rigid, which Philip seemed to take as encouragement; he stepped closer, between her and his brother. "Leave her be," he said again, his voice barely audible. "Mrs. Campbell and I are . . . friends." The delicate pause suggested more. "There is no harm intended between us."

"Don't be a fool." The duke hadn't taken his eyes off Sophie. "She's not your friend. She's not even your mistress, which might at least justify the expense. She merely wins your money."

Sophie's mouth dropped open in fury. "How *dare* you—"

"I can prove it." At long last, the duke looked away from her. He picked up the dice from the table where she'd dropped them. "You wish to play, madam? Then play with me." He put out his hand, and after a moment Philip sullenly gave him a number of markers. Without even looking at them, the duke dropped them all onto the hazard table.

She stared, doing quick mental arithmetic. Almost fifty guineas lay on the table, a princely sum. "You play very high, sir."

"One guinea a round, then," he said coolly. "Or are you afraid of losing the game when your opponent is not a callow young man?"

Lord Philip's head jerked up. He sent a look of scalding hostility at his brother, who ignored it. Sophie saw, though; as much as it had been intended to taunt her, it had been a public humiliation to him.

She knew only one way to deal with humiliation and scorn: by standing her ground. She had faced both many times, from certain snide young ladies at Mrs. Upton's who laughed at her lack of status, from the London matrons who sniffed at her independent ways. To slink away was weakness, and as the duke had insulted her very publicly, it would also tar her reputation. He'd implied she was a confidence artist, if not an outright cheat. Of course Sophie liked to win—she had to, to support herself—but she played fairly, lost her share of games, and was always gracious. And in this case, where she'd been trying to discourage Philip in her own tempered way, she felt the injustice of the duke's words like a slap in her face.

"Afraid?" She drew herself up in her haughtiest imitation of Mrs. Upton. "Of you?" She paused and gave him a pointed look. "Why on earth would you think that?"

A sharp, vindictive grin spread over Philip's face. A muscle twitched in the duke's cheek. "Then play."

She was mad to do this. Mad, and reckless, and probably stupid, but Sophie had done worse. If he wanted to play a few rounds of hazard, nothing would please her more than beating him at it.

Among the few things she remembered Philip telling her about his brother was that the duke didn't gamble—in fact, he disapproved of it strongly. That meant he would play like a rank amateur. The Duke of Ware had been rude and insulting, and she was not above retaliation. She felt a wholly unwarranted solidarity with Lord Philip, and a driving desire to trounce his insufferable brother.

She stepped back to the table, dropped a marker

for a single guinea, and raised the dice. "Seven." Her voice rang in the hush that had fallen around the table, but she barely noticed. The world had shrunk to the two of them. Gazing directly at her nemesis, she brushed a taunting, sensuous kiss over the face of the dice before tossing them onto the table.

Chapter 4

SOPHIE KNEW SHE ought to have walked away the moment the duke ordered his brother to stop playing. Hazard was a game of sheer luck, and clearly hers was ebbing tonight. Not only had Giles Carter disappeared, she was now the center of attention thanks to the duke.

If her luck was bad, though, his was atrocious. He lost and lost badly. After the first round, a tiny frown creased his forehead as he studied the table, making him look almost endearingly puzzled, as if the game's rules had changed on him. It gave her a moment of pause; how could she feel badly taking advantage of Philip, then revel in beating a man who had no experience at hazard?

Behind the duke's back, Philip sent her a gleeful look. She couldn't resist a tiny smile in reply, but the duke looked up at that moment and saw it. His jaw firmed. "A professional gamester, I take it."

Sophie flushed with fury. "Perhaps the personification of Lady Luck."

"Lady Luck," he repeated. "And like my brother

before me, you're against me." He picked up the dice again and held them out.

So be it. If he wished to lose, she was ready to win.

She raised the stakes. She began to flirt a bit with some of the spectators, and to ask the crowd, which had grown rather large and quivered with attentive interest around them now, what she should do. They always cried that she should bet more, so she did. Philip moved to her side and recovered his bonhomie, cheering her on every time she won. And consistently her luck was just a little better than the duke's.

It surprised her that he played on, even after she had won a shocking sum of money from him. Even the most bumbling player would have recognized that the dice were not on his side this evening and slunk away with his pockets lighter, though not emptied. Not the duke. And every time he forfeited another marker, something surged inside her.

Finally, though it felt abrupt, the duke put his hands palm down on the table and surveyed the damage. His golden hair had grown disheveled, falling in rumpled waves over his forehead, and he'd unbuttoned his jacket at some point. It made him look far more like his rakish younger brother. "Enough," he said.

She sent a dazzling smile in his direction. "As you wish, sir. And may I say, it has certainly been my pleasure." The crowd rumbled with laughter. A small mountain of markers sat on her side; she'd lost track of the total after it reached two hundred pounds. This was her best night in a year.

At her words, he looked up, visibly irked. His eyes glittered sea blue, and his mouth tightened. "One more round."

She laughed in disbelief. "Such a gambler!" Beside her, Philip snorted with laughter. Philip was enjoying this immensely. Sophie rested her hand on the table to lean closer to him and lowered her voice. "Surely you've lost enough for one night."

The duke's gaze swung toward her, slowly climbing from her hands to her face. Too late she realized her comment, well meant advice to someone on a bad losing streak, had struck him as condescension. "No more paltry stakes."

Her moment of regret ended. Paltry! No wonder Philip despised him. "Let that be a lesson, Philip," she said lightly, without taking her eyes from the duke. "A hundred guineas is a paltry sum."

Philip chuckled. The duke stared at her. A tiny muscle twitched in his jaw, giving the impression of barely leashed emotion. "I stake five thousand pounds." Sophie's mouth dropped open and the crowd buzzed with shock—and delight. Clearly Vega's did not see recklessness on this scale every night. "One round each, played until loss, winner take all. If we both throw out, it's a draw."

Unconsciously her gaze veered back to her prize money. She'd have to wager it all, on one round. If she won, it would be by far the smallest part of her profit tonight. It would also put her almost at her goal of ten thousand pounds saved. Independence would be within her grasp in this one round . . .

But the first rule of gambling was: easily won, easily lost. The duke's luck had been abominable, but that didn't mean her odds had improved. "Not tonight, sir," she said, with more than a tinge of regret. Better to keep the few hundred pounds she'd already won.

"You mistake me. You don't have to risk a farthing." She made the mistake of looking at him again. Indifferent to the onlookers whispering around them, he rose to his full height and folded his arms. It made his shoulders look very broad and his arms very strong, and there was a focus in his face as he watched her that made Sophie's heart patter erratically. She wanted to look away from his sea-blue gaze but couldn't. "One week of your company is what I want."

IF JACK HAD SEEN any other man act the way he'd behaved tonight, he would have suspected the fellow was barking, howling mad.

Since he *was* that fellow, he knew beyond all doubt that he had indeed lost his mind.

He had ignored his own good judgment and caused a scene—and not just any scene, piously preventing Philip from running headlong into ruin, but a scene that would enthrall every gossip in London, no matter what pledges Dashwood exacted from his patrons. Worst of all, he was breaking his own vow to avoid gambling—at *hazard*, the game designed to beggar a man as speedily as possible.

But there was something about this woman that provoked and entranced him beyond all reason. Her hair had come loose as they played, and one curl hung down at her nape, tangling in that extra length of black ribbon. Every time she leaned over the table to collect the dice—or her winnings—his eyes were drawn to that curl, teasing and tempting him to catch it, to bury his face in the mass of her chestnut hair, to inhale her scent. He could almost feel the ripe curves of her body against his. When she smiled after a good roll, he didn't think of the money he'd just lost but of what her ripe pink mouth would taste like.

Utter madness.

He hadn't been affected by a woman like this in years, and was shocked by how powerful it was. Helplessly he gazed at her, fully aware that she was flirting with every scoundrel pressed up against the hazard table trying to peer down her vivid red bodice. She filled it out spectacularly, he couldn't help but notice. No wonder Philip had broken his vow of moral rectitude for her. Jack hadn't missed the fascination in his brother's face as he watched her, and on no account was he going to allow her to make a fool of Philip. He had stepped forward to save his brother from a mercenary temptress, nothing more.

But the moment her gaze connected with his, every thought of Philip vanished from his brain.

Consequently, he went a little mad, taunting her into gambling with him, playing recklessly even when it grew abundantly clear he had no idea what he was doing. He'd thought Philip looked like a fool, but then he'd proven himself one, in front of every avid gambler in town.

A murmur went through the crowd when he made the last outrageous wager. Philip, who had been openly enjoying his humiliation to this point, lurched forward. "What the devil are you doing?"

Jack barely glanced at his brother. "Wagering."

"You can't wager that!"

"No?" He turned to look at Mrs. Campbell. How reckless was she? She was staring at him, eyes wide, her rosy lips parted. The wise move here would be for her to collect her winnings and walk out the door.

"Five thousand pounds," she said, her voice so soft he barely heard it. Her eyes flickered toward Philip, almost in apology. "Against one week of my company."

She was considering it. His heart jolted in his chest. He would probably lose, the way his luck was running, but . . . she was considering it.

With a quick motion she put back her shoulders and stepped to the table. "Done."

The crowd hissed in stunned surprise. Philip froze, his expression terrible. Jack barely registered any of it; triumph shot through him, hot and thrilling. Mrs. Campbell tipped up her face to stare defiantly into his eyes, and he knew, in some deep primitive part of his soul, that he was going to win.

And damn it all if his pulse didn't surge at the thought.

"A moment, Your Grace," murmured someone beside him. Dashwood, the club owner, had sidled through the crowd. "That's a rather substantial wager."

Slowly Jack turned. "Do you think I cannot cover it?"

A nervous titter ran through the crowd. Everyone knew he could cover five times that amount.

"That wasn't my concern," said Dashwood,

unperturbed. "You're not a member and I cannot guarantee anything . . . on either side."

Jack raised his head and gave him a glacial look. "Are you interfering?"

Finally the club owner paused. It probably went against the grain for the owner of a gambling hell to prohibit any sort of wager. "Not if the lady is certain she wishes to proceed." He cocked his head expectantly. "Are you, Mrs. Campbell?"

It was utterly silent. Jack watched the pulse throb at the base of her throat; he studied the color that rose in her cheeks. She was as rosy and delicious as fresh strawberries. He should hope the owner's question gave her time to reconsider and refuse. He was insane to do this. She had bewitched Philip, and seemed in a fair way of doing the same to him.

But he mentally growled in triumph when she put up her chin and said, clearly and boldly, "Quite certain, Mr. Dashwood."

The club owner bowed his head and stepped aside. Jack picked up the dice and offered them to Mrs. Campbell. Her fingertips brushed his palm as she took them, and her gaze jumped to clash with his. Something leaped inside him, and he waved one hand at the table, inviting her to play first.

"Seven," she called, flinging the dice. An eight. She made a face of exaggerated regret and swept up the dice for her next roll. A nine. Grimly, she rolled once more.

Eleven.

Her eyelashes fluttered, but she didn't say anything. Jack reached for the dice. For the first time all evening, they felt light and easy in his hand. He let them rest there a moment, weighing them. He couldn't lose now; if he threw out, it would be a draw and they would both walk away. But if he won . . .

"Six," he said quietly, and flicked his wrist. The dice bounced around before settling into place.

A pair of threes.

Her chest heaved as she stared at them. It was practically the only good roll he'd made all night. The onlookers burst into a seething rumble of whispers and exclamations. Jack turned to his brother, who was staring white-faced at the table. "You're done here. I won't cover another debt from this or any other gaming club."

"Right. Very well." Philip seemed to have difficulty breathing. "I'll agree to that. I deserve that. But don't do this—not her—"

Jack looked at Mrs. Campbell. She still stood as if frozen at the table. Everyone had withdrawn a step, leaving her alone in the center of a small circle. She was staring at the dice, her eyelashes dark against her pale cheeks.

Reluctantly his conscience stirred. His quarrel wasn't with her. He could speak to her privately, in Dashwood's office, and explain why he'd made that wager. He was only trying to save his brother from ruin. Well—his gaze dipped to her bosom for a moment—not entirely, of course, but it was an unimpeachable motive and had the benefit of being true. He would release her from the wager on the condition she swear not to gamble with Philip again. That was his primary purpose— his only purpose, damn it, even though he had to work to keep his eyes off her—separating her and every other sharper from his brother.

Philip pushed past him and took Mrs. Campbell's hand. "Don't worry, my dear," he said to her. "It was a coerced wager. You aren't required to fulfill it." He shot a venomous glare at Jack.

She started as if from a trance. "What?"

"Of course you aren't!" Philip exclaimed. He lowered his voice, but Jack still heard. "He did it to punish me, because of our friendship. He cannot hold you to it—nor will I allow him to, Sophie." Philip clasped her hand in both of his and brought it to his lips while Mrs. Campbell raised her eyes to Jack's.

There was no fear or horror in them—she was furious. And she was letting Philip hold her hand for far too long.

His conscience fell mute. "On the contrary." He tilted his head, and Dashwood, lingering nearby but pointedly looking away, sighed.

"Mrs. Campbell, you lost a wager freely agreed to. It must be paid."

Her bosom rose and fell. Her eyes glittered. "Yes. Of course. I see that. If His Grace will call upon me tomorrow, I'm sure we can—"

"Mr. Dashwood," Jack said, "collect Mrs. Campbell's winnings and credit them to her account." He took her arm and tugged her away from Philip. She hung back and he put an arm around her waist, deliberately holding her to him. It was meant for Philip, but again his heart seemed to stumble over itself at the warmth of her body against his. He started for the door, taking her with him.

"Stop," she gasped. "Wait a moment . . ."

"You wagered and you lost. Everyone at Vega's pays their debts, my dear."

"Yes, but I cannot go with you *now*—"

"You can." There was an outburst behind him—Philip arguing with Dashwood, who was refusing to intervene. Jack felt a dark satisfaction that perhaps now, at last, Philip would believe he meant what he said.

"Tomorrow," Mrs. Campbell protested, but he squeezed her and she stopped speaking.

"What is different about tomorrow? You're trying to think of a way out of it, or stalling for time until Philip can." He looked down at her as a servant went flying for her cloak. "Don't be afraid," he added in cool amusement as he took in her pale, angry face. "I have no designs on you." He lowered his head until his lips brushed the hair at her temple. She smelled of oranges. "Can you say the same of my brother?"

Her face flushed as scarlet as her gown. Jack caught a glimpse down the front of her bodice and felt an answering flush of heat in his own body. *Forget Philip*, he wanted to say. *Let me seduce you instead.* Which was the clearest sign yet that he'd lost his mind.

The servant ran up with Jack's things and her cloak. The instant she took it, he swept her out the door and down the steps. It had begun raining, and Mrs. Campbell huddled against him, throwing her cloak up to shield herself. Philip shouted after them, but Jack ignored it. This was for his brother's own good, and he was not in the mood for any more confrontation tonight.

The Ware coach was waiting where he'd left it, even though he'd been inside much longer than expected. A footman threw open the door, his expression impassive as Jack bundled his companion inside. She scrambled onto the far seat as he shrugged into his greatcoat and gave a few short instructions to his servants.

Philip burst out of the club, hatless and furious. "Don't you dare do this," he spat, standing with his feet apart and his hands in fists. "I will never forgive you!"

Jack gave him a long, ducal stare, the one he'd learned from his father. "If you'd kept your word, it would not have been necessary. Until next week, dear brother." He touched the brim of his hat in mocking salute and stepped into the carriage.

Chapter 5

SOPHIE LANDED ON the plush velvet seat and tried to gather her scrambled wits.

She'd done it now. In the space of a few short hours, she had risked—and perhaps lost—everything she'd worked so hard to achieve. Bitterly she remembered Mrs. Upton's words from long ago: *gambling is the path to ruin*. Tonight she had flagrantly violated every lesson she'd ever learned, and see where it had got her.

The duke stepped into the carriage and took the seat opposite her. The light gleamed on his golden hair for a moment, and then the footman shut the door, closing her in with the duke.

She wished she'd listened better when Philip spoke of his brother. She wished she'd heeded her own instincts to discourage Philip sooner. If she'd only refused him, she could still be playing whist with Mr. Carter, happily and quietly winning another hundred pounds or so for her savings. The duke had tempted her into lunacy with that enormous wager—five thousand pounds!—and it had been her undoing.

But if he thought he had bought her body and soul for a week, the Duke of Ware was going to be sorely disappointed.

"You're completely mad!" Best to start on the attack.

"Mad?" He gave a sharp huff of laughter. "I don't doubt it."

She gripped her cloak with both hands to keep from slapping him. "This is very nearly kidnapping, you know. I lost the wager, but that does not give you the right to haul me out of Vega's like a constable seizing a wanted criminal!"

"What you were doing to my brother ought to be criminal," he returned.

Sophie's mouth dropped open. "Criminal! It's perfectly legal to gamble in London, thank you very much, and your brother went there of his own will—to *gamble*. Why not turn on Mr. Dashwood, for allowing him entry?"

"Philip gave his word just this morning to cease all wagering for one month." The duke's voice was icy cold. "Yet there he was, unable to resist playing hazard because you were there."

She wanted to throw something very heavy at him. "I was engaged in a respectable game of whist with other gentlemen when he arrived. If anything, he disrupted *my* evening, threatening to cause a scene if I did not play with him. And I suggested hazard because I thought it would end quickly."

"With his money in your purse."

"Only because he plays badly," she shot back, incensed. "But I see that is a common family characteristic, for the most part."

He inhaled audibly. She braced herself, but when he spoke, it was in the same even, implacable tone as before. "Yes, there has been an abundance of poor judgment this evening."

Hope made her sit up a little straighter. "It's not too late, you know. Drive me home, and I give you my word I shall never sit across from Lord Philip again at any table, not for gambling, not for dinner, not for bloody tea. In fact, if you supply a list of other friends or family members you wish to preserve from my offensive presence, I shall commit it to memory and avoid all of them."

"That isn't necessary." In the dim light she could barely make out his face, turned away from her to gaze out the window beside him. "Only Philip."

"Done!" she exclaimed. She never wanted to speak to Philip again after this. "Now take me home—"

"No."

She was sure she'd misheard. "What? Why not?"

"You wagered and lost. Members of Vega's pay their debts, do they not?"

The blood drained from her face. For the first time she felt a shiver of fear. She pulled her cloak in front of her protectively, even though it would be no defense. She was at his mercy, alone with him in his carriage, heading heaven knew where, with no one to help her. "You mean to destroy me," she said numbly, and suddenly hoping that was the worst that would happen to her.

He made a scornful noise. "Not at all."

"But you will—you made a public spectacle of me this evening, dragging me out of the club after claiming you wanted only *my company* for a week," she said, a distressing tremor in her voice. Even if he didn't touch her, enough people had seen them leave together that there would be talk. She would be known as the woman who wagered her own body, and her already thin respectability would go up in smoke.

"Yes," he said. "To prevent you from beggaring my brother."

"I played one round with him," she cried. "*One.* I tried to bow out after that, but he insisted on another. If you have such a care for his purse, you should keep him away from Vega's in the first place."

"Would that I could."

Sophie threw up her hands in mock astonishment. "What? You are powerless to influence the actions of your own brother, but you feel no compunction in overruling my will? Why is that?"

"If you didn't like the terms, you should not have taken the wager," he replied. "Why did you, madam? Too tempted by the lure of easy money? Winning from Philip wasn't enough for you?"

Yes. There was no escaping it: his wager had been too much for her to resist. Sophie turned to glare out the window. She ought to have excused herself the moment the duke approached Philip, and even worse, she'd known it at the time. Some perverse little devil in her had kept her there, and then let her get drawn into the argument. Was it her place to intervene on Philip's behalf? No. Philip was a grown man, older than she was, and if he couldn't keep his word to his own brother, that was his fault—and he ought to bear the consequences. Was it her place to taunt the duke? No. Was it wise to respond to his taunting invitation to play? Very definitely not.

She simply had to persuade him it was in his interest to take her home. "My maid will summon the constables when I don't return."

"My footman is no doubt knocking on your door as we speak, informing her that you have been urgently called away and won't be home for a week."

"What—what—" She couldn't speak, she was so angry. "How *dare* you!"

"How dare I not want her to worry that her mistress was set upon by footpads or murdered in the street?" he asked.

"How dare you tell her lies—"

"Lies?" He leaned forward, and light from a lamp on the street outside illuminated his face for a moment. He was as beautiful as Lucifer. "Would you have preferred I tell her the truth?"

No, curse him. Colleen was a good maid, but if she knew Sophie had lost a scandalous wager and been swept away by the Duke of Ware for a week of unknown activities, there was a strong chance she'd tell someone. Even just Cook, whose tongue was looser yet.

The duke sat back. "Tell her whatever story you wish when you return home."

"If we went there now, I could explain to her—" she began, but the duke cut her off.

"No."

Sophie breathed through her nose for a moment, straining to keep her temper. Mr. Dashwood had stood by, as had an entire club of people, and allowed the duke to carry her off like his captive. She needed to be seen in London or even Vega's gossip-averse patrons would begin to talk. She could try to jump from the carriage, but with the turn her luck had taken tonight, she'd break her leg. She pressed her face to the window, considering it anyway. They were moving at a good clip past Hyde Park, a vast dark expanse in the night.

"Where are we going?" she asked, frowning at the rain.

"Alwyn House."

"Where?"

"A country home of mine," he said, as if he had more homes than he could keep count of. "In Chiswick."

Good God. That wasn't even in London. Anything past Kensington was decidedly out of town. She would be marooned there, with no chance of being able to sneak out and walk home. "That's practically abduction!"

"Don't be ridiculous." For the first time he sounded almost amused. "It's barely six miles away."

"Why so far? I've already given my word not to see Philip again—"

"But Philip has not given his word not to see you," he said, his voice hard again. "Not that I could trust it if he had."

"Why am *I* to be punished for that?"

His laugh was bitter. "I assure you, I shall be punished by it far more than you."

She glared balefully in his direction. It was much too dark to see his face again, but an occasional flicker of light would pick out the white of his cravat or the gleam of gold in his hair. Not that she needed to see him to remember his face. How appalling that she'd thought him beautiful. "How typical of a man. You cause the problem and then feel yourself the maligned party. If you do feel punished, I can only say it is richly deserved." She yanked her cloak closer around herself and resolutely turned her shoulder to him.

JACK DIDN'T BOTHER ARGUING. He happened to agree with her.

What devil had possessed him to make that bloody wager?

Jealousy, whispered his conscience. Jealousy over the way Philip held her hand and the way she looked at Philip, flirtatious and trusting and familiar. The way their heads had bowed together, warm and intimate. It was the way Portia had once looked at him before she eloped with another man.

He closed his eyes and let out his breath, irked with himself even for thinking of her. Portia Villiers was many years in his past. She'd taught him a hard—but necessary—lesson about women. Tonight he'd had another difficult lesson, and he could only hope he came out of this one better than before. And to do that, he'd better figure out what to do with Mrs. Campbell.

The drive to Alwyn House normally took little more than an hour. It was ideal for brief escapes from London, as he could come and go with very little preparation. In the summer he went almost weekly. The road as far as Turnham Green was well maintained and macadamized, but when they reached the turn south toward Alwyn, the pace slowed dramatically. Too late Jack realized it must have been raining harder here; the country roads that covered the remaining distance to the house were in far worse shape.

The carriage lurched violently to one side. Mrs. Campbell gave a startled exclamation as she was thrown across the seat. Jack caught her before she could fall to the floor, but a second lurch flung them both against the side of the vehicle.

"And I wondered what else could go wrong tonight," she said breathlessly, struggling amid the folds of her cloak, which had tangled around her.

Jack inhaled deeply of orange water and some scent that had to be her. She had fallen across his lap, and in her scrambling to right herself, her hand landed on his thigh. Rather intimately close to his groin. His blood surged as she wriggled some more, clearly unaware of the position of her hand. "Mrs. Campbell," he managed to say, squeezing his arms around her to prevent that hand from sliding. "Wait a moment." The carriage was still tilted to the side, and she was trying to climb uphill.

"Help me!" she retorted, and obligingly Jack opened his arms and gave her a small push. She landed on the opposite seat with a thump as the carriage swayed back to upright.

"It's only the rain." He flexed his hand under cover of his greatcoat. His palm still sizzled with the knowledge of the curve of her waist.

She sniffed in reply.

Slower than a walk, the coach moved forward in fits and jerks, pitching from one side to the

other and then back again. Jack braced his feet
against the opposite seat and gripped the strap.
At least it was barely a mile from the main road
to the house. Once they made it to the house, he
would hand her over to the housekeeper, and go
dunk his head in cold water until he regained his
sense.

No sooner had he thought that than they
stopped again. The carriage swayed, rocking
back and forth, before settling at a drunken tilt.
Jack's bad feeling about the road grew worse.

The door opened, letting in a spray of rain.
"Your Grace, the carriage is immovably stuck."

God, he reflected, had not waited long to inflict
penance. "What can be done?"

The sodden footman hesitated. "We're less
than a mile from Alwyn House. Jeffers will ride
on and fetch help, but the road's very bad ahead.
Any other conveyance may well suffer the same
fate as this one."

He could not possibly spend the night trapped
in this coach with Mrs. Campbell. Jack leaned forward to peer out the carriage door. His footman's
boots were sunk in mud to the ankles. He girded
himself for a soaking wet ride in the rain. "Send
Jeffers for horses. Don't waste time attempting to
bring a carriage. We shall have to ride."

There was a rustle of movement from Mrs.
Campbell. "Good heavens, is there no other house
nearby?" she asked in dismay.

"No," he said shortly.

"No inn?"

"Not on this road."

"God save us from your idiocy," she muttered,

just loudly enough for him to hear. "This is a very poor kidnapping, Your Grace."

"It is not a kidnapping," he snapped. "You wish to leave?" He shoved the door fully open, forcing the footman to jump backward. "By all means, madam, you are free to go."

"Very well, I will." She pulled up the hood of her cloak and slid toward the door. "Where is the nearest house?" she asked the footman.

The fellow gaped. "Alwyn House, madam. Our destination. Less than a mile ahead." He pointed into the darkness.

Mrs. Campbell threw an irate glance at Jack, who just raised one brow. It wasn't his fault the carriage was stuck. "What about behind us?"

"I couldn't say, ma'am."

She sighed. "Alwyn it will have to be, then. Pardon me." She poked at Jack's knee, which was blocking the door.

"You can't really mean to walk," he said in disbelief.

"If the alternative is sitting here with you for hours, yes," she replied. "It's not that cold, and I shan't dissolve in the rain."

"And the mud?" He swept one hand toward the open door.

She lifted her skirts and surveyed her feet, clad in thin leather shoes. "It will ruin everything I'm wearing. I fully intend to send you a bill for the loss."

"You've no idea where you're going."

She put her head to one side and gave an odd little smile. "That's never stopped me before." Jack stared, and this time she pushed his knee. On instinct he moved, and without another word she was out the door, helped by the startled footman.

For a moment he concentrated on breathing deeply. He should have never left Ware House in London. It would have been better to let Philip beggar himself, to her benefit or to anyone else's. He should have turned and walked out of the club the moment he saw her face and felt a bolt of desire shoot through him. That had been his warning sign, and because he'd ignored it, he was going to have to trudge almost a mile in the rain and mud.

More penance, no doubt.

Grimly he turned up the collar of his great-coat and climbed out of the coach. The rain beat down on his shoulders, stinging and sharp but not cold—as Mrs. Campbell had said. Jack eyed her with disapproval. She had made her way to the front of the coach and was speaking with the driver, one hand clutching her hood beneath her chin. The driver pointed down the road, toward Alwyn, and she gave a decisive nod. A gust of wind caught her cloak and blew it open, exposing the bright blazing red of her gown—a gown soon to be utterly ruined by the weather. Jack waded forward, wincing with each pull of the mud on his feet.

"Unharness the horses," he told the driver, raising his voice over the rain. "Get them and yourselves to Alwyn House. Fetch the coach in the morning." There was no point waiting; the horses were broken to a postilion rider, but it would be madness to try to ride them now, in a storm with no saddles or proper bridles. They stood placidly enough at the moment, but Jack knew better than to risk it. The driver and footman would have to lead them.

"Yes, Your Grace." The man ducked his head and motioned to the footman to come help.

Jack turned to Mrs. Campbell. "If you're mad enough to walk, I shall have to walk, too."

She looked distinctly unimpressed. "Please don't feel obliged."

"You have no idea where the house is, nor is the housekeeper expecting you." He finished doing the buttons on his coat and pulled his hat lower on his forehead. This would be a miserable walk for him; Mrs. Campbell, in her gown and slippers, was going to be wretched. Of course, she had chosen to do it against his advice. "Shall we?"

They started off, heads bowed against the rain. It must have been raining here longer than in London. The road was a swamp of mud, and every apparent bit of solid footing turned out to be a puddle, lurking like a Charybdis in wait for a careless step. Jack forged into the lead, both to show the way and to block the wind. It also kept her out of his view, which made the rain in his face worthwhile. *Penance*, he told himself as water found a way down the back of his collar. He deserved this for being such an idiot tonight, and he began to feel guilty that he'd dragged Mrs. Campbell into it.

But the woman with him never complained. She didn't speak as they trudged down the road, and every time he stole a glance backward, her gaze was focused downward, minding her steps. Her cloak hung in sodden folds; it was a pretty evening cloak, not a thick one. It couldn't offer much protection, but on the other hand it wouldn't be as heavy when wet.

The rain pounded down without pause. He concentrated on not losing his balance and falling flat on his face in the mud, a humiliation he was determined to avoid.

At long last the wrought-iron gates appeared. He turned in, trusting Mrs. Campbell had enough self-preservation to follow, and heaved a sigh of relief when he stepped onto the gravel drive. It was spotted with puddles but far firmer than the muddy road. The rain still beat steadily on his head and shoulders, but the imminent prospect of a hot bath and a glass of brandy cheered him immensely. His steps quickened.

A tug at his elbow made him look down. Mrs. Campbell gripped his coat sleeve, her wide-eyed gaze fixed on the house ahead of them. "That is your house?"

Jack nodded once. "Blessedly, it is."

She blinked several times. Raindrops clung to her long eyelashes and ran down the curve of her cheek. Her cloak gaped open at her throat, and his eyes skimmed down the expanse of pale wet skin. She was soaked. So was he, but suddenly Jack didn't feel it at all. Suddenly it wasn't his own bath that transfixed his mind, but hers—her, in the bath, her hair curling in the steam and her skin flushed pink everywhere . . .

God almighty. He tore his eyes from her and looked at Alwyn. It was a little jewel of a house, built by his great-grandfather in the style of a French château, though on a far smaller scale. As always, his mood improved merely at the prospect of a few days here. "Have you some objection to it?"

She blinked again and released his sleeve. "None at all, if it is warm and dry."

"Good." Without waiting for her, he strode on.

It took a few minutes of pounding on the door to raise a response. Jack hammered the knocker, aware of his companion standing dripping wet behind him.

"Is anyone here?" Mrs. Campbell finally asked.

"Yes. Always." Jack thumped on the door again. "But we're not expected."

"I gathered," she said sourly. "A spur-of-the-moment kidnapping."

"Stop saying that." He glanced at her, irked. "You wanted a bit of adventure and you got some."

"I didn't want it with you," she shot back.

"Let that be a lesson to you, then. Don't make wagers you don't wish to honor." His ears caught the scrape of the bolt, and he stepped back as the door opened.

The butler stared disdainfully at them through the narrow opening. "Who is there?"

"Ware." Jack removed his hat, ignoring the rain. "Open the door, Wilson."

The butler's eyes nearly popped from his head. He threw the door open wide and bowed deeply. "I beg your pardon, Your Grace. We received no notice of your visit—"

"I know." Jack brushed past him. The house, per his instructions, was kept almost at full readiness. Alwyn was his retreat from London, where he could slip away from the relentless pressures of the dukedom for a few days. It wasn't a total escape, as most of the work followed him, but here it was quiet and peaceful. His mother hated the house, it being too far from the society of London, and Philip found it old-fashioned, so he always had it to himself.

Except tonight, obviously. In the middle of unbuttoning his coat, he glanced back to see Mrs. Campbell hesitating on the doorstep. "Come in," he told her. "Unless you've taken a liking to the rain."

Her eyes narrowed and her lush mouth twitched in irritation, but she came inside, allowing Wilson to shut the door behind her.

Jack turned at the patter of footsteps. The housekeeper was all but running down the stairs. "Your Grace," she said breathlessly, making a hasty curtsy. "We didn't expect you—"

"I know, Mrs. Gibbon," he assured her. "It was a decision made on the spur of the moment." He avoided Mrs. Campbell's gaze as he repeated her words, and shed his greatcoat into Wilson's waiting hands. "This is Mrs. Campbell. Draw a hot bath and prepare a room for her. Are you hungry?" He swung around to address his guest.

She looked dazed. There were still raindrops clinging to her eyelashes. "Er—No. Tea would be lovely, though . . ."

"Very good. Mrs. Gibbon, I leave her to your capable care." Jack headed through the door for the stairs. His boots squelched at every step, and he was fiendishly anxious to pry them off.

"Sir!" He stopped at Mrs. Campbell's cry. One foot already on the stairs, he looked back.

She had removed her cloak. As expected, her scarlet gown was drenched and clung to her body from her shoulders to her knees. The outlines of her stays were visible beneath the wet gown, and Jack imagined he could see her nipples, hard and erect. He imagined unlacing that dress and peeling it down, tasting every dewy wet inch of her skin. He imagined drawing her down with him into the large copper tub that was surely being set up even now in his dressing room, and his breath shuddered.

God help him. He was worse than Philip.

"Yes?" he said curtly, fighting the reaction of his body to the unwanted images running through his brain.

"What . . . ?" She made a helpless motion with one hand. "What am I to do?"

Strip off that wet dress. Let down your hair. Smile at me the way you did at Philip.

"Get warm and dry," he said. "After that . . . we shall talk." *And nothing else, by God.* He turned and went up the stairs.

Chapter 6

Sophie barely restrained herself from saying something very rude to the duke's retreating back. He was insufferable.

The housekeeper was waiting, trying to conceal her rabid curiosity. The butler took her sopping wet cloak and quietly slipped away. She gathered herself. "Good evening," she said to the housekeeper. "Mrs. Gibbon, is it?"

"Yes, madam."

Sophie plucked at her wet skirt. The bright crimson cotton had been one of her favorites, and now it was surely ruined, spattered with mud up to her knees. "The carriage got stuck on the road, nigh on a mile away. I imagine it's been raining all day?"

"Since yesterday, madam." Mrs. Gibbon hesitated, then asked incredulously, "Did you walk a mile?"

"Oh yes," Sophie said. "There was no choice. It was rather hard going at times, I must say."

The woman's face softened. "With His Grace you were perfectly safe, although it must have been miserable! This way, madam. We'll get you warm and dry." She led the way up the stairs.

"I'm so sorry for the extra work it must put you to," Sophie said as they climbed the broad stairs of polished wood. She tried not to think of the wet footprints she was leaving on them for some hapless servant to wipe clean.

"Have no worry on that score," the woman assured her. "His Grace always leaves proper orders for the house."

Sophie took another look around her. Everyone kept calling it a house, as if it compared to the narrow brick home she had in Alfred Street. This looked far more like a mansion to her, even more so inside than out. The walls were robin's-egg blue, and parquet floors gleamed in the glow of the housekeeper's lamp. She glanced up and gasped quietly at the high arched ceiling that shone with gold leaf even in the low light.

At the top of the stairs Mrs. Gibbon led her down a corridor into a room that looked sumptuous in the shadows. "I beg your pardon that it's not been prepared, but the maid will be in directly." She pulled the bell rope, then hurried through the room and opened another door, revealing a cozy dressing room, tiled before the fireplace. A large copper tub sat at the back. "It will take a good while to draw a hot bath, but you've got to get out of those wet clothes." She sized up Sophie, who was beginning to shiver in the cool room. "After that . . . well, we'll see what we can do."

By the time Sophie had shed her sodden dress and undergarments and was wrapped in a number of blankets, two other servants had arrived, one of them bearing a cup of tea. Sophie sipped and watched as they started the fire already laid in the hearth, arranged the copper tub and conferred with Mrs. Gibbon in low voices. Someone took her clothing, promising to make an effort to save it.

When the tub was filled with steaming water, she sank into it gratefully. At home she had only her maid, Colleen, and a cook who came in every other day. It was lovely to have a throng of people look after her, although she still felt the duke owed her that much at least, after upending her evening so arrogantly.

The duke. She slid down until the water covered her to the chin, with only her knees sticking out. What was she to make of the duke?

Philip claimed he'd gone to the club to see Mr. Dashwood, and he'd startled like a guilty boy when his brother appeared. Mr. Dashwood had said the duke was not a member, and the duke himself had told Philip he wouldn't pay any *more* gambling debts. Therefore the duke must have been at Vega's to settle Philip's debt. Sophie could understand the duke's anger, if things were as he said.

But why the devil had he turned on her? She certainly hadn't held the debt from Philip, although heaven knew it wouldn't have been difficult. For all she—or the duke—knew, Philip was still at Vega's, wagering madly since he knew his brother was nowhere nearby to stop him.

And now she was stuck here, far from London, with a man she did not know or like. Rain still pattered against the windows, and it would take at least a day of dry weather for the roads to become passable. Sophie had spent the carriage ride thinking rude thoughts about the duke, which was terribly cathartic, but now it was time to address the more practical question of how she should handle him. If only Philip had told her more about him. If only she had been curious to know more.

She swirled her fingers through the water. He was younger than expected, surely not more than thirty-five, which meant he had inherited when he was a young man. What might that do to a person? She wondered how different his upbringing had been from Philip's; they appeared nothing alike, based on her limited observation.

In the end she decided it was a mistake to assume too much either way. She ought to focus on their area of agreement, which was that she would not gamble with Philip anymore, ever. If she proved herself understanding, discreet, and trustworthy, he would be far more likely to send her back to town in the morning.

And it was vital that she return to London as soon as possible. Despite Mr. Dashwood's rule against gossip, this story would leak out. Sophie was well aware of what would happen when it did. If there were rumors that she had made a scandalous wager to spend a week with the Duke of Ware, bolstered by whispers that he swept her away from Vega's that very night, and then she wasn't seen anywhere in London for a week, she would lose her last shred of respectability. Everyone would think her the duke's mistress, and that would destroy any chance she had of finding a decent husband. Sophie refused to let that man ruin her life so carelessly.

Her mind made up, she got out of the tub. Mrs. Gibbon had left plenty of warm towels for her, and she went into the other room—now brightly lit and warmed by a roaring fire in the hearth—feeling revitalized.

Her determination took a blow, however, when the housekeeper said she had been unable to locate any suitable clothing. The only females in the house were two maids, the cook and Mrs. Gibbon herself, none of whom were close to Sophie's size. "We're searching for something suitable," the housekeeper promised, "but I've located something for tonight." She laid a beautiful blue velvet banyan on the bed.

Sophie stared at that dressing gown. "Whose is this?" But she knew.

"His Grace's," said Mrs. Gibbon. "His man gave it to me when I asked what to do for you. By morning, I vow, I'll have proper clothing."

She touched the plush fabric. It was lined with purple silk, so decadent she almost sighed with pleasure just from touching it.

"I beg your pardon, ma'am," added the housekeeper. "I'll fetch one of my own nightgowns for you. It's the best I can do."

She started out of her reverie. "Thank you," she said fervently. "It's very kind of you."

The woman inclined her head in acknowledgment. "His Grace bid me tell you that he will see you in the library, if you wish to speak to him."

She certainly had plenty to say to the duke. It wasn't ideal to face him down wearing his dressing gown, but he was responsible for that circumstance. She stroked the velvet again. "Thank you, Mrs. Gibbon. I will."

JACK FELT GREATLY RESTORED to sense once he was warm and dry again.

He sent Michaels, the footman who attended him in the absence of his valet, to inform Mrs. Gibbon that he would be in the library, if his guest wished to speak to him, and then he sprawled in one of the comfortable leather chairs by the fire. Michaels brought a glass of brandy and left him to his thoughts.

It was much easier to sort those thoughts out now that Sophie Campbell wasn't in the room.

First, and most important, he had done what needed to be done. Philip needed a shock to his system. It hadn't been the most deft or diplomatic maneuver, Jack admitted, but one could never let that prevent seizing an opportunity when it arose.

He rotated his glass and studied the firelight on the amber brandy. The key element of any strategy was always to know what someone else wanted. Philip had demonstrated that what he wanted, even more than the thrill of gambling, was Mrs. Campbell. The way he'd touched her and comforted her made that plain. Short of following him like a nursemaid, it would be impossible to keep Philip from wagering everywhere, which made this the only option with any significance. Jack didn't fool himself it would cure his brother entirely of his bad habits, but it would make a strong impression on him.

As for Mrs. Campbell herself . . . What business did a young and attractive woman have gambling every night at Vega's? There were two likely answers, neither of them flattering. The first was that she was there for the same reason Philip and his mates were, to fritter away a fortune, either her own or someone else's, in pursuit of idle entertainment. Jack felt no regret about his actions whatsoever if this were her motive. He didn't care if she were the richest heiress in Britain; gambling was reckless and wasteful.

The second possibility was that she was looking for something other than the thrill of winning. It hadn't escaped his notice that while women might be admitted to Vega's, not many there were as beautiful or as vivacious as she. Every man in the club had noticed her, in her scarlet dress with that lone tormenting loose curl of dark hair. She could be playing for higher stakes than money. If her intent was to attract Philip as her wealthy lover, Jack would put an emphatic end to that fantasy. A woman like that could bleed a man dry even faster than the hazard table could.

And if by some remote chance he was wrong, he could simply pay her the five thousand pounds after all. That was what she'd wanted, wasn't it?

The door opened behind him, and he sipped his brandy, girding himself for a confrontation. He was not accustomed to apologizing for his actions. In this case, he didn't even regret them. Had she been hideous or elderly, he would have acted just as decisively to keep her from ruining his brother—not, perhaps, in the exact same manner, but just as forcefully. The fact that she was young and attractive only made her more dangerous.

"I do hope you've made a better plan for getting back to London than you made for getting here." She came around his chair toward the fire, and Jack almost dropped his drink as he got a look at her.

Her hair tumbled down her back in loose waves, shining like polished mahogany in the firelight. But it was her clothing that threatened to strike him dumb. The long blue velvet dressing gown brushed the floor as she walked, and the sleeves had been folded back to expose her hands. She'd wrapped the belt around herself twice, emphasizing the slimness of her waist . . . and how beautifully curved the rest of her was. It was the most intimate of undress, even before his stunned brain registered one obvious point.

"That's my dressing gown," he said.

She gave him a saucy look and twitched the too-long banyan around her legs. "It's all they could find for me to wear. The housemaid nearest my size recently gave notice. The clothing of the other housemaids is too small, Mrs. Gibbon's is far too large, and that left this." She swept one hand over the velvet, lingering on the fabric. Jack's eyes tracked her fingers, imagining the feel of the velvet . . . and the flesh beneath it. "Everything I have to wear is soaked and quite likely ruined, thanks to your lunatic desire to kidnap me from London in the middle of a torrential rainstorm."

"I did not kidnap you." He poured more brandy down his throat, trying not to look at her bare ankle, visible below the hem. Was the rest of her bare under the banyan? It was not helping his concentration.

"You didn't let me go home, as I wished." She dropped onto the settee opposite him, and the gown parted, showing one slim leg, naked to the knee. Thankfully she tugged the dressing gown over it before she caught him looking.

Staring, actually. Did they really not have a single item of female clothing in the house?

Insanity seemed to be riddling his brain. What the devil was he thinking, to drag this woman to Alwyn House? He'd never survive a week alone with her. She'd be the death of him, one way or the other.

"What is your plan?" she asked directly. "What do you hope to accomplish?"

"Philip," he said, grasping the thread with relief. "He broke his word to me, and there must be consequences."

"Why didn't you drag Philip away with you?"

Because he hadn't wanted to spend a day, let alone a week with Philip. He tried to squelch the thought. "That would do nothing. He would sulk and glower, then go right back to the tables."

"As opposed to this, where you left him to gamble without even that minor interruption," she said gravely. "I see your reasoning."

He took another swallow of brandy. His reasoning made less and less sense even to him. Was she wearing anything under the banyan? "If you didn't want to be part of it, you ought to have walked away instead of rushing to his defense."

She blew out a breath. "Yes, I really ought to have. But as you said, I was seduced by greed. The prospect of winning five thousand pounds in one stroke was too tempting to resist."

He tilted his glass in mocking salute. "A deadly sin."

She made a noise of rueful agreement. "Is Philip a terrible liar, then?"

Jack gave her a cold look and said nothing.

"Am I overstepping my place by asking that?" She sounded amused, incredibly. "You said he broke his word to you not to gamble. I see him all the time, you know. Mostly at Vega's, but sometimes at the assembly rooms. If you think he's losing all his money to me, you're sadly misinformed."

"I never supposed that." Jack thought of the bank draft he'd just written to Sir Lester Bagwell, and drank the last of his brandy. "How badly *have* you fleeced him, now that you bring it up?"

She glared at him. Jack realized he'd been watching her and got up from his chair. He went to pour more brandy because one glass was clearly not going to be sufficient. On impulse he poured a glass of sherry as well and brought it to Mrs. Campbell.

"Thank you," she said in surprise. She tasted the wine, and her eyelashes fluttered closed in patent delight. She sipped again, and her lips glistened wet with sherry.

Jack stared. God, her mouth. He resumed his seat, eyes trained on her. He was damn near bewitched by everything she did. When she opened her eyes again, he made himself look away from her bare ankle and her shining hair and most of all her mouth.

"A few hundred pounds at most," she said in belated answer to his question. She tilted her head and faced him. "Not all at once, of course, and I do lose to him from time to time."

"But not often, I take it."

She swung her feet up onto the cushion, pulling her knees up under her chin. She took another sip of sherry before setting the glass down. "No, not often. He plays recklessly."

"How so?"

The firelight flickered on her face, giving her a pensive air. Jack tried not to notice that her bare toes were peeking out beneath the hem of his dressing gown. She'd kicked off the plain pair of slippers, which no doubt belonged to Mrs. Gibbon. It was completely unlike the vision he wanted to have of her as a scheming charlatan, angling to seduce her victims into ruin. It could be an elaborate play to persuade him of her innocence, but if so, it was the best Jack had ever seen.

"He never plays the odds," she said after a moment. "He always raises the stakes, even when he should not. And then . . . Well, there's no other way to put it. He's got dreadful luck."

"Not like you," Jack murmured.

Her smile was twisted. "His luck is nothing like mine."

There was an undercurrent in the words he couldn't place. "Then that means he's got no sense, either, if he persists in playing recklessly without even the veneer of good luck to carry him through."

"He persists because he doesn't fear losing." She rested her chin on her knees and smiled at his expression. "I presume that is due to you."

"Not as a general rule."

"The last resort is almost as reliable," she said, unperturbed by his clipped response. "Especially if one knows it will always be there when needed. Gambling is about risk, you know, and a guarantee is rare."

He knew all that. In his younger days, before he was a duke, Jack had been fond of a good wager himself. Never dice, and rarely cards; his wagers had been more personal. Could he beat his mate Stuart Drake in a carriage race from London to Greenwich? Yes, he could, and win twenty guineas in the process. Could he bag more birds on the heath than the other gentlemen out shooting? Yes, he could, for another ten pounds. Could he win a dance with the prettiest girl in any assembly room they passed, without telling her his title—which, Aiden Montgomery had once alleged, was outright cheating? Yes, he could, and lighten every friend's purse by another handful of guineas.

But then he'd inherited and abruptly such frivolous pursuits were beneath him—not that he had time for them anyway. His father had expected to live to age ninety, not drown just shy of fifty. Jack had expected to live the carefree life of an heir, not inherit every responsibility before he turned thirty. Wagering on carriage races became a quaint, almost childish thing.

"Is that what appeals to you?" he asked instead. "The risk?"

She laughed, although without much humor. "Oh no. I prefer to think of it as the chance of winning rather than the risk of losing."

Of course. Jack tore his gaze away from her bare toes again. "Spoken like a true sharper."

"Which you believe me to be." Another twisted smile.

"Are you not?" he drawled. "You frequent a gaming hell and routinely relieve people such as my brother of large sums of money. You admit you were eager to relieve *me* of five thousand pounds."

"You proposed the wager," she said, unrepentant. "I'd like very much to know why."

Hoist by his own petard. Jack drained his brandy and contemplated the empty glass. Two was enough. Any more and his wits—already lacking this evening—might desert him entirely and lead him to do something irretrievably stupid. Her bare toes tormented him. "Nothing but a useful device," he murmured.

"To separate me from Philip?" She scoffed. "If so, it was completely unnecessary. I already told you I didn't wish to play hazard with him. He interrupted my evening and maneuvered me into the game. I know well enough to be wary of Philip."

He gave her a jaundiced look. She hadn't looked wary at all in Vega's, blowing kisses to the dice in Philip's hand.

"I do," she insisted. "Contrary to what you may think, I don't want to beggar anyone, and I don't like watching my friends run themselves into ruin. I consider him a friend, but he's become a bit overbearing lately. If you had simply drawn me aside and asked my help in getting him away from the gaming tables, I would have happily given it." A trace of a mischievous smile touched her lips, and Jack's stomach contracted involuntarily. "For far less than five thousand pounds, even."

She was tweaking him. "Philip fancies far more than friendship from you," he replied, repaying the jab.

Her face froze for a moment. But not in surprise; she knew Philip wanted her. He couldn't tell whether she was pleased or not by that fact, though. It hit Jack that she was very good at hiding her feelings and emotions.

But then in a flash she turned into a cooing society miss. Her eyes widened and a simpering smile crossed her lips. "Does he?" she said in a wondering tone. "Good heavens. I've never discovered a gentleman had warm feelings for me through his brother." She gave him a breathless hopeful look. "Is he madly in love? Should I prepare myself for a proposal of marriage? Shall we soon be brother and sister, Your Grace?"

God no. Jack barely kept his seat at the thought of this woman as his sister-in-law. She would run Philip in circles and he . . . he would end up in an early grave, watching her with his brother. "You'd be a fool to accept him, if he were to propose. He has no fortune of his own, and he wastes his income at the hazard tables."

She laughed merrily. Jack smiled before he

could help it. "Your face! Did you think I meant it?" She shook her head, still smiling. "Of course I would never accept Philip, for matrimony or other entanglements. He'd make a terrible husband and I—"

"Yes?" he prodded when she stopped short.

She licked her lips. "I know he's far above my touch," she finished lightly. "The brother of the Duke of Ware! I would never dream of setting my cap at such an eligible gentleman."

That was not what she'd been about to say. Jack leaned forward to set down his glass, and used the chance to shift in his chair so he could see her better. "Some women would seize their chance to land such an eligible gentleman."

"Would they?" She smiled artlessly and raised one shoulder. "I suppose I'm not like most women."

Yes . . . but why not? What was it about her that teased him and lured him, even when he knew he should be disapproving and disdainful? He had to clear his head about her. He had to clear his head *of* her. "I can see that," he said evenly. "You gamble and freely admit you like to win, but then you say you don't want to beggar anyone. A true gamester wouldn't care. That makes me think you're playing a different game. When I suggested Philip might want more than merely your company, though, you went to great lengths not just to deny it, but to mock the very idea. Too great, in my opinion—it was not a novel thought to you.

"It could be you're not prowling the gaming hells of London in search of a wealthy protector and find the thought offensive or demeaning, but you didn't fly into outrage when I said it. You know he wants to bed you, and anyone watching how you flirted with him this evening would assume you are encouraging him. You've thought about what he would be like as a lover or even as a husband, yet claim to have rejected him on both counts. That leads me to suspect you *are* in fact playing for more than a few guineas at the hazard table, but Philip simply isn't a plump enough target for you." He tilted his head to one side. "Am I wrong?"

She had sat up straighter during his speech, returning her feet to the floor. Now she was staring at him, her lips parted, her eyes dark. "Put a lot of thought into it, have you?"

"Not much," he returned. "I'd never heard of you before tonight." He couldn't stop his eyes from dropping to the dressing gown. It gaped open a little, revealing a tantalizing hint of bosom. His blood surged no matter how he tried to quell it. "But I recognize your kind."

For a moment he thought he'd finally rattled her. Her eyes flashed and she inhaled unevenly, but again she recovered. "Of course you would think so." Her smile this time was forced. "Good night, Your Grace." She rose and sank into a flawless curtsy, and the velvet banyan slipped open a little more. Now he could see the shadow between her breasts.

His mouth dried up. Nothing. She wore nothing beneath it. Mrs. Campbell regally flipped the hem of the banyan out of her way—her legs were bare all the way up, curse it all—stepped into the slippers and walked out of the room without another glance at him.

And even though Jack suspected he'd scored a direct hit with his last remark, all he could think about was her bare feet.

"I see. Tell them to do what they must to repair the axle. Are the horses we arrived with unhurt?"

"One of them picked up a stone, Your Grace, but the groom is tending to him."

Jack gave a nod. "That will be all, Wilson."

"Yes, sir." The door clicked softly closed behind the butler.

Alwyn House was set in a large landscaped park. There were other vehicles on the property, but only ones meant for short distances. With the roads a mess and the coach unable to be driven, he was stuck at Chiswick.

Or rather, *they* were stuck.

As if on cue, the door opened again. Even before she spoke, Jack knew it was Mrs. Campbell. Not only did the air seem to develop a subtle hum, he could see her reflection in the window before him.

"Good morning."

He noticed she didn't refer much to his title. There was no deference in her demeanor, either. Jack had grown accustomed to both behaviors in the last seven years; even before his father's death, he'd been styled the Earl of Lindsay and treated accordingly. This woman, though, treated him as if they were equals.

Actually, she treated him as if he were slightly inferior. It was both intriguing and maddening.

"Good morning, Mrs. Campbell." He turned and watched her cross the room to the sideboard. She walked like a dancer, graceful and light on her feet. She lifted the lids on a few dishes, clearly intending to serve herself, and Jack made a motion to the footman who stood guard over the sideboard. The servant slipped from the room without a word, leaving them alone.

"I see they located something for you to wear," he said.

She selected some toast and a muffin and added an egg, then brought her plate to the table and sat down. "Yes. This stylish ensemble belonged to a former housemaid who left rather abruptly last spring. Mrs. Gibbon apologized profusely for it, but it is clean and dry and fits tolerably well. I am hardly in a position to refuse anything that satisfies those requirements." She smoothed one hand over the plain, dark blue bodice. "Livery, I presume?"

He jerked his gaze away from her hand, still poised very near the shadowy cleft between her breasts. It was a housemaid's dress, but she'd left off the customary kerchief the maids wore tucked into their bodices, and as a result her bosom was perfectly visible. "Yes."

"Very fine wear for livery."

"Is it?" He lifted his shoulder. "I didn't select it."

"Ah." She spread jam on her toast. "Far too mundane a task for a duke."

"Yes." There was no point disputing that.

She looked up at him as she ate. He stood on the far side of the table from her, and the light from the windows—such as it was—fell on her face. "I saw Wilson, your butler, in the corridor. He says the carriage has been retrieved from the road."

"It has been." Jack returned to his chair and reached for the coffeepot. "Unfortunately, with its axle broken. It will take a few days to repair it."

She stopped chewing for a moment, her eyes

widening. Her gaze drifted away to the windows, no doubt observing the rain rolling down the panes. She finished her bite of toast, wiped her mouth delicately, and finally glanced at him again. "We're trapped here?"

"A rather ominous characterization. The roads are a mess, and it would be a dreadful ride back to London in the pony cart or gig that are kept in the stables."

For a long moment she said nothing. He looked up to see she was watching him, a thin crease of bemusement between her brows. She really had the most beautiful eyes, clear and intelligent and frank. And right now she was looking at him as if he were an idiot. His temper rose a little; the weather was not his fault.

"Does it even matter?" he said to goad her. "You did wager a week."

Her knife clattered to the plate. "That bloody wager! You proposed it. Was this what you had in mind?"

Jack opened his mouth to reply, then realized he had no answer. "To be perfectly honest, I fully expected to lose."

Her lips parted in astonishment. "Well—I fully expected to win!"

Against his will he smiled. "Serves us both right."

She made a derisive noise, almost a snort, and rolled her eyes. "Given that neither one of us wanted this, shall we brave the elements and attempt a return to London? It will mitigate the damage for both of us."

I never said I didn't want it. Jack shifted in his

chair. "No. That would be foolish, and almost surely end in failure."

Pique flashed across her face. She jumped up and went to the sideboard to prepare herself a cup of tea. When she came back, her determinedly pleasant expression was back in place. "Then what are we to do, since we're marooned here?"

And that was the moment that Jack realized he was completely at leisure for the first time in years. Normally his visits to Alwyn House were planned, at least a few days in advance; his secretary and estate agent made the trip with him, as did the endless stream of work that was his lot in life. Even here in his private sanctuary he was usually kept busy for hours a day.

But all of that was off in London, and even if it caught up to him tomorrow, it still meant today was devoid of responsibility. He leaned back in his chair, adjusting to the novelty of it. "I've no idea," he murmured, almost in wonder.

Mrs. Campbell shook her head. "This really is the most dreadful kidnapping. I expected more of a duke."

"Oh? What, specifically?"

She thought for a moment, sipping her tea. "Well, have you got a dungeon?" He shook his head. "A torture chamber?"

"Alas," he said dryly, entertained in spite of himself.

She sighed. "You see my point. You've spirited me out of London to a beautiful house full of servants, including a cook who is worth twice what you pay her, whatever that sum is." She lifted the muffin in illustration. "If this is your idea of punishment, I should very much like to see your vision of pleasure."

And I should very much like to show you pleasure. Jack bit his tongue to keep the treasonous thought silent. "It is a beautiful house—my favorite, in fact. But it is fairly new, and I doubt there are any medieval devices lurking in the attics."

"Your favorite house." She arched a brow. Her face was marvelously expressive; he could tell just from that brow that she was laughing at him, even though her tone was politely somber. "Have you got so many there's a ranking of preference?"

"It only takes two to have a ranking of preference," he pointed out.

"Have you only got two?"

"No." He thought for a second. "Five."

Now both her eyebrows went up. "Five houses. Good heavens. How could one possibly choose among so many?"

"Quite easily. This one is the smallest and coziest." He said it to needle her, although it probably was true.

"I see." Her eyes flitted over the room. "And how, pray, would you describe the others?"

"Drafty," he said. "Cold. Dark, for the most part." He turned to the windows and sighed at the vista of iron-gray rain clouds and fog. "On sunny days this room is bright and cheerful."

"I shall have to take your word for it today." She finished her tea and pushed back her chair. "Well. I think I shall explore the house and see why it's your favorite. Since we've neither of us anything more important to do," she added as he turned to stare at her.

It was probably the safest thing he could do with her. And oddly, it appealed. He did like this house, and yet it had been almost two months since he'd been able to visit. "I would be delighted to show it to you."

SOPHIE HAD LAIN AWAKE late into the night, trying to think of a way out of this predicament.

She absolutely had to return to London as soon as possible. Her absence would only confirm the wildest rumors, and there were sure to be some, thanks to the public display she and the duke had made of themselves. The duke claimed he had no designs on her, but he'd been stubbornly dismissive of her promises to avoid Philip. That was worrying. Sophie had learned to live on her personal charm and persuasive ability, and now more than ever she needed to convince the duke to see her point of view.

But he merely sat through all her attempts to reason with him, watching her with those cool blue-gray eyes and a faint smile, pointing out every tiny fault in her argument. The man was infuriating. She had no choice but to continue trying; he was lord and master here, and her only way back to town was by his command.

Exploring the house might allow her to discover more about him. He was unlike anyone she had ever known: reserved, cold, and a bloody duke. She had tried to ignore that last one, as it only reminded her how powerless she was in comparison, but there was no way to ignore the difference in their situations in life.

He led her through the formal entrance hall,

which she had seen by lamplight when they arrived. The clerestory windows let in the gray light of the day, but even so the hall was magnificent. The robin's-egg blue walls must glow like the antechamber to heaven when the sun was out, and the floors were polished to a rich sheen. Her eyes caught on the portrait of a lady in a richly embroidered gown of some antiquated fashion, hung high above the door the duke opened. The woman's face was serene, almost regal. A small dog stood at her feet, the trailing end of her shawl in his teeth. Behind her were rolling hills and a building that was most likely Alwyn House itself. "Who is she?" Sophie asked without thinking.

The duke stopped and looked up. "My great-grandmother. The house was built for her, and she oversaw the planning of the gardens."

"My," she murmured, impressed. "Your great-grandfather must have loved her very much."

"On the contrary," he said. "I believe they disliked the sight of each other. He built this house and exiled her to it."

Disconcerted, Sophie jerked her gaze away from the portrait. "Oh."

Ware clasped his hands behind his back and contemplated his ancestor. "I understand she was much happier here. He gave her free rein to do as she pleased with the house, so long as she remained in it."

"Charming," was all she could think of to say. It sounded like something her grandfather, Lord Makepeace, would do. The duke gave her an unreadable glance, then swept out one hand, indicating she should proceed through the door.

They went through the soaring staircase hall and into another room. "The Blue Room," he said unnecessarily. The carpet was a luxurious sapphire blue, woven with vines and flowers in endless spirals. The woodwork was polished mahogany with gold accents, as was the furniture, which was upholstered in the same deep blue damask that covered the walls. Tall windows looked out onto a garden, now limp and bedraggled in the rain but exquisitely terraced and arranged. Sophie took her time strolling through the room, examining the paintings, all bucolic landscapes.

"Look up," said the duke when she had finished her circuit. Obediently, she put her head back—and gasped out loud.

The ceiling was coffered in alternating octagons and squares of dark wood. That was unremarkable. What set it apart were the carvings. The whole ceiling seemed to be alive, as if a woodland had been captured in polished walnut. All sorts of creatures peered from every cornice, stags and hounds, birds, even mythological creatures. "How beautiful," she whispered, craning her neck to see as much as possible as she circled the room again. "It's incredible! How long it must have taken to carve all these!"

"My brother and I would lie on our backs as boys and try to locate various animals," said the duke.

She gave a disbelieving laugh, as her eyes picked out a thin-faced weasel, a fat cat, and even an exotic elephant. "I don't wonder!" She came around the sofa, still looking upward, and tripped on the fringe of the carpet.

With one quick step forward, the duke reached for her. Sophie yelped in dismay, expecting to hit the floor, only to be hauled up against him instead. She had instinctively grabbed his sleeve, and now their arms were tangled together. For a moment neither moved, and then the duke put her back on her feet without a word. With a murmured apology she stepped back. Her heart raced, both from the sudden near fall and then from the feel of his arms around her. She hadn't realized she was that close to him, and now found it difficult to meet his eyes.

Which was foolish. He had done what any gentleman would have done. Sophie drew a fortifying breath and told herself not to be a ninny. "Which is your favorite?"

He was staring at her and blinked at the question. He clasped his hands behind his back and straightened to his usual poker-stiff posture. "Sorry?"

"Your favorite creature," she said. "On the ceiling."

He looked upward as if he didn't understand what she meant. "Ah—the sphinx. Above the fireplace," he added as she immediately looked up again, careful not to walk. "I believe it has my grandfather's face."

Yes, there it was. Mindful of her steps this time, she went closer. "How clever."

"I always thought it was," he said thoughtfully. "I believe my great-grandmother had his face—and the faces of all her children—carved into the ceiling because she almost never saw them in life."

"Never!" she exclaimed. "Why not?"

"He and his brothers were sent off to school as soon as they were old enough, and he was rarely here. The sisters were sent to live with other well-connected families or to finishing schools. One died, but the other two made their debuts and were married off by the time they were eighteen."

There was nothing except calm contemplation in his tone, but Sophie felt a shadow fall on the room. This beautiful room suddenly became the solace of a grieving mother. "How many children?" she asked softly.

"Six. The daughters were permitted to live with her until they were twelve."

"That's beastly," she burst out. "Who would deny a mother her own children?"

He sighed. "The same sort who would exile his wife, and only visit her once a year for the purpose of siring another child."

Again that brought her own grandfather to mind. He'd disowned his son, Sophie's father, and then exiled her to Mrs. Upton's when she was orphaned. The fact that she was grateful for it didn't change the fact that he'd done it to be rid of her. Her mouth flattened into a grim line before she consciously relaxed her muscles. "I hope the next room is more pleasant," she said lightly. "Or I shall begin to wonder why you like the house."

"Do you find it morbid?" The duke had been watching her, but now he tipped his chin up to study the ceiling again. "It was the way things were done."

"Oh?" She eyed him. "Were you sent away to school then, and Philip?"

"Of course," he confirmed. "Although my father never tried to separate us from our mother."

"Were your parents kind and affectionate?"

This time he hesitated. A shadow seemed to pass over his face, and he didn't reply. He walked on to the doors at the far end of the room and waited for her there. Sophie reminded herself it was not her concern and strode after him.

"The music room," he said, opening the door. That was apparent, from the pianoforte at one side and the harp, under sheets, opposite it. But Sophie was transfixed nonetheless by the beauty of the room. Three sides of the room were tall windows, offering a spectacular view of the park in front of the house. The walls were soft yellow, with long draperies of flowered silk that matched the upholstery on the chairs, and when she looked down, she realized the carpet must have been specially woven for this room. Twined through the pattern was a scroll of music, and at intervals there were whimsical harps and lyres. Someone who loved music had decorated this room.

But the most enchanting thing by far was the pianoforte. It was the most splendid one she had seen in years, the sort a virtuoso would play. Reverently she opened the lid. The nameplate bore the name John Broadwood and Sons, whom Papa had believed made the finest pianofortes in the world. "Do you play?" She touched a key. It sounded a little off tune.

"No."

"Do you sing?" She touched another key, not sure why she was persisting.

"Not well."

She looked up in surprise. "Not at all? I thought all gentlemen were taught music."

Instead of answering, he asked, "Do you play?"

"Yes. This is out of tune, though." She closed the lid over the keys. What a shame, to have such a wonderful instrument in a house where no one played it. "The headmistress of my school insisted all girls learn at least one instrument." She looked around the room. It was beautiful, but it wasn't lived in. There was no music on the pianoforte, the harp was covered, and everything was arranged too precisely. A music lover had decorated it, but all the music had gone out of it. "I take it you don't spend much time in here."

"As I do not play," said the duke, "no."

What a waste, to have such a beautiful room and not use it. If this had been her family home, it would have been the most used room of the house. Her father would have played while her mother sang arias and lieder. For a moment she pictured her family, before the illness that destroyed it, arrayed in this lovely room. Papa at the pianoforte, her mother singing in front of the windows, Sophie reaching up to turn the pages of music for Papa . . .

She blinked to get rid of the image of what would never be. She went to the windows, turning her back on the pianoforte. From here one could see the colonnaded entrance of the house, even more intimidating in daylight than it had been in the dark of night. Sophie studied it, realizing how far they had walked in the rain. Across the graveled drive and manicured grass, the trees they had trudged through in the dark looked very far away. Sophie imagined she could see the wrought-iron gates, as well. It was a sweeping view of the park, but it somehow made her feel lonely. Everything was perfectly lovely but too still, too remote.

Like the duke himself, now that she thought about it.

She turned. "What is your favorite room?"

"The library, where we spoke last night."

"Shall we go there?" If she wanted to gain insight into him, better to visit the rooms where he actually spent time.

With a nod, he led her back through the Blue Room, and they passed into a gallery. The tall, narrow windows didn't let in much light, and the room was dim. "There's little of interest in here."

Her steps slowed as a small framed picture caught her eye. "This is Philip," she said in surprise, regarding a pencil sketch on the near wall. "As a boy."

"Yes." The duke stopped beside her. "I drew it."

She blinked in surprise. The boy in the portrait was unmistakably Philip, several years younger with longer hair and a more innocent grin. He looked joyful, sitting in the crook of a branch. The tree was a faint suggestion around him, but Sophie could just see him, climbing the tree to dangle his bare feet over a lake or a pond while he fished or threw stones in the water.

"He looks so carefree and happy."

The duke gave her a long, measuring look. "It was a long time ago."

"And now he's not?" Sophie studied the sketch. It was drawn with affection. Philip had been laughing at his brother as he drew. "You must have been close as boys."

The duke inhaled a deep breath. "Yes. As boys we were very much alike. We spent hours by the lake. It was our primary escape from lessons."

But as men, they were very different. Sophie's curiosity prodded her hard to keep asking. Why had they grown apart, and when? "I thought you went away to school."

"Of course," he replied evenly. "Between terms there were still lessons. My father insisted."

"Oh?" This was interesting, and it was about him. "What sort of lessons?"

"Crop management. Keeping the ledgers. Architecture, when my father had a bathhouse built." He made a mild grimace. "Very dull sorts of lessons."

"Philip must have hated them," she said with a laugh.

His mouth quirked for a moment. "Philip was excused from most of it."

Ah—those were lessons for the heir. Sophie kept her gaze on the sketch, wondering if Philip had gone off to the lake while his older brother was kept behind to learn crop management. "He must have been required to do something."

"A bit of ledger keeping. We both learned to drive at Alwyn House. Whenever we were here, my mother filled the house with guests, and we were required to participate in any events she held. She finds the country dull and quiet." He paused. "My father liked it here."

"Is that why you like it?"

He studied the portrait of Philip. "I like it for the same reasons he did," he said at last.

There was something in his tone that warned against further discussion of that topic. "It's an excellent drawing," she told him. "You're quite talented."

His expression grew remote. "Thank you, but it was many years ago."

"I'm sure you've not forgotten how entirely." She smiled teasingly as she said it, but his face didn't change. Sophie knew when to cut line; she changed the subject. "Shall we go on?" Thus far she hadn't seen any reason he might prefer this house, unless his other properties were mausoleums. Even though Alwyn House was luxurious and beautiful, the tour so far had only made her miss her own cozy home in London. She had her father's pocket watch and her mother's hair combs there, reminders of happier times that made her smile.

The duke merely bowed his head and opened the door. He took her through the formal dining room, glorious in red damask, with three crystal chandeliers and an enormous painting of the wedding at Cana. "My mother expanded it," he said as Sophie exclaimed over the size of the room in a country house. "She entertained a great deal."

Because she found this beautiful house dull and quiet. Sophie suspected Philip took after his mother; he also was ever in search of society and gaiety, while the duke seemed far more restrained.

She reconsidered that thought when they reached the library. Despite the rain and general gloom of the day, the library was glorious. The room was a large oval, with walls of celery green and white woodwork. A pair of marble columns at either end of the room set off the shelves of books that filled both rounded ends of the oval. Last night it had been too dark, and she'd been too irate, to take it in, but today—

"How beautiful," she burst out. "And I didn't notice any of it last night!"

The duke walked to the tall windows and looked out. "Why is that, I wonder?"

"Well, you were being terribly vexing," she replied absently, wandering about the room in awe. "I was concentrating very hard on keeping my temper."

"Oh?" He leaned one shoulder against the shutter and watched her. "What did you want to say that you didn't?"

She glanced at him, startled. Thanks to the numerous windows in here, the light was better. His gaze was just as clear and focused as the night before, but somehow less piercing. The acid edge of scorn was gone, and it made her unfortunately aware again of how attractive he was.

No. Giles Carter was attractive, with his square jaw and the distinguished touches of gray at his temples. The Duke of Ware was magnificent. If she hadn't landed against him in the Blue Room and felt for herself how alive and real he was, she would have thought him an artist's creation of marble, standing there in the watery light in his perfectly tailored clothing and expensive boots and golden hair that had just enough wave to make him imperfect.

And here she stood in the borrowed dress of a housemaid who'd been sacked. She drew a deep breath and felt the sturdy fabric rasp against her skin, reminding her that she was only a few steps above that housemaid—an immaterial difference to a man like the duke.

"I wanted to tell you to bugger off," she said lightly.

The duke's eyebrows shot up, as if no one in the world had ever told him to bugger off. "Did you really?"

Sophie laughed, resuming her tour of the library. A glass case held an array of miniatures, and she bent down to have a closer look. "I certainly did. How dare you call me a hardened gamester and say you recognized what kind of woman I am? You know nothing about me."

Ware cleared his throat. "I know a little."

Still bent over the case of miniatures, she flipped one hand. "You know a very little—mostly that I cannot resist an enormous wager with someone who seems determined to lose to me."

"That is significant."

"Yes," she acknowledged, "but by no means the sum of my character." She glanced up with a mischievous smile. "I daresay the same could be said about Philip."

"Not to his credit." The duke folded his arms. "How did you meet my brother?"

"At Somerset House." Sophie savored his start of surprise. "The Royal Academy exhibition. Are you astonished I would attend such an event?"

"Of course not."

"You are." She arched her brows in teasing. "Don't worry, I'm not offended. We already agreed you know nothing about me."

"What I thought," he said gravely, "was how incredible it was for *Philip* to attend. I freely admit I do not know you, but I am well acquainted with my brother, and the Royal Academy is one place I never would have guessed to find him."

"Oh." She pressed her lips together in chagrin. "My mistake."

He inclined his head in acknowledgment. "Don't worry. I'm not offended. You know nothing about me."

A wry smile crossed her face as he repeated her own words back to her. "Now you know another of my failings: I am sometimes quick to judgment."

Unexpectedly, he grinned back at her. Sophie took an involuntary step backward. With his face lit by mirth, the Duke of Ware was unbearably attractive. She imagined most women would find him so even at his most severe, but when he smiled . . . Oh, when he smiled, he looked like the sort of man even she could lose her head over. "Something we have in common, Mrs. Campbell."

"Indeed?" she asked brightly, trying to scrub away all thoughts of losing her head over the duke. "How unflattering to both of us."

"And yet proof that we may understand each other better than it seems." Sophie closed her mouth at this subtle but unmistakable reproof as the duke strolled over to stand beside her. He gazed into the case as she stared at him, helpless to stop. It was one thing to find him attractive, in a wholly objective way, and quite another to feel the tug of attraction at close range.

Well . . . the tug was more like a steadily increasing pull. She could see the lock of his hair, tawny gold, that had caught on his neckcloth, curling it romantically upward; he smelled of rich, clean male, with a whiff of coffee. He glanced sideways at her, his eyes vivid blue today, and something elemental deep inside her seemed to swell in anticipation—and even worse, longing.

"What else do we have in common, I wonder?" he murmured.

Sophie tensed. "Nothing."

"Nothing at all?"

He must be standing too close to her; she felt hot and breathless and edged back a step to clear her head. "You sound as if you know something I don't. What do *you* think we have in common, Your Grace?"

His mouth quirked again. "Determination."

"In service of very different goals," she said trenchantly.

"I acted to keep my brother from ruin."

"While I acted—or rather, argued—to save *myself* from ruin. You'll forgive me if I don't prize Philip's survival above my own."

"Survival," he said thoughtfully. "I never thought Philip's survival was at stake, only his good name and credit. Did you really fear yourself at risk?"

She still did. There was a very delicate balance between doing what she had to do to earn her income and maintaining her nominal respectability. "If you knew what it costs a woman to lose her good name, you wouldn't possibly ask that. But then, as a duke, I daresay you could do just about anything and still be welcome everywhere."

"Are you envious of that? Do you also wish to be welcome anywhere?"

He was prying, trying to puzzle her out. That's what she was trying to do to him, and she did not appreciate her own tactic being turned on her. Sophie drifted back another step and gave him an arch look. "If so, it must have worked. A duke was willing to risk five thousand pounds against the mere chance of winning my company!"

"Indeed." His gaze swept over her, fleeting but thorough. It wasn't a cynical glance, sizing her up as a charlatan. It was a glance of male assessment, and her body reacted to it, flushing warm from head to toe. Perhaps she wasn't the only one who felt that pull. "Will that wager close some doors to you?"

She laughed lightly. "It may open the wrong ones."

"So it was a mistake."

"Only because I lost," Sophie shot back, nettled.

He rocked back on his heels. She savored the hit and turned to the shelves. "Do you read? What a fine library."

"Every day," he replied. "Though rarely anything so amusing as that."

She looked closer at the finely tooled binding her fingertips were brushing. The books here must be worth a fortune. Each and every one was bound in leather. "But you own it."

"Owning it is the smallest part of savoring it."

"That is your loss, when the opportunity is always at hand." She selected a book from the shelf and opened it, flipping pages for a moment. "'There is great satisfaction in quarreling with her; and I think she never appears to such advantage as when she is doing everything in her power to plague me.'" She gave him a saucy look. "Perhaps you *should* read more. There's tremendous wisdom in these pages."

A thin line appeared between his brows. He put out one hand, and Sophie obligingly handed over the book. He read the page in silence, then aloud, "'How pleasingly she shows her contempt for my authority.'" He tilted his head and gave her a look. "I see you're familiar with this one."

"I have seen that play performed, yes," she said. Too late she realized her voice had gone breathless and soft.

He slid the book back on the shelf and let his hand linger there, right beside her head. "I don't doubt it." And he smiled.

He stood very close to her, his elbow brushing her arm. She ought to step away again, but somehow she stayed where she was. The duke might claim the wager was nothing but a means to separate her from Philip, but she sensed that he wouldn't mind enjoying her company in more intimate ways.

Men had flirted with her before; some had tried to seduce her. Sophie knew very well when a man's interest had been aroused. Once she had given in to a pursuit, years ago. It had been a heady experience, fraught with youthful passion and the thrill of being so wicked. When her head cleared, she'd realized what a risk it was. Her lover had been generous and kind, but when he broke with her, she'd breathed a sigh of relief that it was over without serious repercussion. Since then she had ignored, deflected, and parried every attempt men made to seduce her. It was safer, if less exciting.

Today she was keenly aware of how *much* less exciting it was. Normally she didn't feel any reciprocal interest, and was a little shocked that she did this time. Even worse, she'd felt it last night, when he was still being condescending and accusing her of trying to ruin his brother. Today he was smiling at her and being charming, and Sophie was discovering that she could ignore her own attraction as long as she didn't like him, but when he smiled and let down his guard . . . That flicker of humor and humanity turned him from a cold, haughty duke into an irresistibly attractive man. A man she was marooned with, in this beautiful house, in perfect privacy and seclusion . . .

She flinched as she realized how wildly her thoughts were wandering. *Idiot*, she told herself. The worst possible thing she could do now would be to let herself be seduced by the duke, a man she didn't know, who thought her a cheat. She had to put a stop to this now, before either of them went too far.

"Enough ponderous philosophy." She beamed up at him. "We must teach you how to gamble, Your Grace."

Chapter 8

Jack had to send for a servant to locate cards. He dimly remembered card tables being set up in the library when his mother hosted parties here, but that had been years ago. He'd never had guests at Alwyn House since his father's death.

He watched Mrs. Campbell make herself at home on the same sofa where she'd tormented him the previous evening with her bare toes. Today she wore a discarded housemaid's dress, a garment devoid of any seductive traits, and yet he felt more fascinated than ever. Who was this woman and why was he apparently helpless to stop her from driving him mad? Michaels returned with a deck of cards, and she thanked him with a glowing smile that made Jack's stomach tighten. He wanted her to smile at him that way.

"You're very adept at this," he remarked as she shuffled the deck with the ease of a croupier. Instead of focusing his mind on how she had learned such scandalous skills, it only made him wonder what her nimble fingers would feel like on his skin.

She smiled modestly, the cards flying as she dealt. "Every woman has a deep well of hidden talents, Your Grace."

A riot of dangerous thoughts sprang up in Jack's brain. What sort of talents did she have hidden, he wanted to ask. He shifted in his seat. "And secrets?"

"As many as men do, I suppose." She set down the deck and motioned to the cards in front of him. "Have you played loo?"

"Yes."

"Unlimited loo?" she asked with a sparkling smile.

Unlimited loo could ruin a man in a night's time. "Already looking for a new victim to beggar?"

She batted her lashes at him as she swept up her cards. By now he recognized it as a warning instead of an invitation. "You know me too well, sir."

He didn't know her, not at all, he was realizing—but his curiosity was growing by leaps and bounds. "We haven't got enough players for loo."

She sent him a stern look over her cards. She was holding them in front of her face on purpose, he thought. "We haven't got money, either. It's a lesson, Your Grace, to preserve you from any further significant losses."

He smiled and finally picked up his cards. "Pass."

"What?" She lowered her cards and blinked at him. Passing ended his role in the game. "No, you may not pass. That ruins the game."

"That also preserves my fortune." He grinned

at her expression, so beautifully nonplussed. "See how easily it happened? I've lost nothing."

"And also won nothing!"

Jack put the cards back on the table. "I don't need to win anything. Why do you?"

"It's quite a thrill," she said after a barely perceptible hesitation. "I understand the concept might be very strange to you, but I recommend it."

"Winning?" He leaned back in his chair. "I won last night."

Pink colored her cheeks. "An occasion I'm sure you regret deeply."

He studied her for a moment. "No," he said slowly. "I don't think so."

She glanced up at him, wary and watchful. "I have failed dreadfully if your victory last night has given you the slightest satisfaction."

It had been far more than slightly satisfying. "It achieved my immediate objective."

Her eyes flashed, and she threw her cards down. "Philip! I vow, one might think he's your son, from the desperate lengths you'll go to for his sake."

Jack thought of what his father might have done, in his place. The late duke had been decent through and through. If he were still alive, Philip would no doubt be sitting here now, penitent and chastened, willingly submitting to whatever the duke decreed his punishment would be. Jack imagined his brother mucking out stalls in the stable, or helping plow a field on one of Kirkwood's tenant farms.

Of course, if their father were still alive, Philip probably wouldn't have fallen into such rakish behavior. The duke had been a patient man, tolerating a fair amount of youthful hell-raising, but only to a point. He wanted his sons to be strong, honorable men, and he would have put a stop to Philip's gambling before it became ruinous—something Jack had failed to do. "Philip hardly views me with such respect."

She met his gaze head-on for a moment, then gathered up the cards. "Perhaps we should start with something simpler." She dealt again, tossing a pair of cards in front of him. "Vingt-un."

"What will I win?" he asked softly.

"Not me," was her swift retort.

Jack grinned again. "How about . . ." He paused, thinking. "Music."

She jerked. "What?"

"A song on the pianoforte."

"It's horribly out of tune," she protested.

He made a dismissive gesture. He'd seen the way her eyes devoured the instrument. Music meant something to her. Even her protest hummed with longing. He said nothing, just waited.

Her gaze dropped to her cards. She reordered them in her hand. "Your ears will regret it," she warned at last, "but if you insist, so be it."

"I accept the risk."

"Then you'd better pay attention and win," she said tartly.

They played for an hour. Jack had agreed to the game only as a means to learn more about her, but he found himself drawn in. He already knew vingt-un, of course; he'd played it years ago, whiling away time when forced to attend balls at his mother's instigation. Back then he'd been relatively adept at it, and even years out of practice, he fell back into a reasonable rhythm with the game. Within minutes, though, he realized Mrs. Campbell was far, far better at it than he'd ever dreamed of being. She smiled and spoke as easily, even as pertly, as ever, but her eyes noted every play. The way her fingers touched the cards was sensual. The way she tilted her head and smiled when asking if he wanted another card was distracting—purposely so, he was sure. And her knack with the game was uncanny. After a time he realized she had to be keeping a tally in her head of all the cards played, increasing her chances of winning.

In short, she played like a professional.

Could that be? Jack tried to keep his attention on the game enough to avoid humiliation even as questions about the woman opposite him sprouted by the dozens in his mind. It would explain how she trounced Philip, who was—as she had said—utterly reckless when gaming. Jack had believed his brother was mostly distracted by her splendid bosom, but now thought there might be more to it than that.

Of course, if she really were as skilled as the men who supported themselves at the tables, why hadn't she beggared Philip yet? She certainly could have. Perhaps it was out of some regard for his brother, but after some thought, Jack got the idea that she wanted to win, but never too large an amount. That would explain her horror at his actions and her angry charge that he was making a spectacle of her. She was a regular at Vega's, everyone knew her and gambled with her, but she did not crave attention. Winning huge sums night after night would make her infamous.

That still didn't explain everything. Jack hadn't kept close track of how much he lost to her at Vega's, but it had been a substantial sum, more than enough to keep a widowed lady in comfort for a year. She said she lost on occasion, but Jack was willing to bet she won significantly more often. Even now, with no money at stake, an intent focus had come over her face. She wanted to win, always.

Debts? Perhaps her husband had left her badly off. Who had her husband been, anyway? Why hadn't he left her better provided for? She must have married as a girl to be widowed so young. Perhaps she frittered money away and had no sense for keeping it. He frowned slightly at that thought; it didn't fit, somehow. She was too aware of everything. What would she be like, he wondered, if she ever let down her guard completely?

It was his distraction that saved him. Too busy thinking of why she needed money, and how he might get around her defenses to learn the reason, he declined another card when he meant to accept it. Smiling slightly, she flipped it over into her own hand—only to blink at it in patent surprise. The six of clubs had put her over twenty-one, ruining her hand.

Jack looked at his own hand, a fourteen, and let out a shout of triumph.

"How—" She turned over the last few cards in the deck. Every one was a four or smaller, and all would have beaten his hand if she'd drawn them.

She mustered a smile. She had made a mistake. "Well played, sir."

"It should have been your hand," he said, feeling magnanimous in his unexpected victory.

She smiled as she gathered the cards. "No, no! Absent cheating, any win is fair."

He believed that. This woman played to win, but she lost with dignity and grace.

"I suppose I shall have to take credit for being an excellent teacher, to have been bested within an hour. Shall I play for you now, or later?" She set the cards aside and faced him, smiling as easily as if they were old friends.

Jack had the most terrible desire to kiss her. In a housemaid's dress, dealing cards like a seasoned gambler, she still managed to sparkle. He hadn't had such a pleasurable morning in years, even with the questions battering at the back of his brain. She was a riddle, a delicious, beautiful mystery, and he was shocked by how mesmerizing he found her. He could easily spend the rest of the day—the rest of the week—trying to puzzle out her secrets, especially the secret of how to make her smile at him in truth.

He doubted kissing her now would help him in that pursuit.

"I would like my song now," he said. "Please."

They went back through the house to the music room. Mrs. Campbell slowed in the doorway. "Oh my."

Jack continued walking. The servants had been in while they played cards in the library, uncovering furniture and dusting. They would be swarming over the house all day, bringing every room to perfect readiness. Normally it was done before he arrived, but this time they'd had no chance. He opened the lid of the pianoforte and waited.

She recovered her aplomb, taking the seat. "Have they tuned it, as well?" she asked pertly.

"I doubt it."

She ran her fingers over the keys familiarly. "Then this may be a dreadful assault on your ears."

Jack grinned. "My ears are not so attuned as yours, so I doubt I'll notice the difference."

She muttered something like, "Be careful what you ask for," and began to play. At first her fingers stumbled a few times, and there were a few notes that twanged, but gradually her confidence took over. He took a seat where he could watch her face, which lost some of its guardedness as she got into the piece.

Jack had learned years ago that it was best to own up to his weaknesses honestly, at least to himself. Mrs. Campbell was rapidly becoming a significant weakness of his—no, strike that. He was thoroughly bewitched by her. He wanted to know more about her, from what made her laugh to what she looked like without any clothes on. He knew either of those desires, let alone both of them, could only lead to trouble.

But by God, right now he didn't care.

She played the first piece, something he vaguely guessed was Mozart. Absorbed in watching her, Jack said nothing when she finished. Instead of rising from the seat, though, she stayed where she was. Her expression changed, becoming almost wistful. A slight smile curved her lips as she played a few trills, and then she began to play again.

He could tell this music meant something to her. The first piece she had played with more spirit than technical skill, but this one moved her. She swayed with the music, and at times her head dipped slightly, and the notes would pause. He could swear she was listening to some accompaniment only she could hear.

"I don't know that piece," he said when the last note had faded into a suddenly melancholy silence.

"It was my mother's favorite," she said softly, her eyes shadowed and focused somewhere far away.

"Did you learn to play it for her?"

She didn't answer. Reverently she ran her fingertips across the keys, so lightly they made no sound. "It's a beautiful instrument, Your Grace," she said at last. "You should have it tuned properly." A fine shudder went through her, and he realized with a small shock that she was on the brink of tears.

Damn. Of course—she'd referred to her mother in the past tense. Jack knew what it was like to lose a beloved parent, and she was even younger than he'd been when his father died.

"I'm very sorry," he said quietly. "That you've lost her."

Without looking at him she gently closed the lid on the keys and rose from the bench. "If you'll excuse me, sir, I feel in need of some rest." She swept that ridiculously ornate but graceful curtsy again and then walked from the room.

Jack followed her, driven by a nebulous desire to comfort her but held back by the fact that he'd been the one to make her sad. She never looked back, and when she reached the stairs she broke into a run. Jack stopped dead and listened to her footsteps echo in the hall above him, feeling like an utter cretin.

Chapter 9

Sophie avoided the duke until dinnertime. By then she'd gotten her feelings under control, and resolved not to play any more music. She didn't know what had caused her to play "The Soldier tir'd" from Arne's *Artaxerxes*. It had been Mama's favorite piece to perform, and the one that won her modest fame across Europe. It must have been the pianoforte, a truly beautiful instrument even if some notes were out of tune. How Papa would have loved to play it, and how Mama would have loved singing in that splendid music room, with the wonderful acoustics.

But she should not have given in to those memories and thoughts. If her parents were here now, they would be shocked by what she'd got herself into. She had always told herself they would understand why she'd made the choices she had in life, but this . . . *predicament* . . . was foolish and needn't have happened at all, if she had been able to keep control of her temper. And the only way to rescue herself from it was to keep her wits sharp and collected.

When she went down the stairs, Mrs. Gibbon was waiting for her. "His Grace is outside," she told Sophie.

She blinked. "What, in the rain?"

The housekeeper smiled. "No, ma'am, under the portico." She led the way through the entrance hall, past the gallery, to a pair of wide doors that stood open. With a murmured thanks, Sophie stepped out onto a flagstone terrace, lit by a quartet of large brass lanterns hanging from the roof of the portico.

The rain had become a thick mist. One could see it falling in bands, almost like clouds billowing down to the ground. The sky had lightened to a shade somewhere between gold and gray, as if the clouds had thinned under the force of the sunset. The formal garden visible from the Blue Room lay off to the right, while directly in front of them stretched a sweep of manicured lawn, dotted with tulip trees in the distance. A stone path wound through the landscape toward a lake, dimly visible in the distance only because of the woods that edged the far banks.

"A beautiful view," she said to the man gazing out at it.

He turned. His gaze moved from her face down to her feet, sending that unwanted shiver of awareness through her again. "Yes." He turned back to the landscape as she came to stand beside him. "The lake is a dammed stream that goes well into the woods. That's where Philip and I used to go as boys. We kept a punt or two tied beneath the bridge and would row ourselves out of sight of the house to swim and fish."

"How delightful."

"It was." He hesitated. "I must apologize for earlier."

She knew what he meant, but she instinctively flashed a bright smile. "For kidnapping me from London?"

He smiled wryly. No, she knew he wasn't sorry for that. "For earlier, when I asked you to play."

"Oh! I did warn you the pianoforte was out of tune . . ." She tried to make light of it, but he looked at her with knowing compassion in his eyes, and she fell silent.

"It brought up sad memories for you, which was not my intent at all. I apologize."

She had to swallow a sudden lump in her throat. "Not at all. You couldn't have known. In truth, I ought not to have played that piece. It's been so long since I sat at a pianoforte . . ."

"You must have lost her as a child," he guessed.

Sophie forced another smile. "Yes. I was twelve."

"How tragic. I'm very sorry," he said with honest sympathy. "Was she musical?"

Her smile turned real. "Yes," she said warmly. "Very. When I was cross or rude, she would sing her scoldings at me. Our house was always filled with music. That was her favorite piece, one I heard her sing many times . . ." Before Mama lost her clear, high soprano. Sophie blocked it from her mind. "I believe it was a cruel disappointment when everyone realized I had no voice and only modest talent on the pianoforte, no matter how much I practiced. And then at school—"

"Did they not have a music master at school?"

asked the duke when she broke off, on the brink of terrible memories again.

"No, they did. But it was not the same," she murmured. No music lessons at Mrs. Upton's could match watching her mother sing for the czar, or spending her evenings fetching ale for the tympanists in the orchestra in Milan. No teacher could give the same feel to music as Papa did, a life and emotion that no one ever learned at a school for young ladies. He could have wrung a performance from that out-of-tune pianoforte that would have left tears in the eyes of every listener, and no one would have heard a single sour note.

"My father encouraged me to draw," said the duke. Sophie glanced at him in astonishment, but his gaze was fixed on the distant lake. "He himself sketched, although his was a more architectural bent. He drew the buildings, I drew the people who lived in them." He raised one hand and pointed to the right. "There, past the corner of the house, is the bathing house he designed."

"Do you still draw?" she asked softly.

His hand fell back to his side. "No."

"Why not?"

A gust of wind blew a spray of rain at them. Sophie couldn't resist the urge to turn her face into it, breathing deeply of the soft, moist air. She would never admit it aloud, but it was a magnificent evening. In London she would have made a grimace at the rain for the damage it would do to her slippers on her way around town. Tonight she could simply stand here and savor the quiet, beautiful landscape.

When she opened her eyes, the duke was watching her as if mesmerized. There was a focused intensity in his face, nothing reserved or cold about it. Their eyes met for one charged second, then he turned back to face the rain. "For the same reasons you stopped playing, I expect. Other things claimed my time and attention."

For a while they watched the rain in silence. "This house has always been my escape," said the duke at length. "Even as a boy when I had lessons to do, there was a lake and the woods to explore when lessons were done. Now that it's mine, it's mine alone—my mother dislikes it, and Philip prefers other entertainments. I am loath to fill this one place of refuge with unpleasantness and anger." He turned to her. "I should not have coerced you into coming here. I was furious at Philip but—well. It's done now, and the rain is beyond my control. Can you accept my apology?" He held out his hand.

Slowly she put her hand in his. He wore no gloves, and she had none. "Yes, Your Grace."

One corner of his mouth crooked up. "Might we dispense with that? Ware will do."

"Very well. Ware." Her smile this time was tentative but real. He still held her hand, and his fingers tightened a fraction before he released her. Sophie hid her hand behind her skirt and wiggled her fingers to erase the warmth of his skin against hers.

"I thought to dine in the breakfast room. The dining room is . . ."

"Much too magnificent for an ordinary supper?" she finished when he hesitated.

"I was searching for a word other than *oppressive*," he replied, one of those true grins lighting his face.

In spite of herself she smiled back. "Too large for two people?"

He laughed. Sophie started in spite of herself. He had a wonderful laugh; it was a pity he didn't do it more often. "Far too large." He offered his arm.

Gingerly she took it. Handsome, attracted to her, and now becoming charming. She would have to be very, very careful to avoid making a fool of herself.

Chapter 10

꧁ ꧂

JACK WAS AT breakfast when Wilson brought the first bit of bad news the following morning. "Your Grace, Mr. Percy is here."

Percy ought to have been working diligently in the Ware mansion in Mayfair at this very moment. Percy knew his place, which meant there was only one explanation for the man's presence at Alwyn. Jack closed the newspaper—Wilson must have sent someone on horseback for it at dawn—and stood.

"Where?"

"The morning room, Your Grace."

Jack glanced at the door. Mrs. Campbell had not yet appeared. He was looking forward to seeing her far too much. "Has Mrs. Campbell awoken yet?"

"I believe so. Mrs. Gibbon has located some garments for the lady, but mentioned they would need some alteration."

Of course; she had no clothes of her own. Jack breathed a bit easier, only now realizing he'd grown tense as the minutes ticked away and she didn't appear. "Very good." The butler nodded, throwing open the door as Jack strode out of the room and went to see his secretary.

Richard Percy stood in the morning room. He had obviously ridden from town, judging from the mud on his boots and his wet and bedraggled clothing. "Your Grace," he said, bowing at Jack's appearance. "I do beg your pardon for this intrusion—"

"But Her Grace my mother is going out of her mind with worry," Jack finished in a dry tone. "Is that it?"

"Yes, sir." Percy's expression eased.

Jack knew his mother's worry didn't spring from fears for his safety. In fact, it probably wasn't worry at all, but anger. Since the moment he inherited, she had drummed it into him that he must be above reproach, morally, financially, and socially. Getting into a very scandalous, public wager with a woman at a gaming club would be just the thing to outrage her notions of propriety, and abruptly decamping for Alwyn House with that same woman would send her into a paroxysm of alarm.

For a moment he wondered what Philip had told their mother. Philip never could resist telling a good story, and the scene in Vega's was unquestionably the most shocking thing Jack had done in the last several years. Of course, telling her would have required that Philip confess he was already playing at Vega's again, explicitly breaking the promise he'd made in exchange for Jack paying his debt to Bagwell. Philip was not fond of confession.

Well. No doubt that would have been overshadowed by the duchess's horror at Jack's actions. It had never been much of a secret that the duchess preferred her second son, the one who took after her, while Jack—the heir—might as well have been solely his father's son.

"You may assure Her Grace I am perfectly well, and will return to town when it suits me."

"Will it be a long stay, Your Grace?" Percy backed up a step at Jack's cool stare. "I ask only for my own knowledge, sir."

"No," he said curtly. "A few days only."

"Of course." Percy wet his lips, then took a sealed letter from his coat pocket and offered it. "Her Grace bid me deliver this."

Jack took it without looking at it. "Wilson will have sent someone to prepare a room. Go get dry. You can return to London as soon as your mount is cared for. I trust you will be able to carry on in my absence for a few days."

His secretary bowed and left. Jack cursed aloud in the empty room. His mother's letter was like an anvil in his hand. He knew what it would say. Since the day he inherited his title, her constant refrain had been one of duty: he must remember his position as duke and moderate his behavior accordingly to honor his father and all the dukes who came before him.

He broke the seal and skimmed the letter. It was as expected, indignant and dismayed, concluding with a stern scolding that he had completely undermined his role as head of the family by engaging in the precise sort of behavior Philip must be persuaded to avoid. His brother, the duchess wrote, was humiliated and stunned by this reversal, and she hinted he would be impossible to govern from now on.

Jack's mouth flattened at that charge. Philip was already impossible to govern, and it had nothing to do with Jack's actions.

Worst, though, was the last paragraph. *Not only was it most shocking that you would do such a thing, but you have left me open to acute embarrassment. I was counting on you to accompany me to the Benthams' ball tonight; I presume from your absence you have forgotten and left me to send my regrets at an unpardonably late moment. Lady Stowe and her daughter will be in attendance, and both were anticipating your company. I had not thought you would abandon them so carelessly or hastily; your father would not be pleased . . .*

That, Jack thought in irritation, was unfair. The Stowe family had been close to his for decades. The late earl had been his father's dearest friend, and Lady Stowe and Jack's mother were inseparable. It was both tragic and fitting that the same boating accident claimed the earl's life and, after a week of illness, the duke's, as well. On his deathbed, his father had begged Jack to see that Lady Stowe and her young daughter, Lucinda, were taken care of, and Jack had promised. In the seven years since, he had done everything for them the moment it was asked. He had never abandoned them.

It was true he'd forgotten about this particular ball. Normally he would have gone, if Lady Stowe and her daughter were to attend. Lucinda was making her debut this Season, and Jack knew his father would expect him to do anything he could to ensure she was a success among the *ton*. The last time he'd seen her, just after Christmas, she'd admitted she was nervous about it.

But his mother was not thinking of Lucinda's nerves, she was trying to shame him into rushing back to London, something he had no intention of doing. Not only was he not accustomed to being coerced and shamed, he still hadn't figured out what to do about Mrs. Campbell—but he found her dangerously exhilarating, far more so than any ball.

He stuffed the letter into his pocket and took his time returning to the breakfast room. There was one sobering note of warning in it that he could not ignore. Of course Philip would discover a way to make *him* at fault, thereby deflecting any blame or reproach from himself. As long as the duchess believed Philip was more victim than scoundrel, she would continue making allowances for him instead of encouraging him to reform his ways. Perhaps Jack ought to open the account books and show his mother exactly how much he'd paid to settle Philip's debts recently; he was certain Philip hadn't told her. His father had believed it was not a woman's place to see any accounting but the household expenditures she supervised, and that she should submit even those to her husband for approval. The late duke had treated his wife and younger son with an indulgence that left them both in ignorance of, and absolved of any responsibility for, the consequences of their actions. All of that had descended onto Jack, and the expectation that he would continue doing everything exactly as his father had done was beginning to wear.

Mrs. Campbell was seated at the table eating by the time he returned to the breakfast room. Today she wore a simple dress of dark green. He wondered where she'd got it, and then reminded himself that he ought not to be thinking about her clothing at all, as long as she was provided something decent. This dress, alas, had a slightly higher neckline than the housemaid's dress of yesterday.

"Good morning," she said with a smile at his entrance.

"Good morning." He resumed his seat at the table. Somehow he must keep Percy from setting eyes on her. Percy had been his father's man before his, and at times Jack suspected his loyalty was more to the dukedom than to the duke, whoever that fellow might be. Percy wasn't blind, and if he reported that Jack had hared off to Alwyn House with a beautiful woman, it would inflame the duchess. Jack didn't bother to think about why he cared. "Would you care to explore the attics today?"

She looked at him in amazement, and Jack realized how odd the question sounded. "You inquired about dungeons and torture chambers, neither of which Alwyn has. The attics would be the closest I can offer. The rain continues, which means we are stuck in the house. I am struggling for anything to pass the time."

Her lips quirked in that sly smile he found so entrancing. "When you present it so appealingly, how could I miss the chance?"

They finished breakfast, and Jack told Wilson to fetch some lamps. He also murmured to his butler that nothing should impede Percy from returning to London as soon as possible. Then he headed toward the east wing with Mrs. Campbell at his side, unaccountably eager to explore the dim, stuffy attics.

"What manner of things shall we find up here?" she asked as he opened the door leading to the attic stairs. A rush of warm stale air hit him in the face as he considered the question.

"In truth, I'm not sure. It's been decades since I went up."

She gathered her skirts and followed him up the stairs. "Another exploit with Philip?"

Jack grinned, glancing back. From this angle he could see down her bodice, and it almost made him miss a step and drop his lamp. "Er—no," he said, trying to remember the question. "Philip once got lost and took such a fright he refused to come up again."

Her hands full of skirts, she looked up, her lips parted in surprise. "No!"

His mouth was dry. Perhaps this was a terrible idea. All he could think of now was being alone with her in the dark. She didn't seem angry with him anymore, and it had been an eternity since he found any woman so tempting . . . "It became my hideaway after that," he said, still distracted by her mouth and the plump curves of her breasts. "Free of mothers and younger brothers and any sort of lesson."

"What did you discover up here?" She was a little out of breath, breathing harder than usual as she reached the top of the stairs. Covertly Jack watched the rise and fall of her bosom, straining the bonds of her drab green dress.

"Old furniture, mostly," he said. Sofas and settees where one might seduce a woman properly. "With the odd suit of armor."

"Oh my." She stepped into the attics. The high mansard roof arched above, invisible in the darkness. The rain drummed down on the slate over their heads, not fiercely but steadily. Thanks to the leaden skies it wasn't hot in the attics, but comfortably warm. "I see what you mean," his guest exclaimed softly.

"Hmm?" She might have been a Madonna, reverently painted by an adoring artist, as she raised her face in awe toward the ceiling so far above them. Her skin glowed like gold in the light of his lamp.

"What a perfect hideaway!" She smiled broadly. "No one would ever find you. And as you said— full of furniture. With a lantern, some biscuits, and a good book, who might not want to squirrel away on a lonely day?"

Jack thought of the decanters of brandy, not books, he'd brought up here to enjoy in secret. There was a good chance the bottles were still up here, where he'd carefully hidden them as a lad. He also thought of doing as she said, hiding away up here all day with her. "Er—yes. Who would not?" He lifted the lamp higher and moved farther into the quiet attics.

They wandered slowly. Like the rest of Alwyn House, the attics were kept in good order, with furniture neatly ordered and stored by room.

Mrs. Campbell discovered an ornate birdcage, and Jack was surprised to remember his grandmother's parrot. "Possessed of a viciously sharp beak," he said with a grimace.

She laughed. "That sounds like you put your fingers through the wires of the cage."

"Why would you think that?" He studied the golden cage, still hanging from its stand. "I remember it being much larger than this. The parrot was enormous."

"No wonder he bit," she murmured. "Any creature trapped in a too-small cage would lash out on those who caged him."

"I didn't cage him," said Jack. "He left a scar." He rubbed his thumb along his forefinger, where there was a faint mark from the bite.

She only smiled. "Imagine how the parrot felt. He was still confined to the cage."

He gave her a sharp glance but she had walked on, her expression clear, already engrossed by a curious chair. Jack remembered that as well—it had once been in the library—and he showed her how to flip the seat up to turn the chair into a stepladder. That led them deeper into the attics until they reached the end of the east wing, and when Jack took out his watch, he was shocked to see they had spent hours rummaging in the dust. And most shocking of all, he would have sworn it had been only a few minutes.

"This is almost as intriguing as the house proper," she said, sitting gingerly on the edge of an old, worn-out settee tucked against the eaves. "It's a history of your family."

"Not quite." Jack stepped over a trunk and

opened one of the tall, narrow windows. It stuck after opening a few inches, but the fresh breeze felt deliciously cool. He could see the stables from here and wondered if Percy had left yet. "You'd have to go to Kirkwood Hall for that. It's been in the family since before Henry Tudor took the crown."

"Goodness! What a lot of history that must be." She leaned toward the window, inhaling the rainy air.

"Due to a compulsion to save everything for future generations. A hundred years from now this attic floor will have broken down and collapsed under the weight of family history."

She smiled, her gaze directed out the dust-covered window. "Only think how fascinating your great-grandchildren will find it."

"To read my old Latin lessons? Unlikely." He had found his and Philip's old schoolbooks, neatly stacked in a desk he dimly remembered from the nursery quarters. Why anyone had kept those was beyond him.

"I don't know," she said wistfully. "They will see your portrait downstairs, pompous and regal. It might please them to no end to discover proof that you were once a boy with poor penmanship who had to write his Latin verbs over and over, just as they might have to do."

Jack ignored the bit about his portrait being pompous. He leaned against a particularly ugly chest of drawers opposite the sofa she sat on. She wasn't guarded now; her expression was nearly the same one she had worn yesterday when he asked about her mother. "It sounds like you've been that child."

"I?" Her lips curved and she heaved a sigh. "No. My parents died when I was twelve. I have almost nothing left of either of them." She hesitated, her gaze distant. "My father was disowned by his parents and I was never able to explore his family home. Everything of his youth was lost to me, but if I had the chance to read his old Latin lessons, to see what he drew in the margins, simply to have something of his . . . I would seize it."

"Why?" She blinked, and Jack realized he'd asked the question rather stridently. He moderated his voice. "Why was your father disowned?"

"For marrying my mother." She lifted her chin. "He never regretted it."

Jack raised one brow. There had been something very like regret in *her* voice as she talked of the family history her father had lost by being disowned.

"He didn't," she insisted. "His father wanted him to marry a girl whose family lived nearby, someone he'd known since they were children. It would have been like wedding his sister, Papa used to say, and it would have given his father—" She stopped, pressing her lips together. Her eyes flashed and she looked quite fierce, despite the smudge of dirt on her chin and the cobwebs on her borrowed dress.

Jack guessed she had no good opinion of that grandfather. "He was fortunate he was free to follow his heart."

She looked at him sharply, but then her annoyed expression melted into one that was almost pitying. "He *chose* to follow his heart. It required certain sacrifices on his part, of course, but he accepted them as part of the bargain he'd made."

"Commendable," replied Jack. Her father hadn't been the heir, then, at least not to any significant estate or title. No heir was permitted to follow his heart unless his heart led him to a lady of impeccable breeding and fortune. "But why was your mother so unacceptable to your grandfather?"

She drew breath to answer, then went still, her eyes focusing on him with renewed wariness. "She was French," she said in the light tone he'd come to recognize as a diversionary tactic. Jack guessed there was more objection to her mother than being French, but he let it go. For now.

"Not Parisian, although I've no idea if that would have been better or worse. She came from Nice," added Mrs. Campbell.

"One supposes it didn't matter, given her inability to be the English girl who lived nearby."

She laughed. "Precisely! And in all honestly, I don't think there's any pleasing my grandfather. He would have found something to disapprove of regardless of whom Papa married."

"One of that sort, is he?"

"When I was a child, I nicknamed him the Ogre," she replied with a cheeky wink.

Jack laughed even as he tucked the fact away in his mind. She'd said her parents died when she was twelve; had her grandfather done something on their deaths to earn her enmity? It wouldn't be unheard-of for a man to cast off an unwanted grandchild, particularly one from a marriage he had opposed. Perhaps Mrs. Campbell had learned to look out for herself from an early age. And then her husband appeared to have been a useless fellow as well, which would only have made her more independent. Who was this woman? Jack was beginning to wonder why she seemed to have no connections at all.

"Since you were not able to excavate your own family attics, I am pleased to offer you mine," he said instead, making a half bow. "Your grandfather sounds much like my great-grandfather."

"The one who exiled his wife here?" She dusted a clean spot on the windowsill and rested her elbow against it as she settled more comfortably on the old settee. The breeze stirred the loose wisps of hair at her temple, almost as if a lover's gentle fingers stroked it. "Why did he do that?"

"I don't think he cared for her, nor she for him." One tendril curled around her jaw, teasing the corner of her mouth. Jack was mesmerized by it, and in the dim attic felt at full liberty to stare.

"One wonders why either agreed to wed the other."

He smiled without amusement. "It was an advantageous match for both. The Dukes of Ware don't wed for trifling matters like affection."

"No?" She seemed genuinely surprised, tilting her head to face him. "Never?"

Jack thought of Portia. He would have married her, as mad in love as he'd thought himself, and it would have been a disaster. "Not to my knowledge."

"And here I thought a wealthy, powerful duke could do as he pleased, wed whom he chose, and no one could say him nay." She shook her head in mock sadness. "Instead you're required to wed a piece of land or a sum of money rather than a person."

His mouth thinned in irritation. "Hardly required."

"Oh." She gazed at him, wide-eyed. "Each generation *chooses* to marry for purely financial reasons, then."

"I've not married anyone," he said. "Obviously." She lowered her eyes and smiled. Too late he realized she'd only been tweaking him. He let out his breath and stared out the window. He could just see her face from the corner of his eye. "I expect I have as much freedom to marry as you do."

Her head came up. "What does that mean?"

Ah, a hit. He lifted one shoulder. "You're an independent widow, able to do as you please and with no one to say you nay."

"Except when I wish to go home," she said with a pointed glance. "Do you think your ancestors were happy, wedding for dynastic reasons?"

"Happy? I have no idea. Satisfied? I believe so. One presumes they found . . . delight in other places." He knew they had. His ancestors were fiendishly organized men, and Jack had seen the records of gifts for mistresses and lovers. His grandfather had kept a house in London specifically for trysts, with instructions to the housekeeper to turn the mattress and place fresh linens on the bed every day.

"My parents loved each other very much," she said softly. "They found delight in each other. Perhaps more practical marriages would have yielded more wealth or property, but I believe nothing could have matched their happiness."

"Is that what you want?"

She met his eyes. "Would you believe it if I said yes?"

"I—" He stopped, remembering how he'd accused her of trying to attach a wealthy husband. "I would."

For a moment she didn't reply. Then a smile crossed her face, and her tone turned light again. "It would be wonderful, but that sort of match seems very rare."

That didn't answer the question. Not that it should matter to him who or why she married, so long as she didn't set her sights on Philip. Which she'd already denied in convincing terms. So what sort of man was she looking for? Jack cleared his throat, wondering how the hell he'd got into this conversation anyway. "Shall we explore the other side of the house while the light is still good?"

She was on her feet before he finished the question. "By all means."

SOPHIE THOUGHT SHE MIGHT be losing her mind. How on earth had she got into a discussion of love and marriage with the duke?

It must be the dark, warm atmosphere of the attics, softening her wits. Or perhaps it was the decades of family history all around her, something she had never had in her life and secretly craved. The thought of finding her mother's childhood doll or her father's first music book made her feel uncharacteristically sentimental. Surely that explained why she had told him, of all people, about her parents' romantic but illicit marriage. Only Eliza and Georgiana knew about that, yet somehow she'd opened her mouth and told the Duke of Ware.

The eastern side of the attics were not as intriguing. Neat rows of crates and trunks lined the walls, and when she managed to pry open one crate, it turned out to hold pieces of metal, wrapped in flannels under the straw.

"A knight's suit of armor and weaponry!" She held up one piece in triumph, a long rod with a wicked hook on one end. "How many enemies do you think your ancestors struck down with this? It looks like a spear."

Ware looked astonished and came over for a closer look. He inspected the spear for a moment, then gave her a strange glance. "It's an old fire fork. Unless our enemies were attempting to invade the house through the fireplace, I doubt it struck down anyone."

She made a face and replaced the fire fork, which really ought to have been a spear. "How ordinary."

He smiled. "I did warn you."

That sapped any interest from opening more crates. Sophie surveyed the trunks nearest them. "What is this?" She touched a small silver badge hammered into the end of one.

The duke brought the lamp and stooped to see it. His shoulder brushed her elbow as he did, sending a charge through her that went right down to her toes. She drew back, unconsciously rubbing the spot. She would have retreated more but there was no room—she was stuck with her back against the crates and his broad shoulders and golden head right in front of her, almost on his knees at her feet. Right at the perfect level for her to plow her fingers into the rumpled waves of his hair.

Horrified, she forced her eyes up to stare fixedly at the rafters above them. He was a sinfully handsome man. He was being very kind today, indulging her interest in rummaging through old furniture. Before she could stop them, Georgiana's words pattered through her mind about making one of the gentlemen she met at Vega's fall in love with her, and she couldn't help remembering that she had met Ware at Vega's.

She had kept the men she wagered with at arm's length for the most part; she didn't want to marry an avid gambler. But the Duke of Ware was not a gambler at all. Nor was he the cold, boring drudge Philip had described. He was almost unbearably attractive, particularly when he smiled, and he was attracted to her. And her body was suddenly warming to the idea of flirting with him up here in this shadowy private world where only the two of them existed . . .

"My grandmother's monogram," he said, making her start. "The *W* for Wilhelmina beneath the ducal coronet." He rose to stand beside her. "She was a capital rider," he remarked. "Even in her old age she kept an excellent stable."

Sophie was endeavoring to ignore how his arm was right next to hers, and how she would be practically in his arms if she made a quarter turn to her left. "Wilhelmina," she said, seizing on any distraction. "What an unusual name."

"Her father was a Prussian archduke. The marriage was arranged because my great-grandfather thought it would curry favor with George II if his son wed a bride from Hanover."

"Of course," she murmured.

He sighed in exasperation. "Yes, it was arranged for political advantage. But I do believe they were fond of each other, and my grandfather never exiled her anywhere. In fact, he indulged her a great deal. Her horses were imported from the finest stables in Europe."

"A veritable love match," she said. "I feel vastly relieved to know it, for their sakes."

He gave her an exasperated glance. "Must everyone have a love match?"

"Of course not. People are free to marry for misery, or for money, or for any reason they choose."

"I suppose you would know," he said. "Having been married."

Right—the mythical Mr. Campbell. During her long trip on the mail coach from Bath to London three years ago, Sophie had created an entirely new history for herself, including a sadly deceased husband. In her mind, Mr. Campbell had been tall and thin, a bit sickly but kind, a scholarly man who could be lamented but not really missed. She told people he was Scottish but had an American mother, to deter any questions about his family.

But the duke didn't need to know any of that. "The vicar doesn't quiz you on your reasons for marriage," she said lightly. "As long as the banns have been called properly, he reads the ceremony."

"You must have been very young."

Sophie's smile grew fixed. "Young but not naive."

"I presume it was a love match." Even in the lamp light, his eyes were so very blue and vivid. "Since your parents had such a blissful union."

She turned away. "I told you before—that sort of marriage is rare." Rare, and not without cost. Her Grand Plan was to find a sensible, kind man of sufficient income. Someone she could be fond of, but not someone she fell in love with. Someone very like her imaginary Mr. Campbell, as it happened. As much as Sophie longed for the devotion and adoration her parents had shared, she wasn't sure she had the fortitude to follow her passion as they had done. Could she give up everything for a man, even a man who loved her? Could she resign herself to scraping for money to pay the butcher, the landlord, the doctor? Her parents had loved each other deeply, but it had cost them—and in the end, it had cost Sophie, as well.

"What is in these trunks?" she asked to divert him. "There are so many."

The duke's gaze lingered on her; he knew she had dodged his question, and for some reason he seemed disappointed. He cared to know her answer. "Clothing, most likely." He pulled out the trunk with the elaborate engraved *W* on the end and undid the latches.

Inside lay a cloud of silver paper, then layers of soft linen. Gently, Sophie lifted the wrappings aside and gasped at the gown that lay below. It was cloth of gold, lavishly embroidered with pearls and dripping with lace. "May I?" She glanced at the duke in question, and he nodded. Carefully she lifted it up, speechless at the exquisite work. It still sparkled and shone, some six decades after it would have been fashionable. "It's beautiful," she whispered. "Stunningly beautiful!"

She wanted to take the gown out of the trunk and hold it in the sun. She yearned for a mirror to hold it in front of herself and imagine, for one brief moment, that it was hers. She glanced at the duke from beneath her eyelashes; he had propped one elbow on the topmost trunk and stood watching her, relaxed but attentive. Perhaps what she really wanted was to pretend that in a gown like this, she'd be a worth a duke's attention . . .

"Perhaps there are some benefits to marrying for wealth and position," murmured the duke wryly.

She flashed a reproachful glance at him. "I never said there were none." She just didn't think they were worth the risk. Reverently she laid the dress back in its wrappings, tucking the coverings securely around it. "It's a treasure chest," she said as she closed the lid.

"That looks like her court presentation gown. There's a portrait of her wearing it at Kirkwood Hall in Somerset."

Another repository of family history. "She must have looked like the bride of Apollo."

"Surely you jest. Apollo would be a mundane husband for a Duchess of Ware," he said with a straight face. Sophie blinked, then burst out laughing. The duke did, too, his face easing into an expression of warm familiarity. He pushed the trunk back into place. "Do you wish to open more?"

Part of her did, to see what other treasures were hidden up here, but she tucked a loose tendril of hair behind her ear and made a face as her fingers came away sticky with cobwebs. "Unless one of the trunks contains a ghost, ready to rise from her rest and rattle chains for our entertainment, I suppose not. Surely we've dislodged enough dust for one day." She brushed at her skirt, belatedly realizing a disadvantage to exploring the attics. She was a mess.

"Alas, another thing Alwyn cannot supply—ghosts," he said in mock chagrin. "Or if there are any about, they must be very quiet ones." He cocked his head. "I never suspected women could be so ghoulish."

"Well." She waved one hand. "Discovering beautiful clothing is even better than finding a ghost."

He grinned and looked around. "I suspect there's enough packed away here to clothe the entire court of St. James."

She thought of her own modest wardrobe in London—now reduced by one bright crimson dress. Mrs. Gibbon had brought it back this morning, stained to the knee, saying there was nothing more they could do for it. The green dress Sophie wore today was another cast-off from one of the maids, she suspected, and now it was covered in grime. Alwyn House had more clothes, of higher quality, than she did.

"If it's all as fine as that gown, I consider it a crime to leave it packed away," she said. "Are your grandfather's ermine-trimmed robes here, as well?"

The duke did not reply. There was a very odd look on his face as he studied her. He reached out and drew his fingers across her cheek, lingering for a moment. Sophie couldn't move; she could hardly breathe. The touch of his fingers on her skin, stroking, the way a man might do to a woman he loved, had ignited that terrible feeling again—the strange pull she felt toward him, and the wholly unwanted longing for him to plunge his hands into her hair and pull her against him and ravish her against these old trunks . . .

He took his hand away and flicked his fingers. "Cobwebs," he said, his voice deep and rough.

Her face burned. She was suffering pangs of desire and he was noticing how filthy she was. *Mad, mad, mad*, she scolded herself. "The perils of exploring!" She swiped roughly at her dress with both hands. "I should wash . . ."

The duke made a noise, low in his throat. "You're a very unusual woman, Mrs. Campbell."

More than you know, Sophie thought uneasily. She summoned a carefree smile. "I choose to accept that as a compliment, Your Grace."

He dragged his eyes up to hers, and she went hot all over at the realization he'd been watching her try to brush the dust from her bodice. "Good," he said in the charged silence. "I meant it as one." And with that he picked up the lamp and headed for the door, leaving her to follow with a pounding heart.

Chapter 11

"I DON'T KNOW ABOUT YOU," Mrs. Campbell announced on the third morning, "but I shall run absolutely mad if I don't get out of this house."

Jack raised one brow. "Into the rain?"

She looked at the windows. "It's more of a light mist today. In Russia they would account it a fine day, nothing to keep one indoors."

"When were you in Russia?" he asked with interest.

Instead of answering, she pushed back her chair and rose. "I think a simple walk in the garden to start and then perhaps to the lake. You did say there is a path. Will you join me, or shall you spend the day lolling on a sofa in the library?"

Jack pushed back his chair as well. "I have not *lolled* anywhere in years, madam."

Her smile was triumphant. "Then let's ask Wilson to find some umbrellas."

She was right about the rain; it barely made a sound against the ground as they stepped out under the portico. Mrs. Campbell drew a deep breath—of relief, he realized—and exclaimed, "How beautiful it is!"

Jack pulled his greatcoat collar closer around his neck and squinted at the sky. It was lighter today, a pale pearl color instead of the sullen pewter it had been. Perhaps that was a sign the rain was ending.

Wilson appeared with two umbrellas, but Jack took only one. He gave the butler a look, and the man promptly bowed and went back into the house, still holding the second umbrella. Mrs. Campbell, gazing at the wet garden, had her back to the door and missed the exchange. Jack opened his umbrella and stepped forward. "Shall we?" He offered his arm.

She looked at him, then at his arm. Her face stilled for a moment before she curled her hand around his elbow. It was the lightest of touches, but Jack felt it echo through every nerve in his body. He raised the umbrella overhead, and they walked out together.

"Who planned the gardens?" she asked as they passed the roses, the petaled heads drooping heavily in the mist.

"My great-grandmother, originally. I confess I don't know much about the gardens. Mrs. Gibbon could no doubt recite an entire history."

"Has she been here long?"

He nodded. "Thirty years or more—as long as I can remember, at any rate."

"How loyal," she murmured.

"Not everyone finds my family appalling."

She gave a gasp of indignation. "I never said that."

"You called my great-grandfather beastly. You remarked with disapproval on my grandparents' arranged marriage. You said my brother would make a wretched husband, and you called me terribly vexing and accused me of kidnapping." Somehow the recitation of charges made him want to smile. Perhaps it was the nonplussed expression on her face.

"Yes," she rallied to say, "one must only suppose you pay extraordinarily high wages, to have such loyal servants."

"So one would work for an ogre, if the wages were high enough?" he asked, affecting deep thought.

"Well, if you can't marry for money, you must work for it." She tilted her head and gave him a saucy look. "Foreign as that thought might be to a duke."

"You're entirely correct," he said. "I work for no wages at all."

She stopped. "I didn't mean—" She pursed her lips, and Jack found himself openly staring. He even found himself thinking how easily he could lean over and kiss her, here in the garden while the rain came down and she stood there looking so beautifully contrite with her mouth perfectly shaped for a kiss. "Philip says you work a great deal."

Mention of his brother doused Jack's contemplation of kissing her. He looked away from her ripe pink mouth. "Yes. Alas, Philip has yet to express any interest in seeing that the servants' wages are paid, or the rents are collected, or any of the other dull things I do."

"I didn't—" She stopped. "I didn't intend any slight," she said in a softer tone. "Quite the contrary! Philip is an irresponsible scoundrel, which makes for an amusing companion but not for an admirable man. I only meant . . ." Again she turned, taking in the house, the gardens, the rain-dewed lawns. "Working for servants' wages is a world apart from this. When one worries about having money for food and shelter and medicine, then . . . yes—one would work for an ogre, if he paid extraordinary wages."

The spark of irritation had faded as she spoke. Jack realized something: she had been poor. What's more, she had worked for wages. She had worried about the cost of food and shelter.

It was not difficult to put together a history wherein her parents died and left her, still only a child, with very little. Her disapproving grandfather—the Ogre, she'd called him—hadn't done well by her, and it seemed her husband hadn't, either. It was odd how she never spoke of him. But it formed a picture of a woman trying to forge her own way in the world by necessity. And gambling, he must admit, was more respectable than some ways she could have earned her keep, particularly when she did it so artfully.

"I try not to be an ogre," he said at last. "Not all the time, at any rate. You must ask Mrs. Gibbon if I ever succeed."

A smile broke out on her face, pure shining relief. "I have no doubt she'll browbeat me for even implying you might be! The evening we arrived, she assured me with great confidence that

I'd been entirely safe with you, walking a mile in the storm."

Safe was hardly what Jack felt right now. He was deep in lust with his unexpected guest, and remembering that he was a gentleman was becoming increasingly difficult. If he spent much longer strolling in the garden with her like this, her hand on his arm and her mouth so temptingly near, he might go mad and do something idiotic like kiss her. But she wanted out of the house, and the carriage axle was still being repaired.

Then it came to him. "Do you ride?"

Her brows went up. "Yes. But I haven't a habit."

Jack noted she was wearing the housemaid's dress again, the one with the low neckline, and nodded once. "I think we can solve that."

It took Mrs. Gibbon quite some time to unearth an old riding habit from the trunks in the attics, but she did it. Jack took himself off to the stables while Mrs. Campbell changed. The days when Alwyn had housed a dozen or more fine horses were in the past, but he still kept a few mounts here.

He was conferring with the groom about where best to ride in the rain when a figure appeared in the doorway. He glanced up and forgot what he'd been saying as Mrs. Campbell hurried inside, brushing drops of mist from her sleeve.

The habit was old-fashioned but fit her perfectly. It was a vivid emerald green, with gold braid on the jacket and a small puff of lace at the collar. The fitted jacket emphasized the curves of her bosom and waist, and the long full skirt swayed appealingly around her hips. She folded her gloved hands and looked up from under the wide-brimmed, round hat she wore, to meet Jack's eyes.

"Will it do?" she asked lightly, striking a pose as if her portrait were being painted. "Or shall your grandmother come back from the grave to punish me for my presumption?"

"No," he said quietly. "If she would punish anyone, it would be me." But it would be worth it. He thought of all the other fine items of clothing that must be up there, and it made his throat close up. Sophie Campbell was a vision in servant's clothing. In a golden court presentation gown, with diamonds in her hair and around her throat, no one would guess she wasn't a duchess herself . . .

Breathing harder than he should have been, he turned back to Owens, the groom, and tried to focus on anything other than his intriguing guest.

"The high meadow," supplied Owens, a taciturn old fellow. "Drains well, level ground."

"Yes. Splendid. Put Mrs. Campbell on Minerva," he said, naming a mare with a mellow temper and a smooth gait. He'd already had them saddle a horse for him. His favorite was still in London, but Maximillian was a good horse, an older gelding who wouldn't mind the rain.

He stayed away while they saddled Minerva and brought her into the wide center aisle of the stable. There was a mounting block there, and Owens was leading Minerva to it, anticipating helping Mrs. Campbell into the saddle. Jack watched her walk toward it, the full skirt caught up in one arm. She looked like she knew what she was about, and probably didn't need his help, and yet his feet started moving on their own.

"Let me," he said, intercepting her before she reached the block. "Minerva doesn't like the block."

Owens gave him a queer look at the lie—Minerva was well trained to stand by the block—but obediently he stopped the horse. Jack laced his fingers together and stooped slightly. With only a brief hesitation, Mrs. Campbell put her foot into his grip and rested her hands on his shoulders. Her skirts smelled slightly musty, but Jack inhaled deeply and gave her a boost. She landed easily in the saddle, but he stood near as she hooked her knee over the pommel and adjusted her skirts. Minerva shifted, and for a brief sizzling moment, Mrs. Campbell's leg pressed against his chest. He could feel her knee, right at his shoulder, and without warning his brain imagined her knees rising beside his waist as he moved above her, tasting every inch of her luscious skin, driving hard and fast into her . . .

God save him.

"Thank you, Your Grace," she said, interrupting his increasingly carnal thoughts. He jerked his head in a nod and swung onto Maximillian's back, discreetly adjusting his breeches once safely in the saddle.

They rode through the stable yard, then turned up the lane that led toward the woods. "The high meadow is beyond the woods," he told her, keeping Maximillian beside Minerva. "Owens says it's fairly firm and should offer a good ride."

"Brilliant." She was riding well but very carefully, he noticed, as if she'd not been on a horse in a while.

"Still, we can't be foolish. It's wet and I won't risk Minerva's legs."

"Of course not." She patted the horse's neck. "I don't wish to humiliate myself by racing madly across the fields and ending on my backside in the mud."

She smiled and Jack laughed, although his stomach had contracted at the thought of her backside, muddy or otherwise. "An easy ride, then," he said, and urged Maximillian into a trot. When he glanced back, she was keeping pace. Her face was alive with joy beneath the brim of her hat.

They rode through the woods, along paths that wove through the trees and avoided any large puddles. When they emerged from the trees and reached the high meadow, Jack realized the rain had actually stopped.

"Goodness," said Mrs. Campbell breathlessly beside him. She pulled Minerva to a stop and gazed openmouthed at the meadow. "Look . . ."

Barley visible, a rainbow shimmered across the far end of the meadow. Jack raised one brow in question at her, and with an eager smile she nodded. They took off, skimming across the field at a canter. The air felt soft and full, and he realized how right she had been to want out of the house. He couldn't regret the day spent in the attics, but this felt immeasurably more alive.

They reached the opposite side of the meadow and slowed back to a walk. "Oh my," cried Mrs. Campbell. She gave a very unladylike whoop. "That was brilliant!"

Her hat had blown off, and tendrils of mahogany hair blew about her face. Her eyes sparkled and her cheeks were flushed, and he thought he'd never seen anyone look so unabashedly happy. It made him laugh, and a thrill went through him that he'd been responsible. "At last! Something you can savor about Alwyn House."

She flicked her crop toward him in jest, but her smile was wide and infectious. Even brighter and more joyful than the one she'd given Philip. "It's a wonderful place because of Minerva. Minnie, darling, you were magnificent!" She leaned low across the horse's neck to scratch between her ears.

Jack turned and looked back; her hat lay forgotten in the trampled grass, a small gray spot in the green meadow. "Minerva follows wherever Maximillian leads. She's quite besotted with him."

"Oh?"

"See how she follows him. Leave your reins slack," he directed, and nudged his horse back toward the hat.

"Unfair!" she cried as Minerva promptly followed.

He grinned. "Because she chooses to follow her heart?"

She rolled her eyes as he teased her with her own words. "Because all this time I've been feeling rather proud of myself for remembering how to ride, when she was merely following you."

"How long has it been since you rode?" They had reached the hat. Jack swung down to the ground and scooped it up. It looked a little damp but otherwise unscathed.

"Oh, years. Keeping a horse costs far more than hiring a hackney."

Maximillian was snuffling at Minerva in a friendly fashion. Jack had chosen this pair because of how well they got on together. "See?" he said, nodding at them. "True love."

"I shall allow that to stand unchallenged, as it proves my greater point—true love is rare, but powerful." She put out her hand for the hat.

"How do you know it's rare?" He held on to the hat. He rather liked the way locks of hair had fallen loose around her face. It gave her a beautifully disheveled air, intimate and arresting. Of course, damn near everything about her was arresting his attention lately, making him crave ever more intimacy.

She wiggled her fingers in appeal. "How many marriages can you name based on true love?"

"Several," he countered, stubbornly holding the hat.

Her brows arched. "But none in your family."

Jack sighed and relinquished the hat. "By their choice."

She took her time resetting the hat on her head, tucking away all those teasing wisps of hair. "I suppose that divides us, Your Grace," she said at last, gathering her reins again. "I think it is rare, and I would not put duty or social advantage above it. Shall we ride on?" She nudged Minerva forward, leaving him standing in the field and wondering why he'd asked that question. Her opinions on love should not matter to him.

THEY RODE FOR A while, tearing across the meadow several more times. It occurred to Jack that she hadn't asked an obvious question: why couldn't they ride back to London? The meadow wasn't as rutted or flooded as the road, but it was remarkably solid, and with care it certainly seemed they could navigate the roads. Given the fresh newspapers lying on the breakfast table every morning, Jack expected Owens had been riding Maximillian to the nearest posting inn with regularity.

But she never asked, and he began to suspect she was enjoying herself. That suited him perfectly, because he was beginning to think a week was far too short a time to spend with her.

The skies were noticeably brighter by the time they returned to the stables, spattered with mud. Owens took the horses, and Jack offered her his arm as they started toward the house. She took it very naturally.

"Thank you," she said. "For taking me riding."

"It was my pleasure, Mrs. Campbell." He was surprised by how true that was. By how much he had enjoyed every day with her, in fact.

"Do you know, I don't think I've spent so much time exclusively with any one person since my parents died," she remarked.

Jack thought of Percy, his secretary, who sat in his study for hours each day as they worked. Percy couldn't count. "It's unusual for me, as well."

"One might also suppose we've come to be friends," she said lightly.

Aside from the fact that he harbored some feelings toward her that one never applied to mere friends, Jack heartily agreed. "One might."

She glanced sideways at him, as if she'd heard his unspoken caveat. "I don't expect it will last once we leave. But perhaps . . . just for now . . . you might call me Sophie." Jack stopped dead. She smiled and waved one hand airily. "I've grown tired of hearing 'Mrs. Campbell,' is all. If you find it objectionable, by all means—"

"No." He put his hand over hers on his arm. "You mistake me . . . Sophie."

Her smile turned brighter, almost too bright. "Very good . . . Ware."

Jack knew that calling her by name breached some barrier from which there would be no going back. *Friends*, she said; *it won't last once we leave.* That sounded like the first step on the road of temptation. Every inch of familiarity would lead to another, and another, and another, because he couldn't see an end to his fascination with her, and damn but he wanted to race through all those inches of familiarity. He knew he was playing with fire, but instead of trying to quench the embers, he squeezed his hand around hers and smiled into her bright sherry eyes.

He'd worry about the danger later.

Chapter 12

❦❦❦

S OPHIE APOLOGIZED PROFUSELY to Mrs. Gibbon for the state of the riding habit after she changed, but the housekeeper waved it off.

"His Grace wanted you to wear it, and what good was it doing anyone in a trunk?" She collected the damp, mud-spattered habit and headed for the door. "I'm to tell you dinner will be ready shortly, and you may go down when you wish."

"Oh," she said in surprise, but the housekeeper was gone, leaving her alone in the room. She stepped in front of the tall cheval mirror to make certain she was as neat as could be in the housemaid's cast-off dress. For a moment she thought of the fine gowns that must be lying in wrappings just above her head. If she could borrow a riding habit, perhaps she could borrow another dress . . .

No. She firmly put that thought from her head. Those were not her clothes, they were the duke's. Just because he allowed her to borrow a riding habit didn't mean he wanted to see her in one of those fine gowns upstairs. And as for herself . . . She was five kinds of fool for wanting to look attractive tonight, when she was already suffering from an overwhelming temptation to flirt with Ware.

She drew herself up in front of the mirror. "Remember yourself," she said sternly to her reflection. She was not a duchess, and she didn't deserve to wear their clothes any more than she ought to consider letting the duke seduce her. It was a good thing the rain had stopped and she would be returning to London soon, where she would go back to her ordinary life and Ware would resume his very elegant one. She gave her skirt one more tug to smooth a wrinkle, then turned and went down to dinner.

They dined, as they had every night, in the breakfast room. It had a different feel by candlelight, and tonight it felt even more intimate. The names, she decided; he called her Sophie, as she had impulsively invited him to do. And she called him Ware, marveling every time that she was on friendly terms with a duke.

After dinner they wandered through the house idly. Ware showed her a few more of his drawings, tucked away in odd corners of the gallery. He was so charmingly modest about them, calling them his scribblings when she thought they were quite good. There was one of a horse—"the best jumper in all of Britain," he said—and one of Kirkwood Hall, his main estate in Somerset. It looked like a palace from the time of the Tudors, and was every bit as intimidating as she had expected a duke's home would be. Now at last she saw why he called Alwyn his favorite of all his houses; the rest of his houses were actual castles.

But she could listen to him talk about it forever. There was something different about his voice now. At first it had been cool and remote, as elegant and aristocratic as could be. Over the last two days, he had become warmer, more animated. He laughed at her teasing instead of giving her a stern look. At first she'd thought he was affronted—as she had intended—but now she thought it was because he wasn't arrogant and dull, and he didn't like her thinking him so. Every now and then she caught him giving her a roguish glance. What had he been like as a young man? she wondered. And what might have happened had she met him then?

Eventually they ended up in the library. By now it was also Sophie's favorite room in the house. She sank gratefully onto the sofa, lounging inelegantly on the silk upholstery. "That was a glorious day," she announced. "You must watch carefully, or I shall be tempted to steal Minnie from your stables."

He had followed more slowly, but now came around the sofa and took the chair. "She would run back the first time you took her out, to rejoin Maximillian."

Sophie laughed. "Ah yes, her true love."

"I understand one should not interfere with it in any way." He set down two glasses and wrapped a towel around the top of the bottle he held.

Sophie sat up, eyes on the bottle. "Is that champagne?"

"Indeed." He uncorked it, filled the two glasses, and handed her one. The bubbles fizzing gently against the crystal. "Wilson says the roads are drying well. The carriage is repaired. If the sun is out tomorrow, we can return to London."

"Oh!" She took a sip, then another. "That's lovely," she whispered.

He looked amused. "Have you never had it?"

"Oh no." She drank some more, reveling in the cool crisp wine. "Far too elegant for my usual haunts."

"Then we shall have two bottles." He leaned back in his chair. "In celebration of the repaired carriage."

And their impending return to London. Sophie raised her glass in salute and drank some more, reminding herself that it was what she'd been demanding for three days. Now that the moment was at hand, she felt none of the relief she had anticipated. Back in London, there would be no more playing cards with the duke, or riding in the rain, or exploring dusty attics. She would go back to the gambling tables, carefully squirreling away shillings and pounds either as a fortune to help her get a husband, or to purchase an annuity to sustain her into old age. She would have tea every fortnight with her friends, listening to Georgiana wax euphoric about Lord Sterling's charm and to Eliza fret about her father's determination that her enormous dowry must attract a noble husband.

Her lips curved at the thought of her friends. How it would amaze them if they knew she was here with a duke, reclining on a sofa in his country mansion and drinking champagne with him.

But her smile faded. She could hardly tell them about this—indeed, if gossip had spread despite

Mr. Dashwood's rule to the contrary, she might not be permitted to see her friends again. Mr. Cross was indulgent and fond of her, but even he would draw the line if he feared Sophie's reputation would tarnish Eliza's. And Georgiana's chaperone had only agreed to their regular teas with reluctance in the first place. One whiff of scandal about Sophie's name and Lady Sidlow would be furious.

No, back in London her life would not be completely the same.

She turned her head to study Ware. He was watching her, and when their eyes connected, a little shock raced through her. All his aloof reserve had vanished; she had thought him implacable and stern, but now it seemed like that had been another man. He sprawled as easily in the chair as she lay on the sofa, his chin propped in one hand and the glass of champagne dangling from the fingertips of his other hand.

"It will be strange to go back to London after this," she said.

"Very," he agreed.

"No doubt in a few days' time it will all seem like a dream. A holiday from the world and its cares."

He made a soft noise of agreement. Sophie finished her glass of champagne, and he leaned forward to refill it. "Are you still eager to return?"

She settled more comfortably on the sofa. Her answer at the moment was a resounding *no*. This moment, right now, was almost perfect. But this moment could not last, and the fact that she wanted it to last meant it was past time to go home. "Of course," she said. "One does what one must."

"Hmm." He slouched deeper into his chair. "You stopped demanding I take you back at once."

"I'm not a fool," she said pertly. "With a broken carriage axle and never-ending rain, I acknowledge that returning at once was beyond even the Duke of Ware."

He smiled. "Yet now the happy moment is approaching, and you aren't dancing with joy."

No. Not only was she less than eager to face the consequences, she was finally admitting to herself that she had enjoyed these few days.

With him. *Because* of him.

"You said you didn't expect to win that wager," she said softly, staring up at the ceiling. It was covered with elaborate scrollwork in gold, with a frieze of mythological beings cavorting around the edges. The chandelier of cut crystal glittered in the lamplight. That ceiling was probably worth more than her entire house. "Why did you propose it?"

He pushed himself upright in his chair and leaned forward, elbows on his knees, and looked down at her. His golden hair was rumpled into waves that made her long to smooth them. "Haven't you guessed?"

She angled her face toward him. "Tell me. I'm no good at guessing."

He let out his breath, his eyes shadowed, and then he bent and kissed her. His mouth was soft, a gentle hint of a kiss rather than a real one. Her eyes drifted closed as his lips whispered over hers, and she moved toward him like a flower seeking the sun. His fingertips touched her jaw, angling her face with the slightest perceptible pressure. A soft sound of pleasure hummed in her throat.

The duke lifted his head. For a moment they stared at each other. "Is that all?" Sophie whispered, belatedly realizing how her heart was thudding. "All you want?"

"No." He traced one finger, as lightly as a feather, down her throat. A shiver rippled over her skin, and her nipples hardened as his gaze swept over her. "Not by a tenth."

She was in no condition to face this decision. Alone with him for three full days, exposed to his dry humor and surprising humanity and unbearable attractiveness, she was virtually defenseless when his gaze connected with hers again, this time hot with hunger. She should think of her reputation, already perilously uncertain after that wager; she should think of Philip, who would view it as a betrayal by both of them. She should think of Giles Carter, who was her best chance for a respectable marriage. She should think of herself, and how she would feel if she succumbed to this strangely potent desire for a man who would never fall in love with her.

But when she opened her mouth—"Show me," she whispered. "Please."

His answering smile was slow and hungry, as if some sort of fire had roared to life inside him, and Sophie felt it all the way to her toes. He had chipped away at her guard by taking her riding, by showing her his house, by letting her tempt him into being silly and then laughing at himself. She had begun to like him, far more than she'd thought possible. But when he looked at her like this, with desire and passion sharpening his features, everything inside her ignited into a simmering lust.

She could blame it on the rain, or the roads, or even the champagne, but the truth was she wanted the Duke of Ware. She wanted him to take her to bed and make love to her over and over until she couldn't remember anything other than the touch of his hands and mouth on her body. She wanted him to make her feel wanted, as desperately as she wanted him.

This time his mouth was firm, demanding. He tipped her chin until her lips parted, and then his tongue invaded, conquering. She went down without a fight, reaching up to push her fingers into his hair and hold him to her as she kissed him back. His fingers slid down her throat to her neckline, along the edge of the fabric until she squirmed and writhed with longing for him to rip it right down the middle and ravish her.

She twisted on the sofa, straining to be closer. His arms went around her, and dimly she felt the sharp tug of buttons being undone. Her bodice came loose, and she arched her back as he pulled it down her arms.

He was on his knees beside the sofa now, still kissing her deeply. Sophie was all but curled around him, her thighs pressed to his side, her arms clinging to his neck. His hand gripped her knee for a moment, then slid up, dragging her skirt with it. He cupped her bottom and pulled her hard toward him, and she moaned as he moved against her, his erection obvious even through layers of clothing.

In fits and starts she shoved and yanked at his clothes. His jacket hit the floor and then his cravat. He pressed her back into the cushions, his lips murmuring over the swells of her breasts as he stripped off his waistcoat. Frantic to feel his skin against hers, she twisted her arms behind her, trying to reach the remaining buttons of her dress.

His breath puffed in a faint laugh on her throat. "Leave it," he whispered, untying the string that held her chemise closed.

"Take off your shirt," she gasped, and he obligingly whipped it over his head.

She spread her hands on his bare chest, almost whimpering with want. God, he was perfect, lean and firm and so hot against her palms. He growled some indistinct encouragement as he tugged the chemise aside and licked her nipple.

"Oh—!" She lurched upward, gripping his arms. His muscles bunched and flexed, and then his hand was on her knee, sliding upward.

"I wanted you the moment I saw you," he whispered, his fingers pausing to tug at her garter. Sophie jerked in disbelief. His expression was fierce, his eyes burning. "I want to make love to you, Sophie, so badly I can hardly bear it."

His heart was hammering; she could feel it beneath her palms. Her blood was running just as hot, and she looked him right in the eyes and said, "Yes. *Yes.*"

The rakish grin flashed across his face for a

moment, and then his hand reached the top of her thigh. His fingers brushed the curls between her legs, and she spread her knees wider. She stared at him, her eyes wide with pleading.

He swore under his breath, then tossed up her skirt as he dragged her to the edge of the sofa. She sprawled wantonly, one foot on the floor, her other propped on the back of the sofa, the duke on his knees between her thighs. He pressed her back again, his big hand cupping her cheek before sliding possessively down her chest, pausing to fondle her breast, then spreading wide across her belly. His eyes were stormy gray as he touched her again, his fingers bold and unhurried, making her writhe and gasp.

Ware's touch seemed electric; she was sure her hair would be standing on end if she weren't tossing her head back and forth, her breath rasping in her throat as he stroked her and bent over her, his mouth on her breast. She flung her arms wide, gripping the cushions, trying to anchor herself as she felt the climax building inside her.

"The way you look," said the duke, his voice guttural. "It could make me come, just looking at you." She pried open her eyes to see him looming over her as he shoved down his trousers with one hand. Sophie caught her breath—he pressed her thighs wider apart as he knelt one knee on the sofa—and when he thrust deep inside her on one hard slide, it pushed her over the brink. She came with a broken cry, her body spasming hard.

"Christ," said the duke hoarsely, his fingers digging into her hip to hold her tight against him.

He withdrew a little, then thrust home hard, eliciting another tremor in her body. "Can you do it again?"

"What?" She could hardly speak; her hair was in her face, and she felt drunk as she gazed at him, above her, inside her, around her.

"Again," he said, his voice taut, and he slid one hand back beneath her bunched-up skirts.

"I—I don't . . ." Her voice choked off as he stroked her. Every muscle in her body twitched, and she gave a high-pitched whimper.

"If timed just right, some women can climax again almost immediately." He pulled back then pressed deep again.

"I don't know," she whispered, her voice shaking. "Try . . ."

He bared his teeth in a feral grin and increased his pace. Sophie wasn't sure she would survive. He was so big and strong, so hard and thick inside her. Her stomach was twisted into a hard knot, and she could hardly breathe. She gripped his arm, braced beside her head, and found his muscle as hard as iron, his skin slick with sweat.

And incredibly, the wave of pleasure rose inside her, faster this time, not quite as intense but still hard enough to catch her off guard. She heard herself sobbing even as her body rose to meet his thrusts, harder and faster than ever until he bore down and went suddenly still. His grip on her hip was painful for a moment. His breath hissed and his head dropped, and she felt his climax deep inside her.

"Your Grace," was all she could gasp.

A laugh rumbled in his chest. He kissed her,

his lips lingering a moment on hers. "I think you ought to call me Jack now."

Her smile felt silly and insanely happy. "Jack."

"Sophie." He kissed her again. "My Sophie."

It sent her heart leaping. "What now, Jack?" Playfully she looped her arms around his neck, marveling at how warm he was. Even with her dress mostly off, she didn't feel the slightest bit chilled.

"Now . . ." He cupped one hand around her breast, spilling over her corset, and rolled his thumb over her nipple. Sophie flinched, and a dark smile crossed his face. "I'm going to make love to you properly."

"Properly?"

"Yes." He bent his head and swirled his tongue over the nipple, causing her to shudder again. "In my bed, with the lamps lit so I can see every flicker of passion in your face, with none of this"—he tugged at the fabric of her skirt, crumpled between them—"in the way."

Yes. Even with her body still humming with pleasure and spent of all energy, something inside her leaped at the thought of what he offered. She wrapped her legs around his hips, reveling in his weight atop her. "That does sound very proper. Very ducal."

His eyebrows went up. "I see. You think I'm too proper. Too ducal." She laughed, but he moved his hips against hers and she stopped. The feel of him inside her made the breath catch in her chest. He rested his cheek against hers and murmured, "If wicked is what you want, wicked is what you shall get."

"How wicked?" she asked, intrigued.

He settled on top of her and whispered in her ear. "I want you naked in my bed, spread like a feast for me. I want you on your hands and knees on the rug before the hearth, where I can watch every flicker of firelight on your skin. I want you in my bathing tub, astride my lap and slippery wet. I want you in my blue banyan and nothing else, with your legs around my waist and your back against the wall."

"Oh my." Her voice faltered as she imagined every one of those couplings, and her blood heated in anticipation. Even she, who frequented gaming hells, blushed scarlet.

"Shall I take you to bed now?" He nipped her earlobe, and Sophie managed a nod. Yes, yes, *yes*.

It took a few minutes to tug their clothing back into some sort of order. The duke—Jack—put his jacket around her shoulders to hide her disheveled dress and undergarments. He tossed his shirt over his head, buttoned his trousers, and put his waistcoat and cravat over one shoulder. He looked rakish and devil-may-care, more beautiful than any man had a right to look, but it was the way he took her hand that made Sophie's heart give an off-kilter thump. His fingers, so much larger than hers, laced perfectly with her own. Stopping only to pick up the half-full champagne bottle, he led her out of the library.

She braced herself for any servants they might meet, but blessedly the corridors were deserted. Jack stopped at a door very near her own and threw it open to reveal a luxurious chamber.

"Why, they put me right near you!" she whispered in astonishment.

His blue-gray gaze slid over her as he closed the door behind them. "Yes. You have the duchess's chamber."

Sophie put her hands on her burning cheeks. "They must have assumed, when we turned up late at night, that we were lovers . . ."

"Given that I wished it were so even then, I had no complaint." His eyes gleamed. "Take off the jacket." She let it fall to the floor. "And now the dress." Deliberately slow, she slid loose the one button holding her dress closed at her back. The fabric slithered down her body, and she stepped out of it. "Everything else," he said, his voice gone rough and low again.

She took a step backward, winding the string of her corset around one finger. "Isn't that your role?"

He pulled his shirt over his head and dropped it on the floor. "Yes. By God, it is."

Chapter 13

JACK WOKE WITH sunlight in his face and a blissful warmth in his muscles. Both were unusual. Normally he woke at dawn, his mind unable to sleep longer under the weight of his daily responsibilities. Normally his valet would be in the room by now, brushing his clothing and heating water for his shave, because a duke could not lie abed all morning. Normally he didn't awake with such a feeling of utter relaxation, but today . . .

A slight movement beside him brought everything back. Barely breathing, he turned his head. Sophie lay beside him, curled on one side with her mahogany hair covering her bare shoulder. Her eyelashes were dark against her cheeks, and her lips were slightly parted. She was so beautiful he wanted to stop time and just watch her.

Making love to her had been electric, the sort of lovemaking that would make a man embrace whatever madness was necessary to maintain it. She met him boldly, unafraid to tell him what she liked, and her gasps and moans had acted like kindling on the burning hunger inside him. It had ruined any thought he had of being able to walk away from her. If she'd only been desirable, he could have; if she'd only been after his title or his wealth, he would have. But she didn't seem to care about any of that. She made him feel like a man, not a duke, and she made him climax so hard he saw stars in the aftermath.

He caught a stray lock of her hair in his fingertips. Thank God for Philip and his intemperate gambling. Thank God his mother had wept and scolded until he agreed to go to the Vega Club. He could almost thank God that his brother had badgered Sophie into gambling with him once more, because otherwise Jack never would have met her. And now he never wanted to let her go.

But the incontrovertible truth was that their idyll was almost over. The sun streaming through the gap in the drapes meant the rain had definitely stopped. The carriage was repaired, and the roads would be firm enough for travel. It was time to go back to London.

For a moment Jack let his mind wander freely down that path. What then? He wanted to see Sophie again. He wanted to dine with her, laugh with her and make love to her again. Surely they could manage that in London, with some discretion . . .

Although. In London there were a thousand prying eyes spying on everything everyone did. In London Percy would be waiting, with all the work of the dukedom. In London he would have to deal with Philip, and with his mother. The duchess would vehemently disapprove of his liaison with a woman like Sophie, but Philip would be apoplectic.

Jack let her curl slip through his fingers and fall back to the pillow. He'd spent the night in bed with the woman his brother wanted. Even though Sophie had assured him all along that she didn't return Philip's interest, that would matter little to his brother. She was right: they had once been close, back when Philip could revel in being their mother's favorite and gleefully escape the requirements of being the heir. The dukedom had become a wedge between them, not because Philip wanted it but because he resented what it conferred on Jack. He would view this affair as another exercise of influence and power.

While Jack had no hesitation admitting that it had begun that way, it had become something very different. He had meant to teach Philip a lesson, but not by coldly seducing Sophie. He might have thought about it during that fateful round of hazard—imagined her in his bed, her hair down and her face flushed as he woke her by making long, slow love to her . . . Yes, he *had* imagined all that, but never as a means of revenge on Philip.

Only because he wanted it for himself.

He watched her sleep, his heart pounding. What he felt for her didn't have one damn thing to do with Philip, but everything to do with his own desires.

But now . . . The rain had stopped. There was no more excuse to keep her to himself in Chiswick. What awaited her in town? *Who* awaited her in town? The memory of the other fellow lurking behind her at Vega's stabbed at his mind; a suitor? A hopeful lover? A deep scowl settled on his face. He had no right to ask, but bloody hell, he wondered.

"Sophie," he murmured, shaking off the thought. If he made her forget every other man in London, it wouldn't matter who that man was. He bent and pressed his lips to that bare bit of shoulder. "Wake up, darling."

Her eyes fluttered open, and a sleepy smile of pure joy bloomed on her face. He kissed her, clinging to that joy for another few heartbeats.

When he lifted his head, it ended. Her gaze veered to the brightly lit windows, then back to him. "The roads will be drying out."

"Perhaps," said Jack with a noncommittal shrug.

She closed her eyes for a moment, then pushed herself upright in bed. "I suppose we should talk, if we're returning to London—"

"Why?" He raised her hand, pressing his lips to the inside of her wrist. "I don't want to speak of it now."

"I don't, either, but—"

He kissed her again, cutting off whatever she'd been about to say. Her arms went around his neck, which was all the encouragement he needed. He bore her back down into the mattress, pulling the linens away until he could hold her flush against him. Then he rolled over, taking her with him, so she sprawled atop him.

She pushed up on straight arms, as if to rise, but he cupped her hips in both hands and urged her against him. "It's not time to dress yet," he whispered.

"I thought you rose with the sun to attend to a thousand duties," she replied, but with a slow smile that made his blood surge in anticipation.

"As it happens"—he raised one knee, separating her legs until she straddled him, her feminine center hot and wet against his erection—"I did indeed rise, but I would not call making love to you a duty."

Her eyes widened for a moment as he continued rocking his hips. She slid one hand down his chest until she took him in her grasp. "If not a duty, then what?"

"The best part of my bloody day," he growled. "Ride me, Sophie."

She blushed. "Like this?" She sat back on her heels and put both hands around his member.

Jack inhaled until he felt faint. Her hands were firm and warm, and he felt the incipient flush of climax. He was about to come in her hands, which was not what he wanted. He held his breath until the feeling receded and then opened his eyes.

Her hair fell around her bare breasts and shoulders, as if he'd caught a nymph of old in his bed. Her sherry eyes glowed with desire, but there was something else—something hesitant—

"You've never done it this way?" He didn't even need to see the color in her face to know he'd guessed rightly. He rolled up onto his elbows. "It's much the same," he said thickly, "as the other way. Spread your knees—wider—take me—guide me—" His voice choked off as she followed his directions, rubbing his head against her cleft in search of the right position. He couldn't stop his hips from jerking on instinct, pushing in an inch.

Sophie went still for a moment. Slowly she sank down, taking him deep inside her. Jack's breath rasped in his chest. "Like this?" She pushed herself up and then slid down again, and his eyes burned as he watched their bodies join.

By God's bloody eyes, he couldn't let her go. Philip could go to the devil. Jack wanted this woman like he wanted his next breath.

He fell back into the pillows so he could put his hands on her breasts, her belly, her shoulders, her face. He would never get enough of touching her. She pressed into his hands, her hips moving against his at her own pace. He didn't want to rush her, he didn't—but he was boiling in his own skin, unable to hold it back much longer. He brushed aside the dark curls between her legs and touched her.

"Come with me," he rasped. He gripped a handful of bed linens, his muscles shaking as he tried to hold back his release.

"Yes," she moaned. "*Jack.*" Her spine flexed, her breath caught, and he felt her body close around his with a powerful pull. Just the sight of her rapturous expression would have been enough to send him over the edge, but her climax felt like an explosion that reverberated through him. He threw back his head and shouted in release, his fingers digging into her hips to hold their bodies as tightly connected as possible.

She collapsed on top of him, her skin damp and hot against his. Still gasping for air, he kissed the top of her head blindly. Why the devil had the rain stopped? He would have welcomed a biblical flood at the moment, anything to keep her here with him, away from the disapproving world. Let that world go hang; never in his life had Jack been so happy as he was now, with Sophie in his arms.

After a while she stirred. "Jack," she whispered, brushing one fingertip over the stubble on his chin. "Your Grace."

That made his eyes open. "I thought we agreed you wouldn't call me that."

She laughed and propped her hands under her chin on his chest. "What happens now?"

"Breakfast?" he suggested. "We don't even need to leave the bed. Wilson will have it served right here."

"Right." She drew her fingers across his collarbone, and he almost moaned in satisfaction. "But after that. When we return to London."

"It might yet start raining again," he said with a hopeful glance at the sun streaming through the windows.

She snorted with laughter. "Jack!"

"You're still determined to return." He made a face. "If we must."

She settled beside him, and he felt almost chilled at the absence of her skin on his. He couldn't get close enough to her, even when he slid his arm around her and pulled her against him again. "I certainly must," she said with a sigh. "I've been away too long as it is . . ."

"Not long enough, if you ask me." He caught a stray lock of her hair and gave a gentle tug. "Where shall we find such privacy in London?"

She seemed to stop breathing, her eyes round with surprise. "You mean—you mean to . . . ?"

He nodded. "Of course I want to see you again."

Her smile was the sweetest thing he'd ever seen. A burst of happiness warmed his chest. God almighty, just making her smile made him feel like a king. "Truly?"

Jack laughed in disbelief. "How can you doubt me, darling?" He ran his hands up her bare back, then down to her splendid bottom. "It will be more difficult in town, obviously, but a little planning ought to suffice. I can let a house, for privacy. Near yours, if you wish, or anywhere in town."

Her face went blank. "A house."

"Near yours." He kissed her neck, ignoring the small jerk as she turned her head away. "I know discretion is vital in these matters. You may choose it, if you like, and do anything you want to it." He tried to pull her closer. They might have to return to London, but not just yet . . .

She resisted, bracing her arms on his shoulders. "I don't want to be a kept woman."

"Then don't be," he said after a pause. "Be as you are now—but slip out at nights to meet me."

"I go to the Vega Club at nights," she began.

"Then in the afternoon. In the morning before anyone else wakes. I can make love to you any time of day."

"It's not that simple," she said, worrying her lower lip.

"It can be." He kissed her shoulder.

"No," she whispered. "No, Jack." She slid from his arms and sat up, her back to him. "It's not. We—we ought to have discussed that before now."

Jack went up on his elbow to watch as she pulled on his banyan, tugging her hair free of the collar and sending the rumpled mass of dark waves sliding over the blue velvet. God, how he liked the sight of her in his dressing gown. "I'm in no hurry to leave. We have time to discuss anything you like."

Sophie stood up and tied the sash. "I never expected anything like this would happen, you know."

"Nor did I." He held up one hand in innocence at the glance she shot him. "I swear it."

She bit her lip. "Then you understand why we can't see each other again."

"Of cour—" He stopped in the middle of blind agreement with whatever she said. "What?"

Color flooded her face. "We can't see each other after this," she said again. "No one must know about . . . this. You know why."

Jack stared. *No*, he wanted to snarl, he did not know.

"If you don't, you will once we are back in town. Philip—" She paused and frowned, without looking at him. "Philip told me enough about you and the requirements of your title, and obviously during our time together I've seen . . . I understand, really, I do. But my position is far more delicate, and I—" She took a deep breath. "I would not fit into your life, nor you into mine."

Jack lurched upright. "Don't be ridiculous. One of the benefits of being a duke, my dear. I can do what I want."

"We both know that's not entirely true," she answered quietly. "You have responsibilities, far beyond saving Philip from himself. But I . . . I cannot do whatever I wish. I also have a reputation to guard, and this . . ." Her voice wavered. "This *interlude* would irreparably harm it. I haven't a title to shield me from ruin."

"Who said anything about ruin?" he demanded.

She paused, blinking several times. "What—what do you mean?"

Yes, what did he mean? He wanted to wake up with her in his bed more often, but there were only a few ways that would happen: if she were his mistress, his lover, or his wife. And only one of those offered no possibility of scandal for a respectable widow.

Jack swung his legs over the side of the bed and stalked to the windows to glare at the bucolic scene below. She'd said she didn't want to be his mistress. She also wouldn't risk being his lover. And that left only one option, which was simply impossible. Because it would be madness even to think of anything more than an affair with a woman he barely knew. Wouldn't it?

Wouldn't it?

He flexed his hands, thinking about it anyway. It would shock society if he began courting a woman like Sophie. Everyone would accuse her of being a modern Circe, scheming to ensnare a duke. Before long the parade of people who hounded him for something would turn to her, hoping to win her favor so she would use her influence with him. And then she would see him as the duke, a source of wealth and power, and not just Jack . . .

No. He scowled at the thought; she wasn't like

that. If he knew anything about her after these days together, he knew that much.

But for all her independent ways, she wanted to marry someone she loved. He wasn't fooled when she said such matches were rare. Her parents had defied convention and been disowned to be together. Would she go to the same lengths for someone she cared for? He thought she would.

She wouldn't risk anything for him, though. She didn't want to be his lover. She was perfectly ready not to see him ever again, which could only mean she didn't see any possibility of falling in love with him.

Ever.

He should have shrugged it off. Hadn't he told her himself that the Dukes of Ware didn't marry for love? They married for status, for wealth, or for connection—all three, whenever possible— and Sophie Campbell offered none of those. Even if she did, marriage was not something to consider after knowing a woman only four days.

But something inside him rose in denial at the thought of never seeing her again, bringing an instinctive growl of protest to his lips. "There's no need to make a hasty decision."

"Hasty!" She looked at him askance. "It's not hasty if it's the only possible choice! What will change once we return to London? You said yourself you are consumed by duty and obligation. I have my own life, and the circles I move in do not intersect those you move in. In London we have no respectable reason to meet, which means that if we do, it will attract notice." Her voice dropped.

"I cannot weather that sort of scandal. It will be bad enough after the wager."

"Dashwood exacts a promise," he began.

"And the most he can do to punish someone who breaks it is expel that person from Vega's," she finished. "The odds that no one will whisper about it . . ." One hand fluttered helplessly. "I don't risk odds that poor."

Jack's hands were in fists. She was right, but . . . God. These last few days he had felt like a new man, a man he vastly preferred being.

When he said nothing, she sighed. "Promise me, Jack. Please."

"If that is what you really wish." *Say it isn't*, he silently urged. Let her show one little sign of encouragement, and he would toss convention and expectation on its ear, and see her anytime he liked. He was a duke, damn it, and he could do whatever he pleased . . .

When she didn't reply, he turned to look at her. "Is it?"

She lifted her chin and gazed right at him. "It doesn't matter what I want. It's the way the world is."

There was his answer. The possibility of *more* flickered and died like a candle guttering out. "Then I give you my word not to breathe a word to anyone."

THE DRIVE BACK TO London took place in near total silence. She wore her crimson dress again, stained dark from the hem to her knees. Jack hoped she did send him a bill for it.

They sat on the rear seat together, close enough

for him to hear her breathe. Under the folds of her cloak his hand clasped hers. Jack's brain felt paralyzed. In four short days he had grown so attuned to this woman, her smiles, her frowns, her wry little glances that made him want to laugh out loud. He would have been content for the carriage to keep driving all the way to Scotland.

But there was no way to say any of it. In fact, he thought he might be going mad just for thinking it.

Even sooner than expected, she stirred. "I should get down."

"What?" He tensed. "Why?"

"I can walk from here. Tell him to stop."

Jack drew breath to argue, then leaned forward and rapped twice on the driver's window. Of course he couldn't drive her to her front door, after swearing a vow of secrecy. "Stop here," he called. The carriage slowed, creaking from side to side as the driver maneuvered out of the flow of traffic.

"Will you be—" he began, but Sophie cut him off. She put her hands on his cheeks and kissed him. Jack pulled her to him, wrapping his arms around her and hauling her onto his lap.

She rested her forehead against his, her fingers sliding into his hair at the base of his neck. "I'll have to put out a story to explain my absence from town. I think it would be best if no one even thinks I left."

"Of course." Saying the words aloud made him want to punch something, even though he had agreed to it. Before they left Chiswick, he had told the entire staff, under penalty of immediate sacking without a reference, not to mention her presence at the house to a soul.

But he knew. He could never forget that she'd been there, playing his out-of-tune pianoforte, laughing at his ineptitude at cards, making love to him on the sofa in the library. He kissed her again with the desperation of a man who feared he would be bereft once she stepped out of the coach. "If you ever need anything"—*if you ever need* me—"send for me. Write to me."

She touched his lip and mustered a bittersweet smile. "Goodbye, Jack."

"Goodbye," he managed to say.

She brushed her lips against his once more, and then she was gone. He threw up the shade in time to see her tug her hood over her head and join the throng of people hurrying to market. It was still early, and she should be able to reach her home unnoticed.

"Ware House," he murmured, staring at her and not at the footman standing smartly by the door.

"Yes, Your Grace." With a snap, the door closed, and the carriage resumed moving.

Jack let out his breath. She was gone.

Chapter 14

Sophie went to the back of her small house, startling the cook and Colleen at their breakfast when she let herself in through the scullery. "Madam!"

"I'm home," she said with a forced smile. "And in desperate need of a bath." She wasn't really, but it would give her servants something to do and put off their questions. Colleen scrambled up to attend her while the cook went for water, and Sophie breathed a sigh of relief once she was back in the privacy of her bedroom.

"We didn't expect you back for two more days," said Colleen, bustling around the room. "That servant who came said you'd been called away urgently and wouldn't be back for a week."

Her breath hitched at the thought. She might have spent two more days in Jack's arms . . . but no. It was better to be home now, before things could spiral completely out of control.

"He also said it was a very secret reason, madam," Colleen added with evident curiosity, "and that I wasn't to speak about it."

"Oh—Oh, yes, it was very sudden," Sophie said quickly. "A very personal reason, which I would like to keep secret." When she'd hired Colleen, it had been on the understanding that the maid wasn't to gossip about her. That had been to conceal the fact that Sophie was not a widow and gambled for a living, but now it paid immeasurable dividends as her maid rushed to assure her she hadn't said a word to anyone.

"How have things been here?" she asked to change the subject.

"Quiet." Colleen unpinned her hair from its twist and began brushing it. Sophie closed her eyes against the memory of Jack's hands tangled in her hair as he kissed her, his body hot and heavy above hers. "Mr. Carter called and left his card, as did Lord Philip. And there's some letters from Lady Georgiana and Miss Cross."

Nothing out of the ordinary, but a pointed reminder that she had a fine line to tread in the next several days. "Bring the letters after I wash," she directed. "What did you tell the gentlemen?"

"I didn't know what to say, so I told them you were ill. Was I right?"

She let out her breath in relief. "You did very well."

Colleen's eyes met hers in the mirror for a moment. "Are you . . . *well* again, madam?"

No. Jack had upended and jumbled everything in her life, and already she missed him more than she could say. She could still almost feel his freshly shaven cheek against hers. "I'm home again, aren't I?" she said briskly. "That's what matters—and that no one knows I was gone. How did the gentlemen take the news of my, er, indisposition?"

Colleen went to unfasten her dress. "Mr. Carter looked relieved. He sent flowers." Her hands busy with the buttons, she nodded toward the writing desk by the window, where a bright bouquet sat in a vase. "Lord Philip didn't take it quite so well. He demanded to see you, and when I refused, he scowled and muttered about traitors." She motioned for Sophie to stand and take off the dress. "He came twice. The second time I thought he might try to force his way upstairs, but finally he went away when I said you specifically didn't want to see him." She paused. "I couldn't think how else to persuade him, ma'am. I hope I did right."

Blast. She had hoped Philip would leave her in peace now. "Yes, exactly right," she told Colleen. The maid handed her a dressing gown to wear until the bath was ready, and she couldn't help thinking of Jack's blue velvet banyan. Would his next lover wear it, too? Would he take another woman to Alwyn House? *I want you in my blue banyan, up against a wall, your legs around my waist . . .*

"Letters," she said to force her mind away from that. "You said there were some . . . ?"

"Yes." Colleen fetched them. There were three, one from Georgiana and two from Eliza. Sophie took them to the chair by the window to read while Colleen prepared the tub.

I have heard the most alarming rumor about you, began Eliza's first letter. *Can it really be true? After G and I teased you so about Lord Philip, it is incredible you would wager with his brother! Did you really? I did not know you were even acquainted with him. Everyone seems to be talking of it, although your part is overshadowed by that of the Duke of Ware. Papa said he thought the man was made of stone. It has left everyone quite scandalized that he would behave so . . .*

Sophie set it aside and opened Georgiana's note. It was far shorter, only a few lines:

Lady Sidlow says I may write you this once to ask if it is true, that you gambled with the Duke of W. If it is true, I may not be permitted to write again, but I would still cry bravo! I hope you are taking my advice to make one of the patrons there fall in love with you. Ware is the most splendid catch in Britain, and so very handsome—you could not have done better. If it is not true, you must write to me at once, in language suitable for Lady Sidlow, so that I may come to call again and hear the true story—I know you well enough to know something occurred. Reply as soon as you are able, as I am absolutely perishing of curiosity.

She set that one aside as well, but with a smile. Eliza's second letter, though, dated only the day before, erased it.

Since I've not heard from you, I can only suppose something dreadful has happened. No one has seen either you or the duke in society, at least not that Papa has heard. Was he terrible to you? Are you in hiding? We are worried for you, Sophie. Do reply and let me know you are well. If there is to be trouble, you will want friends . . .

The pages fell in her lap. She put one hand to her forehead, feeling as if she'd been wrung out like a wet cloth. It was tempting to soak in the tub and then take a long nap, hiding just a little longer from the ravenous crowd, hungry for any sign of impropriety that would be awaiting her. Vega's infamous promise of secrecy had obviously been strained to the breaking point.

She hadn't exaggerated when she told Jack that she had no rank or fortune to shield her from ruin. She would have to save her reputation one steely word and resolute smile at a time. There was no other choice: no one must know the truth.

Her gaze drifted to the window, wondering if Jack had reached his house yet. He'd spoken of it in such stark terms, even though it was sure to be one of the finest homes in London. She rested her hand against the windowpane. Where was Ware House? He'd never said and she had no idea. Just one more sign that he was gone from her life forever.

By the time she wrote brief, vague replies to her friends assuring them she was well and would tell them all at their next tea, her bath was ready. Sophie stepped into the tub and submerged herself to her shoulders. Part of her didn't want to wash away Jack's touch, but she made herself do it. It was a lark, she told herself as she scrubbed, an affair that ought not to have happened in the first place. The best thing she could do now was to tuck it deep into her heart and leave it there forever.

She slid a little deeper into the water, tipping

back her head onto the rim of the tub. It was impossible not to think of the large tub at Alwyn House—the generous bathing tub in the duchess's chamber. Next to Jack's. She closed her eyes and let herself drift back to that first evening, when she'd been wet, irate, and ready to vent her temper on the arrogant, obstinate duke. A smile touched her lips as she pictured what she must have looked like to him when she stormed into the library, wearing nothing but his own silk and velvet banyan. It was the most luxurious thing she'd ever worn.

That banyan should have told her, above anything else, that he wasn't what she expected. It was too decadent, too indulgent. And the way his eyes ignited when he saw her wearing it should have told her he was a man of deep passion, just waiting to be tapped.

Even more, he'd seen right through her. Sophie lived by her wits, and it was rare that someone left her speechless, but Jack did. Even while he was stealing glances at her bare legs, he was still able to pick her apart and dig right to the heart of her secrets. He saw through her facade and spelled out virtually every bit of her Grand Plan, even if he never knew how right he was.

The smile slipped from her face at the thought of her plan, her precisely detailed plan to achieve respectability and security. Last night she hadn't spent a moment thinking of it. In fact, for a few hours this morning she had let the treacherous thought cross her mind that perhaps she wouldn't need that plan, that perhaps she'd found something worth more than ten thousand pounds and an amiable gentleman. When Jack said he wanted to see her again, she'd thought . . . even hoped . . .

That was nonsense, of course. A duke would have to be mad to marry a woman like her—and indeed, he'd only proposed an affair, with a discreet little house where they could meet until he tired of her. No matter how much she wanted him, that was something Sophie dared not risk. Creating and preserving her reputation had taken diligent effort and care. Losing it would be accomplished in the blink of an eye, and once it was gone, she would never get it back. She passed herself off as a widow in society, but if anyone dug too deeply, they would discover there had never been a Mr. Campbell, only a Miss Graham who somehow became a widow on the mail coach between Bath and London. They might discover that her only legacy was three hundred pounds left to her by Lady Fox, and that the four thousand pounds she had carefully accrued and invested in government consuls had been won from society gentlemen at hazard and whist.

Even though she sensed Jack would be generous, perhaps extravagantly so, to her if she became his mistress, it would only last as long as he wanted her. A mistress had no claim on her protector. Even worse, sooner or later he would marry someone else, a proper duchess, and then she would lose him entirely. Sophie refused to flirt with a married man, let alone carry on an affair with one.

She'd told him the truth: there was no other choice for her. Now that she was back in London, she must not only resume the plan, she must redouble her efforts, to make up for the setback it had suffered.

And that meant going back to Vega's, facing the same people who had last seen her being swept out the door in Jack's arm after that outrageous wager. Facing Philip, who would be angry—and Giles Carter, who might well be disgusted. With a gusty sigh she slid down, letting the water wash over her head.

BY THE TIME THE carriage reached Ware House, Jack had replayed the entire morning in his head several times, with the end result being that his mood was black and surly when he strode through the tall carved doors held open by servants in spotless livery. His gaze fell on a maid, innocently going about her duties, and he scowled. Her plain, dark blue dress was a match for the one Sophie had worn the first day at Alwyn House, and again last night when he made love to her on the sofa.

"Mr. Percy awaits you in the study, Your Grace," intoned Browne, his butler.

"Does he?" Grimly Jack stripped off his coat. Let Percy wait. "Have my horse brought around at once. I want a bath prepared when I return."

Browne blinked, a shocking lapse of form for him. "Yes, Your Grace."

"Has my brother been here?"

"He is with Her Grace right now."

Jack's steps paused, but only for a moment. So Philip was here now, before noon, with their mother. No doubt they would both want an explanation of where he'd been these past few days, albeit for very different reasons. Percy, Jack knew, had returned to London without any real knowledge. Wilson had hurried him out of Alwyn House while he and Sophie were exploring the attics. He thought of the promise he had made to Sophie, that their stolen interlude would remain a secret, and he strode on toward his dressing room. Keep it secret, when she was all he could think of. Not see her again, when she was the only person he wanted to see. A long pounding ride was what he needed right now, to pummel some of the tension from his muscles.

His mother intercepted him on his way out. "There you are, dear. I was beginning to wonder if you'd taken ill, you've been away so long."

"Not at all, Mother." He bowed briefly. "If you'll excuse me, I'm about to go for a ride."

Her dark eyes widened. She had Philip's knack of conveying deep indignation almost without effort. "Out? When you've just returned home after almost a week? You're behaving very oddly."

"Am I?" He took his hat from Browne and tugged on his gloves. "It doesn't feel odd." Going back to his study and closeting himself with Percy again would feel odd, which was why he was going for a ride instead.

Her brows went up in astonishment. "Ware! You mustn't sport with me. I heard there was a scene at that club. It was most unseemly."

So much for Dashwood's pledge of secrecy, Jack thought. Which—damn it—meant Sophie was right to worry about her reputation.

"How could you do such a thing?" his mother added in a tone of mild distaste.

"You begged me to go," he reminded her.

She blinked. "For Philip's sake! I never—"

"Philip played a part in that scene, as you call it. I trust you've scolded him already for breaking his word and returning to the tables at the Vega Club the very same day he promised you he would avoid them for a month."

Her mouth fell open. It occurred to Jack that he hadn't called out her unequal treatment of him and his brother since they were boys. "But—But Jack . . ."

His shoulders stiffened. She generally called him by his title, and had since the day his father died. Using his name was how she escalated her attack.

She stepped closer and put her hand on his arm. "Of course Philip should rectify his behavior. He has been quite remorseful, as you would know if you hadn't disappeared without a word. I was very worried."

He stepped away from her touch and spread his arms. "As you can see, I am home, hearty and hale. And now I'm going riding."

"But dear, it's not merely my feelings you should consider. Lady Stowe and Lucinda called while you were away—"

From the corner of his eye he could see the footman leading his horse. Nero pranced from side to side, restive and ready to run. Good. Jack intended to let him run to Hampstead and back. "I trust they are well. My horse is waiting, Mother. Good day."

"But—but Ware! We must speak about Philip!"

Jack threw up one hand in farewell as he went down the steps. He was done speaking about Philip for now. He took the reins from the footman and swung into the saddle, tipping his hat to his mother, who was so overset she had followed him to the door, her eyes wide and her hand at her bosom. Without another word he rode off, fully aware that his mother was gaping at him in shock.

He wondered if Philip were lurking somewhere in the house, waiting to hear how the duchess's intercession had gone. That was his usual course of action: enlist their mother to plead his case, usually by telling her a highly selective version of the truth. The duchess, who was always quick to trust Philip, was indomitable, and Jack usually acceded to her demands simply to save himself the frustration of being scolded and nagged, since she never gave in without achieving some part of her goal.

Sophie had tried to persuade him too, but he'd never felt browbeaten. She might tease him about something, but she didn't demand.

God. Sophie. Had she made it home safely? He ought to have followed her, to be sure of it. Instantly Jack reconsidered that; if he knew where she lived, he wasn't sure he could keep away from her. Of course it wouldn't be difficult to find out—his footman had discovered her direction in order to deliver a message to her maid after their wager—which meant he must resolutely not try. It had been only an hour since he said goodbye to her, and already he wanted to break his promise and sweep her back to Alwyn House, damn the scandal.

How was he ever to survive the rest of his life without her?

Chapter 15

⟡⟡⟡

THE LAST PLACE Sophie wanted to go that night was to Vega's, but at eight o'clock she walked up the steps.

"Welcome, Mrs. Campbell," said Forbes, the manager, as he helped her out of her cloak. "I trust you're well this evening."

If he were as curious as everyone else would be to know what had happened between her and Jack—*not Jack, the duke*, she reminded herself—Forbes didn't show it. She gave him a bright smile. "Thank you, I am."

He sent the cloak off with a footman. "Mr. Dashwood would like to have a word at your convenience."

"Oh?" Sophie tensed, then made herself relax. She'd never fool anyone if she twitched like a startled mouse every time someone spoke to her. "I am free at the moment, if he will speak to me now."

"This way," he said, and led her to Mr. Dashwood's office. It took real effort to keep her muscles from knotting; what was Mr. Dashwood going to say? Forbes had obviously been instructed to bring her in immediately. Had she breached some rule and was about to have her membership revoked? She had been to Mr. Dashwood's office only three times: when she applied for membership, and the two very happy occasions when she'd won wagers large enough that the owner had overseen payment.

Although, after her time with Jack, Sophie began to suspect that it was more likely her sex and not the size of the wager that had brought Mr. Dashwood into those matters. She had won two hundred seventy pounds from Sir Edward Tisdale, and then almost five hundred pounds from a very drunk viscount who stared at her bosom more than at his cards. Someone confided to her later that the viscount claimed she'd dressed indecently to distract him. Sophie hadn't felt the slightest twinge of guilt over it. Her gowns were no different from any other fashionable lady's, and if a man allowed himself to be that dazzled by a hint of female flesh, he ought to restrict his gambling to male company. Both men paid, though rather grudgingly in the case of the viscount. Mr. Dashwood had made sure of it.

Sadly, she was not in possession of a winning marker this evening.

Forbes knocked at the last door. "Mrs. Campbell, sir," he called, then nodded in apparent response to a reply. He stepped back, opening the door wide for her. "Mr. Dashwood will see you, ma'am."

"Thank you, Forbes," she murmured, pressing her hands flat against her skirt to steady them. Lifting her chin, she walked into the office.

Mr. Dashwood was on his feet, coming around his desk. "Mrs. Campbell. How good to see you back at Vega's."

"Yes," she said with a smile, as she dipped a shallow curtsy. She had practiced that gracious, unperturbed expression until it came effortlessly, but tonight it was difficult to hold. "It is good to be back."

He tilted his head, giving her a sharp look. Everything about Dashwood was sharp: his mind, his features, his ambition. He was a ruthless shark in gentleman's clothes. "You caused a commotion when you left the other evening."

Sophie drew a quick breath and clasped her hands. She'd known this was coming. "I am sorry for that—"

"No doubt," he said, cutting her off. "That's not the sort of wager I want in my club."

Her face heated. "Nor is it the sort of wager I delight in making. His Grace insisted, as you heard—"

"But you agreed." Dashwood folded his arms and leaned one hip against his desk. His piercing gaze was almost physically uncomfortable to endure, and he wasn't letting her put out any of her practiced excuses.

"I did," she conceded in a low voice. "It was a mistake."

"I hope you won't make the same mistake again. If that's the sort of wager you're after . . ." He shrugged. "There are plenty of places to make them. But not at the Vega Club."

Sophie's breath rasped in her throat. Her spine was as stiff as an iron spike, and her face was surely three shades of scarlet. "Nor do I. It—it was a momentary madness, certainly on my part and, I believe, on His Grace's. It was not a serious bet—I had never met His Grace before that night. I suspect he only proposed such a wager to prevent me from playing hazard with his brother, Lord Philip. I believe there had been some unpleasantness over a debt that caused tension between them, and the wager was made in a moment of anger."

Dashwood cocked one brow skeptically. "A harsh punishment for you. Not so harsh for Lord Philip."

She blinked rapidly. "As you can see, it was not fulfilled."

Something like sympathy drifted over his face for a moment. "You've not been here since then."

"I was indisposed," she said. Colleen had told two people she was ill in bed, which was as good a story as any. Her hands were gripped together so tightly, she couldn't feel her fingertips. "I struck a bargain with His Grace. In exchange for my promise not to wager with Lord Philip again, he took me home." That was true, even if it left out mention of the fact that it happened only this morning. "I took a chill in the rain that night, and was confined to bed for a few days."

He didn't look convinced. "Rumors are slippery beasts, madam, hard to cage and even harder to put down. I suggest you avoid His Grace so as not to provide succor to any beastly rumors."

"I assure you, sir, I have no intention of doing anything remotely similar ever again." But her heart was hammering wildly.

"Very good, Mrs. Campbell," he replied after a moment. "See that you don't—not here, at any rate."

"Of course not," she said through dry lips. And then, because she couldn't let a single instance of suspicion go unchallenged, she added, "I trust your code of conduct for members will cover this."

He knew what she meant: the embargo on speaking of what happened at Vega's. "It does, and I will enforce it to the best of my ability." He gave her a speaking look. "I am not God, Mrs. Campbell. If the truth is at odds with rumor, you would be wise to promote the truth at every opportunity."

She bowed her head in acknowledgment of the warning. "I shall."

Mr. Dashwood went behind his desk again. "One more thing, Mrs. Campbell. Your account."

"Yes?" Her stomach threatened to revolt. What was wrong with her account?

The club owner gave her a long look. "You won over six hundred pounds from the Duke of Ware. I did as he directed and credited it to your account. If you'll sign here, I'll make the funds available." He pushed a slim account book across the desk surface and held out a pen.

Sophie let out her breath. "Of course," she murmured, dashing her signature across the page. Six hundred pounds. It was a fortune, more than she'd ever won before, and it left her cold. What would Jack think when he had to pay it? Would he even notice?

Her head felt hot and fuzzy as she left the office

and followed Forbes back to the main salons of the club. She was walking on thin ice already, and now it felt like it was cracking beneath her feet. She flexed her shoulders, trying to relieve some of the strain in them, and a dull ache shot up her neck toward the base of her skull. This evening was already very trying, and she hadn't even entered the club.

There was a brief hush when she strolled into the salon. No one stared openly, but she caught a few veiled glances of rabid curiosity. Graciously she nodded to the people she knew, repeating over and over in her mind that she must behave exactly as she normally did. Most people returned her nod, some with speculative looks that only increased her tension.

She started when someone spoke at her shoulder. "Good evening, Mrs. Campbell."

"Mr. Carter!" Her laugh was almost a gasp of relief. "How delightful to see you again."

"Yes, it has been a few days." He bowed, but his expression was unreadable.

She summoned an apologetic smile. "Unfortunately, I was unwell. A chill from the rain. I was quite miserable and am so sorry I was unable to receive you when you called."

"Your maid seemed rather nervous when I called."

"Was she?" Sophie affected mild surprise. "I can't imagine why. Perhaps it was your handsome face, sir." She smiled.

He studied her for a moment; he wanted to believe her. Sophie couldn't bear it. He was a decent man. She *liked* him, and now she had to lie to him.

She dropped her gaze and squeezed her hands together. "No, you must know the full reason why I stayed away. I—I was mortified by how I behaved that night. I lost my temper and allowed myself to be goaded into things I ought not to have done. That kept me from returning to Vega's before tonight." She looked up at him. "I hope you can understand and forgive me."

His expression had softened considerably. "I do understand." He hesitated. "Then the duke did not . . . ?"

"He allowed me to go home and apologized for causing such a public spectacle. I believe both of us regretted that dreadful wager as soon as we left Vega's." She shook her head, picking her words carefully to escape further outright lies. Lies by omission and suggestion were unavoidable. Jack had indeed let her go home and offered an apology. She simply couldn't tell Mr. Carter it had happened this morning, and not four nights ago.

"Ware also disappeared for several days."

"Did he?" She tried to look blank. "I had never met His Grace before that night. I've no idea what his habits are."

Carter shifted. "Well, he's not often about in society. Now that I think of it, I've only ever crossed his path twice. Perhaps it was coincidence."

Sophie said nothing. Against her will, her memory was conjuring up images of Jack stretching his neck as he untied his cravat, touching her under the chin before he kissed her, the way his fingers tangled in her hair. She knew *some* of his habits.

Abruptly she jerked a little straighter and inhaled in dismay. Across the room Lord Philip

Lindeville had entered, his hair ruffled, his expression moody. His dark eyes roved around the room. She ducked her head and prayed he wouldn't spot her.

"What is it, my dear?" Mr. Carter leaned toward her.

She mentally cataloged the endearment: a positive sign. "Lord Philip has arrived."

Mr. Carter's mouth flattened.

"I do not wish to see him," she said with unfeigned vehemence. Not only had she promised Jack, she had lost most of her sympathy for Philip. He was reckless and irresponsible and he'd deliberately used her to taunt Jack, making far more of their friendship than there was. In time she might forgive him, but for now she still felt the sting of his actions too plainly.

Carter shifted to block her from sight. "Then you shall not."

They made their way to a quiet table, sheltered from full view of the room by a stand of plants, and Mr. Carter called for cards. Sophie didn't feel like playing but knew she had to. This was why she came to Vega's, after all, and it would attract notice if she did not. Besides, nothing about her Grand Plan had really changed.

Sophie was too distracted by Philip's presence to play her best, but she still managed to take some tricks, and she lost only ten pounds. Carter gave her a swift glance as he totted up the score, then pushed back his chair. "Perhaps you would care for a glass of wine, Mrs. Campbell?"

Gratefully she rose. She had taken the first step by returning to Vega's tonight. That was

enough for now. Tomorrow some of the surprise
would have died down, and the day after, even
more; soon she would be treated more normally
again. And leaving now could be excused not
as cowardice—which it was—but as a lingering
weakness from her fictitious malady. "You are so
kind to offer, Mr. Carter, but I think I ought to
return home. It seems I'm not as recovered as I
thought. I feel a headache coming on."

"Of course. You look rather pale." He offered
his arm, which she gratefully took, and they circled the room, heading discreetly for the door.
Philip was nowhere to be seen, to her immense
relief. He must have gone into another room.
Jack would be furious at him—but that was not
her concern or her problem to solve. Sophie just
wanted to go home. She really might be falling ill
this time.

They had nearly reached the stand of palms
near the manager's office when someone stepped
in front of her.

"There you are, Mrs. Campbell."

She jolted and barely restrained a small scream
of surprise. Philip Lindeville gave a bow so defer-
ential it was almost mocking. He'd spoken loudly
and warmly, and she heard the pause in the room
noise as everyone turned to look. She had no
choice: face him or risk another scene. Gritting
her teeth, she curtsied. "Good evening, sir."

"Indeed it is, to see you." His gaze flicked to
the man beside her. "Good evening, Carter."

He gave a tight nod. "Lindeville. You must pardon us. I was about to see Mrs. Campbell home."

His eyebrows rose in exaggerated surprise.

"Home? Surely not. It's not even ten o'clock, and the lady hasn't been at Vega's in several nights. Don't deny the rest of us the pleasure of her company."

"You flatter me, sir," she said, smiling as best she could. *Act normally.* "But to my great regret, I feel unwell."

"Good heavens." He rocked back on his heels. "After you've been ill these last several days? I'm growing concerned, Mrs. Campbell."

And the eavesdroppers were growing interested. How cruel it would be if she single-handedly brought down Vega's pledge of secrecy by being so scandalous no one could resist gossiping about it. "How kind of you, my lord, but unnecessary. It is nothing more than a headache," she said firmly, keeping her voice low. "I'm sure a good night's sleep is all I need."

"No, no, a glass of wine shall restore you." He reached for her arm, subtly edging Giles Carter aside. "Say you'll stay."

Sophie stubbornly resisted and looked him full in the face—his face, enough like Jack's to make her heart twist. "Not tonight, sir."

"The lady said no, Lindeville," said Carter quietly.

Philip's eyes grew dark and turbulent, and his mouth pulled into a hard line. "Perhaps we should send for a doctor. It seems very serious, this illness—it's lasted several days, and it came upon you very suddenly, didn't it?" He cocked his head. "Right about the time my brother appeared." A sardonic smile crossed his face. "Although I find his presence also makes me feel ill of late."

"Oh no," she said, pretending he hadn't spoken suspiciously and angrily. "I wasn't seriously ill— only a cold, miserable as they are. I may have overtaxed myself by coming out tonight."

Philip glanced at her companion. "Carter, be a sport and give me a moment with Mrs. Campbell." When Carter scowled, Philip laid one hand over his heart. "I've been worried about her."

He was going to make a scene; he was already making one. Sophie gave Mr. Carter a slight nod, and after a moment he stepped backward and bowed. His expression was inscrutable. "I see. Good evening, Mrs. Campbell."

With a sinking heart, Sophie watched him walk away. She turned to Philip and reminded herself that she could not slap him, no matter how much he deserved it. How had she let this spoiled, arrogant young man have such sway over her life? "My head is aching already, and I haven't the strength to argue with you."

He looked offended as he pulled her hand around his elbow. "There won't be an argument. I only want to talk." He led her to one of the small sofas at the edge of the room. It was still in the main salon, but far from the hazard and faro tables, where the crowd was concentrated.

"Lord Philip," she began as soon as she took a seat, "this cannot contin—"

He raised one hand in a gesture so like Jack, she stopped midword. "Answer one question. I have to know. Did my brother do anything offensive to you?" His tone implied suspicion of all manner of abuse and humiliation.

She snapped her mouth shut before she could

give herself away by springing violently to Jack's defense. "No."

"Nothing?" He pressed her hand between his. "If he did, I will make him regret it."

Sophie tugged her hands free of his grip. "Philip, this is madness."

He scowled. "What?"

"You're making a spectacle of me," she said bluntly. "Of yourself. Please stop."

"Mrs. Campbell—*Sophie*," he protested. "I would never do such a thing."

She looked at him in reproach. "Think, my lord. You insist I stay and talk with you. You turn away Mr. Carter, who was merely escorting me to the hall so I could have Mr. Forbes summon a hackney. The other night you interrupted a perfectly cordial game of whist I was playing with Mr. Whitley and Mr. Fraser and insisted I play hazard with you instead."

For a moment he looked shocked, but then a penitent smile curved his mouth. Again he looked like Jack, and again it made her chest ache. "I hadn't realized, but now I see you're right. I'm sorry."

"I enjoy your company very much," she told him, "but you must understand my position. Even I have to mind my reputation."

He laughed. "Must you? Reputations are such tiresome things . . ." She lifted one shoulder as if in resignation, and he ran a hand over his head, ruffling the dark waves. "It's a good thing my brother is such a dry stick. If it were anyone else, I'd never believe him indifferent to you."

She never knew if he meant it to be a trap, but

if so, it was an effective one. At this unexpected mention of Jack, her mask slipped; something must have shown on her face, for Philip—who was watching her closely—grew suddenly grim. "What did he do?"

Sophie's temper was fraying with every word. She had enjoyed Philip's company, laughed at his wit, been flattered by his attention. But she had never encouraged him to think she wanted more. She was too mindful of what it would cost her to step over the line. Everyone believed her a respectable if somewhat high-spirited widow, which gave her some license to have companions like Philip and Mr. Carter, but she did not want society to believe her a very *different* sort of widow.

And Philip, who had appeared to respect the boundaries earlier in their friendship, was all but proclaiming her his, which was not and would never be true. In truth, Sophie thought his behavior was really more about his brother than about her, but it was incontrovertible that her reputation was the one that would suffer if he persisted in this.

She looked him squarely in the face. "What I do is not your concern, my lord."

He blinked. "I only want to know about my brother's treatment—"

"No! I am not answering. You have no right to question what I do." She drew a deep breath. "If you wish to know about your brother's actions, you should speak to him. Perhaps he will feel obliged to answer. I do not."

For a moment there was silence. Philip was

clearly struggling to master his own temper; suspicion and uncertainty flashed across his face in rapid succession. "I beg your pardon," he said at last. "I was concerned for you."

"Thank you, but I am fine." She got to her feet. "I am tired, I have a headache, and now I am going home. Good night."

He followed her out, an uneasy frown on his brow. Sophie tried to ignore him. Now she did feel unwell, cold and clammy and her heart racing. She squeezed her bloodless hands together as Mr. Forbes sent someone to fetch her a hackney. Mr. Carter had disappeared, and she couldn't even regret it. She only wanted to go home, get into bed and pull the covers over her head.

Frank, the servant who monitored the cloak room, brought her cloak, and Philip waved him off, taking the cloak and draping it around her shoulders himself. "Let me take you home," he said. "To be sure you're well."

If she left with him tonight, after the way she'd left with Jack a week ago, she would never recover. "Thank you, no," she told Philip coolly. "I can manage on my own." She faced away from him, all but giving him the cut direct.

"Very well." His voice was also chilled. "I shall see you another evening, madam."

She nodded once. "Good night, sir."

It was almost four minutes later when the hackney arrived. Sophie knew because she could see the clock on the mantel of the small fireplace at the side of the reception hall. It seemed an eternity because she could also tell Philip hadn't budged. He stood behind her, silent but looming, and it made her want to spin around and tell him off properly.

Instead she clenched her teeth shut and watched the mechanism on the clock tick away the seconds. When Forbes finally came to say her hackney was waiting, she all but ran out the door. She didn't mean to look back, but as she stepped into the carriage and gave the driver the direction, she caught sight of Philip, on the steps of Vega's, watching her moodily.

Oh dear.

Chapter 16

"THERE IS A lady to see you, Your Grace. She refused to give her name, but sent in this." The butler held out his tray.

Jack's gaze jumped to the note on the salver. It had been almost a week since he last saw Sophie—five days, to be exact. For five days he had personally inspected every item of his correspondence on the slim chance there would be something from her. He had no idea of her handwriting, and yet somehow he knew from looking at it that this came from her. Unconsciously holding his breath, he picked up the note and broke the seal.

I must see you about an urgent matter. —S.

"Show her in," he said to the butler. "Percy, that will be all for now." His secretary looked up from his station at the far end of the room, startled. Jack gave a curt nod: *Go.* Percy gathered his papers and bowed out of the room after the butler, closing the door behind them.

He got to his feet and paced around his desk,

trying to calm the ecstatic leaping of his pulse. What could she want? He reminded himself it was far more likely to be bad news than good, but even that couldn't quiet the thudding of his heart. She was *here*, in his house . . .

The door opened. "Your Grace," said Browne in starkly disapproving tones. "Your visitor."

He turned. She wore dark gray, a black veil over her bonnet, but as soon as the butler closed the door she threw it off. And Jack felt like he could breathe again, for the first time in five days, at the sight of her face.

"Your Grace," she murmured, dropping her extravagant curtsy.

"Mrs. Campbell." He bowed. As if they were polite acquaintances, not one-time lovers. "Won't you come in?"

"Thank you for seeing me. I am sorry to disturb you." She came into the room and removed her bonnet. Her hair was pinned up in a severe knot, and he longed to pull out the pins and see it streaming down her back again.

He cleared his throat and tried to banish the image of her with her unbound hair spread across his pillows. "Not at all."

She faced him, somber and beautiful, and his knuckles grew white, gripping the edge of the desk behind him. If he didn't anchor himself somehow, he would never be able to keep his distance from her. "Something must be done about Philip."

Jack thought he'd misheard. "What about him?" he growled.

"He will not leave me alone," she said, her

voice tight. "Everywhere I go, he appears. I have told him several times I won't wager with him anymore, so he merely follows me. He gambles wildly, and I suspect he's losing a great deal. The other night I heard him blame his bad play on the loss of Lady Luck's affections, and then he turned to look quite pointedly at me—causing everyone else to look at me, too. He is making me and himself objects of gossip and speculation."

Jack let out his breath. Curse Philip. "I will speak to him."

Pink rose in her cheeks. "I'm not certain that will be enough. I tried speaking to him, and then I tried *not* speaking to him. Others have tried to reason with him as well, all to no effect. He is angry, and he's not making any effort to hide it."

Jack wanted to know, intensely, who else had spoken on her behalf. "And you think my words will have no greater impact."

She hesitated, wetting her lips. Helplessly he watched, wishing he were the one tasting her mouth. "He's angry at you," she said softly.

"That is normal." Philip was usually annoyed at him over something.

"No." Sophie shook her head, seeming to understand what he meant. "He is jealous. He demanded to know what happened between us."

His muscles tensed. "What did you tell him?" His brother—the world—mustn't know the truth, and yet something deep inside him rebelled at the thought of saying nothing had happened between him and Sophie. Damn it, he wanted her and he wanted everyone to know she was his—

Except that she wasn't. And he had given his word.

"I told him it was none of his concern!" she exclaimed. "He came to call twice at my house while I was . . . away. My maid told him I was ill, but he wasn't fully convinced. He makes insinuations and suggestive comments, fishing for information. I have tried my best to avoid him, but he's persistent."

"What does he hope to achieve?"

"I have no idea!" She took a deep breath and lowered her voice. "He is making me an object of speculation." She nibbled her lip, then continued, looking deeply uneasy, "He implied I had been your whore."

Jack came off the edge of the desk, hands in fists. "When?"

"Last night. He was drinking. I don't think anyone else heard, but it's only a matter of time—"

"I don't give a damn what his excuse is," he retorted. "That is utterly unacceptable."

For the first time a tremulous smile appeared on her face. Jack's fury subsided, and he was beside her before he even realized he was moving. "It won't happen again," he said, and then—unable to resist any longer—he smoothed a loose wisp of hair from her temple. "I give you my word."

"How?" Her eyes were warily hopeful. "Can you keep him from Vega's?"

Jack wound the tendril around his fingertip. He probably couldn't bar his brother from Vega's, not without posting a servant outside the club with orders to physically restrain Philip from entering.

Dashwood might not be pleased about that. "I can prevent him bothering you. You may depend on that." He had no idea how, but right now all that mattered was reassuring her.

The tension went out of her. Her smile grew radiant, and she gazed at him with open adoration. "Thank you. I didn't know what else to do."

God. It hadn't even been a week, and it felt like a decade. He touched her chin, then tipped her face up to him. "It's the least I can offer." And he kissed her, cupping his hands around her face when her mouth softened under his.

She went up on her toes, clinging to his arms, and kissed him back. Something in his soul stirred possessively. He had not got over her at all. Perhaps he never would.

"I've missed you," he breathed in her ear, brushing his lips over the pulse throbbing faintly at her temple.

"And I you," she said on a sigh. "Oh, Jack . . ." Her arms went around his neck, and she threaded her fingers into his hair.

Jack gathered her to him. The feel of her body, the scent of her skin went straight to his head, like the most potent whisky drunk too quickly. But no—that wasn't right. This wasn't a passing condition that would be cured when he woke up in the morning. He'd been waiting five long days for that to happen, and when it hadn't, he burned for an excuse, any at all, to see her again. Not even Philip's appalling behavior could make him sorry that she was here.

He reclaimed her mouth, coaxing her to open to him. She moaned, and he urged her back a step, then another, until they reached the desk. He put his hands on her waist and lifted her, heedless of the papers being disarranged. His stomach flexed in eagerness and anticipation as her knees rose beside his hips. Five endless days . . .

Jack caught her knee, hiking it up to his waist so he could move fully between her thighs. Sophie arched her back, and her fingers dug into his nape, urging him on. Still kissing her deeply, he flicked open the top button of her prim dress, then another, then another, until he felt the top edge of her corset under his fingertips.

This was madness. They had said their farewells, knowing it was madness, and still he wanted her, more than ever, more than he cared for the dignity of his father's house, the obligation of his title, the fact that the door was unlocked. He needed her. Jack ignored every argument against it and bent his head to press his lips to the pulse beating rapidly at the base of her throat. She whispered his name again, clutching his head to her with one hand and bracing herself with the other hand.

The tap at the door sounded like a clap of thunder. Sophie gave a violent start, almost toppling over, and seized his shoulders to catch herself. "Stop," she gasped. "We can't—I have to go."

Jack held her a moment longer, resenting the interruption, but another knock sounded. He felt the weight of duty drop heavily back onto his shoulders, and he pushed himself away from the desk. Sophie slid off, frantically buttoning her dress. Her face was flushed with desire, and her mouth still looked soft and inviting, and he had to step back and turn away to master himself and put down the urge to bolt the door and make love to her on the sofa, on the desk, on the damn floor if necessary.

"I will see to Philip," he said, breathing hard. His body ached with frustration. "He shan't bother you again."

"Thank you." Her buttons done, she retrieved her bonnet. With jerky motions she tied the ribbons. Before she flipped the veil over her head, she glanced at him, filled with longing and regret. "I wish I hadn't had to trouble you—"

"You must not apologize for coming to me." He managed a tight smile. "Never."

"I won't," she murmured. She pulled the veil down, and her hands shook. Even that sent a charge through him; if he *had* bolted the door and carried her to the sofa, she would have welcomed it.

He walked ahead of her to the door, opening it to see his butler waiting. "Yes?" he snapped.

"Her Grace your mother requires an urgent word with you, sir," said Browne, his face impassive.

Jack's jaw tightened. Browne never would have disturbed him on his own; he was an excellent butler. That meant his mother had forced him to do it, to knock not once but twice on his study door. Of course, his mother could only have known about his visitor if Browne had told her, which made the butler complicit. "I will see her later," he said coldly and turned his back in dismissal. "Come, madam," he said to Sophie, hovering uncertainly.

"Let me escort you out." He offered his arm and walked her through the house.

Neither said a word. The last time they parted, they had both thought it was forever. He'd watched her go that time with despair. But this time . . .

When they reached the door, she dropped a quick curtsy. "Thank you, Your Grace," she murmured, and then she was gone, hurrying without a backward glance out the door held open by the footman.

Jack watched her go. Seeing her again had torn off the veneer of resignation and obligation. He had acted to save Philip, both by whisking Sophie away and then again when he gave her up.

But his brother couldn't leave anything be, nor heed any warning. After all Jack had done to fulfill what was expected of him, he was damned if he wouldn't do something for himself now. He turned to the servant. "Send for my horse."

HE WAS SHOWN IN almost at once, despite the early hour and the fact that the club was not open to guests. Dashwood was hurriedly shrugging into his jacket when the manager opened the door. Jack strode in. "I understand my brother has been at your tables again," he said without preamble.

Dashwood paused, then gave his jacket one last jerk into place. "I don't discuss my members' habits."

Jack leveled a stony look at him. "It was not a question."

"He is still a member," said Dashwood in oblique acknowledgment.

"He is still wagering and losing vast sums of money at your establishment—money he does not have, and will not receive from me." Jack tilted his head. He'd thought very carefully about how to approach Vega's owner. "I believe your rule is 'pay your debts.'"

"It is."

"I am warning you that my brother will soon be unable to pay any debts. Cut him off. Revoke his membership."

A humorless smile crossed Dashwood's face. "Then he'll have to deal with the consequences, as a gentleman."

He hadn't expected Dashwood would agree to that, but it had to be attempted. "Then admit me to your club."

The other man blinked, his only sign of surprise. "There is a procedure, Your Grace . . ."

"Which you can circumvent at will, I have no doubt—as the owner."

Slowly Dashwood nodded, obviously doing some rapid thinking. His face seemed to grow hard and cold for a moment, and Jack had the feeling he was seeing the real Dashwood, not the debonair club owner who mingled with his wealthy patrons. He was counting on that man to see the benefit of admitting the Duke of Ware.

"If you will not cut off my brother from your tables, he risks ruin," Jack went on. "I cannot stop him from degrading his own name and prospects, but I will not stand by and see him become a stain on my name. Admit me to your club, so that I can keep an eye on his activities and intervene as necessary to prevent him losing what he cannot pay to your other patrons."

Dashwood didn't bat an eye. "I could be persuaded to allow it—on your own merits, of course. There is one matter, though, which gives me pause."

Jack had a good guess what the matter was. He propped one hand on his hip to hide how it had curled into a fist. "Oh?" he drawled.

The club owner looked him in the eye. "Mrs. Campbell."

That was the one. Jack kept his face impassive. "Who?" he said in a tone of mild scorn.

"The lady you gambled with—very inappropriately—the last time you were here, Your Grace." Dashwood's smile was thin but dangerous.

Jack dismissed her with a flick of his fingers. He mustn't give any sign that he even remembered who she was. "Ah. Her. I acted only to separate her from my brother, whom she appeared intent upon fleecing."

"She is still a member of this club. I won't have you harassing her or any other lady here."

Jack drew himself upright and glared at the man with all the ducal arrogance he possessed. "You forget yourself, Dashwood."

"That's my condition," replied Dashwood, relatively unperturbed. "I don't want that kind of wagering in my club, not from you or anyone else. And you'll keep your distance from Mrs. Campbell in particular."

"Obviously," he said, the word like frost on his lips. If only Dashwood knew—Jack was tolerating this insulting conversation solely for Sophie's sake. He'd let Philip twist in the wind, if his brother would show some basic honor and leave her alone. "Then we are agreed." He picked up his hat and turned to go. "I shall attend this evening."

"I'll see that Forbes has your name."

Jack gave a nod and left. Not until he swung into the saddle and headed home did he allow himself to think about the very much intended consequence of this maneuver. He had got himself admitted to Vega's, where he would be able to keep an eye on Philip and prevent him from harassing Sophie. And to do that . . .

He would get to see her, as well.

Chapter 17

Sᴏᴘʜɪᴇ ᴡᴀʟᴋᴇᴅ ᴛʜʀᴏᴜɢʜ the doors of Vega's two nights later with some trepidation. She was not hopeful that Jack would have persuaded Philip to leave her in peace. Every time she went, he'd been there, as if waiting for her, watching everything she did.

It was both alarming and puzzling. Surely he couldn't have felt such an attachment to her based only on their convivial habit of gambling together. As Jack had pointed out, she won more from Philip than he won from her. He himself had been the cause of the scene that led to Jack's outrageous wager. If anything, he ought to have apologized to *her* when next they met.

Instead he was suspicious and possessive in a way he had never been before. It all made her believe that his anger was more at Jack than at her. Sophie had never had a sibling, and a small piece of her heart ached that the two brothers seemed permanently at odds now, after a close youth. Unfortunately, she couldn't say any of that to Philip without belying her claim to have been ill in bed instead of off in Chiswick making love with his brother, and since that prospect was what had enraged him so . . . She was helpless.

Tonight she headed for the whist tables. Hazard had lost all appeal, and faro was nearly as bad. Whist was quieter, and somehow more peaceful—she had to keep her mind focused on the cards to play well, which prevented her thinking about Jack, and how he had crossed the room in two strides to take her in his arms and kiss her, and how she would have begged him to make love to her one last time there on the desk if someone hadn't knocked on the door and startled her out of the haze of desire. She'd thought, after a few days apart, that her attraction to him would have lessened, or at least been manageable. Instead, it flared hotter than ever the instant she set eyes on him.

"Mrs. Campbell!"

She gave a violent start at the exclamation. "My goodness," she gasped, clapping one hand to her breast. "You startled me, sir."

Fergus Fraser grinned. He was charming enough, though terribly shallow. His grandfather was a Scottish lord, and Mr. Fraser had been living on that connection as long as Sophie had known him. She suspected his purpose at Vega's was similar to her own—to win a fortune, or at least a decent income. "'Twas not my intent. I only came to deliver a message from a mutual friend."

She tensed. They had several acquaintances in common, but chief among them was Philip Lindeville. "Oh?"

He handed over a folded note with a flourish. "I'm to bid you to read it privately, and if you wish to send a reply, I shall be pleased to deliver it."

It was Philip's handwriting on the front, spelling out her name in swooping letters. She tapped it against her palm and gave Mr. Fraser a smile of dismissal. "Thank you, sir. That is very kind of you."

With a lazily elegant bow, he excused himself and wandered away. Sophie watched where he headed from beneath her eyelashes. The vingt-un room, one of Philip's favorites. Stepping closer to the wall, she broke the seal on the note and read it.

It might have been from a different Philip. *I have been a fool*, he wrote. *Through trying too hard to be your friend I have lost your favor, and now feel lost without your company. Say you forgive me, dearest Sophie, and we shall be as we ever were—for now. You must know I care for you, but I am prevented from even speaking to you by one who has neither of our interests at heart. No one shall ever keep my thoughts from dwelling on you. Ever your servant, P. Lindeville*

One who has neither of our interests at heart . . . Heart suddenly leaping, she edged closer to the vingt-un doorway. It was relatively early still, but several tables were full. After a moment she picked out Philip, his dark gaze moody as he tossed aside a card and motioned for another. But behind him . . .

Stood Jack.

He wore his more forbidding ducal expression, his sensual mouth flat, but he was here. And Philip hadn't dared approach her.

Her heart swelled until she gave a little gasp. Jack hated gambling, despised Vega's, and yet here he was. And it could only be for her. For a moment she couldn't keep herself from gazing at him, wishing she could cross the room and thank him—acknowledge him—throw herself into his arms and see him smile down at her before he kissed her—

"I heard the Duke of Ware had applied to become a member, but I didn't expect to see him here," remarked Giles Carter beside her.

Sophie hadn't even heard him approach, and almost jumped out of her skin at his voice. It was a blessing in disguise, for it gave her a chance to cover her lovesick gazing at Jack. "Has he?"

"Apparently it was granted on the spot." Carter gave a humorless huff. "Privilege of a dukedom, I suppose."

She managed to smile wryly. "Then he'll be here regularly?"

"No doubt." Mr. Carter turned probing eyes to her. "Does it distress you or please you?"

She froze in apprehension. "What do you mean by that?"

"I mean you and he had a very public scene, which ended with him sweeping you into his carriage. And neither of you was seen for several days afterward."

"I was home," she said carefully. "Ill in bed. I told you."

He nodded. "You did. And I believed you. But just now . . ."

"What?" she asked sharply. "What are you suggesting, sir?"

He held up one hand. "Only that his presence here again might be an unforeseen opportunity to you."

No. It was an unforeseen torment, a reminder of what she could never have. And no one must ever know that she even dreamed of it, let alone that once he *had* been hers. She forced her shoulders to relax. "An opportunity to humiliate myself again?" She shook her head. "I have learned that lesson the hard way, thank you."

He was silent for a moment. "Women are mysterious creatures to me," he said at last. "I have three sisters and four nieces, and I never can guess what any of them are thinking. The slightest things become tragedies worthy of Shakespeare, whilst weighty matters are brushed aside as piffle. When I met you, I thought you were nothing like them. Sensible and intelligent, I thought to myself, a woman with whom a man can be at ease instead of constantly on guard."

She should be falling over herself to reassure him she *was* like that. She should be pleased to hear he had regarded her with such esteem, and doing everything possible to restore that esteem. After all, three weeks ago she'd put Giles Carter on top of her list of possible husbands. He was a gentleman, and she was a gentleman's daughter with four thousand pounds. He didn't know that last bit, but she'd been very careful to project an image of a woman with some money of her own. There was a very real possibility that Mr. Carter would marry her.

Jack never would.

Sophie knew this; she'd known all along. Not

only was it utterly unthinkable for a duke to marry a woman who gambled for her living, Jack himself had said and done nothing to suggest otherwise. He'd told her directly that dukes, especially Dukes of Ware, didn't marry for affection. He might still want her—and wicked woman that she was, Sophie felt an irrational burst of longing at the knowledge that he did—but only as his lover. At best, as his mistress. She was every kind of fool to want him anyway, even without accounting for her goal of marrying a respectable gentleman who could give her the security and family she craved.

With some effort she hardened her heart to her visceral reaction to the sight of Jack. The time for being foolish had ended the moment they drove through the gates of Alwyn House on the way back to London. "I fear you are about to say your feelings have changed on that," she murmured.

"I am no longer as certain as I once was," Mr. Carter acknowledged. "Not because of the scene at the hazard table—I was witness to it all, you remember, and I know the duke was provoking and rude. Any man would have drawn his cork, and I don't know many who could have resisted his goading challenge. But since you've returned to Vega's . . ." He paused. "You're not quite the same," was his final conclusion.

It was stupid to lie. "No," she agreed softly. "I suppose not."

He gave a lopsided smile. "Then the only question is how you've changed. It might give a woman ideas, gambling with a duke. It's not so different from a young lady scheming to dance with one,

I suppose. Who knows what might result, once a man's attention is snared, and dukes—even the Duke of Ware—are men of flesh and blood like the rest of us."

Before she could stop herself, Sophie stole another glance into the vingt-un room. Jack was speaking to another man, one shoulder elegantly propped against the wall. He smiled slightly at whatever his companion said, and glanced her way. For the briefest second their gazes connected, with the same lightning-sharp jolt of awareness that she'd felt at Alwyn House. The world seemed to fall away for that second, leaving just the two of them, two complementary pieces of one whole. *I'm in love with him*, Sophie thought with blank surprise.

Then Jack looked away, his expression unchanged. Sophie made herself do the same, turning back to Giles Carter. "If you're asking if I harbor hopes of attaching the Duke of Ware," she said evenly, "the answer is no. The very thought defies belief. His presence here is very much a surprise to me. The last thing I want to do is cause another scene and revive any unpleasantness. I am thoroughly aware of how rashly I acted that evening, and have resolved never to do so again."

Mr. Carter listened attentively. Sophie's heart twisted; he was a good man, one for whom she had hoped to develop true affection. If Philip hadn't been so stubborn . . . if Jack hadn't swept in, furious and out of patience . . . if she hadn't lost her temper and given in to the temptation of winning all that money . . . she would probably still be doing her best to flirt with Mr. Carter and bring him up to scratch. He met all of her husband requirements, and she genuinely liked him.

But he was not Jack, and he never would be. Those few fleeting days at Alwyn House had changed something inside her, like clay being fired in a kiln, and she couldn't go back to the way she was before. She didn't have it in her to deceive Mr. Carter any more than she had room in her heart for anyone but Jack. Perhaps in time that would relent, but for now . . .

She made herself smile. "You asked how I have changed. I believe I've become more calculating. Tonight I feel like winning a great deal of money, and I like you far too much to make you my prey. Shall we say farewell until a more genial evening?"

His face eased, and he even laughed. "I might say that's proof you hold me in high regard," he teased. "Warning me away to spare my purse—and my pride!"

"The very highest regard, sir!" She tapped his arm with her fan. "Although you do lose so graciously . . ."

"Only to you." He offered his arm. Sophie took it and let him lead her to the faro tables. Whist was too tame after all; tonight she did feel restless and reckless, and damn anyone who got in her path.

Her luck held through the evening. By the time the clock chimed two, she had won a tidy sum, just over one hundred pounds. She should have been pleased, and instead she only felt drained. It was time to go home. She bade her companions good night and headed to the reception hall to send for her cloak and have Forbes summon a hackney.

The hall was quiet at this time of night. Vega's doors were open until dawn, but most people who meant to play tonight were already in the main salon. The hardened gamesters in search of excitement had usually departed for more depraved haunts by now, and the competition for hackneys at this end of St. Martin's was minimal. The front door stood open, and a fresh breeze swept through the elegant hall as she entered. Sophie took a deep breath gratefully. "Mr. Forbes," she began, approaching the tall, fair-haired man with his back to her.

He swung around. She stopped in her tracks with a gasp. It was not the majordomo.

Jack's face was as still as marble. "Mrs. Campbell."

Of course. She mustn't know him and he mustn't know her. "Your Grace," she murmured, dipping a curtsy. "I beg your pardon."

"Forbes has stepped out to summon a hackney. They seem in short supply in this street." His tone was cool and remote—ducal.

She flushed. "Yes, they often are."

They stood in awkward silence for a minute. She longed to say something to him, anything, but didn't dare. All it would take was one overheard word, one sign of connection, and the rumors would roar back to life. And yet . . . standing here so near him was almost more than she could bear, especially tonight.

Fortunately Mr. Forbes stepped back inside, his

brows rising at the sight of her. "Mrs. Campbell! Are you in want of a hackney?"

"Yes."

He nodded once. "I'll send for one immediately. Your carriage is waiting outside, Your Grace." He motioned to Frank, the servant in charge of the cloakroom who was just hurrying back into the hall with a greatcoat over one arm and a hat in the other hand—Jack's, no doubt. "Fetch Mrs. Campbell's cloak," Forbes told him.

Jack shrugged into his coat and took his hat from Frank. "Nonsense," he said coolly. "The lady must take the hackney."

Forbes bowed. "As you wish, sir. I shall summon another at once."

"No." Jack set the hat on his head. "I find that I am in want of some fresh air. I shall walk."

Sophie kept her chin up, but her gaze carefully away from his face. "That is very kind of you, sir."

He tipped his head in regal acknowledgment as he tugged on his gloves. Without another word or glance he strode out into the night. Sophie inhaled sharply as the breeze swirled around him, carrying the faintest whiff of his shaving soap back to her.

"Are you well?" asked Forbes, watching her far too closely. "Was His Grace importunate?"

"What? No." She gave a quick shake of her head. "I'm merely tired. His Grace was very kind to let me take his hackney."

Forbes didn't look entirely convinced. "If you're certain . . ."

"Yes." She smiled in genuine relief as Frank reappeared with her cloak. "Quite certain. And now I shan't have to wait while a carriage is summoned, which makes me feel even better." She tied the ribbons on her cloak, and Forbes offered his hand to escort her down the steps to the waiting hackney.

A covert glance up and down the street revealed no sign of Jack. Sophie stepped into the hired carriage, thanking Mr. Forbes for his assistance with a silver crown. The carriage started off, and she tried to calm her still-leaping pulse. She would have to get used to seeing him, if Giles Carter were correct that he had become a member. When she had asked him to stop Philip harassing her, she hadn't guessed he would do it personally. If she had known, she wasn't sure she would have asked. It was a great relief not to see Philip watching her all the time, but it would be even more unsettling to catch fleeting glimpses of Jack. She leaned her head against the narrow window, thinking how farcical her life had become lately.

The hackney turned onto the main road, and abruptly she jerked upright, then lunged forward. "Stop a moment!" she cried to the driver. He slowed the horse, and she groped for the handle. She pushed open the door just as the hack drew even with Jack on the pavement.

He stopped and faced her. Breathless, gripping the handle for dear life, she stared back at him. "This was meant to be your carriage, sir."

"Yes," he said.

"I would not have accepted your offer of it if I had suspected it would force you to walk."

He took a step closer and laid his hand over

hers on the door handle. "Perhaps we might . . . share the carriage."

Her mouth was dry. She smothered the little whisper in her head, warning that this was a mistake. Jack's voice had lost the cool, aristocratic drawl. Once more he sounded like the man who'd laughed with her at Alwyn House, and the way he looked at her made her heart leap. She nodded *yes*, sliding over on the seat to make room for him.

Chapter 18

She barely heard Jack tell the driver to drive on; her heart was pounding so hard she could feel it in her throat. The hackney started forward with a small lurch, and it unstuck her tongue. "I was told you're now a member of the Vega Club."

"Yes." Under cover of her cloak, his hand slid over hers on the seat between them. His fingers rubbed across her knuckles before drifting to her wrist, where he slipped loose the buttons of her glove. "It was the only way I could keep my word to you."

"That's far beyond what I expected," she said unsteadily. He was peeling the glove from her hand, sending tremors through her whole body.

"It shouldn't be."

"I know how you feel about gambling . . ." The glove came off, and his bare skin was against hers. When had he removed his own glove? Sophie's voice choked off as his fingers speared between hers, his palm to hers.

"No one said I must gamble while I'm there," he murmured.

"It must be a terrible inconvenience. I cannot ask—"

He squeezed her hand. "Perhaps I wanted an excuse to be there." He glanced at her, his eyes catching the light of a street lamp as they passed it. "Despite what people say about me, I am not made of stone, and it's been a miserably long week."

She made an odd gasping noise, hardly aware she'd been holding her breath. *Even dukes are men of flesh and blood.* Her own blood seemed to sizzle in her veins. "It has."

His hand tightened over hers, his thumb stroking her knuckles.

She was a fool. Not only had she gone and lost her heart to the wrong man, she didn't care. If this moment with him, with no more contact than his hand around hers, cost her every hope of a respectable marriage, she couldn't regret it. Sophie had lost too many people she loved to take any second of joy for granted. She turned her face into his shoulder, breathing deeply to imprint the scent and feel and warmth of him indelibly on her memory.

All too soon the hack stopped in Alfred Street. Jack opened the door and stepped down, reaching back to help her. He gave her his arm and walked her the few steps to her door. He tipped back his head, studying her house and glancing left and right to take in the street. It was modest but clean, and relatively safe. "So this is where you live."

"Yes." She took out her latchkey, trying to prolong the moment. "I thought you might have found out."

"No." He gave her a searing look. "If I'd known where to find you, I never could have stayed away."

God help her. All her resolve to move on, to keep their days together a secret hidden in her heart, drained away. "Come inside," she whispered before she could stop herself. "Stay with me."

His fierce smile sent her heart soaring. "One moment," he said, turning on his heel. Sophie jammed the key in the lock as he spoke to the hackney driver, who snapped his whip and drove off just as she got the door open. She turned, but Jack was already behind her, his expression taut. He pressed his finger to her lips and slid one arm around her waist as he urged her over the threshold before closing the door and sliding home the bolt. He put his cheek next to hers. "What about your servants?" he breathed.

"There's only one," she replied. "My maid, Colleen. She can hold her tongue . . ."

"Excellent. Where does she sleep?" His lips were brushing the sensitive skin below her ear, and Sophie felt in very real danger of swooning.

"Upstairs. She'll be sound asleep now . . ."

She caught the white flash of his teeth as he grinned, just before he kissed her. Her key made a tiny ping as it hit the floor. She clung to his jacket, holding him to her as she returned his kiss. Her entire being seemed to light up with pleasure as his fingers—both hands bare now—cupped her jaw as his tongue met hers. When he lifted his head, she swayed and almost stumbled, drunk on the taste of him.

"Take me to bed," he whispered, his teeth grazing her earlobe. "I told the hack to return in two hours."

Because he could not stay. It should have slapped some sense into her, but instead she took his hand and led him up the stairs. There was no time to waste.

She barely got her bedroom door closed before he caught her again. With one hand he untied her cloak and let it fall to the floor. "Do you know," he asked as he removed her bonnet, "how close I came to ravishing you on my desk when you called?"

"I wouldn't have objected." Her efforts to strip him were hampered by the frequent touches of his hands on her skin. Her pulse was leaping so erratically it was a wonder she hadn't fainted.

Jack's laugh was quiet. He let her push off his greatcoat and jacket, then spun her around to start working at the fastenings of her dress. "It was damned difficult to see you walk away from me yet again. I nearly didn't let you." Her bodice sagged loose and he pressed his lips to the back of her neck. Sophie put her hands on the wall in front of her for support; her bones seemed to turn soft when he did that. "Every day I look through the post, hoping there will be a message from you," he went on, his voice low as he divested her of the gown. "Every time I go out, I can't help hoping to catch sight of you."

Her breath shuddered as his arms went around her and his body pressed against hers. "We agreed—" she choked, trying to cling to sanity. "It's not wise for either of us—"

"No, it isn't, but I don't bloody care," he growled. "My God, Sophie, I want you more than ever."

She let out a whimper; her skin prickled, and her heart wobbled in her chest. *I love you*, she thought again, helplessly. She turned in his arms and seized his waistcoat in both hands. "I don't bloody care, either."

His mouth was on hers almost before she finished speaking. With urgent fingers they stripped each other before falling into bed. Jack's weight atop her made Sophie wild with hunger. His hands ran roughly over her skin as if he couldn't believe she was real. She unabashedly parted her legs and wrapped them around his hips, straining toward him.

He resisted her efforts. "I thought of having you like this the moment our eyes met at Vega's," he whispered. One by one he extricated her arms from around his neck and spread them wide, clasping her hands as he levered himself above her. "You were with another man, and it took all my control not to march over and knock him senseless."

"A friend," she gasped. "Nothing more." She could never marry Giles Carter now.

"Hmm." Jack didn't sound convinced. "Does he know that?" He kissed the side of her neck, right where her pulse throbbed, his lips sucking at her skin until she felt faint. "I wanted him to know. I wanted everyone to know you were mine." He moved, sliding over her in an imitation of lovemaking.

It was the perfect invitation to ask what he meant by that. It was rapidly becoming clear to her that they couldn't stay away from each other, nor did they want to. Philip and his jealousy could go hang; Giles Carter and his honorable intentions would have to slip away. This man was in her head, in her heart, and she wanted to be with him. Lover, mistress, or something else, she didn't care, so long as they were together.

But that was too somber for the moment, when her body ached for his. "Jack," she pleaded. "Make love to me." She rocked her hips upward again, and his breath caught with a perceptible flinch.

"Have you thought of me?" He held her pinned to the bed, although his mouth wandered all over her face and neck. "Like this?"

"Yes." Her breath was coming in ragged gasps now. His hips were sliding against hers, hard and slow, but denying her what she wanted. "All the time. You know I do . . ."

"Good." He adjusted his weight and pushed inside her. Sophie sucked in her breath and dug her heels into the mattress, wanting to draw him into her so completely, he would never leave. He released her arms and cupped one hand behind her nape until she focused her gaze on him. "I can't stop thinking about you." He withdrew, only to thrust home again, harder and deeper this time. "I can't stop wanting you." Another slow withdrawal, another strong thrust. She clasped her hands on his backside and tried to urge him faster, harder, deeper. Instead, he pushed himself up on straight arms, his electric blue gaze boring into hers. "I'm utterly mad for you." One hand stole between them, his thumb gliding between her legs. Just that light, probing touch sent a shudder through her that got stronger and stronger until it crested and broke like a wave over her.

Jack cut off her sobbing gasps of release with a deep kiss, his body driving urgently against hers until he threw back his head and went stiff in his own climax. And when he rolled onto the bed beside her, gathering her tightly against him with still-trembling arms, she rested her cheek against his chest, listened to the pounding of his heart, and silently mouthed, *I love you.*

"If every night at Vega's ends this way, they won't be able to keep me out," he muttered.

She giggled. "It's the first time I've ended an evening at Vega's in bed with a duke."

He started plucking at the pins in her hair, which was in a terrible state. "As long as I am that duke, I heartily recommend you do it more frequently."

She smiled, but with a tiny clutch of apprehension at her heart. She put back her head so she could see his face. "What does that mean? We agreed it was over when we left Alwyn House."

"Yet here we are." He'd got all the pins out, and now he swept them off the mattress onto the floor. Her hair unbound, she settled more comfortably against him, her cheek pillowed on his arm. "It means . . ." He paused, searching her face. "It means what we want it to mean," he finished. "What *you* want it to mean. I've already admitted I have no command of myself where you're concerned. Whatever you will give me, I will take."

The words *Take all of me* blazed across her mind, but only for a moment. Her sense and reason were slowly reasserting themselves as the fever-tide of passion receded, and she chose her words with care. "I want to see you."

"Done," he said at once, a lazy smile softening his face.

"As often as we can manage," she went on. "I realize you don't wish Philip to know—"

Pique flashed over his features. "Only for your sake. For my own sake, and for his, I don't give a damn." Her eyes widened, and he brushed a stray wisp of hair from her temple. "I am well aware that this is not so easy a choice for a woman. The only thing that would keep me away from you is fear of what consequences you would suffer if it were well-known. Philip's pride will mend in time, but I won't let him ruin your reputation in a fit of bitterness."

Her reputation mattered because she was trying to attract a respectable husband. If she became Jack's mistress, that would no longer be an option. Even though she had already dismissed that idea, it swirled around her brain like a fog, obscuring all reason and logic. Perhaps her Grand Plan would never come to fruition; perhaps she would be happier as Jack's mistress than as the wife of any amiable squire. Would she spend the rest of her days regretting it, if she gave up Jack in hopes of a respectable but passionless marriage?

Sophie didn't know. She had trusted her own instincts since she was twelve, but no longer felt sure of anything. Follow her heart and hope all turned out well? That begged the question of what "turning out well" would mean in this case. She'd spoken truly when she told Mr. Carter she had no expectation of snaring herself a duke. A duke would not marry a woman like her, a woman with a false name, an imaginary late husband, and a deeply ingrained sense of survival. Georgiana had moaned about her chaperone's strictures on her behavior enough for Sophie to understand just how far on the fringe of respectability she was already. To boldly step off that edge by becoming a mistress, even Jack's mistress . . .

Could she risk it?

Jack was not promising her anything more than an affair. Sophie made herself face that plainly. He—like she herself—wanted their affair to continue, but as it had at Alwyn House, a hidden private thing. Even as she admitted that it was too tempting to refuse—like that wager—she reminded herself she must savor it without expecting anything more.

"Sophie," Jack said softly. She blinked, realizing her thoughts had veered off course. "Whatever you're contemplating, stop. You look so grim."

She spread her hands on his bare chest. *Savor this.* He was back in her arms, and she would drive herself mad if she dwelt on how and when it would end. "You don't appear frightened off."

His grin flashed again. The lamp Colleen had left beside the bed lit his face with a warm glow and turned his hair to burnished brass. "On the contrary, my dear. It only makes me determined to make you forget whatever it is."

If only he could. She swirled her fingers over his bare chest, her somber thoughts fading as she refocused on having him near again. "It's not the sort of thing I could forget." She ran her hands up his arms to link her fingers behind his neck. "I was only scheming how I might maneuver to meet you outside Vega's every night . . . how we might share a hack or chance to walk the same way and wind up here, like this, every night."

He laughed again, the low wicked laugh that made her toes curl. "I shall contrive to make it exactly as you say." He flipped her onto her back and rolled atop her. "Beginning now."

He made love to her again, slowly this time, until her mind was blissfully blank. She drifted off to sleep, curled against his chest with her cheek over his heart and his arms around her, and only woke when he slid from the bed. She made a quiet sound of discontent as he separated his clothing from hers in the garments scattered on the floor and began dressing.

"The hack will return soon."

"I wish you wouldn't go," she whispered without thinking.

Jack's head came up, and his fingers paused in the act of buttoning his shirt. His eyes met hers, and for one endless, charged moment he stared at her as if waiting for something, some word or expression that would keep him here. In that moment, the familiar calculations and consequences ran through her mind once more, and this time she wavered in her determination. Just as she drew breath to say the fateful word— *stay*—he looked away.

"I must." He reached for his neckcloth and looped it around his collar.

The reckless fluttering in her chest stopped. She let out her breath silently, thinking that he had saved her from herself. "I know."

She stared up into the dark and listened to the

quiet sounds of him dressing. The floor creaked faintly when he stepped back over to the bed. "When will I see you again?" He sat on the edge of the mattress and leaned down to kiss her, his hand falling on her bare breast for a lingering caress. "Give me a time and day, darling."

"Jack." Sophie pushed herself up on the pillows to ward off the temptation to pull him back down with her one more time, the returning hack be damned. "I go to Vega's most nights between eight and nine o'clock."

His blue eyes were fixed on her. "When do you leave?"

"Usually not before three o'clock." His fingers were playing along her ribs, and she shivered. "But that is quite late. I've been considering leaving sooner . . ."

"One o'clock," he whispered. "Leave at one. I'll find my own way here."

"What if . . . ?" she began.

"You don't want me?" He smiled ruefully. "Don't leave at one. Leave earlier or leave later, and I will know not to come."

"How will you know when I leave?"

He touched one fingertip to her lips. "I pay attention—especially to you. It's not hard to watch someone else when you're not watching any cards."

Sophie pursed her lips and kissed his finger. "You might consider playing a hand now and then. It's a gaming club, and you'll be thought odd if you never play at all."

He arched one brow, amused. "Will I be?"

"I don't mean you should wager heavily," she

added, "only that it will attract notice if you never wager at all."

"Thank you for the counsel. I shall consider it." He kissed her again, first lightly, then deeper and harder until she sighed in pleasure.

She had to get up to walk him out and bar the door for the night. Wearing only her dressing gown, she followed him down the narrow stairs into the tiny hall. There he took her into his arms and simply held her. She pressed her cheek to his chest, once more covered in perfectly tailored linen and wool, and felt her heart swell.

"Good night, darling," Jack whispered, his lips against her forehead. "Until tomorrow night."

"Good night, Jack." She let him out, watching for a moment as he strode away, tall and far too elegant for her modest street. She closed the door and shot the bolt again.

It was only an affair. It would last only a short while. But by God, she would try to savor every blissful moment of it.

Chapter 19

J ACK MET THE waiting hackney in Tottenham Court Road, around the corner from Sophie's house. Her little home was on a quiet street, and he didn't want to attract any notice. It had been years since he'd been out in London so late. He leaned back against the thin, shabby seat, and a smile spread over his face at the memory of Sophie in her flower-printed dressing gown, with nothing underneath. He much preferred her in his banyan. Perhaps he ought to send it to her . . .

He stopped that thought. Of course he couldn't do that. This liaison between them was to be a secret. Only an idiot could have missed the way her mood dimmed abruptly when he said he would accept any condition she set upon their affair. She didn't want anyone to know about them because it would spoil her reputation; she still hoped to marry someone else. His mood dropped another notch at the thought of her in another man's arms, a man she loved. And he would have to sit by and watch it happen.

But he had promised to keep their relationship

secret. It was becoming clear to him that Sophie kept many secrets.

He muttered a heartfelt curse in the silence of the hackney. Gaining admission to Vega's might prove to be the death of him. Philip had been furious to see him arrive, but two short sentences put his brother in his place. As much as Philip might chafe at his presence, Jack made it clear he wasn't budging. Philip could avoid him by avoiding Vega's.

His brother's eyes had narrowed, and he'd leaned closer. "You're here because of *her.*"

"Do you mean Mrs. Campbell?" Jack had coolly replied. "Yes. I've heard rumors you are making a spectacle of yourself chasing after her, and that must stop—as must your losses. If you can't keep yourself away, I shall do it for you."

His brother had glared and muttered, but in the end he hadn't gone near Sophie. Jack had kept Philip in view all night, so he was certain of that much. And eventually, as hoped, he'd spied Sophie herself. The charge that went through him at the sight of her lasted only a moment, though, because there was a man with her. A man who stood familiarly close, who spoke to her and made her smile. A man who offered her his arm and escorted her away, out of Jack's view, causing a tidal wave of black and bitter jealousy to rush over him.

It took only a few subtle hints to elicit the man's name: Giles Carter, a gentleman of respectable family and fortune. No one had an unkind thing to say about him; in fact, he was well-regarded by the patrons of the Vega Club as honorable, sensible, and even somewhat witty. He had seen with his own eyes that the fellow wasn't ugly or misshapen, and he made Sophie smile. Jack positively ached to punch him in the face. And even though she claimed Carter was merely a friend, that would change in the blink of an eye if she encouraged the man. Carter's interest was patently obvious, even from across the room.

Jack might ignore the marriage mart on his own behalf, but he knew perfectly well how it worked. A man like Carter was an eligible match, especially for a woman who seemed to have no family or connections and a reputation that balanced precariously on the edge of respectability. He knew Sophie had secrets; he told himself he had no right to demand them. For a brief affair at Alwyn House he could ignore that, but now . . . he wanted more, of everything about her. Her company, her time, her attention, her trust.

How was he to persuade her to give him more?

The carriage stopped near Ware House, and he stepped down and paid the driver. The wheels clattered loudly on the cobbles as the hack drove away through the quiet night, and he walked the rest of the way home.

Even at this hour, a servant was waiting for him, ready to sweep open the door as he climbed the steps. Jack shed his coat and hat and sent the footman off to bed. For a moment he lingered in the silent hall. The house was as quiet as a tomb at this time of night. Restlessly he picked up the lamp and walked the corridors, finally turning into his study. He poured a glass of brandy but abandoned it after one sip. What was Sophie hiding?

He'd already guessed she was gambling to build a fortune. It wasn't above reproach, but neither was it criminal.

He suspected she was on the hunt for a husband. As were so many other women in London.

Nicholas Dashwood warned him off speaking to her. Yet she found him and invited him home with her, breaking her own decree that they mustn't see each other.

But there must be something lacking in his understanding. If she wanted a fortune, she had only to ask and he'd lavish her with luxury. She must know that; he'd offered to give her a house. Instead, she asked for his promise not to speak of their affair at Alwyn House nor even to see her again . . . only to take him back into her bed tonight. He was already mad for her, but this might drive him to Bedlam.

Was this all a great scam? Had he fallen into the hands of a truly skilled schemer and swindler? A woman in need of money, casting out lures to men she gambled with, rejecting the men who didn't have independent fortunes, making love to him and then declaring their affair over, but conveniently circumventing any obstacles between them when it suited her? Her every action had only made him want her more; had that been her intent? Was he being drawn into a pursuit where he was unwittingly the hunted instead of the hunter? Was he about to be used and humiliated again by a woman?

With a flinch he swore and ran both hands over his head. He was doing it again, seeing shades of Portia where there probably were none. What an idiot he would be if he let her haunt him forever. In truth, he hadn't thought much about her in recent years. But here he was, suddenly ascribing the same motives and intentions to Sophie, on very slim evidence.

The key was in his desk. It took him a minute to find it, but then he turned to the large chiffonier between the windows. He set the lamp nearby, turning up the flame, and unlocked the top cabinet. It took a few minutes to find the miniature. It was smaller than he remembered, the delicate silver frame a bit tarnished after all these years. Jack held it by the flickering lamp and stared at the face of his first love.

She looked so young. In his memory she was a woman, as beautiful and deceptive as Eve, but in this tiny portrait she looked barely more than a girl. It surprised him. He tilted the frame and studied her round cheek, her tiny rosebud mouth, her golden curls. He'd been taken with her almost at first sight, and thought the same had happened for her. She welcomed his attention, smiled at everything he said, even let him kiss her. Being with her was not like being with other young ladies, who were all too obviously sizing him up as a potential husband. Portia didn't seem to care two farthings for that.

She'd seemed perfect: beautiful, vivacious, unconventional. She liked horse races and art. She learned Russian instead of French, like most young ladies, because she read about the czar's court and found it more interesting. She was every bit of his class and the world he knew, and she still managed to be a breath of fresh air. Jack's father approved of her, and Portia's parents actively encouraged him. Somewhat to his surprise, Jack found himself agreeing with all of them that he probably ought to marry her. He even fancied himself in love.

That was when she eloped with another man. One night she danced three times with him at a ball, causing a flurry of whispers and expectations, and the next day she slipped out the back of a milliner's shop while buying bonnets with her maid and into a waiting carriage to flee northward. Only later did he learn that she'd had a secret, unsanctioned engagement to a rising naval officer all the time she'd been flirting with him. Her father, the Earl of Farnsworth, disapproved, and maneuvered to have the young man sent away to sea. He told his daughter to find someone more appropriate. Portia found Jack and used him for her purpose: fooling her parents while she made plans to run away with her lover to Scotland, where she could marry him without banns or her father's permission.

She begged his pardon in the note she left behind, but it took little time for Jack to hear the whole truth. She had never cared for him at all. In her eyes, he was an idle young man who would become an idle old man waiting to inherit his title. There was a war going on, and her naval officer was already famous for a daring raid on a Spanish port. Portia saw herself sailing the world with him, a decorated hero and fearless adventurer. She'd scoffed with her friends about how no one would ever know Jack's name; he'd be nothing but a numeral in the line of Dukes of Ware. She wanted a man of action, not someone who would inherit everything that made him desirable.

Carefully Jack restored the miniature to the cabinet. He'd long since gotten over the shock that she wanted another man. She was heartless and calculating to use him as she did, and he'd thought himself brokenhearted, but that faded in time. The scar Portia left on him was not a broken heart, as the ignorant gossips thought; it was the realization that no one would ever want him for himself. Less than a month after Portia's elopement, the eighth Duke of Ware, Jack's father, died. At the age of twenty-four, wholly unprepared and unready, Jack inherited the sprawling estates, massive wealth and heavy responsibility of the dukedom.

His more fortunate friends, the ones who either had not yet inherited their titles or who had no titles in the family to inherit, teased him about it. Now there were no tedious limits on his behavior or spending. Now he could have any woman he wanted, they said, with knowing winks and ribald laughter, and carouse as much as he pleased. That was small consolation, when the one woman he'd thought he wanted ran off with another man, and his carefree life as an heir had been crushed beneath the mountain of duty and obligation of a duke. Any woman he approached now saw not him, but a duchess's coronet.

Sophie Campbell was the first woman since Portia to make him think she didn't care for his title. For a moment the thought that had tantalized him at Alwyn House—why couldn't he call on any woman he chose?—beat at his brain. He didn't need to marry for money or consequence, so why couldn't he break several generations of tradition and marry a woman just because he wanted her? Assuming he wanted to marry her.

Did he? Could one even decide such a thing in the space of a few weeks?

You don't really know her, hissed his conscience. He'd thought the same about Portia, but she'd been deceiving him. He clearly didn't know much about women. No matter how deeply Jack felt that Sophie was not like Portia, the fact remained that she had secrets. Secrets she seemed determined to keep.

What was Sophie hiding?

Chapter 20

⌘⌘⌘

FOR THE NEXT fortnight Jack steadfastly ignored those secrets and what they might mean about Sophie.

He kept to his plan of shadowing Philip. When his brother went to Vega's, so did he—until a quarter past one o'clock. At that time he left, occasionally with a mocking salute from Philip, who had grown to accept his presence but not with particularly good grace. Jack no longer cared either way. Mr. Forbes, who was remarkably observant of patrons' habits, soon had a hackney waiting for him when he walked into the reception hall. Every night Jack took the hack to Tottenham Court Road and walked to Sophie's neat little house in Alfred Street so as not to disturb—or alert—her neighbors.

Those stolen hours in the dark of night fed something deep in Jack's soul. Every time she opened the door to let him in, his heart leaped at the sight of her face. When they hurried up the stairs, hand in hand, he felt more alive than ever before in his life. And when her bedroom door closed behind them, and he could kiss her and strip her bare and make love to her until they lay twined around each other in bed, hearts pounding and skin damp from exertion, he allowed himself to think again about his position.

He was the ninth Duke of Ware, with relations and connections to every noble house in England and half the royalty of Europe. He hardly needed to instill more respectability or status into the family.

He was one of the richest men in Britain. He did not need to marry an heiress.

He sat in the House of Lords, as his ancestors had all done, but politics was not his passion. He had no urge to make a politically powerful marriage.

In short, there was no reason he couldn't marry an ordinary woman.

They talked in bed, sometimes silly conversations that left them both shaking with laughter, sometimes more thoughtful conversations that left him quietly impressed. She had seen something of the world—more than he had—and she had an appreciation for small things that surprised and humbled him. Her curtsy, for instance; that grand elaborate motion that looked like a ballet in one movement had been taught to her when she was eight by a Russian ballerina. She drolly recounted how she had practiced and practiced in front of a mirror, anticipating her presentation to the czar—which of course never came. But the curtsy remained because it reminded her of that ballerina, who had refused to wear anything not made of red silk, who kept a pet mongoose, and who had been kind to a little girl.

Jack wondered why she'd been in St. Petersburg in the first place, but she never said. He found he cared less and less what Sophie's secrets were, but more and more what her feelings for him were.

She wouldn't be a conventional duchess, but that hardly mattered. The Duke of Exeter had wed a country vicar's widow and the world had not ended, not even the toplofty little world of the *ton*. And really, wasn't his opinion the one that mattered? Wasn't his preference paramount as to who stood by his side at balls and had her portrait in the gallery at Kirkwood and bore his children? As Sophie lay curled against him one night, relating another silly story from her childhood about some pastries in Vienna and the stray cat she'd tried to hide from her parents, Jack listened with a faint grin and thought to himself, *I don't give a damn what anyone else thinks. She's worth it.*

His growing feeling that he should follow where his heart and mind were urging him to go lasted until his mother joined him for breakfast one morning, three weeks to the day after Sophie had come to Ware House.

"Good morning," she said as the footman pulled out her chair.

"Good morning." Jack watched with mild surprise as she seated herself. The duchess usually took breakfast in her room, and not at this early hour. Her appearance this morning was decidedly unusual.

By the time the servant had fetched everything

she wanted and arranged it at her place, Jack was nearly finished with his meal. His regular habit, before Sophie, had been to go to his study for an hour before taking a morning ride in the park, depending on the demands of the day. Now, since Sophie, he had put Percy to handling more of the routine matters. Now he rode every day, rain or shine, and today he planned to stop by the boxing saloon for the first time in years. He wasn't ready to climb in the ring again, but it felt good to get out of his study and do something. He pushed back from the table. "If you'll excuse me, Mother."

"Are you well, dear?"

The question, asked in such a gentle tone, caught him off guard. "Perfectly," he told her, thinking that he'd never been better. "What makes you ask?"

Concern creased her brow. "You've not been yourself these last few weeks. Neglecting your work, going out every night and staying out until dawn . . . It's not like you, this wildness. Of course I wonder."

It wasn't as wild as the way he had behaved before his father died, and it didn't hold a candle to Philip's regular habits. "Percy is handling things well. Father ought to have trusted him more. There's no need for me to personally approve every purchase at Kirkwood House or review the plan for repairing the ice house at Alwyn." He cocked his head when her reproachful expression didn't abate. "What worries you, Mother? What friend has come to you, faint with horror over the hours I keep?"

"Don't be ridiculous," she said. "I'm your mother. My concern springs from my own observations. And I cannot help noting that you have changed your habits very dramatically since the *incident* at that club."

The Duchess of Ware never said the name Vega's, not even when she was imploring him to save his brother from it. And Jack bit back a grin at the way she referred to his wager with Sophie. She had no idea how much he'd changed since then. "Perhaps it shook me out of my calcified ways," he said mildly.

"Not for the better!" she exclaimed. Her butter knife clattered on the plate. "How can you go to that wicked place every night?"

"Wicked? I go with Philip. Are you equally worried for his habits?"

Her eyes flashed. Jack had long known Philip was her favorite son, and it did not surprise him when she refused to address that. "We were discussing you, not your brother. Are you neglecting your duty because of him?"

Jack wanted to laugh. Philip had provided him an excellent excuse to see Sophie, and he was very grateful for that. "I'm not neglecting my duty at all. In fact, one might say I am observing my duty—the duty *you* pressed upon me—by keeping an eye on my brother and preventing him from ruining himself at the tables."

Now she was piqued. "Stop blaming Philip," she snapped. "I wasn't speaking of your duty to him, but of your duty to Ware. Your father would be gravely disappointed."

Jack said nothing. For seven years he had done everything possible to make his father proud, and never once had his mother complimented him on it. She only mentioned how disappointed his father would be whenever Jack refused to do as *she* wished. And Jack had long since given up trying not to disappoint his mother.

"There." Her tone softened at his lack of argument. "Leave Philip to his own devices tonight. I am sure he cannot get into very much trouble in the span of a few hours. Come with me to the theatre."

"The theatre," he repeated in surprise. This was new, this gentle entreaty.

"Yes." She sipped her tea. "I have already invited Lady Stowe and Lucinda to share my box. They will be so delighted to see you at last."

But he would be more delighted to see Sophie. Lady Stowe talked a great deal and laughed even more, a high girlish titter that made his head ache. Jack couldn't fathom spending three hours trapped in a theatre box with her. "Not tonight, Mother."

The duchess sighed. "Wait." She motioned to the footmen, who silently left the room. "Let us be plain with each other, dear. You are being unpardonably rude to Lucinda and Lady Stowe."

"Rude!" Jack began to wish he'd taken breakfast in his study. "How have I been rude to Lucinda?"

His mother gave him a severe look. "You have avoided her all Season when you ought to have been doing the precise opposite."

"I have not avoided her," he said. "I have been otherwise engaged. And more to the point, why on earth should I seek her out? That is what you mean, isn't it?"

"You know very well what I mean. Everyone expects you to propose marriage to her this year."

If the ceiling had caved in on them, Jack couldn't have been more astonished. "Propose? Marriage—to Lucinda? She's just a girl," he protested, incredulous.

"She's eighteen," replied his mother, unruffled. "And you gave your father your word, as he lay dying, that you would marry her. She's grown up expecting your offer, and now you're haring about London like a boy just out of university without a care in the world when you should be courting her."

Jack was dumbfounded. It was true he had promised his father that he would look out for Lucinda, but . . . marry her? No, he most certainly had not promised that. He glanced at his mother, hoping to see some trace of hesitation, but she was wholly serious. Good God. Did she really think he had engaged himself to a child, seven years ago . . . ?

He leaned back in his chair, suddenly filled with suspicion. "Mother, I never vowed to marry her. She was a child when Father died."

"And he begged you to look after her, the daughter of his dearest friend."

"Right. 'Look after her'—that's what he asked, and that's what I promised. And I have."

The duchess waved one hand. "A few bills paid! That's not what your father meant, and you know it."

It had been far more than that. Jack knew Percy had been acting virtually as Lady Stowe's man of business for the last seven years, letting her houses, hiring her servants, arranging for everything a household could need in London. Knowing Lady Stowe, he'd probably paid a great many bills of hers, as well. Jack was sure the new Lord Stowe, younger brother of the late earl, appreciated that very much, as his sister-in-law was not known to be a thrifty woman.

But Jack had been glad to do it. It was the last thing his father had ever asked of him, and he would have walked through fire to keep his promise. He remembered the day his father and Stowe, friends since Eton, had set out on the duke's yacht, *Circe*. There was a brisk wind, a few raindrops now and then from the gray sky above, but nothing ominous in the air. A good day for sailing, the duke had declared. Sailing was his passion, and the river near Kirkwood was wide and smooth.

Stowe hadn't wanted to go. Lady Stowe was unwell, expecting a child, and she wanted Stowe to attend her. He still didn't have an heir, only a daughter, Lucinda. She was a quiet, bookish girl, tall and gangly at eleven, her wiry red hair always falling over her face, at least in Jack's memory. He had been home only because his favorite horse had developed a foot infection and the grooms at Kirkwood were the best in England. And by that unfortunate stroke of luck for his horse, Jack was there when his father and Stowe climbed aboard the *Circe* with a pair of servants and set sail.

The storm hit suddenly, blowing up the river in a matter of hours. It passed just as quickly, but when the sun came out again, the *Circe* limped back to shore, her main sail ripped and trailing in the water. A swell had almost capsized the boat, and Stowe was swept overboard. In horror, the duke had dived in after his friend, to no avail. The servants and the duchess had to drag the duke to his bed. By the next day he had a raging fever, and Lord Stowe's body washed ashore not far from the house.

It took four days for the duke to succumb to the fever. The doctors came and bled him several times before saying there was nothing else they could do. Privately Jack thought Lady Stowe's screams of grief, and the news that she had lost her unborn child, had made his father want to die. *I killed him*, the duke repeated over and over in delirium. *I killed Stowe.* The night before he died, he'd grasped Jack's hand and made him swear he would look out for Lady Stowe and her daughter. Unnerved and frightened by his father's weakening health, Jack swore it.

But that promise had not been to *marry* Lucinda. He narrowed his eyes at his mother, guessing what she was up to. "If he had asked for my promise to marry Lucinda—who was, as noted, merely eleven years old at the time—I would have refused, not only for my sake but for Lucinda's. She deserves to have some say in her husband. You and Lady Stowe have decided I ought to marry her, haven't you?"

"It would be for your own good," she replied, unrepentant. "You've gone completely mad lately. Your father would be appalled if he heard half the things you've done in the last month. Trust me in this—marry a proper young lady, one who's grown up preparing to be your duchess, and it will restore you to your right self."

"My right self," he echoed in disgust.

"Precisely." She nodded once. "You are a duke, a Lindeville, and must live like one, with a respectable duchess. It's time you saw to your duty to have an heir."

Jack barely heard that last shot about duty. His mind had belatedly stuck on one thing his mother said: Lucinda had grown up believing he would marry her. Christ. Was that true? It would put him in a terrible spot if so. Even though he'd never mentioned marriage to her, even though she'd never hinted she expected him to, if she believed they were informally engaged, and had been for years, what could he do? He had taken care of her and her mother as if they were family. If everyone in town believed he and Lucinda were betrothed . . . if *his own mother* and Lady Stowe had been telling people there would be a marriage . . . everyone would believe it.

Even worse, Lucinda might believe it. She had made her debut this Season, the only child of the late earl with a handsome dowry. All of London would expect her to make a splendid match this year.

And Lucinda herself . . . They'd always got on well. If Lucinda expected to marry him, she'd never said a word, not even in jest. But perhaps she'd not thought about it. She was a pretty girl, and an eligible one. Had she really been preparing to be his duchess since she was eleven? Had she turned down offers of marriage because she expected one from him? Jack rubbed his suddenly damp palms on his knees. Bloody hell.

It wasn't merely that he didn't trust his mother not to manipulate things to suit her. It wasn't even that he didn't wish to marry Lucinda, who was more of a younger sister to him than a desirable woman. It was that he'd damn near decided he wanted to marry *Sophie,* her secrets and mysteries be damned. He wanted her. He wanted to be with her, all the time. He was falling in love with her.

What would he do about Sophie, if he found himself unwittingly engaged to marry Lucinda Afton?

Chapter 21

Sophie knew she was running a tremendous risk by continuing to see Jack. Every night that he came to her door was another chance for a nosy neighbor to spy him and start malicious rumors that could upend her life. She'd already had to tell Colleen, after Jack left his gloves in the hall one night and Colleen discovered them the next morning, and even though the maid promised to be discreet, Sophie was acutely aware that most servants gossiped. More than once she told herself to make a clean break with him, for her own good and for his.

But then he would tap on her door, and she would fling it open without hesitation, her heart soaring as he slipped in and caught her close for a passionate kiss. It was enough to make her abandon her own rules, despite the risks. Love might be making her stupid, but it was also making her the happiest she'd been in many years. At times she felt like she was glowing with joy, just thinking of him, and therefore she resolutely refused to think about how or when it might end.

There was one test she dreaded, though, and before long it arrived. Sophie had put off her friends again and again. She knew they had heard something of her scandalous wager. At first she had brushed their questions aside, calling it a momentary and mortifying lapse in judgment. That was true, and it aligned with the story she put out to everyone else. Once Jack began spending almost every night in her bed, though, she couldn't maintain the lie, not to her dearest friends—but neither could she settle on what *to* tell them. She postponed their regular tea and responded to their letters without mentioning a word about Vega's or Jack or much of anything, really; she wrote of the weather and the new shoes she bought.

It wore on her. She didn't want to lie to Eliza and Georgiana, but neither did she want to drive them away by being distant and secretive. When Eliza sent a note asking if they would take tea together as usual after several weeks, she replied in the affirmative. The gossip about her wager seemed to have died down. No one in London seemed to know about her affair with Jack. She could only hope her friends had lost interest in the whole thing. And if they hadn't, and asked directly about the wager or Jack . . . she would have to remind herself that it was for their own good that she didn't tell them everything. The Countess of Sidlow was very vigilant of Georgiana's associations, and even Mr. Cross, who had been such a friend to her, might balk at letting his only daughter spend time with a loose woman.

She went down to her tiny drawing room when

Colleen announced Eliza's arrival. "Eliza! It's so good to see you again."

The other girl smiled and returned her embrace. "And you! I've been perishing of curiosity to hear from you, and you've been a terrible correspondent of late."

She had been, deliberately. But if she meant to continue seeing Jack, she'd better learn how to carry on with her life and still keep her secret.

Sophie flipped one hand carelessly and took a seat. "I'm much the same as ever. How have you been? I trust your father is well."

"Papa is very well," said Eliza, beaming now. "As am I. Oh heavens—I can't keep my news secret any longer! Sophie, I've met a gentleman!"

Sophie gasped. "You have? Eliza, how wonderful!" It was clear from Eliza's flushed happy face that she had more than *met* a gentleman. Eliza had met many gentlemen . . . who were all well aware of that fact that she was sole heiress to her father's considerable wealth. None of them had made Eliza blush and smile as she was doing now. "Who? When did you meet him? How have you not said a word about him before?"

Eliza laughed. "He's wonderful! He really notices me, Sophie. He's engaged in some business with Papa, so he comes to call regularly, and he pays attention to me as no one else ever has." She rolled her eyes and gave an embarrassed laugh. "Of course, he's so charming, he may treat every young lady that way, which is why I didn't say anything sooner . . ."

Sophie scoffed. "Only if they are as sweet and kind as you, but so few are. I don't see how all the decent gentlemen in London don't fall in love with you."

Her friend blushed. "That's ridiculous and you know it. But . . . oh Sophie, I'm in love!"

Even though she felt genuine joy for Eliza, even though the starry look in Eliza's eyes made her truly pleased, Sophie felt a sharp pang in her chest. She couldn't say that she too had fallen in love, because her love was not the respectable kind that might lead to a happily-ever-after. Her throat felt tight and her smile a little wistful as she said, "Tell me everything."

Eliza didn't need to be begged. She moved to the edge of her seat, her eyes shining. "Everything! There isn't much to tell, not really. I thought he was merely another of Papa's business partners when he first came to call, but before long he began making a point of seeing me—just politely, you know—when he came to see Papa. One day he arrived early, while Papa was still out, and we walked in the garden for quite a while, talking. I'd no idea how fast the time had gone by until Papa came and said he'd been home and waiting for half an hour! And then he apologized so handsomely, even Papa couldn't be annoyed, and you know how he dislikes waiting."

Sophie laughed. "He does!" When she spent holidays at the Cross home, she had learned not to be even a moment late to dinner. "Does your father know you care for him?"

Her friend's cheeks grew even pinker. "He does. Papa approves. And—and Papa hinted that His Lordship has spoken to him about me. Sophie . . . I think he's going to propose!"

Sophie clapped her hands together, beaming helplessly at Eliza's joy. "Oh Eliza—how thrilling! But wait—you've not said his name! Who is to be my almost brother-in-law?" she teased.

"Oh!" Eliza laughed, blushing at her own omission. "How could I forget? Hugh Deveraux, Earl of Hastings," she recited, each word soft with love.

Sophie blinked in surprise. "Indeed," she said after a pause. "The Earl of Hastings?"

"Yes." Eliza's green eyes grew dreamy at the mention of his name.

Colleen brought in the refreshments then, giving Sophie a welcome moment to think as she poured the tea and offered her friend some cake. She knew that name. Lord Hastings was often at Vega's. He was handsome and genial, but Sophie had never sat at a table with him because he played for far higher stakes than she dared attempt. She knew nothing else about him, but it put her on guard.

But surely Mr. Cross did. Edward Cross always seemed to know everything about everyone, and there was no way he would allow a reckless gambler, let alone a ramshackle fortune hunter, to spend a minute alone with his daughter. Mr. Cross wanted nothing but the best for Eliza, even to the point of helping her friends. He'd taken in Sophie with open arms when Eliza invited her to their home at holidays; he'd vouched for her when she applied to Vega's. Sophie knew he'd even looked the other way when Eliza urged her to take all her pin money, in the threadbare days when she'd first come to London. The man missed nothing.

Lord Hastings must be perfectly acceptable

then, despite the whispers Sophie had heard about large losses. The earl didn't look like a man in dire straits, and he certainly didn't act like one. Mr. Dashwood would have revoked his membership if he lost more than he could afford, which must mean he was well able to afford any losses. Or perhaps he won a great deal.

Thank heavens; she'd never seen Eliza so excited and happy about a suitor. That was the main point here, and she was happy to return to it. "I suppose your father gave his blessing."

Eliza laughed. "Of course he did. Lord Hastings invited me to call at Hastings House, and presented me to his mother the countess. She was so kind and gracious. I've not met his sisters yet, but . . ." She shook her head, her face glowing with happiness. "I never knew my mother," she added softly. "To fall in love with a gentleman, and gain not only a husband but a mother and sisters . . . Could I truly be so lucky?"

Sophie squashed her doubts. "Of course you could! Of course you *should* be. You're quite the kindest person I know, Eliza, and Lord Hastings is the lucky one if you've fallen in love with him."

The other girl wrinkled her nose and laughed again. "I can only hope he agrees! Oh, Sophie, I wish you could be so lucky too, to find someone to love."

"Pssh! Luck is a myth," Sophie said with a slightly forced laugh.

Something in her face must have given her away, for Eliza's smile dimmed. "What's happened?"

She sipped her tea and glanced at the windows. "Nothing! But where is Georgiana? She's extraordinarily late, even for her. Have you told her about Hastings?"

"Oh." Eliza went still. "I—I forgot. Georgiana won't be able to join us today, but she does send her best regards."

"No? Is she ill, or . . . ?" Sophie's voice died away as she took in Eliza's clenched hands and unblinking expression. Her spirits deflated as she guessed what had kept Georgiana from calling. "She isn't allowed to come, is she? Lady Sidlow won't let her."

Eliza rolled her eyes. "Lady Sidlow won't let her attend Astley's for fear it's too stimulating. She had an appointment with the modiste, or some such thing. She sent me a note yesterday and asked me to tell you when I arrived . . ."

"Eliza." Sophie waited. "You don't have to lie."

The other girl pursed her lips and looked out the window for a moment. "No, Lady Sidlow won't let her come," she said at last. "Now that they're making plans for the wedding at long last, Lady Sidlow says she must be far more vigilant about anything that might offend Lord Sterling or anger Lord Wakefield. But Sterling loves her. He knows you are her friend, and he's never once objected. And it's not as if his soul is noble and pure! He gambles, too, and he used to go to immoral houses from time to time—" She blushed as Sophie gaped at her. "Papa said so. He adores Georgiana, you know that, and he wanted to be certain Sterling was a good match for her. He had someone look up the viscount."

Sophie shifted uncomfortably at the reminder

that Mr. Cross didn't merely know things, he investigated people. Which meant that he would hear about the slightest misstep she made with Jack.

"Lady Sidlow's a strict old crow!" exclaimed Eliza, mistaking the reason for Sophie's silence. "Georgiana ranted at some length about her in the letter she sent me. She thinks it's a lot of rubbish, as if Wakefield would care now, when he's never cared tuppence before for anything she's done. You've been making wagers at Vega's for years, and Wakefield never said a word to prohibit Georgiana from calling on you."

Sophie pleated her dress against her knee. "Those wagers were for money."

"Wasn't this one?" her friend asked in surprise.

A week of your company is what I want, echoed Jack's voice in her head. A vise seemed to tighten around her chest for a moment as she thought of those days at Alwyn House, the fascinated way he looked at her, the desire in his eyes when he finally kissed her.

"You didn't say much in your note," Eliza said when Sophie fell silent. "I know *something* happened, or you would have dismissed the entire thing as the most incredible farce."

She shot a wry glance at her friend. "It's less believable than a farce."

"Don't you want to talk about it? Perhaps I can help."

Sophie studied the crease she'd made in her skirt to avoid Eliza's loyal offer of help. There was no chance of that. Eliza couldn't make her fall out of love with Jack any more than she could make

Jack fall so desperately in love with Sophie that he threw aside his entire ducal history and expectations and married her. "What did you hear?" she asked instead, then rephrased the question. "What did your father hear?"

Faint color marked Eliza's cheeks again. "He said the Duke of Ware offered you a notorious wager involving a large sum of money, and you agreed. Papa said he understood why," she quickly added, as if Sophie would be upset by that characterization. "Papa's a member at the Vega Club, too, you know, and he said it was one of the largest wagers proposed this year, which might have tempted anyone."

One corner of her mouth lifted. "It did."

"Was the duke rude to you?" Eliza persisted. "Papa feared he might have been, to provoke you into accepting. I know you don't want to be notorious, Sophie, and are never reckless. And Ware is known to be rather cold and reserved. For him to engage in such unusual behavior shocked everyone, even Papa."

Jack isn't cool or reserved, she thought with another pang. "No, he wasn't rude."

"Georgiana's theory is that the duke fell in love with you at first sight and made an outrageous wager because he went mad with passion for you." Sophie jerked up her head, and Eliza gave her a little shrug, smiling in her gentle teasing way. "Which story is closer to the truth, Georgiana's or Papa's?"

Slowly she set down her cup. The tea must be cold by now anyway, since she hadn't touched it in several minutes. "The truth might cause your father to forbid you to see me, as Lady Sidlow did Georgiana."

"Papa is a very keen judge of character. He's not swayed by idle gossip and savage rumor. He always wants to know the truth before passing judgment." Eliza's voice was firm. "He didn't object when I told him I was coming to see you today."

She nodded, smoothing the crease fiercely. Mr. Cross had heard the terms of the wager—so much for Vega's vow of silence—yet Eliza was here anyway.

"Does it make you uneasy? Sad? Afraid?" Eliza guessed. "You look tense enough to snap, which doesn't suggest it's a happy thing. You know I would keep it secret until I died." She paused, but Sophie still couldn't answer.

She should not speak of it. Eliza was kind and conscientious, and had certainly never done anything half so scandalous. Would Mr. Cross forbid their friendship if he discovered just how much wickedness Sophie engaged in? Georgiana's chaperone had already done it. She did not want to lose both her friends.

But on the other hand, Eliza knew her better than anyone—and Sophie desperately needed someone to talk to. Eliza would listen with sympathy, if nothing else. Since the age of twelve, she had heeded her own counsel, but this time she was utterly at sea.

"You're right—something did happen," she admitted. "I couldn't put it in a note. And you must swear not to tell anyone."

"Not even Georgiana, if you don't wish her to know," Eliza vowed.

"I don't even know how to put it into words!
It all began so innocently . . ." Sophie grimaced.
"Well, perhaps not entirely innocently."

Eliza was listening with compassion. "I gather
it did not remain innocent, or there wouldn't be
rumors furious enough to throw Lady Sidlow
into a fit."

Sophie blushed. "I made a mistake about Philip
Lindeville. You remember Georgiana teased me
about him? I thought he was a flirt—amusing but
harmless."

"You said he was charming."

"He was, but growing less so." Again she
thought of all the trouble she could have avoided
simply by being colder to Philip sooner. But then
nothing would have happened between her and
Jack, either, and she couldn't regret that. The
whole thing made her head ache. "But I was loath
to lose a friend, *any* friend, and so I ignored his
hints that we could be more than friends."

"Forgive me for asking this," said Eliza, "but
would that be so terrible?" She and Georgiana
were the only people in the world who knew her
Grand Plan, and from a distance, Philip looked
like the perfect solution: handsome and charming, with impeccable connections.

"Yes," said Sophie at once. "Beyond terrible.
He's too reckless. A reckless friend can be amusing, but a reckless husband is ruinous. And his
behavior of late does nothing to recommend him.
It was his insistence that I wager with him that
began the trouble. I suggested hazard—"

"Hazard!" exclaimed Eliza in dismay. "You
never play hazard!"

Sophie put her hands over her face for a moment. "I thought it would teach him a lesson. He wagers so wildly, he was sure to lose. If he lost, he would go home and leave me be sooner."

"Gaming hells must bring out the worst in people," said her friend hesitantly. "Georgiana says he's so charming and handsome . . ."

She sighed. Eliza was too romantic for her own good, having been sheltered and protected by her doting father. Sophie, however, saw a very different side of gentlemen than her friends did. Men who would treat Lady Georgiana Lucas with respectful decorum had no hesitation leering down Sophie's bodice every chance they got. Men who knew Edward Cross would take off their heads for any impropriety toward Eliza felt no qualms making indecent innuendos to Sophie over cards. "I know. But he insisted I gamble with him that night, and I gave in."

"But how did you begin wagering with the duke?"

"He had come to Vega's to pay off a debt for Philip. It must have been large, because Philip vowed to quit the club for a month, a vow he broke within a day of making it. The duke was furious to see him at the hazard table. He ordered Philip away from Vega's."

Eliza's eyes widened. "In front of everyone?"

"Yes," she said ruefully. "It wasn't well done of him. He admitted as much later." Deep interest filled Eliza's face. Sophie braced herself. "When Philip refused, the duke forced his way into the game. I—I may have spoken somewhat impertinently to him, and he said I should stop fleecing

Philip and gamble with him instead. In pique I agreed."

"Georgiana will be so very sorry she missed this tale," murmured Eliza. "Papa didn't tell me even half of it."

Sophie hoped that was true, but she forged onward. "And he lost very badly, which piqued *him*, and then he made that outrageous wager and like a fool, I agreed again." Sophie shook her head. "It was too good to be true—five thousand pounds! Against a week of my company. I should have known I'd lose."

Eliza's mouth fell open. For a moment the room was entirely silent, until the mantel clock chimed the hour, making both of them start. "Sophie, what were you thinking?"

"I was thinking of the five thousand pounds," she admitted. "I thought I would win. He had the worst hand at hazard of any player I've ever met."

"So you lost? And had to spend a week with him?" Eliza goggled at her. "I can't believe it. You wrote to me that you were sick in bed!"

Sophie's vision blurred. Her chest felt tight. She thought of Jack frowning in concentration at the cards when she tried to teach him vingt-un. Of his laugh when they rode in the mist and her absurd borrowed hat blew off. Of his smile when she woke to see him lounging in bed beside her, wishing for the rain to begin again. She sniffed, and it turned into a lump in her throat. "It began as scandalously as you heard, but Eliza—Eliza, it's so much worse. I've gone and fallen in love with him, and I don't know what to do."

Eliza jumped up and ran to her side, throwing

her arms around Sophie. "Oh, my dear! But why is that so terrible? If you lost your heart to him, he cannot be the cold, calculating man rumor says he is. I know you—you would never care so deeply for someone heartless or dismissive."

"He's not cold or calculating. He's decent and kind and wonderful," she said, her voice wobbling. She groped for the handkerchief Eliza held out. "But it's doomed. He's a duke, and I'm a woman who lies about her name, gambles every night, and has no connections."

"I suppose it depends on how much he wants *you*," Eliza said. "Papa is fond of saying nobility can do anything if they want to desperately enough."

She swiped at her eyes. She'd thought so as well, but it either wasn't true, or Jack didn't want her enough. "That's not encouraging."

"Well, where do things stand now?" asked Eliza with her usual sensibility.

"An affair," Sophie confessed in a small voice. "It's a complete secret. I know I should stop, and yet I can't. He was at Vega's one night and even though I know it would be ruinous to connect our names again, I invited him to share my hackney, and then I invited him in and asked him to make love to me."

"Oh my." Eliza released her. Sophie realized too late she had said far too much. "Have—have you done that before?"

"No!" she exclaimed. "It's utterly unlike me. I know it's dangerous and could ruin everything I've worked for. So why can't I stop myself from thinking about him?"

Eliza squeezed her hand. "Because you're in love with him. When you're in love, you lose some sense, I believe, and do things you wouldn't consider doing otherwise. All you can think of is him, and when you'll see him, and how you'd give anything for it to be sooner than expected. Love can make one a thorough optimist that everything will—*must*—work out well, because how could such happiness be denied?"

Her voice had grown soft and dreamy again as she spoke, enough to make Sophie's heart contract in anguish. Eliza was speaking of Lord Hastings, not Jack; she had met a gentleman the proper way, and he had conducted a very proper courtship. Sophie was happy for her friend, she truly was, but at the same time it made her own situation even more stark.

"What do you want to happen?" Eliza prodded, obviously putting Lord Hastings from her mind. "Perhaps he's the solution to your Grand Plan."

Sophie sighed. "I doubt it." Jack felt the weight of his heritage and duty very keenly, and the Dukes of Ware did not marry for affection, as he had told her himself. Philip had once said his brother would be sure to marry the most boringly proper woman in London. Would he even imagine marriage to someone like her? It seemed unlikely, not least because he had never mentioned it.

Only once, on that last sunny morning at Alwyn House, had she thought for even a moment he might consider it: he'd snapped that their association needn't lead to ruin. It had made her hope that he might want more, as she did. But when she cautiously asked what he meant, he turned his back and walked away. The only thing he did was ask if she really wanted it to be over, and with little other choice, she assured him she did.

Obviously she had lied. She wanted more, but Jack held all the say in that. When he agreed that he wouldn't see her again, that he would pretend they had never been lovers, it told her all she needed to know. She still wanted him enough to overrule her own good sense and carry on an affair that could only end with her heart broken, but she wished he'd made even the smallest attempt to persuade her that he cared for her more deeply than that.

"Do you want him to be?" Eliza squeezed her hand. "If he did propose, would you accept?"

"Yes," she whispered without thinking. The longing in the word surprised her, but obviously not Eliza, who was nodding.

"You made your plan to find a husband. Why can't he be it?"

"He's a duke," she pointed out again.

"And you're the granddaughter of a viscount."

"The disowned granddaughter of a misanthropic viscount," she corrected. "With scandalous parents and only the fortune I've won at the tables. Even if my connection to Makepeace were known, it would do me no good because I'm just as dead to him as my father was."

"If the duke loves you, he won't mind," persisted Eliza.

"And I gamble every night," Sophie went on. "He dislikes gambling."

"If you married him, you wouldn't need to gamble again. Would you give it up?"

She gave a dispirited laugh. Some nights it only felt like she went to Vega's to pass the time until Jack knocked on her door. She hadn't even checked her account there in a fortnight, something she'd never overlooked before. "Yes. But—"

"Sophie." Eliza pressed her hand again. "If you love him, you must tell him the truth."

"That I love him?"

"No, about you. No love can flourish and grow without honesty."

If Sophie had any secret that she kept more hidden than her affair with Jack, it was her history. She pulled free of Eliza's grip. "Honesty could also be fatal." She jumped up from her seat and paced to the window. "I fear he doesn't want more than what we have now. Telling him everything would only confirm that I'm not fit to be a duchess." Telling him everything might also cause him to reconsider their whole affair, and deep down Sophie feared that most of all. She had already accepted that she would never be a duchess, but now that she had embarked on this doomed, wonderful, secret, passionate affair, she wanted it to last as long as possible.

"Well." Eliza gave her a sympathetic look. "You know the only way to find out. You must ask him—after you tell him the truth about yourself."

Sophie folded her arms and gazed out at the street. Almost unconsciously her brain started asking what the odds were. Jack never asked about her family, but he listened to her stories of her childhood with a fond smile. That boded well. He never said anything against her attendance at Vega's, possibly because he was there himself every night. That also helped. And, as strange as it seemed, she felt they were equals in their affair. *Whatever you will give me, I will take*, he'd said. What if she offered him her heart, along with all the rest of her? Perhaps the chances weren't so negligible after all . . .

There was a rustle of cloth as Eliza came to stand beside her. "When I told you about Hastings, you assured me he couldn't fail to love me. That's quite ludicrous for you to say, as you don't know him at all. Why do you dismiss it so quickly when I suggest the duke might fall in love with you?"

"Because I'm not as sweet as you are."

"Rubbish," declared her friend. "You've endured more than I have. You're stronger and more resourceful and cleverer—"

"No," she protested.

Eliza nodded stubbornly. "*Far* more clever, and more beautiful. I'm sure His Grace can see all that just as well as I can. You must give him a chance."

Sophie made a face, but her brain was being won over by Eliza's argument. Jack knew what she was—not every detail, but enough. If she wanted a chance at real happiness with him, she would have to tell him everything. If he recoiled in disgust and stopped coming to her, then she must accept the fact that his feelings weren't as deep as hers. Perhaps it would be the spur she needed to end things.

But if he didn't recoil . . .

"Yes," she said softly. "You're right." She took a deep breath and nodded once. "I'll tell him."

Chapter 22

JACK SPENT THE day trying to determine whether or not Lucinda might consider herself engaged to him.

It had to be investigated with extreme discretion. As certain as he was that it was all a scheme his mother had concocted with Lady Stowe, if word got around that *he* was discussing it, everyone would believe it was true, or that he was on the brink of proposing and making it true. If all of London believed them engaged, he would be in an impossible situation. When engagements were rumored but then failed to occur, it was widely presumed that either the lady had declined the offer of marriage, or something had changed the gentleman's mind about making the offer at all. The latter would spread a rash of unfair whispers about Lucinda, which Jack had no wish to do; but the former would put the matter entirely in Lucinda's hands. And if she had indeed grown up expecting—wanting—to become a duchess . . . he could very well find himself caught, with no honorable way out.

He made very little headway in either direction, though. His solicitor assured him that legally he was under no obligation to a woman until settlements had been negotiated. But Percy produced records showing the extent of his "looking after" of Lady Stowe and her daughter that surprised even Jack. He had approved everything at the time, but only when he saw the sum of it over seven years did he realize how devoted it appeared.

In desperation he called upon a man he knew only slightly. Once upon a time, before his father died, Jack had run with a crowd of hell-raising rogues. The wildest of them all had been Lord David Reece. He doubted Reece would have anything helpful to add—Reece still possessed a wild streak and would never be called discreet—but his elder brother was a different story. The Duke of Exeter, Jack dimly remembered, had been supposedly engaged to a society lady when he suddenly presented an entirely different woman to the *ton* as his bride. The new duchess had set tongues wagging; she was a commoner, the widow of a country vicar, and London seethed with curiosity to know how on earth Exeter had ever met such a woman, let alone married her.

Since Jack was considering doing very nearly the same thing, he felt a fiendish desire to know how Exeter had managed it. Fortunately the duke was in when he called.

"I have a rather intrusive question," he began after being shown into Exeter's private study. "One I would like to keep utterly private between us."

Exeter's dark brows went up. "How intriguing."

"Once upon a time it was rumored you were betrothed to Lady Willoughby."

The polite interest in Exeter's face died, and his expression grew forbidding. "There was no betrothal," he said coldly.

Jack nodded. "I never meant to suggest otherwise. It is the rumors I am concerned with—specifically how they affected Lady Willoughby when proven untrue."

For a long moment the other man glared at him. Jack remembered David Reece saying his brother's stare could turn a man inside out, and thought that it might be true. Jack, however, was far too desperate to know the answer to his question, and simply waited. Finally Exeter spoke. "Dancing attendance on rumor will drive a man into an early grave."

"Right." He wished intensely there was anyone else he could ask. But he'd lost touch with most of his mates from years past, and was only realizing there was almost no one he could approach about this. "I would not ask if I did not find myself potentially entangled in a similar knot, utterly without warning or action on my part."

Finally Exeter's face relaxed. Something like a smile crossed his lips. "Ah. I know one thing—marriage to someone else puts a quick end to the matter."

His heart jumped at that thought. "But the lady presumed to be your fiancée . . . how did you tell her?" He could not leave Lady Lucinda to face a storm of whispers about why he hadn't married her. If, indeed, everyone—or anyone—thought he was about to.

Exeter turned and gazed toward the windows. The casements were open slightly, and the faint sound of a child's voice, raised in excitement, drifted into the quiet study. "I believe she read it in the newspapers," he murmured. "It was . . . regrettable, but as I said—there was never an engagement between us."

Jack let out his breath in disappointment. He couldn't possibly do that to Lucinda.

"I always thought it ludicrous that society took such an interest in my bride," remarked Exeter idly. "As if my judgment could be trusted in the House of Lords to steer the course of Britain, but my choice of wife must be approved by all of London." He glanced at Jack. "There are undoubtedly some among the *ton* who believe any man with a title and fortune rightly belongs to one of them, and they take his marriage to someone outside their society as a personal affront."

"But you did it," said Jack in a low tone.

An honest smile bloomed on the other man's face. He rose from his seat behind the desk. "I did. Would you care to step into the gardens with me?"

Mystified, Jack nevertheless bowed his head in agreement. Exeter had been remarkably forthcoming on a very private topic. It hadn't helped him on the question of Lucinda, but it did add to his growing belief that he was willing to chance a scandal to have Sophie.

That belief only grew as they went into the sunlit gardens. Exeter House, as one of the older great houses in town, was a small estate in the middle of London, not hemmed in by neighboring houses as Ware House was. A formal garden lay behind the house, and as they skirted a bed of roses, a little girl with long blond curls bolted toward them. "Papa!"

The change in Exeter was startling. His cool reserve vanished, and a warm smile lit his face as he caught the child up in his arms. "Molly, dear, you must meet my guest. His Grace, the Duke of Ware." He set her back down on her feet. "Ware, may I present my stepdaughter, Miss Molly Preston."

She wobbled into an off balance curtsy and recited, "It is a pleasure to make your 'quaintance, sir."

Jack smiled at her, his heart swelling at the thought of another little girl, practicing her curtsies in front of the mirror. He bowed. "The pleasure is mine, Miss Preston."

She gave him a wide smile before turning back to Exeter. "Mama caught a butterfly. Come see it!"

Exeter smiled at her. "In a moment. Are there a great many butterflies out today?"

"*So* many!" she cried, before turning and running down the path toward a dark-haired woman. She wore a very fashionable gown, but wielded a long-handled bag-net.

"Thank you, Exeter. It had been illuminating." Jack inclined his head in farewell and turned to go.

"Ware." Exeter's voice made him pause. "Marrying the right woman is worth a scandal," murmured the duke, his eyes on the woman catching butterflies. "Worth *any* scandal. I cannot give you better advice than that. Good day." He turned and walked away, toward his duchess with the insect net and his stepdaughter, who was climbing on top of a bench and reaching for the butterflies that fluttered above the profusion of roses.

A servant stepped forward to show him out. Jack went, unable to shake the image of Exeter's face. The man had been pleased when he saw the child, but when he saw his wife . . . It was as clear as day that Exeter loved her, passionately and deeply.

Worth any scandal, indeed.

PHILIP WAS WAITING FOR him in the hall at Vega's that evening. "Dear brother," he said with false cheer. "Might I have a word in private?"

Jack repressed a sigh. He had hoped to intercept Sophie before she reached Vega's, to no avail. Though no closer to a solution to the question of Lucinda, he was desperate to see her. Marrying the right woman puts an end to any rumors of other engagements, Exeter had said, which Jack was beginning to think a sensible choice. If he whisked Sophie to the nearest church and married her by special license, it would put a quick end to the problem, scandal be damned. He just needed to know if she would have him.

However, he'd been expecting this confrontation with Philip. He hadn't done anything other than keep his brother in sight at all times, but he suspected that was unnerving Philip more than if he'd scolded and harangued him to stop gambling. "Of course. Lead the way."

They went through the main salon, down a corridor lined with several doors. Philip opened one for him and then closed the door behind himself. They were in a small room with a table and two leather chairs, with a sideboard nearby waiting to hold decanters and the smell of smoke lingering in the room. This must be where the high stakes private games were played.

"What the devil do you want from me?" Philip demanded.

Jack folded his arms. "I've only made one demand."

"Which I have followed to the letter!"

"To the letter," he agreed.

"Then why are you still here?" his brother exclaimed. "Why are you following me like a nursemaid?"

"Because your promises have not always been reliable."

Philip threw up his hands. "One bloody time!" Jack gave him a speaking look, and Philip flushed. "One time when you cared."

"You mistake the matter," Jack corrected him. "I cared every time you broke your word. That time was simply once too often."

"No," Philip growled. "You cared more than usual that time. Because of *her*."

His whole body tensed. "Don't be ridiculous."

"Ridiculous!" His brother snorted. "That would describe *you*, playing hazard. At first I thought you did it simply to humiliate me, but you've never cared that much before, to risk your own reputation and funds. And you hate gambling! You've lectured me far too many times about it for there to be any doubt. No, you wanted Sophie— Mrs. Campbell—and you maneuvered to take her away from me."

Jack wanted to snarl back that Sophie had never been Philip's, and had never wanted to be Philip's.

Again the urge to declare her *his* rose inside him, and again he had to push it down. He'd given his word. "She was not yours."

Philip scowled. "She was—"

"She was *not* yours," Jack repeated forcefully. "I asked her, Philip, and she denied it. How dare you suggest I would contrive to steal a woman's affections from you? What sort of brother do you think I am?"

"You wanted her!" Philip charged.

"Suppose I did." Jack knew he was doing a dangerous thing, but he was boiling with frustration already, and someone had to make Philip see reason. "Would it matter, if she'd wanted you instead? Wouldn't she be the one to decide?"

His brother glared at him. "Of course."

"And what did she say to you?" He put his hands out. "She's at perfect liberty to bestow her favor where she likes."

He knew very well what Sophie had told Philip. And as hoped, some of Philip's fury faded. He scowled at the floor. "You took her away to punish me."

"I did," Jack baldly admitted. "Nothing else I did got through to you. Philip, you're flirting with ruin. I'm not speaking of Mrs. Campbell, but the gaming. A public spectacle and the loss of her company are small prices to pay if you quit the tables now."

"Quit!"

"At least moderate your play," Jack argued. "For your own sake, but think of Mother, as well. She indulges you, but even her patience will run out eventually."

"Moderate!" Philip flung himself into a chair moodily. "What does that mean? If I stop when I lose, it will only ensure I never win it back."

"It astonishes me that I'm about to say this," Jack said, thinking of what Sophie had said about Philip's play, "but you might try learning more skill. You play poorly, and then you become reckless, and that's why your losses are so crippling."

His brother's mouth dropped open. "Are you suggesting I take lessons? For hazard and vingt-un?"

"Think of it as improving your odds."

Philip was still staring at him as if he'd sprouted horns and a tail. "Are you mad? A *gambling* tutor?"

"Are *you* mad, to keep playing as lackadaisically as you have been?" Jack shot back. "What do you expect will happen? Playing badly time after time after time doesn't give you a chance to win back your stake, it causes you to lose more and more. If you won't give it up entirely, or even moderate your wagering, at least learn to play the bloody odds!"

There was a moment of stunned silence. Then, as Jack began to think the gambit had failed utterly, Philip muttered, "Well, I suppose a little practice couldn't hurt."

Jack ignored the fact that he had just encouraged his brother to become a better gambler, which would only lead him to wager more often instead of less. "Of course not. Buck up, man," he said bracingly. "It's not like learning Latin all over again."

That elicited a sharp bark of laughter from his

brother. "Thank God for it." He looked at Jack without animosity, for the first time in weeks. "How does one locate a gambling tutor?"

Jack thought of Sophie patiently listing the odds of hazard rolls, and watching the cards so intently in vingt-un. He lifted one shoulder and turned toward the door. "Ask a clever player."

Philip laughed. "I know just the one! Mrs. Campbell plays better than any bloke I know. I'll ask her."

The name caught him off guard. "No," he said instantly. "Not Sophie."

"I knew it." Philip leaped to his feet. "This *is* about her."

Damn it. He'd given himself away by saying her name. Slowly Jack turned around to face his brother again. "No," he repeated. "You're not to speak to her."

Philip gave a bark of incredulous laughter. "I'm not to speak to her, even about something like cards—you stand over my shoulder every night to make certain I keep my distance—but not because you have any interest in her! No, you goaded her to play hazard with you after humiliating me in front of the entire club, then you whisked her out of the club and set tongues wagging about her morals." He shook his head in disgust. "Lie to yourself if you want, but don't tell me you don't want her."

"That is not your concern," Jack bit out.

"No?" Philip scoffed. "She was my friend before you ever set eyes on her. How do you have more claim on her than I do?"

"Not one more word about her." His temper

was hanging by a thread. He turned on his heel and reached for the door.

"She deserves better, Ware."

He stopped. His brother's voice rang with warning. Philip stood like a fighter ready to box, feet wide, hands loose at his sides. "You're hardly the one to decide what she deserves."

"Neither are you!"

Jack recoiled.

Philip glared. "You've already done enough to her, don't you think?"

"What the hell does that mean?" he growled.

"Dragging her off to Alwyn House like a Roman with a Sabine woman?" Jack gave a small but perceptible start. "I'm not the only one who doubts the story she spread, although I may be the only one who knows you like to slip away to Alwyn for a few days now and then. Very conveniently near, for a secluded seduction."

Jack took a step toward his brother. It had been years since they fought physically, but his hands were in fists and his muscles were taut. "Close your bloody mouth."

"I have a bit of advice for you," his brother continued, "since you've been so generous with yours today. Sophie Campbell isn't going to be your mistress, so you can give up hope there."

"Shut it," he growled.

"No, I will not," his brother snapped back. "Give her up. And do it before you announce your engagement, for God's sake."

Jack froze. "What?"

His brother shook his head, scorn written on his face. "Mother told me about it. Sophie won't have anything to do with you once she knows. She turns away every married man who approaches her."

"I am not engaged," said Jack, his heart beginning to thud.

Philip raised his eyebrows in patent skepticism. "Almost engaged is nearly the same as married, among the *ton*. You know that."

Damn it. Damn it to hell. Jack concentrated on breathing deeply as his thoughts caromed from his mother to Lucinda to Sophie—Sophie, who would feel cruelly betrayed if she heard that rumor. He had to put a stop to this nonsense before it got out of control and ruined whatever chance he had to persuade her that he hadn't deceived her and wanted her, not Lucinda or any other woman. "You should avoid idle gossip," he said coldly.

His brother spread his hands. "Idle? Mother says it will happen, and we both know you always let her have her way in the end. She'll spread the news all over London within days, if she hasn't already, and I know you—you're too honorable to throw Lucinda over then." Philip leaned forward, his dark eyes deadly serious. "I'm offering you some well-intentioned advice—forget Sophie. Leave her alone. You ruined my chances with her—fine—but she deserves better than you, too."

Chapter 23

Eliza's words played over and over inside Sophie's head.

She had formulated her Grand Plan at the age of eighteen or nineteen, while darning Lady Fox's best lace mitts for twenty pounds a year as a hired companion. Sitting quietly behind Lady Fox, watching her flirt and have affairs with men half her age, Sophie had distilled her own goals into a short, simple list: security, companionship, and a family. She hated worrying about how she might keep a roof over her head if her elderly employer died. She hated watching other young ladies her age smile and dance with gentlemen before becoming wives and mothers, while knowing such a fate was unlikely for her. She hated being alone. Her friends were wonderful and loyal, but Sophie knew very well it would not be long before Eliza and Georgiana both had husbands and children of their own. Having lost her only family at the age of twelve, Sophie could think of nothing she wanted more than a comfortable home with a husband who was fond of her and a child or two to brighten her life.

To have a family, she needed a husband. To get a husband, she needed a fortune. To gain a fortune, she turned to the card tables. And so far, everything had been proceeding according to that plan . . . until Jack.

Eliza suggested he could be the solution to her Grand Plan. Even as Sophie denied it, the idea didn't need much encouragement to take root and flourish in her mind. Why couldn't he be? The odds might not be high, but they weren't zero. Sometimes one had to chance long odds, when the reward was tantalizing enough.

When the clock struck one, she rose from the whist table at Vega's and collected her winnings, fending off protests at her early departure with a smile. Without fanfare she went and collected her cloak, asked Mr. Forbes to fetch her a hackney and left, exactly as she did every other night. At her house she let herself in and waited, pacing circles around her parlor.

She would start with the worst—her gambling— and progress from there. Eliza was right, and she either needed to trust him enough with the truth, or break things off with him because she couldn't trust him.

Within minutes there was a soft knock upon the door. Her heart jumped into her throat as she hurried to open it. He stepped over the threshold and caught her in his arms.

"I've been watching the clock for hours," he whispered, his hands in her hair. "I thought it would never reach one o'clock."

Her pulse beat wildly. She cupped her hands around his jaw and kissed him, her lips lingering on his. To hell with the odds. She loved him—she trusted him. Eliza was right. If she wanted more from him, she had to be honest. Flushed, nervous and hopeful at the same time, she put her hands on his chest. "Nor did I. I've been waiting all day to talk to you."

He stiffened with a perceptible jerk. "Oh?"

The wariness in that word gave her pause, but Sophie banished it and forged on. "There is something I must tell you, before things grow even more complicated between us."

Instead of answering, he closed his eyes and pulled her close again, holding her as if they were about to be parted. "Must you?" he whispered, his lips against her forehead.

Her mind raced and her heart sank. What did that mean? He was clearly dreading it. "Do you not want to know?"

His chest heaved with a silent sigh, then he released her. "Anything you want to tell me, I want to know."

Sophie didn't move. "Jack, what is wrong?"

He took her hand and studied it, stroking his thumb over her knuckles. "It's been a trying day." He flashed her a wry smile, looking for a moment as he had at Alwyn House. "Thanks to my mother and Philip, not you."

"Oh." She exhaled and gave a small laugh in relief. "I'm very sorry to hear they made life difficult."

"Now that I am here with you, I don't give a damn about them." He pulled her into his arms and kissed her temple, and they walked into the parlor and sat on the sofa, never letting go of each other.

"I think you have suspected me of having secrets for some time now, and you're right—although perhaps not for the right reason," she began. "I have not been completely honest with you."

Jack cleared his throat. "Secrets."

"Yes." She hesitated. "The first one is that my name isn't Campbell. Mr. Campbell is a myth, as well." She watched his face closely but saw no sign of horror or disgust there. "I invented him because I wanted a fresh start when I came to London, and a widow is allowed so much more freedom."

"A fresh start," he repeated. "From what, if I may ask?"

Her face grew warm. "I was companion to an older lady in Bath. She left me three hundred pounds in her will, and I took my chances and came to London with it."

"Ah." A thin frown creased his brow.

"I wanted to be independent," she explained. "My family . . . You know my father was disowned when he married my mother. His father was a—a viscount. Papa was not the oldest son, but he would have had a generous inheritance. But he fell in love with my mother, and my grandfather vehemently disapproved because she was an opera singer. My father gave up everything to marry her." A smile crossed her face, thinking about her parents again. "My mother sang in every court in Europe. It was just the three of us, traveling from city to city, as she got engagements. It became harder as the war spread, and then Mama got sick.

"We had to come home to England," she said, her words growing softer. "Mama lost her voice and Papa had to support us. He . . ." She hesitated. "He did so at the gaming tables. I helped him practice."

"And that's where you learned to play," he murmured.

Sophie nodded. "I have a knack for cards—of all the silly talents to have. That's why Vega's was a crucial part of my plan. I never would have been accepted as a member there if I'd been a spinster, which was another good reason to become a widow."

He said nothing for a moment. "You've won a good sum at Vega's, haven't you?"

Sophie nodded. "Approaching four thousand pounds, after expenses, in three years. I want to be independent."

Jack's eyebrows went up. So far her story aligned reasonably well with what he'd already assumed. Nothing she said had changed his mind about her—if anything, he had to admire her pluck. This was a real plan, and she'd executed it well. The contrast between his brother's careless carousing and Sophie's methodical pursuit was impossible to ignore.

She blushed under his regard. "I play to win because I have no other means of support. You accused me of being a hardened gamester. I suppose I am, although I truly don't try to ruin anyone. It's true I won from Philip, but never very much. I don't want to beggar my friends, and I did think very highly of Philip until—"

Until Philip became possessive and troublesome. Jack resolved to revisit that point with his brother until Philip understood how loathsome his behavior had been. Incredibly, he found it all a massive relief. When she'd begun so somberly, he had feared there was something far worse. But this . . . it was nothing like what Portia had hidden from him. Sophie was as he had thought: independent, determined, and fundamentally true. His heart lifted at the realization that he'd been right about her, which meant he was free of any doubt about what to do next . . .

"How very sensible," he said to change the subject.

She started. "Sensible! You think it's sensible?"

He shrugged. "How many gentlemen with empty pockets have the same plan? Excepting the fictitious spouse, of course. And, no doubt, any actual employment."

"Yes, well, gentlemen seem to have different rules," she said wryly. "I wouldn't dare do some of the things men at Vega's have done."

He acknowledged the point. "Have you any other support? Surely your grandfather would step in if he knew." He found himself hoping she named the old tartar. Jack wanted to give the man a stern word about abandoning orphaned grandchildren.

Her eyes sparked with disdain. "No, my grandfather won't lift a finger to help me. He disowned me as thoroughly as he disowned my father.

I'd sooner starve than ask his help—not that he would give it even if I were starving."

"Perhaps a cousin, or an aunt—your mother's family—"

She gave a tight shake of her head. "No. My father had a brother, but said he was just as surly as my grandfather. I don't want to know him, either. And I haven't had contact with my mother's family since we came home to England. I wouldn't even know where to look for them. I have preferred to be on my own."

Jack let it go. "It doesn't matter. You're of age, after all."

"There is more." She took a deep breath. "I confess I—I had hoped to find a husband," she said, avoiding his gaze. "Someone respectable, who could offer me a good home and a chance to have a family." Her voice grew wistful, and his stomach tightened. He burned to banish that lonely tone from her voice forever. "I haven't had anyone since I was twelve. My grandfather—the Ogre—is worse than having no one. A penniless woman with no connections is hardly likely to attract a respectable man, but I thought, if I had some small fortune saved up . . ."

It took all his restraint not to growl at that. Sophie had no idea how appealing she was. Once more he thought of Giles Carter, who'd been with her at Vega's, the man who made her laugh and took her arm. That man, he knew, was attracted to her, and Jack doubted her four thousand pounds had anything to do with it.

"I wanted you to know, so that you may walk away," she said, interrupting his thoughts.

"Do you think I wish to walk away?"

Color rose in her face. "I hope not," she whispered.

He raised her hand to his lips and pressed an openmouthed kiss to her palm. "Are those all your deepest secrets?"

"No," she whispered, watching with dilated eyes as he made love to her hand. "There is one more . . ."

"Tell me, darling." He didn't think there was anything she could say that would change his mind now.

Her lips parted, and she raised her gaze to meet his. "I love you."

His heart jumped in his chest, and for a moment he forgot to breathe. "Sophie . . ."

She pressed her fingers to his lips. "I didn't say it in expectation you would feel the same."

"No? Then you hope I don't?" He removed her hand from his face and bent her backward on her tiny sofa.

"What? Well—no . . ." Her breathing grew uneven as he hooked one finger into the neckline of her dress and tugged the fabric down to bare her shoulder.

"Good." He shifted his weight until she was beneath him. His luck, so poor all day, had undergone a sea change. *She loved him.* He felt bold and invincible, and his next move seemed so right, he wondered why he hadn't already made it. "I've been falling in love with you since you stormed into the library and called me a lunatic. You were entirely correct, and I wanted to say that it was because of you—blowing kisses to the dice at hazard, declaring you would walk to Alwyn through the mud and the rain, taunting me with your bare feet while you wore my banyan." He pressed his lips to the soft skin atop her shoulder. "You drive me mad, Sophie, and I never want it to end."

Her fingers plowed into his hair as he kissed his way along her collarbone. "Madness is not something to crave . . ."

Jack lifted his head. "For me it is—your kind of madness. My father, like his father and his grand-father and undoubtedly several other generations before them, married for sane, calculated reasons. Some of their unions were civil and harmonious, some were not, but I can't imagine one of them felt as I do when I'm with you. Marry me, Sophie."

Her eyes flew wide open.

"I want you, darling," he breathed, skimming his palm up her waist. Exeter had shown him how to cleave the knot: marrying someone else would put paid to any rubbish rumors about an engagement. Tomorrow he would call on Lucinda and make it clear there was no understanding, no promise, no betrothal. He was prepared to do almost anything else in his power to see to her comfort and safety, for the sake of the promise he'd made to his father, but he would not marry her. *Worth any scandal*, echoed Exeter's words in his mind.

Then he was going directly to Doctors' Commons in pursuit of a special license. Sophie wasn't the woman anyone would expect him to marry, and it would astonish, if not scandalize, most of London. But she was the only woman he could imagine spending his life with, and by God he meant to have her—in his life, in his bed, in his heart.

She put her hands on his face and searched his eyes. "Jack—no, you can't mean that. I have nothing to offer you that's worthy of a duchess—"

Jack made a scornful noise low in his throat. "Only a duke can determine that, and I have determined that you offer everything I want in my duchess. Will you have me?"

She surged up and kissed him, her mouth soft and hot. Jack kissed her deeply, shuddering when she sucked on his tongue. "I will," she whispered. "With all my heart and soul."

"And body, I hope." He began drawing up her skirt. "I intend to have you here and now."

Her eyes shone dark with desire. "Yes."

"Do you know, I've thought about making love to you on a sofa again ever since we returned to London."

"Have you?" Her eyes drifted closed and she arched her back, pressing up into him.

"Every night." His hand reached the garter tied above her knee. He tugged it loose and hooked his fingers under her knee, urging her to put her legs around his hips.

"Then . . . I hope you do . . . every night."

He grinned at her breathless reply. "Nothing would give me more pleasure." Jack's heart beat so hard he was sure she would feel it. He wanted her to feel it. It never beat that way before her, and he thought it might stop beating altogether if he ever lost her.

He made love to her on the sofa, and then he

took her upstairs and made love to her again, leisurely this time, in her bed. When Sophie had fallen into an exhausted slumber, draped over him, and his muscles felt as though they wouldn't support him if he tried to stand, Jack wound a lock of her hair around his finger and dismissed any thought of sneaking home before dawn.

He was home. And he wanted the world to know.

Chapter 24

~~~~~~~~~~

LADY STOWE HAD let an elegant house in Berkeley Square, facing south across the garden at the heart of the square. Jack fleetingly wondered how much of the rent he was paying before dismissing the thought. After last night, when Sophie whispered that she loved him over and over as he moved above her, joining his body, heart and soul to hers, he'd pay the rent on every house in this street and thank Lady Stowe for it. He tied up his horse and rapped the knocker.

His arrival caused a bit of a flurry inside the house. The butler showed him to a bright morning room while the sounds of running feet echoed upstairs. He strolled to the window and watched the traffic roll by outside as his mind drifted to Sophie—his love. He wanted to spoil her with every luxury he could. Perhaps he'd whisk her back to Alwyn for a month after their wedding.

The door behind him opened. "Your Grace," cried Lady Stowe. "How delightful of you to call."

Jack turned. The countess curtsied, a rather rigid motion compared to Sophie's flowing one.

"Good day, Lady Stowe. I called in hopes of having a word with Lady Lucinda."

Her face brightened. Lady Stowe was a petite woman and had been a beauty in her youth, with pale blond hair and wide blue eyes. Now her hair was turning to silver and there were lines around her eyes, but Jack was not fooled. The countess might look like a china doll, but she was cut from the same iron-willed cloth as his mother. "My daughter will be down soon to receive you. She will be most delighted you've called." She came into the room, a proud smile on her face. "Won't you be seated, sir?" She went to the sofa, and Jack obediently took a chair. "I hope the duchess your mother is well?"

"She is." Jack thought she must know how his mother was even better than he did, especially since he'd been avoiding his mother since their conversation about Lucinda.

"I am delighted to hear it," said Lady Stowe warmly. "Family is so important."

Sophie wanted a family. She'd had no one since she was twelve, not even a managing mother or an irresponsible sibling. Jack, who had never been free of family duty and obligations, thought he would also like a family, one of his own making. His lips curved at the thought. His sons would be better cardplayers than Philip; he had no doubt about that. His daughters, too. Sophie would see to it.

"My husband's brother, Lord Stowe, is in town at present, as well. Are you acquainted with Stowe yet?"

Jack's polite expression felt as stiff as a mask.

If he had been about to propose marriage to Lucinda, he would have to receive her guardian's blessing. But he wasn't about to propose, and he had no interest in speaking to Lord Stowe. "I am not."

"Stowe is very fond of my Lucinda," the countess went on. "He treats her quite as if she were his own child! I'm sure I couldn't ask for a better guardian for her, since her own dear father is no longer here."

"I'm delighted to hear it," he replied. He glanced around the room, determined to change the subject. "My man Percy tells me you have had no complaints this Season with the house."

"Oh no," she said at once. "This house suits us very well. It is too small to hold a ball, of course, but your own mother—such a kind lady!—has offered to host one in Lucinda's honor." She gave a little peal of laughter. "But naturally you must know all about it, since it will be held in your very own home!"

There was no doubt in Jack's mind that his mother had been actively scheming with Lady Stowe to make that ball a betrothal ball for him and Lucinda. "I'm afraid not," he said. "My mother does not always keep me apprised of her plans, and I rarely attend balls."

She paused, her expression turning sharp and frustrated for a brief moment before she smiled again. "I hope you will make an exception to attend this one. It would mean so much to Lucinda, and to your mother, I imagine."

He tipped his head. "Perhaps." He'd attend that ball only with Sophie on his arm, as his duchess.

Otherwise, a regiment of soldiers couldn't make him walk through those doors.

Lady Stowe pursed her lips. "Where is Lucinda? Normally she is so punctual, Your Grace." She reached for the bell rope and gave a hard yank. "I'm sure she'll be so distressed to have kept you waiting."

The door flew open then to reveal Lucinda, pink cheeked and flustered. She hurried into the room and almost stumbled into a curtsy. "Your Grace, Mother," she murmured breathlessly.

"There you are at last, dear. Come, ring for refreshments for His Grace," said her mother, patting the seat next to her.

"Actually," said Jack as Lucinda flushed at her mother's criticism, "I wonder if Lady Lucinda would care to take a turn about the square with me. It's a very fine day out, and I confess I long to feel the sun."

Lady Stowe blinked, then let out another peal of her tittering laughter. "Why, that's a splendid idea! It's been ever so rainy lately, a breath of fresh air would be delightful. I fancy a turn about the square as well—"

Jack cleared his throat, and she stopped speaking at once. "If I may, Lady Stowe, I have something particular to discuss with Lucinda and wonder if we might speak alone."

The countess shot a look of triumph at her daughter. "Of course, Your Grace."

But Jack was watching Lucinda, to see if she shared her mother's delight. If she did, he couldn't tell; Lucinda's expression didn't change, for better or for worse. Since he'd seen ladies' faces brighten simply at the sight of him approaching, he took this as a positive sign. If she'd been waiting eagerly for his proposal, as his mother claimed, he would expect to see some indication of gratification. Instead, Lucinda continued looking slightly nervous, fidgeting with a ribbon on her dress.

When she caught him watching her, she dropped the ribbon and blushed. "Yes, Your Grace. That would be lovely." She curtsied again.

Lady Stowe swept out into the hall, where the butler was waiting. "Lady Lucinda will be walking out, Wilkes," she told him before turning back to Jack. "I will have refreshments waiting when you return."

He sincerely hoped there was no reason for him to come back into the house. If Lucinda broke down weeping and he had to escort her back to her mother, it would be awful. He turned to Lucinda, who was tying her bonnet ribbons, and offered his arm. "Shall we, Lady Lucinda?"

They strolled across the street to the large central garden, through a gate in the iron railing. Directly across from them stood Gunter's Tea Shop, with a cluster of carriages sitting under the shade of the trees nearby and more people sitting on the benches in the park. Jack steered Lucinda toward a quieter part of the square, wanting a little privacy. "Have you been enjoying your Season?" he asked politely.

"Yes, Your Grace." Lucinda was a tall girl, as slender as a reed with a mop of wild red curls. Or rather, she'd had wild red curls as a child; today her hair was scraped back from her face into a braided knot, now hidden beneath her bonnet.

"Very good." They walked in silence for a moment. "I asked you to walk with me because I have something of a delicate nature to discuss with you," Jack said.

"No," she blurted out.

Jack stopped in surprise. "I beg your pardon."

Lucinda flushed deep pink. "My mother told me what you are going to ask, and as honored as I am, I must decline."

"Must you?" he murmured, his mind racing.

She released his arm and took a step away, wringing her hands. "I must. I know you made a promise, and you have been so very generous and good to me and my mother since Papa drowned, but I am afraid I absolutely cannot marry you."

"Ah." He was so relieved he felt dazed. "Cannot?"

Her mouth opened in dismay. "Oh—I meant I don't want to!"

Jack began to smile. She looked so horrified and then embarrassed as awareness of what she'd said sank in. Yet it was beyond anything he'd hoped to hear from her, and in spite of himself he began to laugh.

"Oh please." Lady Lucinda was the color of milk, clutching her hands to her stomach as if she would be sick. "Please forgive me—I ought not to have been so rude. Please, Your Grace, let me explain—"

He recovered enough to speak. "Set your mind at ease. I am not offended. Quite the contrary, as it happens. That was the matter I wished to discuss with you"—she made a low moan of anxiety—"but your answer does not surprise me."

Her eyes darted from side to side. "It doesn't?"

He shook his head. "I gather our mothers have been plotting a match between us, entirely without my knowledge. I presume your mother spoke to you about it."

"Well." She bit her lip hard. "Yes . . ."

By which Jack guessed Lady Stowe had talked of little else this Season. "Did she never ask your opinion of the matter?"

Lucinda blushed bright pink. "No," she whispered.

"Then there is really nothing more to explain." He offered his arm again. "Shall we enjoy the rest of our walk? It really is a fine day out."

She goggled at him for a moment, then slowly put her hand back on his arm. "You're not angry?"

"I suppose it's somewhat lowering to be told a woman absolutely doesn't want to marry me, but I am not angry." Vastly relieved, in fact.

Lucinda's brow knit, and for a moment she looked to be thinking very hard. "I don't suppose you actually wanted to marry me. Mama said you had given your word to do so, but that was years ago, and I can't imagine you knew what you were promising."

"I gave my very solemn vow to look after you and your mother," he replied. "I shall not break that promise. As for marriage . . . It would be unconscionable for any man to swear to marry a girl who was too young to have any say in the matter. You were scarcely eleven years old."

Her fingers twitched on his arm. "When my papa died."

"Yes."

She was quiet for a moment. "You never promised to marry me, then."

"No," he admitted.

Lucinda exhaled loudly. "Thank goodness! Oh, Your Grace, that is such a relief to hear. My mother told me it was my duty to accept you, so that you could keep your vow—vows being vitally important to gentlemen—and I've been dreading your call for so long! When you left town a few weeks ago, I even began to hope you wouldn't return this Season at all, and I wouldn't have to do anything about it."

A few weeks ago he'd left town with Sophie. A small smile crossed his face. "I considered not returning at all."

"I wouldn't have minded," said Lucinda frankly. "Every day my mother has reminded me that it's my destiny to be a duchess, and all I could think was how terrible that sounded."

"Why?" This was far more entertaining than expected.

She wrinkled her nose. "First, a duchess is so proper! I should dread everyone watching me to see what I wear and how I behave. It's bad enough when my mother does it. And then you're so old—" She froze, her eyes widening. "Oh dear—oh no—"

Jack was losing his battle with laughter. To her he must appear ancient, even though little more than a dozen years separated them. "No, no, I quite understand. Go on."

"I meant so much older than I," she said, her face cherry red. "Very kind, of course, and so good to Mama and me, but . . ." She bit her lip before rushing on. "But the most important reason is that if I become a duchess, I shan't be able to go to Egypt, and that is my fondest wish in the world."

He wondered why she thought a duchess couldn't travel, but let it go. "Lady Lucinda, you have astonished and delighted me. Shall we get some ices, and you can tell me why Egypt is your heart's desire?" Still blushing, she agreed, and he escorted her to a bench near Gunter's and hailed a waiter who had just served several ladies in a carriage nearby. He ordered some lavender ices, at Lucinda's eager request, and said a prayer of thanks that Gunter's was one of the few places he could be seen with a lady and not be presumed to be courting her.

It turned out Lucinda had got her hands on some volumes of *Description de L'Egypte*, the observations and pictures created by Napoleon's army in Egypt. She convinced her mother it was to improve her mastery of French and pored over every inch of them. Lucinda was entranced, especially by the Egyptian writing, which she described as artful little drawings.

"What do they mean?" Jack asked as they ate.

"No one knows! I wish I had been able to study Greek or Latin and have some chance at deciphering them." Lucinda could hardly sit still, she was so animated. "But the country sounds so exotic, so foreign and so beautiful. It's my dream to travel there, to see the monuments and the wide expanse of sand, barren of trees or other greenery. Can you imagine anything so magnificent here in England, where it rains so often?"

Since his week at Alwyn House with Sophie, Jack had been feeling much more fond of rain. "I cannot."

She spooned the last of her ice and set down the dish. "I don't think I shall be able to go until I am twenty-one. My mother will never let me leave before I'm of age. Her only thoughts are of hairstyles and fashion and how well I can embroider, and no one cares about any of that. But Egypt is like a new world, only very old, and so full of mystery and treasure. There is nothing in England like it."

"Undoubtedly that is true." Jack nodded to a hovering waiter, who rushed forward to take their empty dishes. "What shall you tell your mother?"

Lucinda scuffed her toe in the grass. "She would never approve of my traveling to Egypt."

"Are you certain? It's quite the thing, now that the war is over. Travel is much safer, as well. I daresay you could go, eventually, if you put your mind to it."

"Do you really think so?"

He smiled. "I would never underestimate a woman with a plan."

Lucinda brightened. "That's so! She's told me I don't need to know much beyond keeping household accounts and planning menus, but I want to know so much more. It is so frustrating to feel ignorant. Perhaps I could travel with a scholar and help fund his explorations in exchange for lessons. Do you think anyone would agree to that?"

"The scholars I have known are always eager to find someone to fund their expeditions." Jack knew Lucinda was heiress to a sizable fortune.

She would certainly have the funds when she came of age.

"That's it, then!" She beamed at him as they strolled back toward her home. "Thank you, Your Grace," she added shyly. "I cannot tell you how vastly relieved I am. It's been weighing on me for weeks what I should do, but now I feel so much more hopeful."

Jack felt bloody pleased himself. Lucinda didn't want to marry him, and she'd saved him from having to tell her that he didn't want marry her, either. "I quite agree. Your mother won't scold you, will she?"

Lucinda made a face. Her anxious air had vanished completely. "Of course she will. She scolds about everything. But I am determined, and since I've already given you my firm answer, there's nothing she can say. I plan to study everything I can find on Egypt and leave her to fretting about fashion and gossip. I want to *do* something with my life."

"I hope you do," he told her honestly. "Will you write to me when you are a famous explorer in Egypt?"

She laughed. "Of course! I shall send you an artifact, too, if I discover any."

"Very kind of you." He winked and raised her hand for a kiss. She really was a charming girl, now that she'd got over her dread of having to marry him. "Until later, Lady Lucinda."

She curtsied politely, but her smile was infectious. "Until later, Your Grace."

He waited until she ran up the steps and back into the house, touching the brim of his hat when she waved once in farewell. Her mother would be unhappy—as would his—but Lucinda's happiness was more important. He made a note to send her some lithographs and travel diaries from Egypt, and mounted his horse.

His happiness was also more important than his mother's disappointment. It was time to choose a ring for Sophie.

Chapter 25

❦

Sophie slept late and woke with a smile on her face.

Jack had stayed far later than usual. Dawn was breaking over the rooftops when she bid him farewell on her front step, this time careless of who saw him or her or the silly smile on her face as he walked down her quiet little street. It was almost too good to be true, she thought as she went back upstairs and crawled into her bed, still warm from his body. She'd taken an enormous risk, and could hardly believe that it had paid off beyond her wildest dreams. He wanted to marry her and could overlook her shabby past. For the first time in a dozen years, someone cared for her above all others.

She lingered over breakfast, and was writing to her friends with the happy news, prone to staring out the window with a smile on her face every now and then, when Colleen came in.

"There's someone to see you, ma'am." The maid handed her the calling card.

Sophie inhaled sharply at the name on it: *Vis-*

count Makepeace. She thrust it back at Colleen. "Throw him out."

The girl blinked. "Ma'am?"

"Throw that hateful old man out of my house," she repeated in a low voice. She never wanted to see Makepeace again. What could he want? She'd changed her name to sever any remaining connection to him.

"But he's not that old," protested Colleen. "He was quite civil to me, as well. Are you certain?"

She paused. "Not old?" Her grandfather must be nearly eighty. Colleen shook her head, wide-eyed in amazement. "And civil?" Her maid nodded. Sophie didn't think her grandfather had it in him to be civil, and certainly not to servants.

She laid one hand on her throat. It could only be her father's older brother George—her uncle. Papa hadn't spoken fondly of him, saying he was just as cold as their father. Sophie had never met him, as he'd been away during the horrible spring when her father's solicitor had brought her to Makepeace Manor after her parents died. If her uncle were styling himself Lord Makepeace, that must mean the heartless ogre of Sophie's memory had died.

But . . . what could *he* want?

Warily she walked to the parlor. He might be just as cruel and spiteful as his father, come to call her an abomination and worse. He'd never showed any interest in her before. When Papa was banished from Makepeace Manor, he had left nearly everything about it in the past. He rarely spoke of his family, who hadn't been a warm or loving lot. The main thing she remembered Papa telling her, in fact, was that he'd named his father her guardian in his will. He'd been so desperately ill, coughing up blood until she feared he had none left in his veins, but he'd wanted to explain to her why he did it. Makepeace had money; Makepeace knew his duty to his family, and he could see that she was provided for when Papa was dead.

Her mother had already died, a week earlier, and Sophie had sobbed that if Papa died, she wanted to die, too, to be with him and Mama. She would never forget how he squeezed her hand and told her never to say that again. "You must live for her now," he'd whispered, his rich tenor voice destroyed by the consumption. "And for me. Makepeace is not a gentle man, but you're stronger than he. Don't let him cow you. You're a Graham, and Makepeace will see that you're treated as one."

Well. Her mouth flattened to a thin line at the thought of her grandfather, glowering and growling that he had no desire to raise a granddaughter. The only indisputably good turn he'd done her was to abandon her at Mrs. Upton's Academy. If her uncle was anything like him, she would throw him out, no matter how civil he'd been to Colleen. Girding herself for confrontation, she turned the knob on the parlor door and went in.

The man waiting inside looked up at her entrance. He rose to his feet, tall like Papa but portly, although he looked far too young to be her uncle. His hair was sandy brown, not fair like her father's had been, but his eyes were Papa's—and they were kind. She stopped cold, suddenly unsure.

"Mrs. Campbell." He bowed and gave her a small, tentative smile. "I am Lord Makepeace. I—I rather think I'm your uncle."

She wet her lips. "What makes you think so, sir?"

"Were your parents Thomas Graham, of Lincolnshire, and his wife, Cecile?" he asked, adding apologetically, "Cecile was French, but I've forgotten her surname entirely."

The air seemed to grow thin for a moment. He knew her parents. "Yes," she managed to say.

A smile creased his face. "Then I most certainly am your uncle. Well, I knew it as soon as I saw you! You've got Tom's look. I met Cecile only once, but you've got her coloring."

"Why are you here?" she asked unsteadily. "I've had no contact with your family since the viscount stopped paying my tuition at school several years ago."

Embarrassment flicked in his eyes. "Yes, that. My father was a stubborn man. When he died, I discovered a thick stack of letters from Tom in his papers. All neatly boxed, and I don't think he replied to one of them."

Her heart was about to pound out of her chest. What had Papa written to his father? *When* had he written? He'd always sworn never to speak to Makepeace again unless the viscount welcomed and accepted his wife and daughter. Sophie had presumed that never happened. "Not that I ever knew," she murmured.

The new Lord Makepeace nodded. "He and Tom went at it hammer and tongs more than once. I'm not so keen on that m'self, and, why,

Tom was a good brother to me. I knew he had a child, but my father never would say anything about you. The last time I asked, he said you'd been at school but had run away." He squinted at her uncertainly. "I came to see that you're well, ma'am. You're the only family I have left now."

Slowly she came into the room. Her knees were about to give way; he was nothing like she had expected. She gestured at the sofa and sank into a chair as her uncle resumed his seat. "Forgive me, sir—I know almost nothing of my father's family. Lord Makepeace was the only person I ever met, and it was not a warm and tender reunion. My father hardly spoke of his family at all."

He chuckled. "I don't doubt why! An old tartar he was, my father. George was the same, but Tom and I . . ." He shook his head. "I hope I can do better."

She stared at him, jolted. George? George was Papa's older brother, who taunted and teased her father over his musical studies, who mocked him for refusing to go see the bearbaiting in the village. Frantically she searched her memory. It had been so long, and Papa had never said much, but hints of it were coming back to her . . . "You're Henry," she blurted.

He grinned proudly. "I am! Tom must have said something of me."

"He did." She frowned, rubbing her forehead. Henry was Papa's half brother, younger by several years. Papa had spoken of him as a child. "It was so many years ago . . . You kept a pet hedgehog."

"Humbert," he said with affection.

"You fell off your pony when you were eight," she added with growing enthusiasm as bits of stories surfaced in her memory. "And broke your leg! Papa had to help you with your lessons for a month while you were abed."

"He tried," said Lord Makepeace with a laugh.

Sophie laughed, too, then clapped her hand to her mouth to stop it. "What happened to . . . ?"

"My father? George?" Her uncle nodded, unperturbed. "George died a few years ago. A cancer, the doctor said. My father breathed his last right after Christmastide. It's taken me a while to get things in order, and then I wasted time searching for Miss Graham. I'd no idea you married," he added apologetically.

"You were looking for me?" she repeated in wonder.

"Of course." He looked at the floor. "I found the bills for your school and wrote to the headmistress. Mrs. Upton, her name was. She's quite fond of you and gave me a direction in Bath. Well, you weren't there anymore. Lord Fox told me his aunt left you some funds, and it made sense you'd go to London. I had to hire someone to ask about in town."

Sophie could hardly breathe. "Why?"

He pursed his lips. "I thought I'd like to know how you are," was his reply after a moment. "I haven't got children—never did find a wife, either, a younger son with no expectations. I know my father didn't take well to Tom marrying Cecile, but I didn't do much better. I only wrote to him a few times, being a young idiot, and never managed to come see him after he came back to

England. So I thought I owed something to Tom's daughter, if she needed anything."

Numbly she shook her head. If she had known she had an uncle—a kind uncle who might take an interest in her, she could have had somewhere to go when she left Mrs. Upton's Academy.

"Well. Good. I'm glad you're getting on all right." He rubbed his palms on his knees. "I've got no experience at this, but if you'll welcome me, I thought I'd call on you now and then. Make certain you still don't need anything." He shrugged. "Tell stories on Tom, if you want to hear them. He was a dozen years older, but I remember him well. I was twelve when he met your mother and left."

"Yes," she whispered. "I would like that very much, my lord."

"Uncle Henry, if you wish," he said, almost shyly.

She beamed. "I do."

It looked like her uncle blushed. He told her where she could find him in London, then got up and bowed in farewell and put on his hat. He let himself out and went down the step to where a handsome roan stood waiting. Sophie followed, still dazed by the visit. He was gathering the reins when something struck her. "Uncle Henry," she called.

He looked up, waiting.

"Are there attics at Makepeace Manor?" she asked. "Crammed with old furniture and perhaps some of Papa's things from when he was a boy?"

"There are attics," he said in surprise, "although I've no idea if there's anything of your father's up there. You . . . you are welcome to visit and see, if you like."

She thought of that rainy afternoon with Jack, up under the eaves of Alwyn House. Perhaps he would come with her to rummage in her own family's history. "Thank you. I think I might."

Uncle Henry grinned, touched the brim of his hat, and rode off.

She closed the door and leaned against it. She had family. Just an uncle, but one who seemed kind, who didn't disdain her or her parents. Who asked to call on her and tacitly offered his support.

Her breath caught. She had *family*. Connections. With her four thousand pounds and a viscount for an uncle, she was no longer nobody; she was almost . . . eligible.

Jack might say he didn't care, but other people would. London society would look down their aristocratic noses at the just-barely-respectable woman who'd snared the Duke of Ware. She dreaded being snubbed and suspected of tricking Jack into wedding her. It was very easy to say one didn't care what other people thought or said, but to spend the next several decades of her life atoning for doing what she had to do to survive . . .

But now she didn't need to. As niece to Lord Makepeace, and with her modest fortune, she had claim to being one of the *ton*. Good enough to be a duchess. Her heart lifted at the thought of telling Jack tonight.

Her joy lasted all of two hours and twenty minutes. She finished her letters to Eliza and Georgiana, greatly expanded to include the news of her uncle's visit, and sent Colleen off to post them. Georgiana's letter she enclosed with Eliza's, since Lady Sidlow was intercepting Georgiana's messages and would confiscate anything from unapproved persons—namely Sophie. She felt an extra burst of vindication that soon Lady Sidlow's objections would melt like ice in the summer sun. Not merely the niece of a viscount, but a future duchess, as well. She couldn't wait to see Georgiana again.

So it was a great surprise to hear a rapid knocking on the door, and open it to see Georgiana herself, flushed and flustered. "What—?" she began, astonished.

"Sophie, listen to me," said her friend in a great rush. "I'm not supposed to be here—I promised Nadine all my pin money for the next month not to tell Lady Sidlow we came here instead of going to the lending library. Eliza wrote to me about you and the duke. Are you still in love with him?"

She blinked at the intensity of the question. "Yes, but Georgiana—"

The other girl closed her eyes. "That *scoundrel*. You must refuse to see him again, Sophie, for your own sake. Trust me in this!"

"Why?" Sophie reached for her hand. "I was just writing to you—about him. Georgiana, he asked me to marry him. Can you believe it?"

Georgiana's eyes flashed. "No," she said grimly. "I cannot. Oh, if only Lady Sidlow hadn't refused to let me come to tea! I could have saved you—"

"What?" Sophie asked when she compressed her lips into a fierce scowl. "Saved me from what?"

"From falling for him." The plain-faced maid

loitering several steps away coughed, and Georgiana flapped one hand at her in irritation. "Another minute, Nadine!" She turned back to Sophie. "I've been hearing little bits of rumor about Ware," she said, low and fast. "Gossip that he would marry Lady Lucinda Afton, whose mother is such bosom friends with the duchess—everyone knows both mothers are in favor of the match. But he rarely goes to balls, and no one had ever seen him dance with her, let alone show any other sign of interest, so I dismissed it. But we were at Gunter's today, enjoying ices in the shade, and there he was!"

"Jack?" said Sophie in confusion, as Georgiana paused to draw breath.

"Ware!" Georgiana gave her a deeply disapproving look. "Don't think of him as Jack. He was in Berkeley Square just today with Lucinda Afton on his arm."

She shook her head even as a shiver of dread crept up her spine. "It doesn't mean he's going to marry her."

"I didn't see him go down on one knee and propose," retorted Georgiana, "but they were arm in arm. They sat on a bench in the square not far from Lady Sidlow's carriage and talked for some time, quite cordially and intimately. He ordered an ice for her from Gunter's. Lady Capet, one of Lady Sidlow's gossipy friends who was with us, couldn't stop remarking on it. She said Ware is very somber and proper, but there he was smiling and laughing with Lady Lucinda. Lady Sidlow said an engagement announcement was surely imminent, and I was so outraged I asked why she thought so."

Sophie said nothing. The shiver had turned into a sharp chill. She folded her arms around herself and listened even as protests screamed through her mind. She knew Jack. He would never do something so heartless and cruel as ask her to marry him when he meant to marry someone else . . . a proper young lady of his own class . . . of whom society and his family would happily approve . . .

"Lady Sidlow said it was because his father caused Lady Lucinda's father's death," Georgiana went on, "and that the Afton ladies have been under the duke's protection ever since. She said there is a longstanding agreement that Ware would marry Lucinda. She'd heard it from Lady Stowe herself, who has pointedly discouraged other suitors for her daughter. Lucinda is quite an heiress and rather lovely, and normally she would have a number of gentlemen vying for her attention."

"Then why hasn't he already married her?" Sophie argued. "There's nothing stopping him, if he wants her."

Georgiana gave her a look of pity. "Lucinda's much younger than he is. She's only eighteen. I daresay he wanted to wait until she was grown and had her presentation at Court."

Nadine the maid coughed again, with more vigor this time. Georgiana flung out her arm angrily. "One minute!" She turned back to Sophie. "I cannot stay—we shall have to run as it is, to make it back to the lending library before Lady Sidlow's carriage returns for us. Will you listen to what I said? Sophie, I can't bear to see you humiliated and brokenhearted."

"I always listen to your advice," she said softly. "Thank you, Georgiana."

Her friend gave her a hasty hug. "Goodbye. I hate to be the one to tell you, but I couldn't wait. I'll write more when I know more, and have Eliza send it. Goodbye!" She hitched her shawl back up her shoulder and hurried off with the impatient maid.

Sophie watched them go in silence. Georgiana was a reliable witness, and she wouldn't have dared risk Lady Sidlow's anger for anything less than a dire emergency. The trouble was, Sophie couldn't believe it. It was impossible. Jack wouldn't have lied to her that way. She would have to hear him admit it before she believed that he'd betrayed her that badly.

No. She gave herself a sharp shake. It was ridiculous. Georgiana must be mistaken. Jack had proposed and then made love to her all night long until she fell asleep in his arms. He stayed until morning, when anyone could have seen him leaving her house. He wouldn't have done that if he intended to throw her over for another woman, if—she staggered as something even more horrible struck her—he had been engaged to Lady Lucinda all this time.

Breathing hard, she steadied herself against the door. She trusted him. She was mad to let rumor and a chance sighting at Gunter's obliterate everything she believed about him.

Still . . . Sophie had met many liars in her life. Some she'd seen through at once, and some had got the better of her, but she learned something from every encounter. When someone was caught in a big enough lie, he usually lied again to hide it. If Jack had led her on, saying he wanted to marry her when in reality he planned to marry another woman, there was no reason to think he'd be honest with her now. Georgiana said Lady Sidlow believed it to be a very longstanding betrothal, which meant she ought to be able to find independent confirmation . . .

Her heart sank as the answer came to her. Philip. She would have to ask Philip, tonight at Vega's.

Chapter 26

⊱❦⊰

She climbed the club steps earlier than usual that evening. Jack usually arrived later, as Philip kept his word and stayed away from her. Sophie had been grateful for that at first, but tonight she walked through the entire club looking for him.

When she finally spotted him, lounging in an armchair with a glass in his hand, she walked right up to him. "Good evening, Lord Philip." She dropped a curtsy.

He sat up straighter, then leaped to his feet and bowed. "Mrs. Campbell. What an absolute pleasure." One of his mates nearby snickered, and Philip made a rude gesture at him. "Let us talk somewhere else." One corner of his mouth quirked up. "Since I presume you've not come to invite me to play hazard again."

"Never hazard again," she said lightly as she took his offered arm. "I only wanted a private word, if I may."

"Always," he said. They walked through the still-quiet club until they came to an unoccupied sofa. Sophie seated herself, and Philip sat an arm's distance away. "What troubles you?"

"I would like there to be peace between us," she said.

His brows descended. "Have we been at war?"

"I don't think so," she said honestly, "although things became a bit tense."

He heaved a sigh and stared across the room. "Was I really that obnoxious to you?"

"Well . . . yes." She gave a little nod as he glanced at her in astonishment. "You followed me about like an angry thundercloud, scowling and muttering. It would strain anyone's nerves."

"I am sorry for it." He dropped his head and ground his palm against his forehead. "I was so worried when my brother swept you away—the thing is, I know him, and you don't. You said *I* made a spectacle of you, when he was the one who carted you away like a prize of battle."

This was what she wanted to discuss, but her mouth still went dry. She wet her lips. "What do you mean, you know him and I do not?"

He gave a sharp huff of bitter laughter. "I know him! Have my whole life. He used to be a capital fellow, open to adventure and daring. Sometimes I think that fellow must be deep inside him still, but he never shows it."

She thought of the pencil drawing at Alwyn House, of a young Philip laughing in the tree. It was difficult to fight back the urge to defend Jack, to say that he still had that adventurous, caring side, and that he would prefer to be close to his brother rather than constantly at odds. "Why not, do you think?"

"Because he's the bloody duke, obviously." Philip's eyes flashed. "Too important to come out to the theatre or a boxing match. Too noble to play cards or do anything sporting. He's become a raging bore—well, until that night, clearly, when he seemed pleased enough to toss aside all his vaunted dignity and decorum."

"Not all of us are carefree, with an income and the freedom to do as we please." Philip shot her a sharp look. Sophie smiled artlessly. "I mean you're very fortunate you haven't the responsibility for a dukedom. It must be . . . demanding. I only know about running my small household. There must be so much more to an estate."

"There is." Philip gave a gusty sigh and leaned forward, propping his elbows on his knees. "I know there is. And you're right, I am fortunate not to be the duke, for I'm no good at being responsible." A devilish smile played at his mouth. "I'm terribly good at being adventurous, though."

She laughed. "Well do I know it! Although I suggest you try being less daring at the tables."

"You too?" He eased a bit closer on the sofa, stretching out his legs. "Someone told me the other day I ought to improve my play at cards. Have you any advice? You seem to do quite well."

"Hmm." She tilted her head as if in thought. "I suggest you avoid hazard. It's the devil's game." He laughed. "The rest is practice. Study the rules, learn the odds of each play, and keep your mind on the cards or the dice—not on flirting with your opponent," she finished with a speaking look.

He laughed again. "Well, it didn't help me." He

shot her a sideways look. "It never would have, would it?"

She hesitated. He didn't mean at hazard. "No. Not with me."

"Did that happen before or after my brother swept you away?" He asked it simply, directly, without suspicion.

"Before," she said lightly. "Long before. You're far too adventurous and daring for me, you know. I fear I'm really a dreadful bore at heart, as well."

Philip looked at her. Suddenly she realized he *knew*, somehow, about her and Jack. "You're nothing like him, Sophie."

Her face burned. "Like who?" she tried to ask innocently, but Philip's expression had changed. He leaned back on the sofa and gave her a weary look.

"I know there's something between you and Ware. He gave himself away the other night, when I told him he ought to leave you be."

Sophie said nothing. She couldn't speak.

"I understand why you want it kept quiet," Philip went on. "And I don't begrudge you taking up with him, by the by. You're certainly not the first to spot a chance and try for it. But you've got a kind heart and a sensible head, and . . . well, I care about you, even if you won't flirt with me and win my money anymore. Trying to capture Ware's heart is a fool's game."

She wanted to slap his face for saying such things about Jack. *But what do you know?* she reminded herself. This was why she'd sought him out. "Good heavens, Philip, you make me sound like a hunter and your brother my prey."

He snorted. "More than one woman has felt that way about him! He's so damned aloof, and women find that infuriatingly appealing . . . but Ware hasn't got a heart anymore. He fell in love years ago—wildly, exuberantly, you'd never know it was the same man—and the girl jilted him. She ran off with a war hero or some such fellow, and he never got over it."

Years ago, she wanted to repeat. If Jack still nursed a broken heart, he never showed her any sign of it. "Surely a duke must marry, to have an heir." She shouldn't have started this conversation. Philip was in a mood to talk, but he wasn't helping her, and was only making things worse. Jack had never mentioned another love.

"Oh, he'll marry," replied Philip with a snort. "But for duty, not for frivolous reasons."

Frivolous reasons like love. Her hands shook until she squeezed them together in her lap. "I heard a rumor," she said, her voice as careless as possible. "About him and Lady Lucinda Afton. That they've been engaged for some time." The words were like ashes in her mouth, but she had to know . . .

Philip glanced at her, his eyebrows lifted in mild surprise. "You heard that? Well, well. He promised our father on his deathbed that he would take care of her forever. As I said, duty. One feels a bit of sympathy for Lucinda, but she'll make it her own, being a duchess. She's a clever girl, and as a child she always knew her mind."

And just like that, he robbed her of breath. Sophie swayed in her seat and had to clutch the cushion to keep her balance. She raised her stricken gaze to Philip, who was watching her with all-too-knowing eyes. "Are you certain?"

"My mother says they'll be wed by the end of this year," he said. "Lucinda's mother wanted her to have a Season first."

She's only eighteen, echoed Georgiana's voice in her head. "Does he love her?" she asked, clutching at straws.

"Lucinda?" Philip looked surprised. "I doubt it. The men in my family—the heirs, anyway—make prudent marriages, Sophie. Always have, probably always will." He gave her a sympathetic glance. "That never stopped any of them from having plenty of mistresses and lovers on the side, but when they marry, it's for power and for money. I would have warned you earlier, if I'd been allowed to speak to you. I suppose I see now why he forbade me doing that."

Her heart was pounding erratically, and her head felt light and dizzy. She might be ill. Jack had said as much to her—*the Dukes of Ware don't marry for love*—but then he'd said she was everything he wanted in his wife. He'd asked her to marry him. Who was wrong? Georgiana, who had seen Jack laughing arm in arm with Lady Lucinda? Philip, who knew things about his brother and his family she couldn't possibly know? Or Sophie, who had broken her own rules time after time—making love to Jack, carrying on with their affair after they returned to London, losing her heart to him, even falling for his shocking proposal of marriage?

"Thank you, Philip," she said unsteadily. "It has been illuminating."

"Sophie." He caught her hand as she rose. "I know I behaved like a nodcock earlier—jealousy of Ware for having had you to himself, even if not by your choice." He tried to smile but stopped as she stared at him, probably looking like wild-eyed Ophelia in her madness. "I apologize, and swear to you it won't happen again. Can we be friends once more?"

She tugged free of his hold. "Perhaps." *No*, she wanted to cry—not when his face would always remind her of Jack's. "Pardon me—" She turned and hurried away, barely keeping her expression composed. She slipped into the first empty room she came to, closing the door behind her and sagging against it.

The air burned in her lungs. Oh God. Had she really been such a fool? Had she really thought her luck had changed so dramatically? From counting cards and playing for guineas to being the Duchess of Ware? "Idiot," she whispered to herself. She should have known when Jack—Ware—kept looking at her bare legs that first night at Alwyn House. It hadn't been love or marriage on his mind. Lady Fox had warned her about that: *When a man wants a woman he shouldn't have, he becomes a dangerous creature*, she'd said.

But Sophie, foolishly, fell for everything because she'd wanted him. And for those few glorious days, she'd thought he was hers.

She swiped the back of her hand across her burning eyes. No tears. She'd made mistakes before, and had to pick herself up and dust off her pride; she would recover from this, too. It would hurt, much worse than the time she'd miscalculated her odds and lost four hundred pounds in one night. Much, much worse than when her one previous lover broke with her. At least he'd never proposed, only gave her a very handsome diamond bracelet as a parting gift. She'd sold it for two hundred fifty pounds, a plump addition to her nest egg.

So it would hurt, and her heart might never recover fully, but she would carry on. She had no choice. Perhaps she'd take a holiday to visit Makepeace Manor, as her uncle had offered. Her few memories of it were dark and grim, but this time she might be able to recover some bit of her father and his childhood, before he'd thrown it all away for love . . .

As a girl she'd thought her parents' story was beautifully romantic. Now she realized how truly lucky they had been. Papa loved her mother just as much as ever when she lost her voice to a persistent cough and could no longer sing. Mama loved him even when he was unable to win enough at the card tables to support them. Their love had survived heartbreak and hardship and endured to their dying days, and Sophie had somehow thought all love could do the same.

Papa, she thought hopelessly, *I wish you had warned me how terrible love can be.*

JACK ARRIVED AT VEGA'S later than usual, but in a buoyant mood.

He had a special license in his pocket. It had taken a few hours to procure, but he'd assumed his most ducal demeanor and sent clerks scurrying until he got it.

He had a ring in his pocket as well, a flawless ruby set in a golden band; he liked Sophie in red.

The main reason for his tardy arrival was his mother, who had alternately scolded, wept, and pleaded with him to change his mind. Lady Stowe had broken the news to her earlier, no doubt in a hysterical letter, but Jack still had to weather the storm of her disappointment. When the brunt of it had passed, he told her he was unable to marry Lady Lucinda for two reasons: first, that Lucinda didn't want him, and second, that he wanted someone else.

"Lucinda will see reason," she cried, trailing after him as he went down the stairs.

"She wants to go to Egypt." He grinned at the memory of her enthusiasm.

The duchess looked blank. "Egypt? Don't be ridiculous. Of course she doesn't. What sort of idea is that for a young lady? She will stay right here in England and do her duty."

Jack, ready to leave for Vega's, slid his arms into his coat as Browne held it up. "Her duty does not include wedding me."

"But your duty is to wed her!"

"No," he said firmly. "It is not." She opened her mouth to argue, and Jack held up one hand. "I vowed to Father that I would see that she was cared for. I have done that—she and her mother have always had a comfortable home, a well-stocked larder, the latest fashions. But she is grown now, with thoughts and ideas of her own, and she does not want to marry someone as old and boring as I."

"She is still a girl and will heed her mother's guidance!"

"No, she is a young woman who deserves a chance to choose her own husband." He gave his mother a quelling look. "That is the end of the matter."

The duchess's mouth pinched, and she closed her eyes for a moment. "You're being hasty and rash, and it's not like you, Ware. Throwing over Lucinda for a common cardsharp!" She nodded even as he shot her a dark glance. "Of course I heard about that foolish wager—of course I know you went off to Alwyn with her, and of course I know you're still seeing her. You've been quite unlike yourself lately, and I have no illusions why. Men are the most predictable creatures on earth when it comes to their baser needs. But to bring that woman into this house would shame your father, your grandfather, and every other ancestor who knew his duty and treated marriage with the gravity it deserves."

He took his hat and gloves from Browne. "Good evening, Mother."

"You cannot ask me to receive that woman," she pleaded. "A woman of no name, no connections, no character!"

"That woman has a name, I don't care about connections, and she has more fortitude and character than half of society put together." He set the hat on his head as a footman swept open the door. "And if you don't wish to receive her, have Percy take a new house for you. I expect to bring my bride home within a fortnight." He ignored her gasp of shock and went out, down the steps and into the carriage waiting for him. He cast a glance at the opposite corner and remembered Sophie, indignant and flustered, badgering him from that seat. His pulse leaped and a slow smile crossed his face at the thought of what he'd do the next time he had her in the carriage with him.

He strode through the door of Vega's, hardly stopping to leave his coat and hat. Where was she? Tonight he didn't care a fig for the promise Dashwood had extracted. After tonight, the only gossip that might accrue to Sophie's name would be about her new place in society, as his wife. After tonight, Dashwood could ban him from Vega's for life, and Jack wouldn't give a damn.

A brisk patrol of the club didn't reveal Sophie, though. He frowned when he reached the main salon again, wondering if she'd stayed home this evening. He'd sent his carriage away, but he could hail a hackney, as he usually did when headed to Sophie's house . . .

"Here I am." His brother stepped in front of him, arms open wide.

"I'm not looking for you."

"No?" Philip affected surprise. "Was that not your sole purpose in joining the Vega Club?"

Jack was beginning to envy Sophie her lack of family. "Philip, I am not in the mood for this."

"Oh." His brother perked up. "Fancy a hand of cards, then? Fraser and Whitley would surely make up a table with us."

"No doubt," he said dryly. Fergus Fraser never had two shillings to rub together, and Angus Whitley was Philip's most useless friend. "Perhaps another time. I'm looking for someone."

"Who?" Philip fell in step beside him when he started to walk away. "I can help you locate him."

Jack gave him a narrow-eyed look. "Why are you so accommodating this evening?"

"A renewed spirit of brotherly love."

"No, really, why?" Jack moved past the hazard table. No gleam of mahogany hair caught his eye.

"Perhaps I'm keeping an eye on you tonight."

"What?" He could barely attend to what Philip said. Was she really not here? Surely she would have mentioned it last night, if she planned to stay home.

"To keep you from any awkward situations with people who don't desire your company."

He looked at his brother, perplexed, and finally took in Philip's expression. "What are you talking about?"

Philip's gaze darted left, then right, and he lowered his voice. "Sophie knows about Lucinda."

"What?" A nearby table looked around at his sharp exclamation. Jack also lowered his voice. "There's nothing to know!"

Philip threw up his hands in protest. "She asked me. Whoever told her you were going to marry Lucinda, it was not I."

"And did you deny it?" he whispered harshly. "I am not engaged to Lucinda, I never was, and if you told her I am—God help me, Philip—"

His brother put down his hands. "Deny it? When my own mother said it was true? Ware, everyone believes you've been promised to Lucinda for years—"

With a curse, Jack turned and stalked off. Philip dogged his heels, seeming to understand that their conversation was too public. As soon as they reached a quieter spot, Jack whirled on his brother. "I told you that was idle rumor, no matter what Mother wished," he said between his teeth. "The mythical engagement was cooked up by her and Lady Stowe. No one even asked Lucinda her opinion, which turns out to be that she'd much rather traipse off to ancient Egypt than marry a dull old man such as I."

Philip grinned in delight. "She said that? I always liked Lucinda."

"And I'll happily send *you* to Egypt, never to return, if you told Sophie I was marrying another woman." Jack glared at him. "I'm in love with her, damn you. She said she loves me, too. If you have ruined this for me, Philip, if you have broken her heart by telling her rubbish . . . as God is my witness, you shall never draw another farthing from Ware, nor be welcome on any property I own."

"Love?" His brother goggled at him. "You—in love?"

He stared at his brother, who had once looked up to him and trusted him, even when they were lads and Jack told him tall tales and scary stories. It was like a different person in front of him, someone who believed him capable of seducing one woman with false promises while betrothed to another woman. Someone who believed him incapable of any deeper feeling than distaste for large gaming debts. *His own brother.*

He swore under his breath. This was a waste of time, scolding Philip when he should be looking for Sophie and assuring her it was all false, that the only truth between them was what he had told her last night: that he loved her and wanted to marry her. Sophie was all that mattered to him, not his mother's disapproval and not his brother's dislike. "Never mind." He brushed past his brother, but Philip caught his arm.

"Ware. *Jack.*"

He paused, glaring icily at the hand on his sleeve. Philip released him and edged back a step. "I didn't know."

"How could you, when you were sulking that I'd spoiled your bid to make her your mistress?"

His brother flushed at his scathing derision. "For what it's worth, I actually do care for her. When you carted her off, I'd no idea what you meant to do, and I worried for her."

Jack gave him a look of pure disdain. "You have an odd way of demonstrating your affection and concern."

"I might say the same," retorted Philip. Jack jerked, and his brother took another step backward. "Do you really love her?"

"Desperately." He hesitated. "I asked her to marry me."

Philip exhaled. "I suppose she said yes." Jack nodded once, unable to speak. His brother seemed to wilt for a moment, then he took a deep breath and straightened his shoulders. "Since we're both miserable at this, I guess we had better work together. One of us might as well be happy. Come, I'll help you find her."

Chapter 27

⚜⚜⚜

SOPHIE DID NOT want to be alone.

After Philip confirmed what Georgiana had seen, her first thought was to go home, climb into bed and pull the covers over her head, and stay there for the rest of the year. How could she have been so wrong about Jack—so foolishly, spectacularly wrong? How could he have lied and deceived her so brilliantly? Everything he did had been perfectly designed to work upon her weaknesses, dismantling her rules one by one until he smashed her world to bits. How long would he have continued telling her he loved her? she wondered numbly. How long would he have continued charming his way into her bed? She pressed one hand to her stomach and thought the real question was, how long would she have continued to believe him?

But crawling into her bed would only remind her more of Jack, and how he had held her there and whispered that he loved her. She would only think of how his big body felt lying beside her, moving above her, and it would only make her misery more profound.

The cure was to do something to keep her mind off him. When Sophie walked out of that small private room, her heart was in pieces but her resolve was back in place. She took a glass of wine from a waiter and surveyed the room before setting her sights on Anthony Hamilton, sitting by himself with a snifter in one hand.

Mr. Hamilton was one of the more notorious gentlemen in society. He was heir to an earl, but refused to use his courtesy title. Rumor had connected his name with half the ladies of the *ton*, and it was a mystery to all why he hadn't been called out over any of those affairs. He was enigmatic and reserved, the sort of man everyone seemed to talk about but no one spoke to.

But most important for Sophie's purposes, he gambled ruthlessly, and no amount was too dauntingly high for him. Her stomach fluttered as she made her way through the room toward him. She'd heard he had once wagered everything he owned, including the clothes on his back, at the hazard table—and won. Normally she avoided playing with people who could tolerate that kind of risk, but tonight she needed something to distract her. She would either win a great deal, salving the open wound on her soul, or she would lose a great deal, and have something more important to worry about than handsome, lying dukes.

"Good evening, sir." She swept a deep curtsy as Mr. Hamilton looked up, his dark brows lifted in surprise. He'd been watching the play at the nearby hazard table, a calculating look in his eyes.

Now he rose. "Good evening, Mrs. Campbell." They'd never been introduced, and her stomach fluttered again that he knew who she was.

"I hope you will forgive my boldness," she said with a bright smile, "but I was told you are by far the best piquet player in London."

He smiled. "Flattery, ma'am? Or condemnation?"

She laughed. "Admiration! Is it true?"

"I cannot possibly answer that. I've not played with everyone else in London." He cocked his head slightly. "I've not played against you."

It was the opening she wanted. Her heart gave a hard thud of warning against her ribs. Sophie widened her smile and ignored it. "Perhaps you would care to remedy that?"

He seemed amused. His mouth curled into a reluctant smile that never touched his eyes. "What stakes?"

"Ten guineas a point." Scoring in piquet could vary immensely. Sophie knew she was risking a thousand pounds, if not more.

However, piquet had been Papa's favorite game. When he lost, it was at other tables. Sophie could play piquet since she was a child. It was a complicated game of strategy and skill, not merely luck of the draw, and it would require her full attention—exactly what she desired. It also had the potential to pay a handsome reward.

Mr. Hamilton held out one hand. "After you, madam."

She located a small table at the back of the

room, sheltered from view by some of Vega's famous palm plants. A servant brought a fresh deck of cards, and Sophie set aside her wine.

She won the cut and elected to deal first. She shuffled the cards several times, mindful of Papa's opinion that the cards weren't completely unordered until they had been shuffled repeatedly. Mr. Hamilton watched with a hint of his amused smile. She dealt the hand, and they settled in to play.

There were six hands played in a *partie* of piquet. After a bad beginning, she pulled almost even by the end of the fifth hand. She'd been right about him; playing against Mr. Hamilton required all her concentration. He played with the steeliest demeanor she had ever seen, despite lounging in his chair as if he hardly cared.

She was preparing to deal the final hand when a footman glided up to Mr. Hamilton, leaned down and murmured something to him. He looked startled, then rose from his seat. "Mrs. Campbell, my apologies. I must step away for a moment."

"Of course." She put down the deck. "Shall you return to finish the *partie*?"

He hesitated. "I believe so." He smiled briefly. "I hope so." He gave a little bow and walked away.

Sophie reached for her wine. She must either play much better in this final deal of the cards, or much worse. Her score hadn't yet reached one hundred points, which meant her loss—if she must lose—would be less than if she played well enough to score one hundred but still lost. Sophie rarely played to lose, but sometimes it was the right tactic. She was contemplating her odds when Mr. Hamilton pulled out his chair.

"Good evening," said the wrong voice.

She jerked upright in her chair. It was not Mr. Hamilton who had returned, but the man she'd spent all evening trying to forget. Perfectly attired in evening clothes, he was as blindingly handsome as ever. Her throat closed up as he smiled at her, so damnably, appealingly rueful, when she knew he was the worst sort of liar.

"I've been looking for you," Jack added.

She swept one hand in a mock salute. "Here I am. What do you want?"

"To speak to you. Sophie—"

"Don't," she snapped. "I don't want to see you tonight, let alone speak to you."

Jack paused. "You deserve to be angry."

Any flicker of hope she had that there was some incredible misunderstanding died in a burst of flame. "You must pardon me, sir. I am already *engaged* at the moment," she said acidly, hoping the double meaning of that word hit him in the head. "My companion will be returning soon, and I wish to continue my game of piquet with him."

"You mean Hamilton?" Jack leaned forward, resting one elbow on the table. His eyes were such a soft blue, she had to look away. "He won't be back."

"What?" She looked past him in angry alarm. "Why not? What did you do to him?"

"Nothing. Philip's having a word with him." He reached for the deck of cards in the center of the table. "Play a hand with me instead." He glanced at her. "I was told it's what people do here."

Her face felt hot. "Not with me."

"Why not?" He cut the cards and shuffled. "I've been practicing. I shan't lose every hand this time."

She bared her teeth in a smile. "You know very well why not."

"Oh?" He shuffled the cards again, his enigmatic gaze fixed on her. "Do explain."

Sophie was having a hard time keeping her temper. It was bad enough that she had to see him here, where she needed to be but he came for no apparent purpose. It was awful enough that she had to imagine him with his bride, some lovely, elegant creature of a rank and family fit to be a duchess. She could not sit across from him and pretend none of that mattered, that he hadn't driven a spike through her heart.

She couldn't take it, not now. "Mr. Dashwood explicitly warned me against associating with you, Your Grace." She bit out the honorific, trying to remind him of his place. Of her place.

"Did he?" He nodded sagely. "Dashwood warned me about you, as well. But he shan't interfere this time. Don't worry, you won't lose your membership for playing a hand with me."

She was going to do something unpardonable in a moment—fly into a shrieking fit, snatch the cards and throw them into his face, even burst into tears. "Go away," she said, enunciating every word. "Please."

"Why?"

"Because this isn't a decent place for a man of your stature," she said in the same low, hard voice.

He glanced over his shoulder. "There is an earl playing hazard at this moment, if it matters that much to you."

She pressed her fingertips to the bridge of her nose. "*Please*."

"Sophie." He spoke softly. "Let me explain. I know what you heard—"

"Jack," she said wearily, "it's over. It's for the best."

He exhaled. "Then play." With surprising dexterity, he dealt a hand of piquet.

"Not tonight." She pushed back her chair and rose. Where had Mr. Hamilton gone? There must be someone she knew close by who would rescue her. Perhaps tonight was the night she should bring Giles Carter up to scratch; she didn't love him, but he was a good man. Perhaps that was what she needed—a sharp, clean break from this ill-fated, doomed love she'd developed for the Duke of Ware. Filling her thoughts and time planning a life as Mrs. Carter would distract her. It had to. Nothing else had, but if she married Giles, she would force herself to think only of him, to throw herself into making herself care for him. She would firmly block every thought about the Duke of Ware and the way he'd once kissed her and laughed with her and made her knees go utterly weak with desire.

Jack laid a stack of markers on the table. "I stake five thousand pounds on this hand."

Her stomach dropped at the amount. He'd wagered that huge sum once before, and she'd lost—not just the wager but her heart, in the end.

"If you win, it will be a wedding gift," he went on, "enough to set you up quite nicely with Carter or some other chap, as you'd be a wealthy woman and sure to have several suitors."

Sophie knew she should walk away, but somehow when she opened her mouth to say so, instead she asked, "Against what?"

He leaned forward. His hair was burnished gold in the chandelier light. "If I win . . . you'll marry me instead, as you promised."

Her mouth fell open in shock. How dare he? He was going to marry Lady Lucinda Afton. Georgiana and Philip had told her so.

"Do you agree to the wager?" he prompted.

She stared at the cards, then at him. He had hurt her and lied to her, and now he treated the entire thing as a game. Very well—she could do the same. Piquet was a challenging game, and she knew he didn't play often. After the night of intense joy followed by a day of crushing heartbreak, she deserved to win five thousand pounds from him. She sat down and reached for the cards. "Only a fool would wager on marriage, but if you're foolish enough to risk five thousand, I'll be pleased to win it from you." She inspected her deal. "I have *carte blanche*, and I will exchange five."

Jack nodded once. "I am indeed a fool. I should have mentioned Lucinda sooner—"

Sophie didn't even want to hear the other woman's name. "How many cards are you exchanging?"

He exhaled. "Three."

"I suppose you didn't mention her sooner for fear I would refuse to have an affair with an engaged man. You were correct." Sophie flipped her cards quickly onto the table, just long enough for him to see she did have *carte blanche,* then scooped her hand back up. She was already ten points in the lead, simply by having no court cards.

"I didn't mention her because I was not engaged to her," he said.

"Oh?" She selected five cards from her hand, set them aside, and drew five replacements from the cards still in the talon. It was a good draw, as she had expected, full of high cards. "A bit odd that your own family thinks you are."

Jack tossed aside three cards from his hand and took the remaining talon cards. "My mother hoped I would marry Lucinda, but that is all it ever was—*her* hope."

"Is that why you took her for ices at Gunter's?" Sophie widened her eyes while keeping her attention on her cards. She would not fall for him so easily again. "I have a point of six."

Jack's lips tightened. "Good," he said tersely, admitting he did not have six or more cards of the same suit.

Sophie added a six to her score.

"I had to speak to her and be certain Lucinda also knew there was no betrothal between us," he added. "Her mother had been telling her for years it was her duty to marry me . . ."

Sophie's vision burned red around the edges. *"Sixième,"* she said coldly. She had clubs from seven to queen.

"Good," said Jack again, after a slight pause. He did not have a longer sequence than six in his hand.

She smiled without meeting his eyes. "That's a *repique* for me." And another thirty points, on top of the sixteen for the *sixième*. She was at sixty-two before play even began.

"Lucinda couldn't wait to say that she did not want to marry me," Jack said in a low, urgent voice. "She even hoped, when I left town a few weeks ago, that I would never come back and she wouldn't have to see me." Unthinkingly Sophie glanced at him. He looked pale, but his blue eyes were steady. "I wish we'd never come back from Alwyn House, either."

Her breath faltered. She had also wished they could have stayed at Alwyn House, just the two of them, forever. She forced her eyes back down to her cards. "But we did," she pointed out. "Because of duty."

"Damn duty," he said with sudden fierceness. "Do you really think I would have proposed that you marry me if I were engaged to Lucinda?"

Her chin quivered before she could stop it. "Philip said you've been promised to her for years . . ."

"Philip," Jack bit out, "is an idiot."

Her vision blurred, and she had to blink several times. "He said you'd got your heart broken years ago and never recovered. He said you would marry for practical reasons."

"He was right about that." Jack dropped his cards. "I think it eminently practical to marry the woman I want to see every morning when I open my eyes. The woman with enough nerve and cleverness to come to London and expect to support herself playing cards, of all the cursed things to depend on. The woman who would get out of a carriage and walk a mile in the rain and mud, and then ask where the dungeons are. The woman I want to have on my arm at balls and soirees, because she'll make me laugh through the endless tedium. I think it's the best idea I've ever had, marrying you, because it suits my every desire. I love *you*, Sophie—only you."

Sophie was stunned into silence, which was a good thing; it let her mind start working again. The first time he kissed her, *she* was the one who invited him to make love to her. Back in London, *she* had broken their promise not to see each other again by seeking him out. When she asked for his help regarding Philip, he went to great lengths to do so—personally. He hadn't asked to resume their affair in London, she had invited him to share her carriage and then to stay the night with her. In everything, he had followed her lead, and now she had repaid him by believing the worst of him.

She looked at him, at his perfect face and his elegant clothing and the intense, anguished gaze he leveled at her. Slowly she put down her cards.

She thought about her uncle, admitting he'd never got around to finding a wife because he had no expectations. Of Giles Carter, who seemed so eligible and kind but was also still unmarried, whiling away his nights at the card tables. And of her father, walking away from his family, rank, and wealth because he'd met her mother, standing by her through poverty and sickness and never uttering a word of regret.

Finding someone she loved as much as she

loved Jack was a rare stroke of luck. If Sophie knew anything about luck, it was not to waste it.

"You win," she said, lashing out with one arm to sweep the cards and markers off the table.

Jack was out of his chair and around the table before they hit the floor. He pulled her up and into his arms, capturing her mouth in a scorching kiss.

Sophie thought she might combust right on the spot. She arched against him, winding her arms around his neck so she could kiss him back with equal passion. He growled low in his throat and licked her lower lip until she opened for him. His fingers plowed into her hair as his kiss deepened until she lost all sense of where they were. In her world there was only Jack, and he loved her— *only her.*

Finally he lifted his head and clasped her to his chest. Sophie felt the rapid thud of his heart against her temple, and it made her own chest unbearably tight. "Right," Jack muttered, breathing hard. "Enough of this place."

His arm still around her waist, he headed toward the hall, carrying her along with him, just as he'd done once before. This time Sophie went willingly, almost running to keep up with his stride as she clutched at his jacket for balance. Dimly she realized people were watching them— staring in astonishment at them, actually—but this time she didn't care at all. Let them stare. She caught sight of Philip and Mr. Hamilton sitting at a table with a bottle of port between them; Mr. Hamilton lifted his glass in salute, but Philip didn't even look at her.

"Damnation," said Jack under his breath. Face dark with disapproval, Mr. Dashwood was striding toward them, Forbes at his heels.

Sophie flushed as she recalled the stern warning Mr. Dashwood had given her. "We're about to be scolded."

"Not much," returned Jack, his pace unchanged. They reached the hall, and he turned a look of ducal command on a wide-eyed Frank. "Fetch Mrs. Campbell's cloak and my things." The servant gulped and ran to do as ordered.

"Jack, Mr. Dashwood made me promise not to wager with you," Sophie whispered. Jack still held her tight against him, almost as if he feared to let her go. Her heart swelled; he needn't worry. She wasn't leaving his side again, even if Mr. Dashwood threw her out and banished her for life.

"Did he? Thank God you ignored him." Jack raised his voice as the club owner reached them. "Dashwood."

"Your Grace." The other man gave a short bow. "Might I have a word?"

"No," said Jack. "I am leaving."

Mr. Dashwood didn't look pleased, but Jack's cool, aristocratic tone brooked no argument. The owner's gaze moved to Sophie, who knew her face must be four shades of pink. "Mrs. Campbell. I trust you've not forgotten our agreement."

"No, sir. But I must assure you, I have not lost a wager with His Grace tonight—"

"On the contrary. She's won everything I have." Jack finally released her to take her cloak from Frank and swing it around her shoulders. "You may strike my name from your rolls. You may also strike Mrs. Campbell's name. If she wishes to remain a member, you shall have to enroll her under her new title, Duchess of Ware."

That stopped Dashwood's reply, whatever it was to have been. His face froze somewhere between grim disapproval and astonishment. Jack looked past him. "Forbes, I want a carriage. Now."

"Yes, Your Grace." Without looking at his employer, Forbes bolted by them and out the door.

Sophie summoned a smile. "Thank you, Mr. Dashwood. I have been very pleased to be a member of your club. But I think . . ." She glanced up at Jack, whose expression softened as he gazed down at her. "I think I am through with wagering," she finished. "I apologize for any uproar I may have caused."

Mr. Dashwood had recovered his aplomb. "It looks as though you've played your cards exceptionally well, madam. I wish you joy." With a wry glance, he turned and left, just as Forbes rushed back in to say a carriage was waiting. Frank handed Jack his hat and coat, and they went out the door of Vega's—perhaps for the last time, Sophie thought with a start. As a duchess, it would be unseemly for her to gamble, and she wouldn't need the money. She would have to learn a great deal about her new life.

Jack helped her into the hackney and climbed in beside her, but the instant the carriage moved forward, he hauled her into his lap and wrapped his arms around her. "Much better," he growled, pressing his lips to her neck.

"We'll be scandalous," she said on a sigh, tilting her head so he could do it again.

"We'll be happy, which will bore the gossips into an early grave." He untied her cloak and tugged it out of the way so he could slide his arm around her waist inside the garment.

"Jack." She twisted to face him. "My uncle came to see me. The Ogre died, and my uncle wants to be cordial. He . . . he's a lord—Viscount Makepeace."

He didn't even blink at this revelation that she had aristocratic connections. "He shall be welcome, so long as he is cordial."

"But—don't you see? I am not a nobody with no family now. I never would have said Makepeace's name aloud while my grandfather was still living, but Uncle Henry—well, he seems kind, like my father."

Jack touched her lip with one finger. "Sophie. You misunderstood me. I don't care if your family is royalty or itinerant cardplayers. I want *you*. I love *you*. Your uncle, and any other family and friends, are welcome in my house so long as you wish to invite them."

"Itinerant cardplayers?" She rolled her eyes even as she smiled. "Society would never accept such a duchess."

"Hang them all," he said. "Have you a dress to be married in?"

"Well—yes, but I ought to get a better one—"

"I have the special license in my pocket." He nodded at her gasp of astonishment. "I browbeat every clerk in Doctors' Commons until they produced it. We only need a vicar and a church. Does tomorrow suit you?"

"Surely a duke doesn't marry in such a hasty

fashion!" She pushed back from him, just enough to see his face. "And you were presumed engaged to someone else just this morning."

"*Presumed*," he stressed. "Only by my mother, who was incorrect."

"Still, you might have warned me," she said in reproach. "I was going to beat you at piquet and win your money, just to repay the anguish I suffered when Philip told me about her. Why didn't you tell me—?"

"I knew I'd only win if you wanted me to." He stopped her question with a kiss. "And you should never listen to anything Philip says, ever again. I promised to take care of Lucinda after her father died when she was a child. My mother decided I ought to marry her, not I."

"Philip says she's a clever, pretty girl . . ."

Jack smiled, pressing his forehead to hers. "She is. Clever enough to want to go to Egypt and discover antiquities, rather than marry a stuffy old duke."

Sophie raised her brows, unable to stop smiling. "You?"

He gave her his wicked grin, the one she was increasingly certain he reserved for her alone. "I'm afraid so."

She laughed, and he grinned before shifting his hold on her, until her back was against his chest and her legs straddled his. "Do you know what I thought of doing on that long, long ride to Alwyn House?" he murmured against her nape.

"You said . . ." Her voice broke as his hands skimmed up her thighs, over her belly, to settle around her breasts. "You said you only wanted to teach Philip a lesson . . ."

"Hmm? Oh, yes. The lesson was that he should not interfere in my seduction of you." He eased the dress off her shoulder with one hand and pressed a hot, openmouthed kiss on her bare skin.

Sophie quaked. "Was that your plan?"

"Plan?" He laughed softly. "I had no plan. Was it the driving thought I couldn't keep from my mind, no matter how hard I tried? Absolutely. Even when you wore a housemaid's dress and had cobwebs in your hair."

She thought of that moment in the attics, when he had brushed close by her and her body had all but gone up in flames. "Did you know I wanted you then?" she whispered, letting her head fall back as his wicked hands ravished her.

His hands paused. "I think we shall live in Alwyn House," he said after a moment. "Fill it with children and laughter and happiness, so that someday, our great-grandchildren will explore the attics and marvel at how deeply the ninth duke loved his wife." He kissed the back of her neck, his lips lingering. "My future duchess."

"Jack." She gave a little sigh. "My future duke."

"Until the end of time," he agreed.

Epilogue

Six weeks later

"Hold still, Sophie."

"I am."

"No," he said, with a crease of exasperation between his brows, "you're not. Your hand is brushing your bodice and it's driving me mad."

Sophie laughed. "Like this?" She ran her fingers over her breast, arching her back as she did so.

Her husband's eyes riveted on her hand. For a moment she thought he would act on the desire she could read in his face, but after a moment he gave his head a small shake and turned back to his sketch pad. "You're the one who asked me to draw you."

She smiled. She had, but he was the one who told her to recline on the library sofa in this artlessly seductive pose. Her skirts were pulled up to expose her bare feet, and her hair tumbled loose and free over the arm of the sofa. Merely lying here made her think of the first time he'd made love to her, and how easily he could do so again, now that they were married.

But it was true that she had encouraged him to draw. "I only suggested you draw me because we've been alone at Alwyn this past month," she remarked. "Unless you wish to sketch Wilson while he polishes the silver, I'm the only person who can sit for you."

"I have no interest in sketching Wilson or anyone else polishing the silver." His golden hair fell forward over his eyes as he rubbed out something on his pad. It had taken her this long to persuade him it wouldn't be ridiculous to try his hand at sketching again. But once he picked up the pencil and paper, his reluctance faded away and his face grew intent and absorbed. Her heart felt so full it might burst.

"No?" She grinned. "That ruins my plan to polish your mother's epergne without any clothes on."

His pencil stopped moving. Jack drew a deep breath and glanced up at her. "You're about to be ravished, madam. And doomed never to have a sketch of yourself that anyone else may see."

Sophie laughed again. She crossed her legs, giving her skirts a little kick to get them out of the way so she could wiggle her toes at him. Jack dropped his sketch pad and pencil on the floor and crossed the room in one step, going down on his knee beside her.

"Heartless wench," he murmured. "Teasing your poor husband like that . . ."

She wound her arms around his neck. "I humbly apologize. How shall I console him?"

"Oh no, I'm going to repay you. Be careful what you wish for, my dear . . ." His hand closed on her ankle and slid up her leg. "I was drawing you naked, and now I'd like to see you that way."

Sophie gasped, then laughed, and then caught her breath as he lowered his head and pressed his lips to the pulse at the base of her throat. Wordlessly she clutched his head to her bosom, embracing the tide of heat rushing through her body. Both his hands were under her skirt now, plowing upward, and a tremor went through her. Five weeks of marriage had done nothing to diminish her craving for his touch. Everything else about her new life felt strange and awkward still—from her mother-in-law's cool regard to her splendid new wardrobe to the way servants bowed when she walked by—but when it was just the two of them, she and Jack, everything felt right.

There was a knock at the door. Wilson had walked in on Jack kissing her rather passionately one morning in the breakfast room, and now he never entered a room without knocking. Sophie appreciated that even if Jack, who'd had servants every day of his life, saw no need for it.

This time they both ignored it, but a moment later the knock came again. When it sounded a third time Jack lifted his head, his eyes blazing with irritation, and barked, "Yes?"

Sophie, her dress now unfastened and disarranged, lay still and quiet out of sight on the sofa as the butler opened the door. "Your Grace, there is a young woman insisting on seeing the duchess. Her name is Lady Georgiana Lucas." Sophie gasped, and Jack pressed lightly on her chest to quell it.

"She is quite agitated, Your Grace," added Wilson. "She says it is urgent."

Sophie gripped his wrist in wordless anxiety. A muscle tensed in Jack's jaw. "Show her to the Blue Room and assure her the duchess will see her soon."

"Very good, sir."

The door closed with a click, and Sophie scrambled up from the cushions. "What can Georgiana be doing here?"

"What, indeed?" Jack watched mournfully as she pulled her bodice back up and began trying to fasten it.

Sophie shook her head. "She would never come without warning unless it was truly, desperately urgent—especially here. What can it be?"

"Trouble with her fiancé," he guessed, reluctantly helping with her buttons.

"Perhaps." Sophie was doubtful. Lord Sterling would have to do something very terrible indeed to spoil Georgiana's regard for him, and he didn't seem that stupid. Sophie had finally met the elusive viscount after her wedding to Jack; as predicted, Lady Sidlow's objections to Sophie's company had melted away once Sophie outranked her. Lord Sterling had come to call at Ware House with Georgiana, the very vision of a suave charmer. He'd expressed his envy that Jack had been able to whisk Sophie to the altar in a matter of days, while Georgiana's brother, the Earl of Wakefield, dragged out the negotiation of their wedding settlements for an eternity. Sterling had held Georgiana's hand and looked like a man in love.

"Family," was Jack's next idea.

Sophie shook her head. Georgiana knew her family was eccentric and sometimes stuffy, and she laughed at them affectionately. "I can't imagine what would bring her running to Chiswick."

"Then I suppose I cannot keep you from her." Jack pulled her close and kissed her hard. "Go, my dear. I shall sit here and work on my sketch."

"Without me posing for you?" She affected disappointment as she wound her hair into a knot.

Her husband winked and released her. "I have it fixed in my head, precisely how the sketch should look."

"Have I got any clothes on in this sketch you can see in your head?" she asked with a laugh.

"Not a scrap." He scooped up his pencil and pad. "Hurry back and allow me to check my memory."

Still shaking her head and smiling, Sophie hurried to the Blue Room. Unlike the first time she'd seen it, today the room glowed like a sapphire in the sunlight streaming through the tall windows. The garden was a riot of color outside, and just stepping into the room made her smile. But the expression quickly died when Georgiana turned to face her.

"What's wrong?"

Georgiana rushed across the room. She looked wild, her eyes red-rimmed, her hair swinging free in a braid and her pelisse buttoned wrong. "You've got to come back to town with me, Sophie. It's Eliza."

Her heart stopped. Eliza should be at home with her own new husband. A fortnight after

Sophie wed Jack, Eliza had become the Countess of Hastings, radiant and blushing with joy. The three friends had shared a wonderful moment of tearful happiness, reflecting on how splendidly things had worked out for each of them in love. A dozen years ago, playing illicit card games at Mrs. Upton's, Sophie never would have guessed they would all find such happiness at the same time.

"What's happened to Eliza?"

"I don't know," cried Georgiana, wringing her hands. "She didn't say, and Lady Sidlow won't allow me to go on my own. I'm so very sorry to intrude on you, when you and Ware must be so cozy and happy away from London, but I've no one else I can ask! Please, Sophie. We have to find her."

"Find her?" Sophie repeated sharply. "Georgiana, explain!"

Her friend drew a deep breath. "I saw Eliza just two days ago at the Montgomery ball. She was radiant, happy, and looked the picture of bliss. I even saw her dance with Hastings, and I swear they gazed at each other with stars in their eyes. But this morning—" She broke off and dug in her reticule. "She sent me this."

Sophie took the crumpled note and recognized Eliza's handwriting. She read the two sentences it contained, then read them again. Stunned, she looked up at Georgiana.

Georgiana nodded grimly. "She's left her husband. And no one knows where she's gone."

Adrienne Basso crafts a spellbinding tale of suspense, mystery, and unexpected passion along the elegant salons and ballrooms of Regency England . . .

Blessed with beauty, fortune, and noble birth, Lady Meredith Barrington puzzles the ton by choosing to remain single. Then a roguish bet placed by her younger brothers leads Meredith to impulsively flirt with—and boldly kiss—the handsome, brooding Marquess of Dardington. A threatened scandal results in a hasty wedding. Their is a marriage of convenience, and Meredith is determined to maintain her unusual independent ways. Then an apparent accident nearly takes her life, and Meredith, shaken, finds herself turning again and again to her husband for comfort, reassurance . . . and more.

Trevor Morley, Marquess of Dardington, is less than pleased when he's forced to wed, and vows to avoid his lovely wife—no matter how tempting that soul-stirring kiss in the garden. But when the *ton* is rocked by a string of savage murders, Trevor comes to realize the killer has targeted Meredith. He ensures he's always at her side . . . day *and* night. Their intimacy ignites a fiery passion between them, and both are stunned to discover that what began in rueful obedience to Society's dictates has become a love match. But can Trevor protect the woman he cherishes from deadly harm?

Books by Adrienne Basso

HIS WICKED EMBRACE

HIS NOBLE PROMISE

TO WED A VISCOUNT

TO PROTECT AN HEIRESS

Published by Zebra Books

TO
PROTECT
AN HEIRESS

Adrienne Basso

ZEBRA BOOKS
Kensington Publishing Corp.
http://www.kensingtonbooks.com

ZEBRA BOOKS are published by

Kensington Publishing Corp.
850 Third Avenue
New York, NY 10022

All Kensington titles, imprints, and distributed lines are available at special quantity discounts for bulk purchases for sales promotion, premiums, fund-raising, educational, or institutional use.

Special book excerpts or customized printings can also be created to fit specific needs. For details, write or phone the office of the Kensington Special Sales Manager: Kensington Publishing Corp., 850 Third Avenue, New York, NY 10022. Attn. Special Sales Department. Phone: 1-800-221-2647.

Zebra and the Z logo Reg. U.S. Pat. & TM Off.

First Printing: July 2002
10 9 8 7 6 5 4 3 2 1

Printed in the United States of America

In Memory of Kyle Moten Disch, daughter, sister, wife, mother, friend.
Taken far too young, her valiant spirit lives on in those of us who were lucky enough to have known and loved her.
Dear friend, I mourn and miss you.

One

The whispers were not whispers at all, for they could be heard clearly among the fashionable guests preening about the lawn at the Duchess of Suttington's afternoon garden party.

"She might be worth nearly five thousand a year, but the Earl of Portersville said he wouldn't take her if she were a royal princess—with ten thousand a year. Too much spirit and opinion for a *proper* young lady," a portly matron declared vehemently.

Her female companion nodded enthusiastically. "I heard she actually had the audacity to correct the Duke of Hastings last week when he was showing her the latest acquisition to his art collection. Claimed it was most likely a fake and that he had been swindled. Utterly shocking!"

Eighteen-year-old Lady Meredith Barrington, the subject of this disapproving conversation, sat only a few feet away. She tossed her blond curls regally over her left shoulder with feigned indifference, determined these old biddies would not have the pleasure of seeing how deeply their criticism wounded her.

Their conversation continued, and Meredith forced

herself to ignore the words, to treat them as only irritating sounds, not spiteful slander. She felt the onset
of a numbing headache and longed to retreat inside
the castle, away from the guests, yet she stood her
ground, trembling but calm.

"What else can one expect from the Earl of Stafford's daughter? He has always been far too scholarly
and outspoken for my tastes. One can learn to excuse
that sort of behavior in a man, but certainly not in a
young woman."

Meredith's concentration slipped as she compre-
hended the last statement. Her first inclination was to
turn and snap at these catty gossipmongers, but that
sort of scandalous behavior would only lend credence
to their lies.

Dear Lord, would they never leave her alone? Was
it not enough that she was considered unacceptable,
branded a bluestocking because she had the effrontery
to offer up an intelligent opinion that often differed
from that of her male escort? Must she constantly be
maligned also by the members of her own sex, too?

Deep within her, Meredith seethed with the injustice
of it all. Her father's differences were labeled eccentric, while hers were considered unacceptable. And,
yes, she had indeed told the Duke of Hastings his Venetian goblet had most likely not been owned by Pope
Pius II, since that holy man had lived and died nearly
100 years before that particular shade of green was
being blown by Venetian artisans.

Meredith's reason for divulging this fact had not
been to showcase her knowledge, nor to embarrass the
duke, but instead to distract him. The man had cleverly
managed to get her alone and was in the process of
making the most improper advances toward her at the
time she sputtered her revelations.

It was either wound his pride or wound his person.

Meredith gritted her teeth, now regretting her decision to wound his pride. A swift kick in a most indiscreet location would certainly not have been so eagerly discussed by the duke to his cronies. Perhaps then this latest tale never would have come to light.

But the duke's unwanted advances had been deliberately left out as these two matrons recounted the episode, giving credence to the theory they had no idea what actually occurred.

In an odd way, Meredith was almost disappointed. Revealing the true nature of the duke's behavior might produce a scandal of such magnitude Meredith would be placed solidly beyond the pale and thus put an end her disastrous debut into Society.

For the simple truth was that Meredith had never been more miserable in her entire life. She had started the Season with such high expectations. As the beautiful daughter of a wealthy and noble family, she had initially been embraced by the *ton.* However, that acceptance quickly turned to disapproval.

And it was not a one-sided disillusionment. Meredith equally disliked the *beau monde,* with its rigid rules that seemed designed to exclude anyone or anything that had a slightly different view of the world. She had quickly and disappointedly learned that if one did not embrace Society in its entirety, one was systematically shunned.

"Ahh, so that is where you have gotten to," a musical female voice declared. "I've been looking everywhere for you, Lady Meredith."

Meredith lifted her head and smiled. Lavinia Morely, the young Marchioness of Dardington, came gliding gracefully toward her, arms outstretched in greeting.

"How lovely to see you," Meredith said truthfully

as she embraced her friend. "I was unsure if you would be in attendance this afternoon."

"Oh, we would not miss today's little gathering," Lavinia replied as she returned the hug. "The Duchess of Suttington is my dearest Trevor's godmother. She would be crushed if we did not make an appearance at her afternoon soiree. The moment we arrived she spirited Trevor away to discuss a matter she proclaimed to be of utmost importance.

"I have a feeling it has something to do with the latest horses she purchased at Tattersall's. The duchess really is horse mad, yet she lacks the good sense to trust her own judgment. Poor Trevor. I promised to go and rescue him if he does not reappear within the hour."

"What a noble wife you are, Lavinia." Meredith clucked her tongue in mock horror. "And so very unfashionable to be seen so often in your husband's company."

Lavinia gave an exaggerated sigh. "We are quite the pair, are we not?"

"Indeed." Meredith leaned forward and whispered in her friend's ear. "You are the envy of every woman here because you have such a handsome, dashing husband who is totally besotted with you, and doesn't care in the least who knows it."

Lavinia smiled charmingly. "Well, not every woman envies me. I daresay your mother enjoys equal devotion from your father. And they have been married nearly twenty years."

Meredith lowered her chin. "Yes, my parents are unusual in many regards, including the loving state of their marriage. Something I believe the *ton* fails to understand at all."

"That is because loyalty, devotion, and true love are foreign ideals to most of them." Lavinia cocked her

head, her rich brown eyes alight with suspicion. "That scowl marring your lovely brow has me worried. I suspect it has nothing to do with your parents. Don't tell me the Duke of Hastings has had the audacity to approach you again?"

Meredith's head swung around sharply. "Is he here?"

"Isn't everyone?"

Meredith choked down a laugh. "I wouldn't know. I've been here nearly two hours and on;y a handful of people have actually spoken to me—though I cannot help but notice they have spoken a great deal *about* me."

"Vicious swine," Lavinia muttered. She linked her arm through Meredith's. "How quick they are to sit in judgment of others, having no qualms at finding fault. Yet all the while they are busy skulking about searching for juicy tidbits of gossip. It can be quite maddening."

Just then the two gossiping ladies who had so enjoyed discussing Meredith called out a greeting to the marchioness and gestured for Lavinia to join them. Meredith was pointedly excluded from the invitation.

The young marchioness' eyes narrowed on the pair and she favored them with a barely perceptible nod. Meredith felt a rush of gratitude as the portly matron's smile slipped a fraction.

Lavinia tightened her grip on Meredith's arm. "Come along now, Merry. 'Tis time we mingled."

Meredith smiled. There was comfort in that strong grip, and genuine friendship. She once again said a short, silent prayer of thanks to whatever God had seen fit to bring her and Lavinia together. For Meredith, the only bright spot in this otherwise dismal coming out Season had been her newly formed friendship with Lavinia.

It had been an unexpected delight to find such an open and honest young woman who was happy to offer her friendship for no other reason than she liked Meredith.

The two woman circulated among the guests, chatting about the weather, the lovely party, and the latest fashions. With Lavinia by her side, Meredith was quickly acknowledged, though not warmly greeted. Not that she really cared.

Within minutes she was bored to tears by the dull and tedious topics of conversation, and it took a great effort to keep a pleasant expression plastered on her face. She suspected Lavinia was equally bored, but the young marchioness somehow managed to display interest in the discussions without appearing fawning or condescending.

Meredith admired her friend's social skills and poise. At times it was difficult to remember that Lavinia was only a few years older than she. Perhaps the security of a loving husband who clearly demonstrated anything his wife did was exceptional had contributed to Lavinia's remarkable self-confidence.

"What is your response, Lady Meredith?"

Meredith squinted noncommittally at the small, squat woman who addressed her, fearing to make any sort of remark. She had been woolgathering for the majority of the conversation and had no earthly idea what the Countess of Ridgefield had asked.

Trying to play it safe, she muttered an affirmative, sympathetic remark.

Lady Olivia Dermott raised a gold-rimmed quizzing glass and looked disdainfully at Meredith. "That is all you have to say about the matter? I find that a rather shocking reaction from a refined young woman."

"Nonsense," Lavinia interrupted icily. "That is a logical, honest reaction. If you will excuse us, ladies."

Meredith quickly rallied her senses. With the boldness she instinctively knew was required, she followed Lavinia's lead, turned on her heel, and walked away. Meredith could practically feel the annoyance sweep through her friend at each step they took.

"Spiteful witch," Lavinia muttered beneath her breath, when they had gained a fair distance. "She's jealous because she's heard Julian Wingate offered for you. She's been trying all season to bring him up to scratch for that mousy daughter of hers and having no success."

"Is that what they were discussing? Julian Wingate?" Meredith was almost glad she had been ignoring the conversation. "Lady Olivia is more than welcome to him. For the life of me, I cannot understand his great popularity. I find him boorish, conceited, and possessing of a negative opinion about everything. Except himself. It took every ounce of willpower not to run screaming from the room each time he came calling for me."

"Most women find his charm nearly irresistible." Lavinia struck a pose of contemplation, then grinned. " 'Tis rather remarkable that you aren't considered a great social success, yet you have managed to garner three proposals of marriage."

"Four, if you include Wingate. But I am not so foolish to think anything but my vast fortune has attracted their attention." Meredith smiled despite her grim words. "There are still a few more weeks left until everyone retires to the country, or follows the Regent to Brighton. I fear that number will increase before I can escape."

"We should make a game of it and see how many proposals you can accumulate," Lavinia said smoothly.

Meredith's spine went stiff. She turned to her friend in astonishment, but the mischievous twinkle in Lav-

inia's eyes let Meredith know she was only jesting. "I suppose if I managed an even half dozen, that would put a flea in Lady Olivia's ear."

"Most definitely."

The two women exchanged a sly glance, then burst into merry laughter.

"We need to find you someone like my Trevor," Lavinia declared when the laughter subsided. "The problem is, there is simply no other man in England quite so perfect."

As if somehow aware he was the topic of their conversation, the Marquess of Dardington appeared within the scope of their vision. Meredith spotted him first, but she knew it would be only a moment before Lavinia saw him, too.

The marquess was conversing with several gentlemen of various ages. Though not the tallest of the group, he was the one Meredith's eyes were drawn toward. Golden-haired, with a fine sharp profile, broad shoulders and an undefinable dash of charisma, he enraptured those around him.

He was dressed more conservatively than his companions, in buff breeches, a patterned waistcoat, and jacket of navy superfine, yet it wasn't his imposing handsomeness Meredith found so extraordinary. There was an underlying strength of character in Trevor Morely that had always intrigued her.

His mannerism, his attitude, his conversation all indicated he was a man who could be depended upon in times of crisis. Having grown up with a father who adored her but was hardly known for his sense of responsibility, Meredith found this a most admirable quality.

That, along with his obvious love for and devotion to his wife, made him one of the few men in Society

with whom Meredith was truly interested in forming a friendship.

"Trevor."

The sound was a mere whisper, but the emotion in that single name told Meredith Lavinia had indeed seen her husband. Meredith knew it was impossible, but somehow the marquess either heard or sensed his wife's voice, for his head turned away from his male companion and toward Lavinia.

His attention grew fixed, centered completely on his lovely wife, though he stood several yards away. Meredith watched in fascination as the couple's eyes first met and then held. For an instant, something dark and intense burned in the marquess's gaze.

Blushing, Lavinia lowered her head.

Meredith abruptly glanced away. The emotion and longing on the marquess's face had startled her, and she somehow felt as though she had intruded on a very personal, private moment—which was rather ridiculous, considering the number of people surrounding them.

Though she had witnessed it many times in the past, Meredith was once again struck by the closeness the pair radiated, even when standing so physically far apart.

Still, a slow smile spread over Meredith's face. She might not entirely understand their relationship, but it made her happy to see the lightness that seemed to lift Lavinia's heart whenever she saw her husband.

"My goodness, I just felt you shiver." Meredith reached out and grasped her friend's arm. "Are you cold, Lavinia?"

"Not at all." A host of emotions crossed her face. " 'Tis Trevor. My husband can reduce me to a puddle of shivers with a single glance. Isn't it marvelous?"

Truthfully, Meredith thought that sounded rather ri-

diculous, but she wasn't about to hurt her dear friend's feelings by saying anything. "Actually it sounds rather uncomfortable. Here, take my shawl. 'Tis a warm afternoon, but there is a bit of a breeze. Those short puffs of sleeves on your lavender gown are charming, but offer no protection."

"I'm really not cold," Lavinia protested, refusing the garment.

Meredith sighed, but did not press the matter. She heard Lavinia catch her breath as a second shiver went through the marchioness. Meredith turned her head, scanning the faces of those who ambled by, pretending to be completely absorbed by the strolling crowd. It seemed a better alternative than watching the woman at her side turn into a shivering puddle of lust.

However, at the marchioness's third shiver, Meredith found she could no longer ignore the situation.

"Lavinia!"

"All right, I'll take your shawl."

"We both know that is not the cause of your shuddering," Meredith retorted, her eyes narrowing.

Lavinia fixed her with an innocent look. "Nevertheless, it would not hurt to take special care of myself. Trevor is most solicitous of my health these days."

"Have you been ill?"

"Goodness, no." Lavinia waved away Meredith's obvious concern as she adjusted the distinctively patterned silk shawl around her shoulders. "I have never felt better. Nor been happier." The marchioness grinned slyly. "It appears I am in an interesting condition."

Meredith frowned. "Interesting?"

"Rather interesting."

Meredith's frown deepened, as Lavinia stared expectantly at her. She knew the marchioness was trying to

tell her something, and by the look of her it was a fairly significant something. Yet Meredith was completely puzzled.

After a few moments of silence, Lavinia rolled her eyes good-naturedly and laughed. "For an intelligent, quick-witted young woman, you can be a real slowtop at times." The marchioness pressed her hand gently against her stomach. "An *interesting* condition."

Meredith's jaw dropped. "Good lord!"

A dreamy expression flitted across Lavinia's lovely features. "Isn't it miraculous? A baby. Trevor and I have been congratulating ourselves all week for being such a clever pair." She sighed deeply. "We haven't told anyone yet. It has been our own wonderful secret. But we are dining tonight with Trevor's father and can hardly wait to inform the duke."

Meredith's throat tightened. "I am honored you saw fit to share this news with me."

Lavinia tilted her head in surprise. "You are my dearest friend. Of course I would share my special secret with you." The marchioness linked her arm with Meredith's as the two woman began to stroll toward a cluster of guests. "I know I can count on your discretion. While I am thrilled about my condition, I prefer not to share it with the world.

"The rules restricting the movements of expectant mothers in Society are every bit as ridiculous as all the others. My doctor has informed me my condition will not become obvious for several months. As long as I continue to feel well, there is no reason not to enjoy the rest of the Season."

Meredith flushed with guilty relief, pleased to discover Lavinia had no immediate plan to withdraw from Society. It would be intolerable trying to endure the final weeks of the Season without her friend attending at least some of the events.

"I am very happy for you, Lavinia. You shall make a wonderful mother."

"Thank you." Lavinia's eyebrows raised. "Oh, dear, Lady Tolliver has spotted us and is gesturing for us to join her. I know how much she grates on your nerves, so I will not ask you to accompany me while I give her my regards."

"You are a true friend."

"Yes, I am." The marchioness glanced anxiously among the guests. "Will you be all right on your own?"

"Stop worrying about me," Meredith said, though her stomach tightened momentarily at the idea of being alone.

"We can meet near the Grecian folly on the other side of the ornamental lake," Lavinia suggested. "In an hour?"

"Perfect."

"Don't forget your shawl." Lavinia began removing the lovely garment from her shoulders but Meredith held up her hand.

"No, you wear it. There is bound to be more of a breeze near the water." She winked at her friend. "After all, we must keep you in the best of health."

The marchioness's twinkling laugh lingered long after she strode away. With a small sigh, Meredith turned and lifted her parasol onto her shoulder, positioning it at the exact angle to protect her face from the sun. She wasn't especially interested in preventing the warmth from reaching her skin, but the device helped shield her from prying eyes.

Assuring herself there was no reason for her heart to race and her nerves to twitch, Meredith moved forward to stroll with the other ladies and gentlemen over the gravel walks and sections of lawn. She returned

the cool regard she received with a haughty watchful-
ness, the grip on her parasol tightening with each step.

"Lady Meredith. What a delightful surprise."

Lord Jonathan Travers stepped directly in her path,
neatly trapping her. Two large trees flanked them on
either side, making it impossible to go around him.
After a fractional hesitation, Meredith returned the
young man's greeting.

Though the number of her male admirers had dwin-
dled during the Season, there were still those who
thought her a challenge. Or a curiosity.

She had yet to decide Lord Travers's motivation. He
was a rather serious young man who put far too much
stock in the opinion of others and could always be
counted upon to supply the dullest of conversations.

Still, Meredith could think of worse things than
spending a few moments in his company. She resolved
to be pleasant and took comfort knowing she could
escape in an hour and meet Lavinia by the water. With
a glazed eye and a contrived expression, she turned
her attention to Lord Travers.

"Are you enjoying the afternoon, Lord Travers?"

"All the more now that I have found you, Lady
Meredith."

Meredith gave him a distant smile, not wanting to
encourage him in any way. She and Lavinia might
have joked about it earlier, but the very last thing
Meredith wanted was another marriage proposal.

Resolved to keep the attention away from herself,
Meredith found she had little difficulty getting her escort to speak of other subjects—or offer his opinion.
She wisely declined to offer hers, since it so seldom
agreed with his.

With her fingers resting lightly on his arm, the pair
strolled amiably in the sunshine.

The scream pierced the glib conversation with

alarming suddenness—high pitched, female, and drenched in sheer terror.

"My God," Meredith whispered. She turned in the direction of the sound, then back to her male companion. "What was that horrible noise?"

Lord Travers blanched under his tan. "It sounded like an animal caught in a trap."

"It couldn't be."

Without conscious thought, Meredith moved forward, following the crowd that hurried across the lawn, then through the large cluster of trees. Men were yelling and running about, shouting questions and instructions with equal excitement.

Most of the women were staying deliberately out of the fray, though a few were bold or curious enough to follow the ever growing crowd. As they reached the small clearing and veered left, Meredith at last realized where they were heading. The lake.

Her step quickened as her heart began to pound with fear. She was to meet Lavinia at the lake in less than fifteen minutes' time. A eerie vision slipped into Meredith's head, weaving through the fear in her mind. A body, lying prone on the bank. Still. Unmoving.

Meredith gasped. Her heart slammed against her ribs. She dropped her parasol, lifted her gown above her ankles and quickened her pace. Dodging the slower walkers, she weaved among the crowd, gaining speed with each step. By the time she reached the muddy edge of the lake perspiration dampened her skin and her gasping breathing burned in her lungs.

"What has happened?" she asked in a breathless whisper.

A colorfully garbed dandy she did not recognize tried to block her view. "There appears to have been an accident."

"Who is it?" another man cried out. "Do you know who has been hurt?"

"The Marchioness of Dardington," a third man replied. "Her husband is with her."

No! Meredith began shaking with a terror that ran all the way down her body to her toes. For an instant she could not move, could not think, could not feel. Then, with strength born of primal fear, Meredith pushed her way through the men ringing the edge of crowd.

She dimly felt the touch of a hand trying to hold her back, but she shook it forcefully off and emerged but a few feet from a waking nightmare.

A moan escaped her lips. There, on the edge of the grass near the Grecian temple lay a body. A female body, clothed in lavender. It was not moving.

Meredith swallowed a shriek and fought to control her breathing. Stumbling forward, she came closer to the inert form. There were three men surrounding the body.

They were as still and silent as the form that lay at their feet.

Meredith struggled to master her emotions. Lavinia needed her to be calm. An hysterical female would only be in the way. But a cool, composed lady would be an asset. Resolutely she stepped forward. Saying nothing, the three men allowed her to pass.

Trevor Morely was kneeling beside his wife. His head was bent, yet Meredith could almost feel his whole being vibrating with suppressed emotion.

Her lips pressed stubbornly tight, Meredith knelt on the other side of Lavinia, facing the marquess. She tried to gaze down at the body, but could not bring herself to look. She did notice, however, that the marquess held his wife's hand gently in his own.

They stayed that way for what seemed like an eter-

nity. At last, he raised his head, but he did not release his wife's hand.

Meredith watched him in silence, the muscle flexing and unflexing in his jaw. He said nothing as the speculative conversation surrounding them grew in volume and intensity.

"What a tragic accident! Her neck's broken. She must have tripped and fell and fatally injured herself when she hit the ground."

"Perhaps she was frightened by something," a male voice muttered. "Why else would she have screamed?"

"A good fright would explain both the scream and the fall," the third man interjected. "It might have been an animal. But what?"

"There are no wild beasts in the duchess's folly. It wouldn't be allowed."

The speculation and muttering continued, but Meredith turned her attention away from it.

She looked again at the marquess and the grief inside her returned, stifling in its intensity. His face mirrored her own emotions of shock and pain, and she could see the faint trace of tears shimmering in his eyes.

Trembling, Meredith reached out to offer him comfort, but her hand faltered. Instead she grasped the fringed edge of the shawl that now draped Lavinia's lifeless body.

Mesmerized, she slowly moved her hand, gliding it along the delicate silk, remembering how her friend had not wanted to wear the garment, saying there was no need.

The baby! Stillness gripped her as she recalled Lavinia's joking and laughing about being extra careful of her health. *Merciful God, that tender little life was gone now too.*

Tearful, Meredith raised her chin. The marquess was no longer staring at his wife but looking straight at her. She couldn't avoid his eyes.

Questioning, hollow, lifeless.

Meredith's composure shattered. She lifted the edge of the shawl and stuffed it in her mouth, struggling to quiet her heaving sobs.

From the covering of trees, the man watched in silence. His breath blew out in panting gasps. His heart raced with a strange rush of exhilaration. He pressed his damp palms together and cast an approving glance at the scene before him.

He was close enough to hear their conversation, their speculation. He had done his job well. They were convinced it was an accident, a cruel stroke of fate. It had been difficult, but he had not demonstrated any savagery when he performed his task. The young woman barely had time to be frightened before his hands had stolen around her neck.

Her soft eyes had widened in surprise, then panic and finally pain. She had lost consciousness quickly and it had taken only a quick snap to break her neck.

For him, killing was a compulsion. A necessity, like food and water and air for other men. He had long ago ceased trying to understand it, for it had always been a part of him, cleverly and successfully concealed from the world.

This woman was unlike his usual victims. Female, of course, but of a far different class. He preferred the young assistants in the shops on Bond Street or the fresh-faced serving wenches at the taverns, working girls who fought with fear and determination to escape their fate.

Yet this particular woman had been chosen for a reason. A very personal reason.

His senses gradually began returning as the rush of excitement and exhilaration began to ease. He peered again through the leaves to savor the death scene one last time and became aware of a woman kneeling beside the body. She lifted her head, and he sucked in his breath in astonishment.

It was impossible! He had just killed this woman! He blinked vigorously, then carelessly pushed aside a branch for a better view.

There was no mistake. The woman sobbing so pitifully beside the body was Lady Meredith Barrington. Cursing soundly, he realized he had not taken full measure of his victim's face. He had seen the distinctive shawl and stalked his victim patiently. The moment she was alone, he had sprung, attacking from behind, turning her to face him only at the last instant, so he could relish the final moments of her life as he hastened its end.

Lady Meredith bowed her head. Her hands stole around her waist and she clutched at her stomach as if in great pain.

His anger began to ease. She was suffering. Horribly. Perhaps this was better. Her death would have been a swift punishment for her sins. The death of someone she clearly cared for would bring her years of pain and anguish.

He dragged in a breath, his chest swelling. His skin began prickling with enjoyment as he savored this strange twist of fate.

Perhaps all had not gone precisely according to his original plan, yet he was pleased with the final result.

For now.

Two

"I thought by now you would finally comprehend that it is beyond foolish to place a wager when you do not possess the coin to pay if you lose," Lady Meredith Barrington admonished forcefully. "Nor the legal means to obtain it."

She assumed what she hoped was a grave expression of disapproval and glared at the two gentlemen who were sprawled on the patterned brocade sofa in her drawing room.Identical in golden coloring, with sharp handsome features that were also nearly the same, they gazed back at her with matching green eyes that held a hint of boredom, a reaction hardly befitting this serious matter.

She had hoped her lecture would inspire regret or remorse or even repentance. Yet that seemed unlikely.

With a forlorn sigh, Meredith admitted her younger brothers were no longer a pair of lanky youths who grew still and quiet when she raised her voice. Those skinny, boyish limbs were now muscular arms and wide shoulders, clothed in the finest garments Weston could produce. And when they were not being lectured

by their older sister, she knew those brilliant green eyes burned with youthful zeal and a passion for life.

It did not, however, disguise the fact that her younger twin brothers, Jason and Jasper, were without question the most mischievous, irritating, frustrating, and charming men in all of England. Meredith was also firmly convinced they were responsible for the gray hairs she had discovered in her hairbrush this very morning.

"I don't understand why you are getting so distraught over this matter," Jasper grumbled. He leaned back and casually rested his left ankle atop his right knee. "It is not an overly large wager."

"Nor have we lost it," Jason added in a deliberate tone.

"Yet," Meredith said in her sternest voice. She huffed dramatically, folded her arms across her chest, and used her considerable height to her advantage. Unfortunately, neither man was looking directly at her, so the effect of glaring down upon them was lost. "I told you most emphatically two weeks ago I would neither intercede on your behalf with father's man of affairs to advance your quarterly allowance, nor would I make you a loan from my own meager funds."

"Meager!" Jasper hooted. He shifted position swiftly, placing both booted feet firmly on the carpet. "Saints above, Merry, you've got more money than anyone else I know, male or female. I'd wager you could lend the Bank of England funds if it was needed."

"The Bank of England?" Jason rubbed his chin thoughtfully. "A solid, reliable institution, with sound collateral and a sterling reputation. I know Merry has a pretty bit of coin put aside, but it can't possibly be as much as the bank. Or could it? An interesting notion. I believe I shall accept that wager, brother."

"Oh, for heaven's sakes, will you both stop it?" Meredith nearly stamped her foot in frustration. This was ridiculous. Would they never stop, never learn? She loved her brothers to the extreme but was hardly blind to their faults, the principal one being their over-zealous enthusiasm for gambling.

At twenty-two years of age, the twins were a pair of spoiled, privileged gentlemen, reckless, overindulged, and self-centered. Meredith's parents were of little use when it came to controlling their sons. The earl and his wife were often out of the country, pursing some archaeological find or scholarly relic that had captured the earl's fancy. They were, for the most part, blissfully unaware of their sons' extreme antics.

Yet even when they were in town, they did nothing to curb the twins' wild behavior. The earl was of the opinion his sons would eventually grow out of their high spirits. Consequently, he allowed them to live their lives entirely as they wished. No matter how outrageous the circumstance, the earl gave no censure to his sons.

Initially Meredith had tried to follow her father's lead, but she soon discovered that, left to their own devices, the twins would run totally wild. She had tried to be a steadying influence on them, but more and more that task was requiring stronger measures. They no longer easily followed her direction nor listened to her advice or opinions with solemn, wide-eyed regard.

As they grew older, it seemed the harder she tried to control them, the more they resisted. Each time Meredith vowed she would not intercede at the next crisis, yet she found it impossible to follow her own advice.

She partly blamed herself for the current state of affairs, admitting she had bailed her brothers out of

so many scrapes over the years that they no longer fully considered the consequences of their escapades before acting.

They knew if things went awry, she could be counted upon to somehow set everything to rights, for she had taken the task of watching over them very seriously. It was a role she did not relish, yet she knew she must often seem like an avenging angel, refusing to let any real harm come to her wayward siblings, especially when it was within her means to prevent it.

Despite everything, she loved her brothers deeply and knew they held her in equal regard. However, at moments such as these, that was occasionally difficult to remember.

"It never ceases to amaze me that given the vast amount of time you waste with your endless gaming and wagering you are both so exceedingly poor at it," Meredith said tartly. "One would think you could at least improve over time."

" 'Tis just a run of bad luck," Jasper declared stoically. He was the older twin by several minutes, and thus the heir to his father's title.

That gave him a distinct advantage over his brother, for as the future earl he was afforded more privileges and considerations. Chief among them was a larger line of credit from merchants, moneylenders, and his gaming partners.

"Why, only last week I won a shockingly fine pair of matched bays from Lord Darby," Jasper continued, "at the turn of a single card. It was the talk of the club for several days."

"And I won them from Jasper only three days later," Jason said in a cheerful tone.

"You cheated." Jasper flicked a small bit of lint off his breeches and glared at his brother. "Though I cannot prove it, I am convinced you marked those cards."

"Sore loser." Jason smirked. "You are loath to admit it, but my skill at piquet exceeds yours. It always has."

"It never has," Jasper stated emphatically. "The only possible way you could have won was by foul means."

Jason shrugged his shoulders. Her brother's total lack of offense at the suggestion he had cheated had Meredith convinced there might be some truth in the charge. She only prayed he practiced such foolishness with his twin and not with other gamesters. Cheaters often came to a swift and unpleasant end.

Though her brothers were nearly identical in face and form, there were distinct differences in their personalities. Jason was by far the more congenial of the twins, quick with a smile, always eager for a new experience, a new challenge. Yet Meredith had recently begun to notice a reckless streak in Jason that worried her greatly.

"If the horses are as prime as you say, then you should sell these magnificent beasts to cover your current gaming debts and wisely hold aside enough coin to make good on this latest wager," Meredith said, as she diverted the conversation back to the current problem at hand. "If you lose this newest bet, of course."

"I'm afraid that is impossible." Now it was Jasper's turn to smirk at his brother's expense. "Jason lost the bays only last night. In another game of piquet."

"Good lord." Meredith collapsed onto an upholstered chair. "Those poor animals are being shuttled all over London as half the bucks in town win and lose them. Have you no conscience at all for their well being?"

Both men gave her an equally puzzled expression.

"They are fed the finest grain, housed in the cleanest stables, exercised in the choicest fields," Jasper said. "I daresay those less fortunate souls in the East

End of London would envy the treatment these horses receive."

"A most pitiful comment on the state of our society," Meredith said dryly, but the blank expressions on her brothers' faces told her it was pointless to continue in this vein. This was most definitely not the time for her to begin a lecture on the responsibilities and duties of a privileged man in Society toward those who were less fortunate.

"We can discuss your ideas for political and social reform later, Merry," Jasper said smoothly. "But first we would like to talk about a more pressing problem. Of a personal nature."

Meredith's brows arched upward. Perhaps she had underestimated her brothers' shrewdness. At least they were aware of her opinions, even if they did not share them. "I have already told you I will not lend you any money, and I have no intention of changing my mind, no matter how eloquently you state your case. Therefore, we have nothing to discuss."

Meredith regained her feet and strode restlessly to the other side of the room, deliberately keeping her back to the twins. When they turned pleading, sincere eyes toward her, it was much harder to stand firm, and Meredith was determined not to relent in this matter.

"We are not asking you for money," Jasper said in an indignant tone. "You have obviously misunderstood the entire situation."

"We have come to ask your help in winning a wager that could restore those long-necked bays to us," Jason added in a righteous voice. "Won't you at least do us the courtesy of listening to our plan before you dismiss it?"

Meredith sighed as her shoulders sagged. "Jasper initially won these poor horses from Lord Darby, then

Jason won them from Jasper, and last night Jason again lost them in still another card game." She rubbed her temples in an effort to ease the steady pounding in her head. It was not successful. "I fail to see how I can assist you in the matter. I don't even play piquet."

"Don't be ridiculous, Merry."

"I was being sarcastic."

"Oh."

Silence fell. Meredith raised her eyes toward the gilt porcelain clock resting on the marble mantel above the fireplace and slowly counted to ten.

"All we ask is that you listen to us. With an open mind. Please?" a voice which could have belonged to either brother entreated.

Against her better judgment, Meredith slowly turned around. Both men immediately flashed her their most winning smiles. Merry gritted her teeth, refusing to be charmed.

Then Jason invitingly patted the seat beside him. Merry's mouth quirked faintly, but her gaze was sharp as she took the place so solicitously offered by her brother.

"All right, out with it. I know I shall not have a moment's peace until you have revealed your latest plan." Meredith primly folded her hands together and placed them in her lap. "I'm listening."

Jason leaned forward eagerly. "We have devised a most clever way to ensure we win this latest wager. All we require is a bit of help from you—in a very limited role."

"For once my brother does not exaggerate," Jasper agreed heartily. "It will take very little effort for us to be victorious, and the best part is that we will walk away not only in possession of the bays but with a tidy sum in our pockets."

"More than enough to last until we receive our regular quarterly allowance," Jason said.

"I hardly dare ask, but with whom have you placed this oh-so-easy-to-win wager?"

"The Marquess of Dardington," both men said simultaneously.

Color flared high on Meredith's cheeks and she had difficulty catching her breath. The Marquess of Dardington! The last time she had set eyes on Trevor Morely was at Lavinia's funeral, eight years ago. He had stood beside the black-silk-draped coffin stiffly, without a trace of emotion marring his handsome features, as his young wife was entombed in the family vault.

The grief of the day had nearly shattered Meredith's own heart. She had worn a dark, heavy veil to hide the constant flow of tears that would not cease. The sadness had seeped inside her very soul and would not abate.

Eventually time had lessened the pain Meredith felt, but somewhere inside she knew she would always grieve for the friend she had so abruptly lost.

Jason and Jasper had been away at school that ill-fated year Meredith made her debut into society and knew nothing of her friendship with Lavinia. They knew of the tragic, accidental death of the lovely young marchioness, for that harrowing tale had reached even the halls of Eton, but they had no idea of its impact on Meredith's life.

Immediately after the funeral, the marquess had disappeared from Society entirely. Rumors abounded as to his fate. Some said he had joined the army, others said he had shut himself away in one of his father's remote estates and nearly gone mad with grief. There were even hints that in a raging fit of madness he had taken his own life.

It was all nonsense, of course. Trevor had emerged again among the *ton* two years after Lavinia's death and became a formidable presence among the rogues and rakes who existed on the fringes of society. Meredith often wondered how she would feel, how she would react, if she once again met the marquess, but their paths never crossed.

She attended fewer and fewer Society events each Season, and apparently the marquess went to even less. By all accounts, he seemed to prefer the company of men, those who had reckless and daring reputations that equaled his own, and women who were known for their beauty, not their moral character. It surprised and worried Meredith to realize that Trevor was an acquaintance of her brothers. She wondered what a jaded, worldly man like the marquess would find interesting or even amusing about her younger siblings.

Meredith struggled to control her emotions, but when she spoke her voice was nearly a whisper. "I know the marquess has a reputation as a reckless gamester, but he is not a fool. Why would he make a wager with you that can be so easily lost?"

"He does not realize how clever we are." Jason slapped his thigh gleefully. "That is the true beauty of our plan. By the time Dardington discovers we have tricked him, it will be too late. The wager will have been lost, and we will already be in possession of our winnings."

Meredith sincerely doubted it would be as easy as her brothers insisted, but she needed to know the details of this ingenious plan, so she kept that opinion to herself.

"What precisely is the wager?" she asked. "A horse or a carriage race?"

"No. We are not foolish enough to bet against the marquess in a race," Jason stated emphatically. "I have

never heard of Dardington being beaten on horseback nor when racing his phaeton. He has nerves of steel, and even with disaster only a hairbreadth away, he won't pull up or hold back.

"I once saw him balance his carriage on its two left wheels as he shot around a narrow curve and overtook his rival. They were so close the men could have touched whips, but the marquess never faltered. His steady hand and boundless courage won the day."

There was no mistaking the admiration in her brother's voice as he related the tale, and that troubled Meredith deeply. The marquess was hardly the type of man she wanted her brothers' to emulate. They already had enough bad habits to overcome.

"If the wager does not concern racing, then what is it about?" Meredith asked again.

"Women," Jason admitted with a sly grin.

"Women!" A spot of color flared high on Meredith's cheeks. "When it comes to experience with the female sex, I am certain the marquess is far more knowledgeable than either of you." *Or both of you combined,* Meredith added silently to herself.

"Oh, no. In this instance the marquess just *thinks* he knows more," Jason said. He paused briefly for a moment as if he were carefully considering his words. "When the subject came up late last night, a rather heated debate ensued."

"A debate about women?" Meredith squeaked, fearful the gist of the discussion was about to take a most embarrassing direction. While she certainly did not consider herself a prude, there were some subjects she preferred not to discuss with her younger brothers.

"Our conversation turned to unmarried ladies, specifically those who are placed firmly on the shelf,"

Jasper explained. "Dardington insisted a spinster has no passion lurking within her soul, and I disagreed."

"As did I," Jason added. "Several other opinions were offered, and in the end Dardington proposed a wager. He said it would be impossible to get a confirmed spinster to passionately kiss a rake, but if we somehow managed it within the week, he would pay us each five hundred guineas."

"And if the spinster was passably pretty, he would throw in the bays for good measure," Jasper concluded with an eager grin.

Meredith nearly sighed with relief. Clearly the marquess was jesting with her brothers. "Getting a rake, a man who has an extremely limited moral code, to kiss a woman, spinster or otherwise, hardly involves any effort. I imagine a true rogue would kiss his horse and not think twice about it, if the poor animal was female."

Jasper and Jason both grinned.

"You are missing the subtle nuances, Merry," Jasper said, a smile still brightening his face. "Everyone knows a rake is a connoisseur of women and, given the opportunity, will chase nearly anything in skirts, even a woman who is firmly on the shelf.

"To win our wager, the woman must be the one who pursues the gentleman. She must be the one who initiates the kiss. That is the essence of the challenge."

Jason leaned closer to her. "And it must be a real kiss, lips firmly locked upon each other. A full, passionate embrace, given freely and with no regret."

"It appears you have given this a considerable amount of thought," Meredith stated dryly. " 'Tis a most frightening notion knowing that men of wealth, rank, and privilege spend their nights concocting these outrageous wagers. I can assure you almost no one

else cares in the least about spinsters and rakes kissing each other. Passionately or otherwise."

"There were some that felt far more physical involvement was necessary to prove our point. However—"

A fierce glare from his twin abruptly ended Jason's confession.

Meredith gritted her teeth, having a fair idea of what her brother had nearly revealed. "So you believe I should commend you for your restraint in limiting this wager to a single kiss?" Meredith asked, her brow raised.

"It is just a harmless bit of fun that won't hurt anyone," Jasper insisted hastily, glowering over her head at his twin.

"I'm not sure your poor, unsuspecting spinster will feel that way," Meredith retorted sharply.

She had always heard the betting book at White's was filled with absurd, ridiculous wagers concerning just about anything—the color of the coat worn by the third gentleman to enter the room, the exact time it began to rain on a particular afternoon, the number of flies on the wall. This preposterous wager her brothers had accepted amply demonstrated that point.

"No one will be harmed," Jasper said in a smooth tone. "Especially if you agree to help us."

For an instant Meredith was struck dumb. Then angry color flooded her cheeks. "You expect me to find and then persuade some unfortunate, unsuspecting woman to aid you in winning this ridiculous wager? For the love of God, have you lost all sense of decency?"

"You have misunderstood us completely," Jasper yelped as he sprang to his feet. "We would never think of, let alone ask you to perform, such a distasteful task."

"Never," Jason stated emphatically as he stood beside his brother.

Meredith stared at them for a long, hard moment. When she concluded the expressions of surprise, shock, and indignation on her brother's faces were genuine, her anger slowly disappeared.

"Then what are you asking of me?" she asked with a puzzled frown.

Jasper's eyes suddenly had great difficulty meeting her own. Meredith swung her gaze toward Jason. She saw his finger creep up to his cravat and tug insistently at it, attempting to adjust the fit around his neck. A nagging suspicion snaked through her mind.

" 'Tis me," she said in a voice of soft wonderment. "I am to be the spinster."

"Don't look so distressed," Jasper admonished. "It's a clever, flawless plan. Dardington will never suspect you."

"Never," Jason repeated enthusiastically. "In fact, I'm not even sure he realizes you are our sister." Jason rubbed the palms of his hands together gleefully. "The best part is that everyone in Society knows what a beautiful woman you are, so Dardington will have to pay out on the second half of the wager and give us the horses, too."

"Is that how you see me? A beautiful spinster-" Meredith choked off her words, unable to continue.

"For pity's sake, Merry, we would never call you a spinster," Jasper said, his expression suspiciously innocent. He moved the tip of his polished boot back and forth across a small section of the carpet. "However, you are well past the age when most women marry, and it seems unlikely you will form a union anytime soon."

A chill skittered along her spine. True, she was twenty-six years old and unmarried, with no immedi-

ate prospects to change that situation. But that was *her* choice.

Over the years she had lost count of the men whose marriage proposals she had rejected. Why, only last year the Earl of Monford had offered for her. He was a well-established nobleman in his early fifties, possessing an important title and an adequate income.

She had been both kind and gracious when refusing his offer, mentioning neither his lack of personal hygiene nor his inclination for conversation so boring it could be classified as mind-numbing as her main reasons for refusing his suit.

Meredith had always known she was different from other women of her class. At first the difference had confused her, but over the years she had learned to embrace and even celebrate her independence. She said it often and believed it totally—the opinion of others did not matter to her.

Yet why did it hurt so much to discover her brothers thought of her as a woman firmly on the shelf? A spinster!

"We thought you might find the wager amusing," Jason said. He glanced worriedly over her head at his twin.

Concern flickered in Jasper's eyes. "Your helping us win was meant to be a bit of fun. A lark."

Meredith suppressed the exasperated reply that sprang to mind and instead searched her heart to find the humor in this situation. Yet she was still feeling too ruffled to find any.

"Since you have already decided I would be the perfect spinster, I assume you have also selected the rake I am to kiss?"

"We would hardly allow our sister to kiss someone

we did not approve of," Jasper said with a great show of indignation.

"How comforting to know I can count on your diligent vigilance of both my person and reputation," Meredith said. "It warms a sister's heart to know how highly she is regarded by her brothers. So who is it to be?"

Her expression remained frozen as she jerked her head back and forth to stare at the men seated on either side of her. They both looked sheepishly back.

"Dardington proposed the terms of the wager," Jasper finally replied. "We thought it only fitting he should be the man who is kissed."

"Very clever." Meredith sniffed in a most unladylike manner, hardly surprised by the answer. "I applaud your ingenuity. If Dardington is the man kissed, there shall be no quibbling over the completion of the wager. I was wondering how you were going to prove the task had been accomplished, but frankly was afraid to ask."

She sucked in a painful breath. "However, I feel compelled to mention some flaws in your otherwise sterling idea. For example, what if I object to kissing Dardington?"

Jasper and Jason's immediate scowls gave Meredith a wicked sense of satisfaction. Apparently this contingency had never even been considered.

"He is a very handsome, well-turned-out gentleman," Jason sputtered. He looked at his brother in confusion.

"I'm sure you would like him," Jasper added.

Meredith tilted her head to one side as if she were carefully considering the matter. "And if I do not?"

"I suppose you could chose another man," Jason replied slowly. "But he must be a rake. Are you acquainted with any?"

"Gracious, how and where would an old, on-the-shelf spinster such as myself have the opportunity to meet a gentleman with an unsavory reputation?"

There was no mistaking the embarrassment etched on Jasper and Jason's faces. Yet their clear discomfort did not completely ease the hurt she felt.

"You have made your point, Merry," Jason declared stoically. "We apologize."

"As well you should." Meredith bristled as she arranged and then rearranged the folds of her skirt. She tried holding on to her anger, but their guilty remorse ate at her conscience.

Their plan might be outrageous, but she had done far worse than kiss a gentleman of questionable reputation over the years to shield and protect her brothers.

"Instead of going through with this ridiculous scheme, why don't I purchase the bays from the marquess? I'm sure he will accept a fair price for them." Meredith suggested. "I will, of course, retain ownership of the animals so the poor creatures cannot again be used as gambling collateral, but would keep them here in London, at your disposal, to be used whenever either of you wished."

The twins looked appalled at the notion. "The horses are part of a standing wager. You cannot simply buy them."

"Why not?"

"It just isn't done," Jasper insisted.

Meredith shook her head in puzzlement and rose to her feet. As far as she was concerned the discussion was ended. In a moment of weakness, she had offered to acquire the horses her brothers seem to covet so keenly, but they had rejected her offer in favor of some antiquated male code of gambling honor she could not begin to understand.

Meredith strode to the door, then paused to look back at her brothers. "I politely suggest you both now turn your efforts toward a way to legally obtain the coin needed to cover this bet. For it seems rather certain that despite your *flawless plan* to emerge victorious, you shall instead be the losers in this wager."

Three

"What are you doing?" the sultry redhead asked as she turned her head languidly on the pillow.

Trevor Morely, Marquess of Dardington, stiffened slightly at the sound of her voice. Yet he never hesitated as he tugged on his black evening trousers and began to calmly button them, half hoping if he ignored her, she would remain silent.

"Darling, come back to bed," the female voice insisted. "It won't be light for hours, and my dreadful husband never returns until the dawn has broken."

Trevor lifted his head and gazed with a practiced eye at the naked woman sprawled among the bed linens. Lady Melody Ramsey was a sight to behold, with her tousled red hair, flushed face, and creamy white skin. It was rumored among the *ton* that she was able to do most anything a man could want or even imagine. After tonight, Trevor could testify that claim was not an exaggeration.

Lady Ramsey's expertise in the bedroom went beyond mere skill. She was inventive, aggressive and incredibly lovely. So why was he donning his trousers instead of removing them?

" 'Tis late, Melody." He smiled gently, hoping to avoid a scene. "And I'm tired."

Trevor shifted restlessly, searching the moonlit room

for the remainder of his clothing. He discovered his silver patterned waistcoat and linen shirt draped over a chair back, but could locate neither his stockings nor his shoes.

"You shall hurt my feelings if you leave so soon," Melody pouted. Her voice was playful, but there was expectation in it, too. She rolled off the bed in a quick, efficient movement and walked toward him, her heavy breasts swaying.

Trevor grinned despite his mild annoyance. Her athletic mobility was one of the reasons he had found her such an exhausting bed partner—that, along with her seemingly insatiable sexual appetite.

For a man who had spent the last eight years of his life intent only on forgetting, on living life for the moment, she was the perfect match. As with most of his women, she required little effort. No sweet phrases or coy wooing, no grand seduction or forceful embraces were needed to get her on her back.

And yet after spending two nights in her bed, Trevor was already feeling restless—bored, almost, though given Melody's inventive nature that seemed a ridiculous notion.

She must have sensed his distraction. As she came within reach, Melody struck a provocative pose and gave a low soft moan. Instinctively Trevor braced himself, thinking she was going to fling herself at him.

Instead she gracefully extended her arms, her eyes glittering with seductive intent. She touched his naked chest with the tips of her fingers, slowly gliding them down his torso until they came to rest on the top of his trousers.

Trevor drew in a sharp breath when those nimble fingers stroked him through the fabric. With practiced efficiency, Melody slipped the first gold button free, then the second and third. Trevor's mouth twisted, and

he wondered how he was going to escape without mortally offending her.

But the handsome marquess was too long in making up his mind. Without the protection of his garments, he was an easy target and Melody took full advantage of it. She greedily reached inside his open trousers with both hands, drawing him out. She stroked him slowly with her palm, finding his most sensitive places with unerring accuracy.

"It appears you are not so *very* tired," Melody pronounced with relish as she cupped his testicles, squeezing gently.

Trevor shut his eyes. He briefly entertained the notion of stepping away from his insatiable partner, but she had dropped to her knees before him. One vigorous pull of her mouth destroyed any thoughts of leaving. She blew a stream of hot breath over his straining penis and the marquess groaned at the sensation. His hands fell to her head, spanning her skull and holding her firmly in place.

He took a deep breath, his chest heaving with the effort. Trevor gave himself up to the passion, reasoning that if he brought Melody to whimpering pleasure, rode her hard and long, she would fall deeply asleep, and then he would be able to make his escape in blissful silence.

"You are late."

Forcing himself to a civility of tone he was far from feeling, Trevor replied calmly, "Yes, I am. Would you like me to leave?"

He struck a casual pose and waited. Trevor's father, the Duke of Warwick, flicked a chilly gaze over his son.

"Sit down," the duke commanded after only a brief

hesitation. "It has already taken you three days to answer my summons. If you leave now, lord only knows when you will see fit to return."

Deciding it would be in his best interests not to provoke the duke further, Trevor complied, though he wondered at his father's fairly mild response. In the past, a battle of wills between the duke and his heir would not have been so easily conceded.

Yet as he settled himself in an upholstered gilt chair near the blazing fire, Trevor remained wary. Though he saw his father rarely, it seemed each time he did, the duke was increasingly ill-tempered and petulant.

"The weather is exceedingly fine this afternoon," Trevor said conversationally. "I noticed many green buds on the trees as I rode through Hyde Park. Perhaps we shall have an early spring."

"I did not ask you here to discuss the damned weather!" The duke cast him a glare that would have withered a lesser man, but Trevor returned the stare with equal measure.

"I was merely trying to engage in polite conversation," Trevor said evenly. "We speak so rarely I thought it might be refreshing to begin our discussion on a civil note for a change."

The duke grunted. "You're a fine one to be speaking of civility and polite conversation. Those ruffians and reprobates you spend your days and nights carousing with wouldn't know a civil discussion if it came up and bit them on the arse."

"And therein lies the essence of their charm," Trevor replied. He settled himself back against his chair, crossing his booted feet at the ankles. No matter how cruelly provoked this afternoon, the marquess was determined not to be baited.

"Have you eaten?"

Trevor blinked in surprise at the unexpected ques-

tion. A grumble from his empty stomach gave the answer before the marquess could voice it, and the duke nodded his head in understanding.

Instead of ringing for a servant, the duke walked to the door and opened it. A footman stationed outside snapped to attention. "Tell Cook the marquess is hungry. I want a meal served to him here within the hour. A combination of hot and cold dishes will be fine, but make certain to include a lemon cake for dessert. 'Tis his lordship's favorite." The duke glanced back at Trevor. "And tell Harper to bring up another bottle of wine."

The servant bowed deeply and rushed off to do his master's bidding.

"Thank you, sir," Trevor said cautiously. He suspected his father had ulterior motives for demonstrating such benevolent concern, but surprisingly his suspicion left Trevor feeling a distinct sense of guilt. "I find that I am rather hungry."

"I doubt you can remember the last time you had a decent meal," the duke grumbled as he crossed the room to stand near Trevor's chair. "I don't know why you insist upon living in those squalled rooms on St. James Street when you have a perfectly fine home right here."

"My quarters are hardly squalid," Trevor replied. "Especially if one takes into account the substantial rent I pay. More importantly, the size and location of my rooms suit my needs perfectly. I want for nothing else."

"I still say it is unnatural to prefer them to all of this," the duke proclaimed, lifting his hand in a sweeping gesture. "If you lived in a proper establishment, you would be taking better care of yourself. You are far too thin."

It galled Trevor to realize his father was correct. He

had lost weight this past winter after suffering from a nasty cold and had yet to regain it. But he was determined to make light of the situation.

"A man of fashion cannot have a protruding stomach. It totally ruins the smooth line of one's waistcoat," Trevor replied airily.

"Prinny's stomach protrudes noticeably and he fancies himself a real connoisseur of fashion," the duke said.

Trevor smiled in private amusement. "That is true. However, it is my understanding that the Regent does not button his waistcoat completely unless he is wearing a corset."

"He is still a fool, no matter how he is dressed," the duke grumbled.

He took the chair opposite his son and glowered. Trevor wasn't certain if his father's annoyance sprang from his dislike of the Regent or his disapproval of his son, yet he realized philosophically it was most likely a combination of both.

A silence settled over the room. Trevor regarded his father patiently, knowing the duke would reveal the true reason for this summons when he was good and ready and not a moment sooner.

Despite his age, the duke was still an impressive, aristocratic presence, possessing towering height and a sharp, authoritative voice that could reduce many a servant, male and female, to trembling tears.

Trevor had feared his father when he was a young boy, held him in awe as an adolescent, and grown to respect and admire him tremendously when he reached adulthood. Yet that, like so many other aspects of Trevor's life, had changed dramatically at Lavinia's death.

"I won't bother to ask what has kept you away from my house for so long," the duke began. "I am well

aware you spend your time and money in all manner of salacious pursuits. I shudder to imagine the depths to which your debauchery has sunk.

"Drinking, gambling, womanizing." The duke shook his head. "With all the advantages you have been given in life, the rank, privilege, and wealth, you choose instead to live the life of a ne'er-do-well, without purpose, without restraint, without basic morality. I raised you to be a noble gentleman, a peer of the realm, and this is how I'm repaid for my efforts."

He regarded his son shrewdly. Trevor held his ground beneath that razor-sharp gaze. He also wisely held his tongue.

"I expected more from my only child than a son who's retreated from the world," the duke concluded. "Who has retreated from me."

Trevor's fists clenched, but he forced himself to remain calm. Father and son had already had this discussion many times, and the end result had never changed. Trevor continued to live his life exactly as he pleased, and his father continued to vehemently disapprove.

"You have accused me of being an overly licentious man, yet that is clearly an activity I certainly cannot pursue without venturing forth into the world." Trevor slowly released his clenched fist. "Please do make up your mind, sir."

The marquess's response squarely hit the mark, but his father had no opportunity to vent the anger that visibly rose to the surface, for a knock sounded at the door.

"Enter," the duke called out.

The butler appeared, leading a procession of footmen, each carrying a silver tray. He bowed solicitously

toward his employer, then gave a polite nod of greeting to Trevor.

"Would you care to eat by the fire, Your Grace, or do you prefer the window overlooking the south garden?"

"The fire."

The first footman set down his laden silver tray and stepped forward. Under the keen eye of the butler, the servant efficiently moved a round wooden table near the fireplace and positioned it between Trevor and the duke.

The moment it was set properly in place, the next footman moved ahead. His arm muscles bulged under the weight of the tray he carried, which held an assortment of china plates, linen napkins, silver cutlery, and crystal goblets.

The table was quickly laid out with the proper plates, cutlery, and glasses for a five-course meal. There was even a small cut glass vase filled with fresh flowers to serve as a centerpiece. Trevor watched in slight amazement as the staff bustled about with deft precision. He knew his father had a well-trained staff and Harper, the butler, was known to be a hard, yet fair, taskmaster.

Yet the proficiency displayed came not only from good and proper training, but from experience. Obviously the servants had performed this task numerous times before, for no detail was left to chance.

But why would they be serving meals in the drawing room when the house boasted a formal dining room, two smaller dining salons, and a breakfast room? Did his father dine alone so often that he had begun to forsake the vast, cold formality of the dining room? Were the even slightly smaller dining salons so unwelcoming a place to partake of a meal on one's own?

Could his father possibly be lonely? The thought

forced a rather distressing observation on Trevor's conscience.

To distract himself from these unsettling thoughts, the marquess turned his full attention to the servants as they uncovered the various dishes.

A savory soup of fresh vegetables, tender chicken stewed in wine and flavored with thyme, thick slices of cured ham, poached Dover sole, creamed potatoes, peas, marzipan tarts, strawberries, and the requested lemon cake were all displayed with dignified formality.

Trevor attacked his meal. The food was piping hot, perfectly seasoned, and delicious. Though he would never admit it to his father, the marquess realized it had been a long time since he had eaten such fine food. He soon found himself savoring every forkful.

When he joined his male companions for supper, they were far more interested in the quality of the brandy, the quantity of wine, and the availability of the serving wenches for entertainment after the meal than the variety or quality of the food.

Realizing he could not possibly swallow another bite, the marquess at last settled his fork upon his plate. He looked up and leaned back in his chair with a satisfied sigh. The duke had apparently finished. His plates and cutlery were already cleared from the table. All that remained before the duke was a half empty goblet of wine.

The footmen removed Trevor's dishes, but at the duke's command left a second bottle of wine and the goblets. As he faced his father across the table, Trevor realized his apprehension as well as his hunger had been appeased. Partly due to the excellent bottle of wine he and his father had consumed, no doubt.

"I want you to attend Lady Dermond's ball tomor-

row evening," the duke announced abruptly. "There is someone I'd like you to meet."

Trevor blinked. The goblet in his hand began tilting. Catching himself before the red liquid spilled out and stained the linen cloth, he set the crystal to rights. "I have already made plans for tomorrow evening."

"Break them."

"I could not possibly on such short notice."

"If you had answered my summons immediately, as I requested, you would have had ample time to make your excuses." The duke scowled. "I have told several people, including the hostess and the lady you are to meet, that you will be in attendance. I want you at that ball."

"Matchmaking, sir?" Trevor arched his brow at an insulting angle. "I thought only desperate maiden aunts and scheming mamas indulged in that distasteful task."

"Don't turn your nose up at me, boy," the duke responded with an indignant sniff. "You were singing a far different tune when I paired you with your first wife."

His wife! The unexpected mention of Lavinia caught the marquess unawares, igniting once again the tormenting ache in his heart he tried so desperately to control.

A rush of painful memories flooded Trevor's mind. Her sweet smile, her merry laugh, her loving embrace, the pale, cold stillness of her lifeless body. The endless questions and recriminations that had haunted him for years once again felt fresh and raw.

He drew in a deep breath. Over the years, Trevor had kept well hidden from his stoic father the suffering and heartache, the agonizing guilt he felt every single day.

"I am not interested in acquiring a wife," Trevor

stated forcefully. "Besides, you know well my opinion of these unmarried young women. I have no intention of wasting an evening by furthering the acquaintance of this year's crop of shrews, ninnies, or milk-and-water misses."

"The woman I have in mind for you is older, more mature," the duke countered. "And she is no fool."

"Ahh, that means she must be formal and cold." Trevor shuddered visibly. "I repeat, I am not interested. In the least."

Ignoring the disgruntled expression on his father's face, Trevor rose to his feet. "I thank you for your hospitality this afternoon, but you must excuse me, sir. I am already late for another appointment. Please extend my compliments to Cook. The meal was delicious."

The marquess bowed formally, then turned on his heel. As he exited the room, Trevor told himself the expression of hurt and disappointment on his father's face was merely an act, an attempt at manipulation that was going to fail.

The marquess repeated those words in his mind as he walked through the long picture gallery, while a multitude of ancestors and former dukes stared down disapprovingly at him from their gilded frames.

His feet moved rapidly down the winding staircase, increasing speed with each step. Upon reaching the cavernous entrance hall, the marquess told himself yet again that his father's distress was feigned, his lack of protest at Trevor's refusal to attend the ball merely a ploy to prey on Trevor's guilt.

It was not until he burst outside into the fading afternoon light and filled his lungs deeply with a breath of cool, fresh air that Trevor was able to admit the truth.

Despite the discord, strain and general imperfection,

the relationship he had with his father was something the marquess valued greatly. And though he was loath to admit it, his father's opinion mattered. Strangely, it mattered very much.

Lady Meredith Barrington sat alone in Lady Dermond's ladies' retiring room, staring doubtfully at her reflection in the mirror. She adjusted her diamond ear-bobs, then lifted her neck to admire the matching diamond necklace that graced her throat. The jewels were her mother's, borrowed for this madcap evening. Meredith had hoped they would lend an air of sophistication to her evening ensemble. She realized belatedly what she really needed was a dose of courage.

Her new gown was a deep shade of blue, cut daringly lower than any other she had ever worn. It was gathered beneath the bodice and flowed down the lines of her body with simplicity and grace. Despite the changing fashion, Meredith had insisted the skirt of the gown be left unadorned.

She had always preferred simple styles without the fripperies of lace, bows, embroidery, or beading, but it had taken her years to convince her modistes she was not trying to economize on her outfits by leaving those items off.

Yet tonight Meredith almost wished she had a few rows of lace or a collection of bows to draw attention to the skirt of her gown, for the simple, unadorned style made her look taller and more curvaceous. With a sigh, she stood up and twisted from side to side, critically observing the sway of material as she moved.

The fabric was sheer, and if viewed in the gleaming candlelight at a particular angle, the distinct shadow of her body could be seen. Meredith let out a nervous

giggle. It was most definitely not the type of ensemble worn by a spinster.

Knowing she had stalled long enough, Meredith prepared to leave. She had just begun to tug on her evening gloves when the retiring room door suddenly opened. Meredith spun around in surprise at the interruption.

"Oh, I am sorry. Did we startle you, Lady Meredith?"

"Not at all," Merry replied breathlessly. She inclined her head politely toward Mrs. Fritzwater and her daughter. Alice? Allyson? Meredith had met the young woman only once and could not recall her name.

"My dear Alice had a slight mishap while exiting the carriage," Mrs. Fritzwater explained as she held up a length of lace with several bows dangling from it. "I had hoped one of Lady Dermond's maids would be in attendance here so it could be repaired."

Meredith glanced down at the skirt of Alice's gown. There were several rows of lace adorned with both rosettes and bows along the hem. Meredith looked carefully, but it was impossible to tell where this section had been torn.

"You cannot even notice anything is missing," Meredith said.

"Really?" Mrs. Fritzwater bent down to examine the skirt. "You're right. It doesn't appear that the fabric has been ripped. Still, I would feel so much better if the dress was properly repaired."

Mrs. Fritzwater leaned toward Meredith and whispered, "I just want everything to be perfect this evening. This is Alice's first ball."

Meredith cast a sympathetic eye toward Alice. The young girl's eyes were wide and round and her complexion looked very pale. Clearly all of her mother's

nervous fluttering was not helping her daughter conquer her own fears.

"I shall have a maid sent in directly to assist you," Meredith said.

"How very kind of you, Lady Meredith," Mrs. Fritzwater replied with obvious relief.

"I hope you enjoy your first ball, Alice," Meredith said as she jerked open the door. "You look lovely."

Alice blushed shyly and modestly bowed her head. As Meredith started out the door, she saw Mrs. Fritzwater adjust the stray curl that lay against Alice's cheek, then deliberately tug the scooped neckline of the girl's bodice up a full half inch.

For a moment Meredith felt a sharp pang of longing for her own mother. Though they had difficulty understanding each other, the Countess of Stafford had always loyally supported and defended her daughter.

Meredith was unsure what her parents would think of this current situation. She secretly doubted they would agree or approve of what she was about to do, but she knew they would never voice that disapproval to anyone outside the family.

It took only a few moments for Meredith to locate a footman. She quickly told the servant of young Alice's plight. He bowed and assured her a maid and a sewing basket would be sent immediately to the ladies' retiring room.

Her task completed, Meredith next turned her eye toward the grand ballroom on the second floor. The strains of music could be clearly heard, along with the sound of muted conversation and twinkling laughter. Though it was not yet ten, the ball was already crowded—a rare occurrence, since these events usually began later in the evening.

Meredith hesitated at the bottom of the steps, knowing in her heart she shouldn't be here. Yet she had

promised her brothers she would make a valiant effort to win their ridiculous bet.

She had been prompted by a rash impulse, but once she had given her word, Meredith felt compelled to keep it. The biggest obstacle she faced now was her own good sense. Fearing it would prevail before she reached the entrance, Meredith forced herself to begin the long climb up the staircase, ignoring completely the voice in her head that insisted she should turn on her heel and depart.

For four days, Jason and Jasper's silent pleas, forlorn looks, and heavy sighs of disappointment had driven her to distraction. And it was said that women were prone to dramatics!

She had resisted with a gritty determination, telling herself over and over again she would not even entertain such a preposterous notion. Besides, she reminded her brothers each afternoon at tea and each evening at dinner, how was she going to kiss the marquess if she never saw him?

He apparently did not attend many *ton* functions. The only place in Society he was seen on a regular basis was Hyde Park. Yet a chance encounter where the nobility spent the afternoon riding about in open carriages and on horseback was hardly the opportune moment to try to kiss the marquess passionately.

This practical dilemma had kept the twins busy scheming and plotting for two days. Time on the bet was running out, and Meredith had begun to congratulate herself on so neatly diverting her brothers' attention. However, her smug attitude of success was apparently premature.

Late last night the twins had wakened her from a sound sleep to gleefully report that the marquess was indeed about to attend a society function that would afford her the perfect opportunity to win the bet.

So here she stood, ready to enter Lady Dermond's ballroom in search of the Marquess of Dardington, with the sole intention of luring him to a secluded location and then kissing him in a most passionate manner. Madness, it was pure madness!

"Good evening, Lady Meredith."

That shrill female voice could belong to only one individual. With a cool smile, Meredith turned and faced the Duchess of Lancaster, one of the most ignorant, annoying, and petty females of the *beau monde*.

"Your Grace. Lord Byrd." Meredith dipped a slight curtsy toward the duchess and her escort. "How pleasant to see you both."

"This is a surprise," the duchess declared with a haughtily raised eyebrow. "I was unaware you had come to town this Season."

"I've only recently arrived," Meredith lied smoothly. She felt the woman's keen gaze skim her from head to toe. The glint of jealousy that flashed in the other woman's eyes was brief, but distinct.

Meredith nearly sighed. She had hoped that with time the duchess would eventually forget Meredith had rejected marriage proposals from both the duke and Lord Hawke, a former lover of the duchess. Apparently she had not.

"You appear to be without escort this evening," the duchess observed slyly. "Perchance have you come as a chaperon for one of the younger ladies? Or perhaps you are serving as a companion for one of the elderly dowagers?"

"You are so witty, Your Grace." One corner of Meredith's mouth turned up. "I am neither a chaperon nor a companion. My two *male* escorts await me inside the ballroom."

"Really?"

"Yes."

"Then we shall take you to them," the duchess declared.

"You are too kind, Your Grace," Meredith said. She turned toward Lord Byrd with a deliberate smile of encouragement. "I have a small errand to attend to first. It should take me no more than ten minutes. Will you wait for me here?"

"Of course," Lord Byrd answered. He bowed low to better ogle her bosom and offered her a sly wink.

Meredith somehow managed to keep a half smile on her lips. In her opinion, Lord Byrd was the worst sort of male. He had married an heiress to obtain control of her fortune and now kept his meek, frail wife hidden away on his country estate.

It was said the only time he ever visited the poor woman was to get her with child so she would be forced to remain in the country. The rest of Lord Byrd's time was spent in London, in pursuit of any and all selfish pleasures.

"Did you say ten minutes, Lady Meredith?" the duchess inquired, tapping her fan rapidly against her palm.

"At the very least," Meredith replied smoothly.

"Perhaps it would be best if we went on without you," the duchess decided.

Meredith inclined her head graciously, pleased to see the pursed expression on the duchess's face. The pair bowed and left her, but Meredith knew her fate was sealed. She could not possibly leave without entering the ballroom, or else the duchess would believe she had somehow managed to force her away.

Still, Meredith was determined to make a her initial entrance as quietly as possible. She waited a full fifteen minutes and then quickly climbed the stairs to the second floor.

With a deft movement, Meredith was able to avoid the pompously garbed majordomo loudly announcing each guest's arrival. Thus she slipped into the crush, scarcely noticed by anyone.

Her brothers had escorted her to the party, but she knew she would not find them in the ballroom, dancing attendance on any of the females. Instead they would be barricaded in the card room. Meredith decided she would find them at the first opportunity and insist they each engage young Alice Fritzwater in a dance. It was the very least they could do.

For once Meredith was not averse to her brothers' great regard for gambling. She was nervous enough about this evening. Having the twins scrutinizing her every move would be most unsettling.

Meredith began a slow circuit on the perimeter of the ballroom, positioning herself so she had a clear view of most of the guests. An odd shiver marked its way down her back as she suddenly spied the marquess across the room.

Trevor had always had a certain style of dress that was distinctly his own. Though garbed similarly to the other gentlemen in a black evening coat, embroidered silk waistcoat, and knee breeches, there was a certain casual elegance about the marquess's attire that eclipsed those around him.

He was engaged in conversation with Lady Ann Towers, a leggy brunette who was rumored to have been his mistress last year. Or was it the year before? Meredith couldn't remember. Dardington's name was linked with so many different women it was difficult to keep them all straight.

It seemed as though nearly every married and widowed woman in Society beneath the age of forty had been thought to be his mistress at one time or another.

Meredith inwardly grimaced. If only half the gossip

were true, the marquess would undoubtedly be the most exhausted man in all of England.

Yet he did not look exhausted. He looked fit and trim. Certainly older than the last time she had seen him, but that was to be expected.

She continued to observe him from afar and noticed his eyes darting about the room. Poor Lady Ann. Though possessing both a lovely face and figure, she clearly did not have the necessary wit to keep the marquess entertained for any length of time.

To her credit, it did not take much longer for Lady Ann to apparently reach the same conclusion. With an aristocratic tip of her chin, she turned on her heel and stalked away from the marquess. He barely seemed to notice.

The moment he was alone, Meredith made her move.

Four

Trevor had deliberately positioned himself on the left side of the ballroom with a clear view of the grand staircase. Though he tried hard not to make it very obvious, his eyes were constantly drawn to the staircase as each guest was announced.

The marquess had arrived at the ball unfashionably early, hoping his father would do the same. He had sent word to the duke this morning, informing his father he would be in attendance at Lady Dermond's ball. There had been no reply to the message, but Trevor had not expected any.

He still could not say for certain whether a moment of madness or guilt had brought him here this evening. Although he was at a loss to explain his motives, Trevor acknowledged he was now committed to the endeavor and must see it through.

". . . and that is when I told the fellow he was all wet," the Earl of Kendale declared loudly.

There were titters from the ladies and bellows of laughter from the gentlemen who stood within the circle of conversation. Trevor turned his head away from the milling scene in the ballroom and attempted to look interested in the discussion.

There had been many surprised looks sent his way when he first entered the room. He had ignored them

and intentionally joined a small group of males and females brought together by a single bond—their love of gossip.

Trevor reasoned his unexpected appearance would make him the natural topic of whispers and speculations. And so it had. Yet by ingratiating himself within the group that thrived on it, he had managed to shift some of the attention away from himself.

This select group might be a rude, stuffy, and possessing an inflated opinion of their importance, but there was not one among them, male or female, who possessed the courage to repeat any unsavory speculation about the marquess while he was standing in front of them.

"The earl can be most tedious at times," the woman at Trevor's side remarked as she leaned into him. "But he does tell the most amusing tales."

She spoke in a flirtatious whisper that Trevor found oddly annoying. Though accustomed to female attention, this young matron surprised him with her boldness, for her husband stood directly across from them.

For a brief second he debated walking away, but then realized he would just be forced to join another equally annoying group of individuals.

He blew out a breath and wished he was holding a tall glass filled with whiskey. It was a humbling and not altogether pleasant realization to admit how much he felt the need for a drink. He had limited himself to a half bottle of wine with his dinner and had downed only one glass of whiskey since his arrival. Clearly that was not a sufficient amount of alcohol to sustain him through the evening.

An elderly couple emerged from the crowd and strode toward him.

"Dardington? Is that you?" the gentleman called out in amazement.

Trevor smiled faintly in greeting. He recognized their faces, but could not for the life of him recall their names. Yet their timing could not have been more fortuitous. The flirtatious matron by his side whispered something vulgar under her breath and quickly took her leave.

"Good evening," he said pleasantly, presenting a polite bow to his rescuers.

They chatted briefly, then left to greet other friends. Trevor felt a slight flush of embarrassment as they left, for he was still unable to recall precisely who they were.

Yet he was pleased to finally be alone. Restlessly the marquess observed the preening young ladies, blustering men, and scheming mamas who stood amongst the crowd, and concluded once again what he really needed was a large glass of strong spirits to deaden his brain.

Alas, that would not be possible until after he left the ball. Trevor was resolved to be on his best behavior this evening. He would ignore the smug smile that was certain to be on his father's face when he greeted him, be charmingly polite to the woman the duke insisted he should meet, ask her to dance once and only once, and when that arduous duty was completed he would take his leave. Immediately.

Thus he would fulfill his familial obligations and perhaps avoid his father's censure for a few weeks. Or maybe even months.

But where the devil was his father? He could hardly perform this act of generosity if the duke did not make an appearance soon. With the woman he hoped to marry off to his son.

Frustrated, Trevor again glanced at the main staircase. He saw a tall, curvaceous woman dressed in blue avoid being announced by cleverly stepping behind

the majordomo and gliding down the stairs. Her reason for anonymity intrigued him, yet her breathtaking beauty kept his eyes upon her as she attempted to melt into the crowd.

Her pale lustrous skin glowed in the candlelight, her simple unadorned gown showcased full breasts and a lovely neck. She was taller than most of the women and many of the men in the room, so it took little effort to follow her progress, even though she kept to the edges of the ballroom.

Something about her seemed oddly familiar, but at this distance Trevor could not be certain he knew her. She seemed more like a dream conjured up from his adolescence, an ethereal beauty who was the very picture of grace, elegance, and raw sensuality.

"I heard a rumor you were here, but needed to see the proof of it with my own eyes before I could believe it to be true."

Trevor turned to find one of his former lovers, Lady Ann Tower, standing beside him. Dark-haired and dark-eyed, Ann was pretty and intelligent, a widow who enjoyed her independence. Their affair had been brief and torrid, and she was one of a select few Trevor chose to remember with affection.

But not at this moment. His eyes and mind had been captivated by the blond beauty. Fortunately Lady Ann was intelligent enough to realize that Trevor had other, more pressing matters on his mind. After exchanging polite greetings, she made no further attempt to invade his privacy and merely smiled at the distracted farewell the marquess bestowed upon her when she left.

Frustrated, Trevor once again searched the crowd for the blond beauty. He felt a surprising amount of regret when he could not find her, but she seemed to have vanished.

He turned to lift a glass of champagne from the

silver tray of a passing servant and then, miraculously, unexpectedly, she stood before him. His breath caught. Odd that lately he felt indifferent to the charms of so many females, and yet the sight of this particular woman could affect him so completely.

She nodded regally in his direction, then dipped a low, graceful curtsy. As she regained her feet, her blue eyes flashed, and he suddenly recognized her. His back went stiff with shock. With painful clarity he recalled precisely who she was and exactly how he had come to know her.

Trevor's need for a tall glass of whiskey increased tenfold.

Steadfastly ignoring the flitter of nerves in her stomach, Meredith approached the marquess. Her progress across the room drew little attention among the crowd, though several male heads turned as she glided gracefully past them.

He was not looking in her direction when she approached. For a moment she wasn't certain how to best gain his attention. Meredith was about to loudly clear her throat when she realized her knees were shaking.

Good heavens, she had not felt this nervous when she had been presented at court.

As she struggled to control the knocking of her knees, the marquess lifted a glass of champagne from a passing servant, then turned toward her. His initial gaze of curiosity and delight turned to puzzlement, and then utter surprise.

"Meredith," he whispered.

"Good evening, my . . . my lord."

Meredith wished she had the nerve to address him

as Trevor, but it seemed far too presumptuous despite all they had shared in the past.

Though the years had wrought changes, he was still a commanding man. Handsome seemed too mild a word to describe his looks. He was like some golden god, spun from brilliant sunlight, created by magnificent sorcery. Yet for all the beauty in his face and form, it was his eyes that spoke to her. Despite his youth, they were old. Old and filled with a weariness buried within their depths she had never seen.

"Champagne?" he asked, lifting a second glass from a servant who stood silently near.

Though her mouth was dry, Meredith refused the drink. The marquess shrugged his broad shoulders. Instead of returning the untouched flute of bubbling wine, he lifted it to his lips, tilted his head back, and emptied it in one long swallow. He quickly repeated the gesture with the goblet he held in his other hand.

Meredith glanced at the silver tray the footman held. Among the empty glasses were three crystal flutes filled to the brim. The marquess placed his goblets on the tray. His hand moved fractionally toward one of the filled flutes, then hesitated.

As if sensing her intense regard, his head turned toward her.

Their eyes met. She lifted her brow fractionally, almost daring him to pick up another glass. A ghost of a smile appeared at the corner of his mouth.

"No words of disapproval?" he asked in a daring tone.

" 'Tis hardly my place," she replied demurely.

"That rarely stops a female from commenting with a scowl of her brow and a click of her tongue."

Meredith smiled. "I am not like other women, my lord."

"I remember."

She blinked at him, suddenly uncertain. For a brief second, there had been a glimpse of the man she had known, carefree, fun-loving, mischievous. The man Lavinia had loved so completely.

It hurt to remember. Meredith expected it would feel strange to see him again, but she had not known how hard it would be.

"It has been a long time," he said, forsaking a third goblet of champagne.

"Eight years," Meredith whispered. She looked over at him.

His face was carefully expressionless, but she had the distinct feeling he was about to rebuke her. With a start she realized he must be experiencing the same feelings of loss and regret and pain that she felt. It was as if this meeting had brought to the forefront a wealth of shared memories of Lavinia—tragic, sad memories.

Dimly Meredith heard the strains of music as the orchestra began to prepare for the next dance. She assumed the marquess would be most anxious to depart from her company, for she now understood why her unexpected presence could be considered unwanted and unwarranted.

She nearly let it happen. Yet before the back of her throat closed completely with emotion, Meredith blurted, "Will you dance with me, my lord?"

The marquess said nothing. His head tilted, his golden brows pulled together in puzzlement.

"I own I consumed a fair amount of wine with my dinner, a drink of whiskey upon my arrival, and two glasses of champagne, yet I am not so far gone I cannot remember the rules of polite society. Ladies do not ask gentleman to dance."

His frown deepened. "Or has there been some cataclysmic event that has changed everything we know

to be proper and correct? If that is true, I am damned sorry to have missed it."

"Neither of us have ever subscribed to the dictates of polite society. Besides, you just said *damn* in my presence, proof positive you do not think of me as a lady. And if I am not a lady then I am not bound by any silly rules of convention." She slowly let out her breath and slanted an amused look in his direction. "So, my lord, will you dance with me? I believe the next set is to be a waltz."

"You always had a reputation for being unconventional, Lady Meredith, not scandalous. Shall I assume from your current behavior you plan on changing?"

"If you dance with me, sir, perhaps you will learn the answer."

It was an invitation no man could resist. He extended his gloved hand. She placed her fingers lightly in his palm, and the marquess escorted her onto the dance floor. He chose a position on the far side of the room. Deliberately? So they would not be so clearly in view?

Meredith suspected that was his motive, but whatever the reason she was grateful. The extra steps provided a little time for her to compose herself.

They made their proper bow and curtsy just as the dance began. Meredith felt the marquess's hand tighten around her waist, and her hard-won composure slipped fractionally. She rested one hand ever so lightly upon his broad shoulder and obediently linked the fingers of her other hand with his.

Meredith felt the warm contact through their gloves. She worried for a moment that he was aware of the tension that had gripped her the instant they touched, but Meredith had no time to ponder the peculiar sensations afflicting her, for the dance had begun.

She believed she was prepared for it, but her breath

caught as they revolved and whirled down the floor. She kept her gaze fixed over his shoulder and her lips pressed tightly. The marquess held her at the proper distance, yet why did it feel so intimate?

They remained silent through the first part of the dance. Meredith could feel his eyes on her, studying her intently with a highly charged gaze. Her stomach knotted and twisted, and she chided herself for such a foolish reaction.

She was not a young debutante, wide-eyed with wonder at her first ball. She had danced with countless gentlemen in her life. Men who flattered her outrageously, pledged undying devotion and love, threatened to do themselves bodily harm if she did not look upon them with favor.

Yet she found none of these bucks as compelling as being held in the arms of the Marquess of Dardington. That surprising realization troubled her greatly.

"You disappoint me, Lady Meredith. Luring me onto the dance floor with subtle hints of outrageous behavior and then retreating behind a wall of proper silence. 'Tis most unfair."

She gave him a tentative smile. "Please, forgive my proper, reflective behavior. I shall endeavor most studiously to utter something of monumental impropriety the moment I catch my breath."

"Excellent."

"Ahh, now I am truly feeling the pressure to be sparkling and witty." She felt his shrewd eyes on her face, but surprisingly her nerves began to ease. He led her into a graceful turn and her mouth curved broadly. "You must allow me a moment to marshal my composure, or I shall trod upon your shiny shoes. It has been a long time since I danced a waltz."

"I do not believe you."

" 'Tis true." She paused a moment, allowing the

enchanting music and graceful rhythm of the dance to lull her. She felt like she was floating as the cool air rushed by her cheek. "I spend the majority of my evenings at home. There is hardly anyone appropriate to waltz with, though I suppose if I were desperate I could ask one of the footmen. I am, however, uncertain if they know the steps."

"Are you as much of a recluse from society as I?"

"Nearly. I find I attend fewer and fewer events each year," Meredith admitted. "I do not enjoy the activities of the Season, nor the company of many of the esteemed members of Society."

"Why?"

Meredith gave a shrug of nonchalance. "I fear I have never been able to discuss feminine pursuits with much authority, and my competence in business affairs long ago labeled me a bluestocking."

"What has saved you from utter ruin?"

"My outrageous sense of propriety?"

"I think it is more your ready sense of humor." His hold around her waist tightened fractionally, drawing her closer.

Meredith smiled. "Alas, my unusual appreciation for the absurd has offended more than one self-centered, overblown aristocrat."

"You have easily described half the people in this room."

"I think two thirds is a more accurate count. Many object to me and my odd ideas on principle alone."

The marquess shook his head. "And yet you hold no grudges?"

Meredith lifted her chin. "I react without malice to their slights, for that only frustrates them more. It was a trick Lavinia taught me, though I know in my heart I shall never achieve her grace and charm and kind-

ness with such easy fluency. She was a dear friend, and one of the finest women I have ever known."

"That is because conversation and wit came naturally to her," the marquess answered readily. "As well as her affinity for society."

" 'Tis true. Her natural gifts made her a well-respected and sought-after addition to any social gathering." Meredith felt a tug at her heart, remembering her friend. "I, on the other hand, must work very hard at being amusing and entertaining."

"Not so very hard, I think."

"You are being kind, my lord."

The marquess's gaze clung to hers and it was dark with emotion. "I am being honest."

The unexpected compliment startled Meredith and she nearly missed a step. He held her tightly as she swayed unsteadily, and she could feel the heat of his body, the raw strength in his arms.

She fought to hold herself stiffly, for the sudden urge to mold her body softly against his was overwhelming. Her heart jolted at this thoroughly disconcerting notion.

Meredith's cheeks went warm. Though she knew he could hardly read her thoughts, she worried he had somehow known what she felt, for his gaze was probing and far too perceptive.

They finished the waltz as they had begun, in silence. The music ended with a resounding crescendo and the dance was done. The marquess turned his head and scanned the crowded ballroom with great interest. Meredith felt herself blushing. While not being precisely rude, it was obvious the marquess had dismissed her from his thoughts.

Meredith held her smile steady, trying to ignore the unwelcome bite of disappointment. It was usually she who sought refuge from an ardent male, not the other

way 'round. Was she truly becoming the undesirable spinster her brothers thought her to be?

Meredith knew within moments the marquess would bow stiffly and escort her off the dance floor. It seemed unlikely he would seek out her company again, and Meredith was unsure if she possessed the courage to approach him a second time.

If she had any hope of winning that ridiculous wager and proving to herself she was not set firmly upon the shelf, she would have to act now.

"The room is warm, my lord," Meredith said anxiously. "Shall we take a stroll in the garden for a refreshing breath of air?"

He raised an eyebrow at her, and Meredith once again marveled. There was something so striking about him. Even his smallest gesture or expression seemed important.

"Are you not engaged for the next dance, Lady Meredith?"

"I have danced with only you this evening," she said very quietly.

The marquess tensed, and his expression became guarded. She could almost sense the wariness that filtered through him. He remained silent for so long she was certain he was going to refuse her suggestion of a walk outside. Then he silently held out his arm. She grasped it eagerly, and they paraded across the room in full view of any who cared to be interested.

And many were. She was very aware of the speculative glances thrown their way, but Meredith took her cue from the marquess and ignored them all.

It was a moonless night. Only a few couples milled about in the corners of the large patio. Servants had lit torches on the perimeter of the slate terrace, and the light they cast was sufficient to see the shapes of

the neatly tended bushes and rows of blooming flowers that comprised the garden.

The night air felt damp, but there was no mist. Instead layers of shadows spread over the gardens, curling around the gravel paths, casting strange shapes into the far corners.

A light breeze blew, ruffling the stray curls that had escaped from Meredith's tightly coiled hair. She resisted the temptation to set them back in place, afraid the gesture would bring more attention to herself.

"Have you filled your lungs sufficiently with fresh air, Lady Meredith?"

The marquess sounded bored. She stiffened her spine and lifted her head, reminding herself the bet he had made with her brothers revealed much about his attitude and opinion of women. If nothing else, it would give her a great sense of satisfaction to make a sufficient adjustment to that pompous attitude.

Abruptly she cleared her throat and waved vaguely at the French doors leading to the ballroom. "Please don't feel obligated to stay out here on my behalf, my lord. I understand perfectly if you wish to return to the party."

She suspected that was the last thing he wanted to do, but he was unpredictable enough to call her bluff.

When he did not reply, Meredith decided to tempt the fates once more. She moved forward slowly, then called over her shoulder to the marquess, "The enchanting fragrance of the garden beckons, my lord. I fear I must indulge myself."

She sailed blithely down the stone steps, listening intently for the crunch of his footsteps behind her. As the silence lengthened, Meredith slowed her gait, but she resisted the urge to turn around.

She might be stubborn and occasionally willful, but she had her pride. If the marquess followed her into

the darkness of the secluded garden, she would make every attempt to kiss the man senseless and win this outlandish wager. And if he did not, well, perhaps the loss of this bet would make an impression upon her brothers as to the fickle nature of gambling.

And perhaps pigs would learn to fly!

Meredith sensed a restless shifting behind her, then breathed a sigh when she heard the telltale crunch of a shoe upon the gravel. He was following her!

Eyes alert, Meredith strolled along the path. The marquess kept silent pace behind her. They did not speak, and she was glad, for she had long since run out of conversation.

What Meredith sought was privacy, for to be caught in the act of kissing the marquess would be disastrous for them both. A vague recollection of a pretty gazebo tucked away in a secluded area of the lawn had Meredith eagerly scanning the shadows with each step she took.

She nearly cried out with delight when she at last spied it. Meredith lifted her skirt and trod up the wooden steps of the structure, ducking her head to avoid becoming tangled in the hanging vines. She took a seat on the wicker sofa inside and waited.

He did not immediately follow her but instead stood outside the open-air gazebo. Through the silence of the still night, Meredith could clearly hear the sound of her own breathing.

"Tired, Lady Meredith?"

"A bit."

She heard the note of sarcasm in his voice, and oddly understood it. Viewing the situation from his side, Meredith admitted her behavior the entire evening had been somewhat vexing. Mysterious and flirtatious, she had been poking him, jabbing at him, prodding him like a sleeping tiger.

With each request, each offhanded suggestion she had tweaked his curiosity, then resorted to silence. It was only a matter of time before the beast within him awoke and roared, and Meredith knew she must be prepared to jump out of harm's way or be devoured.

The marquess at last climbed the steps to the gazebo and took a few short steps inside. He folded his arms over his chest and glared down at her. Even in the semidarkness she could see his confusion.

Meredith turned her head and stared out into the darkness. She clasped her hands together tightly, wiggled her fingers free, then clasped them together again.

"Why are we here, Lady Meredith?"

"To enjoy the night air, my lord."

"I think not." The marquess lowered his head wearily and moved forward.

He took a seat on the wicker sofa and Meredith slid over to allow him room. A tension permeated the air. Meredith admonished herself to behave with sensibility and calm, though there was little of that regarding what she was about to do.

It had been at least a year since she had been kissed. She struggled to remember the subtle approach used by the many men who had wooed her, who had attempted a seduction and received a cool set down for their efforts.

Sweet, flowery phrases and forceful embraces would hardly work in this instance. What was needed was directness, yet the very idea nearly gave her hives.

She risked a glance at him. He appeared not to notice, for the marquess gave a small sigh and stretched out his long legs. For a moment she relaxed. *All I need to do is wait. Before long he shall lean toward me, pull me into his embrace, and kiss me.*

The notion was equally thrilling and comforting.

But then Meredith clearly remembered the subtle nuances of the bet. It must be the spinster who kissed the rake. If that aspect of the wager was not met, she could not claim victory.

She turned expectantly toward him and her heart lurched. When she had lured him out here, her mind had been fixed on winning that ridiculous bet and proving to herself that she was not a prim and proper spinster. She intended only to steal a hearty, passionate kiss and then flee into the night before the marquess had time to recover his wits.

But as she gazed at his handsome profile in the semidarkness, she found herself wondering what it would be like to really kiss him, deep and slow and tender, with an intimate coupling of their tongues—to hold nothing back, to surrender completely to the hidden passion that lurked within her soul.

Knowing she had to act quickly, before her courage failed, Meredith moved closer to him. Her eyes remained fixed on his lips. He opened them to speak.

"Would you care to—"

Meredith lurched awkwardly forward and cut his words off with a kiss. For an instant she felt him stiffen—in surprise she fervently prayed, not revulsion.

She tried to keep the kiss light and soft, but she quickly found herself giving in to the temptation of his masculine beauty, sinking into the embrace, giving herself over to the emotions and excitement.

The marquess slanted his head to fit them closer together. Then his hand cupped the back of Meredith's neck, drawing her forward. His hard lips softened, then opened slightly, allowing her to deepen the kiss.

Titillated at the invitation, Meredith slid her tongue inside, tasting the warmth of his mouth. A faint moan escaped. His? Hers?

She tried to ignore her quickening breath, the flush

of desire that rushed through her. Her breasts began to swell, and a damp, tingling sensation fluttered between her legs.

In her heart, Meredith knew she should end the kiss. The bet had been well and truly won. There was no need to continue the physical contact.

Yet the event seemed to have taken on a life of its own that had nothing at all to do with the wager. As Meredith pressed her lips urgently on his, her hand reached up to touch his face. Her fingertips glided over the smooth line of his recently shaved jaw, enjoying the feel of his skin.

He gasped at her intimate touch. Meredith felt him tug urgently on the bodice of her gown. The marquess loosened several buttons and it gaped open. She cried out as he lowered his head and took the nipple of her left breast into his mouth. He tasted, licked, and suckled. Liquid heat curled though her body as his mouth and tongue feasted on her exposed flesh.

The faint sound of laughter and muted conversation drifted through the stillness of the night and reached Meredith's ears. *Good heavens, what am I doing?*

"My lord! My lord!" Desperately she fought to retain a piece of her sanity, a modicum of her pride and dignity. The marquess lifted his head briefly, nuzzling the sensitive hollow of her neck. His lips moved higher, once again finding hers in a long, slow, thorough kiss. The heat inside her grew. Reality seemed to fade away. When he finally drew back, Meredith nearly forgot why she was trying to end this incredible interlude. "My lord . . . my lord . . . please, oh, please . . . Trevor . . . stop, we must stop or else we shall be discovered."

He paused for a moment. His breath was coming in shallow gasps, and she noticed with awe that the

hand reaching out to caress her cheek trembled slightly.

"You are a lovely surprise, Lady Meredith," he whispered, his tone laced with wonder. "Your flesh feels like silk beneath my fingers, so soft, so smooth, so perfect. What a heady temptation you are, my dear, passionately responsive, sensually giving, a delight far too tempting to ignore. Are you certain we must stop?"

His eyes moved with undisguised longing over her still exposed breasts. Heat flooded Meredith's cheeks. She was an idiot! How pompous and naive she was to think she could control a man of his sexual appetite and experience. She felt like an utter fool for allowing her wits to be swept away on a sea of pure desire.

"We could be discovered," she whispered.

For a moment she thought he would argue the point with her, but then he nodded. "I shall have my carriage summoned so I may escort you home."

"No!" Meredith declared.

Traveling alone with him in a dark, secluded carriage was unthinkable. She might as well lean back against the sofa and allow the passion stirring between them to ignite into full desire. The marquess was far too tempting and she was feeling too strange and puzzled by the encounter to risk being alone with him in such a private, intimate setting.

"You cannot return to the ball." He reached for her.

"Don't." She drew back in alarm.

He straightened and pulled away. Meredith got the absurd impression she had somehow insulted him. "I'm only trying to help, my dear."

She followed his pointed gaze and looked down at her chest. The bodice of her gown gaped open. Her naked breasts were completely exposed. Her hands, clumsy with nerves and embarrassment, fumbled with

the fastenings. In the end it seemed easier to allow him to aid her.

Silently he tied the ribbons of her chemise and buttoned her bodice closed. Oddly, it felt almost as intimate as when he had unfastened her garments.

"Thank you." Meredith rose unsteadily to her feet.

It felt cowardly and rude to leave so abruptly. But she did. Against the protests of the marquess, with her pulse galloping and her head whirling, Meredith raced along the winding walkway, through the garden, and beyond the tall hedge.

She reentered the house by a side door. Thanks to the crush of people, she was easily able to slip into the crowd. Her aim was to find her brothers and insist they leave immediately.

However, too late, Meredith drifted by one of the many gilded mirrors that lined the edge of the ballroom and caught a glimpse of her reflection.

Her cheeks blushed bright with color. Her lips were red, ripe and swollen, her eyes bright and feverish. Tendrils of her normally tightly wound chignon were curling haphazardly about her face. But worst of all, the exposed area of flesh above breasts was flushed and marked.

By the marquess's possession.

In the mirror, Meredith met her own eyes and grimaced. She should have listened to him and avoided the ballroom. Desperately she glanced at the French doors on the opposite side of the room. It was the closest means of escape, yet at this moment they seemed very far away.

Knowing she had no choice but to brazen it out, Meredith moved forward. Keeping her head low and her feet swift, she chose the most direct path, circling around the dancing couples. As she neared her goal, Meredith dared to let out a soft breath, thinking she

had made it, vowing to herself she would never again do anything so dim-witted.

Her hand reached out eagerly for the brass handle, but then a shrill female voice filled the air. The Duchess of Lancaster stood directly in her path. Meredith nearly shouted out loud at the unfairness of it all.

"We meet again, Your Grace," Meredith said evenly. Her hand fell to her side and she straightened her spine. "Are you enjoying the ball?"

"Apparently not as much as you are, Lady Meredith." The duchess wrinkled her nose, then frowned. " 'Tis not difficult to know precisely what you have been doing tonight. However, I would very much enjoy knowing with *whom* you have been spending your time and bestowing your favors."

Five

Trevor leaned back against the wide seat, enjoying the plush velvet and thick padding beneath him. The elegant coach was a vehicle he seldom used, for it was too large and luxurious for just one person. And it carried his coat of arms brazenly upon the door, which made discretion about town a near impossibility.

Yet he was glad he had decided to take this monstrosity to the ball this evening, for it provided a much needed means of escape at the most fortuitous of moments.

"Are you going to speak to me, or sit there glowering for the entire journey to your home?" Trevor inquired of the tight-lipped female who sat across from him.

"I thought you would prefer a silent glower over a heated lecture," Meredith replied stiffly. "But if you truly wish to hear my thoughts on this matter, I should be pleased to oblige you."

Trevor coughed softly, lifting his hand to his mouth to hide the brief smile that emerged. He had thought her beautiful in the ballroom, exquisite in the evening shadows of the garden, but now she was beyond equal as she sat across from him, wearing her indignity like a royal badge of honor. Though it was dark, he could

see the fire of anger she cast his way, and it set his blood racing.

"I fear you are overreacting to the situation, Lady Meredith. 'Twas just a stolen kiss."

"A stolen kiss!" Meredith's lips tightened. " 'Tis not the incident but rather the discovery of it that has me all tied in knots. The Duchess of Lancaster is a mean-spirited gossip who thrives on the misery of others. She despises me, which will make the telling and re-telling of this sordid tale all the more enjoyable for her." Meredith paused and took a deep breath. "This, my lord, is a full-blown scandal."

"You exaggerate." Trevor frowned skeptically. "However, if you had done as I asked and left with me from the gardens instead of returning to the ball-room, all this could have been easily avoided."

"How gallant of you to point that out to me, sir, at this late juncture," Meredith huffed. She tilted her chin in the air. "If I had listened to my innate good sense, this unfortunate incident would never have occurred. But that, as the saying goes, is water under the bridge."

"You insult me, Lady Meredith."

"How so?"

"Labeling my kisses, my caresses, an unfortunate incident is a serious insult to my manhood. Is that perchance a challenge to best my performance in the gazebo?"

"Don't be an ass."

This time he did allow his laughter to escape. She was nothing short of magnificent. The cloak she wore was unfastened, leaving her gown exposed. She still had the glow of a woman who had recently enjoyed a passionate embrace, and that mussed, slightly di-sheveled look had kept the erection in his trousers throbbing ever since they had entered the carriage.

Wisps of blond hair were falling around her face and the tops of her breasts seemed ready to spill out of that sparkling blue gown at any moment. Trevor silently cursed the driving skill of his coachman, for if they hit a particularly nasty rut the force might succeed in jolting that pair of beauties free of their confines.

The very idea put a fine sheen of sweat on Trevor's brow.

"I am sure this will all be forgotten by tomorrow evening," he said smoothly. "The most appealing element of any gossip is its newness. This little tidbit will be dropped the moment the rumormongers discover new grist to run through their mill."

"This is not a mere tidbit of gossip, this is a banquet," Meredith snapped. Her mouth twisted one way, then another. "All possibilities of a quick ending to this little drama vanished the moment you stood by my side to defend me. Until your appearance, all the duchess had was suspicions."

"We were seen dancing together a mere three quarters of an hour before you returned to the ballroom," Trevor replied, wondering why he felt such a need to defend his actions. "The duchess is a woman of only moderate intelligence, but even a lackwit would be have been able to determine I was the person who put you in that most charming, disheveled state."

Meredith ducked her head. For a moment Trevor thought she was blushing, but when she lifted her chin, her eyes were blazing with emotion.

"Suspicion is one thing, proof another," she insisted.

"Proof? What proof?" Trevor asked. "We were not caught in a compromising situation."

"Exactly. If you had not come to my defense, I could have brazened it out, left the duchess with only

suspicions of what I had been doing and no idea of with whom." Meredith turned her head and groaned. "Your defense of me ruined everything."

"I cannot imagine what came over me," he said, fixing her a look of mock dismay. "The duchess was clearly doing her best to humiliate you, and I thoughtlessly intervened to prevent it. In retrospect that was a very uncharacteristic action, for I am constantly told I seldom behave with even the slightest degree of honor. Therefore, I extend my apologies."

"Would you kindly do me the courtesy of waiting until I have left before indulging your off-color sense of humor? Unlike you, I do not find this situation in any way amusing." She rested her head against the cool glass of the carriage window and sighed.

Normally such a scathing set down would have had him answering her in kind. Yet she seemed genuinely upset, and for some ridiculous reason Trevor's conscience pricked at him.

"Is it really all that horrible?"

"I am a strong, forceful person in many regards, yet I posses one keen weakness—a great horror of scandals." She closed her eyes and sighed again. "A scandal of this ilk has far-reaching consequences, my lord. It can be detrimental in ways we have yet to discover. The perception of our discretion can have even more harmful effects, not just for us but for various members of our family."

He grimaced. "When you speak of your family, I presume you are referring to your husband?"

"My what?" She sat up suddenly, nearly knocking her head on the window latch in the process.

"Your husband, Lady Meredith. When this scandal reaches his ears, will he be very cross with you?"

She gasped and gave him a strange look, then opened her mouth to reply. She closed it abruptly,

without uttering a sound, opened it a second time, closed it yet again, this time biting her lips together so tightly they turned white.

"Who told you I was married?" she asked at last.

"No one. I just assumed." A gnawing anxiety sprang to life in the back of his mind, but he cautioned himself against overreacting. Neither her attitude nor her kisses were those of a maiden. Of that Trevor felt very certain.

"You are a very beautiful woman, Meredith. I remember well the year you made your debut in Society, and despite your unconventional demeanor, you were much sought after by the young bucks. And the old men. And most other males in-between.

"I knew you had turned down many proposals that year, but I naturally assumed you had married sometime in the interim. It was a long time ago."

"I am not that old," she cried out with indignity.

"Old?" Trevor smiled faintly. "You are far from a crone, and yet even you must concede you are hardly in the first blush of youth."

"I am twenty-six years old." Meredith snorted. "Four years younger than you, my lord."

"And well past the age of marriage." His eyes met hers. "My assumption was a natural one."

"Your assumption was an insult." The look she shot him was one of pure disgust. "And speaks of your contemptuous regard of women. I can assure you if I were pledged to another man, wed before God, I would not have been kissing you in the garden. I would honor my vows, especially that of fidelity."

Trevor's eyes narrowed with suspicion. Why had she kissed him? Unmarried women of society guarded their reputations and persons most diligently. Unless they were seeking a husband.

"I believe you owe me an explanation, Lady Meredith."

Her eyes flashed, but instead of a scathing retort she gave him a smile filled with irony. "The kiss we shared was part of a wager. A wager you have now lost."

Her tone had him tensing while her confidence made him even more edgy. "I can assure you, Lady Meredith, I make countless wagers each day. You must be more specific if I am to recall a particular one."

She looked on the verge of shouting, but somehow managed to resist the urge to scream at him. "Last week, while dining out with my brothers, you declared, most vehemently, that a spinster harbors no passion in her soul. My brothers disagreed with this notion, suggesting the opposite. The challenge was put forth to find a spinster who would kiss a rake, of her own volition, with passion and ardor."

"You are the spinster?" he asked in an incredulous tone.

"I am. And you are the rake." Even in the glittering light, he could see the spark of satisfaction in her eyes. "So the challenge has been met. You, sir, have lost the wager."

Her words might have angered him. Or made him cry foul, for it felt very much like he had been well and truly fooled. Despite her age, she was hardly the type of female he had in mind when he spoke of spinsters.

Even by his rather lax standards, her behavior had been highly improper and exceedingly daring. Yet the marquess wisely swallowed that observation and instead offered another.

"I must correct your assumption, Lady Meredith. I might have lost some coin and, if I recall clearly, an incomparable pair of matched bays. However, after

kissing you, I strongly contend I am the true winner of this wager."

On the opposite end of town, the moonless night provided a cloak of anonymity for the man who waited in the shadows of a tavern. There was little chance of being recognized by anyone on the street, for he seldom frequented this rather seedy, rundown area of London, yet caution was needed.

The man had entered this establishment two nights prior, in search of a pretty barmaid. He had found precisely the type of woman he was looking for—buxom, fresh-faced, and young enough to be missing the tired eyes and downtrodden spirits shared by so many others in her profession.

He had given her a handsome tip and a friendly smile, knowing she would remember him. He had hoped to see her later that evening, but the tavernkeeper, a barrel-chested man with large hands and a cynical attitude, had taken notice of him. Knowing it was foolish to tempt fate, the man had left, frustrated and angry.

For two long days he had thought of little else but this woman, and tonight he had been driven to return. To finish his task.

In the distance he heard the toll of the watchman's bell. Two clangs. Good. The tavern would be closing soon. Another ten minutes passed, and then the lights were gradually extinguished inside the building. A few moments later the front door opened and a woman emerged. His woman.

The man blew out his breath. His luck was holding. The young barmaid was alone. Head down, she jumped across a large puddle, then hurried across the street.

The man stepped out of the shadows, directly into her path. The young woman gasped with fright and held her arm up in a protective gesture. Then slowly her expression changed from one of fear to relief.

"Oh, 'tis only you, sir. You gave me a grand fright, that's for sure."

"I apologize." He bowed gracefully, and she tittered with delight. Women of the lower classes, he had discovered, were easily led to ruin by displaying simple manners and common courtesies toward them. "May I see you home?"

Her eyes narrowed slightly. "I live with me Mum and brothers and sisters," she answered. "I'm sure at least one of 'um is waiting up for me to get home."

"I only wish to walk with you," he said gently. "If you have no objections."

He could see the indecision clearly in her face, so he gave her a brief smile. It had the desired effect. She smiled back, then nodded in agreement.

"Thank you, sir, for your kind offer. 'Tis nearly twenty blocks to our flat. I shall be glad of the company."

They walked for several blocks in silence. He did not offer her his arm, fearing to touch her too soon. It was the right decision, for of her own initiative she left a respectable distance between them as she walked. He knew she was shy of him, for she spoke only briefly when answering his many questions and initiated no conversation.

He found her reticent nature charming, her natural shyness exhilarating. Forward, aggressive women had always angered him.

As they walked, he became dimly aware of the passage of time. Soon, it must happen soon. Eagerly, his eyes scanned ahead, watching for the perfect spot, the perfect moment. When it came, he was ready.

He stumbled on a piece of uneven cobblestone, pretending to lose his balance. The young woman stopped immediately and offered her arm to him in assistance. With a wicked smile of satisfaction, he grasped her arm, righted himself, and then yanked her into the small alley between two tall buildings.

"No, please," she cried, as he jammed her against the wall with his body. She pushed against his chest with the heels of her hands, struggling to get away from him. But he was too strong.

He caught her flaying arms, swiftly tying the wrists together with a silken cord he had brought specifically for this purpose. She gave a choked cry as he shoved a scarf in her mouth, muffling her screams.

Slowly, almost reverently, he placed his hands around her neck. He leaned his full weight against her, waiting for the fright to fill her eyes, followed quickly by dread and fear. She did not disappoint him.

She began to struggle immediately, arching her back, bucking her torso, twisting and turning her body sharply in a vain effort to free herself. After only a few minutes, he could tell she was beginning to tire, but she fought on, the sharp edge of her elbow digging into his side.

He gloried in her fear. He felt his body harden and his groin grow thick and heavy with desire as a muffled groan slipped through the gag. He allowed her to struggle a few more moments, savoring each sharp twist of her body. Then he increased the pressure around her neck until her eyes bulged and her complexion took on a faint purplish hue. Finally she slipped into unconsciousness, her eyes fluttering closed.

Once she stilled, the fierceness left him. He squeezed her neck only until he felt the breath leave her body. Then he calmly allowed her inert form to slump to the ground.

He took a moment to enjoy the surge of emotion, the sense of completion that filled him. A deep primal instinct invaded his being. He wanted to throw back his head and howl, but he controlled that impulse, fearing discovery.

Breathing hard, he dragged the body to the far corner of the alley. After untying her wrists and removing the gag from her mouth, he hid the corpse beneath a pile of rubbish. With luck she wouldn't be discovered for many days, until the flesh on her bones began to rot.

He felt bubbles of saliva that had gathered at the corners of his mouth ooz onto his face. With a grimace, he removed the neatly pressed linen handkerchief from the pocket of his trousers and carefully wiped the moisture away.

Ever fastidious, the man straightened his spine and began to right the rest of his appearance. He shook out his rumpled greatcoat, adjusted his misaligned cravat. His hat had been knocked off in the ruckus. Bending low, he retrieved it, then ran trembling fingers through his hair before placing it neatly upon his head.

He walked to the edge of the alley and peered first to the left, then to the right. After assuring himself no one was about, the man slipped from the shadows, proceeding quickly down the street. When he judged he had gone far enough from the crime scene, he hailed a hackney.

Tucked safely inside the darkness of the cab, he allowed himself a moment to relive each delicious nuance of the kill, savoring the details with gruesome joy. The coach stopped abruptly, and with a start the man realized he had reached his destination. Grosvenor Square.

He paid the driver, then entered the quiet, darkened house by a little used servants' entrance. Thanks to

deliberate caution and the lateness of the hour, he encountered no one.

He felt tired and drained, but performed his usual, lengthy preparations before retiring to his bed. The instant his head rested upon the pillow, sleep claimed him. It was deep, peaceful, and dreamless.

Evil, in its purest form, had returned to London.

The pounding in his head kept perfect cadence with the steady knocking upon his bedchamber door. Trevor turned onto his side, winced, then growled, "Go away."

The noise did not stop. If anything, it became louder. Trevor groaned and buried his head under the pillow. The knocking became muffled but was still audible.

He opened a bloodshot eye and groaned again, realizing his tormentor wasn't going anywhere. It took far to much effort to yell again, so Trevor sat up and waited. He was trying unsuccessfully to hold his aching head together when his valet, Everett, entered the darkened room.

"I do beg your pardon for disturbing you, my lord," the servant said as he approached the massive bed, "but it could not be avoided. The duke is here."

"The duke? What duke?" Trevor attempted to lift his head, and the thumping in his brain increased.

"The Duke of Warwick," the valet hissed, adding for good measure, "your father."

The mention of his father's title jarred a vague memory of last night's ball, a moonlit kiss, a scandalous scene, and a fascinating carriage ride, all the components that accounted for the perfect excuse to get falling-down drunk the moment Lady Meredith had

been safely deposited at her home. An idiotic, yet perfectly understandable way to end the evening.

The stabbing pains behind Trevor's eyes increased tenfold as his energetic servant began bustling about the bedchamber, retrieving the haphazardly strewn articles of clothing that littered the carpet. The marquess heard a distinct *tsk* of disapproval the moment before his valet pulled back the heavy tapestry curtains and flooded the room with light.

Trevor slumped back in his bed, using one hand to shield his eyes from the sudden sunshine. "My head is pounding far too much to be amused by your little jokes, Everett. The Duke of Warwick would sooner eat nails than step foot inside my humble rooms. Now, close those draperies at once. Then go fetch me some coffee. A large pot, if you please."

"I would never joke about such a serious matter, my lord," Everett insisted with his usual display of haughty dignity. He poured hot water into a bowl and began to methodically sharpen the marquess's razor. "I informed the duke you would attend him the moment you completed dressing."

Trevor barely managed to resist barring his teeth in an angry snarl as the servant hovered expectantly beside the bed, ready to render assistance.

"My father is truly here?"

"Yes, my lord."

"I am not receiving visitors this morning," Trevor declared. "Tell the duke to call back another time. Preferably next week."

Trevor rolled lazily onto his side and buried his aching head into his pillow. He could almost hear his valet working himself into a snit. In Everett's rather stuffy, proper mind, one did not eject a duke from the premises.

"I could not possibly tell his grace you refused to

see him." The valet sputtered with astonishment. "It would not be polite. Or proper."

" 'Tis most improper to call on people without warning at such an ungodly hour of the morning," Trevor groused.

"It is three o'clock in the afternoon, my lord."

"Oh." Trevor muttered under his breath, then sat up gingerly. He cradled his head in his hands, hoping the throbbing at his temples would not increase to unbearable levels now that he was upright. "The hour of the day is immaterial. I have never had uninvited afternoon guests to my rooms."

"I imagine, just this once, you could make an exception for a family member," the valet replied blandly.

And a person of such noble rank. The valet did not speak the words aloud, but Trevor knew they were very much a part of the servant's reasoning.

It was a delicate decision, considering the state of his head and the exhaustion of his body. Yet Trevor realized his father would have to be faced eventually. Perhaps it would be best to get it over with now.

"Allow me a few minutes of privacy to attend to personal matters," Trevor said, motioning toward the chamber pot. "Then you may escort the duke in here."

"Here?"

"Yes."

The valet's jaw dropped. "There is no proper sitting area in your bedchamber. What will you have his grace do? Pull up a chair next to the bed as if you were an invalid?"

"Why not?"

" 'Tis most undignified."

Trevor wanted to bellow, but he selfishly realized that would only make his head ache more. He glared

at his valet. Everett returned the stare. They were at a standoff.

With ill grace, Trevor threw off the bedcovers. He stumbled off the bed, nearly landing in his valet's lap. Although knowing it was not the reason his valet was so appalled, Trevor concluded it wouldn't be prudent to receive his father while he lay abed with a monumental hangover.

The marquess made no further protests as his valet set about grooming him. Thirty minutes later, Trevor entered the small but tastefully furnished antechamber that served as his parlor.

The duke stood near the window, avidly watching the traffic below.

"At last." The duke spoke without turning his head. "I knew if I waited long enough you would finally realize any attempts at avoiding me would fail."

Trevor nearly turned around and walked back to his bedchamber. His brain was foggy from lack of sleep and too much whiskey. "I can hardly be accused of avoiding you, since I've only just discovered you were here, sir."

Though the blood was surging through his veins, Trevor calmly took a seat.

"What the devil happened last night? You promised to be at Lady Dermond's ball, yet I never saw you."

Trevor smiled brashly as his father finally turned to face him. "I arrived early, sir, in hopes of concluding my duties in a reasonable amount of time. Alas, I found the affair so impossibly boring that after waiting nearly three hours for you to arrive, I gave up and left."

The duke's eyebrow rose shrewdly. "Is that what caused all the ruckus with the Barrington chit? Boredom?"

Trevor's mouth twisted derisively. It appeared the

gossiping tongues had been most busy today. "Are you referring to Lady Meredith Barrington, perchance?"

"Don't take that innocent tone with me. I'm not one of your lackwitted cronies to be so easily put off by a show of indignity." The duke gave a disgusted shake of his head. "I've heard all manner of outrageous tales about last night. That's why I've come here. To learn the truth."

"Right from the horse's mouth," Trevor said mildly.

"Horse? If only part of what's being said is true, I would liken you more to a jackass." The duke's mouth twisted tauntingly. "She's the Earl of Stafford's daughter, isn't she?"

"I believe that is correct."

"And you ravished her in the garden?"

"What!" Trevor felt the pounding in his head return with colossal force. "I merely kissed her. If truth be told, she initiated our embrace."

The duke gave a humorless smile. "You shared nothing more than a kiss? That certainly doesn't sound like you."

Trevor felt some of the tension leave his face at his father's unmistakable mockery. "Impossible as it may seem, sir, I can occasionally show some restraint of my carnal and depraved nature. When necessary."

"That is a relief," the duke replied in a matching tone. "Since it was only a little kiss, there is no need to make amends. Though Stafford is an earl, I've never liked the man. Too forward thinking for my tastes, allowing his daughter to run amok the way she has all these years— although his wife is a fine looking woman. In her younger days she could rival her daughter in beauty."

Trevor's mouth tightened. "The thought of making amends to Lady Meredith never entered my mind until you mentioned it."

"Good. Forget I ever said anything." The duke made

a move toward the door. "I'll expect you for dinner Friday evening. I'm having a small supper party. 'Tis only three days from now. I'm sure if you exert a supreme amount of effort, you can manage to stay out of trouble until then."

"I make no promises," the marquess retorted grimly.

The duke paused and turned toward Trevor. "Don't be too hard on yourself," he said, in an uncharacteristic display of sympathy. "Your various exploits are often overlooked by Society. I'm sure this too shall be eventually forgotten."

He gave his father a look of mock disbelief. "I am not interested in the opinion of Society."

"Well, you should be," the duke barked. A frown creased his brow. "You have made your position on this issue clear to me for several years and I know I will never be able to change your mind. Yet if you do not wish to guard your own reputation, will you at least have a modicum of concern for mine? This scandal will be forgotten if you behave yourself for the next few days. By the end of the week, the brunt of the attention will shift away from you and fall on the Barrington girl."

His father's comment roused the edge of Trevor's conscience. It was true he was nearly immune to the censure of Society, having little regard for others' opinions. But it was different for a woman.

Though it was well known to all that Lady Meredith had never been completely accepted by the *beau monde,* a breath of true scandal had never touched her. Until now.

Though he was loath to admit it, Trevor knew he would have to do whatever was reasonable to help her rectify that problem. And he was honest enough with himself to admit it frightened him to even think about what that might entail.

Six

Meredith had trouble sleeping that night. Her thoughts were consumed with the events of the evening and their possible consequences. As she listened to the clock strike each hour, she tried to assure herself all would be well. Yet as the morning sun invaded her bedchamber, she was not feeling as certain.

It was not only the kiss she had shared with the marquess and the possible consequences she might face because of her actions that disturbed her thoughts. It was knowing she would have to face them entirely on her own.

Though she prided herself on being a forthright, independent woman, Meredith was honest enough to admit that every so often she felt lonely for the comfort, company, and strength of a male confidant, a male champion.

Though in her head she knew the existence of a man who would accept her and all her eccentricities was more a product of her wishful imagination than a reality, her heart could not help but long for his discovery.

Yet on this morning after, Meredith had no intention of succumbing to the blue devils. With her usual forthright determination, she resigned herself to throwing

off her melancholy mood as effectively as she threw back her bed covers.

She spent her morning in the usual manner, purposely adhering to her comfortable routine: breakfast in quiet solitude in the cozy informal dining room, a brief consultation with Cook over the day's menu, a meeting with the butler to discuss a nagging problem with a member of the household staff.

Then it was off to her father's study, where Meredith read through the monthly financial statements she received from her solicitor. After completing her daily correspondence, which included a rather lengthy letter to her childhood friend Faith Linden, now the Viscountess Dewhurst, Meredith decided to indulge in one of her dearest passions. Reading.

Relaxed at last, she was so engrossed in her book of poetry she did not at first hear the butler enter the library.

"I do beg your pardon, Lady Meredith," the butler said in an apologetic tone. "There has been a delivery of flowers for you. Would you like them brought in here, or shall I have them sent to the kitchens so Mrs. Hopkins can arrange them in vases?"

"Vases?" Meredith's brow quirked. "Is it a particularly large bunch of flowers?"

"Several of them are quite large. The rest are of a more modest, appropriate size," the butler replied dryly.

"Precisely how many bouquets have arrived?"

"Ten."

"What!" Meredith stood so quickly her book fell to the carpet. She ignored it and instead accepted a pile of engraved cards the butler silently offered her.

Heart racing, Meredith quickly shuffled through the heavy vellum notes. The Earl of Botsworth, Lord Chillingham, Mr. Julian Wingate! Men she had not

seen for an age. She did not even know they were all in town.

With a more considering eye, Meredith looked through the cards a second time. There were a number of mature bachelors, several married gentlemen, and quite a few old admirers. She frowned slightly, realizing she had not been plagued by so much male attention since her first Season.

Yet one name was noticeably absent—the Marquess of Dardington. Meredith surprised herself mightily by even noticing.

"The flowers, Lady Meredith?"

Meredith looked at the butler blankly for several seconds. Then his question penetrated her jumbled thoughts. "Please ask Mrs. Hopkins to arrange them for me," she answered calmly. "Then place them throughout the house, in any room except my bedchamber."

"Very good, my lady." The butler bowed respectfully, but did not take his leave.

"Was there something else?"

" 'Tis early in the day. If additional flowers arrive—"

"Have Mrs. Hopkins sort it out," Meredith interrupted. She drew in a deep breath and modulated the tone of her voice. "Just make certain I receive the cards accompanying each bouquet."

This time the servant did not hesitate. He left the room the moment she ceased speaking. Meredith sighed. Perkins was a competent butler. He had been with the family for almost twenty years. The very last thing she wanted to do was upset him.

She wondered what subtle thing she could do to smooth his ruffled feathers. Though the feelings of one's servants were hardly a weighty problem, Meredith indulged in sorting through options to over-

come it. For it kept her mind focused on other, less personal matters.

But she had little time for contemplative thinking. Throughout the morning she was interrupted by either the butler or a footman informing her of a delivery of flowers. An even dozen bouquets, with accompanying cards, had arrived by luncheon, fifteen by early afternoon. Meredith smiled wanly each time a servant entered the drawing room, determined not to take her agitated mood out on the messenger.

"A caller, Lady Meredith," the butler announced in a stiff tone that let her know he had not yet forgiven her for her earlier actions.

Meredith went still and frowned at the butler. She gingerly lifted the gold embossed name card resting ominously in the center of the silver salver. Her fingertip flicked the turned down edge of the card, signifying that the caller was in fact here and had not sent a servant in their stead to deliver a message.

Lady Olivia Dermott. Meredith nearly choked when she read the name. "Has she been here long?"

"She just arrived."

"Tell her I will see her shortly," Meredith instructed. "Then wait a full ten minutes before showing her in."

Meredith picked up the book of poetry she had begun reading earlier and tried to once again immerse herself in the words. She was not successful.

"How good to see you," Lady Olivia proclaimed, approaching Meredith with a blatantly false, sugary smile pasted upon her face. "I know it is early for afternoon callers, but I confess I was hoping to catch you alone. Now we shall have a chance for a little private tête-à-tête. There is so much to talk about!"

Meredith nearly laughed incredulously. Lady Dermott had always been one of her most vocal critics. With three daughters to marry off, the older woman

had viewed her as a rival and an irritant. In fact, two of the three men who had eventually married her daughters had first proposed to Meredith.

And, if Meredith remembered correctly, Lady Olivia's third son-in-law was one of the many gentlemen who had sent her a bouquet of flowers this very morning. Indeed, Lady Olivia was the very last person Meredith would ever consider sharing a confidence with or revealing anything of a personal nature.

"I suppose I must consider it flattering to be an object of such interest to you. One would think you had more important and significant issues to occupy your thoughts." There was no mistaking the mockery in Meredith's voice, but Lady Olivia was not a woman known for her wit or wisdom, and the barb fell short of the mark.

"I am not the only one with an eye on you, Lady Meredith." Lady Olivia cast a sly glance about the room. "I gather from the many bouquets of fresh flowers decorating the hall and the drawing room that you have attracted a gaggle of male admirers. Or are they perhaps all from one special gentleman?"

"One admirer? He would have to be either very rich or very overbearing," Meredith mused.

Lady Olivia tittered. " 'Tis said the Marquess of Dardington can be most forceful—if necessary."

A wave of frustrated anger washed over Meredith. She suspected the news would spread quickly, but had valiantly hoped there might be some other juicy scandal that would at least share the spotlight. Instead it seemed as if all the attention would be centered squarely at her.

Meredith knew charm could be a formidable weapon. She had seen other women, most notably Lavinia, use it to their advantage many times before. Yet Meredith knew herself well enough to realize she

had neither the stomach nor fortitude to try and charm Lady Olivia.

"For the life of me I cannot understand why you would care, but if you really must know, I received no flowers from the marquess today. Nor yesterday," Meredith quickly added, before the question could be asked.

That statement stopped Lady Olivia cold. Her eyebrows lifted at least half an inch as she viewed a lush bouquet of roses in full bloom. "These are all from other gentlemen?"

"Yes."

"It would seem a person in your position would be more mindful of the risks they were taking."

"Risks?" Meredith leveled a somber look at the older woman. "Whatever are you implying?"

A snide little smile spread over Lady Olivia's face. "Even a woman of your advanced years must be concerned with her reputation. 'Tis bad enough you arranged an assignation with the Marquess of Dardington in Lady Dermond's garden last evening. It would not be in your best interest to now encourage the attentions of so many different men. It gives rise to all sorts of unsavory speculation."

"Speculation?"

"As to your character," Lady Olivia replied promptly. "And your morals."

Meredith's ears burned at the condemnation. What was even more distressing was knowing she had no plausible defense of her actions to offer. She *had* lured the marquess into the garden last evening. The fact that Lady Olivia was apparently unaware of the reason Meredith had wanted to be alone with the marquess offered up only a tiny bit of solace.

Swallowing hard, Meredith felt her palms begin to dampen. *Stop it!* Now was not the time to become

panicky. She must face this head on and emerge the victor, or else her disgrace would forever taint the family's good name. Though she cared not overmuch for herself, Meredith did not want her parents or younger brothers to suffer for her foolishness.

What she really needed was a few moments of solitude so she could better consider her current difficulties. Yet Meredith keenly realized nothing short of crying fire would effectively clear Lady Olivia from the room. Meredith instead plastered a relaxed smile upon her lips and casually turned the page of the book of poems she had been reading as if she had not a care in the world.

After counting silently to twenty, she looked up, pinning Lady Olivia with a deliberate stare.

Meredith knew the older woman was watching her closely, aching for a glimpse of her true feelings. Did she feel remorse for her indiscretion? Embarrassment? Delight? Though she was resigned to this most unwelcome scrutiny Meredith was as equally determined to let no hint of her inner self betray her.

"Long ago I resigned myself to enduring the unfair and unfounded arrows of jealousy slung in my direction. In all these years, not a breath of scandal has ever crossed my path, though many have tried to lay disgrace upon my doorstep. Small minds and plain faces are a most lethal combination, are they not, Lady Olivia?"

The older woman's snide smile quickly disappeared. She hesitated, clearly trying to decide whether or not she had been directly insulted. Meredith thought it best not to give her adversary too long to dwell upon the matter and hastened toward the door.

"I greatly appreciate your call this afternoon, Lady Olivia. You have no idea how enlightening I found our conversation."

Lady Olivia stiffened fractionally, but after a forceful nudge in her back, stepped forward.

"Good day, Lady Meredith."

"Farewell."

Only with the door shut firmly did Meredith allow herself to crumple. For a moment.

Even as she had kissed the marquess last night, she had realized life as she had known it would never be the same. Yet that did not mean she had to succumb to the inevitable. She had endured the censure of Society during her first Season and had survived the ever present undercurrent of disapproval since that time.

"Are my brothers still abed?" Meredith asked Perkins the moment the butler answered her summons.

"Yes, I believe Lord Fairhurst and Mr. Barrington have not yet left their chambers." The butler hesitated and then added, "Considering the lateness of their arrival home last evening, it is hardly surprising."

"Kindly inform Lord Fairhurst's valet that I require my brother's company in one hour's time. I wish to go for a drive in the park, and I need his lordship to accompany me."

The servant turned to leave, and Meredith hastily added one final order. "Oh and, Perkins, I am not at home to any more callers this afternoon. No exceptions."

"I understand, my lady."

This time when the door closed, Meredith felt less agitated, more in control. Somehow she would figure out a way to escape this disaster. With fortitude, courage and determination, this too could be overcome.

The morning rain had washed the London streets clean of their usual debris. For now, the air was sweet smelling and fresh, the thoroughfare just beginning to

once again team with life. As they clipped along in the open phaeton, Meredith wished she could enjoy the smell of freshness, but her mind was too focused on the task ahead to indulge her senses in her surroundings.

"Do be careful," Meredith calmly said to her brother Jasper, who was holding the carriage reins nonchalantly. "There are hidden dangers in these rain puddles—deep ruts and broken cobblestones. A fractured carriage wheel will no doubt cause us a great deal of aggravation, as well as drawing an inordinate amount of unwanted attention."

Jasper skittered sideways, neatly avoiding an ominous looking puddle. "I know what I'm doing," he replied, crinkling his nose in disgust at the admonishment. "I've been driving a carriage in London for years."

"You have also had more than one accident, if I recall," Meredith said pointedly.

"I've never overturned a vehicle when I was sober," Jasper retorted.

Meredith bit her bottom lip and held it tightly between her teeth until they rounded the next corner. Now was not the time to begin a lecture on responsibility and acceptable behavior, especially given that her behavior last night was the reason she needed to make this fashionable appearance at the park.

So she focused her gaze instead on the high-stepping horses pulling the coach and realized she had never seen the pair before. "I do not recall seeing these animals in the stable. Are these the infamous bays you won in your bet with the marquess?"

"The very same," Jasper replied cheerfully. "Dardington had them brought 'round first thing this morning. Aren't they beauties?"

"Lovely," Meredith responded dryly. "I assume I

have your word as a gentleman that you will never again wager away these poor beasts?"

Jasper slanted her a jaded look. " 'Tis hardly necessary to harp upon the matter, Merry. Jason and I have already agreed we would share the horses, therefore making it impossible for one of us to sell or otherwise dispose of them."

Meredith turned to her brother with a cool smile. "Agreements between you and Jason are like the wind. They blow hot and cold with unfailing regularity."

Jasper shrugged. "I cannot help it if my dear brother shows, on occasion, an utter lack of common sense. As the elder it is my responsibility to set him to rights."

Meredith could not contain the grin that widened her smile further. "That is a fairly accurate and wholly frightening notion."

She shook her head. If Jasper, who more often than not showed a lack of judgment and maturity when making a decision, was indeed the more responsible of the twins, then Jason should probably not be let out of the house without a keeper.

"I noticed the front parlor and entrance hall, not to mention the breakfast room and drawing room, resembled a flower shop," Jasper said. "Could not one of your afternoon callers have taken you to the park? I assume you had several offers."

Meredith turned to give her brother a sharp retort, reminding him that winning that ridiculous bet for him last evening was the catalyst for all of her current woes. But she caught him gazing rather wistfully at the cavalcade of horsemen riding toward the park and quickly swallowed her remarks.

"I understand escorting an old spinster sister is hardly befitting your image as a dashing rogue, but I need to be seen and acknowledged today. Since, as

you so recently pointed out, you are the more responsible and respectable of my brothers, I felt the task should fall to you."

"I will repeat, for the last time, Jason and I do not think of you as a spinster," Jasper insisted.

"How quickly you change your tune, dear brother. Why only last evening I was considered enough of a spinster to win that ridiculous bet."

"Ah, so that is your plan. You are determined to shed any vestiges of the spinster image and thrust yourself into the social fray on this rather soggy afternoon. That is the real reason you have dragged me out to the park today."

Meredith felt a jolt of surprised embarrassment. Her brother's assessment of the situation painted her in a frivolous light, and though it was completely incorrect, she realized it might be preferable to the truth.

"We are here today because I suddenly find myself to be the object of great interest, the majority of which is unfavorable. The events of last evening, specifically my kiss with the marquess, is providing the *ton* with an endless stream of conversation and speculation.

"The many bouquets of flowers you saw is only a prelude to the propositions I am certain will follow, now that I am thought to be easy prey to any number of unscrupulous males. That notion must be immediately dispelled."

"What!" Jasper nearly lost control of the bays as he reacted to her disclosure. "If any of your gentlemen callers were disrespectful, you should have summoned me at once."

"There were no gentleman callers," Meredith stated flatly. "After a thoroughly unpleasant and enlightening visit from Lady Olivia Dermott, I realized I was the sensation of the hour. I therefore refused to see anyone. Better to deny them the chance to imply I am no

longer respectable, that my *incident* with the marquess has somehow left me tainted. In this instance I thought it prudent to lead the attack instead of waiting for more scandal to touch upon me."

Jasper's indignant expression turned to one of admiration. "Leave it to you, Merry, to know exactly how to manage the situation."

Jasper's approval boosted her confidence, yet Meredith knew there could be several pitfalls of disaster awaiting her. "The plan is sound, but hardly foolproof. Only the proper execution of it will deem it a success or failure."

"Then we must make certain all goes well." He tipped his hat to a pair of ladies who were riding in the opposite direction. They smiled cordially in return.

"Bring the carriage round to the other entrance," Meredith instructed as they reached the park. "I want to greet the Duchess of Barlow and her friends first. If she acknowledges me, others will quickly follow."

Meredith discreetly pointed to a trio of ladies promenading on the gravel path. Their heads were bent close beneath their fringed parasols, which did not obstruct the view of their chattering mouths.

It seemed as though the instant the carriage entered the park, all eyes turned in their direction. It took a concerted effort not to squirm in her seat, but Meredith managed. She gave her brother a quick glance, yet Jasper seemed oblivious to all the scrutiny.

"Ladies, I bid you a pleasant afternoon," Jasper called out. He expertly guided the carriage alongside the trio of elderly women. "I hope you are enjoying the sunshine."

"There has not been a ray of sunlight the entire day, Lord Fairhurst," the duchess replied sternly. "The thick clouds are effectively obstructing all attempts at the sun breaking through."

"Are they?" Jasper tilted his chin toward the sky. "I had not noticed the clouds. Probably because you bring the sunshine wherever you go, Your Grace."

The duchess's eyes narrowed noticeably. The two women flanking her drew closer to her side, in a protective solitary gesture.

"Flattery, young man? To a woman of my advanced years?"

"Truthful observations, Your Grace."

The duchess raised her eyebrow. "You have your mother's charm, sir." A smile grudgingly appeared at the corner of the older woman's mouth. "And your father's good looks."

"Please, Your Grace, you'll put me to the blush."

The duchess laughed. After a moment's hesitation, her two companions joined her. "You are a naughty boy, Lord Fairhurst," the duchess declared, her eyes sparkling. She tipped her head in a girlish manner, but her expression sobered noticeably when her eyes lit upon Meredith.

"Mischievousness in handsome young lords is to be expected," the duchess continued in a lecturing tone. "But it is neither accepted nor tolerated in unmarried ladies. Is that not correct?"

The duchess's two elderly companions nodded their heads in enthusiastic agreement and glanced pointedly at Meredith. She could practically hear the clucking of their disapproving tongues, nearly read the censure in the sharpness of their gaze.

"A sad, though true comment on our society," Meredith said. "Women have long been denied the freedoms men enjoy, even when we are older and wiser."

"Hmmph." A mulish expression crossed the duchess' face, but to Meredith's relief the older woman did not leave. "At least you have the good sense to allow

your brother to bring you to the park. He is a far more appropriate escort than the company you have been keeping."

"I quite agree, Your Grace," Meredith replied.

" 'Tis good to know that you have recovered some of your senses," the duchess huffed.

"Whatever could you have been thinking, dear girl, to be so wildly indiscreet?" the woman standing beside the duchess asked. "I was all aflutter when I heard."

"I can assure you whatever you heard is a vast exaggeration of the truth." Meredith lowered her head and made a muttering sound, hoping she appeared sufficiently contrite.

The duchess sighed heavily. "I daresay this new sensation you've created will quickly become an old one. Why, I heard this very morning that Lord Robertson's daughter was enamored with her dancing instructor. Not only is he completely unsuitable for the girl, he's a Frenchman to boot!"

Meredith slowly began to release the breath she held so tightly in her lungs. All would be well. She would endure the admonishment of the duchess and her circle with a contrite expression, leaving them with the impression she was remorseful and planting the seed that she was also not entirely guilty.

Satisfied with the results, Meredith waited anxiously for the appropriate moment to depart. She knew this moment was critical. A slight misstep at this stage would quickly undue the strides she had made.

The sudden squeak of a carriage coming to a halt invaded her concentration. All eyes turned. To Meredith's astonishment, she saw the vehicle stop in the center of the road. It was an open curricle, harnessed to a magnificent pair of pure white horses. The lively

animals stomped their feet impatiently on the ground, huffing in displeasure at being forced to stand still.

Slowly, carefully the carriage pulled beside their own, effectively jamming all the traffic behind it. The driver subdued his spirited horses, then turned toward her.

The Marquess of Dardington stared at Meredith with clear blue eyes, a bemused expression on his handsome features. "Good afternoon, Lady Meredith. I called on you earlier today, but you had already left for the park. Since I was unable to escort you here, I do hope you would consent to allowing me to drive you home."

The scrutiny Meredith had felt so keenly when first entering the park increased tenfold. Hordes of interested spectators seemed to press forward, attuned to her every word, observant of her slightest expression.

She deliberately avoided the marquess's eyes as she tried to formulate an appropriate response. If she gave a direct cut, that might give rise to greater speculation about the relationship between them. Yet she could hardly greet him as a friend, or even a warm acquaintance.

"My sister prefers the company of her family," Jasper said. "It is, after all, the proper and correct behavior for a lady of her stature."

She glanced beneath her lashes, trying to gage Trevor's reaction to her brother's comments. He seemed to be fighting back a smile. Meredith frowned slightly, hoping he would let the matter pass.

"Lady Meredith's behavior is always above reproach," the marquess countered. "Yet she has the intelligence, wit, and character to ignore the rigid dictates of a stuffy, hypocritical society when it suits her needs. This strength has always been one of her greatest assets."

Meredith was speechless. Stunned, actually. All of her hard work was ruined in a single moment. In any other circumstance, she might have been flattered by the complement, for he uttered it with such conviction. But this was hardly the appropriate instance, especially when she had been so close to convincing the duchess she was a contrite, remorseful woman.

Meredith had done everything in her power to downplay the association between her and the marquess, and in a few sentences he had ruined it all.

But it seemed Trevor was not content to leave well enough alone. For he next drew his carriage even closer to hers. Before she had a chance to reason a reply, he reached over and grabbed her hand. He bowed his head, and Meredith watched with tingling anticipation as his lips brushed across her glove.

It was an intimate, familiar gesture that brought forth a gasp of astonishment from the duchess and her companions. Recovering her composure, Meredith tilted her head at a challenging angle. This time she met his gaze directly. "I hardly think a man of your reputation is a fair judge of the character of others." She folded her hands deliberately in her lap, yet she could still feel the burning imprint of his lips. "You must excuse us, my lord. I find I tire of the open air. Good afternoon, Your Grace. Ladies."

Their unenthusiastic replies were drowned out by the crunching wheels of the vehicle as it maneuvered down the path.

Trevor watched with an admiring glare as the carriage turned the corner and disappeared from view. He gradually became aware of the swell of nearby conversations, as those who had been listening to the exchange gleefully shared their impressions with each other.

"She sure is a beauty. I'd wager a gold sovereign

that blond hair of hers reaches below her waist. Must be a glorious sight to see her shaking it free, to watch it tumble down to her bottom."

Trevor twisted his neck and looked over at the man with exasperation. "I'll remind you only once that you are speaking of a *lady*. One who is far too good for the likes of you, Mallory."

"I meant no offense. I would never dream of poaching on your territory." Lord Mallory pulled a handkerchief from his coat pocket and pressed it to his brow. He was a stout fellow, prone to drink and occasional mean-spirited barbs, yet he usually lacked the backbone to do any fighting.

"We all know you are bound to get tired of her eventually, Dardington. You always do. That will leave the road clear for the rest of us to make a play for the lady's affections and favor."

Trevor had never considered himself to be an overly violent man. Yet the urge to smash his fist into Mallory's nose and watch a spurt of blood stain that white handkerchief was nearly overpowering.

Yet he did not act upon his emotions. He held them in tight rein. Yet he was so close to Mallory, he knew the other man must feel the waves of anger emanating from his body.

"Lady Meredith is the daughter of an earl," Trevor said. "She is a creature of delicate beauty, upstanding character, and refined sentiment. You, sir, are not fit to wipe her shoes."

The last comments were hardly necessary. The expression on his face must have clearly conveyed his meaning, for Mallory got rather red in the face, began sputtering like a lackwit, and at the first opportunity took off like a shot.

Seven

Trevor waited two days before he called upon her. He deliberately arrived early in the afternoon to avoid the possibility of meeting anyone else. The gossip about their relationship had not abated. New tidbits of outrageous speculation had reached even Trevor's ears. And there had been a note from his father reminding the marquess to stay away from the girl until the furor died down.

Which, of course, made Trevor realize it was essential that he visit Lady Meredith. The door to her family's Grosvenor Square home was answered by a meticulously dressed butler possessing a most dour expression.

"Lady Meredith is not at home, my lord," the servant insisted the moment the marquess gained entrance to the establishment.

Trevor grinned charmingly at the expected response. "Perhaps Lady Meredith will change her mind when she reads my card." The card he casually slipped into the butler's reluctant hand was accompanied by a gold sovereign.

The servant's eyebrow's raised fractionally as he studied the gold-embossed name. Then the coin disappeared from view. "I'll see what I can do, my lord."

The marquess was kept waiting no more than a min-

ute. Trevor looked up expectantly, but to his great consternation saw another gentleman approaching from the second floor.

"Ah, so that's the way the wind is blowing," the other man said. He nonchalantly smoothed the lace of his cuffs over the back of his well-manicured hands, then smiled broadly. "Though I've naturally heard all the rumors, Lady Meredith failed to mention you were among the current admirers she receives at home. As much as it pains me to lose her, it is far from a disgrace to be beat out by you."

Trevor stared hard at Julian Wingate. He had a narrow, arrogant face many women considered handsome, though Trevor thought there was an air of superiority about him that detracted from his features. Wingate was a military man, assigned to Wellington's own staff, yet his civilian dress of breeches, half boots, and a smartly creased coat suggested otherwise.

"I did not know you had returned to town," Trevor commented.

"I've been back a fortnight," Wingate replied cheerfully. "I resigned my commission last month. 'Tis good to be home."

Any further conversation between the two men was interrupted by the reappearance of the butler. "This way, my lord."

"Good luck, Dardington. Unless her ladyship's mood has improved considerably, I fear you shall need it."

The marquess watched the other man saunter casually down the hall and make a leisurely exit out the front door. Trevor was now completely unsure what to expect and was heartily relieved to find the drawing room contained only one person, Lady Meredith. Her back was toward him as he entered the room, but she whirled around at the sound of the door opening.

"Good afternoon, Lady Meredith."

For a moment her eyes looked blankly into his. Then she lifted her hand, rubbed her temple furiously and muttered something beneath her breath. "Apparently my butler has difficulty interpreting my orders. How much did it cost you to gain entrance?" she asked.

"Pardon?"

"My butler, Perkins, is still somewhat distressed over an incident that occurred several days ago. Your presence, along with that of Julian Wingate and Lord Fairchild, indicates Perkins has not yet forgiven me." She crossed her arms and stared at him with compressed lips. "Though well paid for a man in his position, I cannot imagine he would have the fortitude to forgo this sort of money making opportunity. How much?"

The marquess smiled. She looked stunning, as always. The simple pink-striped, high-waisted day gown highlighted the glow of her alabaster skin and neatly showcased her long-limbed beauty. "A gold sovereign," he reluctantly admitted.

"Ah, you are either more generous or more desperate than my other callers. They paid only half a guinea."

"It was worth every last cent," Trevor said honestly. Though he had seen her only a few days ago, he felt this sudden strange longing to be near her. He was in the process of taking a step forward when he realized his intentions. Fighting the pull, he stiffened his spine and rocked back on his heels.

"Perhaps it would be best if you had a word with Perkins," Trevor suggested. "I'm sure if you spoke to him sternly enough, he would not dare to cross you."

"And ruin his windfall?" Meredith laughed lightly. "That would be very cruel. At this rate he should be

able to comfortably retire back to the country before the year is out."

"I would never stand for such insolence from a servant," Trevor declared firmly, though in truth he knew his own valet could be positively tyrannical at times. "You might even consider sacking him. Or at the very least demoting him."

She smiled, very slowly. "Perkins is employed by my father and therefore answerable only to him. I have neither the authority nor the inclination to terminate his employment.

"Besides, he has done us a great favor by coming to town. He usually oversees our ancestral estate in Yorkshire, which he has often remarked is a far grander position. Perkins has only recently come to London to assume the duties here when our former butler became gravely ill."

The marquess was not impressed. "I would be concerned about such disloyalty within my household."

"You should be pleased at Perkins's display of insubordination. If he was a more scrupulous servant, you would have never gained entrance to my drawing room."

Trevor could feel the rush of heat in his cheeks. *Good lord, was he actually starting to blush?* "I suppose it is rather ungrateful to denounce my cohort." Trevor assumed what he hoped was a wounded, contrite look.

Meredith's eyes darted knowingly back and forth between his. Trevor resisted the urge to tug at his cravat, which suddenly felt a bit tight and constricting.

"You must tell me, my lord, what urgent matter required your corruption of my staff."

"Certainly." The marquess gestured toward the sofa. "May I?"

"If you must," Meredith replied, biting the words

through clenched teeth. She moved aside so he could gain entrance to the center of the room. "I had hoped you would not be staying long enough to require a seat."

He paused, tilted his head back, and gave her a smoldering smile. The backs of his calf touched the edge of the settee, yet Trevor deliberately remained on his feet.

"Oh, for heaven sakes," Meredith huffed ungraciously and flopped into a chair.

He marveled that her graceful beauty was still evident, even when she was trying to be a bore.

"Why was Julian Wingate here?"

"That is none of your concern."

Her voice was strong and steady, but he caught the unease quiver in her eyes and realized her bravado was a mask for her nervousness.

"I thought Wingate was engaged to be married," Trevor said.

"He is, and to a woman of my acquaintance. She is the sister-in-law of my oldest friend, which makes the situation even more awkward."

"How so?"

Meredith shrugged nonchalantly. "Though the notion might be considered old-fashioned, or even stuffy, I feel his intentions toward me are hardly appropriate for a man about to be married."

"Do you believe he will renounce his fiancée if you favor his suit?" Trevor scowled as an even more unpleasant thought came to mind. *"Do* you favor his suit?"

Meredith rolled her eyes. "Mr. Wingate was not offering me marriage."

Trevor shot to his feet. Annoyance billowed through him. "He shall answer to me for such insolence."

"Oh, do sit down, my lord." She crossed her arms

over her chest. "What did you expect? After your little display at the park the other afternoon, I have been on the receiving end of several less than reputable propositions. At the theater last night, not one respectable woman spoke directly to me. It was as if I were invisible."

"Your reputation?"

"In shreds, I fear. Though it might be restored in time. One can never tell with this sort of thing." She ran her tongue thoughtfully over her upper lip. "Not that I mind all that much. Truly. I have never overly enjoyed society, though I confess I prefer having the option of rejecting the *ton* instead of the other way round.

"However, I am very concerned about how this will impact my brothers. Already there are several fathers who have made rumblings that they do not wish their young, impressionable daughters to associate with them."

Trevor huffed. "Your brothers are both far too young to be considering marriage."

"Perhaps. Yet I have learned through years of observation that doors closed are seldom reopened. I would not wish that to be my brothers' fate."

She lowered her eyes, and he noticed she was fidgeting with the single flounce on the skirt of her gown. Though she was trying valiantly to make light of the situation, it was clear she was unhappy. And regretful.

"Do you know what you need?" he asked, gazing at her steadily. "A little reminder of what landed us in this hornet's nest in the first place."

He reached out and curled a stray wisp of blond hair around her ear. She looked up, clearly caught off guard. A wave of tenderness and desire surged though him. Taking her lovely face gently between his hands, he held her head still and pressed his lips upon hers.

He wasn't sure she would accept his kiss. He felt her stiffen, hesitate, but then, to his great joy and relief, her lips parted to welcome the thrust of his tongue.

The sweet taste of her nearly made Trevor dizzy, bringing forth a rush of pure pleasure to every nerve in his body. He slipped one arm around her back, pulled her closer to him, and continued to kiss her mouth slowly, intimately, until he heard her moans of excitement. She was a passionate creature, and he yearned for her in a way he almost could not understand.

He softened his lips and moved over hers in gentle, exploratory touches. His fingers lightly caressed the delicate, vulnerable place where her neck and shoulder joined, and then the tip of his tongue followed the same path. She moaned louder and curled her arms around his neck, straining upward toward his heated body.

Trevor inhaled her warm, womanly scent, and his spiraling arousal reached the heights of sweet desperation. He felt as though he were standing on a cliff and the ground was slowly giving way beneath him.

Suddenly, he pulled his lips away. He could feel her trembling in the curve of his arm, yet he knew if he allowed this to go any further, he would end up seducing her on the drawing room settee.

Their eyes met and held, mere inches apart. In that instant she was so open, so beautiful it nearly made his heart stop. Trevor cleared his throat.

"In the midst of all this misery and scandal you have overlooked the simplest, most direct way to end it all."

"I have?" she whispered.

"Yes." Unable to resist, he nuzzled the side of her throat. "We could get married."

She jerked in response and stared at him incredulously. "You are joking."

"I am alarmingly serious."

This was hardly the first proposal of marriage Meredith had ever received. In her coming-out season alone, there had been an even half dozen offers for her hand. Lovestruck youths on bended knee, mature widowers who spoke of companionship and security, accomplished rakes who smoothly vowed to forsake their hedonistic ways and transform themselves into pillars of society, had all crowded this very drawing room.

There had been endless praise of her beauty, her spirit, her womanly charms. The proposals were as varied and unique as the men who made them, yet they shared one very important trait. They each had left her feeling slightly queasy and completely disinterested.

Yet the marquess's remark, spoken in an almost offhanded manner, had not brought forth the usual reaction. His words had opened up a well of endless possibilities within Meredith's soul. They had miraculously struck a chord somewhere deep within her.

She dared to look into his blue eyes, and for just an instant felt herself falling into them. But she could not! It would be disastrous for them both. Meredith shook her head slightly and resolutely put her attraction to him aside.

"That is a most impossible suggestion, my lord."

He leaned down and kissed the top of her hand. "Are you very certain, Meredith? I promise it would not be all that grim to be married to me. I am hardly a man who would insist upon obedience and submissive behavior from you."

"Therein lies the dilemma, my lord, for I would expect that of you."

"Submission? Or obedience?" He smiled softly, and Meredith realized he did so rarely. Perhaps that was for the best. The devastating charm his relaxed smile evoked played havoc with her peace of mind.

Before she realized his intent, he kissed her again. Deeply, passionately, and with such gentle eroticism her lips tingled. He kissed the edge of her temple, the side of her cheek and the corner of her mouth. She put her hand on his chest and felt the solid wall of muscle beneath. Her thought was to push him away, yet the unbearable tension knotting inside her left her feeling almost too weak to accomplish the task.

Instead Meredith's traitorous body strained toward his, seeking the intimate pleasures he was offering. Trevor's fingertips drifted down her throat to the swell of her breasts. Reverently he cupped them, one in each palm. She closed her eyes and sighed as he stroked and teased the nipples until they ached and hardened.

He murmured something low and urgent and then lifted her onto his lap. She knew she should protest, tell him to cease at once, but her voice could not be found. Her cheek turned against his shoulder, her rapid breath fanned his heated flesh. His legs shifted so that the hard bulge beneath his breeches was fitted against her womanhood.

A heavy, sweet ache formed inside her as Trevor began a rhythmic rocking motion, pressing his hips into hers. Meredith's body jolted alive. *This is madness!*

The heartbeat drumming in her ears was suddenly threatening to drown out all sense of reality. Abruptly Meredith pulled away. She rose, frightened and confused, nearly stumbling as her weakened knees began to collapse.

A shaken sound escaped her lips, and she struggled to control her labored breathing. In this emotional and

physical state it was difficult to think clearly, but Meredith gave it a valiant effort.

A marriage between them could never occur. She began to list the objections to the match in her mind and found she could not form a single coherent thought.

But she must. Meredith forced herself to ignore the great heat that seemed to be emanating from him, despite the distance between them. Nearly every inch of her skin felt on fire, but she did not allow herself to think of it. Now, more than any other moment in her life, she must remain clearheaded and logical.

How could they possibly marry? Once the passion was purged from her body, she would find herself trapped, married to a man who had no real interest in her, no true regard for her. Meredith could not imagine a more miserable experience.

She knew Trevor possessed the ability to love a woman well and completely, for she had witnessed the remarkable happiness he had shared with Lavinia. Yet Meredith entertained no illusions about the possibility of rekindling that degree of love and devotion in Trevor toward herself.

He had changed much in the years since Lavinia's death and not for the better. The Trevor of today would be a most unsatisfactory husband.

And what of herself? Though she did not like to dwell upon her shortcomings—after all, what person did?—Meredith feared she would make an equally unsatisfactory wife.

"I appreciate your honorable solution to my current difficulties, yet there is no need to sacrifice ourselves to the dictates of a society neither of us respects," Meredith said, focusing her eyes upon the spot just above his left ear. "It would be foolish if we allowed this scandal to bring us a lifetime of unhappiness."

"A lifetime, dear Meredith?" His mouth twitched. "That is a bit overdramatic. A simple no to my proposal would have sufficed."

Her common sense told her she had done the right thing, had given him the only reasonable answer possible. Yet why did she feel like such a coward? There was a mocking half smile upon his lips, but for just an instant she thought she had seen a flash of hurt—or maybe it was disappointment—in his eyes.

She put her tongue firmly between her teeth and held herself rigid as the marquess stood. He kept his eyes pinned to hers as he deliberately adjusted his clothing, the clothing she had mussed during their kisses. To her dismay, she found it necessary to blink several times in order to contain the sudden emotion that had sprung to her eyes.

"I thank you for your visit today, my lord." She dipped into a low, graceful curtsy.

He shot her a searching glance. When she failed to respond, Trevor gave a curt nod of his head, turned on his heel and left the room without a backward glance. She listened intently until she heard his footsteps fade from the hallway, strained mightily to hear the front door being opened and then closed behind him.

She wondered if and when she would see him again and realized it might not be for a very long time. And if they did meet by chance, it would certainly be in a room filled with people. In all likelihood, she would never again be alone with the handsome, dashing marquess.

Strange. The reality of that made her feel hollow and empty, almost to the point of desolation.

Hoping to settle her nerves, Meredith took a long, hot soaking bath after dinner. Reclining lazily with

her head propped on the edge of the porcelain tub, she let the steaming water seep into her bones in an effort to ease some of the tension. But while the soothing waters had some effect on her body, they could do nothing to ease the torment that clouded her mind.

She sought her bed soon after her bath and drifted through hours of fitful slumber, until a noise outside her bedchamber drew her awake.

It began as a low rumble, then escalated to a persistent drone. Meredith rolled over on her side and tried to ignore the sounds, but they persisted. It was a conversation. Low and hushed and whispered, but echoing through the cavernous hallway and into her room. Puzzled, Meredith looked toward the bedchamber door, and heard it again.

There were at least two, perhaps three different voices. She thought one of them might be her maid, Rose, but could not be certain. Tired and out of sorts from lack of sleep, Meredith pushed back the coverlet, climbed from her bed, and padded barefoot to the door to investigate.

She yanked open her door, fully prepared to chastise whoever stood in the hallway at this unmentionable hour of the early morning, but found it empty. Frowning, she poked her head out and glanced furtively up and down the corridor.

There was no one in sight. Questioning her eyesight, as well as her hearing, Meredith squinted intently into the darkened hallway.

"Who's there?" she called out suddenly, nearly jumping when she heard the loudness of her own voice breaking through the quiet.

There was no answer. Meredith blinked, then saw a shadow move at the end of the hallway. A cold shiver of apprehension ran up her spine. "Show yourself at

once!" she commanded, thrusting her hands deep into the pockets of her nightgown to hide their trembling.

"Beg pardon, my lady," a quivering female voice replied. " 'Tis only me, Rose."

"Who is with you, Rose? Will they not show themselves too?"

Rose turned her head and whispered something to her companion.

" 'Tis me, Lady Meredith," a proper male voice announced.

"Perkins?" Meredith stepped back into the shadow of her doorway to avoid being seen by her butler in her nightgown.

"I apologize if we woke you," Perkins said.

Meredith moistened her dry lips with her tongue. There was something in the butler's tone and manner that disturbed her. "Is something amiss?"

"Oh, my lady." Rose rushed forward, her face a mask of fear. " 'Tis Lord Fairhurst and Mr. Jason."

Meredith stepped forward. "What has happened?"

"Nothing," Perkins said, as he too came forth. "A harmless incident below stairs has been given far too much attention and dramatic interpretation."

Perkins gave Rose a pointed stare, and Meredith saw the glimmer of fear in Rose's eyes flare.

"Please explain," Meredith demanded.

Perkins sighed. "Apparently a member of the staff noticed your brothers leaving the house a half hour ago and became concerned. The ensuing commotion woke several other servants, and I was called upon to set things to right. I assure you the matter is under control."

"Leaving the house? Surely they were mistaken. This is the time of the morning my brothers generally return home."

The butler gave her a strange half smile and

shrugged his shoulders. Meredith quickly glanced over at her maid. Rose's hands were by her sides, but they were clenching and unclenching fistfuls of her skirt.

"What are you not telling me?"

"There's going to be a duel!" Rose blurted out in a horrified whisper. "Lord Fairhurst and Mr. Jason are going to avenge the insult to your honor. One of your brothers will fight the Marquess of Dardington and the other will act as his second."

"Rose!" Perkins cast a sharp look of reprimand at the maid, but the maid appeared too distracted to notice.

"George, the stable boy, heard Mr. Jason's valet tell the coachman and he told Roberts, the underfootman, and he told—"

"Idle kitchen gossip," Perkins interrupted. "I instructed Rose not to disturb you with such drivel. I apologize for interrupting your sleep, my lady."

Meredith barely heard the butler's apology. Could this possibly be true? Her brothers were not known for their level heads, but even they would not be so foolish as to engage in an illegal and possibly deadly ritual. Meredith looked sharply at her maid. Rose was in most instances a levelheaded woman, yet she was on occasion prone to exaggeration. And she did have a real love of gossip.

Still, there was no doubt the maid's agitation and fear were very real. Meredith's stomach tingled with the rush of sudden fear. "Is it true that my brothers have left the house, Perkins?"

The butler nodded solemnly.

"Where have they gone?"

"I do not know."

There was a crack in the butler's rigid countenance, and Meredith's fear heightened. "Well, someone in the household must know their whereabouts. I want every

servant questioned. Immediately." She turned to her maid. "Rose, you must help me dress. Assemble the entire staff in the drawing room. By the time I appear below stairs, I want to know exactly what is going on."

Fighting her rising panic, Meredith allowed Rose to dress her, but the haste in completing her toilet made no difference. All that could be confirmed after questioning the entire staff was that the duel was to take place at dawn. None of the servants had any idea where.

"I am sorry, Lady Meredith," Perkins said regretfully. "Perhaps Lord Fairhurst or Mr. Jason's valets could have been of some assistance, but they are well and truly gone. I checked their sleeping quarters myself."

Raw emotion filled Meredith's heart as a feeling of total helplessness swept over her. But she tamped down the emotion. She must think! Lives depended on her acting quickly and rationally. "I must do whatever I can to stop this lunacy. Where, in your opinion, is the most likely location for this . . . this event?"

Perkins looked miserable. "Since the activity is not looked upon with great favor, these incidents often occur on private estates. Considering the hour of the morning the gentlemen left the house, they could not have been traveling too far out of London. There might be time to catch them, if you knew where to look."

"Then I must discover where to look," Meredith declared grimly. "And quickly."

She summoned the coach and waited impatiently for it to be brought out, all the while trying to decide who she could call upon for help. Her mouth curved in an ironic frown when she realized her first instinct was to call upon the Marquess of Dardington.

A chill went through her as she stepped onto the

deserted street. Meredith's eyes hastily scanned the quiet, sleepy mansions that lined the square and came to rest on an impressive stone structure three doors down.

It belonged to the Duke of Shrewsbury, but Meredith distinctly remembered that Julian Wingate had told her he was residing with the duke, who was his maternal grandfather, while in town. Did she dare call upon him at this uncivilized hour?

Meredith's coachman's knock upon the front door of the duke's home was answered by a hastily garbed butler who looked most annoyed at the interruption. Peeking behind the drawn shade of the carriage, Meredith held her breath as the two servants exchanged words.

"Mr. Wingate is not at home, but his valet has agreed to speak with you," the coachman reported when he returned to the coach. Meredith let out a sigh of relief.

After what felt like an eternity, the valet at last appeared, with a mulish expression and a scornful attitude. Meredith's hopes plummeted, but she refused to be defeated. Opening the carriage door wide, she graciously invited the valet inside the coach.

"You are so kind to see me," Meredith said softly. "I'm afraid I must beg your indulgence in a most delicate matter, Mr.—"

"Hawkins, my lady," came the stiff reply.

Meredith folded her hands in her lap and looked steadily at him. "Do you have any siblings, Mr. Hawkins?"

"A sister," the valet answered in a surprised tone.

Meredith let forth a small grin of relief. "Ah, then you understand the obligations of family. I love my twin brothers dearly and fear they have put their lives in grave danger. I've heard rumors of a duel that is

to take place sometime this morning, involving my brothers. I was hoping Mr. Wingate might be able to tell me where this will occur."

Hawkins' eyes narrowed. "My employer does not engage in illegal activities."

"I apologize if you misunderstood," Meredith added hastily. "I never meant to imply Mr. Wingate was involved in any way. Yet I would suspect a gentleman of Mr. Wingate's stature certainly knows about such things. And you, as his valet, would naturally be privileged to the same information."

"I might." The servant's chest puffed out slightly.

Meredith nearly screamed with worry. She was well aware the servant was under no obligation to tell her anything. Her fingers clutched the small leather pouch of coins she held in the palm of her hand, but for some reason she resisted offering him the money.

While she knew from experience that many of her own servants would easily respond to a monetary inducement, she suspected Wingate's valet would not. He seemed a man more interested in his importance. Fearful that if she insulted him he would stalk away without revealing anything, Meredith took a deep, calming breath and forced herself to proceed slowly.

"I know I can rely only upon a man of your stature and importance to assist me in this most delicate matter." Though her stomach was churning with emotion, she managed to gave him a wavy smile. "Will you help me, sir?"

The valet's expression never faltered. In desperation, Meredith began pulling out the bag of coins from her pocket, but before she could offer them the servant spoke.

"I suspect if you drove to a large clearing on the south edge of Hyde Park, my lady, you would find something of keen interest."

Meredith sagged forward. "I am forever in your debt," she whispered emotionally.

The valet inclined his head and exited the coach. The moment he stepped down, Meredith gave the coachman their destination and the carriage raced off.

The first streaks of dawn were beginning to light the distant horizon. Meredith remained glued to the window of the carriage, watching with mounting concern as the deep gray of night gave way to a lighter hue. Then shafts of pale yellow, red, and blue began to emerge.

On any other day, she would have enjoyed watching the brilliant colors of the morning begin to light the sky. But today the coming dawn meant she was running out of precious time.

They could be mortally wounded. It was far too easy to imagine one of them with a gaping black bullet hole in his chest, lying in the grass, still and silent as his life's blood stained the ground a shocking crimson red.

It could be any of them. Jasper. Or Jason. Or Trevor. Meredith closed her eyes and shuddered, then firmly repressed the pain she felt.

At long last they reached the park. As they rounded the corner, Meredith craned her neck out of the window, desperate for a better view. Her eyes darted across the horizon, as swirls of fog and mist obstructed her sight.

"There!" she shouted. "On the edge of that secluded stretch of lawn. Do you see them?"

"Aye, my lady," the coachman grunted. "Hold fast."

Meredith gripped the edge of the seat as the coach lurched awkwardly to one side. Pulling herself up, she straightened and looked out the window. Hope stirred within her breast. There was a group of men milling

about on the crest of the hill. All were standing up-right—for the moment.

"Let me out here," she called, fearing it would take too long for the cumbersome vehicle to gain the top of the knoll.

Gradually the carriage began to slow. Giving no thought to her own safety, Meredith leaped from the still moving vehicle, landing upon the soggy grass with a loud thud. The moment her feet touched the earth, she picked her skirts up above her ankles and broke into a run.

Eight

Trevor Morely, Marquess of Dardington, was in good spirits as he stood on the damp grass in Hyde Park. The dawn was just beginning to appear on this cool, slightly wet morning and the brilliant colors of the day reminded him of his favorite painting, a pastoral landscape done by a unknown artist more than a century ago.

There were ten other gentlemen convened with the marquess on the grassy knoll. Most were conversing in quiet, civilized tones—except for the two youngest men, who were engaged in a serious and often times ear-splitting discourse over which of them would be granted the privilege of defending their sister's honor.

"I am the elder. It falls to me to preserve the family position and reputation."

"Yes, you are the elder, Jasper. And the heir. Therefore it should be I who risks his life. My death would have a small impact upon the family."

"Don't be an idiot. Meredith would never forgive me if anything happened to you. Besides, I have no intention of getting killed or wounded—yet another reason why I should be the one to fight. You shall be my second, Jason."

Jason responded with a jeering noise. "I put forth the challenge to Dardington."

"You did not!"

"I did so!"

Jasper paused for a moment and flexed his fingers. "Even if that were true, it makes no difference. I have decided I will be the duelist."

"You have decided! 'Tis not your decision to make."

The bickering between the two brothers continued at an even higher volume. In the gray half light and swirling mist, Trevor had difficulty telling the twins apart, yet it was clear each was filled with passion over the rightness of their cause.

"Perhaps it would be best to let the two of them duel with each other first," Julian Wingate observed. "Then you could challenge the winner. I fear we shall miss breakfast and luncheon if we wait for these two young pups to make a decision."

"I am in no great rush." Trevor took a step back and frowned at Wingate. He was not certain how the man came to be a member of the party, for he had not invited him along. Yet as Trevor took a closer look at the throng of interested male spectators, he realized that aside from Viscount Aarons, who was acting as his second, he knew only one other gentleman in attendance.

"If it were me, I'd prefer to face the younger brother, Jason," Wingate added. "He is rumored to be a keen shot, but his emotions are clearly riding high. With a steady arm and careful aim, you could hit him the moment the signal is given to fire."

Trevor's lips curled in distaste. "You have been too long on the battlefield, Wingate. 'Tis well known that in a duel, honor can be served without killing someone."

Wingate shrugged. "Honor is only a part of this

ritual. Equally important is the need to prove one's superior manhood."

The last comment was apparently heard by the twins, for they ceased arguing with each other, turned, and gave Wingate a nearly identical cool, arrogant stare. Trevor had to bite his lip to keep from smiling. The two brothers were filled with a vibrant, self-possessed attitude clearly reminiscent of their sister.

"Now that they have ceased fighting for a moment, let me see if I can do anything to expedite this matter," Viscount Aarons said.

Taking his duties as second most seriously, the viscount strode off purposefully to confer with the twins. Trevor watched as the viscount's solemn expression changed to one of impatience and then finally annoyance. This time Trevor could not suppress his smile when the viscount sighed heavily before withdrawing a coin from his pocket.

"Is it finally decided?" the marquess asked, when the viscount returned.

"At last," Viscount Aarons answered with a bit of impatience in his tone. "I forced them to flip a coin. It was the only solution I could contrive. Lord Fairhurst will duel and Mr. Jason Barrington will act as his second. I assumed you would not be inclined to issue an apology, so I've already rejected Barrington's suggestion. All we need to do now is load and inspect the pistols. Then we can finally get started."

"Splendid." Trevor smiled, then handed the viscount the engraved dueling pistol he had just finished cleaning.

Though the other men in the gathering were clearly annoyed by the many delays, Trevor had found it most amusing. He had been impressed by the heated discussion between the twins and wondered how much

of it had been real and how much had been for the benefit of the crowd.

For, unbeknownst to any of those in attendance, the outcome of this morning's duel had already been determined.

The brothers had been genuinely distressed over their sister's disgrace and the part they had played in it. They had approached the marquess last night in hopes of finding an agreeable solution.

Previously, Trevor had thought them to be a rather reckless, irresponsible pair, but he had been moved by their devotion to their sister and their determination to somehow set things to rights. After sharing several glasses of fine French brandy, the marquess surprised himself by revealing that he had in fact asked Lady Meredith, on that very afternoon, to become his bride. But she had adamantly refused his offer.

"Does not shock me at all," Jason had replied. Though his words were slightly slurred, the marquess had understood them. "Merry would never agree to the obvious and easiest solution."

"Goes against her nature, I think," Jasper added.

With a commiserative shake of their heads, all three men poured another round of spirits and discussed an alternative solution. Thanks to the strong drink and lateness of the hour, the marquess could not remember which twin had suggested a duel.

Yet once mentioned, the idea was seized upon with great zeal. If nothing else, a duel between the marquess and one of the brothers would shift the focus of the scandal. It might even garner Meredith some much needed sympathy from the female population. And it would certainly put an end to the unwanted male attention that now plagued her.

The impatient grumbling of the crowd of spectators quickly fell to a hushed silence as the duel at last

began. The marquess nonchalantly accepted his now loaded pistol from his second and took up his position, his back toward his adversary. He refrained from looking at either Jasper or Jason, knowing at this point he needed to keep his full focus on the business at hand.

His glance fell momentarily upon the surgeon, medical bag in hand, who was present. If all went according to plan, the man's services would not be needed. After a lengthy, private discussion, the marquess and the twins had agreed it would not be necessary to draw blood in order to preserve Meredith's reputation.

Even a well-placed shot in the leg or arm could fester and cause unbearable pain, or possibly fatal consequences. No, 'twas far safer for each duelist to take fair aim and shoot wide, missing his opponent by a clear margin.

Trevor straightened his spine and strode carefully as Julian Wingate called out the regulation number of steps. Then he turned, stood sideways, raised his arm and took careful aim. Knowing his opponent had no intention of harming him made it a bit easier to stare down the end of the opposing pistol barrel with a steady glare.

He was relieved to note that Jasper looked equally calm. Trevor cocked the hammer of his gun, awaiting the signal to fire. The silence among the spectators became an almost tangible thing, as they waited with respectful quiet for the battle to begin.

The marquess's concentration was so focused that he did not at first hear the distraction on the sidelines. He turned his head and saw Julian Wingate hold up his hand in a firm staying gesture. Then Trevor heard a voice, high, breathless and female.

"Stop! For the love of God, stop this madness at once!"

Under his breath, Trevor swore colorfully. He knew that voice could belong to only one female, one head-strong, obstinate woman who had a knack for picking the most damnably inconvenient times to show up.

The marquess saw his opponent waver for a moment, an expression of incomprehension on his young face. Trevor relaxed his stance, but did not lower his arm. For some perverse reason, he did not want to deprive Lady Meredith of the full effect of the duel.

"Deuce take it! What are you doing here?" Julian Wingate called from the sidelines. "You are an unwanted and inappropriate distraction, Lady Meredith. Please return to your coach and leave the premisses at once."

Wingate's voice was joined by those of several other spectators, all jeering the untimely interruption of the morning's fun.

Lady Meredith silenced them all with a single withering glare. Trevor observed that her cheeks were flushed with emotion, but they had paled noticeably when she had reached the top of the knoll and saw clearly how close he and Jasper stood, pistols drawn and aimed.

That momentary look of an uncontrolled frenzy was now gone, replaced once more by the calm, collected air that announced to all Lady Meredith was once again in charge of herself.

"Have you all lost complete control of your senses?" she shouted, her eyes glinting dangerously. "This will solve nothing."

"Wingate is right, Merry," Jasper declared. "This is no place for a lady. 'Tis men's business. You must go home immediately."

"I will leave only if you and Jason accompany me," Lady Meredith retorted, planting her feet firmly in the grass.

"Meredith, please." Jason strode toward his sister.

Her chin rose. Trevor felt a jolt of sympathy for Jason, knowing there would be little chance the man would succeed in getting his sister to do his bidding.

The marquess slowly lowered his right arm. He could feel the tension lock along his shoulder; the strain of keeping his arm raised was too much. He noticed Jasper doing the same, a silent acknowledgement there would be no duel this morning.

After shrugging into his waistcoat and coat, Jasper joined his twin at Meredith's side. The men stood close together, their bodies shielding her from the questioning eyes of the crowd. Unfortunately they could do nothing to modulate the volume of her voice. Her words rang out loud and clear for all to hear.

"I told you repeatedly that the marquess offered me no insult, but you would not listen. If you felt it necessary to defend my honor, could you not have settled upon a less lethal manner?" Lady Meredith asked. "You boast constantly of your sparring skills, honed to near perfection at Jackson's boxing salon. Would not landing a blow to the marquess's jaw or nose have appeased your inflated sense of honor?"

"What? Are you suggesting I should have planted a facer on him in the middle of White's?"

"That is certainly preferable to a bullet through the heart." Meredith hmmphed. "Of course, little damage would have been sustained if the shot struck you in the head. There is naught between your ears but a lot of empty space, Jasper."

Trevor smiled inwardly. Though he suspected he might make this volatile situation even worse, he found it impossible to hold his tongue. "Perhaps this discussion would best be continued in private," he suggested, coming forward until he was standing almost toe to toe with Lady Meredith.

Meredith jerked her head around and gave him a glare that could wilt a hothouse rose on a winter's day. "Your opinion is not required, my lord. This is a family matter. It is most inappropriate for you to interfere."

"You are hardly one to be speaking of propriety," Trevor said. "It might amaze you to know this, Lady Meredith, but there do exist women who know their proper place in the world. Women who know how to be submissive and obedient."

"I shall say a prayer for these unfortunate souls in church next Sunday," she retorted, before turning her back on him in an obviously dismissive gesture. "If you will kindly excuse us, I shall escort my brothers home before any other idiotic male ideas for preserving our family honor are presented."

" 'Tis not completely our fault," Jasper sulked as he trailed languidly behind his sister. "Dardington gave you an opportunity to end this without bloodshed, yet you refused him."

Meredith stopped walking. A wary look passed through her eyes. "I do not know what you mean."

"Have you forgotten our conversation yesterday afternoon already, Lady Meredith?" Trevor closed the distance between them and placed a hand on her shoulder. "I am crushed."

Her head swung around. "He told you?" she asked her brothers. "About yesterday?"

"Yes," Jasper replied.

She turned completely around and faced the marquess. For an instant her face looked naked and vulnerable, her eyes haunted with doubt and confusion. "Why?"

"They wanted to know what my opinion of you was, so I enlightened them," Trevor replied. "I saw no harm."

"You are speaking in riddles, Dardington," Julian

Wingate interjected. He had come, unnoticed, to stand beside them all and apparently eavesdrop on their conversation.

Trevor ignored Wingate. The marquess had not taken his eyes off Meredith. She stood very still and very straight, her hands clasped against her cloak. He wished he had some idea of what she was thinking, but her expression gave no indication of her inner emotions. Trevor wisely kept his mouth shut and waited.

"If you must know, the marquess is referring to the proposal of marriage he made to me yesterday afternoon." Lady Meredith waved one careless hand. "Not that it is any of your business whom I marry, Mr. Wingate."

"Devil take it," Wingate said, scratching the side of his head. "If you are going to marry Dardington, why are your brothers dueling with the man?"

"Why indeed?" Meredith gave an irate sniff and pointed her nose in the air. "It is, I grant you, a most peculiar way to welcome someone into the family. But surely you must have heard that we Barringtons are an eccentric, unconventional lot."

The twins turned and looked at the marquess with identical expressions of shock and incomprehension on their faces. Trevor imagined his own face contained the exact reaction.

For it appeared Lady Meredith had just announced, in a most forthright manner, that she was going to marry him. Fancy that!

It was a most unusual wedding, considering the stature and rank of the bride and groom. A hastily contrived service, taking place in the bride's home, with only her brothers and a handful of loyal servants as

witnesses. There was no one in attendance on behalf of the groom.

The special license had been obtained by the bride's brothers, who had a rather busy day by any gentleman's standards: a near duel in the morning; rushed, secretive wedding preparations until noon; and a private late afternoon nuptial ceremony for their only sister.

As Meredith watched her two brothers share a toast of fine French champagne with her new husband, she told herself she had made the only decision possible. Marrying the marquess would keep the twins safe from duels defending her honor. Accomplishing that task alone justified the sacrifice she had made.

She had never known greater fear, nor felt such a depressing sense of helplessness as she had early that morning, witnessing Jasper and the marquess standing so straight and calm, their pistols pointed at each other's hearts. The sight was mesmerizing, in a terrifying, helpless way, and she had nearly fainted when she first viewed it.

To think her careless actions had brought the twins to such desperate measures was a somber, heart-stopping realization. She knew in that moment she would have to concede, would have to marry the marquess to save them all from the possibility of grief.

Meredith looked down at the nosegay of violets in her hand. The simple bouquet had been a gift from the marquess, presented with casual sincerity just before the wedding ceremony began. The romantic gesture had pleased her greatly, and she had felt the faint warmth of a blush creep on the back of her neck when she accepted the flowers and then stammered a quiet word of thanks.

"Come join us for some champagne, Merry," Jasper

called out gaily. "Dardington had a case of the stuff sent over, and we've only polished off one bottle."

"Yes, join us," Jason insisted. "If we cannot put a respectable dent in the case we shall we forced to bathe in it. Just like Brummel."

"You've got that wrong," Trevor interjected. "Brummel does not bathe in champagne, but 'tis said he has his boots cleaned in it."

"Really?" Meredith smiled and moved forward. "That seems like a ridiculous waste of good wine."

"Indeed." Trevor filled a crystal flute and placed it in her hand. All four clinked their goblets together, then exchanged a hearty laugh. Meredith took a large sip of her wine and felt a surge of optimism. Even though there had been long stretches of silence before and after the ceremony, the prevailing feeling had been one of ease.

There was some tension. How could there not be, given the circumstances of the wedding? Yet there were no barbed undercurrents. This unexpected and most welcome sense of serenity gave Meredith reason to hope.

Yes, she had undertaken this marriage partially for the sake of her brothers, to save them from future foolishness. She had also done this partially for the marquess's sake. Though she still doubted her abilities to be the type of wife he might expect, she felt confident she could at least provide some of the essential elements of a comfortable marriage.

Companionship, if he so desired, lively conversation, a warm, welcoming home, perhaps even a child or two someday, if the marquess wished. She remembered the strength of his kisses, the heat of his caress, and her heart skipped a beat at the thought of creating that life.

And so that was the last bit of truth. She had mar-

ried him in part because of her brothers, in part because he needed someone to take care of him, and in part because she knew her feelings for him went beyond mere concern. Beyond mere attraction.

She was in love with him. Unexpectedly, inexplicably and foolishly in love with him. Meredith had been deeply afraid to acknowledge that truth to herself because she had been frightened of the implications.

Yet she could not hold back her emotions when it appeared the marquess might not live to see another dawn. If that happened, Meredith conceded it would be nearly impossible to face each day that remained of her life.

And now, if given the chance, she could make him and herself very, very happy. Meredith took another large gulp of her champagne and nearly laughed out loud at her own sense of arrogant self-importance. Though a part of her acknowledged it was comical to believe she could control the world when she lacked the power to command her wayward heart, she was nevertheless determined to try.

She was not like other brides, filled with false illusions about a lifetime together that would be filled with only love, happiness, and good fortune. She was prepared to face the challenges of the difficult and uncertain times that lay ahead.

Meredith's gaze was pulled to her new husband. He had dressed formally in a dark coat, knee breeches, silk stockings and black shoes. The embroidery on his waistcoat was an exquisite creation of wildflowers done in threads of gold and silver. The sight was mesmerizing.

Her mouth had momentarily fell open when he swept into the room earlier. Fortunately she managed to snap it closed quickly, hopefully before he noticed.

"More champagne?"

Startled, Meredith abandoned her thoughts and extended her empty goblet toward her husband. She tilted her chin so she could gaze fully upon his handsome face, then muttered a quiet, "Thank you."

The marquess returned her perusal. His expression was set and locked, almost grim. She could feel his eyes searching her face and had no idea what he saw. Her feelings were such a mass of contradictions that she knew no one emotion could be clearly displayed.

Then he lifted his glass fractionally, smiled and wet his lips. The small edge of fear that she might have made a monumental mistake by marrying him vanished. Meredith imitated the marquess's gesture, emptying her glass in the process.

No matter what occurred, she would do all that was within her power to make the best of it.

The first test of her union came less than an hour after she had spoken her vows, when Jason innocently inquired where the newly married couple would reside.

"I no longer keep a house in London," the marquess answered slowly. "However, I do own three estates, two of which are of considerable size. The nearest is in Devon. Would you like to take up residence there?"

"Today?"

"We could leave within the hour." The marquess stroked his chin thoughtfully. "Though I rarely visit Hawthorne Manor, I employ a full staff that prides itself on always being ready to receive me with no advance warning."

"How long would we stay?" Meredith inquired.

Marquess shrugged. "Indefinitely. However if Hawthorne Manor is not to your liking, you may travel to Chester House. Or Billingsworth Castle."

"Are these properties close to each other?"

"Not exactly. Billingsworth Castle is very pictur-

esque, if you enjoy the country." A puzzled expression appeared on the marquess's face. "Do you enjoy the countryside? It occurs to me you might prefer to stay in town, at least for a few more weeks. The Season has yet to reach its full height."

"The activities of the Season do not hold great appeal for me," Meredith answered truthfully, wondering if it would be a wise or foolish thing to leave London. "However, I would not like to give the impression we are running away from anything by suddenly going off to the country to rusticate."

The marquess's eyebrows drew together. "You are now my wife, under my protection, and, as the Marchioness of Dardington, are therefore above the petty gossip that so amuses the *ton.*"

With effort, Meredith bit back her cynical retort. She suspected just the opposite was true, and she would in truth be the object of much gossip and speculation. Yet she had no wish to start an argument with her husband, especially in front of her brothers. "I see no pressing need for us to remain in town. I can be ready to leave for Hawthorne Manor whenever you wish."

"Fine. I shall be pleased to escort you there and leave instructions with my staff that you are to be brought to the other properties if you so desire."

"Will you not accompany me if I travel to the other estates, my lord?"

The marquess gave her a questioning look, but said nothing. Meredith faltered. His silence clearly meant something significant, yet she refused to believe the obvious.

The air in the room suddenly felt icy. "You plan on returning to London without me?" she finally asked.

"Of course."

"When?"

"I am not sure." He continued, ignoring her sharp intake of breath. "Most likely in a week. Two at the most."

"And I am to be left behind in the country? At Hawthorne Manor?" There was an uncomfortable churning in her stomach and a bitter taste in her mouth.

"Don't look so stricken, my lady. I assure that it is a fine estate," Trevor said in a level tone. "And I have already given you my permission to move to the other estates if you feel the need."

"What if I wish to return to London?"

Trevor frowned. "You just said there was no pressing need to remain in town."

"What if I wish to remain with my husband?" she asked curtly. "What if I object to being left in the country while you spend your days and nights in town? Without me."

"You just said the social activities of the Season are of little interest to you."

"And so they are, but I must confess your activities are of interest to me."

He was clearly taken aback by her blunt response. "It makes little sense to journey to the countryside if neither of us has any intention of staying for any length of time. We might as well remain in town."

"Fine." The strain of keeping her tone even and steady was difficult. "Since you have no appropriate lodgings, I shall have rooms prepared for us here. I am certain we can make you comfortable."

Meredith turned her head swiftly and glanced over at the twins. Their eyes were filled with sympathy. She smothered a sense of anger and irritation. More than anything, Meredith hated to be pitied.

"I will not impose upon the hospitality of my newly acquired in-laws as though I were some indigent fortune hunter," the marquess snapped. "Especially when

your parents are not available to grant their permission."

"Oh, for pity's sake, we are all family now," Meredith cried out. "If you require permission, my lord husband, then I will grant it to you."

The moment the words fell from her tongue Meredith wished she could call them back. The thunderous expression on the marquess's face let her know this was not a solution he found acceptable.

"We need stay only until your man of affairs can locate a property in town for us to rent," she added hastily.

Chilled by the mask-like expression of determination on the marquess's face, Meredith wisely made no more additional suggestions.

"Instruct your maid to pack your clothing."

To Meredith's ears the words sounded all the more forceful because they were spoken with such quiet, stubborn authority.

She made a slight curtsy before quitting the room. Yet Meredith made a point of returning quickly, dressed in her newest walking cloak and matching bonnet. "I told Rose to pack a smaller case with any garments that are needed for a few days. The rest of my clothing and personal items can be sent for later."

The marquess looked startled when she made her announcement. Meredith nearly smiled. Had he expected her to refuse? To delay until the hour became impossibly late? Or to defy him and lock herself in her room?

Suddenly it was time to go. There were hugs and kisses of farewell for her brothers. Meredith clung to them tightly, surprised at the depth of emotion she was experiencing. She never thought it would be this hard to leave them.

"We wish you joy," Jasper said softly in her ear.

"But if you ever have a need for us, for any reason, send word. You are our sister, and we shall always love you."

"I know."

She gave Jasper's broad shoulders a final squeeze, then turned away. The marquess was looking at her expectantly.

"I am ready, my lord." Meredith straightened her shoulders and lifted her chin.

"Then come, my lady. The hour grows late and we have a very great surprise to bestow upon my noble father."

Nine

Any regrets the marquess had felt over his impulsive, hastily orchestrated marriage to Meredith increased tenfold as their carriage pulled up to his father's front door.

"Is the duke expecting us?" Meredith inquired curiously as an army of footmen and underfootmen, dressed in formal livery, scurried to assist them from the coach.

"I do not believe so," Trevor replied. "There was no opportunity to inform him of our arrival. Or marriage."

The last statement was uttered in a dull whisper as they crossed the threshold of the mansion. Trevor heard his bride catch her breath. Then she turned to him, her eyes wide with astonishment.

He held her gaze with a steady, lazy look, almost daring her to create a scene in front of the many curious servants. She studied him hard, then had the audacity to appear amused.

"Coward," she muttered.

The marquess found himself swallowing a smile as he trailed obediently behind his wife. They were led directly to his father in the green salon, so named because of the many shades of that color dominating every scrap of fabric, inch of carpet, and length of

drapery in the room. As a child Trevor had found the effect caused his head to swim, just like the light-headed feeling he achieved when holding his breath for a long period of time.

He bowed in polite greeting to the duke and admitted reaching adulthood had not altered his reaction to the sea of green dancing before his eyes.

"You're early," the duke said impatiently. "Though I suppose it is better than being fashionably late. Or not coming at all." The duke moved forward, then stopped suddenly. The look of surprise on his father's features told Trevor the duke had only just noticed his son had not arrived alone. "I was not informed you were bringing a guest to my dinner party."

The blasted dinner party! How could he have forgotten that stellar event was being held this evening? Trevor nearly kicked himself at this unlucky turn. The timing for announcing his sudden marriage could not have been worse, for this was the very night his father expected to introduce the marquess to the woman the duke deemed to be a suitable bride for his son.

Trevor never had much use for panic, but it was the dominant emotion that now embraced him. Until he resolutely pushed it aside.

"We have not come to attend your dinner party, sir," Trevor said.

"Why not?" the duke bellowed in an exasperated tone. "I told you of its importance three days ago."

The marquess shrugged, conveying clearly that the duke's dictates meant little to him.

"Beg pardon, Your Grace," the butler interrupted the escalating tension with a respectful bow. "Mrs. Pritcher would like to know to which chambers you wish the luggage be brought."

"Luggage?" The duke's brow lifted and a slow smile spread across his face. "You brought luggage

with you? Are you planning on moving back home?" Darting a joyful glance at his son, the duke continued, "I feared you might never come to your senses and return where you belonged. Now, don't go all pucker-faced on me, Trevor. 'Tis splendid news, my boy. Splendid."

Trevor tried to hide the edge of panic that once again crept forward. The situation was rapidly deteriorating. "We shall decide about the luggage later," the marquess said, waving the butler to the door.

The moment the servant left the room, Trevor stepped over and grasped his wife's hand. Despite the pleasant warmth of the room, her fingers felt cold. "We have come to share some rather important news. Lady Meredith and I were married a few hours ago."

"What?" The duke's eyes were round and horrified. "You have gone and married this woman after I expressly told you to leave her alone? Are you incapable of heeding my advice on any matter? Or are you determined to drive me to my grave, a broken and unhappy man?"

"I am no longer a boy, sir, but a man of thirty years. Your approval is neither sought nor necessary for any of my actions. I thought only to give you the courtesy of hearing the news from my lips instead of reading of it in the *Times*. Perhaps I was mistaken in my judgment."

"Well, perhaps not only your judgment has been hasty in this matter." The duke's eyes dropped pointedly at Meredith's stomach. "What is the real reason you married so swiftly? And in secret?"

Trevor felt a sudden clenching in his gut. For an instant he worried that Meredith might flounder before the duke's obvious disapproval, but the sparkle in her eyes revealed only her pride and determination.

"It might be wise of you both to remember that I

am neither deaf nor dumb and standing but a few feet away, hearing every disagreeable word spoken about me," she declared in a steady voice. "Fortunately, I am a practical woman who did not expect a welcoming embrace from my new family.

"However, I would appreciate it if you would at least do me the courtesy of ceasing to discuss me as though I were across the ocean and unable to take offense at your numerous unkind remarks and unfounded accusations."

"My comments are hardly unfounded," the duke retorted. "You spent time in the garden alone together during Lady Dermond's ball, returning unkempt and disheveled."

"Gossip and innuendo, Your Grace. We were not seen by anyone in the garden."

The duke compressed his lips. "Are you certain?"

"Yes. Absolutely," Meredith replied, as she boldly met his gaze. "Though you may not be pleased that I am now your daughter-in-law, at the very least you owe me and your son your support against those who would slander our good name. *Your* good name."

Meredith's rebuke was so surprising it shocked the duke into silence. Trevor watched in amazement as his father sputtered, then turned a deep shade of red. The marquess realized, with some amusement, it was the first time in his life he had ever seen his father *blush*.

The marquess gazed at his wife, and a sense of pride washed over him. If nothing else, his father must allow that he had excellent taste in women. She was poised, beautiful and in total control, a rare combination of elegance and feminine perfection.

"This is a family matter, miss. Nothing to concern your pretty head over."

"I thank you, Your Grace, for the compliment about

my pretty head." Meredith, it appeared, was making no allowances for temper. She folded her arms beneath her breasts and stood at a challenging angle. "If you would please listen for a moment the marquees will explain everything."

"Oh, will he now?" the duke asked, in a voice laced with sarcasm.

"Actually there is nothing to explain." Trevor felt his own temper begin to rise. He would not stand here and be treated like a wayward child, nor would he subject his wife to such unpleasantness. "I asked Lady Meredith to marry me immediately, she agreed, and we decided today would be the perfect day. I am sorry if that offends you, sir, but it cannot, and will not, be changed."

The duke's body went stiff. The marquess swallowed the bitterness that rose to his mouth, then whirled around to leave. A part of him had hoped his father would accept this marriage, but that appeared vastly unlikely. Better to go while he still retained a modicum of dignity.

"May we stay for dinner, Your Grace?"

The soft tones of Meredith's sweet voice rang through the room. Trevor opened his mouth to recant the request, but felt her fingers give his arm a strong squeeze. He watched the duke's jaw work rebelliously and braced himself for the inevitable set down.

"My butler said you brought luggage with you. Seems to me you were intending to stay for more than just a meal."

Meredith's nostrils curled. "It would be rude to make assumptions or foist ourselves where we are not wanted. That is why I asked about the dinner party."

"This is your home," the duke said gruffly. " 'Tis insulting to imply that a formal invitation must be extended."

"My lord?" She turned to the marquess in a display of wifely deference that seemed genuine, though greatly out of character. Trevor found it oddly intoxicating.

He pushed his fingers through his hair, puzzled. Given the reaction to the announcement of their marriage, he would expect Meredith to bolt for the door the moment the opportunity presented itself. Yet for some reason she seemed determined to stay. "We would be honored to join you and your guests for dinner," the marquess replied.

"The luggage?"

"And to take up residence in the mansion. On a temporary basis," Trevor added.

A surge of relief and triumph flitted across the duke's lined face. In that single moment of clarity the marquess realized something about his father that was almost shocking. The duke might not be pleased with this marriage, but he really wanted them to stay.

Yet he knew not how to ask, he knew only how to command, and that approach had never been successful with his equally strong-willed son.

"Dinner is at seven o'clock," the duke announced. "I am an old man. I keep unfashionably early hours."

"We shall be ready, sir." Trevor turned to look at his bride with a thoughtful expression. "The early hour for dinner suits us admirably. After all, this is our wedding night."

Meredith's head snapped around. She stood perfectly still for a moment, her face inscrutable. Then she jutted her chin out and strode toward the door with a carefree attitude, as though his words were as casual as announcing they were serving roasted fowl for dinner.

For the first time in many years, Trevor smiled with true delight.

He caught up to her in the main foyer.

"You might have warned me," she whispered beneath her breath as he grasped her elbow in a solicitous gesture.

"About what?"

"Your father." She looked neither agitated nor angry by the omission, just slightly put out. "He does not like me."

"He does not know you," Trevor replied airily.

"Precisely." She flashed a smile that turned quickly into a frown. "I am not so naive as to have expected a loving embrace from the duke, given the unorthodox circumstances of our marriage. Yet I feared he would next ask me to use the servant's entrance so as to ensure no one saw me in his, or your, company."

Trevor's brows knit together in confusion. "If he made you so uncomfortable, why did you ask to stay for dinner?"

"Because it seemed so important to him that you attend this party."

"Why should that matter to you?"

She gave a look that made him feel like a backward child. "He is your father. 'Tis your duty, and now mine, to try and please him, especially if it can be done with such ease."

The marquess stared pensively down at his bride. "The reason he invited me to this soiree originally was to introduce me to the woman he deemed suitable to be my wife."

Her shocked reaction brought the amusement back to Trevor's eyes.

"How very medieval," she clucked. "To choose a bride for his son."

Her sarcastic tone allowed him to relax. He had half feared once she knew the truth she would demand they leave.

But she said no more as they made their way down the long corridor of the east wing of the mansion—the wing that had been designed and maintained for the heir. Him.

Years ago the duke had this area remodeled and redecorated in anticipation of his son and future daughter-in-law taking up residence, but Lavinia had died a few months before the quarters were ready. Trevor had since resisted any attempts the duke had made to entice him to live there.

Until now. Though he had not traveled the length of these halls for many years, he caught glimpses of elegant furnishings he vaguely remembered Lavinia selecting. They had her stylized mark—unique, tasteful, and of the highest quality.

He tensed briefly as the housekeeper, Mrs. Pritcher, opened the door to the master suites, expecting to be flooded with a rash of memories. But the elegant rooms, decorated in shades of blue, gold, and ivory, were not in the least familiar.

"You might remember, my lord, there are separate bedchambers for each of you, as well as a sitting and dressing room for her ladyship and a dressing room and small study for you." Mrs. Pritcher fluttered nervously about the rooms, opening and closing doors. Meredith dutifully peered inside, but said nothing until the tour ended.

"The rooms are in excellent condition, Mrs. Pritcher," Meredith told the fidgeting servant. "I commend you and your staff for keeping them so fresh."

"Thank you, my lady." The plump housekeeper dipped a hasty curtsy. She bit her lower lip anxiously, glancing at the marquess. "If you would permit, I would like to offer my congratulations and felicitations to you both on the occasion of your marriage."

Trevor turned stiffly toward the servant. Mrs.

Pritcher looked around desperately for a moment, then lowered her eyes to the exquisite Aubusson carpet. He felt like a cad for making the woman feel so nervous, but her reminder of his newly married state when he was being confronted with such potent memories of his first, wildly happy marriage threw him off balance.

"You are very kind, Mrs. Pritcher." Trevor cleared his throat. "Lady Meredith and I appreciate your good wishes."

A sunny, though quivering smile, broadened the housekeeper's face. "Her ladyship's maid is down in the servant's quarters having a spot of tea. I'll send her up, along with two of the housemaids, to unpack your clothes. Do you require anything else?"

"I cannot think of anything, but I have no doubt you shall efficiently provide whatever I deem necessary," Meredith said.

The words and tone smoothed over the awkward moment. Mrs. Pritcher bobbed up and down twice, then exited the room, this time wearing a genuine smile.

"Are the accommodations to your liking?" Trevor asked.

"They are splendid." Meredith strolled casually about the perimeter, then froze in the act of reaching for one of the porcelain figurines that graced the marble fireplace mantel. "Are these the same rooms you shared with Lavinia?" she asked in a troubled tone.

"That was our original plan," Trevor said carefully. "However, when in town we lived in a house on Berkeley Square I purchased shortly before we wed. These rooms were being made ready for us when she died."

"I remember your home in Berkeley. Lavinia called it her haven from the bustle and noise of the city. What ever happened to it?"

Trevor gave an uncomfortable shrug. He had not thought about that charming home for many, many years. "I sold the property the week after Lavinia died. It was impossible for me to cross the threshold without her."

Meredith pressed her lips together. "If it troubles you, I am sure we can stay in a different section of your father's house. I would be happy to make the arrangements with Mrs. Pritcher, if you prefer not to be bothered."

She was trying to make this easier for him, and for some strange reason that angered the marquess. This was not supposed to be easy. "Lavinia was my wife. We cannot erase all memory of her existence now that you are in her position."

Meredith gave a deep sigh. "She was my dearest friend, my lord. I loved her, too. I would never want either of us to forget her."

The silence in the wake of those gently spoken words was thick and heavy. He saw how pale Meredith's face had become, how the emotions she was feeling turned her beautiful eyes into bottomless pools. He was struck suddenly with the urge to reach for her, to hold her in his arms, to accept and give the comfort they both seemed to need so desperately.

Yet he could not. Ignoring the stabbing of his heart, Trevor willed himself to remain impassive. He had married Meredith to avoid a scandal, to set to rights the part he had played in her fall from grace. It would benefit neither of them to let these raw emotions cloud their relationship.

Trevor reached for the door that led to his chambers, but experienced a moment of acute discomfort. The expression on her lovely face haunted him. "I shall call for you in two hours, so we may go downstairs together."

"I will be ready."

Keeping his back to her he added, "I have no doubt you will charm and dazzle them all tonight."

Trevor heard her sigh softly. "Including the duke?"

"Especially the duke."

The rustle of silk alerted the marquess that she had come closer, but he still refused to turn around and face her. He waited with both dread and anticipation for her hand to fall upon his shoulder, but she resisted touching him.

"And what of the duke's brooding, wild, hedonistic son?"

Bloody hell, she is relentless. Trevor clenched his teeth. "The marquess would never have taken a bride who was not worthy of his regard."

This time he did not hesitate, but turned the knob and fled to the sanctuary of his rooms.

The duke's party was hardly the small, intimate gathering Meredith had expected. Though she had spent most of her life among the aristocracy, she had forgotten that dukes did most things on a grander scale than other peers. There were forty-nine guests for dinner. The inclusion of the marquess and his new bride brought the number of people seated around the table to fifty-two.

At the start of the meal, the duke stood and made an appropriate though not overly enthusiastic toast to the health and happiness of the bride and groom. Given his attitude toward her and his initial reaction to the marriage, Meredith felt it was more than adequate.

This announcement was met with flurries of whispers and glances of speculation, but no one dared to

make even an insinuation of an insult while in the ducal residence.

As the only female relation, Meredith was seated to the duke's left. There was a brief moment of awkward tension when she was introduced to Lady Anne Smithe, the attractive woman seated on the duke's right. Meredith quickly deduced this woman was the true reason for the party that evening, for she was the one handpicked by the duke to marry Trevor.

Lady Anne was a slightly built woman in her late twenties with pleasant features, lovely dark hair, and a full, lush figure. As much as she hated to admit it, Meredith was curious about this woman the duke had selected. While the formally garbed footmen, dressed in their silver livery and powdered wigs, served course after course of rich, elaborately prepared food, Meredith observed her rival.

Lady Anne had a quick wit, a keen mind, and an ease of social graces any woman would envy, including Meredith. She graciously included all those around her in every conversation and encouraged lively, appropriate debate.

Yet the true test of her character came when a footman, in the act of refilling her wine goblet, upset the glass.

"Fool!" the duke yelled, startling the servant further. "How dare such a clumsy imbecile serve at my table? You are sloshing wine all over Lady Anne!"

The young man glanced down with beseeching eyes and made a fateful grab for the crystal goblet. The duke's outburst had attracted the attention of many of the guests and they all turned to stare in fascinated horror as the red nectar spilled over the tumbling goblet, staining the stark white linen of the tablecloth and soaking Lady Anne's fingers.

"My apologizes, my lady," the servant stammered,

as he hastily tried to wipe away the evidence of his mistake.

"There is no cause for alarm," Lady Anne said in a mild tone. "The wine barely touched me. I commend you, young man, for catching that goblet so quickly. If not, I might have ended up with a lap filled with wine. Would that not have been a sight to behold, Your Grace?"

It seemed as though the entire dining room held its collective breath as they waited for the duke to react. The older man muttered something under his breath about hiring more competent servants. "He's not fit to serve in my household if he can't pour a simple goblet of wine without making a mess of it," the duke said.

"Nonsense, Your Grace," Lady Anne interjected. "I have already said no harm was done. May I have some more wine, please?"

Meredith saw Lady Anne give the footman an encouraging nod as she held out her glass. His sagging shoulders straightened and he filled her goblet without spilling a drop.

The move succeeded in diverting the duke's attention to other matters, and he was soon engaged in conversation again. As the footman retreated respectfully behind Lady Anne's chair, Meredith thought she heard him whisper, "Thank you, my lady."

The rest of the meal concluded without incident. When it was time for the ladies to withdraw so the men could indulge in port and cigars, Meredith conceded that her new father-in-law had excellent taste in women. Lady Anne would have been a good match for the wayward marquess.

Once in the drawing room, the women separated into groups. Tea was brought in and served to those who desired a cup, cozy clusters of friends settled into

smaller circles to visit and gossip, and others congregated around the pianoforte. Discussion among the mothers as to which of their young, eligible daughters would play and sing first became a heated debate that soon threatened to become uncivilized.

Meredith, in the process of supervising the tea service on the other side of the room, tried to hurry across the room to intervene, but Lady Anne arrived first. She diplomatically managed to sooth all the ruffled feathers and organize an order of performance that was agreeable to everyone.

"She is rather a marvel, our Lady Anne," a deep male voice whispered in her ear.

Meredith shivered. She need not turn around to identify the speaker. It was now easy and quick for her to distinguish Trevor's voice among all other men's.

"Lady Anne is a virtual paragon," Meredith intoned, trying hard to fight the jealousy she felt, for she truly liked the woman. "You would have done well to heed your father's advice and consider making a match with her."

" 'Tis not necessary for my father to chose my women," Trevor said. She felt his hand close around her elbow.

Meredith turned and angled her head to look up at him. The marquess gave her a wicked half grin. For some bizarre reason, the force of that gaze made her press her knees tightly together in a combination of fear and anticipation.

The words he had spoken to the duke earlier in such a cavalier manner echoed through her head: *This is our wedding night.*

"There are several young ladies who are eager to showcase their musical skills," Meredith said. She

licked away the dryness of her lips. "I imagine the entertainment will continue well into the night."

"We certainly cannot be expected to stay," Trevor said gruffly. He backed her against the wall and swiveled so he stood with his body nearly touching hers. A heavy, sweet ache formed inside Meredith. She strained toward him, wanting desperately to mold herself against his large muscular form.

"It will cause a great deal of commotion if we leave now." Her breasts rose as she breathed in deeply.

"Then we must be very clever and slip away without being noticed." He spoke quietly, his warm breath caressing her face.

"How?"

His eyes deepened to a stormy blue. "Do you think you can find your way to the third floor landing of the main staircase?"

Though it was difficult to concentrate with these feelings of shimmering tension between them, Meredith forced her mind to recall the layout of the mansion. "Yes, I believe I know how to find it."

"Good. I want you to exit the room in five minutes. I shall follow after another five have passed. There is a portrait gallery on the west wing of the third floor. Wait for me there."

She held his gaze for an instant. Then she nodded her head unsteadily. Once he had her agreement, the marquess turned and walked away. His abrupt departure deflated her, but she kept her features bland, in case they were being observed.

Meredith dared not move from her secluded location against the wall, fearing to be drawn into a conversation that might delay her departure. She forced herself to wait five minutes and then an extra minute for good measure before discreetly slipping out the door.

Grinning like a giddy schoolgirl, she scurried down

the hall, around the corner and up the main staircase. Though there were many servants positioned in various locations along her route, no one questioned her. Her heart thundering with nerves and excitement, Meredith proceeded to the third floor to meet her fate.

Ten

In the luxurious gold, blue, and ivory bedchamber, Rose helped Meredith prepare for bed. She was glad the young maid had accompanied her, for Rose's friendly face and usual chatter helped calm Meredith's nerves.

The servant provided a much needed connection to her past, and that was a comfort to Meredith as she prepared to move toward her future. Tonight she was going to start to make a new life for herself, to assume a role she never honestly thought she would achieve: wife.

Trevor had been moodily silent on the walk to their rooms earlier, and Meredith was at a loss to understand why. She had hoped for a kiss when they met on the third floor gallery, conspirators sharing the victory of their escape. But the marquess had only nodded his head in greeting when he found her waiting exactly where he requested and had moved quickly forward.

Thankfully she was tall and long legged, or she would have been forced to run to keep pace with him. That would have almost been too humiliating to bear, for she got the distinct feeling he wasn't hurrying to get to their bedchamber, but rather hurrying to get away from her.

Gone was the look of potent sensuality he seemed to delight in bestowing upon her, replaced by an impassive look that grew distant and tense with each step they took.

Something seemed to happen to Trevor as they walked down that long corridor, and it disturbed Meredith greatly, for she felt incapable of reversing the coldness that had come upon him. He had left her alone to prepare for bed, as any considerate husband would do for his bride, yet it had not felt like consideration. It had felt like abandonment.

Meredith shook her head at her fancy wonderings. Her nerves must be making her melancholy and overly dramatic. It was far too soon to worry if Trevor would ever reciprocate her feelings. If she continued with these gloomy thoughts, she would never be able to survive the night to come. What could be more depressing than facing a bleak, loveless future?

Meredith forced her mind to change directions. This was her wedding night! It was hardly necessary for Trevor to lose his head over her. His kisses and caresses had aptly demonstrated his desire. For now she possessed more than enough love for them both.

"You look beautiful, my lady," Rose said with a trace of awe.

Meredith smiled her thanks and glanced in the mirror above her dressing table. The pale blue silk nightgown was of simple design, low cut and sleeveless, with an open front guaranteed to tempt any warm blooded male to reach inside and explore. In a show of bravado, Meredith declined the matching robe, clearly shocking her maid.

"I will see you in the morning, Rose."

"Late morning, I expect." Rose giggled briefly at her own daring and hastily left the room.

Meredith's nerves kicked up again once she was

alone. She glanced at the door along the far wall, the one that led to Trevor's sitting room, but it remained shut tight. Sighing, she picked up her silver-handled brush, sat before the dressing table, and rhythmically stroked her hair.

He arrived suddenly through the connecting door that linked their rooms. Though she had been expecting him, she nearly jumped when he appeared as a glimmer of movement in her mirror.

"Should I have knocked?"

"Of course not." Rising from the padded seat, she turned to face him fully.

He wore a brocade dressing gown of sapphire blue, loosely belted at the waist, that accented the width of his shoulders and the broadness of his chest. His feet were bare. She could not see much beyond his ankles, but surmised he wore nothing else beneath the garment. The flickering candlelight flattered his fair complexion and refined facial features.

Meredith nearly sighed. He was such a compelling, handsome man. The intensity of his gaze made her heart begin to thud. Yet his face could have been carved from stone, for he showed not a hint of emotion.

"Your maid?"

"Rose has retired for the night."

"Good." She felt his gaze travel over her, taking in every detail of her revealing attire. With effort, she was able not to flinch. "I assume you are a virgin?"

There was a long pause as Meredith told herself not to be insulted or angered by the question. "Yes. Does that disappoint you?"

His expression broke and he grimaced. Yet he did not answer her question but instead said, "Your mother is not here to offer you advice or address any of your

concerns. Is there anything you would like to ask me?"

Ask him? About what? Though she had vowed she would not, Meredith felt a blush creep into her cheeks as she finally caught his meaning.

"My mother already explained . . . that is to say, I already know . . . I mean I am aware—"

Abruptly she stopped, not believing how flustered she felt by this discussion. Taking a deep breath, Meredith tried again. "I am very aware of all aspects of marital relations. Physical relations. My mother has always felt it was most important that a woman not remain ignorant of such matters, so she took it upon herself to enlighten and explain everything to me when I reached my eighteenth birthday."

"Everything?" The notion seemed to amuse him. "Hmmm, now *I* am nervous."

Meredith felt herself relax. It was going to be all right. Trevor seemed to be in the grip of some strange emotion, but it no longer frightened or disturbed her.

She lacked the nerve to suggest they move to the bed, so instead of speaking she acted. Rose, or some other servant, had drawn back the spread. Meredith could feel the coolness of the satin sheet against her bottom through her sheer nightgown as she sat in the middle of the bed.

As she waited for him to follow, she admitted she was looking forward to this aspect of their relationship. He had already demonstrated his passion for her with his soul-melting kisses and languid caresses.

She had always been curious about the physical side of the male/female relationship, but never more so since the marquess had kissed and caressed her. Even that first night in the garden she knew there was something different about him, different about them.

The intimacy they were about to share would create

a bond between them, a bond that would grow stronger as the days and weeks passed.

Meredith was not a love-struck fool. She did not believe this would instantly solve all the obstacles they now faced. But it could be a start. A most important, pleasurable start.

But still she waited. The marquess had not moved from his position. He seemed to be wrestling with some internal dilemma, some indecision. He turned and Meredith nearly cried out, for she thought he meant to leave.

She quieted when she saw him unbelt his dressing gown, then inhaled slowly as he removed the robe. As she had thought, he was naked beneath and achingly beautiful. Hard, solid muscle, broad shoulders and chest, narrow waist, long, fit legs.

The mattress shifted slightly as he sank down beside her. His nearness brought on a longing and hunger that started somewhere deep inside her. Never had she been so acutely aware of her body.

"Are you still nervous?" Meredith asked with a small smile.

"Terrified." His expression was so serious it made her heart ache. Something *was* troubling him.

Tenderly she raised her hand and laid it on his chest. "I promise I will not bite you, my lord."

"Regretfully, I cannot make the same vow, my lady."

Her fingers strayed to his hair, caressed the outline of his ear, then moved to the back of his neck. "I do not mind in the least," she whispered in a sultry voice, pulling his neck forward.

Arching against him, she drew him into a deep, warm kiss. He remained totally still for a moment. Then he ran his tongue along her lips. Eagerly

Meredith parted them, and his tongue sank inside to tease and tangle with hers.

It felt so good, warm and sensuous and wild. Their mouths fit perfectly. Trevor's tongue began plunging slowly in and out, and Meredith became lost in the wonder of it as she tasted him fully.

Trevor placed his hands on either side of her face and gently pulled back from the kiss, his mind in complete turmoil. She leaned forward, pressing every part of her scantily clad body against his. His arms encircled her and she settled herself beneath his chin, burrowing closer. Then Meredith lifted her lips and pressed them gently to the pulse that beat rapidly at the base of his throat.

It was a gesture of trust and caring that rocked the marquess to the core of his being. His heart swelled with a deep, painful yearning he had previously associated exclusively with his relationship with Lavinia.

The urge to protect and cherish grew strong, and he nearly laughed out loud of the absurdity of his predicament. For the one he needed to protect this delicate creature from was himself.

He had bedded many women in the past eight years, more than he could count. More than he could remember. At first he had been mistaken in believing that his passion for Meredith was yet another of his typical reactions to a woman of such beauty, charm, and spirit.

Now he knew better. He knew he was not prepared to be the type of husband she would demand. She had told him that before when she refused his proposal of marriage, but he had not heeded her warning.

She would not allow herself to be ignored, though in the end it would be best for both of them. Was it fair or honorable to allow himself to feel only desire

for her? Would that not make an already difficult situation nearly intolerable?

Trevor lowered his chin until it rested on the top of her head and sighed. He felt a surge of guilt as his conscience warred with his sexual desire. Before entering her bedchamber tonight, he had resolutely put his attraction to his wife aside. That resolve had already been sorely tested when she looked at him with such open longing. And yet he had managed to control his urges, had managed to refrain from unleashing the pent-up passion that was tormenting him. Thus far.

"Is anything wrong, my lord?"

Her caring tone made him feel vulnerable, an emotion he despised.

"Lie back on the bed, Meredith."

He felt her hesitation, her reluctance to leave the warmth of his arms, but she obeyed him without comment. Her breasts rose and fell with her harsh breaths, whether from excitement or fear he could not be certain.

He closed his eyes briefly and fought for mastery over himself, pushing aside all the wild, erotic things he wanted to do with her. He almost wished she was lying stiffly, fists clenched and eyes pinned to the ceiling, awaiting her fate with the martyred indignity of an aristocratic princess.

Then he could lift the hem of her nightgown, move her thighs apart, and couple with her, swiftly and fiercely.

But she was neither stoic nor shy, his exquisite bride. And she seemed incapable of keeping still. Her questing fingers searched through his chest hair and found his nipples. Using the flat of her fingertips, she gently circled the outer rim, then pulled on the puckering buds.

"Our bodies are not completely so different, are they?" she said in wonderment.

"You had best wait a few moments before making such rash statements," he replied.

Trevor lowered his head and nuzzled her neck and jaw. The sheer joy of discovery in her eyes was too much to endure. He felt his cock twitch, then harden further as she slid her hands along the side of his hips and down his thighs.

He knew he should discourage her, but her touch felt so good, so right upon his burning flesh. Ever bold, she closed her wandering fingers around the base of his stiff erection and squeezed experimentally.

Hot waves of hunger poured through his body. "You must remember, I am rather nervous," he said hoarsely, as he reached down and pulled her hand away. "And shy of you."

"Shy?" Meredith laughed, throwing back her head and exposing the column of her long neck. "You do not feel shy, my lord."

He smiled, despite his determination not to enjoy himself. Her innocence and enthusiasm were beguiling. He dipped his mouth to her breasts, kissing her erect nipples through the silk sheerness of her nightgown. Meredith drew in a sharp breath and arched her back.

Trevor moved his hand down below her waist, found the entrance to her body and circled it lightly with his finger. She made a small sound of pleasure deep in her throat and lifted her hips. The hot wetness at the juncture of her thighs let him know she would be able to accept his length with a minimum amount of pain.

He gathered her close, shutting himself off to all emotions except the relentless drive of his passion. Somehow her nightgown had become tangled around her waist. There were no impediments as Trevor

opened her legs with the thrust of his knee and placed himself between them.

He entered her partway, then drove forward slowly. Meredith struggled, her legs shifting restlessly around him. He paused.

"Does that hurt?"

"It burns, stings." She bit her lower lip, then tossed her head back and forth on the pillow. "Don't stop. Full. I feel so full and stretched."

He rocked his hips forward and she whimpered. "Better?" he asked.

"Hmmm." Her face and neck were flushed, her eyes wild and wanton. He adjusted their bodies, trying to keep his strokes slow and shallow, but soon found himself pressing against the resistance of her maidenhead.

"Try not to tense your muscles," he whispered. He held her hips steady in his hands and thrust forward, piercing the membrane, penetrating her completely in one deep stroke.

She cried out again, a mixture of shock and wonder. He expected her to stiffen and lie still or try to pull away from him. Instead she lifted herself up so she could press tender kisses to his cheek and jaw and throat.

His senses exploded. No longer capable of thrusting into her with detached control, he gripped her hips hard, thumbs digging into the soft, tender flesh, and he pumped vigorously with almost mindless, insistent urgency.

The pressure built to unbearable heights, and then Trevor felt the shudder begin, the blessed release. His entire body strained and convulsed as the climax overtook him, spilling his seed violently deep inside her tender flesh, nearly at the opening of her womb.

He tried not to collapse on top of her, to spare her

his crushing weight, but she hugged him so fiercely he fell forward. For a long moment he lay there, the sound of his ragged breathing echoing through the room.

Gradually he came to his senses. Trevor raised his head slowly. A span of several heartbeats passed before he found the courage to gaze at the woman sprawled beneath him—his wife, now in body as well as name.

A blush of color stained her pale cheeks and her eyes were half closed. He brushed the hair out of her face, wondering if she was still in pain, hoping he had not embarrassed or upset her too much.

Her eyes fluttered open. "Is that it? Is it over?"

"Yes." He rolled off to the side. Her simple questions confirmed what he expected. What he intended, really. She had not reached climax.

She was too inexperienced to realize it, of course. Proof of that came to him when she turned and snuggled close to him and sighed contentedly. He had brought her some measure of pleasure, some measure of enjoyment, but not the ultimate release, the ultimate intimacy.

For he knew that by satisfying one need he would be creating another.

" 'Tis late," he said softly. "I should leave you to your rest."

"No!" Her arms tightened around his neck. Then she lowered her head in embarrassment. "Please, stay a while longer."

His fingers trailed over her bare shoulder. Her skin was so soft and smooth, so daintily white and unblemished. Trevor ran his hands through the lengths of golden hair that hung down her back. He caught a whiff of the lust that hung heavy in the air and felt his body begin to stir. He should leave, before she

managed to arouse him once more. Yet he made no move to abandon his pleasant bower, allowing her to intertwine her leg intimately with his.

He felt her fingers twisting through the hair on his chest as he began to drift off to sleep. Unconsciously, his arms tightened around her. His eyelids closed as emotions and fatigue claimed him.

Meredith watched him sleep. When the slow rise and fall of his chest became a steady rhythm, she propped her elbow at an angle and rested her head upon her hand to gain a better view.

She gazed at him for a long time, like a love-struck fool, warning herself again and again not to wish for the stars or expect the impossible. The marquess was a difficult man to love, and the road she had chosen would not be an easy one to travel. Yet stubbornly she refused to give up hope.

Coming to his father's house had taken a toll on his emotions. Even in slumber his handsome face seemed drawn, flushed with weariness.

Meredith leaned forward, dropped a quick kiss on his shoulder, then carefully slid from the bed. Her body ached in odd places and her inner thighs were sticky with his seed. She went to the washstand and poured a small amount of water into the porcelain bowl.

Meredith soaked a linen cloth, then carefully cleansed herself. Her body still throbbed from his possession. Yet as she ran the cloth over her tender flesh, she could not dispel the restless feeling that there should have been more.

There had been joy and wonder in their lovemaking, but there had also been an urgency, a frantic sense of reaching for something—something that was not there. Love? Meredith was unsure. It could hardly be

Take A Trip Into A Timeless World of Passion and Adventure with Kensington Choice Historical Romances! —Absolutely FREE!

Let your spirits fly away and enjoy the passion and adventure of another time. Kensington Choice Historical Romances are the finest novels of their kind, written by today's best selling romance authors. Each Kensington Choice Historical Romance transports you to distant lands in a bygone age. Experience the adventure and share the delight as proud men and spirited women discover the wonder and passion of true love.

4 BOOKS WORTH UP TO $23.96— Absolutely FREE!

Take 4 FREE Books!

We created our convenient Home Subscription Service so you'll be sure to have the hottest new romances delivered each month right to your doorstep — usually before they are available in book stores. Just to show you how convenient Zebra Home Subscription Service is, we would like to send you 4 Kensington Choice Historical Romances as a FREE gift. You receive a gift worth up to $23.96 — absolutely FREE. You only pay for shipping and handling. There's no obligation to buy anything - ever!

Save Up To 30% On Home Delivery!

Accept your FREE gift and each month we'll deliver 4 brand new titles as soon as they are published. They'll be yours to examine FREE for 10 days. Then if you decide to keep the books, you'll pay the preferred subscriber's price. That's all 4 books for a savings of up to 30% off the cover price! Just add the cost of shipping and handling. Remember, you are under no obligation to buy any of these books at any time! If you are not delighted with them, simply return them and owe nothing. But if you enjoy Kensington Choice Historical Romances as much as we think you will, pay the special preferred subscriber rate and save over $7.00 off the bookstore price!

PLACE
STAMP
HERE

Ill..l..lll..ll.l.l.l.l.l.l.ll.l.l.l.ll.l.l.l.ll..l

KENSINGTON CHOICE
Zebra Home Subscription Service, Inc.
P.O. Box 5214
Clifton NJ 07015-5214

necessary to be in love to achieve complete sexual fulfillment.

Her dashing husband was the perfect illustration of that theory. He most definitely was not in love with her, yet he had experienced something far more earth-shattering than she. Perhaps only men so easily achieved this blissful state?

Yet Meredith distinctly recalled that during that embarrassing and rather graphic conversation her mother had initiated about marital relations, there was mention of mutual pleasure and mutual enjoyment—passion so intimate it could make the body sing, surrender so complete one lost all sense of self-protection and simply gave and gave until they were free and satiated.

That was the sort of physical intimacy Meredith was hoping to someday achieve with her husband. Given his rakish reputation and experience with the female sex, she suspected he knew precisely how that was accomplished. All she need do now was somehow convey her desire to him.

With a philosophical frown, Meredith returned to the bed. Trevor stirred, but did not awaken as she climbed in beside him. For a moment she was disappointed. If he woke up, they would be able to engage in more lovemaking, perhaps this time reaching the heights of that elusive shattering pleasure.

Blushing at her wanton thoughts, Meredith laid back against her pillow. She turned and took up her favorite position, with her head resting comfortably against the solid muscle of Trevor's chest. He shifted, then wrapped his arms securely around her. She smiled. A part of him must truly want her, even if the waking side of him had yet to realize it.

All was quiet and still around them. Beneath her cheek Meredith could hear his heart beating. The comforting sound lulled her into a peaceful sleep.

* * *

Meredith awoke alone. It was not a great surprise, but rather a big disappointment. Her mouth set in a thin line as she lay in the bedchamber flooded with morning sunshine, trying to decide if she should take breakfast in her bedchamber or brave the dining room.

Eating in the dining room would increase the chances of seeing her husband. It would also increase the chances of seeing her new father-in-law.

Deciding there was really no way to achieve one goal without facing the consequences of the other, Meredith rang for her maid. She did not linger over her morning toilet, but took care to select one of her more flattering gowns, a simple muslin creation of sapphire blue that set off her eyes.

Once Rose had helped her dress, Meredith descended the stairs in search of breakfast and mentally prepared herself to tangle with the two new men in her life.

As she expected, the duke was seated at the head of the breakfast table, coffee cup in hand, a newspaper spread across the table. There was no sign of the marquess.

"I had not thought to see you this morning," the duke exclaimed. "Or even for the rest of today."

Meredith took a much needed deep breath. "I was hungry and in need of a stroll. I hope you do not object if I join you."

She stood with her head high and waited for the footman to draw out the chair beside the duke. Her father-in-law seemed startled by her choice of seats and quickly scooped up the paper to make room for the plate of food another servant placed in front of Meredith.

"Take this away, Higgins," the duke commanded, thrusting the waded sheets toward a footman.

"Oh, please, do not abandon your paper for me."

The duke eyed her suspiciously for a moment, as if testing her sincerity. He must have reasoned she meant what she said, for he slowly dropped the crumpled mess back onto the mahogany table.

"There's an announcement of your marriage in the society section," he said wryly.

Meredith nodded. She spread a thin, even layer of raspberry jam on her toast, then lifted her head. "Trevor must have instructed his secretary yesterday to make sure it was done. The marquess can be extremely efficient in certain matters."

"When it suits him," the duke remarked with a frown.

Meredith raised an eyebrow. She felt the duke's keen gaze upon her. Sensing he was testing her, Meredith refused to rise to the bait. As much as she felt she needed an ally in this house, she was not about to take sides against her husband in the battle with his father.

"Good morning."

Meredith looked up to see the marquess enter the room. He was dressed for riding, and the sheen of sweat upon his brow suggested he had already been out putting his mount through its paces. Meredith cautioned herself not to react. Though it was rather lowering for a bride to be left for a horse, it was even more disgraceful to let others know she was hurt.

Trevor's voice and manner were very matter-of-fact, but she could feel the highly coiled impatience in his body as he waved off the eager footman and went to the sideboard to serve himself some breakfast.

"Ah, good morning, Trevor," the duke called out. "I was just telling Meredith that I did not expect to

see either of you today. Or tomorrow. 'Tis your honeymoon!'"

Meredith had no idea how these words affected her husband, for he concealed his reaction admirably. And he completely ignored his father's comments.

Trevor circled around the table to take the chair beside her. Meredith's skin tingled when Trevor accidentally brushed against her back while taking his seat. Thinking it best not to meet his eyes, she kept her own firmly directed at her plate.

"The butler has informed me that numerous invitations addressed to us have been received this morning," the marquess said. "Have you had an opportunity to sort through them, Meredith?"

Startled, she glanced up. "No. I have not even seen them."

The marquess impatiently drummed his fingers upon the table. "I already have plans for this evening that were made weeks before our sudden marriage. I suppose if there are events you wish to attend tonight, I can prevail upon Viscount Aarons or Mr. Doddson to escort you."

Meredith felt herself flushing, which she particularly hated doing in front of both her husband and father-in-law. In an uncharacteristic fit of pique, she decided Lady Anne Smithe was probably never flustered or blushing around her male relations.

"It is hardly necessary for you to fob me off on your friends, my lord. I assure you, I can take care of myself."

Trevor's burning eyes suggested he was not pleased by her show of independence, but Meredith was beyond caring. He regarded her with a frown for what felt like an eternity, then finally said, "As you wish."

It was exactly the opposite of what Meredith wished, but she would cut her tongue out before saying so.

The duke looked as if he were bursting to voice his opinion on the matter, but he must have understood the silent plea she cast his way, because he remained quiet.

Trevor's rejection stung. Yet if the marquess did not want her to be a part of his life, she would not beg for his attention or even demand it. Years of observing males had taught Meredith one very important lesson. Most of them did not react well to being prodded or nagged.

Conversation among them resumed. As befitting the members of a civilized society, they spoke of inconsequential matters in modulated tones, though the tension was thick and oppressive.

When the pile of food from Trevor's plate had disappeared completely, he rose. "I wish you both a pleasant day. And evening." He inclined his head and stepped away from the table.

Not trusting her voice, Meredith merely nodded her head. Though she wanted nothing more than to retreat to the privacy of her chambers, she sat and sipped her tea.

"It would seem to me your new husband is not all that interested in spending time in your company." The duke brushed his linen napkin fleetingly across his mouth. "What are going to do about it?"

I do not know! Those desperate words rattled around in Meredith's mind, but she refrained from speaking them. It made her feel weak to admit she was so easily defeated. " 'Tis the fashion for couples to lead separate, independent lives."

"A day after they are married?" The duke snorted. "So that's what you are going to do? Close your eyes, grit your teeth, and grimly endure?"

Meredith bit her bottom lip until she tasted blood.

"Those who want to survive must learn to adapt, Your Grace."

"What nonsense," the duke scoffed. "I thought you had more backbone than that, young lady."

Meredith's nostrils flared with indignation. "If memory serves me, there will be an operatic performance of *Don Giovanni* at the Haymarket this evening. I presume you have a box at the theater?"

"Of course I have a box." The duke frowned. "Haven't used it in years, though."

"That hardly matters. Do you like opera, Your Grace?"

"I never took to it. And I could never understand how a bunch of men and women prancing around on a stage, screeching and carrying on, making enough noise to wake the dead was considered entertaining."

"Opera is a pure expression of music and emotion," Meredith insisted, though secretly she thought the duke's description had merit. "More importantly, half the *ton* will be in attendance, ogling each other rather than looking at the stage or listening to the singers. Since I find myself free for the evening, you may accompany me to the performance."

The duke's eyes darted to the footman who was clearing the table, then returned to Meredith. "I just told you I cannot abide all that noise they make."

"Then I shall bring an ample supply of cotton to stuff in your ears to muffle the sound."

The sputtering sound of the duke's continued indignation gave Meredith a very small measure of satisfaction as she left the room.

away from the fact that her husband, the dashing new
groom, was never seen in public socially with his
wife.

Meredith was exquisitely turned out, wore a brilliant
but dazzling smile as she began the promenade

Eleven

In the two weeks that followed her marriage,
Meredith once again created a sensation among the
ton, for she was seen everywhere with the same escort—balls, parties, dinners, musical evenings, the
theater, even the occasional afternoon at the park.

Tongues were wagging and speculation ran high, yet
the gossipmongers soon discovered it was difficult to
find fault with the new marchioness. When in public,
she always conducted herself with style, grace, and
good humor. Her escort was not always as circumspect, but allowances were made, for he was a tall,
handsome, distinguished man of noble rank who appeared to hold her in some affection. He was also her
father-in-law.

It was quickly noted that Lady Meredith seemed to
enjoy the duke's company a great deal, though she
spent much of her time at various social occasions
circulating among the other guests. Yet she arrived and
departed each event with her head held high and her
arm locked securely around the duke's arm.

It was also noted that when dancing took place she
again allowed herself only one partner: the duke.

This behavior was not, as some believed, a well-
thought out, deliberate plan of Lady Meredith's, designed with the sole purpose of drawing attention

away from the fact that her husband, the dashing marquess, was never seen anywhere publicly with his wife.

Meredith nearly laughed out loud when a high-stepping dandy had slyly complimented her on her cleverness for concocting such a brilliant strategy. The situation she now found herself being applauded for had evolved out of desperation, not planning.

It had begun the morning after her hasty marriage and come to fruition late that night as she waited in vain for her husband to come to her bed. In the wee hours of the early morning, before sheer exhaustion claimed her, Meredith had reviewed the possibilities of her future.

She had thought of becoming a recluse. She had pondered retiring to one of the country estates her husband had been so keen on sending her to. She had even considered claiming an illness to avoid appearing in Society.

Yet each idea fairly smacked of cowardice and, though humiliated, Meredith was not about to compound her shame by hiding herself away. Instead she began to accept a select number of invitations. Because she needed support, needed someone to stand beside her, she had coerced the duke into accompanying her.

Dancing only with the duke was again a happenstance. Desperate to avoid such intimate contact with other men, she refused all invitations to take to the dance floor one night at Lady Chester's ball. But when the duke had asked her to partner him for a quadrille, she had felt it her duty to agree.

The same thing happened the following night, and this occurrence did not go unobserved. Soon it was the talk of the evening. Since Meredith found it was the perfect way to distance herself from the rakes and

rogues who were eager to work their wiles and charm upon such an obviously neglected wife, she continued with the practice and let the wagging tongues have their say.

To her surprise, Meredith discovered she actually enjoyed dancing with her father-in-law. He was a tall man, well over six feet, and she did not have to hunch her back to be comfortable when in his embrace.

On this particular evening, she favored him with three dances, then decided she had enough frivolity for one night. The ducal carriage was summoned and a footman assisted her and then the duke inside. Once they were settled comfortably, the carriage lurched forward, taking the unlikely pair home.

Though only a short distance, these drives often took longer because of the crowded streets. Meredith never minded. It gave her time to recall the evening's activities with the duke. It also gave her time to collect her emotions, gather her strength, and don her shield of polite indifference on the off chance that she would encounter her seldom seen husband when she arrived home.

"That was a crush," the duke said as he gingerly adjusted his position on the velvet seat to ease the pain in his knee. "Leave it to the Countess of Tewskbury to invite five hundred people when her ballroom can accommodate only half that number. The woman is a ninny."

" 'Tis no secret that the countess has a great fear of being a failure as a hostess," Meredith observed. "Therefore she invited an overly large number of guests to ensure a success even if many decided not to attend."

"Judging by the size of the crowd, I would venture to say everyone of consequence accepted her invitation."

Meredith sighed. With a most notable exception, she remarked silently to herself. The Marquess of Dardington was conspicuously absent.

"Yes, the countess seemed pleased," Meredith commented. "I would qualify the evening as a success. I believe I shall write to her tomorrow morning and tell her how much we both enjoyed ourselves."

"Such open approval from you will certainly elevate her status as a first-rate hostess." The duke hunted in his waistcoat pocket and drew out a cheroot.

"How ridiculous." Meredith laughed. "I was always considered something of a social pariah, yet now that I am your daughter-in-law, my opinions suddenly matter."

" 'Tis the way of the nobility," the duke declared. He lit his cheroot and took a puff. "Did you know the countess's grandfather was a merchant? There are some who say she still carries the taint of the shop."

"A most unpardonable sin."

"It certainly can be." The duke lowered the carriage window to let out the smoke. "She might be a ninny, but there is not a cruel or mean bone within her body. Your support and approval would be a boon to her."

"Then she shall have it."

The coach rocked to a stop. Meredith glanced out into the moonlit street, but did not recognize the surroundings. They had not arrived at the duke's residence but instead were caught in traffic. She leaned back against the comfortable, plush squabs and rested her eyes, not minding the delay. After all, it was not as if there was anyone waiting for her at home except her maid.

"You should have heard old Monford tonight," the duke said. "He nearly had a fit of apoplexy when we started our third dance. Just isn't done, you know. He later told Billingsly that I orchestrated your marriage

as an excuse to keep you in my company and in my home. Can you imagine such drivel?"

Meredith smiled in the darkness. "The Earl of Monford has never been known for his tact or intelligence. Still, you sound far too flattered by the comment for it to be such a ridiculous notion."

"I'm not dead yet," the duke huffed. "Is it so impossible to speculate that a man of my years could keep up with a young woman like you? The rumor could be true."

"Most assuredly. You have done a fair job of keeping in step so far." Her eyes glinted with mischief. "However, you must learn to pace yourself. There are quite a few more weeks of frantic socializing to endure."

"Endure? Do you really dislike it so much, Meredith?"

"It can be a trial at times," she admitted softly as the gentleness in the duke's voice prompted an honest answer.

"Why do you do it?"

" 'Tis expected."

The duke sputtered loudly. "What rot! You, my dear child, have never done what is proper or expected. What is the true reason?"

Meredith shook out the folds of her skirt. Keeping her head lowered, she muttered, "It passes the time, helps keep the loneliness at bay. I fear I might lose my mind if I stayed in my rooms all day and night."

"Ahhh, as I suspected." There was a pause as the duke took a final drag on his cheroot, then flung the remaining piece out the open carriage window. "When was the last time you saw my son?"

Meredith's head shot up. She cleared her throat, then swallowed. "I am not certain. Three or four days ago, I believe."

"It was four days," the duke said calmly.

"Are you spying on me?" Meredith asked in astonishment.

"It is hardly necessary when you live beneath my roof."

Meredith folded her arms beneath her breasts. She had underestimated her noble father-in-law. Though he had shown her kindness and empathy, he was still a duke, with a need to manipulate and control everything he possibly could.

It was dark in the carriage, yet he must have sensed her agitation.

"I am concerned," the duke added.

"Then speak with your son," she replied bitterly.

"I have."

Meredith groaned. She felt the warmth of a blush cover her cheeks. "What did he say?" It hurt her pride to ask, but she was too desperate for news to care.

The duke shifted uncomfortably. "Nothing of substance or consequence. Though he did mention a town house property for lease that his secretary had located. It wasn't in a very fashionable section nor in the best condition, but I got the impression he might be interested in taking it. Has he discussed this with you?"

"No." Meredith turned her head, becoming very interested in the fringed shade of the carriage. "Though it does not matter. I will not move even if the marquess has leased the property." A sudden thought occurred. "Unless you wish me to leave?"

"You may stay as long as you desire." The duke cleared his throat. "I confess to becoming used to having you around."

"Rather like a pet dog?" she interjected wryly.

The duke laughed heartily. "I have grown fond of you, Meredith, as you are no doubt well aware. I will

admit, however, that was not always the circumstance."

The tension eased and Meredith smiled also. "Why did you dislike me so much? I do not recall ever meeting you until Trevor introduced us the day we were married."

"Ahhh, but we had met. Three years prior at a ball. When I went into the supper room, I noticed you immediately. You were surrounded by several men, all of whom were hanging upon your every word. I thought you were a beautiful young woman, flirting and flattering with her many suitors, but as I strolled past I heard you spouting advice about making an investment in the Lowry shipping company."

"What was I saying?"

"A bunch of nonsense."

Meredith frowned as she tried to recall the particulars. "As best I remember, I have never invested any money in a shipping firm of that name."

"Well, some of us did." The duke's mouth curled in self-derision. "Lost a fair amount of coin, too. How in blazes could you, a mere slip of a girl, know the investment was ill advised?"

Meredith's brow furrowed as she tried to remember the details. "I always investigate a business opportunity thoroughly before committing any funds. There must have been something about this firm . . . wait! I remember now. It was the captain of the largest schooner. He drank heavily. It was obvious he could not be trusted. I concluded his successful trading runs of the past were merely luck and assumed his luck would eventually run out."

"It did," the duke grumbled. "Along with a good portion of my money."

"You should have listened to my advice," Meredith

countered, trying to keep the smug edge of satisfaction from her tone.

"Investment advice from a woman? A young woman?" The duke shook his head. "Ridiculous."

"I know 'tis practically a crime for a female to have a functioning brain that she often uses—"

"It is a serious liability," the duke interrupted. "However, given the challenges you and my son are facing, I am hopeful that in your case it will prove to be an asset."

Meredith was momentarily shocked into silence. His confidence in her was both humbling and frightening. If only she possessed the same degree of hope concerning the state of her marriage. The coach halted a final time and Meredith realized they had arrived home. The duke escorted her up the main staircase.

"Good night, sir. Sleep well." Meredith leaned forward, raised herself to the tips of her toes, and kissed the duke's cheek. This too had become a nightly ritual.

"Good night." The duke turned toward his sleeping quarters.

Meredith smiled wryly as she began the lonely, solitary walk to her rooms. That nightly kiss was the only one she bestowed upon any man these days, unless her brothers came to call.

She turned the final corner on her meandering journey and immediately noticed something amiss. The door leading to Trevor's rooms stood open. How odd. In the past weeks, the door had always remained closed. Why was it open now?

Nervous energy surged through her as she cautiously passed it. The hall was lit with candelabra set on various pieces of furniture, as well as several sconces. In comparison, the marquess's chambers seemed dark, lit by three single candles, each placed in the darkest corners of the large room.

Though the light was poor, Meredith was unable to resist pausing so she could look inside. To her utter shock, she saw a male figure sitting in a wing chair near the window. Trevor?

She must have whispered his name, for the man looked up at her. Meredith gasped.

"Ah, there you are at last," the marquess called out. "Come in."

When she made no move to comply with his command, he stood up and walked to the threshold. Meredith found herself staring into his blue eyes. She had never known a man with eyes so extraordinary, so beautiful. They were perfectly formed, fringed with dark lashes and the color of a sun-kissed sky.

"Come in," he repeated softly.

Meredith pulled her gaze away and licked her suddenly dry lips. She made a move forward, then stopped. The marquess had invited her inside, yet he blocked the entrance.

He seemed amused by her dilemma. She angled her shoulder and tried again. Her back brushed against his front. Meredith stifled a tremor of anticipation, angry with her traitorous body for feeling such an extraordinary rush of pleasure.

"Is there something in particular you wish to discuss?" she asked formally.

"Must a husband have a specific reason to speak with his wife?"

"In our case, yes."

"Perhaps I want to change that situation."

Meredith blinked, taken aback by his answer. "Do you?"

His jaw clenched. "Why else would I be here? Waiting for you?"

Meredith shrugged her shoulders expressively. Was that what he had been doing? Waiting for her? It

seemed impossible. Or did it? Meredith shook her head. She had long since given up any hope of understanding the complex, moody man she had married.

Looking about, she took in the decor of his bedchamber. Her eyes came to rest upon a wooden table set next to the wing chair. It held an open decanter of spirits and a nearly empty crystal goblet.

He did not seem to be in his cups, but obviously Trevor had been drinking. This might not be the most appropriate moment to have an important discussion, Meredith concluded.

Leave, her mind screamed. *Leave before he makes a complete fool of you.* It was the cautious, wise choice, yet her wayward heart would not obey. Each day since her wedding, Meredith had hungered for a glimpse of him, a chance to have a conversation—any sort of conversation—with him.

If he was sincere about effecting a change in their relationship, she was more than anxious to listen. Yet hope was a frightening commodity and something she could ill afford. Her heart was already bruised, her self-confidence on the brink of falling apart.

"Will you take a seat?" He indicated the chair opposite his.

"No, thank you. I prefer to stand."

"I would think your feet are tired from all the dancing you did tonight."

There was a long pause. The marquess settled himself in his chair and stared at her expectantly. He wore a starched white shirt, a perfectly tied silk cravat, black knee breeches, white silk stockings, and black shoes polished to an impeccable gleam, but no waistcoat or evening coat. She was unsure if he had recently returned from an evening on the town or was preparing to go out.

Meredith came closer to him. Her senses were as-

saulted by the distinctive scent of soap and mild co-
logne that was unique to him. She closed her eyes and
breathed deeply. It was erotic and mildly disturbing.
Her poise began eroding rapidly.

"I danced but three times tonight," she whispered.

"All with the duke?"

Her lips twitched in amusement. "So you have
heard about that?"

"Ad nauseam." He lifted the glass off the small table beside him, drained it, then held it in her direction.
"Would you be so kind as to pour me another?"

A scowl settled over her features. Was that why she
was here? To act as his servant? Or to listen to him
complain about her social activities with his father?
Meredith was of a mind to empty the contents of the
decanter directly into his lap, but at the last moment
refrained from giving in to her temper.

It gave her the oddest feeling to lean toward him
and pour a thin, steady stream of liquid into the glass.
He watched her intently as she performed this simple
task, and she, in turn, felt unable to drag her eyes
from his.

"Thank you."

Shivers trickled down her spine. The mood had
changed noticeably—tense and charged. More than
anything she wanted to lean even closer, to press herself against his solid warmth. Yet she did not dare.

Keeping his gaze firmly locked with hers, the marquess put his glass back on the table without taking
a sip. Then he reached forward and took the decanter
out of her hands, setting that beside the glass. Her
entire body felt singed by the look he gave her.

His hand thrust out suddenly and grabbed her wrist.
She realized she was still bent over him and tried to
straighten herself. He tugged harder and she lost her

balance, falling forward to land in his lap. She tried to push herself away, but he held her wrist.

Mere inches separated their lips. A tide of sexual awareness swept over her. Something hard and masculine pressed insistently against her soft lower belly.

He smiled at her. Wickedly, sensually, irresistibly. The impact felt like a blow. Her heart thundered painfully in her chest. Though they supported only a small part of her weight, Meredith's legs began to tremble.

She felt the warmth of his breath skimming her face. It filled her with a mixture of elation and excitement, yet also dread. For if he did not kiss her now, she would surely wither and die.

As if reading her desperate thoughts, he closed the slight gap between them. His lips brushed lightly against hers. She whimpered softly as the sensations strummed through her body. He released her wrist, but she did not move away. Instead she moved her mouth against his, her tongue stroking his lower lip.

The marquess reached out and cupped her face. He tilted her head, positioning her to accept his kisses, which grew progressively deeper, more intimate. His tongue parted her lips. He tasted of wine and sin. The fingers of one hand threaded through her tightly coiffed hair, while his other hand rested against her bottom.

Trevor then began to stroke her with that hand—pet her, really, like a purring kitten. Across her shoulders, down her back, a tight squeeze on her bottom. Then back again. She felt her body begin to heat, to ready itself for him.

Meredith arched into his palm as he shifted his fingers to the front of her body. Sighing with pleasure, she pushed her full breast into his hand. His fingers were teasing and exciting, but the silk of her gown was a barrier that frustrated her. Hastily she tugged at

the low-cut bodice, yanking it away along with the thin chemise, exposing herself to the waist.

His eyes traveled over her bared flesh and she could see the raw need in his eyes. He buried his face against her throat, kissing his way downward. She leaned forward, and he took her bare nipple between his lips.

The sensation was almost more than she could stand. She clutched at him, clasping his head tighter. The tip of his tongue circled lazily, tasting, teasing. Then he placed the entire nipple inside his mouth and sucked. Hard. Then slowly. Then faster.

Meredith struggled to breathe. It felt so *good*. The scalding touch of his mouth and tongue made her shudder with longing. She squirmed against him restlessly, acutely aware of a primitive ache in her, a desperate need to fill the emptiness inside.

He encouraged her passion. Pulling his mouth away, he bit playfully at her throat and earlobe.

"Move your legs so I can lift your skirts," Trevor whispered sensually in her ear.

Blindly Meredith followed his instructions, hardly blushing at all when he pushed aside her undergarments and placed his hand between her thighs, on her bare flesh.

With agonizing slowness he circled the most sensitive, intimate part of her, his fingers teasing and tangling in the curls of her womanhood. Meredith's pulses leaped as desire, wild and passionate, lanced through her.

Her hand came up between them, pressing against his chest. She could feel her body yielding to him, submitting to the mastery of his caresses. A part of her rebelled at this easy acquiescence, but she quickly shut it down.

Ever since her wedding night, she had known there was more pleasure to be discovered when making

love. Trevor held the key to that pleasure, and for the moment seemed most intent on sharing it with her. She would be a fool to turn away from him now.

His clever, questing fingers urged her thighs farther apart. Parting the thick folds of skin, Trevor brushed against her swollen center, then slowly slid one finger deep inside her. Heat blossomed in every part of her body.

Meredith gave a strangled moan and turned her face to his for a kiss—a deep-throated, full-bodied kiss. The glide of his tongue in her mouth felt heavenly. She thrust her hips mindlessly forward and he stroked and probed until she was frantic.

Suddenly Meredith felt the escalating tension begin to crest and break. She arched upward with a keening groan, and Trevor kissed her full on the lips, swallowing her cries of pleasure.

That was it! The mystery of her wedding night had been solved in a most delicious, delectable manner. He continued to stroke her as the shudders subsided, almost as if he were calming and soothing her passion. She smiled lazily.

Drifting on the lingering swell of pleasure, Meredith sprawled inelegantly in her husband's lap, until she noticed he had withdrawn his hands and was trying unsuccessfully to right the skirt of her evening gown.

Gathering her courage, Meredith opened her eyes. Trevor's expression was guarded, but there was a glint of masculine pride in his eyes, the knowing glance of a man who has just pleased a woman.

It had been truly wonderful, a remarkable sensation superior to any other she had known. And yet still she was not completely satisfied. On their wedding night only Trevor had achieved this bliss. Tonight she had been the benefactor. The throbbing, pulsing erection

poking insistently against her hip let Meredith know the marquess had not yet found fulfillment.

What heights of passion could they reach if they both experienced this ultimate release together? She could scarcely imagine, but Meredith decided she was quite eager to try.

With a sultry smile she tentatively reached for him, setting her hand on his muscular thigh. Imitating his actions, she began a tantalizing caress with her fingertips, drawing small, tight circles that inched forward toward his groin. "Please, allow me—"

The marquess groaned as if in pain, clasped her wrist, and pulled her hand away, while trying to stand up at the same time. Since she was lying in his lap, it was nearly impossible.

"I am fine, Meredith. There is no need for any of that." He practically pushed her off his lap.

Slowly, Meredith straightened. Her body tingled, still riding on the currents pleasure he had given her, yet her mind was beginning to clear.

"Why?" she asked simply.

" 'Tis getting late." He turned his head away, and she felt the sigh he tried to suppress. "Perhaps it would be better if we spoke in the morning."

"I do not plan on doing much talking tonight." She reached again for him. "Or listening."

He stiffened and lowered his head. "I am rather tired."

She sucked in a breath. He was rejecting her, deliberately turning away from her passionate overture. Color flooded her face. But she would not look away or bow her head. He would succeed in humiliating her only if she allowed it. She had nothing to be ashamed of, had no reason to feel embarrassed or distressed by what they had just done, by what she wanted to continue doing.

For heaven sakes, they were married. To each other!

He was looking at her now, staring down at her with a wry expression. She noted a flush still lingered on his cheekbones. Her palm itched to cradle his face, to run her thumb along the seam of his sensuous lips, to tease and tantalize him with mindless passion.

A shiver of goose bumps flashed along her arms and neck, and Meredith realized with a start she was still bared to her waist. This wanton state of undress should have embarrassed her, but somehow it felt wickedly right.

Meredith casually slipped her arms through the sleeves of her gown as if she were donning a bonnet instead of covering her breasts. The marquess's eyes remained on her face. Once she felt her breathing was under control, she asked, "Why did you really ask me in here tonight?"

"I wanted to remind you that you are still my wife."

"How presumptuous of you, my lord." She swallowed back her angry retort. "I was not the one who had forgotten."

She turned on her heel and headed for her room, pausing only to slam the door resolutely shut as she left.

The harsh sound echoed through the chamber. Trevor swallowed back the thickness in his throat, determined not to give in to his emotions. The ache in his groin was an acute pain. His erection was hard and swollen and pressing against the fastenings of his breeches. He could barely shift in the chair without feeling a burst of discomfort.

He had not handled that at all well, certainly not as he intended. She did not understand why he had sent her away. Misleading Meredith was not his aim, yet he was not up to explaining. That exhilarating sexual encounter they had just shared had drained his energy,

weakened his resolve, and left him aching and slightly confused.

It was very plain she thought he had rejected her, and he supposed on the surface that was partially true. Though he desired her greatly, more than any woman of recent memory actually, Trevor was determined not to use her body, even though she was his wife.

He had more respect, more regard for her. He knew what she wanted from him. Love, devotion, fidelity. Trevor smiled and reached for the goblet of brandy he had set aside earlier. Perhaps the alcohol would help take the edge off his discomfort. He took a long sip, then smiled again.

How ironic. Of the three, love, devotion, and fidelity, the only one he felt capable of providing to his wife was fidelity—a lowly state of affairs for a confirmed rake.

Life had settled into a pattern that was not much different than before he married. He had the same friends, same club, same late hours, same drinking, same wagering, same reckless fun.

One notable exception was the lack of females in his bed. Though he insisted to himself it was not because of any chivalrous sense of duty, Trevor found the idea of breaking his vow of fidelity repugnant.

If he were incapable of giving Meredith what she truly desired, the least he could do was be faithful to her. Tonight he had wanted to discuss moving to a new London residence, a town house his secretary had located, with Meredith. Perhaps if he were away from so many reminders of Lavinia, he could find his way in this new marriage.

Yet the moment he had seen the flare of passion glaze Meredith's eyes, he knew living in these apartments of his father's house was not the problem. The memories of Lavinia, the life and the love they had

shared and the unquestioning pain and despair he had suffered at her death would follow him wherever they lived.

And thus was the crux of his torment.

Twelve

The marquess suspected there might be dramatics and even tears to contend with at breakfast the next morning. But he never thought they would be coming from the usually composed housekeeper, Mrs. Pritcher.

As Trevor entered the dining room, he found the housekeeper sitting at the table, hunched over and sobbing into a crumpled square of white linen. Meredith stood beside the servant, her hand resting solicitously on the older woman's shoulder.

"What has happened?" Trevor asked.

Both women turned to him in surprise.

"My lord!" Mrs. Pritcher made a move to rise from the chair, but Meredith's hand pressed down on her shoulder.

"Mrs. Pritcher has received some terrible news this morning," Meredith said. "Her niece, her sister's oldest daughter, has died most suddenly."

"Such a lovely creature she was, too." Mrs. Pritcher blew her nose loudly into the handkerchief. "Only seventeen years old and pretty as a picture. I don't know how my sister will manage without her. It breaks my heart just to think of it."

Mrs. Pritcher pressed the linen to her trembling lips and began to weep again.

"You have our deepest sympathies, Mrs. Pritcher," Trevor said helplessly. Emotional women were hardly his forte, especially older women.

"You are too kind, my lord," Mrs. Pritcher said with a sniff. "And my lady, too."

"Dear Mrs. Pritcher." Meredith patted the housekeeper's shoulder. "How I wish there was more we could do to ease your suffering." She turned to Trevor. "I was just telling Mrs. Pritcher she should take the day off and go to her sister's home at once. A family needs to be together at such a difficult time."

"Yes, of course." Trevor nodded his head vigorously. "Where does your sister live?"

"Here, in town, near Hampstead."

"Then there is no need to delay your departure—though it would probably be best if you took someone with you." The marquess looked at the frightened young faces of the two serving maids who had crept into the room and concluded they would be of little help.

There were no other female senior members of the staff. Perhaps Meredith's maid could be of help, but she barely knew Mrs. Pritcher. "Since I insist you do not go alone, Lady Meredith and I shall escort you to your sister's home, as soon as you are composed and feel ready to make the journey."

Meredith lifted startled eyebrows. Trevor's lips curled. It was obvious poor Mrs. Pritcher needed their assistance. Was it really so impossible to imagine he would offer to help? Did she think him a complete monster, devoid of all feelings of decency?

"I could never impose on your kindness, my lord," Mrs. Pritcher said as she blinked at him though watery eyes.

" 'Tis hardly an imposition," Trevor said. "As Lady Meredith said, your sister needs you. Though it will

be difficult trying to manage the household for the next few days without your expert guidance, I feel certain the staff will do their best."

"A few days?" The housekeeper's eyes widened. "What will the duke say if I am gone for so long?"

"You will leave the duke to me," Trevor declared firmly. "Go and pack your satchel. I shall have the coach brought round to the front."

Meredith helped the housekeeper gain her feet. Mrs. Pritcher dropped a respectful curtsy to him and then shuffled away, the serving maids bustling in her wake. Trevor sank down in a chair and allowed a footman to serve him breakfast and hot coffee. As he began eating, he noticed Meredith take the seat to his left.

"You were very kind toward Mrs. Pritcher," Meredith said. "Thank you."

Trevor raised his head. "You seemed rather surprised by my actions at first."

"Well, it is a bit unorthodox for a man of your rank and position to bother with the problems of a servant."

"Mrs. Pritcher has taken care of my family for over twenty-five years. She deserves our consideration at such a desperate time."

"I could not agree more."

Trevor caught Meredith's eye, and a moment of silent understanding passed between them. He could almost feel her admiration and regard for him, her pride in his decision. The sounds of the footman moving about the dining room faded, and for just an instant nothing existed except the two of them, sharing this moment together.

He remembered how she had felt in his arms last night, so giving and sweet, so incredibly hot and willing—the taste of her mouth and tongue, the hardness of her nipples, the slick dew of excitement that soaked his fingers as he rubbed her feminine softness.

His loins tightened, but Trevor steeled himself against the tempest of desire rising through him. Though he knew she could never really understand it, for he barely understood it himself, the respect he felt for her overruled his sexual drive.

Since he felt incapable of providing her with the level of love and commitment he knew she craved, and, yes, so richly deserved, he would not exploit her natural sensuality.

Though by all the saints in heaven, she was temptation beyond imagining.

"More coffee, my lord?"

Reality returned in a rush. Trevor tapped the edge of his cup and the footman obediently poured.

Mrs. Pritcher's sister lived in the northern section of London, in a respectable middle-class neighborhood of clerks and tradesmen of steady, modest means. Though the housekeeper did an admirable job of keeping her composure during the short carriage ride, she became visibly emotional when they arrived at their destination.

"I think it would be best if I accompany her to the door," Meredith said as she scrambled out of the carriage. "To make certain she is all right."

"I might as well come also," Trevor decided. "I can convey our condolences to the family."

Meredith nodded. Flanked on each side by her noble employers, Mrs. Pritcher made the short walk to the front door. The woman who promptly answered their knock bore little resemblance to the housekeeper, but her hysterical outburst and subsequent embrace left little doubt as to her identity. Somehow, amid the weeping and sobbing, Meredith became swept up by the two sisters and was whisked off to a room toward the back of the small house.

Trevor soon found himself standing alone in the

cramped foyer. He was about to return to the carriage and wait for his wife when a young voice called out.

"Who are you?"

The marquess looked down and found a pair of bright, inquisitive eyes staring up at him. They belonged to a young lad of perhaps ten or eleven years old, who must have slipped into the space during all the hysterical commotion. Deciding it would be best to keep his answers simple, Trevor replied, "I came with your aunt."

The boy took a step closer. He was dressed in what was most likely his Sunday best, a pair of black knickers, white stockings, cumbersome shoes, and a white shirt. A black armband threatened to fall below his elbow and he had a smudge of dirt on the cuff of his left sleeve.

"The buttons on your coat are very fancy. Are you the duke?"

Trevor smiled. "No."

The child seemed disappointed by the answer. He hung his head and scuffed the tip of his shoe against the wooden floor. "My sister's dead."

That calm, matter-of-fact announcement startled Trevor, but then he realized it must be the way of children. To treat something they did not truly understand with commonplace normalcy.

"I am sorry for your loss."

The child shrugged. "Mum just keeps crying and crying. Buckets full of tears." He frowned, then sighed. "Didn't know that a body had that many tears. Wanna see her?"

"Your mother? No, I believe I'll wait here. Better still, I'll wait in my carriage. Kindly tell Lady Mer—ah, the lady I came with where I am."

"I wasn't asking you to see Mum," the child said in an exasperated voice. "I was asking if you wanted

to see Betsy. She's laid out in the drawing room in her best dress, the one she and Mum made last year with the pink flowers embroidered all over it."

The marquess had difficulty hiding his shock. The body. The lad was asking if he wanted to view the deceased. What he initially thought was going to be a brief stop now had the mark of a prolonged visit. "I am not sure it is proper. Perhaps we should wait for your mother."

"All she'll do is start crying again. Come on."

The lad grabbed Trevor's hand and tugged. Reluctantly the marquess ascended the stairs to the drawing room. The parlor faced the street, and even the heavy drapes could not completely muffle the bustling sounds of activity outside.

The sofa had been pushed to one side to make room for the trestles that held the coffin. It was a simple pine box, flanked on each side by unlit candles.

"She looks like she's sleeping," the child whispered. He scrambled up on a chair and leaned over the open coffin."But Mum says she'll never wake up again."

Curious, the marquess approached. He gave a cursory glance inside, only enough to catch a fleeting impression of pale white skin and golden hair. Though the look had been brief, Trevor was struck by how young and frail Betsy appeared, hardly older than the boy who gazed at her with such rapt fascination.

"She was very pretty," Trevor commented.

The child nodded. "Mum tied the scarf around her neck real careful. To hide the ugliness."

Puzzled, Trevor looked again inside the coffin and noticed a white scarf wrapped around the young woman's neck. For modesty's sake? But the rounded neckline of the gown she wore rode high on the collarbone. The boy reached down and gently tugged at the carefully wound fabric.

"See," he whispered solemnly. "It's ugly."

Trevor gasped. Vivid marks of deep blue and purple marred the fragile paleness of Betsy's lovely long neck.

The air tightened around the marquess's lungs. He had seen bruises almost identical to these—on Lavinia the day of her burial. Had this poor young girl also met with a terrible accident?

"What happened to Betsy?" he asked.

"I'm not supposed to know," the boy confided. "But I heard Da talking this morning. Betsy didn't come home from work yesterday. We waited and waited until supper got cold. Da got mad and said he never should have allowed her to work in the glove shop in the first place and he was going to make her quit. Then he told us to eat our dinner.

"But even after we were done and the dishes were put away she still didn't come home. It was real dark outside and Mum said she was scared, so Da went to look for Betsy. He came home crying. There were a bunch of men with him. They were carrying her body. They didn't have a cart with them and Da wouldn't leave Betsy, not even for a minute.

"They found her in the alley, right near the shop where she worked. One of the men said she had been strangled. And another man said they had found two other girls last month the same way as Betsy, only outside of different shops. Guess strangled means you hurt your neck real bad, right?"

Every nerve in Trevor's body began to quiver. Strangled? He looked again at the marks on Betsy's neck, then forced his mind to remember Lavinia. Time, shock, and sorrow had dulled much in his brain, but the memory of his beloved in death was a sight he saw as clearly as though it were yesterday.

Vivid lines of dark purple streaking across the

creamy whiteness of Lavinia's elegant female neck that rested at an unnatural angle: the result of a broken neck. Deliberately done? By whom?

"Harold? Harold? Where are you? Come down at once and say hello to your auntie."

Harold raised his head in alarm. "My Mum's calling me."

"Then we had best go downstairs and see her," Trevor said calmly.

Thoughts of the pitiful corpse resting in the drawing room began to fade slowly from his mind as the marquess descended the staircase. He gave the appropriate condolences to the grieving family, which now included Betsy's father, then escorted Meredith out to their coach.

The ride began in a strained quiet, broken only by the crunching of the carriage wheels.

"Did Mrs. Pritcher or her sister say anything about how Betsy died?" Trevor asked.

"No. Considering how young she was, I merely assumed it was an illness. Consumption, most likely. Why do you ask?"

"No particular reason."

Yet Trevor's mind could not relinquish the picture it carried of Betsy's bruised neck. The stunning reality of violence that had been visited upon her person was a brutal reminder of the fragility of human life. Had she indeed been murdered—strangled, as young Harold suggested?

It was almost too horrible to conceive of such a frightening end for an innocent young woman. The grief visited upon the family was doubly understandable under these circumstances.

And what of the striking similarity of these bruises to Lavinia's? In the anguish and grief over his wife's death nearly eight years ago, had he somehow missed

an important clue? Was it even possible to consider that Lavinia's sudden, shocking death had not been an accident, but rather a deliberate act of murder?

Yet perhaps the most chilling aspect was young Harold's mention of two other women who had recently come to a similar end. If there were truly a connection between the deaths of these young shop girls, would more now follow?

"John Coachman wishes to know if you want to return to the house or if you prefer to be dropped at your club." Meredith's gentle voice cut through the marquess's musings.

"I have no specific plans for the day." Trevor frowned. "Is there anywhere you wish to go? Bond Street, perhaps, for some shopping?"

Meredith sighed. "After the morning we have had, I am hardly in the mood for something as frivolous as shopping."

Trevor rapped on the roof and the coach slowed. He lowered the window and bellowed up to the driver, "Take us out to the park. Her ladyship and I would enjoy a slow turn around the paths." Trevor glanced over at Meredith. "Unless you object?"

"This is a most unfashionably early hour to be driving in the park, my lord."

"You should know by now that I never like to follow the dictates of fashion." Trevor watched his wife for a moment. "Therefore I would very much appreciate if you would please address me by my Christian name. You are so formal at times I half expect you to start curtsying when I enter a room."

Meredith's eyes flared and Trevor felt a jolt of satisfaction. Good. At least he had managed to wedge a crack in her infernal composure. It was starting to get on his nerves.

"I was under the impression you preferred formality

between us. Your behavior, *Trevor,* since our marriage has certainly told me you wish to have as little to do with me as possible. I was merely following your wishes."

"You have rarely, if ever, followed the dictates of any man," the marquess replied. "You do it to annoy me. Or garner my attention?"

She almost leaped across the coach in protest. "Balderdash! I own that I can be stubborn and foolhardy at times, but I would never stoop to such unsavory tactics and push myself on a man who does not want me. You proved that point most admirably last night in your bedchamber."

"I would like to explain about last night, Meredith."

"That is hardly necessary." Her eyes became slits of blue outrage. "You did not wish me in your bed. I understood that very clearly."

"You were mistaken."

She shook her head and gazed steadily into his face. "Since our marriage you have treated me with nothing but apathy and disinterest. Or do you deny you have shown more deference to the servants than to me?"

"I had my reasons," he said.

She looked caught off guard by his admission. "They must be fascinating."

Trevor smiled wryly. Even while he was trying to distance himself from her, his admiration for her spirit and strength grew. Most women had been taught from the cradle to placate a man. Apparently this was a lesson Meredith never took to, for she showed not a bit of apprehension at challenging him.

It only furthered his opinion that she deserved far more than he could give her. It was time for him to be blunt.

"Sex between a man and a woman can often be a physical release for one or both of them. Nothing

more. It is not, as the poets suggest, woven together in an unbreakable bond with love."

Meredith had ceased squirming in her seat and was now regarding him with a look akin to amazement. Encouraged, Trevor continued.

"And yet there is a sort of madness connected with sexual desire and fulfillment that can lead a person to forget everything that matters, everything they hold dear within themselves. They reach a point where they would say anything, do anything, risk anything to please and pleasure their partner."

"Is that not love?"

"No," he answered vehemently. "Many often confuse it with love, and therein lies the tragedy. This sexual obsession is a momentary flash. It burns fierce and bright and menacingly hot and then fades and fizzles just as quickly, leaving behind hurt feelings, anguish, even heartbreak for one partner."

"Me?" she whispered.

"I fear so," he replied, though in the back of his mind the voice of truth shouted, *Liar. You are just as susceptible to this heartbreak as she.*

"If you find I have been distant and cautious these last weeks, 'tis because I fear if we let passion rule, you and I will find ourselves in this hopeless situation."

"If you knew this to be the predicament, why did you marry me?" she asked.

"I was an idiot, blinded by some primitive need to bend you to my will," he said. "Selfishly, I did not recognize the truth of our situation until it was too late."

She sagged against the seat, her brow furrowed. She was staring at him intently, but her gaze seemed unfocused. "Are we beyond all hope, Trevor?"

He felt a trickle of shame at the sad confusion that

laced her tone. "Now that you are aware of the consequences, perhaps we can eventually resume marital relations. But you must fully understand that all I can offer you is physical pleasure. Nothing more."

"Is more necessary?"

"It should be for a wife."

She flinched. "I had no idea you were such an incurable romantic. I thought most men felt exactly the opposite when it came to marriage, expecting nothing more than a woman of breeding, civilized conversation, and children. Good looks would be a plus, but hardly a requirement. And passion? Is that even a consideration between a man and his wife?"

" 'Tis your passionate nature that brings us to this juncture," Trevor said. "It flows so easily from you, and I am merely a man, struggling to resist your allure."

"I am your wife. Why must you resist me?"

"I thought you would want more between us than rough, hard, meaningless sex."

He thought he might have finally succeeded in shocking her. She looked as though she was about to roar with fury.

"Is that what you are offering me?" she inquired with a chilly smile.

"Is that what you are asking of me?"

"You arrogant cur. I am not a complete ninny. I did not expect our union to be without its challenges. I admit I have been distressed to learn how very little you care about me. Despite what you may think, I have long accepted you would fail to love me. Ever. But it goes beyond that. Can you not be truthful with yourself? Apparently you do not even like me."

"Just the opposite is true. I like you very much. Far too much."

Irritation flashed over her lovely features. "You have a most peculiar way of showing this regard."

"In lieu of true affection, would you prefer I seduce you with passion?" He kept his voice reasonable, hoping to emphasize his sincerity. "Forgive me, but I know that is not enough. You deserve better than what I can give you."

"Ahh, but we seldom get what we deserve in life, do we, Trevor?" He felt a warm caress of air as she blew out her breath. Meredith's foot began tapping an impatient rhythm, and her expression became pensive. "You have overlooked the obvious. There are practical reasons for having marital relations."

"Are you referring to children? You never mentioned them before." He stroked his chin thoughtfully, trying to imagine her slender form swollen with his babe. The notion brought on a tender, pleasant feeling. "Do you have an overwhelming desire to be a mother?"

"It would please the duke to have an heir," Meredith answered.

The marquess's hands clenched into fists. "An excellent reason to remain childless."

"For once I quite agree. The one child we already have in the household is sufficient."

"I assume you mean me, madame?"

She raised a haughty brow. "How very astute you are, Trevor."

He had no witty reply. She was right. He was acting childish, but the riff between him and his father went back many years. She did not understand the complexity of the issues nor the degree of his hurt. "I must commend you for your expert handling of my father. You two have become rather cozy in a short period of time."

Meredith sighed. "Though your tone implies you

believe otherwise, I can assure you I have not done this to make you angry. Or to garner your attention." An ironic smile flitted uncertainly across her lips. "The duke has been kind and attentive toward me. I appreciate his company."

"He can be most charming when the occasion or circumstances suit him. But I warn you, his favor can be quickly lost and his wrath a monumental fury."

"Rather like his son?" she remarked with innocent sweetness.

"I am a mere amateur compared to the duke."

Meredith's lips pressed together in a line. "I recall a time when you and your father were good friends. What is the reason for this great quarrel, this constant friction between you?"

"Lavinia."

Meredith frowned. "But the duke adored her. It was common knowledge among those of Society. I cannot imagine her ever doing anything to displease him."

Trevor felt the familiar surge of pain overtake him at the stirring of this long-buried memory. "The morning of her funeral we quarreled bitterly. He demanded I remove her wedding band, informing me it was a family heirloom that had been worn by the wives of the dukes of Warwick for six generations. It was far too valuable and rare to rot in a crypt."

Meredith gasped. He saw her glance down at her gloved left hand, then nervously hide it beneath her reticule. "I am sure he did not mean to sound so brutal. Yet his actions prove that the duke can be a hard, unsentimental man. He was wrong to deny you in your time of sorrow."

Some of the coldness inside the marquess evoked by this bitter memory began to slowly fade. He had been crazed, nearly out of his mind with grief, and his father's words had pushed him beyond civility. He

had said unspeakable things, had vowed never to forgive and never to forget.

Yet perhaps it was time to consider letting go of the past, to look forward instead of back.

Trevor peered from beneath slightly lowered lids and watched Meredith fiddling with the elegant band of gold and diamonds she wore beneath her glove. "You need not worry. The ring you now wear was purchased from a jeweler on Bond Street the morning of our wedding."

"And the other ring? The great heirloom?"

"Rests on Lavinia's hand for all eternity, as it should."

"I'm glad."

He felt vindicated by her response. The battle with the duke had been one worth fighting and winning. A bit more of the pain of the past subsided, and Trevor's mood changed. In the soft light that filtered through the carriage window, Meredith's face took on an ethereal glow. She did not cast her eyes away or try to hide from the emotions he was sharing. Her gaze was direct and steady and intelligent.

She was also exceedingly attractive. She had worn a modest gown, appropriate for the manner of their morning call, with a high scooped neckline. The temptation was strong, oh so strong, to reach across and draw her into his lap, then settle her bottom on his thighs.

He would next bend his head and touch the tip of his tongue to the bare skin at the top of her cleavage, slowly stroking downward until her breasts swelled and firmed, until she lifted her head back and offered herself to him like a pagan goddess.

All manner of thoughts raced through Trevor's head as a thick rope of desire twisted deep inside his gut.

He fought the hunger, determined to master himself, to prove he could control the passion.

She blushed and smiled fleetingly, as if she somehow knew the lustful direction of his thoughts. He shifted his gaze, overcome with a sudden wave of protective feeling for her—and completely disgusted with himself when he realized *he* was still the one she needed protecting from.

Thirteen

Something changed during that afternoon carriage conversation. In the days that followed, the marquess was still rarely seen by his wife. She did not share his bed—yet. And when Meredith thought about the state of her marriage, she could ascertain no visible improvement.

Still, she felt more comfortable with her position as his wife and as marchioness, and her confidence and spirit began to renew. Trevor's explanations for his behavior had been complicated and confusing, but he had succeeded in one very important area. She did not take his rejection so personally. It was a ridiculous notion, yet when examined within the context of their very unorthodox marriage, it made perfect sense.

"When the dancing begins tonight, will you follow your usual form and dance with no other man but your escort, the Duke of Warwick?"

The amused male voice that whispered in her ear was a familiar and welcome sound. "Jasper!" Meredith turned enthusiastically and embraced her brother warmly. "How wonderful to see you! And what a surprise. I thought a ball given by a stodgy, elderly member of the *ton* was the last place I would find you."

"We live but three doors away. It seemed utterly rude not to attend for at least a portion of the evening."

Jasper tossed his head and assumed a haughty manner. "Besides, a true gentleman must learn to be comfortable and accepted anywhere in Society, not only among his male companions."

Meredith nearly dropped her fan at the statement. She was about to congratulate her brother on his amusing mimicry when she noticed he had not broken into a smile. In shock, Meredith determined he was serious.

Her fan immediately lifted to hide the grin that formed on her lips. This sober, mature countenance of Jasper's would take a bit of getting used to, and while slightly affected, it was in many ways an improvement over the reckless, irresponsible behavior he'd exhibited in the past.

"Is Jason here also?" Meredith asked, looking past her brother's shoulder to search for his twin. "I would like to greet him."

"We arrived together, but he is off somewhere sulking." Jasper sighed. "We agreed to allow ourselves only three hours in the card room, and Jason is angry because when the time limit was reached he was on a winning streak. It took me several minutes to pry him away without causing a scene. He was not at all pleased."

Meredith cleared her throat, then coughed. But her astonishment did not easily vanish. Her brothers were now voluntarily limiting their time gambling? Was that truly possible? "I am pleased to discover you are both trying to master some self-discipline," Meredith said slowly.

"It was actually Dardington's suggestion." Jasper smiled pleasantly and bowed low to an elderly couple who strolled near. Then he turned back toward Meredith to resume the conversation. "The marquess thought it was time we began to broaden our social

horizons. And when he ascertained we had no wish to marry anytime soon, he advised us to attend as many functions as we could tolerate that would showcase the new crop of debutantes."

"Really? To what end?"

"Knowledge, of course." Jasper clucked his tongue as though it was a most obvious connection. " 'Tis sound advice. Learning the subtle way to negotiate the marriage mart and those carefully laid traps set out by scheming mamas and desperate chaperons will stand us in good stead in the future. No sense getting caught in the parson's mousetrap unless we are ready. Or nearly ready."

"Wise advice," Meredith retorted. Too bad the marquess had not followed it himself. Damnation! Meredith mentally shook her head. Must every conversation she had eventually lead back to the marquess and the state of her marriage?

With effort, Meredith retreated from the direction of her thoughts. "Have you and Jason been spending a great deal of time with Dardington?"

"A fair amount." Jasper's eyes sparkled. "Though we travel in slightly different circles, we share many of the same interests, frequent many of the same clubs."

Meredith's face clouded. "I can well imagine what those finer male interests entail. Horse racing, boxing, aged brandy, loose buxom women, and high-stakes gambling. Oh, and let us not forget the odd duel now and again. You three are a deadly trio set loose upon an unsuspecting city."

" 'Tis not as bad as all that, Merry. The marquess is changing. Everyone has noticed it. He is slow to anger, thoughtful before he takes action, more considered of his activities. Many have lamented he is more

settled these days, less haunted, at times even down-right somber."

Surprised, Meredith considered her brother's words. Jasper was making her husband sound like a wise old man. Responsible, levelheaded, even sober.

"You sound as though you like him."

"I do. Dardington's a capital fellow," Jasper promptly replied. "He keeps his own counsel, lives his life with-out being overly concerned about appearances. He is much admired, much revered among many of my friends and acquaintances. I confess I, too, admire him greatly."

Meredith could barely credit what she was hearing. Jasper was apparently afflicted with a terminal case of hero worship. "How quickly the worm turns. A few short weeks ago you were facing each other with pis-tols drawn, yet now you are the best of friends." Meredith rolled her eyes heavenward. "And they say women are fickle."

"The duel never took place, as you are well aware." Jasper shrugged. "Besides, we are family. 'Tis bad form to quarrel publicly with your relations."

"I must be sure to remind you of that the next time you and Jason start up with your customary bicker-ing," Meredith said.

Her eyes lit with mischief as she spied Jason strid-ing toward them. It was good to be among the twins again, and almost shocking to admit how much she had missed seeing them on a daily basis. Though they had caused her numerous amounts of grief and worry throughout the years, she loved them both dearly.

"At last I have found you!" Jason executed a hasty bow, then swept her up in a comfortable hug. "I've been searching all over for you, Merry."

"Have you?" A wave of spicy scented soap and fine brandy washed over her, such a pleasing and familiar

odor that Meredith closed her eyes for a moment to relish it. "I confess it is wonderful to see you again, yet knowing you have been searching for me has caused a nervous shiver to run down my spine." She laughed lightly, then pulled away and observed her brother keenly.

Jason was dressed to perfection in black evening attire, complete with a snowy lawn shirt, silver patterned waistcoat, black knee breeches, and a matching black coat. The severe outfit should have looked somber as he stood beside his identical twin, who was garbed in garments of richly hued blue tones, but somehow Jason had the slight advantage.

Meredith at first attributed it to the fine tailoring of his garments, but then decided it was the gleaming devil-may-care sparkle in his eyes that set Jason above his twin.

"Your words wound me, Merry."

"Hardly." Meredith ignored the look of stricken indignation she felt certain was feigned and kissed Jason's cheek. "Are you enjoying the ball?"

A momentary frown marred the twin's handsome brow. "I was having the most incredible run of luck with the cards, winning more this evening than I have in a fortnight." He thrust an accusing finger at a clearly bored Jasper. "Unfortunately, my delight was abruptly cut short when I was unceremoniously yanked from the tables by my brother."

"You might as well save your breath." Jasper replied smugly. "Meredith already knows of our pact to limit our gambling at parties and balls. Needless to say, she approves heartily."

"That is no surprise." Jason sulked for a mere instant, then turned to his sister with a charming smile."You will no doubt be pleased to note, then, that I have admirably managed to control my disappoint-

ment at this unlucky turn of events and vow at the next ball I shall play faster so I may win more."

"Your fortitude astounds me," Meredith said, with a small inscrutable smile.

"It is a marvel, is it not?"

"I think I'm going to be ill." Jasper folded his arms across his chest and gave his twin a disgusted look.

"It irks you no end to be continually reminded that I am the favored brother." Jason's handsome face brightened and the moment his brother's back was turned he winked broadly at Meredith.

"Shall we get a drink?" Meredith suggested, fearing Jasper's earlier vow not to quarrel with a family member in public was in grave jeopardy of being broken.

"There isn't time for drinks," Jason insisted. "I spied the most angelic creature when I was leaving the card room. Fair of face, lithe of form, and in all likelihood newly arrived from the country. She possesses a starry-eyed gleam of provincial naivety in her eyes that is enchanting."

"She sounds far too innocent and honorable for the likes of a scoundrel such as you," Jasper interjected.

"She is a delight and certain to be the toast of the Season," Jason stated firmly, pointedly ignoring his brother's jibes. "A mere glimpse of her and my heart has been soundly pierced by Cupid's arrow. You must find out who she is and introduce me to her at once, Merry, before my sweet young beauty is surrounded and bedazzled by a flattering horde of young bucks."

Jasper laughed. "You are slipping, brother. Whenever a female catches your eye you usually waste no time in presenting yourself."

"True. In the past that method has been most effective. Most women like a man who is bold and assertive. But this woman is different." Jason's lips twisted in a rueful smile. "Unfortunately, she is also

accompanied by a harridan of a sister who is acting as her chaperon. I heard she nearly boxed the Earl of Aubrey's ears for being presumptuous enough to request a waltz before learning if the girl had been granted permission for the dance."

"Cowed by a mere female, brother." It was a challenge, not a question. "How disappointing."

"Trust me, there is nothing *mere* about this chaperon. She seems to have perfected a fine-tuned ability to scare away every potential suitor within a hundred miles. I believe a simple stare from this gargoyle would freeze a man's ballocks."

"Jason!" Jasper's eyes shot darts of censure at his brother.

"What?"

"Watch your tongue. There is a lady present."

" 'Tis only Merry," Jason exclaimed. "She's heard far worse from both of us over the years and has yet to be offended. You forget, she is a married woman now and therefore even harder to shock."

"Meredith is a lady who would naturally find offense at such off-color language. But her reaction is only a part of the problem." Jasper glanced about meaningfully. "What if someone had overheard you? Language of that sort is far better suited to Gentleman Jackson's boxing salon, not a ballroom."

"Reforming one's character is a noble effort, but you are fast becoming a prig of the first water," Jason ground out.

The men turned toward each other and stood toe to toe. While Meredith had initially enjoyed the distraction of their bickering, she determined it was time to intercede.

"Ah, look—there's a waiter with a tray of filled champagne glasses. Would you fetch me a glass please, Jasper?"

Neither brother moved. Nor blinked.

"Please, Jasper," Meredith repeated. With obvious reluctance he shifted his attention to her. Yet he did not move so much as an inch.

Jasper's stony glare told Meredith he wanted nothing more than to refuse her request, but she had not successfully managed her high-spirited brothers for so many years without learning a thing or two. Meredith kept her expression innocent, yet determined. In less than twenty seconds Jasper strode off to do her bidding.

"I'm sorry." Jason's face assumed a baleful look. "I did not mean to insult you with my coarse language."

"In truth, I was not offended, but please do not tell Jasper, else he shall start lecturing us both." Meredith bent her head and murmured in her brother's ear, "If he keeps this up, he will be impossible to live with by the end of the Season."

Jason broke into hearty laughter. "You are a gem, Meredith. Most women would be near to fainting at our behavior tonight. Dardington's a damned lucky man to have a woman as fine as you for a wife," he said sincerely.

Meredith worked to muster a smile, biting back the taste of regret, not wanting to dwell on whether or not her husband believed himself to be a lucky man. "Supper will be served within the hour. You must tell me all you know about this incomparable young woman you are determined to meet. If we can manage an introduction soon, you might be able to escort her to supper."

Meredith's distraction worked exactly the way she had hoped. Jason soon dropped any discussion of her husband and waxed eloquent about the young woman.

" 'Tis just my luck this beauty has such a diligent

watchdog," Jason said in a disgusted tone. "Why is it that the more alluring females are never accompanied by elderly, nearly deaf matrons who prefer to gossip amongst themselves before overindulging in the rich food on the buffet? Then two glasses of champagne later they are dozing off in a corner while their charges are left to fend for themselves."

Meredith shrugged her shoulders indulgently. "I promise I shall do everything in my power to win over this chaperon and allow you a clear shot at the young miss. Ah, here is Jasper with our drinks. Let us all down a fortifying glass of champagne, and then we shall go in search of this paragon."

All three clinked their goblets together in a toast.

"Good hunting, brother," Jasper said.

Jason's mouth edged up. Then he gulped back the bubbling wine. Meredith was sipping hers in a more reserved manner when Jason grasped her arm, demanding her attention.

"There she is, Merry. The blond vision in the aqua silk gown standing beside the marble pillar. Is she not perfection?"

With great interest, Meredith angled her neck and eyed the diminutive blond who had so enraptured her brother.

"Good heavens, I know that woman," she exclaimed.

"How? I am certain she is newly arrived in town."

"She is from the country, as you suspected," Meredith said. "Your lovely young miss is Elizabeth Sainthill, the youngest sister of Viscount Dewhurst."

"Dewhurst?" Jasper rubbed his chin thoughtfully. "Isn't he the chap who married your good friend Faith last year?"

"Yes." Meredith finished her drink and handed the empty glass to Jason, who promptly found a footman

and passed it off. "I met Elizabeth last fall when I went to visit Faith. Dear Elizabeth was a resounding success the night of the local harvest ball, yet all that attention only made her uncomfortable. She is a charming, genuine young woman who enjoys the simple pleasures of life. Her head will not be easily turned by your slick town manners, Jason."

"Egad, Merry. It sounds as though you are having second thoughts about introducing me," her brother replied in an indignant voice.

"I might." Meredith paused, then stared meaningfully into Jason's eyes. "You must promise me you will do nothing rash. I would be horribly disappointed in you if you did anything to upset Elizabeth."

"I just want to meet the girl, Merry. Not seduce her," Jason said. " 'Tis a certainty her chaperon will have my head on a platter if I make so much as a false step. I freely admit I am too much of a coward to brave that female's wrath."

Meredith flicked a glance at the older woman who stood beside Elizabeth, but it was hardly necessary. Only one woman would stand guard over the lovely young blond with such fierce protectiveness—Harriet Sainthill, Elizabeth's older sister.

"Well, at least I can credit you with understanding that situation correctly, dear brother." Meredith took a deep breath. "Any sensible man would give that chaperon a wide berth. Unfortunately, you will never get near the rose unless you risk getting pricked by the thorns of her protector."

"You express sympathy, yet your tone is amused at my plight. Since you know my fair Elizabeth, am I correct in assuming you also know the gargoyle who guards her?"

Meredith nearly burst out laughing. It was a cruel, though apt analogy. Harriet Sainthill was not known

for her sweet temper or her meek countenance. She and Meredith were the same age and had made their debut into Society the same year.

It had become an instant rivalry, though in truth Meredith had never understood why the other woman had disliked her so much. 'Twas not till years later she learned Harriet had fallen in love with Julian Wingate, one of the many men whose proposal of marriage Meredith had soundly rejected that year.

Meredith was always unsure if Harriet had ever forgiven her for rejecting Wingate or if she was miffed by the attention he had lavished upon her. This dislike and distrust Harriet harbored within her still existed despite the fact Harriet had in fact become engaged to marry Wingate several Seasons later.

This animosity had extended beyond Meredith and included Meredith's dear friend, Faith, who was a neighbor of Harriet's. When Faith had unexpectedly married Harriet's older brother last year, Harriet had done all she could to make the new bride's life a misery.

Fortunately, it appeared the two sisters-in-law had somehow worked out their differences. Faith was so in love with her husband and delighted over being a mother to his young son it seemed not much upset her.

"I give you fair warning, dear brother, Harriet will be the very least of your problems if Elizabeth comes to any sort of unhappiness," Meredith cautioned. "You will answer to me first and then be forced to confront her brother. Viscount Dewhurst spent many years captaining his own shipping vessel in the colonies. He is not a man to trifle with, and he is very protective of his women."

"Is he here this evening, too?"

"No, Faith was unable to make the journey to town

this Season." Meredith bowed her head to hide a telltale blush. "She is increasing."

As she spoke the words, Meredith was again in wonderment of the news. Faith having a child! It seemed an impossibility, given the tumultuous start to her marriage, and yet there had ultimately been a happy conclusion, as her current condition implied. Was it possible to believe somehow her own marriage would reach at least a level of comfort? Meredith was almost afraid to hope.

"I suppose Elizabeth is just beginning her sojourn into society," Jasper commented, "though I think she picked a most unusual event to make her debut. Our host, the Duke of Shrewsbury, is hardly a social leader."

"Must have been the older sister, Harriet, who made the choice," Jason surmised.

Meredith jerked her chin up. "How foolish of me not to have remembered. Julian Wingate is a grandson of our host, so naturally Harriet and Elizabeth are in attendance this evening. After all, Harriet is engaged to marry Mr. Wingate."

"Wingate is going to marry that sourpuss?" Jason let out a low whistle. "Her facial features seem to be fixed in a permanently pinched and unhappy expression. I almost pity the man. She must have buckets of money. And property. Or both."

" 'Tis my understanding Harriet has a modest dowry, as does Elizabeth."

"Then Wingate will be in no rush to say his vows," Jasper observed dryly.

Meredith shrugged, silently agreeing with her brother. "They have been engaged for several years. I am sure now that Wingate has returned from the Peninsula and resigned his commission, a wedding date will be set."

"I cannot fathom such a ridiculous match."

"Don't be so unkind," Meredith scolded lightly. "I know you will find this difficult to believe, but Harriet is a very attractive woman. Well, she can be an attractive woman when there are no deep scowls marring her features. She also possesses a sharp wit and an even sharper tongue, so I caution you both to be very careful."

With that final ominous warning, Meredith led her brothers across the room. As they drew closer, Meredith was forced to agree Elizabeth did indeed eclipse her older sister in both beauty and demeanor. It was no mystery why Jason was so captivated by her. She looked exquisite in her gown of aqua silk, with her blond hair artfully arranged in ringlets.

In contrast, Harriet was dressed in a modest gown of deep blue, her brown hair pulled back in a severe chignon. Neither the dress nor the hairstyle enhanced the older woman's looks.

Her eyes darkened as they approached and Meredith hesitated, unsure of the type of reception she would receive.

"Lady Meredith!" Elizabeth's voice rang out with genuine delight. She rushed forward and embraced Meredith in a jubilant hug. "I am so happy to see you. I had hoped you would be here this evening, but Harriet cautioned me not to count upon it."

" 'Tis a joy to see you also, Elizabeth. And looking so beautiful." Summoning up her charm, Meredith turned and inclined her head politely at Harriet, who watched her with an expression of wariness. "Hello, Harriet. I am pleased you and Elizabeth have arrived. Faith wrote me that you would both be coming to town. Are you enjoying London?"

"I find it very much the same as I left it several years ago, filled with self-important people who spend

their days idly preening for each other and gossiping endlessly," Harriet replied with her customary bluntness. "I do not know how you tolerate it year after year."

Meredith exchanged a warning glance with Jason.

"I suppose it does take a bit of getting used to," Meredith said. "Please allow me to present my brothers, Jasper, Lord Fairhurst and Mr. Jason Barrington. This is Miss Harriet Sainthill and her sister, Miss Elizabeth."

The twins stepped forward and bowed elegantly—briefly to Harriet, but noticeably longer to Elizabeth. She blushed prettily at the attention, then raised her chin and smiled.

Her blue eyes widened. "Oh, my, you are—"

"Twins," Jasper interjected smoothly. "Though I am the elder by several minutes and by far the more charming."

"Poppycock!" Jason nudged his brother aside. " 'Tis a poor fellow indeed who must boost his regard by telling everyone how charming he is supposed to be."

" 'Tis not boastful if it is the truth. Do you not agree, Miss Sainthill?" Jasper's eyes twinkled as he stared at the diminutive blond.

"Just look at them," Harriet exclaimed. "Scrapping like a pair of dogs over a bone. We have been in town less than a week, and already I am exhausted from trying to keep Elizabeth from falling prey to a steady stream of charming rogues. The *ton* is fairly crawling with them."

"Elizabeth is a sensible girl. It will take much to turn her head." Meredith lifted her fan to her lips and whispered behind it. "And I have heard from a most reliable source you are doing a more than adequate job of keeping the worst of them at bay."

Harriet smiled. "Thank heavens." She touched her nose with her lace handkerchief, and a whiff of lavender perfume drifted toward Meredith. "Faith told us you had gotten married rather suddenly. I confess I was shocked. When you visited us but a few months ago, you so adamantly declared you would remain single and independent."

Meredith felt the tips of her ears begin to redden as she silently cursed Harriet for having such an excellent memory. "Circumstances change, sometimes beyond our control. I married the Marquess of Dardington a few weeks ago."

"A rather surprising turn of events. I don't believe I've ever met the marquess. Would you be so kind as to introduce us?"

Meredith stiffened. Harriet had already loudly complained about the endless gossip of the *ton*. She must therefore be very aware of the state of Meredith's much talked about marriage. "My husband seldom attends these evenings."

"Pity." There were a few moments of strained, awkward silence. "Are you not going to ask me about my fiancée?"

"No. That would be cruel." It was, of course, exactly what Meredith wanted to do, but already knowing the answer was too much like rubbing salt in an open wound. Any doting or even interested fiancée would at least be in the vicinity of his intended, yet Julian Wingate was nowhere to be seen. Since they were at the home of one of his relatives, it was certain he was in attendance—and pointedly ignoring his fiancée.

"I fear you and I have more in common than either of us would care to acknowledge, Harriet."

"Gracious, you have done it again!" Harriet exclaimed.

"But I said nothing—"

Harriet held up her hand to forestall any protests. "Precisely. 'Tis bad enough your beauty attracts men of all ages while I have the sort of face one forgets even while looking at it. But you also show empathy and consideration to those who clearly do not deserve it. In my eyes, that has always been your worst fault, Meredith. You are better than I." Harriet gave a self-deprecating laugh. " 'Tis rather maddening."

The odd, uncomfortable silence returned. Thankfully Jasper interrupted by asking Harriet to dance. Since Jason was already leading Elizabeth out to the dance floor, Harriet eagerly seized the opportunity to keep a close eye on the younger girl.

Meredith's mood calmed and settled once she was alone. She took a moment to survey the room, to admire the lovely glow from the beeswax candles that made everything sparkle and shimmer. It was all part of the illusion, for this fragile appearance of glistening perfection would disappear as soon as dawn approached and revealed all the true imperfections of the room and the people within it.

A sudden twinge caught Meredith unaware, that shiver of heightened awareness she sometimes experienced in a crowded room when she was standing alone. Meredith shifted her feet and looked about cautiously, expecting at any moment to meet the eye of a bold rake or disapproving matron pointedly observing her.

But there was no one. All the guests she saw were involved with others and focused on their own conversations. She took a deep breath and let it out slowly, hoping to chase away the flush of uncomfortable emotions. Was this a belated reaction to her conversation with Harriet?

Meredith rejected the notion nearly as quickly as

she had thought of it. Given her past history with her former rival, this had been a calm, almost pleasant meeting.

Meredith pressed her gloved hand to her forehead. It was damp with perspiration, though the room was not overly warm. For one insane moment, Meredith thought Trevor was at the ball, for being within the same room as her husband often brought on a similar shimmering of awareness.

Yet as Meredith again scanned the room anxiously, she revised her opinion. That pattering of excitement, that burst of anticipation when Trevor was near her was markedly missing. She felt deep in her bones that the marquess was not here.

Yet the unease of being closely watched persisted.

Her eyes darted anxiously about the room, but no one appeared to be paying her the least bit of attention. Meredith's chest grew tight and she found herself clenching her fan so tightly one of the fragile wooden slats snapped in half.

Shaking off her nervous twittering, Meredith struggled to focus her thoughts and calm her emotions. She was acting like a ninny! She was standing in the midst of a crowded ballroom, surrounded by more than a hundred people. It was perfectly safe. There was no one to harm her.

The strains of instruments being tuned caught her attention and provided the perfect diversion. A new set of partners would soon be forming in the center of the ballroom. Filled with resolution, Meredith went in search of the duke. It was time for her to dance.

He stood behind the marble column and watched her twitter and shake. *She knows she is being observed! And it disturbs her. How marvelous.*

Her fear and discomfort brought him a moment of pleasure on this otherwise dismal night. He had felt restless and edgy, a need he recognized within himself, a need that cried out to be assuaged. But he could not leave the mansion. The duke's ball had filled every inch of the house. There were too many people about, guests and servants, too many eyes that might see what was none of their concern.

There would be dancing until well into the morning, keeping him a prisoner inside the house, for he could not risk being seen either leaving or returning. This made him angry, more driven to act.

He had not felt settled for the past week. The last girl had been a grave disappointment. He had made her acquaintance at the glove shop only a week prior to killing her. She had been shy and stammering, just as he preferred. A sweet innocent, too trusting to know evil when it had embraced her.

Yet she had died that way too—with no fight, no spirit. Her struggles had been minimal, her cries and pleas nearly unheard. It brought him so little pleasure he briefly considered stopping before the job was finished, but he knew that would be foolish.

The shop girl knew his face, could identify him to the authorities. The chances of his being located were very slim, and if that somehow miraculously occurred he would, of course, insist the girl was mistaken. It would come down to his word against hers. He had no doubt he could win such a battle, could convince other men he was innocent and she was merely being a vengeful female.

Had he not proved how clever he was all these years by walking among them, the frivolous society of well-bred ladies and gentlemen? And they suspected nothing.

Yet in this case he could not afford to take the

chance. Other female bodies had been discovered in town, young women who had died in a similar manner, with the deep marks of his hands upon their necks.

So he had finished killing her, wringing out a small bit of delight at the stark look of horror in her eyes seconds before they closed for all eternity. He sighed deeply at the memory. So much effort for so little satisfaction was surely a crime.

A swirling mass of color fluttered before him, jarring him back to the present, back to the ball. He saw Lady Meredith in the center of the dance floor, prancing delicately in front of an older, distinguished gentleman. Her father-in-law, the Duke of Warwick.

The man snorted. He was not as easily fooled as the others. She had attracted much attention with this behavior, been applauded for her virtue, for rising above any scandal. Yet the fact remained she had made a hasty marriage to a man who now neglected and ignored her.

He knew that hurt her. He had seen it in her eyes the morning of the duel. She had been frantic with worry to stop the duel, not only to spare her precious brothers, but to spare the marquess any harm. He had never suspected she cared for the marquess so deeply. It was amazing to see the truth revealed, to learn this most important secret of her heart.

'Twas just and fitting revenge that she who had caused such humiliation to others would in turn be treated with scorn and little regard. How wonderful that this ice maiden who was so beautiful and cold, who had rejected honorable offers of marriage from so many men who were superior to her in every way, was now tied to someone who had no regard for her. Who showed her no respect and no consideration.

The man smiled wickedly at the mystery of fate's

justice. Lady Meredith had become the most pitiful of all society's creatures—the neglected, forsaken wife.

He knew it must rankle her pride, wound her heart to be treated in such a disgraceful manner. That was good. For as long as Dardington ignored her, she would suffer. And as long as she suffered, she would be allowed to live.

Fourteen

Some women felt incomplete without a man by their side. Meredith had always prided herself on being beyond that, on feeling she alone knew what was best when it came to managing her life. Yet as she lingered the morning after the ball in her sitting room, staring at an uncompleted letter she was composing to her friend Faith, Meredith conceded what she really wanted was to discuss the unsettling feelings she had experienced last night—with a man.

Her father-in-law was the natural choice. He was kind, levelheaded, and very much concerned about her. If the opportunity had presented itself, Meredith probably would have mentioned it to him, but the carriage ride home from the ball last night had been unusually brief.

She could always call upon her brothers and solicit their opinion, but she hesitated. She had been impressed by their recent signs of maturity, but they still tended to overreact to a situation. If she confided that she thought she was being watched by someone, they would no doubt raise a cry of alarm.

When considering that reaction, it was logical to conclude the ideal person to ask would be Trevor. He was intelligent, worldly, and calm in the face of danger. Yet it behooved her to remember her husband pre-

ferred to have as little to do with her as possible. That thought stayed with her all through the night, making her decision not to say anything to her husband an easy one.

Meredith's gaze shifted back to her unfinished letter. If only Faith were in town, Meredith could discuss with her good friend the fear and unease that had caused her such a restless night. She had barely slept, plagued by half-formed disturbing dreams that kept her tossing and turning in her bed.

Given the chance, she would even reveal her concerns to Faith's husband, if her friend thought that would help. Unfortunately, this was not the sort of problem one could easily explain in a letter.

> *We had a lovely time at the ball last evening. I so enjoyed seeing Elizabeth again, and even Harriet managed to behave herself. My brothers are completely taken with Elizabeth, while totally fearful of Harriet, the ever present chaperon. Oh, and by the by, I have a great anxiety about being followed and observed by an unseen stranger that I can neither prove nor adequately explain.*

Meredith threw down the quill in frustration. Was she making too much of all this? Probably. Heaving a sigh, she picked up her pen and dipped it in the ink. Bending her head, she set herself to the task of completing her letter, without any mention of her wild imaginings.

Meredith was concentrating on keeping the tone of her letter light hearted and amusing when the hairs on the nape of her neck lifted. Then she heard a footfall behind her. It was Rose's half day off, so she knew it could not be her maid. And the chambermaids had already cleaned and aired her bedchamber.

Meredith had not rung for any servants. There would therefore be no reason for any of them to be in her rooms. Besides, a servant would knock before entering her private quarters.

"I had not expected to find you at home at this time of the day."

Meredith spun around, her pulse beating in an uneven rhythm. Trevor stood in the doorway, his expression openly curious. Meredith swallowed hard. "Goodness, you startled me."

"I can see that." He crossed his arms over his chest and leaned casually against the door frame. "For a moment you looked absolutely terrified."

"I have been a bit jumpy as of late," Meredith admitted. "And you are, of course, the last person I expect to see in my rooms."

He grimaced, and Meredith regretted her choice of words. Steeling herself for his scathing comeback, she put down her quill and faced him fully.

"Do you have plans for the afternoon?"

She bit the inside of her cheek to hold her reply until she could speak in a tone devoid of amazement. He never asked about her plans. "I have nothing specific to attend to today. Is there something you need me to do for you?"

"Actually, I was wondering if you would like to accompany me to a horse race."

There was a short silence. Taken aback by this sudden offer, Meredith's befuddled brain was slow to react.

"I have never been to a horse race," she finally said, wondering if she sounded as much like a simpleton as she felt.

"Why does that not surprise me?" He gave her a wry grin. "I think you might enjoy it. 'Tis a beautiful sunny day, and the weather promises to remain warm. The fresh air will do you good."

It would be wonderful, Meredith thought, and the sudden quickening of her pulse confirmed the idea. An entire afternoon with the marquess by her side. How could she possibly refuse?

"Are you certain you wish me to accompany you?"

" 'Tis just a horse race, Meredith. There's no need to look so astonished. By your reaction, one would think I have asked you to frolic naked in the fountain outside Prinny's palace."

She tilted her chin and gave him a wide-eyed innocent stare. "Is that how you celebrate the end of the race? By romping *sans* clothing in a fountain?"

Trevor laughed. "You'd cause a riot."

" 'Tis better than causing a scandal, sir."

"And a far more pleasing sight." He flashed her a sensuous, disarming glance. "Though I prefer privacy when viewing your *au naturel* womanly charms, my dear."

Flustered, Meredith turned back to her letter. His potent physical presence was beginning to dominate her, and that warm, inviting look in his lovely blue eyes was playing havoc with the speed of her heart. "To avoid the crowd, we would have to swim at night," she ventured.

"That rather defeats the entire purpose, don't you agree? Daylight is far more sensuous."

Her face was flaming red, her breath shallow. Heat prickled across her skin. The erotic thoughts that popped suddenly into her head were so vivid they were almost disturbing. But she wasn't about to be outdone.

She turned back around and faced him. "Must it be Prinny's fountain? The garden here contains several lovely fountains. The one near the boxwood maze is particularly enchanting—and private."

His eyes darkened with a sensual desire that sent a shiver of anticipation up her spine.

"How wrong for society to label me the wild one," he said softly. " 'Tis you who possesses the erotic soul."

For one frantic moment Meredith thought he was going to move toward her and gather her in his strong embrace. Every instinct she possessed urged her to press herself forward, but she knew that would be wrong. No matter how difficult it might be, she had to wait for him to come to her.

He hesitated, and Meredith's heart sank. If he thought too long about his actions, he would not follow his inclinations. As she expected, he made a muffled comment about seeing her later and quit the room.

Disappointed but not defeated, Meredith returned to her correspondence. Though she had longed to feel his strong arms about her, had wished for his lips to press against hers, she accepted it was not going to occur—right now.

There was an entire afternoon to look forward to, and Meredith was very determined to make sure there would be several opportunities for exchanging kisses. And maybe even a dip in the fountain!

It was a lovely day to be out-of-doors. Meredith had difficulty containing her smile as she perched beside the marquess on his curricle's box seat. She was glad he had decided to take the open two-seater carriage. It allowed no room for servants, affording them more privacy.

Meredith enjoyed watching Trevor drive. He handled the reins as he did most things, with ease and accomplishment. Though they did not converse in the carriage, Meredith felt relaxed and hopeful. She determined this would be an enjoyable afternoon. Even the weather seemed to be cooperating. The sun was partially screened by drifting clouds, making the temperature pleasantly cool.

They drove to an area on the outskirts of town that was unfamiliar to Meredith. It was less crowded, more rural in nature, with a main road that led past small brick houses, shops, and stables. They rounded a curve and came to a crossroads with an inn on one side and a church on the other.

The marquess hesitated for an instant, then turned past the church. Meredith edged forward in her seat as the muttering sounds of a boisterous crowd grew louder and the smell of fried pies caught at her nose.

"This is not the type of outing you are used to attending." A shadow came over his face. "The crowd can get a bit rough at times. Are you certain you wish to see the races?"

Meredith turned her head sharply. "You promised me a new experience, and I fully intend to keep you to your word. Besides, I am perfectly safe with you by my side."

"We can leave the carriage here," Trevor decided. He deftly maneuvered the coach beside a fancy barouche. "The racecourse is just beyond the lawn."

Trevor secured the horses, then assisted her from the carriage. The breeze fluttered her bonnet ribbons. Meredith unfurled her parasol and lifted it to protect herself from the sun, which was now out in full splendor.

The marquess reached inside the boot of the carriage and drew out a small basket. He started toward her, then stopped.

"I give you fair warning, madame, if the wind carries that bit of lace and ruffles away I am not going to chase after it."

"I understand." She twirled the parasol smartly, then grinned. "If I lose it in the wind, you may simply buy me another."

He frowned, but said no more. Meredith led the way,

her heart pounding with eager excitement. In the distance she could see a haze of dust surrounding the course, could hear the sounds of laughter and shouting. The air fairly crackled with a light, festive mood.

As they neared the other spectators, the marquess extended an arm. Meredith took it, grateful for his steady presence to help her negotiate the occasionally rutted lawn, which was particularly challenging in her walking slippers.

It also gave her a feeling of safety to stroll through this mostly male crowd under the obvious protection of her husband. Even though he was elegantly garbed in a brown tailcoat, tight buckskin breeches, and knee-high boots, the width of his shoulders and the muscles in his arms proclaimed him a highly fit gentleman.

Meredith saw many faces she recognized, but more that she did not. Surprisingly, there were few females among the throng and those she did glimpse were dressed in colorful garments that were fashionable yet daring. Some even sported cosmetics on their faces.

Meredith struggled not to stare or be too obvious in her curiosity about these women. However, she was not the recipient of equally good manners. She could hear distinct whispers as she walked by several gentlemen. One dandy in an appalling jacket of canary yellow turned his head so quickly in her direction that he winced with pain, while another fumbled anxiously for the quizzing glass that hung from a black ribbon around his neck.

At last successful, he raised it to his eye and peered at her speculatively in openmouthed astonishment. More than anything, she wished she possessed the nerve to lift her chin and stick her tongue out at him.

Meredith could not determine if the astonishment she was receiving was because these men were unused to seeing true ladies at these events or because it was

an amazing sight for the Marquess of Dardington to be seen escorting his wife *anywhere*.

"I see some people I know, but far more who are unfamiliar. Especially the women. Are there any . . ." Meredith's voice trailed off as she sought to find the appropriate word.

"Mistresses, loose women, prostitutes among the crowd? Absolutely." She heard Trevor's low chuckle of mirth. "I venture to say you are the most respectable woman here, my lady."

"Goodness, this is a fast crowd." She could feel his eyes upon her, studying her. Waiting for an outburst of indignity? It would never come. Meredith was hardly in a position to pass judgment on any female, and well she knew it. She dragged in a steadying breath. "May we see the horses before the race?"

"The stables are this way."

They progressed to an area of temporary horse stalls that were bustling with activity. Riders, grooms, and trainers were busy preparing the first set of horses for the race. There were to be five running in the initial heat. Meredith stared with full appreciation as the horses were led toward the starting line, snorting and stamping their hooves in anticipation. With their sleek coats glistening in the sun, Meredith thought they were all magnificent.

"Which horse do you favor to win the contest?" Meredith asked.

"The handsome long-necked bay. He is a stallion with spirit as well as heart. They call him Rascal."

Meredith smiled. "Is that not an unusual name for a racehorse?"

"I like it. Come, let's take a seat." The marquess guided her to a shaded area, then up the steps to the grandstand. He selected a row that held no other oc-

cupants. "Since I own the animal, my opinion of his name is really all that matters."

"I was unaware you owned racehorses."

"Rascal is the first. Consequently, this is also his first competitive showing. The trainer assures me he is ready." Trevor settled in his seat. "I can only hope he has a respectable finish."

"By respectable, I assume you mean winning."

"What else?" He grinned enthusiastically. "Actually, since I have so recently acquired him, I've never seen the horse run against others. But your brother Jason insists Rascal is a prime animal."

"If there is one thing that Jason knows well, 'tis horseflesh," Meredith agreed.

"True. I feel lucky he was willing to part with the horse."

Meredith's spirits deflated. Both Jason and Jasper had been so sincere about trying to change their gambling habits. She had almost begun to believe it was possible, thanks to Trevor's encouragement. Yet it seemed all three men were still very much involved with high stakes betting. It was a most disheartening admission.

"So you are now wagering to win racehorses as well as carriage horses," Meredith commented dryly. " 'Tis a step up, I suppose."

"Wager?" The marquess shook his head. "I did not win Rascal in a card game. I bought him."

"From my brother?"

"Yes."

"Truly?"

The marquess narrowed his eyes. "I detect the beginnings of a scowl on your face, madame. Do you doubt my word on the matter? Would you like to see the bill of sale?"

"That is hardly necessary," Meredith replied. She

knew she should make some sort of apology for her ungenerous remark, but the marquess's righteous indignation rankled her. After all, it was not as if he had never won and then lost a pair of prime cattle on the turn of a card. She knew for a fact he had done both.

"The horses are nearly at the starting line, but there is still time to place a small wager." He glowered at her. "Unless you object?"

"I am not such a prude as to make a fuss over a side bet of a few shillings," Meredith retorted.

"I am pleased to hear it." He stared hard at the racecourse. "So whom do you chose to win?"

Meredith looked down in dismay at her reticule, which contained a second pair of gloves, smelling salts, and a linen handkerchief. "I brought no coin with me."

"I shall advance you a stake. You may reimburse me from your winnings."

Meredith could not contain her laugh. "And if I lose?"

His eyes searched hers. Then his lips curled in a devilish grin. "I imagine we can devise some other form of payment."

His head was bent low, his face close enough that she could feel his warm breath upon her cheek. It was too tempting not to risk it. Meredith tilted her chin and let her lips settle on his.

She could feel his initial jolt of surprise at her action, but there was no resistance. Instead, he parted his lips and opened his mouth to her. The kiss deepened. Softness and warmth spread through her, making her heart beat faster and her insides quiver.

Yet it was Meredith who reluctantly ended the kiss, mindful that they were in a most public place.

"A bonus for the crowd today," she whispered.

"They get several exciting horse races along with a show from the Marquess of Dardington and his bride."

The look he gave her sent a thrill along every inch of her skin. "Blushes from a woman who challenged me to frolic naked in a fountain? You are a fraud, madame."

With a seductive wink, the marquess backed away. Blushing anew, Meredith reached for the parasol she had set beside her, but found it missing. How strange. Leaning over, she glanced at the grass below to see if it had fallen. It was no where in sight.

"Is anything amiss?"

Meredith somehow managed to swallow her scream of fright. She straightened and faced her husband. "How did you manage to place our wagers and return so quickly?"

He grinned boyishly. "I have not had the chance to place a bet. You never told me which horse you wanted to wager upon."

"Rascal, naturally."

"An optimist. I like that in a woman."

She swayed toward him, for one wild moment thinking he might kiss her again. Their gazes remained locked, but then sanity prevailed. Pulling back before making an utter ninny of herself, Meredith lowered her eyes. "Hurry, or else you will miss the race."

Only when she was certain Trevor had gone did Meredith lift her head. As she combed the foggy recesses of her confused mind trying to understand her husband, she remained certain of only one thing. Invitation. It was there in his eyes, in his smile, in his heated body and teasing words.

Just a few days prior, Trevor had spoken so openly about passion and physical desire, had adamantly insisted their relationship remain at a physical distance until it could be managed. Yet it that today he had not

let one moment pass when an invitation had not been clearly issued to her.

A sexual, sensuous invitation.

She was acting just as bad, teasing and flirting with him for all she was worth. Yet she knew what she was about, knew her actions had been deliberate. Ever since her wedding night, Meredith had wanted nothing more than to break through the wall of indifference Trevor had erected between them.

She felt as if she had finally managed to chisel away a few of those staunch bricks. And the afternoon was not yet over!

The marquess returned just as the race began. The starting gun sounded and Meredith stood in excitement as the animals leaped forward, manes flying, hooves thundering along the hard-packed earth.

"Looks like our boy is making a slow start," Trevor observed. "He's dead last."

"They have barely rounded the first turn," Meredith protested. "Give him a chance."

The horses turned into the back stretch, a jumbled mass of glistening coats and long powerful legs. Meredith stretched forward as they approached the next turn, amazed that the animals could endure such a difficult pace.

"It looks like he might be gaining," Trevor declared.

"Then he still can win."

"It all depends on how he runs the final stretch."

Meredith bit her lip as she saw the pack approaching the finish line. One horse, a sturdy looking black, was clearly in the lead, but Rascal was next and moving up with impressive speed.

Meredith grabbed Trevor by the arm and squeezed, her nervous excitement escalating as the crowd set up a cheer.

"We won!" She turned to him, laughing with delight. "How marvelous! We won!"

"So we did."

"I never knew it would be so rousing," she yelled to be heard above the shouting. "This is wonderful."

"Winning always is." The marquess reached into the basket he had carried from the carriage and pulled out a bottled wrapped in a white napkin. Holding it under his arm, he rummaged with his other hand for the goblets.

"Can I help?"

"Hold these."

Meredith obediently accepted the glasses. She watched with undisguised glee as Trevor expertly popped the cork on the champagne bottle. Her laughter bubbled over as the foam spilled down the side of the bottle.

"Steady," Trevor cautioned as he filled each goblet. With a smile, he handed her one. "To Rascal."

They clinked glasses, then sipped. The wine slid down her throat, the effervescence delightfully tickling her nostrils. "Delicious."

Trevor took another sip. " 'Tis refreshing, though I prefer my champagne served a bit colder."

Meredith rolled a mouthful around on her tongue, then swallowed. "We are celebrating Rascal's win. It tastes like ambrosia."

"Victory is always sweet." His gaze was intense, yet oddly tender. "Yet never more so than when it is shared."

That look sent a funny little flutter to her stomach that she deliberately ignored. She marveled anew at how her husband's mercurial moods could have such a strong hold on her emotions.

And she wondered again why he bothered, when he claimed to be devoid of feeling for her. Was it simply

something he could not control? A man of his experience, his reputation, had no doubt been with scores of other women. By his own admission, he was a rogue and a womanizer. Was this heat and invitation he seemed to be casting her way such a part of him that he did it without thinking? Without considering who she was? Or was it more?

The crowd let out another loud cheer, breaking into Meredith's musings. She looked onto the course and saw Rascal being brought before the crowd. It seemed as though everyone wanted to celebrate the stallion's victory.

"Thank you for bringing me today," Meredith said. "I cannot remember the last time I had so much fun."

"It feels good to scream and shout, does it not?"

"Oh, yes." Her heart tugged oddly. "Tell me, whom do you favor to win the next race?"

By the end of the afternoon, Meredith's reticule was weighed down with pound notes and coins. She had wagered, and won, on each race. Never again would she so forcefully criticize her brothers for their gambling indulgences, for she now understood how exhilarating the experience could be.

The crowd had begun to thin as everyone made their way home. While Trevor stopped for a moment to receive congratulations from a group of high-spirited young men, Meredith proceeded to the carriage. It had been a glorious afternoon. The tip of her nose felt a bit tight, for without her parasol she had nothing but the poke bonnet to shield her face from the sun.

She imagined her nose must be pink, perhaps even red, but it did not matter. Nothing could spoil her delight and enjoyment of the day.

The marquess's carriage was easy to identify among the many coaches sequestered in the area. Its sporty yellow wheels stood out among the more somber black

conveniences. Deciding she had had enough exposure to the sun already, Meredith moved to wait in the shade.

As she did, she noticed something in the carriage seat. *How strange, I am fairly certain we left nothing behind.* Curious, Meredith took a step forward. Then another. Her heart began a thunderous pounding when she realized what is was—or rather, what it had been.

Her parasol. That colorful bit of silk and lace that had mysteriously disappeared just before the first race began was now wedged on the carriage seat at an obscene angle. It fluttered gently in the slight breeze, jagged edges of fabric and lace hanging disjointedly from the exposed frame.

Meredith's stomach clenched in a knot and her vision blurred as a wave of cold fear washed over her. Someone had savagely and violently ripped the parasol to shreds, then deliberately left it here for her to find.

"Harper mentioned you were looking for me earlier. Is there something we need to discuss?"

Trevor looked up as his father sauntered into his private sitting room. He shuffled the papers crowding the table where he sat, more for effect than organization. He had been trying to read them for over an hour, with little success. The profits of his country estate were the last thing on his mind.

Upon returning home from the racecourse, Meredith had gone to her room to rest. After her initial outburst of distress, she had said nothing else about her mangled parasol, dismissing the notion as a childish prank.

Trevor did not know if that was a good or bad sign. He only knew the sight of such a personal article of Meredith's viciously destroyed nearly beyond recogni-

tion disturbed him greatly, enough so that he welcomed an opportunity to discuss the incident with his father. The marquess's lips twitched. Fear made strange allies.

"I am glad to see you," Trevor said. "Please, sit down."

"You are glad to see me?" The older man hesitated. "I never thought I'd hear you say those words unless there was a gun pointed at your chest." The duke pulled up a chair and sat facing him across the table. "What is wrong?"

" 'Tis Meredith. I took her to a horse race this afternoon, and she had a most unsettling experience."

"Did you run into one of your mistresses?" The duke snorted. "A wife can find that to be a rather lowering occurrence."

Why must he always think the worst of me? Though he wanted nothing more than to hotly refute the statement, Trevor held his tongue. He had been a less than perfect husband thus far. The duke's scorn was not entirely misplaced.

"Not that it is any of your business, sir, but I have given up my mistresses."

"Frequenting the brothels, then? Whores can be less tedious in the long run, yet even the best houses have women who carry diseases. I hope you are careful."

"I have not set foot inside a brothel in years." Trevor sighed. It appeared this conversation was going to be far more difficult than he feared. " 'Tis only because of my concern for my wife that I will allow you to insult me, sir. Yet I warn you even I have limits."

"All right, all right. We shall save the discussion of your flaws for another time." The duke tapped his fingers impatiently on the table. "What happened to Meredith?"

Thankfully the older man listened attentively while Trevor described the incident.

"Horse racing attracts all sorts of characters," the duke said. "This could be the jealous reaction of a rival owner whose horse lost to yours, or a disgruntled gambler who placed a wager on one of the animals that Rascal beat. Or it could just be some youthful mischief."

Trevor shook his head. He had already considered and discarded many of the same possibilities. "There was something very deliberate about this act, something almost personal. It was as if this individual wanted to taunt Meredith, to specifically frighten her."

"Did he succeed?"

"Though she insists otherwise, I believe she was frightened. Very frightened."

The duke clucked his disapproval. "She is a stubborn woman, with a will of iron. It would take a great deal to rattle Lady Meredith."

Trevor could find no words to protest. "Though I have tried very hard to be logical about all of this, I cannot shake aside the feeling she is in danger."

"Danger?" The duke did not appear to put much stock in that theory. "Are you certain? I think it might be something else entirely. When you speak of her, you have the look of a possessive man—or a smitten boy. I cannot decide which."

" 'Tis neither," Trevor insisted adamantly. Perhaps too adamantly. Tempering his tone, he continued, "I am concerned my wife may very well be facing some sort of threat to her person."

The duke's gaze told Trevor his father was not convinced. "What are you going to do about it?"

Trevor leaned forward eagerly. He had given this much thought. "I believe it would be wise to hire

some men to keep an eye on her, to make sure she comes to no harm."

"I suppose that could be arranged." The duke rubbed his chin. "It might also be a good idea to tell Harper, so he can alert the other male servants. Best to have all eyes alert to the possibility of any mishaps."

The marquess let out a breath of relief. Life went so much smoother when his father was in agreement with him. "That is a good suggestion. I also think we should not tell Meredith about this just yet. There is no need to frighten her more, especially if it all comes to nothing."

The duke grimaced. "You realize, of course, there are some places where these bodyguards cannot go without attracting considerable attention. We plan to attend the theater tomorrow evening. Since you are so worried, it might be wise for you to join us."

Trevor considered the request carefully. "I shall arrive at the family box before the curtain rises."

"I am sure it will be a delightful surprise for Meredith."

Trevor nodded. Yes, of a certainty it would be a surprise, yet he was unwilling to speculate if his wife would think it was delightful.

Fifteen

The three tiers of private boxes where the wealthy and nobility sat during a theater performance were crowded and noisy. The Marquess of Dardington, occupying one of them, stirred uneasily in his chair. Though velvet padded, he found it firm and uncomfortable against his back.

Trevor glanced down into the pit, where the orange girls were selling fruit and running about trying to avoid being grabbed or pinched by the worst of the boisterous, rowdy dandies, and grimaced. His unease at the moment was not caused solely by his chair. This colorful assortment of onlookers, people ranging from the lowest to highest social order had taken on an almost sinister character—for any one of them could be intending to cause his wife physical or mental pain.

His gut knotted at the very idea. That someone should harm her, hurt her, frighten her, brought forth an almost overwhelming impulse to shield and care for her. How ironic that he had now willingly cast himself in the role of Meredith's protector, a role he took most seriously.

A movement off to the side caught his attention and Trevor saw her then, walking through the curtain of the box clutching the Duke of Warwick's arm. The sight of these two, appearing so natural and uncon-

cerned, eased a lingering worry Trevor had not realized existed.

Meredith looked exceedingly beautiful dressed in a gown of shimmering gold silk that matched the color of her hair. It was cut daringly low over the bosom, exposing a good deal of cleavage. Resting gracefully around her neck was a sparkling necklace of diamonds that looked oddly familiar.

Trevor stood politely as they entered the box. She noticed him before the duke did, and her whole body seemed to tense.

"Trevor, my goodness, this is a surprise. Your father did not mention you would be joining us this evening."

Her hand reached up to her throat and she clutched at the necklace nervously. The action brought his attention again to the gems she wore, and he suddenly remembered it had belonged to his mother . . . and then later to his wife. His first wife.

The marquess braced himself for the reaction to set in that would surely result from seeing Meredith wearing something that had once graced Lavinia's slender neck. Yet it did not come. Perhaps the unresolved issues between them no longer seemed so pressing or difficult now that Meredith's safety was his prime concern.

There was no time to answer his wife's greeting, for another party entered, two ladies and a gentleman. Trevor assumed they had stopped on their way to their own seats, but soon realized they had been invited to share the duke's box.

He caught a glimpse of the man's face. Julian Wingate! What the devil was he doing here? Trevor scowled, then felt Wingate eyeing him up and down, all the while looking rather perturbed. He spared Trevor the briefest of nods before turning away.

Apparently Wingate felt the same flash of annoy-

ance at discovering Trevor's unexpected presence at the theater. The marquess almost smiled. At least they were well matched in their disregard of each other.

"I do not believe you have met the ladies, my lord," Meredith said. "They have recently arrived in town to partake of the entertainment of the Season, so I suggested they join us. May I present Miss Harriet Sainthill and her sister Miss Elizabeth. Miss Harriet is engaged to Mr. Wingate."

"Ladies," he said, bowing elegantly, though his actions were automatic and routine. His mind was trying to decipher this ever growing puzzle.

Wingate's fiancée? When had she and Meredith become such close friends? Or was it Wingate who shared that honor with his wife? Trevor seethed at the very idea.

The younger girl, a dainty blond who looked fresh and unspoiled, graciously curtsied to him. She addressed him demurely, sounding sweet and soft-spoken as she exclaimed her delight at attending the performance.

"It was very kind of Lady Meredith to include us this evening," Harriet, the older sister, was saying, "though I would expect nothing less from such a dear friend of my sister-in-law. She speaks often and glowingly of your wife. 'Tis my understanding they have been friends for many years."

Trevor's head turned in surprise. So that was the connection. He wondered briefly who this dear friend was and if Meredith had ever mentioned her to him.

"Have I rendered you speechless, Lord Dardington?"

Trevor glanced down. The others had drifted to the opposite side of the box, but Harriet had stayed by his side. He smiled. The dazzling beauty of the younger sister had made Harriet nearly invisible when

they first entered the box. If not for the fact she was Wingate's fiancée, he most likely would not have given her a second glance.

Yet as he took a moment to observe her now, Trevor noticed the keen glint of shrewd intelligence in her eyes, which were a lovely shade of hazel. They were ringed by long, dark-colored lashes. Her skin was smooth, her cheekbones high, her nose pert with an upturn at the end. She had none of the breathtaking beauty of her sister, but she was attractive in a more unusual way.

And that astute gaze indicated a forthright honesty and strong mind. Trevor immediately decided she was too good for a man the likes of Julian Wingate.

"Forgive my inattentiveness. I fear I was woolgathering." He leaned close, then raised her gloved hand to his lips. To her credit, she neither simpered nor fluttered at the gesture. " 'Tis a delight to meet you, Miss Sainthill. Wingate is indeed a fortunate man to have such a dazzling beauty for his future wife."

She pulled her hand away. Though she refrained, he had a strong feeling she wanted to roll her eyes at him. In disgust. Apparently it took far more than idle flattery and pretty words to impress Miss Harriet.

Everyone settled into their seats. Trevor kept himself deliberately apart from the others, determined to keep his eyes focused on the stage, or on the pit below filled with people. The main purpose of his presence here this evening was to see to Meredith's safety. He felt it only prudent to be on guard against trouble before it occurred, so he could be prepared.

However, throughout the first act, Trevor's vigilance yielded no tangible results except for a painful crick in his neck. He was therefore very glad when the chandeliers were lowered and the candles lit for intermission.

Everyone stood and stretched, preparing to head downstairs for some refreshment and fresh air. Only the marquess remained seated.

"Will you join us, my lord?" Harriet asked.

"Thank you, no. I believe I'll stay here."

Trevor turned his attention back to the now empty stage. Once he heard them all shuffle out, he rotated his aching shoulders and slowly rolled his head, trying to ease some of the stiffness.

"Does it hurt a great deal, my lord?"

Startled, Trevor turned and saw a slender, feminine hand resting on his shoulder.

"I have told you before not to address me as my lord, Meredith."

"Whatever you desire, Trevor."

She had leaned down and whispered her reply into his ear. Her breasts pressed against his back, the soft swells causing an immediate ache and discomfort in another part of his body.

Before he could reprimand her, she began a gentle massage of his shoulders. He tensed against her touch, but she only pressed down harder, digging into the knotted muscles.

Some time during the performance Meredith had removed her gloves. Her bare fingers worked diligently and with surprising skill. Trevor's eyelids lowered as the ache began to lessen.

"Is that helping?"

"Yes." A sigh of pleasure escaped his lips. "Though I do believe the best results of a massage are achieved against bare flesh."

Her hands stilled for an instant, then resumed their magical work. "I would encourage you to remove your coat and shirt, but I fear you would quickly comply. And that sort of activity is best left for the privacy of our chambers."

The marquess's eyes snapped open. He had not meant to make such a suggestive comment about bare flesh. Or had he? It seemed more often than not his famous control was sadly lacking when it came to his extraordinary wife.

Desire, sharp and liquid, spread through him. Desire he could not allow.

He turned and she smiled. "You seem to be in less discomfort," Meredith said. She moved to the chair directly behind his. "I am so glad I could make you feel better."

Her expression was all innocence, but Trevor was not convinced. He had a sneaking suspicion his beautiful wife was relishing the effect she was having on him. Despite his annoyance, he could not help but admire her. She was such a unique person, so unconventional compared to the other women he had known, even Lavinia.

"First a kiss at the racecourse and now a massage at the theater. I am beginning to believe you enjoy making a public spectacle of yourself, madame."

"Does that displease you?"

"Not really." He meant it. The conventional, polite rules of this stodgy society had not held any power over him for nearly a decade. Though he teased her, Trevor acknowledged Meredith had shown far more common sense and discretion with regard to those rules throughout all of her life. "I fancy a bit of fresh air. I believe I will stroll down to the lobby for a few minutes."

Meredith's eyes widened minimally. She said nothing, asked nothing, yet he felt her intense regard. Though he preferred to be alone, Trevor recognized when he was defeated. "Would you care to join me?"

"How lovely."

She rose gracefully. He stepped back to allow her

to precede him, and when she passed, he brushed his
arm deliberately across her breasts. He could almost
feel the faint shudder that traveled through her body,
yet she presented no outward sign of discomfort. Most
likely he was the only person in the theater who knew
she was unnerved. The marquess smiled, pleased at
that exclusive advantage.

Trevor kept a proprietary hand on her waist as they
negotiated the crowded staircase down to the main
level. There were fewer people here, as most were already returning to their seats.

The marquess was about to signal a footman to get
them some champagne when a rumbling noise caught
his attention. Meredith must have heard it also, for
she grasped his arm tightly.

"Is something wrong?" she asked, her brow furrowed.

Trevor grimaced with concern. He heard shouts and
jeers from inside the theater, then the unmistakable
crash of objects being hurled. "It sounds like the
drunks in the pit are losing control. One makes a comment, another disagrees and soon they are brawling
in the aisles. I have seen it happen on several other
occasions, and 'tis not a pretty sight. We had best get
out of here before it becomes a full-scale riot."

Apparently many of the crowd were of a similar
mind. Patrons began leaving in droves, scuttling out
of theater, down the stairs, and rushing for the exits.
There was an unmistakable undercurrent of fear in
their movements.

"We cannot leave without the others," Meredith
cried.

Trevor lifted his head, his eyes darting about,
searching the surging crowd. "I can see the duke and
Miss Harriet on the opposite side. I assume Wingate

and Miss Elizabeth are near them. There is an exit directly to their left."

"What about us?"

"Come. There is a little known exit on the other side."

The marquess had taken only a few steps before realizing Meredith was not beside him. He turned in alarm. She stood but a few feet behind him, white-lipped and stock-still. Then the surging crowd engulfed her, forcing her backward, farther and farther away from him.

"Trevor!"

Her cry of fear was swallowed up by the press of squirming, elbowing bodies. The marquess reacted instantly, but it was like swimming upstream. Within seconds they were separated by a wall of people. Digging in his legs, Trevor somehow managed to propel himself forward, into the crowd. Inch by inch, he made slight progress toward her, his eyes pinned frantically to the gold silk fabric that distinguished her from the rest of the throng.

Then suddenly someone shoved Meredith. Hard. In horror, Trevor watched her stumble, then struggle to right herself. He shouted loudly when she disappeared completely from view. With Herculean effort he managed to push closer. Reaching down, he searched for that distinctive flash of gold silk.

It felt like an eternity till he at last caught a glimpse of what he sought. Head whirling, he wrapped an arm around Meredith and half pulled, half dragged her to her feet. She clung to him tightly.

The relief was so great that he paused for an instant. Beside him a man toppled to the ground. A woman shrieked and fell on top of him. Others surged forward, ready to trample the fallen victims. Terrified screams

from the far side of the lobby suggested some might have already been crushed in the maddening crowd.

Survival instincts prevailed. "We are going this way," Trevor shouted.

He wanted to slide one arm around her waist and haul her to his side, but he knew they would never fight their way through the crowd two abreast.

Meredith obviously understood that he needed to lead, for she clutched his arm tightly. "Go. I shall follow you."

He could feel her fingers digging into his muscles. Convinced she had a strong enough grip, he led her to the edge of the lobby, back toward the theater. The shouts and cursing grew louder as they drew nearer to the escalating brawl, but surprisingly this area held few fleeing patrons.

The marquess never broke stride. Turning left, he headed directly for a door hidden behind a row of velvet curtains. Thankfully it was unlocked. Trevor gratefully pushed it open and they spilled into an alley, filling their lungs with great gulps of fresh air.

Trevor exhaled, closed his eyes, and flopped back against the rough brick wall. His arms were aching from the strain of pushing through the crowd; his head was pounding with shock and the residual rush of adrenaline.

"Are you all right?"

Meredith's trembling voice roused the marquess from his stupor. He paused another moment to catch his breath, then turned. She was slumped, exhausted, against the wall. Her face was ashen, her hair mussed, and a piece of silk had been torn from the bodice of her gown.

"I ache all over, but I am in one piece, with my limbs in working order," he answered. "And you?"

"I'm not sure."

He found her hand, and squeezed it in comfort. She returned the pressure, and he was grateful to feel her fingers were firm and strong.

"Lord, that was awful," he muttered. "I would not be surprised to learn that people were killed tonight."

Meredith made a small sound in her throat and he thought she might burst into tears. "I kept seeing you through the crowd, so close, and yet it felt like you were miles away, for I could not reach you. Then someone shoved me hard, knocking the breath from my lungs. My ears rang and my vision went blurry as I toppled to the ground. I feared I would never regain my feet, that I would be crushed and trampled.

"Then suddenly, seemingly out of thin air, you appeared." In the shadowy light of the street lamp, Trevor saw her bite down on trembling lips. "You saved my life."

Her tone was fervent. Yet it was the look of wonder and amazement on her face that brought forth a surge of emotions in him. Never before in his life had he felt so accomplished, so important, so bloody useful.

It should have frightened him, these feelings that came over him with such unbearable force, yet instead it warmed and soothed him, leaving him feeling strong and important.

Trevor noticed then that Meredith had begun to shake violently. She swayed toward him, and the marquess caught her up in his embrace, holding her tightly, almost savagely against his chest.

Mine, his brain screamed with possessive determination. *Mine to keep safe and protect.*

He lifted her ankles and scooped her up in his arms. "Hold on to my neck. My carriage is at the front of the theater, and there is sure to be a large crowd."

Meredith nodded and settled back, her expression

softer and more vulnerable than he had ever known it.

The marquess was right. There was a large gathering in front of the theater, but the nature of the crowd had once again shifted. Now safe from imminent danger, people were milling around discussing the event. Some were pale and dazed, while others were shouting, trying to locate the members of their party. A few were offering assistance to the injured.

Amazingly, Trevor was able to locate his father. The duke had managed to escape before the worst of the crush had occurred. He had escorted Miss Harriet and Miss Elizabeth safely to Wingate's coach and had come in search of the marquess and Meredith.

"Is she badly injured?" the duke asked in a concerned voice.

"Just shaken. But we need to get her home as quickly as possible."

The duke nodded. "My carriage awaits. I'll have one of the grooms find your coachman and tell him you are returning to the house with me."

A few minutes later, they were climbing into the duke's black barouche. Sitting beside her, Trevor could still feel his wife trembling, could feel the tension in her body. Without saying a word, he shifted in his seat and cradled her in his arms.

The carriage shade was open. He moved to a spot where the moonlight streaked inside. Meredith's impassive countenance was bathed in silver, and for an instant he thought he might have mistaken her fear.

Then, with a small cry of distress, she turned her face into his chest and tightened her arms around his neck. A lump formed in his throat. Her complete trust was humbling, as if she believed there was no one in the world more capable of protecting her than he.

The duke signaled his driver, and the coach lurched

forward. Trevor gathered Meredith closer, and as they traveled the darkened streets he tried his hardest to make her feel safe and secure.

An hour later Meredith was seated in an overstuffed chair in her bedchamber with a glass of brandy in her hand. Though she was trying valiantly to stay calm, she could feel the edges of panic gripping at her composure.

"I am starting to feel better." Meredith smiled wanly at her husband as he paced back and forth. "Truly."

"Drink." He tipped the edge of her glass and forced her to take a large swallow. "Better, my arse. Your face is pale as a ghost and you're still trembling all over."

Meredith wet her lips. She wanted nothing more than to shout a denial, but her teeth were chattering too hard. It all seemed so ridiculous, but now that it was over, she felt even more frightened, more at a loss to control her body and emotions.

"I fear I might have lost one of the diamonds from my necklace." With a shaking hand, she held it up for Trevor to inspect.

"Will you forget about the damned necklace?" He snatched it out of her hands and flung it onto a nearby table. "It does not matter."

Meredith blinked. She would not cry. She would not show weakness. She would remain calm and coherent, for she had something important to tell her husband about this horrible incident tonight. Given his current state of agitation, she suspected he would not be pleased.

"Those are not my personal property, they are family jewels," Meredith said softly. She met Trevor's eyes. "If I have damaged the piece, I want to fix it. 'Tis my responsibility."

The marquess knelt in front of her. He stretched out a hand and lifted a fallen lock of hair back from her face. She could see he was struggling to stay calm. "Since it appears to be so damned important to you, I will make certain the jeweler examines the necklace. If it needs to be repaired, I will instruct him to do so immediately."

"Will you send me the bill?"

"Meredith." He tightened the hold he had on her wrist.

She burst into a nervous giggle. The strain on his temper was showing. Best not to push it past the breaking point. "Thank you, Trevor."

"I need you to tell me everything you remember about what happened at the theater," the marquess said.

Meredith settled back in her chair and took a small sip of her drink. "I'll try, but it all happened so fast. There was the crush of the crowd, that surge that seemed to carry me off my feet. I felt someone bump into me, jostle me from behind. I was so worried about staying on my feet, so frightened that if I fell I would be trampled that I hardly noticed who had shoved me. But it happened again. And then a third time.

"That final impact drove me to my knees. I remember trying to catch myself, but there was nothing steady to grab. It was all a mass of tangled limbs. That's when I felt the hands."

"Hands? You mean my hands, hauling you upright?"

"No." She lowered, then raised her chin. "The hands around my neck."

The marquess leaned closer and for the first time noticed the marks. There were bruises around her throat, deep red marks that were beginning to darken. His face paled as his fists curled in anger.

"Were they the hands of a man?"

"I believe so. I opened my lips to scream, but discovered I did not have the breath to make a sound." Meredith shuddered. "Though I know you do not wish to hear it, I am sure he was trying to take my necklace," she said defensively. "And he nearly succeeded."

The marquess sat back on his haunches. "Was there anything else? Anything that happened before this incident?"

She squirmed in her seat. Finally she whispered, "The stares and scrutiny."

"What?"

How could she possibly explain something she did not fully understand, something she secretly feared was a part of her imagination? Yet a voice deep inside her head urged her to try.

" 'Tis hardly a unique experience for me to be the subject of so much fascination for the *ton*. Over the past few weeks, I have almost gotten used to the stares and whispering. Yet tonight it was greatly heightened. I am convinced we garnered so much attention this evening because we appeared together at the theater." She smiled faintly. "We so rarely attend any of the same society functions, it seemed only natural there would be considerable curiosity and talk."

"I felt it, too," Trevor admitted. "Is it always so intense?"

Meredith shrugged. "Since our marriage there have been times I felt myself being scrutinized by what seemed like thousands of interested spectators. But it is not the multitudes that rattle me. Lately I have had this perception, this feeling, that one single person, one individual is taking an inordinate interest in my movements."

"Do you have any idea who it may be?"

"No." She let out a small laugh. "Which is why I

am convinced I might be imagining it all. And yet . . ."

Meredith looked up. Trevor's gaze was fixed forward, regarding her scrupulously. He appeared to be on the verge of saying something, then shook his head as though changing his mind. "You are a levelheaded woman, not given to imaginings. However, you have had a terrible fright this evening. We shall discuss this again in the morning, after you have rested."

Meredith nodded. Perhaps it would be best to continue the discussion in the morning. Though she did in truth feel exhausted from mental, physical, and emotional fatigue, she wondered how she would possibly sleep. The fear and panic that had overtaken her at the theater lingered still, a dark shadow of fear in the corner of her mind.

"Where is Rose?" Meredith searched the bedchamber for her maid. "She generally waits up for me in my sitting room."

"I dismissed her. I thought she might become frightened at seeing you so upset. Shall I ring for her?"

"Don't bother. If you would just unhook the center buttons at the back of my gown, I can manage the rest."

She stood and presented her back to her husband. The feel of his warm fingers drove away some of the chill. Yet all too quickly he had accomplished his task. She turned, clutching the gaping gown securely to her chest.

It suddenly became difficult to swallow. Meredith wanted nothing more than to beg him to stay with her, yet she could not ask. "Are you going out tonight?"

For a moment Trevor held himself rigid, as if struggling for control. The atmosphere was suddenly charged with a new tension, a different sensation—the alluring pull of sexual longing.

"I think it best if I remain here."

"In my bedchamber?"

The blue of his eyes became deeper, stormier. But he said nothing. Meredith lifted her chin and studied a slight crack in the plaster work on the ceiling. Her anguish must have shown in her face.

"I shall stay until you fall asleep."

The independent, prideful streak inside Meredith fairly screamed at her to object, to deny she needed anything from him. Yet her need for comfort was stronger than her pride.

Silently Meredith went behind the dressing screen to change. She deliberately chose a revealing nightgown of sheer silk, and instead of braiding her hair as usual she left it tumbling wantonly down her back. Pressing her lips together in a tight line, she took a deep breath, then walked boldly back into the bedchamber.

Trevor was sitting in a wing chair beside her bed. His handsome features were composed into an unreadable mask, yet as she brushed near she felt as if he were impaling her with his startling blue eyes.

Meredith's heart skipped several beats as she climbed into the large, lonely bed. Her husband, the man she loved with all of her heart, moved not an inch. In the still silence of the night, he seemed more distant, more unattainable than ever.

Still, he had proven his regard for her most tangibly this evening by risking his life to save hers. His strong, protective presence brought not only a sexual longing, but a deep measure of safety and comfort.

Meredith drew an unsteady breath, determined to overcome the tangled knot of emotions twisting inside her. She pulled the covers to her chin and settled herself on her side, her back to the marquess. She lay there stiffly, willing herself to relax. Though she would never have believed it possible given all that had occurred this night, eventually she drifted off to sleep.

Sixteen

Cold, strong fingers grabbed Meredith's hair, twisting the thick golden tresses and yanking it tight. Her neck was stretched and open, an inviting, vulnerable target. First she felt the menacing grip of his fingers. Then his hands encircled her throat. Closing, tightening, they pressed against her, choking her until she could get no air, could draw no breath.

She fought wildly, thrashing her legs, kicking her feet. Her arms were leaden. She could not lift them. Panicking, she tried to flee, to move away from the attacker, but she could not evade the strong hands so intent on doing her harm. Fear slammed into her chest. She could not escape!

Suffocating her scream of terror, Meredith somehow yanked herself away from the nightmare. She woke up abruptly, her skin cold and clammy, her breathing harsh and shallow.

She sat straight up in bed, glancing hopefully at the wing chair beside her bed. It was empty. No doubt Trevor had kept his word and waited till she fell asleep before leaving, but that thought brought her little comfort, for her bedchamber was now filled with an uneasy, lonely silence.

'Tis just a dream, it cannot hurt you. Meredith repeated the words in her mind as she shifted her back

against the headboard and slowly lowered herself to her elbows.

With determination, she closed her eyes and tried to regulate her breathing, to calm her inner demons. But the images would not abate. Knowing she was clinging to her sanity by the barest of threads, Meredith threw off the covers in frustration.

She slid out of bed and felt her way to the far side of the room. Her fingers found the window latch, and she quietly opened it. The sudden blast of air surprised her, yet it relieved her as well, for the shock made her feel very much alive. She stood there for several long minutes, breathing deeply, hoping the air would somehow cleanse her thoughts. It did not.

Perhaps it was the darkness, so sinister and complete, that was rattling her nerves. Meredith made her way to the low table and fumbled to light a candle. The soft glow momentarily calmed her nerves. She glanced back at her bed. The rumpled sheets and angled pillows were rather unappealing.

Meredith turned in the opposite direction and glanced at the door that connected her bedchamber to Trevor's. There was no light shining beneath the door, no indication he was awake. She tilted her head and listened intently. All was quiet—no snoring, no rustling sheets.

For an instant she panicked, thinking he might not even be in his bedchamber. But no, he had promised her he would stay home tonight, and she believed he would keep his word. He must be asleep.

Meredith chewed nervously at her lower lip. Perhaps if she was very quiet and very careful, she could slip into his bed without waking him.

"That is where I really want to be," she whispered, making up her mind. "Where I need to be."

She did not bother to put on a robe. Padding bare-

foot across the thick carpet, she moved with stealthy efficiency and determination. Once at the door, she turned the latch slowly, so as not to make a sound. Swinging the door open, Meredith took a small step, halting in the doorway.

She extinguished her candle and set it on top of a large dresser. Thankfully, Trevor slept with the curtains of his bed and the draperies of the windows open. There was just enough moonlight streaking through the windows to illuminate the objects in the chamber. If she was very careful, she should be able to negotiate the room without tripping over the furniture and raising a racket.

Meredith waited for a moment to allow her eyes to adjust to the limited light. The shadows were thick, but she could make out the chests and armoires that lined the wall, the chairs and tables positioned around the room.

Trevor lay in the huge canopied four-poster bed, sprawled on his stomach. One arm was flung over his head; the other rested by his side. The sheets were bunched at his waist, revealing the well-defined muscles of his bare shoulders and back.

Meredith assumed he was asleep, though she stood too far away to hear the even rise and fall of his breathing. She needed to be closer. Crossing her arms and hugging herself, Meredith made her way silently to the bed. She hesitated, wavering a bit as she drew near.

Driven by fear, she had felt determined walking in here. Now she suddenly felt unsure at invading the marquess's intimate quarters. What would she do if he refused to allow her to stay? That horrifying question kept her still and quiet for several long moments.

Uneasily, Meredith glanced about the room again. Her eyes had adjusted to the moonlight, and she could

now ascertain more specifically the contents. There were several comfortable upholstered chairs, even a long chaise. She could most likely be content sleeping in one of those for the night if absolutely necessary. It was certainly far more appealing than staying in her lonely, empty chamber.

The sudden chime of the clock on the mantelpiece made her jump. Startled, Meredith's fears surfaced, this time accompanied by anger. She despised these feelings of not being safe, hated the taste of fear. Yet she could not deny they existed so strongly inside her. Would they ever leave?

She advanced five steps closer to the bed, overcome with a strong and painful desire to curl up in Trevor's arms and hold herself close to his chest until all her uncertainties faded.

Holding her breath to ensure she made no noise, Meredith studied him in the moonlight. She briefly considered slipping in beside him, but she loathed to disturb his slumber, uncertain of his reaction if he awoke and found her in his bed.

Trevor's features were oddly commanding, even in sleep. Meredith slowly let out her breath, then drew in another and held it as the seconds ticked away. As much as she might want to, she could not simply stand here until the dawn broke.

There was movement on the bed. Trevor's head lifted off the pillow. "Has something happened?" he asked groggily.

Meredith cleared her throat. "I awoke and found it impossible to return to sleep. I fear the events of this evening have left me excessively emotional."

He studied her, though she doubted he could see much more than the outline of her torso in the moonlight. "You are a woman. It is to be expected."

Normally his words and tone would bring a rise of

indignation from her lips, but she had no right to anger, for he spoke the truth. "I hope I did not wake you," she said.

He raised himself on one elbow, running his hand down his face. "I had only just dozed off myself," he admitted.

"Then I apologize for disturbing you. But I did not know what else to do."

"Do you want me to sit by your bed again?"

"No, for if I awake after you leave the problem will return." Meredith hesitated, giving him a doubtful frown. "I was hoping a different solution could be found."

Taut seconds passed while Meredith gazed into his eyes. Trevor returned her regard, searching her face intently before he looked away. "I suppose you could stay in my chamber."

Meredith blinked. It was hardly the most enthusiastic invitation. "Are you certain?" Her heart stilled, waiting for his answer.

"No. But stay anyway."

She looked around. "Where?"

He let out a loud sigh. "The bed is comfortable. And very large."

"Are you inviting me to sleep in your bed?"

Trevor muttered something about summoning every last ounce of his willpower before throwing back the covers.

The simple gesture seemed to suddenly change the atmosphere in the room from uncertainty to anticipation. Though she had entered the room because of her fear, Meredith realized far more could result from her staying the night in her husband's bed.

Her gaze dropped from his handsome face to his bare chest. She smiled seductively, as though at last acknowledging he was naked. Meredith slowly, sen-

suously slid over the bed, allowing her nightgown to ride up her thigh all the way to her hip.

The marquess's eyebrows slowly rose as awareness flared in his eyes. Meredith could barely breathe. He leaned close and took her hands in his. He felt warm and strong, she thought, momentarily distracted by his touch.

"I prefer the left side of the bed," he said solemnly. "I hope you don't object."

Meredith lifted her chin. "Not at all. Though I will warn you I am a restless sleeper who tends to spread herself all over the mattress. I will probably kick you mercilessly."

He shrugged and gestured broadly. She lifted herself up and climbed in beside him. The motion caused a cascade of golden hair to fall over her shoulder.

"Your hair is exquisite."

Meredith paused in the act of tucking the stray locks behind her ears. "Thank you. I have long thought of cutting it short, in the French style, but worry I might look like a boy."

"Not with those curves."

Meredith ducked her head in embarrassment, yet she was secretly thrilled he had noticed her womanly curves. She settled herself stiffly on her back, careful to keep to her side of the mattress. Stifling a giggle of nerves, she waited with eager anticipation for her handsome husband to turn to her with desire.

The minutes dragged, and nothing happened. Finally, Meredith turned to him in disappointment and frustration. "Are we truly going to sleep?" she whispered.

She felt his entire body tense at her question. He said nothing, but his thrashing legs and restless movements seemed to suggest he was fighting some inner battle. At last he groaned and turned toward her. He

moved closer, nipped her ear, and whispered, "We shall sleep later, dearest. Much later."

He reached out and angled her chin with one hand while the other moved to the back of her head, urging her forward. Then his mouth descended on hers, invading with a possessive claim she found thrilling. His kiss was slow and sensual, his lips brushing back and forth over hers, coaxing them to open for him.

Her hands slid up his hard chest, curving over his shoulders and around his neck. He lifted his mouth a fraction from hers and in a voice thick with desire asked, "Are you still frightened?"

For her answer Meredith kissed him back with all the love and desperation in her heart. Her tongue traced the shape of his mouth, then gently sucked on his lower lip. His response was overwhelming. His mouth became insistent and hungry: his hands wandered possessively over her back and the sides of her breasts.

Meredith shuddered as her body began to respond, began to come alive. For him. She spread her hand over the solid wall of his chest, sliding her fingers through the short, golden matting of hair. His skin felt hot, his nipples hard and tight as she lightly grazed them with her palm.

But it was his kisses that tantalized her so completely. The way he tasted drove her wild. Meredith stretched her neck willingly, offering herself to him. Trevor eagerly complied, pressing sweet wet kisses to her jaw and throat and behind her ear.

Meredith's hand raised and smoothed through his hair. She could feel his warm breath on her neck and upper chest, could feel the heat pouring from his hard body. A shiver coursed through her. She leaned into his strength, savoring his warmth and the excitement it brought to her entire essence.

He shifted, pulling her closer to him. One of his hands slipped down her neck and shoulder, sliding along her side and over her breast. Meredith arched herself encouragingly toward him, eager to leap beyond the languid pace Trevor had set for their lovemaking.

His palms were hot against her cloth-covered skin as they stroked her breasts. She craved his touch with a fierce longing, an almost desperate need. Meredith thrust her chest forward, and her silent pleas did not go unnoticed. Trevor brushed his thumbs over her nipples, teasing those sensitive points until they hardened into tight buds.

Meredith's eyes closed, and a sound emerged from her throat. She fidgeted against the mattress, anticipation building deep within her body. At last Trevor's hands traveled beneath her nightgown and she lifted herself up, encouraging his explorations.

He grasped a bare nipple between his thumb and index finger and applied exactly the degree of pressure she craved. Meredith tipped her head back and inhaled deeply, allowing herself to experience the sexual need.

She tightened her grip around his shoulders and tilted her head for a kiss. Meredith's tongue tangled with Trevor's in a torrid dance, thrusting back and forth in a mating ritual as old as time.

Suddenly Trevor broke the kiss, bent his head, and took one of her nipples in his mouth. Meredith nearly screamed. She shivered with pleasure and shook violently as the tension coiled down through her body, settling between her thighs. She felt the dampness, the surge of fluid that would make her body ready to receive him.

He moved his mouth to her other breast, and she clutched his head, curling her fingers through his hair as he laved that sensitive peak to hardness. It was a

peculiar, almost frightening sensation, for it fed a hunger for something even greater.

Trevor's hand slid down her lower body. He pulled her nightgown up to her waist, baring her, then tenderly stroked her hips, flanks, and upper thighs. Next his questing fingers feathered lightly across her stomach, making the muscles jump in eager anticipation. Meredith gasped loudly when he cupped her moist womanhood with his palm, tangling his fingers in the springy curls between her thighs.

He stroked her softly, intimately, until she became damp and swollen, circling that one special spot that made her entire body shudder.

"Lord, you are so beautiful," he murmured. "And so ready. But first, first I must have a taste."

He bent his head and kissed his way down her stomach, dipping his tongue in her navel, flicking the tip teasingly along the sensitive flesh of her lower abdomen. Her stomach muscles clenched with each wet kiss, yet Meredith was blissfully unaware of the final destination.

His lips nuzzled the hair that guarded her womanly secrets. His breath made her squirm shamelessly. Then he gripped her hips in the palms of his hands and set his mouth to her softness, in the most intimate of kisses.

This time Meredith did scream. Her body jolted in shock, arching and twisting, trying to escape that invading tongue, but Trevor held her down, his hand splayed across her stomach.

His tongue was darting inside her, lapping at the soft folds, laving her gently with quickening strokes until she thought she might go mad from the pleasure. Heat flooded Meredith's every pore as the sharp sensations dipped and climbed.

She struggled to breathe, struggled to ease her acute

embarrassment. It was almost too intimate, too personal an act. Yet while her mind might be shocked and resistant to this, her body was enthusiastic at the notion of experiencing this newly discovered sensual delight.

Within the deep recesses of her heart, she longed for any and all intimacies with this man she loved so dearly, so completely. That love had brought her here, to the point where she trusted him enough to allow him to take any liberty with her body.

There was no time for further contemplation, for the delicious sensations chased every logical thought from her mind. Meredith closed her eyes and let her head fall back against the pillows, let herself feel the shivering thrill of each stroke of that magical tongue.

Trevor's shoulders wedged her thighs even farther apart, and he glided his hands beneath her buttocks to hold her in place. The tension coursed through Meredith as the needs of her body became so strong they nearly overpowered her. The frantic, maddening drive to completion gripped her firmly, and then suddenly Meredith felt it begin to break. She cried out on a sob of ecstasy as she blindly surged against his mouth, her body blazing with heat, her senses exploding.

Meredith was still drifting on a cloud of untold pleasure, her body feeling boneless and sated, when he reached out and began stroking her nipple. The tension started anew, as if she had never achieved release.

"How do you do that?" she asked in amazement.

His answering grin nearly broke her heart. It was boyish and proud and outlandishly sexy. " 'Tis easy with you, dearest. You were made for this, made for me. Only me."

Meredith let out a shuddering breath as his hands

skimmed again over her breasts. "I need to be inside you now," he said hoarsely. "But first this must go."

In a flash he removed her nightgown, pulling it up and over her head in one fluid motion. She gazed at his beloved features. The muscles were tense across his face and shoulders. She found his male beauty irresistible. She reached up and laid her hand on his chest, pulling playfully at the thick mat of hair.

Following the trail of that sexy hair brought her fingers down his abdomen to the throbbing strength of his penis. She stroked the enlarged organ eagerly, then cupped the tender sacs that hung below. Trevor groaned his approval and began flexing his hips in a primitive, sensual rhythm.

With an almost tortured expression, he glared down at her, then roughly pulled her hands off his burning flesh. He parted her legs with his knee, spreading them wide. Meredith's body was trembling when he cupped her bottom and pulled her against him.

Trevor shifted forward and entered her, stretching and filling her so tightly, so completely she cried out from the sheer joy of his possession.

"Lord, I can feel you tightening around me," he said tersely.

" 'Tis wondrous," she agreed.

Meredith cupped his cheek. His jaw felt rough and prickly as her fingers glided over the stubble of his whiskers.

"Wrap your legs around me," Trevor whispered.

She followed his command, tightening herself fiercely around him, clinging to him as if she would never let go. Her fingers, still on his face, now traced over his mouth, and he opened his lips.

Meredith teasingly inserted the tip of her index finger and he greedily sucked on it. She laughed, then lifted her head and kissed him. Trevor returned the

kiss with ardor and excitement. Then he broke away, tilted his head and smiled wickedly. Supporting himself on his forearms, he slowly pulled the length of his hardness out of her.

Meredith protested loudly and raised her hips. Trevor groaned and entered her again, thrusting forward with enough force to make her body arch. A thready sigh escaped her lips as her body welcomed him, the inner muscles clenching tightly as if they feared he would soon abandon her again.

With an expression of pure male need, he began to rotate his hips, creating a friction against the slick bud of her womanhood. The action sent her body quivering but, while mindlessly exciting, the pressure he was exerting was not enough to bring her to climax.

"You are tormenting me," she panted, lifting her hips to show him what she wanted.

"I am prolonging the pleasure," he answered in a voice gone deep and husky. "For both of us."

He teased her but a moment more, then began to thrust urgently into her, his thighs slapping against her, his lower body meeting hers with a searing impact. Meredith's arms came around him, her fingers caressing up and down his back till they came to rest at his hips.

She settled her hands there, digging her fingers into the hard flesh. That seemed to excite him even more, and her breath caught in her lungs as he pushed deeper, pulled back, then plunged again.

The drive to fulfillment soon became too much to withstand. With each hard penetration, the pressure built until she could think of nothing but release. She followed his lead, matching him thrust for thrust, over and over until the sheer joy of the experience was more than she could endure.

She begged him to increase the rhythm, gasping and

writhing on the mattress, half mad with desire as the fire within her began to spiral out of control. Then finally, blissfully, it broke, and Meredith's inner muscles convulsed around him. This ecstatic release was so unexpected, so intense, so emotional that tears pooled at the corners of Meredith's eyes and slid silently down the side of her face, wetting her temples.

Her eyelids flickered closed as her mind and body drifted, lost in a sea of rapture. Only when Trevor again moved his hips did Meredith realized he was still inside her, thick, hot, and pulsing. She surfaced abruptly from her cloud of sated sexuality and glanced up at his handsome face. Their eyes met and the taut line of his mouth gave way to a wicked, sensual grin.

Moved by the depths of emotions still swirling inside her, Meredith arched herself blindly against him. It was all the encouragement he needed. He shifted on top of her, pinning her hips to the mattress as he thrust deeply. Her legs tightened around his waist as he drove feverishly harder, and then the tension suddenly snapped and his body began to shudder.

His head fell forward against her neck. The warm harsh breath of his labored breathing tickled her ear and she smiled. It had been glorious.

Meredith lay limp beneath Trevor's solid weight, trying to absorb the completeness of the moment, trying to understand the array of emotions that invaded her. It was such a beautiful experience. She felt as if she glowed from the inside out. Perhaps they had created a child together this night. That might explain why she suddenly felt bound to Trevor deep within her soul as well as her body.

With a moan, he rolled onto his back, pulling her with him. She snuggled close, folded her arms across his chest; and rested her chin in them. They stared at each other for a long moment, both seemingly at a

loss to explain or interpret the meaning of this frantic, savage coupling.

He reached up and stroked her hair, brushing it away from her forehead. Meredith closed her eyes and tilted her head upon his chest. Listening to his steady heartbeat gave her an odd satisfaction and such a strong sense of being safe and protected that, miraculously, she was able to drift off to sleep.

Trevor cradled Meredith loosely in his arms and tried to recall if he had ever held a slumbering woman. He did not think he had. He listened to her slow, even breathing and decided he was enjoying the experience. She was warm and comforting to hold, all softness and feminine delight.

Meredith stirred unexpectedly and adjusted her position. Trevor's penis, resting inside her body, reacted urgently to this movement by rising with interest. He smiled. Normally an orgasm left him repleted and fulfilled, often sleepy. But not this time.

He felt oddly rejuvenated by their lovemaking. Consequently, he found he could not stop touching her, stroking her, even while she slept. The strange need to share more of this carnal pleasure with her remained and then grew stronger. With a start of surprise, Trevor admitted he wanted her again, writhing and squirming, crying out in ecstasy. For him.

He bent his head and lightly kissed her shoulder, then the nape of her neck and the column of her throat. With each kiss he bucked his hips forward. She mumbled, shifted, but did not awaken.

He was not discouraged. On the sixth thrust Meredith lifted her upper torso off his chest and stared at him in disbelief, her flushed face startled and confused. And heartbreakingly lovely.

Reaching up, Trevor threaded his hands through the sides of her hair. "Are you too sore?"

"For what?"

He placed his hands on her hips to hold her steady and bucked suggestively. "This."

"Oh, my. Me, on top?"

"Are you game?"

"Is it very naughty?"

"Positively nasty. And meant only for women with superior sexual skills."

"Then teach me."

His hands swept up to her breasts, grazing lightly over the nipples that peaked so sweetly for him. She sighed and leaned into him, encouraging the contact. Then he grasped her hips again and shifted her legs until she was pressed against him as close as the position allowed.

She clutched at his shoulders and stared into his eyes. Her face was a mask of concentration as she tried to find the rhythm that would suit them best. He encouraged her with his lips and hands, helping her gauge the tempo, teaching her how adjust the pressure of her hips so he could gain the deepest entry and bring them the greatest amount of pleasure.

This time when she started to come she whispered his name. The sound floated through the air and pierced his heart. It seemed to free something that was deep inside him, tight and twisted and hidden from view. The coldness inside him began to melt at the same time the seed burst from his body.

He reached up and caught Meredith's hand, spreading her fingers as he threaded his own through hers. As he filled her with his essence he pushed himself that final inch closer, spewing himself at the very entrance to her womb. She collapsed against him, leaning her head on his shoulder. He could hear her breath, coming now in little pants.

Trevor could barely breathe himself, but it was not

the physical effects of the moment that had him tied in knots. His head was swimming with a confusing, jumbled mass of revelations and emotions that scared him half to death.

Meredith sighed blissfully. Unable to resist, Trevor lovingly traced her cheek and jaw, then turned her head so he could touch her lips.

Good Lord, how was he ever going to survive this?

Seventeen

Morning sunlight streamed through the curtains, falling across Meredith's closed eyelids. With a wistful sigh of contentment she nestled her cheek against the soft pillowcase beneath her cheek and tried to ignore the beckoning call of morning.

For an instant she thought she was dreaming, as the titillating smell of potent male and sexual fulfillment drifted up to her nose. Opening her eyelids a crack, Meredith beheld a most extraordinary sight. The Marquess of Dardington, naked except for a white linen sheet that rode low on his hips, was slumbering contently by her side.

A swell of emotion tightened deep in her chest. They had shared something monumental in this bed last night, something that went far beyond physical pleasure. Though they had turned to each other again and again during the night, they were not just seeking sexual fulfillment. The connection they had achieved together was almost spiritual in nature.

He might profess otherwise, yet Meredith felt very strongly that her husband was not emotionally indifferent to her. Though he might try to deny it, his actions both at the theater and during the night proved that one fact undisputedly. Trevor cared about her,

worried about her, and was firmly committed to keeping her physically safe and mentally calm.

Yet she was uncertain if his feelings had developed and matured to the state where they matched her own feelings of love. And that haunted her.

Easing her head back on the soft pillow, Meredith stayed perfectly still and simply watched him. Trevor's breathing was deep and even, the rise and fall of his chest a soothing rhythm. She wanted very much to press her cheek to the reassuring strength of that chest, but feared the gesture would wake him.

In sleep, the chiseled lines of his jaw, straight nose, and sculptured mouth had a peaceful, boyish quality about them. With a blush she remembered the wicked things he had done with that mouth and tongue. His hair was mussed, and a golden lock hung over his forehead, yet it hardly detracted from the raw beauty of his face.

He stirred, then opened his eyes. Meredith held her breath. For a moment the silence between them was strained and horribly uncomfortable. She worried frantically that Trevor would withdraw from her, would hide himself away, would reject all outward signs of affection and love.

Though she knew she was a strong woman, capable of doing just about anything she set her mind to, Meredith grew fearful. She had made a vow to herself sometime in the early morning hours that she would not abandon the hope that they could one day achieve the type of loving relationship she so desperately wanted.

Yet as she stared at her beloved's handsome face, Meredith desperately wondered if she would have the strength to endure if everything reverted back to the way things had been—the neglect, the distance, the for-

mality. How would her heart and spirit ever survive such a blow?

The marquess gave her a slumbering smile, and her heart turned over. For the first time she noticed the tenderness touching his eyes, tenderness meant for her.

"Making love in the morning is a singular delight," he said in a serious tone. "Did you know that, my dear?"

Meredith moved her leg restlessly against his thigh, discovering the rampant strength of his growing desire. Her interest was more than aroused. "It feels like a joy I would very much like to experience," she replied, spreading her fingers idly on his chest.

"Then you shall, my lady."

Trevor's voice was husky with awakening desire. He closed a hand on the nape of her neck, tipped her head back, and kissed her as if he were starving. Meredith turned her body to receive his kiss fully.

Her senses were alive to his touch, his nearness, the solid warmth of his bare flesh. His hands raced over her as if he were greedy for the touch of her skin. Meredith felt ensnared in his mesmerizing sensuality, a willing prisoner of his insatiable appetite.

There was nothing delicate or gentle about his lovemaking. He lifted and pulled, thrusting into her mercilessly, pounding her tender flesh, giving her all she could take. It was raw and real and honest, exactly what Meredith craved.

When the last pulse ripped through them, they collapsed against each other, sweating, breathless, and utterly satisfied. In the cozy aftermath, Trevor kissed her shoulder and neck tenderly, then curled himself around her, his chest to her back. Meredith stifled a yawn.

"I have ridden you hard, love." He clenched his

teeth gently over her earlobe and she shivered. "Close your eyes and rest for a few minutes. You have earned it."

The wicked delight in his voice made her smile. She wiggled her bottom suggestively against his groin and he moaned mockingly. "Sleep," he commanded.

She nestled closer and clasped the hand he had placed across her waist tighter against her middle. Trevor pulled one of the blankets over them, wrapping them together in a private, warm cocoon. Meredith sighed with contentment and allowed her eyes to drift shut.

When she awoke the second time, she was alone and in her own bed. Trevor had obviously carried her here, yet she had been sleeping so soundly she had not noticed. Meredith stretched, then sat up and swung her legs to the side of the bed, wincing a little at the soreness. Though it was a decadent indulgence at this hour of the day, Meredith rang for her maid and requested a bath be prepared.

She soaked languidly in the hot water, letting it soothe her sore muscles. Rose bustled about the room, her head buried in the wardrobe as she selected Meredith's clothes for the day. Since it was already past noon, a more sedate afternoon gown had been decided upon by the two women.

Rose had just finished fastening the many buttons down the back of the dress when the marquess sauntered casually into the room. He was dressed for riding and even carried a crop in his left hand. Meredith assumed he had just returned, though he appeared to be wearing a freshly tied cravat and neatly pressed coat.

His gaze swiftly scanned her from head to toe. Blushing, she sat at her dressing table so Rose could arrange her hair, still reeling from the shock of seeing her husband in her chamber. The moment Meredith

was settled he moved in, leaned over, and brushed a chaste kiss to her cheek.

"You've had a bath," he said, his deep whisper tickling her ear.

Meredith's brow lifted in surprise. How had he known? The tub was shielded by a decorated screen, hidden from view. Then she inhaled a deep breath and realized the chamber still carried the floral scent of the steaming water.

"I have just finished bathing. I imagine the water is still warm, if you would like to enjoy it. Or I could order some fresh water to be heated for you." *But only if you allow me to wash you.*

Those wicked words were not spoken aloud, but formed in her thoughts. Meredith caught her breath at the erotic images that invaded her mind. She could easily picture Trevor naked, sliding into the steamy water of his bath. Next she saw herself massaging him, as she had last night at the theater. However, this time his flesh would be bare and she would be able to touch far more than his shoulders.

She would not use a cloth, but her hands, lathering them until they were soapy and slick. Then, slowly, teasingly, she would circle his upper torso until his muscles were straining, his back arching in desire.

His movements would cause the water to slosh up the sides of the tub. Fearing her lovely gown might be ruined, Meredith would next carefully peel down the bodice and her chemise, baring herself to the waist.

She would then lean into his strong back and wrap her arms about him, pressing her naked breasts against his wet warmth. Her hands could now easily reach across to the front of his chest, soaping the golden hair and rinsing it clean. She would cleanse him a

second time, paying special attention to the sensitive peaks of his nipples.

Her questing fingers would then move downward to his waist. Such a delightful position would place her hands in a most interesting location—directly in front of his penis.

Teasingly, she would dip her hands beneath the water, heading straight for that irresistible prize. Boldly she would encircle the shaft of his penis, running it through her fist. Up and down, up and down, stroking and squeezing until it grew larger, harder, hotter. She would make certain to manipulate the sensitive tip, just as he had taught her last night, brushing across that delicate part of his beautiful male anatomy until his hips were thrusting strenuously against her hand.

The surge of pleasure at this forbidden fantasy was so intense Meredith squirmed in her chair. Trevor lifted a puzzled brow and she nearly fainted from embarrassment. Though he certainly could not read her mind, it felt as though he were privy to her most secret thoughts.

"Do you have any special plans for the afternoon?" Trevor inquired.

"I was going to call on Harriet and Elizabeth and Mrs. Danvers if there was time, but have decided instead to write a note of regret for not visiting." Meredith sighed daintily. "I find I am rather tired."

"You should probably take a nap."

"A nap?" Rose snorted with amazement. " 'Tis well past noon, and her ladyship just got out of bed."

In the mirror, Meredith saw Rose lower her head as the marquess gave the servant a censuring stare. "I believe I shall finish arranging my own hair. Thank you, Rose."

"But I always do it for you," the maid replied.

"Since I will remain in the house for the day, there is no need for your special skills." Meredith patted the maid gently on the arm, then turned her back in a dismissive gesture.

With obvious reluctance, Rose put down the hairbrush. "As you wish, my lady." She gave Meredith a brief curtsy, then turned and began to pick up the wet towels that had been left on the floor, the evening gown Meredith had worn the previous night, and several gowns that needed mending.

When Meredith saw the servant reaching for a second pile of garments, she spoke again. "Rose?"

The maid sighed audibly, gave a curt nod to indicate she understood, and then disappeared. Once she was alone with her husband, Meredith turned back to her mirror and attempted to finish arranging her hair.

Trevor watched her every move from a comfortable chair, his eyes reflecting such alert interest she blushed. Her hands were a bit clumsy as she groped for the pins, but they managed to do a respectable job of twisting and securing her blond tresses.

"I believe I prefer your hair unbound, falling over your shoulders and cascading down your back," he said lightly.

"Now you tell me." Meredith swiveled around to face him and smiled.

He returned her smile, and she felt that now familiar sensation of sexual desire begin to tingle along her nerve endings.

"You said you will stay at home for the remainder of the day, but what of this evening?"

"I have accepted an invitation from Mrs. Morten," Meredith replied. "She is hosting a late supper and then a trip to Vauxhall Gardens for dancing and fireworks to support her favorite charity."

Trevor grimaced. "How many are in the party?"

"I am not certain." Meredith frowned. "I imagine fifty or so, including both of my brothers. Miss Elizabeth Sainthill has promised to be there, so naturally Jason will want to attend."

"The gardens are a very public place. The gravel paths are numerous and secluded," Trevor commented. "They can be especially dangerous at night if one encounters an unsavory character. Frankly, I am not comfortable with the notion of you going there."

"Because of what happened last night?" she asked quietly.

They had not spoken again of the incident at the theater until this moment, but Meredith could tell by the flash of awareness in Trevor's eyes that it was still very much on his mind.

The marquess grimaced. "I do not wish to unduly alarm you, but I believe it was more than a mere accident." He leaned back in the chair and paused, seeming to choose his next words most carefully. "I think someone deliberately took advantage of the mayhem at the theater with the intent of doing you grievous harm. We were most fortunate I was close enough to prevent it. My greatest fear is that we shall not be as lucky the next time."

It was a chilling, sobering thought. "What do you propose I do?"

"For the time being, I urge you to accept only a very limited number of invitations. But more importantly, you must not leave the house without me by your side."

His solution surprised her. In one way it was reasonable, in another not so reasonable. She studied Trevor's face. She could see the tension lining his brow as he awaited her response. He was her husband. By law he could command that she do any number of

things, but they both knew she was not a woman who would ever blindly follow any man's orders.

For this plan to work as Trevor intended, she must cooperate. Meredith weighed her decision carefully, considering all the positive and negative aspects, but in the end it was the hint of vulnerability in her husband's eyes that tipped the scales.

Folding her hands in her lap, Meredith fixed him with an earnest look. "I am not certain I agree with your theory. There is no reason for anyone to want to harm me, and yet there have been several unexplained incidents of late that have disturbed and even frightened me. I respect your opinion, Trevor, so I will comply with your wishes, but I refuse to become a prisoner in my own home."

"Of course." The marquess let out a long breath. He seemed very relieved by her answer. "I would be honored to accompany you to any social event you feel you absolutely must attend."

She tilted her head, her eyes steady on him. "I would like to go to the masquerade ball at Lord Linny's next week. It promises to be the crush of the Season, and I have already commissioned a costume for it."

He smiled. "Something daring and provocative, no doubt."

"I am going as Diana."

"The Roman goddess of the hunt?" His eyes traveled over her form with great interest. "A most inspired choice, given your height and coloring. And incomparable beauty."

Meredith lowered her chin modestly at the compliment. "It was actually the duke's idea. With my father's great passion for all things concerning ancient Greece and Rome, it seemed an amusing notion."

"I know you will look enchanting."

Pleasure filtered through her. All of her adult life she had been showered with florid, expressive, and occasionally outrageous compliments on her looks. Yet only Trevor's regard had the power to move her. "I only hope I can wear my Roman gown. The blue silk fabric is fashioned to be held over one shoulder with a gold brooch, leaving the other bare. It will expose a great deal of my neck and throat."

Trevor's eyes darkened. "Are you badly bruised?"

Meredith's hand lifted unconsciously to her throat. "These type of bruises always look worse the following day, when they turn all sorts of nasty colors. There is very little pain, so I know they cannot be too serious."

"I will send for a physician at once," Trevor decided, rising to his feet. "He can be here within the hour."

"No, please. There is no need," Meredith protested. "I had Rose bring me a salve that I used when I finished my bath. After anointing the bruises, I felt much better."

"I am concerned about your health."

"All that is required for my complete recovery is a little rest and time. A physician cannot make the marks fade any faster. Truth be told, he might prescribe a treatment that will make it worse."

Trevor hesitated, and she pressed home her final point. "If the bruises are still evident next week, I will forgo the ball and consent to be examined by a physician. Does that satisfy you?"

The marquess seemed to realize that was the best he was going to get. "I suppose it must. Yet after hearing its description, I confess I shall be very disappointed if I do not see you wearing your costume."

Meredith smiled suggestively. "I will gladly give you a private showing, my lord. Complete with the

crown of laurel upon my head and a pair of sandals on my feet, which are undisputedly the most comfortable things I have ever worn. There is even a small split on one side at the bottom of the dress to allow a glimpse of them."

His expression turned fierce. "Only a glimpse, I trust?"

"Yes, but if I move a certain way, the gown affords a peek at my ankles."

"Hmmm, ankles, too? I shall have to keep a very close eye on you, madame." His eyes took on a teasing manner. "Pity there won't be time for me to have a matching toga made. That would be sure to cause a sensation."

"For the right price, I am certain we can find an industrious tailor willing to try."

Trevor blanched noticeably. "Meredith, please, I was joking about the toga."

She smiled impishly. "I know. But you must promise to make some concession to the occasion."

"I shall wear a black domino with my formal evening attire and follow you about the ballroom like a willing, protective slave."

"What a delicious notion."

"I had an inkling you might enjoy the idea," he said in a wry tone.

A provocative taunt about slaves knowing their proper place rose to Meredith's lips, but after noting the set of Trevor's jaw, she wisely kept it to herself.

There were duties to perform, chores that must be completed, responsibilities of his position that demanded his attention, but the lure of his treasure was like a siren's song, enticing and impossible to resist. Ever alert to the possibility, he slipped away the mo-

ment the opportunity presented itself, stealing up to his room for an irresistible moment of privacy.

His breathing grew rapid and shallow as he carefully extracted his prize from the most clever hiding place, a drawer that boasted a false bottom. Late last night he had wrapped the prize neatly in a clean white linen handkerchief to preserve its essence, and now his fingers trembled as he unwound that cloth.

For several minutes, he kept it clutched within the closed fist of his hand. Then he slowly opened his fingers, like a flower opening its petals, and revealed the treasure. Sparkling, glittering, winking up at him, the diamond that lay in the center of his palm had the power to mesmerize him.

He stared at it openmouthed fascination, trembling with excitement. It was a good size, square cut, perfectly shaped. He turned his hand and watched with glee as the many facets of those clean edges reflected the light that crept through the small window of his quarters with brilliant fire.

He knew the stone had significant monetary value, but that was not what made it so unique, so special, so desperately important. This lovely jewel had once hung around her neck, close to her warm, delicate flesh. It had rested upon the pulse at her throat, had felt the beat of life as it coursed through her body.

And now the diamond belonged to him.

It had been difficult to slip out of the house last night, but he had been determined to get away, so he was successful. He had gone to the theater knowing she would be in attendance with the duke, as always, by her side.

He had purposely selected a seat in that pit the afforded him a perfect, unobstructed view of the duke's private box. Yet this clever plan teetered on the brink

of disaster when the marquess arrived. The last person he'd ever expected to see was her husband.

For an instant he thought she might have altered her plans, but then she entered the box, a look of surprise on her lovely face. He could almost forgive her, for it seemed she had no knowledge the marquess would be at the theater. But as the performance began, they took seats side by side, far too close for his liking.

His eyes never glanced at the stage. They remained trained on her, watching her every move. His excitement climbed when the candles were lit to signal the start of intermission, knowing he might have a chance to brush against her in the crowd.

But to his great consternation, she never left the box! Even worse, she moved herself to a provocative position behind the marquess and began touching her husband's shoulders, rubbing them suggestively, as if they were alone. He had been incensed by this wanton behavior.

It reminded him of the improper kiss she had shared with the marquess at the racecourse. That had also angered him greatly. He had destroyed her parasol that afternoon, shredding it in frustration as a warning that she was stepping beyond what he would allow.

Clearly another message was needed. The sudden, uncontrolled riot had been the opportunity of a lifetime. He had spied her just as the throng threatened to swallow her within its depths. Throwing himself into the fray, he was able to move forward. With supreme effort and tremendous force of will, he somehow managed to make his way to her side.

Once positioned behind her, his hands slipped around her throat, caressing that long white neck, anticipating the moment of utter joy and completion that would come when he applied the pressure that would end her life.

However, the pulsing excitement that sang through his blood ruined his concentration. He was shoved and pushed by the unruly mob and could not retain his balance. She fell to her knees when he unintentionally knocked into her. His hands reached down to hold onto his prize, but his fingers became tangled in the links of her necklace.

She had screamed and struggled, trying to hold herself upright. Her strength was exceptional for a woman, her determination even more so. Sweat broke out on his upper lip as he remembered her fighting valiantly to survive. He knew in that instant he could not kill her then, for there would be no time to savor the event, to enjoy each moment of her violent death.

Lady Meredith, it appeared, was truly the perfect victim. He would be foolish to rush such a rare find. So he pulled back just as the marquess burst through the crowd and lifted her to safety. But he had taken a memento to remind him of the glorious moment—a diamond from her necklace.

A sharp knock at the door sent him cowering into a corner. "You are wanted below stairs. Better hurry."

"I shall be along in a moment." He pursed his lips into a thin line, loath to leave the privacy of his chamber and the visions of his fantasy. But he knew he must.

In a small show of defiance, he lifted the diamond to the light and examined it one last time. Then, carefully, reverently, he wrapped it back in the linen handkerchief and placed it in his coat pocket. Though he had devised the perfect hiding place, he decided that it was too valuable to leave in his room. If someone found it, he would be in grave trouble, for he could not explain how it came to be in his possession.

Yet more importantly, he needed to keep it close to his person, needed to feel the hard edges of the stone

against his flesh. It was a stark reminder that Lady Meredith now belonged to him.

And soon she would know it, too.

Eighteen

Lord Linny's masquerade ball was indeed the crush of the Season, with all who attended agreeing it was a resounding success. Surprisingly, the Marquess of Dardington was among those who voiced a favorable opinion of the event.

Though he privately thought the sight of Meredith in her Roman gown was worth surviving any social occasion of the *ton,* Trevor actually managed to enjoy himself that night.

He had also succeeded in doing what no other man of society had managed, except for his father, the duke—Trevor had danced with the beautiful Marchioness of Dardington.

She had smiled with delight when he presented himself to her, bowing elegantly and asking for the honor of the next dance. Tapping her finger to the side of her cheek, she had feigned indecision, claiming she was uncertain if she knew the identity of the man behind the black domino.

He had allowed her the jest, then swept her up in his arms before she could say another word. The lavish mirrored ballroom, filled with bouquets of white, red and yellow roses, was the perfect setting for this magical night that hinted at endless possibilities.

Though he had not planned it, Trevor was pleased

to discover their dance was a waltz. Just to tease her, the marquess held his wife at the distance that was perfectly correct for the dance. She frowned at him in puzzlement, trying several times to close the gap between them, but he would not allow it.

For Trevor knew such intimate nearness might heat his body to an embarrassing level of arousal. In the crush of the ballroom, other dancers spun past them, but for Trevor it felt as if no one else was there but the two of them. He escorted Meredith into supper at midnight, and they sat cozily together at a corner table, conversing, laughing and sampling delicious morsels of food from each other's plates.

Meredith's brother Jason interrupted them, asking with a polite, pleading note in his voice if he and his dinner partner could join them. Jason had certainly gotten into the spirit of the evening. He was dressed as a pirate, complete with a jaunty eye patch. An impressive-looking crescent saber was tucked into a wide red sash tied about his waist.

His companion, Miss Elizabeth Sainthill, was garbed as a shepherdess. The white ruffles surrounding the sides of her poke bonnet framed her face artfully, and the satin ribbon tied beneath her chin perfectly matched the shade of her eyes. Seated beside Meredith, Trevor could not help but notice Miss Elizabeth looked sweet, innocent, and impossibly young.

"I am sorry to intrude, but I have at last managed to slip away from Elizabeth's sister, Harriet," Jason whispered to Trevor as he took a seat. "Yet I could not indulge in sequestering my lovely Elizabeth at a private table without any sort of chaperon. It would be highly improper."

"I understand," Trevor replied, though he had a difficult time imagining himself in the role of acceptable chaperon.

Why, only a few short weeks ago a young, impressionable girl of Elizabeth's stature would have been forbidden even to be seen in the presence of the scandalous Marquess of Dardington without a bevy of her male and female relatives along.

Apparently that had all changed. His wicked reputation, deservedly earned over the past eight years, was now replaced with one of respectability—thanks solely to Meredith. She had weathered the storm of their scandalous marriage with dignity and grace, refusing to accept anything less than the full acknowledgment of society.

And while Trevor was the first to admit he was hardly ready to cast himself in the role of an elder, stodgy gentleman, it was refreshing to have the choice.

"Are you enjoying the ball, Miss Sainthill?" Trevor asked.

A soft flush rose in the young girl's cheeks. "It has been very entertaining. The decorations are elegant, the atmosphere fun and festive. And there are so many people dressed in a most impressive range of costumes while others are portraying specific historical characters. I have never before seen the like."

Jason smiled enthusiastically. "We have been having a devil of a time trying to decide who is who beneath their masks." He put his hand over Elizabeth's, which was resting on the edge of the table, and squeezed gently.

"Mr. Barrington clearly has the advantage over me in that endeavor, since he is acquainted with far more members of Society," Elizabeth replied. Smiling shyly, she unobtrusively extricated her hand and placed it in her lap.

Jason seemed unaware of her withdrawal. The conversation switched topics and the four began a lively, nonsensical debate about which costume was the most

original, most daring, or most ridiculous. It continued, with much laughter, until the musicians returned and began tuning their instruments.

"You must excuse me." Elizabeth lifted the dance card that hung around her wrist and consulted it carefully. "I need to return to the ballroom. This next dance is promised to our host. It would be rude to force him to search for me in all the rooms on this floor."

Jason immediately stood. "I shall deliver you to Lord Linny personally—if you promise me one more dance later?"

Elizabeth hesitated for a moment, then nodded her head in agreement. The pair said goodbye and melted away into the crowd heading back to the ballroom.

"Jason is certainly smitten," Meredith observed as the two trotted off.

Trevor took a drink of his excellent wine. "Very much so, yet Miss Elizabeth's feelings are not nearly as obvious."

Meredith shrugged. "She is female, cautious and thoughtful by nature. He is a male, headstrong and conceited. Of course they will have differing views on the state of their relationship."

Trevor placed his crystal goblet on the table with a loud *thunk*. "Is that how you see me, madame? A headstrong and conceited male?"

Her eyebrow lifted to a provocative angle. "Headstrong, absolutely. Conceited? Perhaps impossibly arrogant is a better description." She flicked her tongue over her top lip teasingly. "Be quick and finish your wine, sir, so we may also return to the ballroom."

Trevor groaned in exaggerated despair. "Though you are only dancing with the duke and myself, you have already taken the floor several times. Are you not yet tired?"

She shook her head. "I can assure you that thanks to these marvelous sandals I can dance until dawn. Now come along."

Once back in the ballroom, it took several minutes for the marquess to achieve a festive mood. He was again on guard against any possible danger to his wife, observing all those who came near with a suspicious eye. Trevor had taken this duty very seriously, for the need to know Meredith was safe had now become almost an obsession.

He reasoned it was in part due to his feelings for her, feelings he had not expressed in words but rather in physical contact. Meredith had slept in his bed, or he in hers, each and every night since the incident at the theater.

She had welcomed him with an almost fanatical embrace, and Trevor admitted he had been very foolish to deny them both this closeness in the past, especially because Meredith seemed to need and want it so much. When their marriage began, he had believed physical distance was the only honorable course, since he was convinced he could not form any emotional ties to her.

But he was wrong. Those emotional ties had somehow been forged even with only limited physical relations between them. And though neither of them had yet expressed their true inner feelings to the other, the marquess sensed that moment would soon be upon them—at least for him.

It had taken nearly losing Meredith for Trevor to realize she was what he had wanted all along. She gave him a sense of completion that had long been missing from his life. Miraculously, she made him dare to envision that a happy, promising future was indeed possible.

There had been no occurrences since that fateful

night at the theater, but Trevor refused to abandon his mission to protect his wife. True, Meredith had, at his request, severely limited her social engagements, so the opportunities for someone to harm her, if there was indeed a *someone,* were fewer.

More and more of late he wondered if perhaps he had overreacted to the situation. But Trevor then decided it did not matter. Better to exercise caution and be wrong than to relax his vigilance and have Meredith suffer the consequences.

After three more dances, Trevor was finally able to convince his wife it was time to leave the masquerade ball. The duke was also ready to depart, and the three climbed into the ducal carriage for the short ride home.

Trevor accepted his father's invitation of a late night brandy, and the two men seated themselves in the gold salon to indulge. Meredith declined to join them. Instead, she bade them both a charming, sweet good night, kissing first the duke and last her husband. Yet the gleam in her eye and the possessive manner in which her hand fisted so tightly upon his lapel when she chastely pressed against his cheek told the marquess she fully expected to see him later.

Warmth unfurled in his gut and his lower regions. Just knowing she was eager to give herself to him brought on a tantalizing surge of both desire and emotion. Her enchanting Roman costume was a sensuous garment. It draped over her hips and breasts, clinging to every delectable curve of her body.

Trevor could so easily envision himself peeling it from her, inch by inch, exposing the creamy, white flesh he knew was underneath. He remembered how her skin glowed in the light of the candles, how her breasts peaked when he caressed them, how her eyes

seemed to beg him to take her, possess her, however he wished.

"Egad, son, I expect to see smoke curling out of your ears any second," the duke said with a hearty laugh. "Maybe it would be best if you forgo the brandy and head directly upstairs—with your wife."

Though he hardly believed it was possible, Trevor felt the tips of his ears heat. Blushing at his age? Over his wife?

"I am fine, sir," the marquess insisted. He took a large swallow of his drink to prove the point, and nearly started choking.

"Yes, I can see that," the duke replied, grinning.

Trevor let the remark pass. He knew his father was trying to get a rise out of him, so he deliberately refused to be baited.

"Did you enjoy yourself this evening?" Trevor asked.

"Certainly," the duke responded. "Linny always did know how to throw a first-class party, even if he is an idiot when it comes to other aspects of life."

Trevor nodded in agreement. They discussed a few of the other guests and some of the outlandish costumes, shared a laugh over a bawdy joke, then argued over a bill on land reform that the House of Lords was going to present to Parliament.

As he accepted another inch of brandy in his goblet, Trevor admitted he vastly enjoyed having these pleasant, mostly nonconfrontational conversations with his father. It was yet another thing he owed to Meredith. Her presence in their lives had formed the bridge he needed to cross over and reach out to the duke.

"Meredith would like to attend a musical evening at the Duke of Shrewsbury's tomorrow night," Trevor said. "Will you be joining us?"

The duke's dignified features scrunched together in

distress. "Meredith is a wonderful woman, but for the life of me I cannot understand why she likes these musical evenings so much. Screeching singers and whining strings. It drives me positively mad. Did you know she made me take her to the opera once?"

Trevor lifted his glass to his lips to hide his smile. "I recall hearing something about that evening."

"It was awful. My teeth were aching by the time we were able to leave." The duke sighed. "I will therefore be very much in your debt if you can assist me in concocting a reasonable excuse to decline. After all, I do not wish to hurt dear Meredith's feelings."

"She already mentioned to me yesterday afternoon that she fully expects you to find at least three reasons why you cannot be there."

The duke threw back his head and laughed heartily. "Clever girl. She knows me all too well." Sobering, the duke then asked, "Are you still convinced she is in some sort of danger?"

The marquess shrugged. "I am not as certain, but think it would be foolish to relax my guard. Besides, I've discovered I very much enjoy being in my wife's company."

The duke snorted. "It's about time you realized it. The woman is a treasure, a rare jewel that needs to be cosseted and protected."

Trevor regarded his father solemnly. "We are completely in accord on that matter, sir."

The duke smiled slyly at his son. "Well, now that you have finally gotten your marriage sorted out, will there be grandchildren coming along soon? Little mites who will fear my booming voice, my strict demands for proper behavior, but adore how I grant their every wish?"

This time Trevor did choke on his brandy. "I am doing my best."

"Well, get yourself upstairs at once and work on it harder. I'm not getting any younger, you know. I've already decided I want to be nimble enough to chase the little rascals about the room."

By the time they reached the Duke of Shrewsbury's mansion, the number of guests in attendance had swelled to nearly one hundred.

Meredith held out her hand to the footman, who stood politely at the ready to assist her from the coach, but her husband waved the servant off. It was the marquess who possessively took her hand and assisted her down to the pavement.

Meredith stood for a moment and looked up. The mansion was ablaze with lights. Candles glowed from behind each window pane facing the street, and extra torches had been lit on the outside steps to illuminate the way to the front door. Delighted with the twinkling view, Meredith turned to her husband.

"Why are you frowning, Trevor? Is something amiss?"

Behind her, Trevor murmured, "No. I am just surprised so many people are here. I had no idea this sort of evening would be of interest to any but the most ardent of music lovers. To be honest, I expected only a handful of guests."

Meredith quelled a sigh. She had been looking forward to tonight's performance for weeks. It would be a rare privilege to hear the talented singers and musicians the duke had persuaded to entertain, for they seldom left their native homelands in Europe.

"My dear husband, you have yet to hear a note played or an aria sung, so please reserve your judgment." Compressing her lips, she added, "If I wanted

a grumbling man along, I would have asked your father to accompany us."

"He was wise enough to formulate an excuse," Trevor muttered under his breath.

"I heard that," she quipped.

His features grim, the marquess took his wife by the elbow and led her up the stairs. Once inside, Meredith gave her wrap to a waiting servant and allowed her husband to steer her away from the crowd. It was his usual method when they first arrived at an event, so she knew precisely what to expect.

He had told her it was the most practical approach, for he needed to assess the guests and decide if there was anyone around who might pose a threat. However, on more than one occasion, Meredith had caught her husband casting a nasty, possessive growl at any gentleman doing nothing more than showing a flattering interest in her person.

Tonight she wore a red silk evening gown with a neckline that revealed a tantalizing glimpse of her breasts. Hers was hardly the lowest cut dress in the room. In fact, compared to many of the other women, she was almost matronly in her attire.

Yet as they strolled into the high domed conservatory where the performance would be held, Meredith noted Trevor was scanning the crowd with singular intensity, as though he expected her to be accosted at any moment.

"Is everything all right?" Meredith whispered after Trevor had located seats for them.

"I am uncertain. Alworthy has not taken his eyes from your bosom since you removed your wrap."

Meredith felt the heat rise in her cheeks. "I have known Lord Alworthy for many years. I cannot imagine he would cause me harm."

"He is a rake, preying on any female he can corner.

I find his eyes too cool, his gaze too assessing. I do not want him near you."

"Fine. I shall give him the cut direct if he approaches," she said.

Trevor nodded his approval, and Meredith nearly screamed. She had been sarcastic when she suggested snubbing Alworthy, though in truth she doubted the man would have the nerve to come within twenty feet of her with Trevor guarding her so obviously.

Thankfully she spied her brother Jason across the room and signaled for him to join them. He did so eagerly, but his motives were soon clear. He was desperately searching for a glimpse of Miss Elizabeth Sainthill and wanted to know if either of them had had the pleasure of seeing her.

"It is my understanding Miss Elizabeth and Miss Harriet are house guests of the duke's," Meredith replied patiently. "It is therefore reasonable to conclude she will be here."

"Thank goodness."

Jason sighed dramatically and lifted his chin. Meredith soon realized her brother's eyes were trained on the archway entrance and immediately fastened to any female who walked through it.

"Jason," Meredith called.

"Hmmm?"

Her brother never even turned his head in her direction. Apparently it was too much to ask that he break his concentrated studied of the entrance and speak to her using actual words. Meredith scowled. "Though I did not see her when we entered, it is possible Elizabeth is with the duke, greeting the guests."

Jason's head whirled around so quickly it nearly made Meredith dizzy. "Of course! Why didn't I think of it? Thanks, Merry."

The young man dashed off without a second glance.

Trevor grinned wickedly and took his seat beside his wife. "That was well done."

"Oh, be quiet. One difficult man by my side is more than enough for the evening. I shall not allow all these petty disruptions to ruin my enjoyment of what promises to be a spectacular night."

Trevor took her hand and squeezed gently. After a moment she returned the pressure. When the performance began, their fingers were still entwined.

His insides had begun to quiver when he saw her enter the mansion. She was here! For days he had not slept, hoping she would come, fearing she would not. He knew she had not appeared in Society much in the past week, no doubt frightened by his warning at the theater.

But tonight she had ventured out. What unbelievable luck! Nearly everything was ready for her. He needed to execute only a few final details. That must be done soon, for he knew he must strike quickly the moment the opportunity presented itself.

He frowned. It was an annoyance that the marquess had also come to the evening's performance, but that would not change the final outcome of the night. He would have to be cunning and clever to outwit the nobleman, but his arrogant mind embraced the challenge.

Lady Meredith was a prize worth fighting for, and victory would be all the more sweeter if he outfoxed Dardington in the process.

He skirted the edges of the music conservatory, positioning himself in an unobtrusive corner just as the performance began. For several minutes, he merely watched her, sitting slightly forward in her seat so she could see as well as hear the performance.

Her lovely face registered her enraptured delight at the music. Beside her, the marquess looked less pleased. In fact, he looked downright bored. That was a good sign. It meant the marquess would most likely take advantage of the intermission to escape for a few moments. And if he left, there was a very good chance his wife would stay behind.

With a small sigh of satisfaction, he slipped away from the conservatory to set in motion the final pieces of his plan.

Though Meredith kept her eyes on the musicians at the front of the room, she was very aware of the man seated to her left. Trevor shifted, squirmed, crossed and uncrossed his legs, then finally stretched them out.

She cast him a stern glare of silent warning. He shrugged his shoulders and tried to look innocent. She was not fooled.

"The intermission will be starting in a few minutes," Meredith whispered. "Why don't you go to the other room and enjoy a quick brandy?"

"I'm fine," Trevor insisted. "Besides, I do not want to leave you alone."

"You are not fine. You are restless and bored. Now go."

He hesitated, and she glared again. "All right, if you insist. But I shall be gone for only a few moments."

She shooed him away with a dismissive wave, then turned her full attention to the incredible music being played. As the last crescendo faded away, Meredith stood up, along with many of the other guests, and clapped enthusiastically.

"I do beg your pardon, Lady Dardington, but there is a delicate matter that needs your attention."

Meredith lifted her eyes to the man who had spoken. He had moved to stand in front of Trevor's empty chair. She could tell from his garments he was an up-

per house servant, yet for some odd reason he seemed vaguely familiar. "Are we acquainted, sir?"

The man blushed. "I am flattered you would remember me, my lady. We met briefly a few months ago when you sought my assistance concerning a duel."

Meredith's face brightened into a smile. "Of course, now I remember. You are Mr. Wingate's valet, are you not? Wait, don't tell your name." She tapped her foot impatiently as she tried to recall it. "Hawkins? Is that right?"

"Yes, it is, my lady."

She nodded her head in satisfaction. "Without your help that morning, I never would have been able to prevent the duel. I do not forget a kindness, Hawkins. How may I be of aid to you?"

"I do not ask on behalf of myself, but for Miss Elizabeth Sainthill."

"Elizabeth asked you to deliver a message to me?" Meredith asked incredulously. "I find that rather difficult to believe."

His face reddened and Meredith drew back. He looked so fierce and angry for an instant it startled her, but then he hung his head contritely, and Meredith realized he was embarrassed.

"Forgive me, my lady," he said softly. "I did not mean to be presumptuous. Naturally Miss Elizabeth did not ask me to get you. I saw her speaking with one of your brothers a few moments ago. Everything appeared very congenial between the couple, but then Miss Elizabeth suddenly turned and raced away. As she ran up the stairs, I could not help but hear her sobs of distress."

"Goodness, that does sound serious." Meredith bit her lower lip. "Did you notice where my brother went?"

Hawkins's eyes darted away. "No. I have not seen him since the incident."

"Well, you were right to come to me, Hawkins. I am very interested in anything either of my brothers are doing, especially when it involves a young, impressionable girl like Miss Elizabeth."

The servant sighed with relief. "From the direction she fled, I assume she went to her chambers. If you like, I can take you to her. Or I can call a female servant, if you prefer."

Meredith lifted her chin and scanned the room anxiously. Many of the guests had left their seats and were milling about the room. She did not see Trevor anywhere.

"Is there a problem, my lady?"

She shook her head. "I was looking for my husband."

"I believe the marquess is in the green room with several of the other gentlemen." Hawkins bowed politely. "Shall I fetch him for you?"

Meredith hesitated. If Elizabeth was upset over something Jason had said or done, she might want to discuss it. In that case, Trevor's presence would be a hindrance. "I will go to see Miss Elizabeth first. If she asks me to stay with her, will you bring a message to my husband and let him know where I am?"

Hawkins's chest puffed with obvious pride. "As you wish."

Meredith nodded and smiled pleasantly. Then, with her mind focused on poor Elizabeth's plight, she followed Mr. Hawkins from the room.

Nineteen

The hall clock chimed ten as they ascended to the third floor, but Meredith paid it little heed. She was trying to think of how best to manage the coming meeting and wondering why Elizabeth was so distressed.

Meredith had difficulty imagining her brother doing something to deliberately harm Elizabeth. He might be foolish, irresponsible, even thoughtless at times, but his affection for and infatuation with the young girl seemed genuine. Hopefully it was only a silly misunderstanding between the two that had caused this upset and could be easily rectified.

With that in mind, Meredith glanced at her surroundings. They were now in a very old and obviously little used section of the house. There was a musty, stale odor to the air and evidence of dust on the floors and carpet runners. Few candles were lit, casting dark and eerie shadows along the hallway that narrowed, twisted, and turned at abrupt angles.

Even though she was a rather minor guest of the duke, it seemed odd Elizabeth would be housed in such out-of-the-way rooms. Meredith frowned. The prickling of unease grew with each step she took, rapidly growing too strong to ignore.

Yet before she could voice her concerns, they ar-

rived. With a polite bow, Hawkins knocked sharply on the last door at the end of the hall. He did not wait for an answer, but lifted the latch and pushed it open.

Meredith stepped into the room. It was dark, lit only by three candles on a wall sconce. There were surprisingly few pieces of furniture in the room—a large four-poster bed with dark curtains tied back at each post, an armoire with a missing door, a small table.

Meredith noticed Elizabeth was sitting in the only chair, her back to the door. Meredith stepped forward. "Elizabeth?"

Elizabeth's head jerked, but she did not turn around, nor did she speak. Meredith turned in puzzlement to Hawkins, but the servant was no longer there. Meredith moved forward, then gasped.

She understood why Elizabeth had not answered. A scarf was tied across her mouth, effectively gagging her. Horrified, Meredith moved closer and noticed Elizabeth's hands were bound together with a single cord. It was wrapped several times around the girl's wrists, then pulled forward and tied to the bottom rung of the chair.

Meredith stared blindly at the young girl, unwilling to accept what her eyes were witnessing. "My God, who has done this to you?"

Elizabeth's pale blue eyes widened with fright. She shook her head as tears fell down her cheeks, wetting the gag in her mouth.

"Oh, I am so sorry," Meredith said when she realized the girl could not answer her.

Meredith tugged at the scarf, but it did not budge. She next fumbled with the knot at the side, her fingers clumsy and unsteady. Finally she loosened the material enough so she could slide it away from Elizabeth's mouth.

The younger girl took several great gulps of air and

then broke into sobs. Bending low, Meredith hugged her fiercely. "Hush now, 'tis all over."

"He is a madman, a monster," Elizabeth wailed. "I was frightened. I *am* so frightened." She sniffled loudly, then took a shuddering breath. "We must hurry and get away before he returns."

"Before who returns?" Meredith asked. "Who did this to you?"

"That servant, that horrible valet of Julian's. I do not even know his name."

Meredith was speechless. Hawkins did this? But why? And why had he now brought her here to find Elizabeth? It made no sense at all.

"But he led me to you," Meredith said. "Why would he do that if he meant you harm?"

Elizabeth's eyes again welled with tears. "I do not understand any of this, Lady Meredith. He told me Harriet was asking for me and wanted me to meet her; So I followed him here. The moment we were alone, he tied me up. Then he left. I have been so frightened. He never said anything specific, but I know he means to do me harm. Perhaps you also. We must escape."

"She is right, Lady Meredith. You would do well to listen to her."

Meredith looked up to find Hawkins watching them. She had not even heard him enter the room, though perhaps he had never left. She returned his regard with a calculatedly blank expression, hoping to somehow bluff her way to freedom. "Miss Elizabeth and I are leaving," she said, tugging ineffectually on the cord that bound the younger girl's hands.

He smiled then, a feral grin of such evil intent Meredith felt momentarily dizzy. "I knew you had the spirit to fight me," he replied. "But your arrogance

and courage exceeds even my expectations. I am well pleased by it."

Meredith was at a loss. Her defiance seemed to excite him, yet being compliant might put them in even graver danger. "Mr. Hawkins, I am sure we can settle whatever has upset you in a calm and rational manner. There is no need for threats or violence."

Anger blazed from Hawkins's eyes. "I make no threats. I have planned this all so carefully, so thoroughly. There is no need for you to be frightened. Yet."

Meredith swallowed hard. The chamber door was still open. Hawkins stood to the side of the doorway, just inside the room. He was not a tall man. In fact, she topped him by several inches. If she rushed him suddenly, she might be able to knock him down and escape.

Meredith glanced down and gazed at Elizabeth. Though the gag was gone, her hands were still bound to the chair. In the shadowy darkness, the girl's lovely face was so pale it was nearly the same color as her white gown. Her lower lip trembled and tears coursed silently down her cheeks. Meredith knew she could not leave her.

She struggled to contain her nearly paralyzing fear. "You are a very clever man," Meredith said softly.

Hawkins's expression was one of pure triumph. "I spent many hours formulating my plans. I had noticed your husband is often in your company, and I was unsure if I could lure you away. Yet in the end you made it so easy, so effortless."

Meredith took a step back. Hawkins followed, his eyes afire with harmful intent.

"What are you going to do?" Meredith somehow forced the words through her lips.

"Why I shall kill her, of course." Hawkins cocked

his head to one side. "And you shall watch her struggle to take each breath until finally there are no more."

Elizabeth's shoulders sagged, and she whimpered pitifully. Without conscious thought Meredith moved to stand protectively in front of the younger girl. Her mind was racing, her blood pumping hard and fast. "Why would you want to hurt Miss Elizabeth? She has done nothing to offend you."

Hawkins' eyes glittered. "That might be true, but she is clearly someone you care about. Her death will distress you."

A sliver of dread sent shivers along Meredith's spine. "That is your true aim, isn't it, Hawkins? To cause me suffering?"

He smiled at her again, as if she were a clever child and he a doting teacher. "I should not be surprised at how quickly you grasped the reality of the situation. Congratulations, Lady Meredith."

Meredith tried to say something, but her tongue felt stuck to the roof of her mouth. She glanced down and saw Elizabeth struggling against her bonds furiously. When she made no apparent progress, she slumped in the chair, defeated.

Meredith's heart thumped madly. The only chance they had to survive was to stall for time. No doubt Trevor would notice she was gone when he returned to the conservatory. He would not wait long to begin looking for her. Yet it would take time for him to find her, buried back here in such a remote section of the house—if he even thought to search for her within the house.

"I cannot think what I have done to warrant such strong feelings of hatred, Mr. Hawkins. However, I should like to make amends. Will you accept my sincere apologies?"

Her contrite manner seemed to puzzle him. His mouth opened, shut, then opened again. "I shall accept your apologies, Lady Meredith. After all, you are only a woman, weak of mind and body. But I shall still kill Miss Elizabeth."

"What is going on in here?"

Meredith and Hawkins turned in startled amazement toward the female voice. Harriet Sainthill stood in the open doorway, her hands planted firmly on her hips. She saw Hawkins the same instant he spied her. Her mouth formed a perfect O of shock as the valet lunged toward her.

"Harriet, run!" Meredith screamed.

Harriet's face was frozen in surprise. She tried to dodge away, but Hawkins was too quick. In one swift move, he slammed the door shut and captured Harriet. He backhanded her across the face to stun her, then put one strong arm around her shoulders, trapping her against him. He reached for something held within his coat pocket and Meredith sickened when she saw a flash of light reflected off the blade of a long knife.

Her eyes darted around the room, searching for something she could use to attack Hawkins, but the room appeared to have been stripped bare. There was not even a candlestick.

Meredith put her hand to her mouth. Harriet seemed stunned by the blow, but Meredith could not take her eyes off that deadly knife.

"Well, well, things are certainly getting interesting. Somehow I knew I could count on you, Lady Meredith, to keep things lively." Hawkins lowered his head and looked indifferently toward Elizabeth. "It brings me far greater pleasure to use my hands on a female's throat, but I need both of them to accomplish the task."

Hawkins dragged Harriet across the room. Meredith

backed away slowly, pressing herself against the wall beside Elizabeth. He said nothing, only tightened his grip on the now struggling Harriet. When he reached the bound girl, he raised his knife. Elizabeth flinched. Harriet screamed.

"Mr. Hawkins, please," Meredith cried desperately. "Miss Elizabeth is Miss Harriet's younger sister. Miss Harriet is going to marry Mr. Wingate. I dare say your employer will be most distressed if anything happens to his future sister-in-law."

Hawkins's expression turned smugly condescending. "How little you know of Mr. Wingate's true feelings. He does not care a fig for this cow, else he would have married her long ago. He will be pleased by this surprising twist of fate, for it will free him of any obligations toward her. You see, now I shall have to cut her throat, too, since she has seen me."

He pulled Harriet harder against his chest, and she moaned softly. Meredith was unsure if Hawkins's rough handling or his words had wounded the other woman more. She gripped the edge of the window ledge beside her and tried to make her mind function. Somehow she had to keep him talking.

"Why do you prefer to use your hands, Mr. Hawkins? Is it faster that way?" The words nearly made her sick, but Meredith forced them through her lips.

The valet slowly lowered the knife. "What tricks are you playing at, Lady Meredith? No woman of quality wishes to hear of such things."

Meredith steeled herself for what she must do. *They are only words,* she admonished herself silently. *Listening to them will be difficult, yet it might save you all.* "My interest should not surprise you overmuch. You have said I am unlike most other females."

Hawkins's face was a mask of astonishment. He

seemed to be weighing her sincerity, wondering if her interest was genuine. "I use my hands so I can feel the final breaths of life as they leave the body. As I hold the throat between my fingers, life slips away and death takes its place."

Meredith cringed at the pride and excitement in his voice. She did not have to ask another question to prompt him, for it suddenly seemed very important that he explain himself to her, brag about what he had done.

"I choose my women very carefully, you know. The English shop girls are the best. So sweet and fresh-faced, yet they fight and struggle like warrior queens."

"We are not shop girls," Harriet said breathlessly. "We are all women of quality."

"I have killed a noblewoman," he insisted, "though Lady Lavinia died quickly and without the tiniest of struggles. I received little pleasure from it."

Meredith's face twisted with shock. What was he saying? He had killed Lavinia? Was that possible?

Meredith could barely hear his next words, for a sudden pounding had overtaken her head. Her skin grew clammy and the blood drained from her face. Though it might create a much needed diversion if she became violently ill, Meredith did not wish to test that theory.

"You killed the former Marchioness of Dardington?" Harriet asked. "Why?"

"I did not mean to kill her. It was a mistake." He laughed, but the sound was not in the least humorous. "Lady Meredith was meant to die that afternoon, for the insult she had shown Mr. Wingate. She rejected his honorable proposal of marriage most cruelly. I could not let such a slight go unpunished."

His words tore through Meredith, making her stom-

ach roll. She rubbed her damp temples and breathed deeply, trying to quell the dizziness.

"So you came to the duchess's garden party intending to kill me?" Meredith whispered. "How did Lady Lavinia become involved?"

Hawkins's eyes took on a feverish intensity. "She was wearing your shawl. I followed her to the folly, thinking I at last had you alone. I attacked from behind, taking only a moment to enjoy her final gasps of life. It was not until later, when I spied you weeping beside her lifeless form, that I realized my mistake."

"Lavinia died eight years ago. Why have you waited so long to come for me?"

"You were suffering. That pleased me. And then Mr. Wingate left London and soon after purchased his commission. We were out of the country for many years. Yet in all that time I never forgot about you, Lady Meredith."

Hawkins continued talking, fast and furiously, and it was difficult to follow the conversation, to understand his words. When it was necessary, Harriet prompted him with a question and Meredith was grateful for her help. The other woman seemed to understand their only hope of surviving was to keep him talking—for time was fast running out.

Meredith was not in the room. Trevor felt certain of it. The marquess rubbed his brow and leaned against the wall, his gaze glued to the rows of gold-gilt chairs where the guests were seated for the musical performance.

He scanned the rows once, twice, then a final third time, but the results remained the same. Meredith was not where he had left her, nor had she moved to a different seat. At first Trevor reasoned she might have

slipped away for a few minutes, as he had done, but as the seconds ticked away he grew more concerned.

If she had left on her own, she would have returned by now. Something was dreadfully wrong.

"Thinking about making another escape, Dardington?" Julian Wingate asked. "If so, I suggest you make a run for it before the soloist begins. My grandfather adores this woman, but her voice has been known to make grown men weep. In agony."

"Wingate." Trevor favored the other man with a curt nod. "Actually, I was looking for my wife. Have you seen her?"

"No." Wingate raised both eyebrows. "Is she truly missing?"

"Yes." If the situation were not so dire, Trevor might have smiled. The black fear that was rolling inside him was so intense he was now confiding in a man like Wingate on the off chance he would be able to help. "I need to ask the other guests if anyone has seen Meredith, but would prefer to do it without causing a great alarm."

"I will help."

The two men took off in separate directions.

"Have you seen Meredith?" Trevor asked his brother-in-law when he happened upon Jason in the card room.

"No, but 'tis strange you should inquire about my sister. I have been searching for Miss Elizabeth for nearly an hour. Finally, with great reluctance, I asked Miss Harriet where she had gotten to, and she went in search of her sister. But Miss Harriet has yet to return. Now Meredith is missing also. Do you think this is just an odd coincidence?"

Trevor frowned. "I suppose they all could have needed to leave for a few minutes to attend to some

female matter, but I think they have been gone long enough for us to be suspicious."

Jason grabbed the marquess's arm. "Are you implying they might be in danger?"

Trevor's blood ran cold. He was not a man given to panic, but every instinct within him was screaming with fear. "I believe it would be wise of us to locate the women as quickly as possible."

Wingate joined them. He looked at Trevor and shook his head. "I've questioned the servants on this floor. No one has seen Lady Meredith. And yet they are fairly certain no one has left the house, either. She must be here somewhere."

Trevor grimaced. "Miss Elizabeth is missing also. Her sister, Harriet, went to search for her and has not yet returned."

Wingate's brow drew together in confusion. "Harriet is missing, too? I had no idea."

The marquess expelled a long sigh. If the servants said no one had left the premises, then they must assume the women were somewhere in the house. But where? It was a large residence, with many rooms. It would take several hours to search properly.

With growing concern, Trevor remembered Meredith's shredded parasol, the bruises around her neck that night at the theater, the uneasy feeling she experienced at times of being watched. He knew they did not have a moment to lose. If Meredith was in danger, she needed to be found. Quickly.

Fear for his lovely wife made it difficult to think, but Trevor marshalled his wits. He turned in haste to Wingate. "Are you well acquainted with this house?"

"I have lived here for the past two months. And I visited often as a boy." Wingate's mouth curled. "Harriet and Elizabeth are guests of my grandfather. I know

where their chambers are located. Do you want me to take you there?"

Trevor forced his racing heart to calm while he tried to think. "No. Is there an area of the house that is seldom used?"

"The east wing has been closed for years."

He hesitated a moment, knowing if he were wrong precious time would be wasted. "I think we should start our search there."

The marquess was grateful neither man questioned his reasoning, for he was uncertain if he could have formulated a logical explanation for this decision. Silently cursing himself for not taking better care of his wife, Trevor hurried down the twisting hallways, anxiously following on Julian Wingate's heels.

When they reached the east wing the men slowed, and began a careful search of the many rooms. They found layers of dust, mountains of cobwebs, even a few mice, but no missing women. Trevor was beginning to doubt the wisdom of his instincts when the halls echoed with the sound of a terrified female scream.

The three men exchanged worried glances, then broke into a run, stumbling as they raced down the hallway.

"I think it came from here," Jason said, pointing to the last door on the right. He reached boldly for the door handle.

"Wait!" Trevor grasped Jason's wrist. "We don't know what we shall find in that room. It is best to be cautious, at least until we learn what is happening."

Jason pressed his ear to the heavy wooden door.

"Can you hear anything?" Wingate asked.

"Yes, but it is just sounds. I can't make out the words."

"Let me try." Trevor pushed his way forward and

leaned into the door. He squeezed his eyes shut and concentrated completely on the sounds coming from the other side. If he held himself very still, he could hear a male voice speaking rapidly, a female voice answering or perhaps asking a question. The marquess then heard something else. Moaning? Whimpering?

His hand reached down and slowly turned the latch. " 'Tis locked," he whispered.

"I think I can open it." Wingate removed a long, thin implement from his breast pocket and inserted it in the keyhole. He fiddled with the lock for only a moment, then, with a slightly embarrassed grin, sprang the lock.

There was hardly time to question Wingate on where he had learned this rather unsavory skill, yet Trevor could tell by Jason's amazed expression that his brother-in-law was equally scandalized.

"Remember," Trevor admonished. "Be as quiet as you can. An element of surprise might make all the difference."

Yet all their efforts at entering the room soundlessly were for naught. The moment they swung the door open, Harriet screamed.

"Hawkins!" Julian Wingate cried out in astonishment. "What the devil is going on?"

The man Wingate called Hawkins grabbed a fistful of Harriet's hair and yanked her head back. "Make a move toward me and I'll slit her throat."

"Who is this man?" Trevor cried out in anger.

"My valet," Wingate replied.

"What?" Both Jason and the marquess turned in astonishment to Wingate.

The other man shrugged his shoulders helplessly. "Believe me, I am just as shocked as you. Perhaps more. He has never before exhibited such rash behavior.

"Hawkins, step away from Miss Harriet this instant," Wingate commanded.

"My God, he has tied Elizabeth to that chair," Jason declared in shocked tones.

Trevor's eyes frantically searched the room for Meredith. She stood behind Hawkins, directly in front of Elizabeth, who was indeed tied to the chair. Meredith's face was pale in the dim candlelight, her eyes alight with stark fear. She seemed unharmed, but there was a hopeless expression on her lovely face that cut him to the quick.

" 'Tis three against one, Hawkins," Trevor called out in anger. "End it now while you can."

Hawkins's mouth curled in a sneer. "I am the one holding the knife, my lord. And the women."

"Bloody hell, he's your servant, Wingate," Jason said. "Do something."

Wingate drew in a tight breath. "What do you suggest? He has a knife pressed to Harriet's throat. If we rush him, she will be harmed before we reach her side."

Trevor fought the urge to step forward. He knew Wingate was right. And if Harriet were cut, it seemed likely Meredith would be his next target.

"What do you want, Hawkins?" Trevor asked. "Money?"

Hawkins broke into a slow, cruel, taunting smile. "How very foolish you are, my lord. I want only to complete my mission, and nothing any of you do will stop me."

"What is your mission?" Jason asked.

"I punish those who are undeserving."

"You are a coward, full of bluff and pretense," Trevor said with contempt. "I demand you put down that knife immediately and step away from the women."

"Pretense!" Hawkins lifted his head higher and

straightened his spine. His eyes blazed as he pressed the tip of the knife into Harriet's throat. "You are a lackwit, my lord, who does not understand the importance of my calling."

Meredith flung the marquess a despairing look. "Be careful, Trevor. He has killed before. Someone we knew. Someone we loved."

"Yes," Hawkins proclaimed with pride. "Even though it was a small mistake, I took great delight in ending the life of your first wife, Lord Dardington—though I know I shall enjoy it far more when I kill your current wife."

Hawkins's words rang in Trevor's head, and a myriad of questions followed. The man was clearly deranged. Was his outrageous claim the workings of a sick mind?

"It is true," Meredith said in a broken whisper. "He meant to kill me all those years ago, but poor Lavinia died in my place. 'Tis almost too horrible to imagine. Oh, please forgive me, Trevor." Meredith bit back a sob, a mournful sound that tore at the marquess's heart.

He glanced at his brother-in-law. Jason's features were set like granite, but his eyes never strayed from Elizabeth's still form. If only they could distract Hawkins, they might be able to disarm him without the women being injured.

"We need to take control of this situation, Wingate," Trevor whispered. "When I take a step closer, I want you to shove me, but not too hard. If we break Hawkins's concentration, we might be able to overpower him."

Wingate nodded in understanding. Trevor balanced on the balls of his feet, waiting for the other man to act. Everything seemed to move with infinite slowness

as Wingate knocked into him. Hawkins blinked in surprise and relaxed his hold on Harriet.

She bravely took advantage of her captor's momentary distraction and wrenched herself free. Enraged, Hawkins went straight for Elizabeth, who was tied helplessly to the chair. The blade flashed in the candlelight as he menacingly raised his arm. Trevor moved, but Jason was much quicker.

With a cry of anguish, Jason hurled himself forward, thrusting his body between Elizabeth and the knife. Trevor braced himself for the spurt of blood that was sure to follow, but Jason reached up and grasped the villain's wrist with both hands.

The room soon filled with the grunts and groans of the combatants as they struggled for possession of the deadly blade. In a wild tangle of arms and legs, they landed on the floor, twisting and turning as each man struggled for dominance.

It was impossible to tell who was winning. Then, suddenly, Jason yanked his arm free and let fly a hard jab to Hawkins's jaw. It stunned the servant momentarily, allowing Jason, who lay flat on his back, to gain sole possession of the knife.

Before Trevor or Wingate could lend assistance, Hawkins recovered his wits. He gave a roar of pure animal fury and lunged forward to attack. In defense, Jason raised the angle of the knife the last second before impact.

Hawkins screamed in agony, his face registering pain and shock as the blade pierced him through the heart. With a final curse, he crumpled to the ground beside Jason, clutching his chest. It was stained crimson.

The room was still with silence.

"My God, I think I've killed him," Jason finally croaked.

"Good," Harriet declared vehemently as she backed away from the inert form. A darker pool of blood was forming on the wooden floor, encircling Hawkins's lifeless body.

Reacting with primitive need, Trevor raced to Meredith's side, pulling her into his arms. More than anything, he needed to feel the warmth of her flesh against his, to assure himself she was truly unharmed.

She was breathless and shaking. "I knew you would come," she said. "Somehow I knew you would find us. Would save us. I never doubted it, even when I was most fearful."

A shudder ran through her body. Trevor hugged her closer. Meredith lifted her palms to her eyes and pressed hard to keep back the tears. "Oh, poor Harriet," she said when she lowered her hands. "I think she has gone into shock."

The marquess turned and saw Harriet slump down on the floor, wrap her arms around her stomach and rock slowly back and forth. Her hair had fallen forward, hiding her face, but her shaking shoulders were clear evidence of her silent weeping.

"Please, Trevor go to her," Meredith whispered.

He tightened his hold on his wife, not wanting to leave her side for an instant. "Where is Wingate?"

"He has gone to get help. Jason is caring for Elizabeth. Please, there is no one else."

"And what of you?"

She smiled bravely. "I am much better, but Harriet is suffering so much."

Letting Meredith slip out of his embrace took a tremendous amount of courage. Before leaving he bent his head and pressed a kiss to her temple. "If you have need of me, just call."

She nodded. Trevor walked to the opposite side of the room to see about Harriet. She stopped rocking

and lifted a tear-streaked face to him. "Julian?" she asked, her voice choked with tears.

"He has gone for assistance," Trevor said softly. "Please allow me to sit with you while we await his return."

The hesitant way she reached for his hand made Trevor realize Meredith was right. Poor Harriet was on the verge of total hysteria.

Fortunately, help arrived very shortly. A bevy of males entered the room noisily. Several burly servants accompanied Wingate, along with a somberly dressed gray-haired gentleman whom he identified as the local magistrate.

Hawkins's body was removed. Once it was gone, Elizabeth lifted herself off Jason's lap and practically fell into Harriet's arms. The two sisters hugged each other fiercely, crying like young girls. Jason remained at Elizabeth's side, patting her shoulder awkwardly and hovering protectively.

Trevor turned to retrieve Meredith, wanting nothing more than to gather his wife in his arms and get her safely home. Yet as his gaze settled on the far wall, he received a most unpleasant shock. The marquess's heart jolted as bands of panic tightened around his chest until he could barely breathe.

Meredith was no longer in the room. She was gone.

Twenty

Fortunately, the duke's butler was crossing the foyer when the marquess came charging though the mansion's front doors, frantically shouting Meredith's name. The servant calmly informed him his wife had only just arrived and was in her rooms. Without waiting to hear anything else, a much relieved Trevor thundered up the stairs.

The bedchamber was in complete disarray as he burst inside. Gowns, walking dresses, slips, corsets, chemises, gloves, hats, stockings were all piled haphazardly on the bed. He stared at them in surprise, telling himself not to jump to any unfounded conclusions.

Meredith emerged from the sitting room, her arms ladened with a bundle of garments. She froze the moment she saw him, dropping a gown and some fluffy white underthings.

"I am sorry," she whispered. Bending low, Meredith gathered up the fallen garments and pressed them close to her chest. "I had hoped to be finished with all of this before you returned."

"What are you doing?"

"Packing." She dropped the clothes she held in her arms on the bed and turned to the armoire for more. "I promise to be gone by morning."

Trevor's mouth went dry. The fear he had experienced upon learning Meredith was in danger was a mere ripple compared to the wave of terror that now washed through him.

"You are leaving me?"

She would not answer, nor would she meet his eyes. She just kept bringing out more and more garments and tossing them on the bed with frantic, jerking motions. Several strands of hair had escaped from her coiffeur and were dangling against the side of her neck. The gown she wore was wrinkled and slightly disheveled from her efforts.

He stepped directly in her path, blocking her route to the armoire. She shifted left, trying to go around him. Trevor countered to his right, effectively impeding her. She groaned and tried again, but again he prevented her progress.

"I know you must hate me." She paused, then finally lifted her head. Her eyes were dull and sad, her breathing quick and shallow. "I do not blame you for these feelings, yet I cannot stay and be reminded of all the grief I have wrought upon you. 'Tis too much for me to bear."

"Meredith, please. What are you saying?"

"What can I say? You were there. You heard it, too, every horrible, ugly word of truth." He reached for her, but she evaded his hands. "Me, Trevor! It was me Hawkins meant to kill that afternoon at the duchess's party. Not Lavinia. By all rights 'tis I who should be dead, not her."

Just the mention of Meredith's death brought a hot, jabbing ache squarely to his heart. Was that truly what she believed? "I forbid you to speak such rubbish."

"Why? 'Tis the truth."

This time she succeeded in stepping around him to fling another garment on the bed. Tears leaked silently

from her eyes. Trevor wanted only to gather her close in his arms and ease her pain, but the note of hysteria in her voice bade him to be cautious.

"Lavinia was wearing my shawl that afternoon at the duchess's party," Meredith continued in a low, quivering voice. "Hawkins had come to the estate with one purpose in mind, to punish me for rejecting his employer's proposal of marriage. When he saw from a distance a woman wearing the shawl he knew I favored, he attacked."

"That is hardly your fault," Trevor said quietly.

"You don't understand, I made her wear the shawl!"

Trevor was momentarily shocked into silence. He reached again for her, but Meredith shook her head and backed away.

"It was not very cool that afternoon, but Lavinia had been shivering. I was concerned about her health, and the baby's—" Meredith's face suddenly crumpled. "The unborn infant! I had forgotten about that small, precious life. Oh, how can you even bear to be in the same room with me?"

There was no mistaking the agony on her face. He could almost feel the heavy weight of her torment, and it increased the grief in his own heart until it was almost unbearable. "How can you blame yourself?"

"How can I not?" Her lips twisted. "I thought I was so smug, so righteous in my attitude that I was different from other women in Society. I disregarded expectations, flaunted convention, refused so many honorable offers of marriage that first Season. Oh, yes, I happily broke all the rules, yet it was Lavinia who paid the price. With her life."

The marquess could not credit what he was hearing. "You cannot believe that if you had married Julian Wingate this might have been avoided?"

Meredith turned her head and gazed blindly across

the room. "I am not certain. But if I had accepted an offer of marriage that first Season, Hawkins might have forgotten about me. I might not have offended him so greatly, angered him to the point where he would do murder to put me in my place."

"Stop it, Meredith. Listen to what you are saying." Trevor clenched his hands into fists by his side, fearing he would reach for her again and upset her even more. "Your emotions have overridden your common sense. You are not responsible for Lavinia's death."

"I am," she whispered brokenly. "I am."

He laid a finger across her lips. Her body went rigid. "Heed my words, for I speak the truth, Meredith. This was not your doing. Hawkins, and only Hawkins, is accountable to the law and to God for all the horror he has wreaked upon this world. Including Lavinia's death."

Meredith's eyes flared in protest. She stared at him wildly for several long moments, and Trevor braced himself for the arguments that were sure to come. But then her golden eyelashes flickered, her shoulders slumped forwards and without further warning Meredith burst into sobs.

Slowly the marquess edged forward. She cried out when he reached for her, but was too distraught to put up much of a fight. He gathered her in his arms and held her tightly, absorbing her trembling sobs.

Trevor's eyes slid closed. Lord, it felt so right to hold her. He wished he could take away her suffering, could bear the burden of this horrifying pain himself.

"It should have been me," she sobbed.

"Ah, darling. Do not say such things." He tightened his hold as her body started trembling. "It was a terrible, cruel twist of fate. I will not allow you to unfairly blame yourself. Please, Meredith. For my sake, you must put this from your mind."

She lifted her tear-streaked face. "How can you be so kind and comforting to me?"

He pressed his lips lightly against hers. "Dearest Meredith, I have loved but two women in my lifetime. Hawkins took the first from me. I will not allow him to take the second."

There was stunned disbelief in the two watery blue eyes that stared up at him. "You cannot possibly love me."

Trevor's face split into an enormous grin. Revealing his heart had brought him a tremendous sense of peace and joy—and had also managed to stop his wife's tears. Whoever said love could work miracles certainly had it right.

He kissed her forehead and murmured, "Oh, but I do love you, Meredith."

The sorrow and pain etched on her lovely face were slowly replaced by a warm gleam of hope and amazement. "Are you certain?"

"Very." He hugged her fiercely. "Though my behavior since our marriage has hardly demonstrated it, there have always been deep feelings whenever I was near you. I did not understand what they were or why they made me so wild until I realized I might lose you."

"You love me." She repeated the words to herself slowly, and Trevor smiled with tenderness.

"Yes, and because of that love you cannot leave me." He stroked her hair. "My actions of the past have proven me unworthy of your affections, yet I vow I shall do all within my power, for as long as I live, to bring your heart to mine."

The edges of her lips curved up mysteriously. "I cannot give you something that already belongs to you, my lord."

He cupped her cheek with his hand and tilted her

chin until their lips touched. It was a sweet, tender kiss full of love. "Meredith."

"Trevor." She gave him a heart-melting smile.

His chest tightened. "You are everything that was missing from my life. I buried myself away when I lost Lavinia, turning my back on all I had in an effort to forget. Then one evening you lured me out to a secluded section of the garden and kissed me senseless."

Meredith dipped her chin and blushed. "Please, do not remind me. I still cannot fathom what possessed me to help my brothers win that ridiculous bet."

"Fate." He lifted her hand and nibbled gently on each fingertip. "It has given me a second chance at happiness, and I shall not tempt its wisdom."

"Oh, Trevor, what right do we have to happiness considering all that has happened?"

He enfolded her again in his embrace, needing to feel the warmth of her body against his.

"We will never forget the past, but we cannot let it deny our future. Lavinia taught us both what it means to have a giving heart. What better way to honor that legacy than to share our hearts with each other?"

Meredith went very still, then shuddered with soul-deep emotion. The soft light in her eyes reflected her love and her overwhelming need, but most importantly it held the promise of the future.

Trevor bent his head to kiss her cheek, but Meredith deliberately moved, and he kissed her on the lips instead. It was a kiss that was carnal and seductive, speaking of her needs as well as desires. It made Trevor catch his breath.

"I have thrown most of my wardrobe about the chamber and in the process made a total mess of my bed," Meredith whispered when he finally pulled

away. "I doubt we could even find the mattress under that mountain of clothing."

The marquess smiled wickedly at the invitation in her voice. All would be well. Though he suspected it would always haunt her to some degree, Meredith seemed willing to try and let go of the past.

"I recall achieving great success in my bed," Trevor said. He kissed her again, discovering anew in the giving warmth of her embrace why he loved her, needed her, would do all that was in his power to keep her.

What they shared was rare and precious. Trevor vowed never to forget that, never to take for granted this remarkable gift.

Meredith shrieked in surprise as he swept her off her feet. With his wife held securely in his arms, Trevor retreated to his bedchamber, his delighted laughter mingling with Meredith's and echoing through the entire wing of the house.

Epilogue

Hawthorne Manor
Six months later

"I've brought you some hot chocolate and toast, my lady," Rose said.

Meredith glanced up from the small writing desk she was using as she reclined languidly against the many pillows on her bed and frowned. Her maid was practically cowering in the doorway. Her eyes, wide with alarm, darted nervously about the room.

"The marquess is shaving, Rose. In the other room."

"Very good, my lady." The maid heaved a big sigh and finally stepped into the chamber. "Shall I place your tray on the table near the window, or do you want it on the table by the bed?"

"By the bed will be fine. I am feeling lazy this morning."

Meredith watched with amused concern as Rose practically ran across the room. She plunked the tray on the table, dropped a quick curtsy, and left even faster than she arrived.

Meredith sighed. Poor Rose. She had obviously not yet recovered from the incident of last week when a fully aroused, naked Trevor, interrupted while trying

to seduce his wife back to bed in the late morning, had a less than gentlemanly reaction to the maid's sudden appearance.

"Was that Rose?" Trevor asked as he emerged from the small dressing room they shared.

"I believe so," Meredith replied. "Yet she came and left in the blink of an eye, so I could not be certain."

The marquess sat on the edge of the bed. Meredith shifted to the center to allow him room. He was freshly shaven and smelled deliciously of soap. "I was hoping for an opportunity to apologize to Rose again this afternoon. That is, if she stands still long enough for me to speak with her."

Meredith raised her hand to hide her smile. Trevor had been trying since the incident to make amends with the maid, unsuccessfully. It was rather lowering for such a sought-after rogue to now have a woman turn tail and run from him in terror each time he attempted to speak to her.

"I think it might be best if you say as little to Rose as possible." Meredith moved her small writing desk to the side so she could get closer to her ruggedly handsome mate. "She will eventually adjust to you."

Trevor snorted. "I have my doubts."

Meredith smiled. He resembled a petulant child, in a temper because he was being unjustly scolded for doing something he felt was right. And yet there was nothing boyish about his square jawline or wide shoulders or muscular chest.

"Rose has no choice in the matter. For you see, sir, I have decided to keep you."

He raised his head and met her eyes. Meredith's breath caught at the stormy, sexy look he gave her. They reached for each other at the exact same moment, as if the pull of their love and desire was too strong a force to resist.

In their passion, they denied each other nothing, kissing and fondling with utter abandonment, touching each other with love and awareness. Nimble, knowing fingers were busy teasing, caressing, and seeking out all those mysterious places that would render the other weak with pleasure.

Their bodies joined together slowly, but the measured pace soon quickened. Their hearts seemed to beat as one as they neared completion, each urging the other to savor the sensations of ecstasy when it at last shattered over them.

In the aftermath of the moment, Meredith could think of nothing but her absolute satisfaction and total love for her husband. A single tear trickled down the side of her face, wetting the hair at her temple. She moved her head to brush it away, then felt Trevor's warm breath against her ear as he murmured her name and his love for her over and over.

More tears threatened, but she blinked them back. At times it was difficult for her to believe how far they had come in their relationship, and each day Meredith could envision an even better future. With Trevor's love and devotion, she truly felt anything was possible.

She tightened her arms around his broad back and hugged him fiercely. He stirred lazily. "Am I crushing you?"

"Hmmmm, it feels wonderful." Linking her fingers with his, Meredith pulled his hand to her lips. She kissed each finger gently, then pressed his hand against her cheek. "Now, we must not fall asleep. I have many things I need to accomplish this morning."

"All right. Then let's start the day."

Neither one moved. Finally Meredith opened her eyes and glanced up. Trevor was gazing at her with a rapt expression of contentment. She raised her head

and brushed a kiss across his lips. "I am famished. I hope you have not spilled my hot chocolate," she muttered. "For if you have, you will be forced to ring for Rose and ask her to bring another tray."

Trevor laughed loudly. "It will take me half the day just to find her. We will perish from starvation."

Meredith rolled carefully to her side, mindful of the tray of food that rested on the table not far from her head. She adjusted her nightgown and robe, resumed a comfortable reclining position on the pillows, folded her hands, and waited expectantly.

Trevor lay sprawled across the rumpled bed, the picture of total relaxation. Meredith moved her foot and gave him a nudge with her toe. He grunted. She nudged him again, this time a bit harder.

"If your frightening growls are going to keep my maid from our room, then you must perform her duties. I am waiting for my breakfast, sir."

The marquess opened one eye and glared at his wife. She smiled sweetly. With a resigned sigh he shifted his position and sat up. He retrieved the breakfast tray, which was remarkably intact, and placed it across Meredith's lap.

"Tell me, what is so important that we must leave our bed this morning?" Trevor asked, as Meredith fed him bites of toast.

Meredith took a sip of chocolate and smiled. "Though it is still several weeks away, I want to discuss the holiday preparations with the housekeeper, butler, and cook. Our first Christmas together should be extraordinary. I want this place alive with celebration and good cheer. I have already made a list of things."

She reached for the paper on her writing desk and read from the list she had been working on. "Roasted goose, plum pudding blazing in ignited brandy with

Christmas holly decorations on it, a Yule log, Twelfth Day gifts, the house smelling of fresh evergreens and spiced treats. I also think it would be nice to have a party for the local gentry. We have yet to do any entertaining since we arrived."

"I am sure the locals understand. After all, we are newlyweds with far more important matters on our minds." The marquess rubbed his hand over his face. "Are your parents still planning on joining us?"

"Yes. Jasper's last letter said they should be returning to England within the week. I am very anxious to see them."

"I look forward to meeting them."

Meredith's expression softened. "I know they will soon grow to love you as much as I do."

Trevor grinned. Then, sobering, he caught Meredith's eye. "My father will be joining us also. And your brothers. Are you sure the house is big enough for so much family?"

"I think we can squeeze everyone," Meredith said, a twinkle in her eye. "Hawthorne Manor does have twenty-four bedchambers."

"Ah, yes I remember. I also remember you can work wonders in each and every one of them."

"Trevor." Meredith tried for a scolding tone but was blushing too hard for it to have much effect. Somehow her husband had gotten it into his head that they needed to make love in every bedchamber of the manor. It had taken them nearly two months to reach this infamous goal, and the marquess took great delight in informing her of that achievement—and in whispering that his other two estates had even more bedchambers. Just thinking of it brought color to Meredith's face.

"I should warn you that my brother Jason is already hinting about staying on past the new year."

"Why would he want to spend so much time with us?" The marquess picked up a lock of his wife's golden hair and studied it lazily. "Not that I mind. I find Jason rather amusing. Besides, I need someone to practice my piquet skills on, since I haven't played a round in months."

"I certainly do not want to encourage card playing in either of you."

"We shall play for buttons or some other frippery. And if you are very good, we shall teach you to play. Remember how much you enjoyed horse racing?"

"I will not allow you to corrupt me, sir," Meredith teased, pulling her hair out of his fingers. "As much as I hate to disillusion you, my dear, I don't think you are the true reason Jason wants to stay with us. He is very aware Faith's baby will arrive sometime after the new year. Naturally he assumes I shall visit her once the child is safely delivered, God willing."

"I had no idea Jason was so fond of Faith."

"He isn't." Meredith shook her head. "Oh, he cares for her, of course, but my dear brother is far more fond of Faith's younger sister-in-law, and apparently most anxious to see Elizabeth."

"I applaud his taste in women. Elizabeth seems like a charming young woman."

"She is a delight, yet I fear that will be a hard road for Jason to travel. According to Jasper, Elizabeth has refused to answer any of Jason's letters."

"How strange," Trevor replied, frowning. "I would think she would be thrilled and grateful to see Jason again. He saved her life."

Meredith shrugged. "He is also a stark reminder of something Elizabeth wants very much to forget. Faith mentioned in her correspondence last month that Elizabeth still suffers from the occasional nightmare."

The marquess reached out and tucked Meredith's

hand protectively in his arm. "I am very glad you have overcome yours."

Meredith's gaze shifted out the window. Thankfully, the nightmares had ceased, thanks in large part to her husband. His strength and confidence bolstered her own. "I sleep beside my protector—though there are nights when I get very little rest."

The marquess lifted his brow suggestively. "Complaints?"

"Never." She laughed and shook her head.

"What of Harriet?" Trevor asked "Does she suffer from nightmares, too?"

"Faith made no mention of any. Though she did have some startling news. Apparently Harriet has decided to strike off on her own."

"What do you mean?"

Meredith shrugged. "She told Faith and her brother, Griffin, that once Faith's child is born she will be leaving them."

"To go where?"

"It has not yet been decided, but Harriet has answered several advertisements for positions of employment far out in the countryside. I think one post was even in Scotland. Two were for families seeking a governess and one was a companion to an elderly dowager."

Trevor whistled. "Though I do not know her very well, I find it difficult to imagine Harriet surviving as a servant. She has too much pride and far too sharp a tongue."

Meredith once again conceded that her husband was an excellent judge of a woman's character. "I think everyone agrees employment as a menial in a household does not suit Harriet. But after that mess with Wingate, I think she feels she needs a fresh start. How

else can one recover when her fiancé abandons her in the middle of the biggest scandal of the decade?"

The marquess snorted. "He really did turn out to be a total cad. She is better off without him. Yet I am not sure she understands all that is involved with being employed."

"It will be difficult, though I remember she was very fond of her nephew, Griffin's natural son. She might do better as a governess. I cannot imagine her at the beck and call of some elderly, spoiled dowager." Meredith shook her head. "Wherever fate takes her, I wish her well."

"That is very generous, considering your past difficulties with Harriet."

"In my position I can well afford to be so generous, for I have everything a woman could possibly want or need."

"Truly?"

Meredith curled her hand along Trevor's cheek and smiling lovingly into his handsome face. "Of course I have everything, my dearest. I have you."

ABOUT THE AUTHOR

ADRIENNE BASSO lives with her family in New Jersey. She is the author of four Zebra historical romances set in the Regency period and is currently working on her next historical romance, to be published in 2003. Adrienne loves to hear from readers, and you may write to her c/o Zebra Books. Please include a self-addressed stamped envelope if you wish a response.

*G*ive in to your Impulses!

These unforgettable stories only take a second to buy and give you hours of reading pleasure!

Go to *www.AvonImpulse.com* and see what we have to offer.

Available wherever e-books are sold.

AVONIMPULSE